**Bayard Taylor** (January 11, 1825 – December 19, 1878) was an American poet, literary critic, translator, travel author, and diplomat. Taylor was born on January 11, 1825, in Kennett Square in Chester County, Pennsylvania. He was the fourth son, the first to survive to maturity, of the Quaker couple, Joseph and Rebecca (née Way) Taylor. His father was a wealthy farmer. Bayard received his early instruction in an academy at West Chester, Pennsylvania, and later at nearby Unionville. At the age of seventeen, he was apprenticed to a printer in West Chester. The influential critic and editor Rufus Wilmot Griswold encouraged him to write poetry. The volume that resulted, Ximena, or the Battle of the Sierra Morena, and other Poems, was published in 1844 and dedicated to Griswold. Using the money from his poetry and an advance for travel articles, he visited parts of England, France, Germany and Italy, making largely pedestrian tours for almost two years. He sent accounts of his travels to the Tribune, The Saturday Evening Post, and The United States Gazette. (Source: Wikipedia)

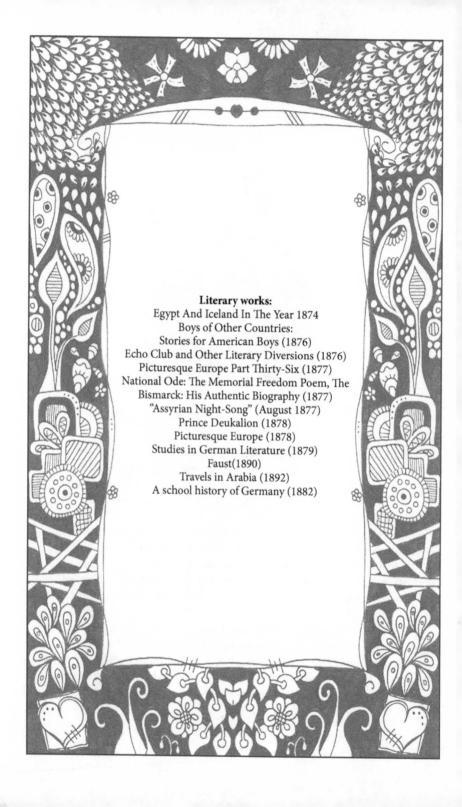

**Literary works:**
Egypt And Iceland In The Year 1874
Boys of Other Countries:
Stories for American Boys (1876)
Echo Club and Other Literary Diversions (1876)
Picturesque Europe Part Thirty-Six (1877)
National Ode: The Memorial Freedom Poem, The
Bismarck: His Authentic Biography (1877)
"Assyrian Night-Song" (August 1877)
Prince Deukalion (1878)
Picturesque Europe (1878)
Studies in German Literature (1879)
Faust(1890)
Travels in Arabia (1892)
A school history of Germany (1882)

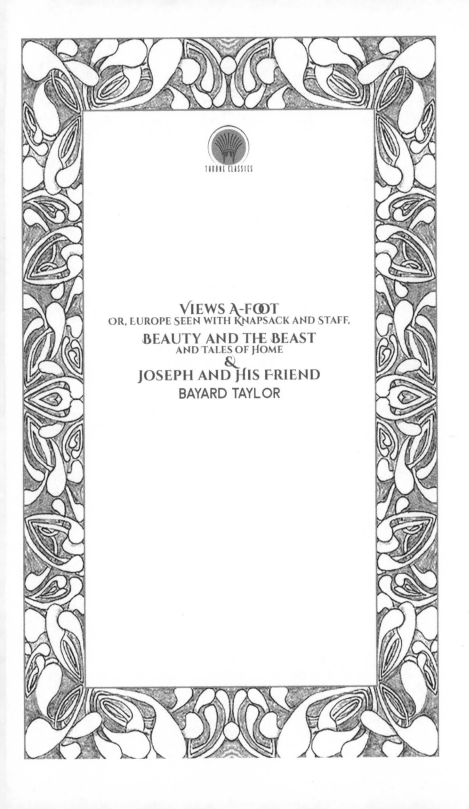

THRONE CLASSICS

VIEWS A-FOOT
OR, EUROPE SEEN WITH KNAPSACK AND STAFF,

BEAUTY AND THE BEAST
AND TALES OF HOME

&

JOSEPH AND HIS FRIEND

BAYARD TAYLOR

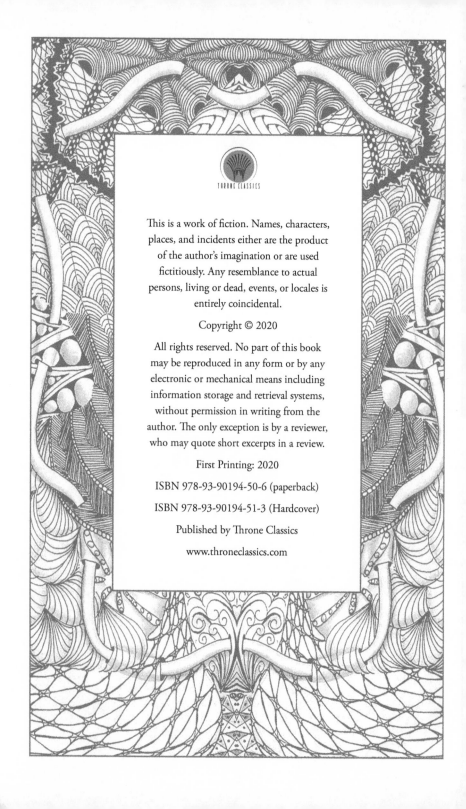

First Printing: 2020

ISBN 978-93-90194-50-6 (paperback)

ISBN 978-93-90194-51-3 (Hardcover)

Published by Throne Classics

www.throneclassics.com

# Contents

VIEWS A-FOOT; OR, EUROPE SEEN WITH KNAPSACK AND STAFF     13

PREFACE.     17

PART I.     23

CHAPTER I. — THE VOYAGE.     23

CHAPTER II. — A DAY IN IRELAND.     30

CHAPTER III. — BEN LOMOND AND THE HIGHLAND LAKES.     35

CHAPTER IV. — THE BURNS FESTIVAL.     44

CHAPTER V. — WALK FROM EDINBURG OVER THE BORDER AND ARRIVAL AT LONDON.     50

CHAPTER VI. — SOME OF THE "SIGHTS" OF LONDON.     59

CHAPTER VII. — FLIGHT THROUGH BELGIUM.     66

CHAPTER VIII. — THE RHINE TO HEIDELBERG.     72

CHAPTER IX. — SCENES IN AND AROUND HEIDELBERG.     77

CHAPTER X. — A WALK THROUGH THE ODENWALD.     85

CHAPTER XI. — SCENES IN FRANKFORT—AN AMERICAN COMPOSER—THE POET FREILIGRATH.     90

CHAPTER XII. — A WEEK AMONG THE STUDENTS.     99

CHAPTER XIII. — CHRISTMAS AND NEW YEAR IN GERMANY.     106

CHAPTER XIV. — WINTER IN FRANKFORT—A FAIR, AN INUNDATION AND A FIRE.     110

CHAPTER XV. — THE DEAD AND THE DEAF—MENDELSSOHN THE COMPOSER.     119

CHAPTER XVI. — JOURNEY ON FOOT FROM FRANKFORT TO CASSEL.     124

CHAPTER XVII. — ADVENTURES AMONG THE HARTZ.     130

CHAPTER XVIII. — NOTES IN LEIPSIC AND DRESDEN.     139

CHAPTER XIX. — RAMBLES IN THE SAXON SWITZERLAND.     148

CHAPTER XX. — SCENES IN PRAGUE.     156

CHAPTER XXI. — JOURNEY THROUGH EASTERN BOHEMIA AND MORAVIA TO THE DANUBE.     161

CHAPTER XXII. — VIENNA.     168

CHAPTER XXIII. — UP THE DANUBE.     182

CHAPTER XXIV. — THE UNKNOWN STUDENT. 188

CHAPTER XXV. — THE AUSTRIAN ALPS. 194

**PART II.** **204**

CHAPTER XXVI. — MUNICH. 204

CHAPTER XXVII. — THROUGH WURTEMBERG TO HEIDELBERG. 215

CHAPTER XXVIII. — FREIBURG AND THE BLACK FOREST. 223

CHAPTER XXIX. — PEOPLE AND PLACES IN EASTERN SWITZERLAND. 231

CHAPTER XXX. — PASSAGE OF THE ST. GOTHARD AND DESCENT INTO ITALY. 240

CHAPTER XXXI. — MILAN. 252

CHAPTER XXXII. — WALK FROM MILAN TO GENOA. 257

CHAPTER XXXIII. — SCENES IN GENOA, LEGHORN AND PISA. 262

CHAPTER XXXIV. — FLORENCE AND ITS GALLERIES. 272

CHAPTER XXXV. — A PILGRIMAGE TO VALLOMBROSA. 283

CHAPTER XXXVI. — WALK TO SIENA AND PRATOLINO—INCIDENTS IN FLORENCE. 290

CHAPTER XXXVII. — AMERICAN ART IN FLORENCE. 301

CHAPTER XXXVIII. — AN ADVENTURE ON THE GREAT ST. BERNARD—WALKS AROUND FLORENCE. 309

CHAPTER XXXIX. — WINTER TRAVELING AMONG THE APPENINES. 317

CHAPTER XL. ROME. 327

CHAPTER XLI. — TIVOLI AND THE ROMAN CAMPAGNA. 341

CHAPTER XLII. — 348

CHAPTER XLIII. — PILGRIMAGE TO VAUCLUSE AND JOURNEY UP THE RHONE. 354

CHAPTER XLIV. — TRAVELING IN BURGUNDY—THE MISERIES OF A COUNTRY DILIGENCE. 365

CHAPTER XLV. — POETICAL SCENES IN PARIS. 371

CHAPTER XLVI. — A GLIMPSE OF NORMANDY. 378

CHAPTER XLVII. — LOCKHART, BERNARD BARTON AND CROLY—LONDON CHIMES AND GREENWICH FAIR. 382

CHAPTER XLVIII. — HOMEWARD BOUND——CONCLUSION. 390

**BEAUTY AND THE BEAST AND TALES OF HOME**       **403**

BEAUTY AND THE BEAST.       405

I.       405

II.       405

III.       410

IV.       417

V.       421

VI.       425

VII.       428

VIII.       432

IX.       437

X.       439

XI.       444

XII.       447

**TALES OF HOME.**       **452**

THE STRANGE FRIEND.       452

JACOB FLINT'S JOURNEY.       474

CAN A LIFE HIDE ITSELF?       497

TWIN-LOVE.       518

THE EXPERIENCES OF THE A. C.       535

**FRIEND ELI'S DAUGHTER.**       **570**

I.       570

II.       573

III.       579

IV.       584

V.       588

**MISS BARTRAM'S TROUBLE.**       **598**

I.       598

II.       606

III.       608

**MRS. STRONGITHARM'S REPORT.**       **615**

FOOTNOTE:       638

## JOSEPH AND HIS FRIEND 641

CHAPTER I. JOSEPH. 645
CHAPTER II. MISS BLESSING. 653
CHAPTER III. THE PLACE AND PEOPLE. 662
CHAPTER IV. MISS BLESSING CALLS ON RACHEL MILLER. 670
CHAPTER V. ELWOOD'S EVENING, AND JOSEPH'S. 680
CHAPTER VI. IN THE GARDEN. 688
CHAPTER VII. THE BLESSING FAMILY. 699
CHAPTER VIII. A CONSULTATION. 711
CHAPTER IX. JOSEPH AND HIS FRIEND. 718
CHAPTER X. APPROACHING FATE. 728
CHAPTER XI. A CITY WEDDING. 738
CHAPTER XII. CLOUDS. 746
CHAPTER XIII. PRESENTIMENTS. 754
CHAPTER XIV. THE AMARANTH. 761
CHAPTER XV. A DINNER PARTY. 771
CHAPTER XVI. JOSEPH'S TROUBLE, AND PHILIP'S. 781
CHAPTER XVII. A STORM. 790
CHAPTER XVIII. ON THE RAILROAD TRACK. 798
CHAPTER XIX. THE "WHARF-RAT." 808
CHAPTER XX. A CRISIS. 814
CHAPTER XXI. UNDER THE WATER. 822
CHAPTER XXII. KANUCK. 833
CHAPTER XXIII. JULIA'S EXPERIMENT. 843
CHAPTER XXIV. FATE. 854
CHAPTER XXV. THE MOURNERS. 864
CHAPTER XXVI. THE ACCUSATION. 874
CHAPTER XXVII. THE LABELS. 882
CHAPTER XXVIII. THE TRIAL. 893
CHAPTER XXIX. NEW EVIDENCE. 903
CHAPTER XXX. MR. BLESSING'S TESTIMONY. 911
CHAPTER XXXI. BEGINNING ANOTHER LIFE. 921
CHAPTER XXXII. LETTERS. 930
CHAPTER XXXIII. ALL ARE HAPPY. 938
About Author 943
NOTABLE WORKS 949

# VIEWS A-FOOT
OR, EUROPE SEEN WITH KNAPSACK AND STAFF,

## BEAUTY AND THE BEAST
AND TALES OF HOME
&

## JOSEPH AND HIS FRIEND

# VIEWS A-FOOT; OR, EUROPE SEEN WITH KNAPSACK AND STAFF

*"Jog on, jog on, the foot-path way,*

*And merrily hent the stile-a;*

*A merry heart goes all the day,*

*Your sad tires in a mile-a."*

*Winter's Tale.*

# PREFACE.

## BY N.P. WILLIS.

The book which follows, requires little or no introduction. It tells its own story, and tells it well. The interest in it, which induces the writer of this preface to be its usher to the public, is simply that of his having chanced to be among the first appreciators of the author's talent—an appreciation that has since been so more than justified, that the writer is proud to call the author of this book his friend, and bespeak attention to the peculiar energies he has displayed in travel and authorship. Mr. Taylor's poetical productions while he was still a printer's apprentice, made a strong impression on the writer's mind, and he gave them their due of praise accordingly in the newspaper of which he was then Editor. Some correspondence ensued, and other fine pieces of writing strengthened the admiration thus awakened, and when the young poet-mechanic came to the city, and modestly announced the bold determination of visiting foreign lands—with means, if they could be got, but with reliance on manual labor if they could not—the writer, understanding the man, and seeing how capable he was of carrying out his manly and enthusiastic scheme, and that it would work uncorruptingly for the improvement of his mind and character, counselled him to go. He went—his book tells how successfully for all his purposes. He has returned, after two years' absence, with large knowledge of the world, of men and of manners, with a pure, invigorated and healthy mind, having passed all this time abroad, and seen and accomplished more than most travelers, *at the cost of only $500, and this sum earned on the road.* This, in the writer's opinion, is a fine instance of character and energy. The book, which records the difficulties and struggles of a printer's apprentice achieving this, must be interesting to Americans. The pride of the country is in its self-made men.

What Mr. Taylor is, or what he is yet to become, cannot well be touched upon here, but that it will yet be written, and on a bright page, is, of course, his own confident hope and the writer's confident expectation. The book, which is the record of his progress thus far, is now cordially commended to the public, and it will be read, perhaps, more understandingly after a perusal of the following outline sketch of the difficulties the author had to contend with—a letter written in reply to a note from the writer asking for some of the particulars of his start and progress:

*To. Mr. Willis,—*

*MY DEAR SIR:—*

*Nearly three years ago (in the beginning of 1844) the time for accomplishing my long cherished desire of visiting Europe, seemed to arrive. A cousin, who had long intended going abroad, was to leave in a few months, and although I was then surrounded by the most unfavorable circumstances, I determined to accompany him, at whatever hazard. I had still two years of my apprenticeship to serve out; I was entirely without means, and my project was strongly opposed by my friends, as something too visionary to be practicable. A short time before, Mr. Griswold advised me to publish a small volume of youthful effusions, a few of which had appeared in Graham's Magazine, which he then edited; the idea struck me, that by so doing, I might, if they should be favorably noticed, obtain a newspaper correspondence which would enable me to make the start.*

*The volume was published; a sufficient number was sold among my friends to defray all expenses, and it was charitably noticed by the Philadelphia press. Some literary friends, to whom I confided my design, promised to aid me with their influence. Trusting to this, I made arrangements for leaving the printing-office, which I succeeded in doing, by making a certain compensation for the remainder of my time. I was now fully confident of success, feeling satisfied, that a strong will would always make itself a way. After many applications to different editors and as many disappointments, I finally succeeded, about two weeks before our departure, in making a partial engagement. Mr. Chandler of the United States Gazette and Mr. Patterson of the Saturday Evening Post, paid me fifty dollars, each, in advance for twelve letters, to be sent from Europe, with the probability of accepting more, if these should be satisfactory. This, with a sum which I received from Mr. Graham for poems published in his Magazine, put me in possession of about a hundred and forty dollars, with which I determined to start, trusting to future remuneration for letters, or if that should fail, to my skill as a compositor, for I supposed I could at the worst, work my way through Europe, like the German hand werker. Thus, with another companion, we left home, an enthusiastic and hopeful trio.*

*I need not trace our wanderings at length. After eight months of suspense, during which time my small means were entirely exhausted, I received a letter from Mr. Patterson, continuing the engagement for the remainder of my stay, with a remittance of one hundred dollars from himself and Mr. Graham. Other remittances, received from time to time, enabled me to stay abroad two years, during which I traveled on foot upwards of three thousand miles in Germany,*

*Switzerland, Italy and France. I was obliged, however, to use the strictest economy—to live on pilgrim fare, and do penance in rain and cold. My means several times entirely failed; but I was always relieved from serious difficulty through unlooked-for friends, or some unexpected turn of fortune. At Rome, owing to the expenses and embarrassments of traveling in Italy, I was obliged to give up my original design of proceeding on foot to Naples and across the peninsula to Otranto, sailing thence to Corfu and making a pedestrian journey through Albania and Greece. But the main object of my pilgrimage is accomplished; I visited the principal places of interest in Europe, enjoyed her grandest scenery and the marvels of ancient and modern art, became familiar with other languages, other customs and other institutions, and returned home, after two years' absence, willing now, with satisfied curiosity, to resume life in America.*

*Yours, most sincerely,*

*J. BAYARD TAYLOR.*

TO

FRANK TAYLOR,

THESE RECORDS OF THE PILGRIMAGE,

WHOSE TOILS AND ENJOYMENTS WE HAVE SHARED
TOGETHER,

ARE

AFFECTIONATELY INSCRIBED,

BY

HIS RELATIVE AND FRIEND.

# PART I.

## CHAPTER I. — THE VOYAGE.

An enthusiastic desire of visiting the Old World haunted me from early childhood. I cherished a presentiment, amounting almost to belief, that I should one day behold the scenes, among which my fancy had so long wandered. The want of means was for a time a serious check to my anticipations; but I could not content myself to wait until I had slowly accumulated so large a sum as tourists usually spend on their travels. It seemed to me that a more humble method of seeing the world would place within the power of almost every one, what has hitherto been deemed the privilege of the wealthy few. Such a journey, too, offered advantages for becoming acquainted with people as well as places—for observing more intimately, the effect of government and education, and more than all, for the study of human nature, in every condition of life. At length I became possessed of a small sum, to be earned by letters descriptive of things abroad, and on the 1st of July, 1844, set sail for Liverpool, with a relative and friend, whose circumstances were somewhat similar to mine. How far the success of the experiment and the object of our long pilgrimage were attained, these pages will show.

*LAND AND SEA.*

*There are springs that rise in the greenwood's heart,*

*Where its leafy glooms are cast,*

*And the branches droop in the solemn air,*

*Unstirred by the sweeping blast.*

*There are hills that lie in the noontide calm,*

*On the lap of the quiet earth;*

*And, crown'd with gold by the ripened grain,*

*Surround my place of birth.*

*Dearer are these to my pining heart,*

*Than the beauty of the deep,*

*When the moonlight falls in a bolt of gold*

*On the waves that heave in sleep.*

*The rustling talk of the clustered leaves*

*That shade a well-known door,*

*Is sweeter far than the booming sound*

*Of the breaking wave before.*

*When night on the ocean sinks calmly down,*

*I climb the vessel's prow,*

*Where the foam-wreath glows with its phosphor light,*

*Like a crown on a sea-nymph's brow.*

*Above, through the lattice of rope and spar,*

*The stars in their beauty burn;*

*And the spirit longs to ride their beams,*

*And back to the loved return.*

*They say that the sunset is brighter far*

*When it sinks behind the sea;*

*That the stars shine out with a softer fire—*

*Not thus they seem to me.*

*Dearer the flush of the crimson west*

*Through trees that my childhood knew.*

*When the star of love with its silver lamp,*

*Lights the homes of the tried and true!*

Could one live on the sense of beauty alone, exempt from the necessity of "creature comforts," a sea-voyage would be delightful. To the landsman there is sublimity in the wild and ever-varied forms of the ocean; they fill his mind with living images of a glory he had only dreamed of before. But we would have been willing to forego all this and get back the comforts of the shore. At New York we took passage in the second cabin of the Oxford, which, as usual in the Liverpool packets, consisted of a small space amid-ships, fitted up with rough, temporary berths. The communication with the deck is by an open hatchway, which in storms is closed down. As the passengers in this cabin furnish their own provisions, we made ourselves acquainted with the contents of certain storehouses on Pine St. wharf, and purchased a large box of provisions, which was stowed away under our narrow berth. The cook, for a small compensation, took on himself the charge of preparing them, and we made ourselves as comfortable as the close, dark dwelling would admit.

As we approached the Banks of Newfoundland, a gale arose, which for two days and nights carried us on, careering Mazeppa-like, up hill and down. The sea looked truly magnificent, although the sailors told us it was nothing at all in comparison with the storms of winter. But we were not permitted to pass the Banks, without experiencing one of the calms, for which that neighborhood is noted. For three days we lay almost motionless on the glassy water, sometimes surrounded by large flocks of sea-gulls. The weed brought by the gulf stream, floated around—some branches we fished up, were full of beautiful little shells. Once a large school of black-fish came around the vessel, and the carpenter climbed down on the fore-chains, with a harpoon to strike one. Scarcely had he taken his position, when they all darted off in a straight line, through the water, and were soon out of sight. He said they smelt the harpoon.

We congratulated ourselves on having reached the Banks in seven days, as it is considered the longest third-part of the passage. But the hopes of reaching Liverpool in twenty days, were soon overthrown. A succession of southerly winds drove the vessel as far north as lat. 55 deg., without bringing us much nearer our destination. It was extremely cold, for we were but five degrees south of the latitude of Greenland, and the long northern twilights came on. The last glow of the evening twilight had scarcely faded, before the first glimmering of dawn appeared. I found it extremely easy to read, at 10 P.M., on the deck.

We had much diversion on board from a company of Iowa Indians, under the celebrated chief "White Cloud," who are on a visit to England. They are truly a wild enough looking company, and helped not a little to relieve the tedium of the passage. The chief was a very grave and dignified person, but some of the braves were merry enough. One day we had a war-dance on deck, which was a most ludicrous scene. The chief and two braves sat upon the deck, beating violently a small drum and howling forth their war-song, while the others in full dress, painted in a grotesque style, leaped about, brandishing tomahawks and spears, and terminating each dance with a terrific yell. Some of the men are very fine-looking, but the squaws are all ugly. They occupied part of the second cabin, separated only by a board partition from our room. This proximity was any thing but agreeable. They kept us awake more than half the night, by singing and howling in the most dolorous manner, with the accompaniment of slapping their hands violently on their bare breasts. We tried an opposition, and a young German student, who was returning home after two years' travel in America, made our room ring with the chorus from Der Freischütz—but in vain. They would howl and beat their breasts, and the pappoose would squall. Any loss of temper is therefore not to be wondered at, when I state that I could scarcely turn in my berth, much less stretch myself out; my cramped limbs alone drove off half the night's slumber.

It was a pleasure, at least, to gaze on their strong athletic frames. Their massive chests and powerful limbs put to shame our dwindled proportions. One old man, in particular, who seemed the patriarch of the band, used to stand for hours on the quarter deck, sublime and motionless as a statue of

Jupiter. An interesting incident occurred during the calm of which I spoke. They began to be fearful we were doomed to remain there forever, unless the spirits were invoked for a favorable wind. Accordingly the prophet lit his pipe and smoked with great deliberation, muttering all the while in a low voice. Then, having obtained a bottle of beer from the captain, he poured it solemnly over the stern of the vessel into the sea. There were some indications of wind at the time, and accordingly the next morning we had a fine breeze, which the Iowas attributed solely to the Prophet's incantation and Eolus' love of beer.

After a succession of calms and adverse winds, on the 25th we were off the Hebrides, and though not within sight of land, the southern winds came to us strongly freighted with the "meadow freshness" of the Irish bogs, so we could at least smell it. That day the wind became more favorable, and the next morning we were all roused out of our berths by sunrise, at the long wished-for cry of "land!" Just under the golden flood of light that streamed through the morning clouds, lay afar-off and indistinct the crags of an island, with the top of a light-house visible at one extremity. To the south of it, and barely distinguishable, so completely was it blended in hue with the veiling cloud, loomed up a lofty mountain. I shall never forget the sight! As we drew nearer, the dim and soft outline it first wore, was broken into a range of crags, with lofty precipices jutting out to the sea, and sloping off inland. The white wall of the light-house shone in the morning's light, and the foam of the breakers dashed up at the foot of the airy cliffs. It was worth all the troubles of a long voyage, to feel the glorious excitement which this herald of new scenes and new adventures created. The light-house was on Tory Island, on the north-western coast of Ireland. The Captain decided on taking the North Channel, for, although rarely done, it was in our case nearer, and is certainly more interesting than the usual route.

We passed the Island of Ennistrahul, near the entrance of Londonderry harbor, and at sunset saw in the distance the islands of Islay and Jura, off the Scottish coast. Next morning we were close to the promontory of Fairhead, a bold, precipitous headland, like some of the Palisades on the Hudson; the highlands of the Mull of Cantire were on the opposite side of the Channel,

27

and the wind being ahead, we tacked from shore to shore, running so near the Irish coast, that we could see the little thatched huts, stacks of peat, and even rows of potatoes in the fields. It was a panorama: the view extended for miles inland, and the fields of different colored grain were spread out before us, a brilliant mosaic. Towards evening we passed Ailsa Crag, the sea-bird's home, within sight, though about twenty miles distant.

On Sunday, the 28th, we passed the lofty headland of the Mull of Galloway and entered the Irish Sea. Here there was an occurrence of an impressive nature. A woman, belonging to the steerage, who had been ill the whole passage, died the morning before. She appeared to be of a very avaricious disposition, though this might indeed have been the result of self-denial, practised through filial affection. In the morning she was speechless, and while they were endeavoring to persuade her to give up her keys to the captain, died. In her pocket were found two parcels, containing forty sovereigns, sewed up with the most miserly care. It was ascertained she had a widowed mother in the north of Ireland, and judging her money could be better applied than to paying for a funeral on shore, the captain gave orders for committing the body to the waves. It rained drearily as her corpse, covered with starred bunting, was held at the gangway while the captain read the funeral service; then one plunge was heard, and a white object, flashed up through the dark waters, as the ship passed on.

In the afternoon we passed the Isle of Man, having a beautiful view of the Calf, with a white stream tumbling down the rocks into the sea; and at night saw the sun set behind the mountains of Wales. About midnight, the pilot came on board, and soon after sunrise I saw the distant spires of Liverpool. The Welsh coast was studded with windmills, all in motion, and the harbor spotted with buoys, bells and floating lights. How delightful it was to behold the green trees on the banks of the Mersey, and to know that in a few hours we should be on land! About 11 o'clock we came to anchor in the channel of the Mersey, near the docks, and after much noise, bustle and confusion, were transferred, with our baggage, to a small steamboat, giving a parting cheer to the Iowas, who remained on board. On landing, I stood a moment to observe the scene. The baggage-wagons, drawn by horses, mules and donkeys, were extraordinary; men were going about crying "the celebrated Tralorum gingerbread!" which they carried in baskets; and a boy in the University dress, with long blue gown and yellow knee-breeches, was running to the wharf to look at the Indians.

At last the carts were all loaded, the word was given to start, and then, what a scene ensued! Away went the mules, the horses and the donkeys; away ran men and women and children, carrying chairs and trunks, and boxes and bedding. The wind was blowing, and the dust whirled up as they dashed helter-skelter through the gate and started off on a hot race, down the dock to the depot. Two wagons came together, one of which was overturned, scattering the broken boxes of a Scotch family over the pavement; but while the poor woman was crying over her loss, the tide swept on, scarcely taking time to glance at the mishap.

Our luggage was "passed" with little trouble; the officer merely opening the trunks and pressing his hands on the top. Even some American reprints of English works which my companion carried, and feared would be taken from him, were passed over without a word. I was agreeably surprised at this, as from the accounts of some travellers, I had been led to fear horrible things of custom-houses. This over, we took a stroll about the city. I was first struck by seeing so many people walking in the middle of the streets, and so many gentlemen going about with pinks stuck in their button-holes. Then, the houses being all built of brown granite or dark brick, gives the town a sombre appearance, which the sunshine (when there is any) cannot dispel. Of Liverpool we saw little. Before the twilight had wholly faded, we were again tossing on the rough waves of the Irish Sea.

# CHAPTER II. — A DAY IN IRELAND.

On calling at the steamboat office in Liverpool, to take passage to Port Rush, we found that the fare in the fore cabin was but two shillings and a half, while in the chief cabin it was six times as much. As I had started to make the tour of all Europe with a sum little higher than is sometimes given for the mere passage to and fro, there was no alternative—the twenty-four hours' discomfort could be more easily endured than the expense, and as I expected to encounter many hardships, it was best to make a beginning. I had crossed the ocean with tolerable comfort for twenty-four dollars, and was determined to try whether England, where I had been told it was almost impossible to breathe without expense, might not also be seen by one of limited means.

The fore cabin was merely a bare room, with a bench along one side, which was occupied by half a dozen Irishmen in knee-breeches and heavy brogans. As we passed out of the Clarence Dock at 10 P.M., I went below and managed to get a seat on one end of the bench, where I spent the night in sleepless misery. The Irish bestowed themselves about the floor as they best could, for there was no light, and very soon the Morphean deepness of their breathing gave token of blissful unconsciousness.

The next morning was misty and rainy, but I preferred walking the deck and drying myself occasionally beside the chimney, to sitting in the dismal room below. We passed the Isle of Man, and through the whole forenoon were tossed about very disagreeably in the North Channel. In the afternoon we stopped at Larne, a little antiquated village, not far from Belfast, at the head of a crooked arm of the sea. There is an old ivy-grown tower near, and high green mountains rise up around. After leaving it, we had a beautiful panoramic view of the northern coast. Many of the precipices are of the same formation as the Causeway; Fairhead, a promontory of this kind, is grand in the extreme. The perpendicular face of fluted rock is about three hundred feet in height, and towering up sublimely from the water, seemed almost to overhang our heads.

My companion compared it to Niagara Falls petrified; and I think the simile very striking. It is like a cataract falling in huge waves, in some places leaping out from a projecting rock, in others descending in an unbroken sheet.

We passed the Giant's Causeway after dark, and about eleven o'clock reached the harbor of Port Rush, where, after stumbling up a strange old street, in the dark, we found a little inn, and soon forgot the Irish Coast and everything else.

In the morning when we arose it was raining, with little prospect of fair weather, but having expected nothing better, we set out on foot for the Causeway. The rain, however, soon came down in torrents, and we were obliged to take shelter in a cabin by the road-side. The whole house consisted of one room, with bare walls and roof, and earthen floor, while a window of three or four panes supplied the light. A fire of peat was burning on the hearth, and their breakfast, of potatoes alone, stood on the table. The occupants received us with rude but genuine hospitality, giving us the only seats in the room to sit upon; except a rickety bedstead that stood in one corner and a small table, there was no other furniture in the house. The man appeared rather intelligent, and although he complained of the hardness of their lot, had no sympathy with O'Connell or the Repeal movement.

We left this miserable hut, as soon as it ceased raining—and, though there were many cabins along the road, few were better than this. At length, after passing the walls of an old church, in the midst of older tombs, we saw the roofless towers of Dunluce Castle, on the sea-shore. It stands on an isolated rook, rising perpendicularly two hundred feet above the sea, and connected with the cliffs of the mainland by a narrow arch of masonry. On the summit of the cliffs were the remains of the buildings where the ancient lords kept their vassals. An old man, who takes care of it for Lord Antrim, on whose property it is situated, showed us the way down to the castle. We walked across the narrow arch, entered the ruined hall, and looked down on the roaring sea below. It still rained, the wind swept furiously through the decaying arches of the banqueting hall and waved the long grass on the desolate battlements. Far below, the sea foamed white on the breakers and sent up an unceasing boom. It was the most mournful and desolate picture I ever beheld. There were some low dungeons yet entire, and rude stairways, where, by stooping down, I could ascend nearly to the top of one of the towers, and look out on the wild scenery of the coast.

Going back, I found a way down the cliff, to the mouth of a cavern in the rock, which extends under the whole castle to the sea. Sliding down a heap of sand and stones, I stood under an arch eighty feet high; in front the breakers dashed into the entrance, flinging the spray half-way to the roof, while the sound rang up through the arches like thunder. It seemed to me the haunt of the old Norsemen's sea-gods!

We left the road near Dunluce and walked along the smooth beach to the cliffs that surround the Causeway. Here we obtained a guide, and descended to one of the caves which can be entered from the shore. Opposite the entrance a bare rock called Sea Gull Isle, rises out of the sea like a church steeple. The roof at first was low, but we shortly came to a branch that opened on the sea, where the arch was forty-six feet in height. The breakers dashed far into the cave, and flocks of sea-birds circled round its mouth. The sound of a gun was like a deafening peal of thunder, crashing from arch to arch till it rolled out of the cavern.

On the top of the hill a splendid hotel is erected for visitors to the Causeway; after passing this we descended to the base of the cliffs, which are here upwards of four hundred feet high, and soon began to find, in the columnar formation of the rocks, indications of our approach. The guide pointed out some columns which appeared to have been melted and run together, from which Sir Humphrey Davy attributed the formation of the Causeway to the action of fire. Near this is the Giant's Well, a spring of the purest water, the bottom formed by three perfect hexagons, and the sides of regular columns. One of us observing that no giant had ever drunk from it, the old man answered—"Perhaps not: but it was made by a giant—God Almighty!"

From the well, the Causeway commences—a mass of columns, from triangular to octagonal, lying in compact forms, and extending into the sea. I was somewhat disappointed at first, having supposed the Causeway to be of great height, but I found the Giant's Loom, which is the highest part of it, to be but about fifty feet from the water. The singular appearance of the columns and the many strange forms which they assume, render it nevertheless, an object of the greatest interest. Walking out on the rocks we came to the Ladies' Chair, the seat, back, sides and footstool, being all regularly formed by the broken columns. The guide said that any lady who would take three drinks from the Giant's Well, then sit in this chair and think of any gentleman for whom she had a preference, would be married before a twelvemonth. I asked him if it would answer as well for gentlemen, for by a wonderful coincidence we had each drank three times at the well! He said it would, and thought he was confirming his statement.

A cluster of columns about half-way up the cliff is called the Giant's Organ—from its very striking resemblance to that instrument, and a single rock, worn by the waves into the shape of a rude seat, is his chair. A mile or two further along the coast, two cliffs project from the range, leaving a vast semicircular space between, which, from its resemblance to the old Roman theatres, was appropriated for that purpose by the Giant. Halfway down the crags are two or three pinnacles of rock, called the Chimneys, and the stumps of several others can be seen, which, it is said, were shot off by a vessel belonging to the Spanish Armada, in mistake for the towers of Dunluce Castle. The vessel was afterwards wrecked in the bay below, which has ever since been called Spanish Bay, and in calm weather the wreck may be still seen. Many of the columns of the Causeway have been carried off and sold as pillars for mantels—and though a notice is put up threatening any one with the rigor of the law, depredations are occasionally made.

Returning, we left the road at Dunluce, and took a path which led along the summit of the cliffs. The twilight was gathering, and the wind blew with perfect fury, which, combined with the black and stormy sky, gave the coast an air of extreme wildness. All at once, as we followed the winding path, the crags appeared to open before us, disclosing a yawning chasm, down which a large stream, falling in an unbroken sheet, was lost in the gloom below. Witnessed in a calm day, there may perhaps be nothing striking about it, but coming upon us at once, through the gloom of twilight, with the sea thundering below and a scowling sky above, it was absolutely startling.

The path at last wound, with many a steep and slippery bend, down the almost perpendicular crags, to the shore, at the foot of a giant isolated rock, having a natural arch through it, eighty feet in height. We followed the narrow strip of beach, having the bare crags on one side and a line of foaming breakers on the other. It soon grew dark; a furious storm came up and swept like a hurricane along the shore. I then understood what Horne means by "the lengthening javelins of the blast," for every drop seemed to strike with the force of an arrow, and our clothes were soon pierced in every part.

Then we went up among the sand hills, and lost each other in the darkness, when, after stumbling about among the gullies for half an hour, shouting for my companions, I found the road and heard my call answered; but it happened to be two Irishmen, who came up and said—"And is it another gintleman ye're callin' for? we heard some one cryin', and didn't know but somebody might be kilt."

Finally, about eleven o'clock we all arrived at the inn, dripping with rain, and before a warm fire concluded the adventures of our day in Ireland.

# CHAPTER III. — BEN LOMOND AND THE HIGHLAND LAKES.

The steamboat Londonderry called the next day at Port Rush, and we left in her for Greenock. We ran down the Irish coast, past Dunluce Castle and the Causeway; the Giant's organ was very plainly visible, and the winds were strong enough to have sounded a storm-song upon it. Farther on we had a distant view of Carrick-a-Rede, a precipitous rock, separated by a yawning chasm from the shore, frequented by the catchers of sea-birds. A narrow swinging bridge, which is only passable in calm weather, crosses this chasm, 200 feet above the water.

The deck of the steamer was crowded with Irish, and certainly gave no very favorable impression of the condition of the peasantry of Ireland. On many of their countenances there was scarcely a mark of intelligence—they were a most brutalized and degraded company of beings. Many of them were in a beastly state of intoxication, which, from the contents of some of their pockets, was not likely to decrease. As evening drew on, two or three began singing and the others collected in groups around them. One of them who sang with great spirit, was loudly applauded, and poured forth song after song, of the most rude and unrefined character.

We took a deck passage for three shillings, in preference to paying twenty for the cabin, and having secured a vacant place near the chimney, kept it during the whole passage. The waves were as rough in the Channel as I ever saw them in the Atlantic, and our boat was tossed about like a plaything. By keeping still we escaped sickness, but we could not avoid the sight of the miserable beings who filled the deck. Many of them spoke in the Irish tongue, and our German friend (the student whom I have already mentioned) noticed in many of the words a resemblance to his mother tongue. I procured a bowl of soup from the steward, but as I was not able to eat it, I gave it to an old man whose hungry look and wistful eyes convinced me it would not be lost on him. He swallowed it with ravenous avidity, together with a crust of bread, which was all I had to give him, and seemed for the time as happy and cheerful as if all his earthly wants were satisfied.

We passed by the foot of Goat Fell, a lofty mountain on the island of
Arran, and sped on through the darkness past the hills of Bute, till we entered
the Clyde. We arrived at Greenock at one o'clock at night, and walking at
random through its silent streets, met a policeman, whom we asked to show
us where we might find lodgings. He took my cousin and myself to the house
of a poor widow, who had a spare bed which she let to strangers, and then
conducted our comrade and the German to another lodging-place.

An Irish strolling musician, who was on board the Dumbarton boat,
commenced playing soon after we left Greenock, and, to my surprise, struck
at once into "Hail Columbia." Then he gave "the Exile of Erin," with the
most touching sweetness; and I noticed that always after playing any air that
was desired of him, he would invariably return to the sad lament, which I
never heard executed with more feeling. It might have been the mild, soft air
of the morning, or some peculiar mood of mind that influenced me, but I
have been far less affected by music which would be considered immeasurably
superior to his. I had been thinking of America, and going up to the old man,
I quietly bade him play "Home." It thrilled with a painful delight that almost
brought tears to my eyes. My companion started as the sweet melody arose,
and turned towards me, his face kindling with emotion.

Dumbarton Rock rose higher and higher as we went up the Clyde,
and before we arrived at the town I hailed the dim outline of Ben Lomond,
rising far off among the highlands. The town is at the head of a small inlet,
a short distance from the rock, which was once surrounded by water. We
went immediately to the Castle. The rock is nearly 500 feet high, and from
its position and great strength as a fortress, has been called the Gibraltar
of Scotland. The top is surrounded with battlements, and the armory and
barracks stand in a cleft between the two peaks. We passed down a green lane,
around the rock, and entered the castle on the south side. A soldier conducted
us through a narrow cleft, overhung with crags, to the summit. Here, from
the remains of a round building, called Wallace's Tower, from its having been
used as a look-out station by that chieftain, we had a beautiful view of the
whole of Leven Vale to Loch Lomond, Ben Lomond and the Highlands,
and on the other hand, the Clyde and the Isle of Bute. In the soft and still

balminess of the morning, it was a lovely picture. In the armory, I lifted the sword of Wallace, a two-handed weapon, five feet in length. We were also shown a Lochaber battle-axe, from Bannockburn, and several ancient claymores.

We lingered long upon the summit before we forsook the stern fortress for the sweet vale spread out before us. It was indeed a glorious walk, from Dumbarton to Loch Lomond, through this enchanting valley. The air was mild and clear; a few light clouds occasionally crossing the sun, chequered the hills with sun and shade. I have as yet seen nothing that in pastoral beauty can compare with its glassy winding stream, its mossy old woods, and guarding hills—and the ivy-grown, castellated towers embosomed in its forests, or standing on the banks of the Leven—the purest of rivers. At a little village called Renton, is a monument to Smollett, but the inhabitants seem to neglect his memory, as one of the tablets on the pedestal is broken and half fallen away. Further up the vale a farmer showed us an old mansion in the midst of a group of trees on the bank of the Leven, which he said belonged to Smollett—or Roderick Random, as he called him. Two or three old pear trees were still standing where the garden had formerly been, under which he was accustomed to play in his childhood.

At the head of Leven Vale, we set off in the steamer "Water Witch" over the crystal waters of Loch Lomond, passing Inch Murrin, the deer-park of the Duke of Montrose, and Inch Caillach,

——*"where gray pines wave*

*Their shadows o'er Clan Alpine's grave."*

Under the clear sky and golden light of the declining sun, we entered the Highlands, and heard on every side names we had learned long ago in the lays of Scott. Here were Glen Fruin and Bannochar, Ross Dhu and the pass of Beal-ma-na. Further still, we passed Rob Roy's rock, where the lake is locked in by lofty mountains. The cone-like peak of Ben Lomond rises far above on the right, Ben Voirlich stands in front, and the jagged crest of Ben Arthur looks over the shoulders of the western hills. A Scotchman on board pointed out to us the remarkable places, and related many interesting legends. Above

Inversnaid, where there is a beautiful waterfall, leaping over the rock and glancing out from the overhanging birches, we passed McFarland's Island, concerning the origin of which name, he gave a history. A nephew of one of the old Earls of Lennox, the ruins of whose castle we saw on Inch Murrin, having murdered his uncle's cook in a quarrel, was obliged to flee for his life. Returning after many years, he built a castle upon this island, which was always after named, on account of his exile, Far-land. On a precipitous point above Inversnaid, are two caves in the rock; one near the water is called Rob Roy's, though the guides generally call it Bruce's also, to avoid trouble, as the real Bruce's Cave is high up the hill. It is so called, because Bruce hid there one night, from the pursuit of his enemies. It is related that a mountain goat, who used this probably for a sleeping place, entered, trod on his mantle, and aroused him. Thinking his enemies were upon him, he sprang up, and saw the silly animal before him. In token of gratitude for this agreeable surprise, when he became king, a law was passed, declaring goats free throughout all Scotland—unpunishable for whatever trespass they might commit, and the legend further says, that not having been repealed, it continues in force at the present day.

On the opposite shore of the lake is a large rock, called "Bull's Rock," having a door in the side, with a stairway cut through the interior to a pulpit on the top, from which the pastor at Arroquhar preaches a monthly discourse. The Gaelic legend of the rock is, that it once stood near the summit of the mountain above, and was very nearly balanced on the edge of a precipice. Two wild bulls, fighting violently, dashed with great force against the rock, which, being thrown from its balance, was tumbled down the side of the mountain, till it reached its present position. The Scot was speaking with great bitterness of the betrayal of Wallace, when I asked him if it was still considered an insult to turn a loaf of bread bottom upwards in the presence of a Montieth. "Indeed it is, sir," said he, "I have often done it myself."

Until last May, travellers were taken no higher up the lake than Rob Roy's Cave, but another boat having commenced running, they can now go beyond Loch Lomond, two miles up Glen Falloch, to the Inn of Inverarnan, thereby visiting some of the finest scenery in that part of the Highlands. It was ludicrous, however, to see the steamboat on a river scarcely wider than herself, in a little valley, hemmed in completely with lofty mountains. She went on, however, pushing aside the thickets which lined both banks, and I almost began to think she was going to take the shore for it, when we came to a place widened out for her to be turned around in; here we jumped ashore in a green meadow, on which the cool mist was beginning to descend.

When we arose in the morning, at 4 o'clock, to return with the boat, the sun was already shining upon the westward hills, scarcely a cloud was in the sky, and the air was pure and cool. To our great delight Ben Lomond was unshrouded, and we were told that a more favorable day for the ascent had not occurred for two months. We left the boat at Rowardennan, an inn at the southern base of Ben Lomond. After breakfasting on Loch Lomond trout, I stole out to the shore while my companions were preparing for the ascent, and made a hasty sketch of the lake.

We purposed descending on the northern side and crossing the Highlands to Loch Katrine; though it was represented as difficult and dangerous by the guide who wished to accompany us, we determined to run the risk of being enveloped in a cloud on the summit, and so set out alone, the path appearing plain before us. We had no difficulty in following it up the lesser heights, around the base. It wound on, over rock and bog, among the heather and broom with which the mountain is covered, sometimes running up a steep acclivity, and then winding zigzag round a rocky ascent. The rains two days before, had made the bogs damp and muddy, but with this exception, we had little trouble for some time. Ben Lomond is a doubly formed mountain. For about three-fourths of the way there is a continued ascent, when it is suddenly terminated by a large barren plain, from one end of which the summit shoots up abruptly, forming at the north side, a precipice 500 feet high. As we approached the summit of the first part of the mountain, the way became very steep and toilsome; but the prospect, which had before been only on the south side, began to open on the east, and we saw suddenly spread out below us, the vale of Menteith, with "far Loch Ard and Aberfoil" in the centre, and the huge front of Benvenue filling up the picture. Taking courage from this, we hurried on. The heather had become stunted and dwarfish, and the ground was covered with short brown grass. The mountain sheep, which we saw looking at us from the rock above, had worn so many paths along the side, that we could not tell which to take, but pushed on in the direction of the summit, till thinking it must be near at hand, we found a mile and a half of plain before us, with the top of Ben Lomond at the farther end. The plain was full of wet moss, crossed in all directions by deep ravines or gullies worn in it by the mountain rains, and the wind swept across with a tempest-like force.

I met, near the base, a young gentleman from Edinburgh, who had left Rowardennan before us, and we commenced ascending together. It was hard work, but neither liked to stop, so we climbed up to the first resting place, and found the path leading along the brink of a precipice. We soon attained the summit, and climbing up a little mound of earth and stones, I saw the half of Scotland at a glance. The clouds hung just above the mountain tops, which rose all around like the waves of a mighty sea. On every side—near and far—stood their misty summits, but Ben Lomond was the monarch of them all. Loch Lomond lay unrolled under my feet like a beautiful map, and just opposite, Loch Long thrust its head from between the feet of the crowded hills, to catch a glimpse of the giant. We could see from Ben Nevis to Ayr—from Edinburgh to Staffa. Stirling and Edinburgh Castles would have been visible, but that the clouds hung low in the valley of the Forth and hid them from our sight.

The view from Ben Lomond is nearly twice as extensive as that from Catskill, being uninterrupted on every side, but it wants the glorious forest scenery, clear, blue sky, and active, rejoicing character of the latter. We stayed about two hours upon the summit, taking refuge behind the cairn, when the wind blew strong. I found the smallest of flowers under a rock, and brought it away as a memento. In the middle of the precipice there is a narrow ravine or rather cleft in the rock, to the bottom, from whence the mountain slopes regularly but steeply down to the valley. At the bottom we stopped to awake the echoes, which were repeated four times; our German companion sang the Hunter's Chorus, which resounded magnificently through this Highland hall. We drank from the river Forth, which starts from a spring at the foot of the rock, and then commenced descending. This was also toilsome enough. The mountain was quite wet and covered with loose stones, which, dislodged by our feet, went rattling down the side, oftentimes to the danger of the foremost ones; and when we had run or rather slid down the three miles, to the bottom, our knees trembled so as scarcely to support us.

Here, at a cottage on the farm of Coman, we procured some oat cakes and milk for dinner, from an old Scotch woman, who pointed out the direction of Loch Katrine, six miles distant; there was no road, nor indeed a solitary dwelling between. The hills were bare of trees, covered with scraggy bushes and rough heath, which in some places was so thick we could scarcely drag our feet through. Added to this, the ground was covered with a kind of moss that retained the moisture like a sponge, so that our boots ere long became thoroughly soaked. Several considerable streams were rushing down the side, and many of the wild breed of black Highland cattle were grazing around. After climbing up and down one or two heights, occasionally startling the moorcock and ptarmigan from their heathery coverts, we saw the valley of Loch Con; while in the middle of the plain on the top of the mountain we had ascended, was a sheet of water which we took to be Loch Ackill. Two or three wild fowl swimming on its surface were the only living things in sight. The peaks around shut it out from all view of the world; a single decayed tree leaned over it from a mossy rock, which gave the whole scene an air of the most desolate wildness. I forget the name of the lake; but we learned afterwards that the Highlanders consider it the abode of the fairies, or "men of peace," and that it is still superstitiously shunned by them after nightfall.

From the next mountain we saw Loch Ackill and Loch Katrine below, but a wet and weary descent had yet to be made. I was about throwing off my knapsack on a rock, to take a sketch of Loch Katrine, which appeared very beautiful from this point, when we discerned a cavalcade of ponies winding along the path from Inversnaid, to the head of the lake, and hastened down to take the boat when they should arrive. Our haste turned out to be unnecessary, however, for they had to wait for their luggage, which was long in coming. Two boatmen then offered to take us for two shillings and sixpence each, with the privilege of stopping at Ellen's Isle; the regular fare being two shillings.

We got in, when, after exchanging a few words in Gaelic, one of them called to the travellers, of whom there were a number, to come and take passage at two shillings—then at one and sixpence, and finally concluded by requesting them all to step on board the shilling boat! At length, having secured nine at this reduced price, we pushed off; one of the passengers took the helm, and the boat glided merrily over the clear water.

It appears there is some opposition among the boatmen this summer, which is all the better for travelers. They are a bold race, and still preserve many of the characteristics of the clan from which they sprung. One of ours, who had a chieftain-like look, was a MacGregor, related to Rob Roy. The fourth descendant in a direct line, now inhabits the Rob Roy mansion, at Glengyle, a valley at the head of the lake. A small steamboat was put upon Loch Katrine a short time ago, but the boatmen, jealous of this new invasion of their privilege, one night towed her out to the middle of the lake and there sunk her.

Near the point of Brianchoil is a very small island with a few trees upon it, of which the boatman related a story that was new to me. He said an eccentric individual, many years ago, built his house upon it—but it was soon beaten down by the winds and waves. Having built it up with like fortune several times, he at last desisted, saying, "bought wisdom was the best;" since when it has been called the Island of Wisdom. On the shore below, the boatman showed us his cottage. The whole family were out at the door to witness our progress; he hoisted a flag, and when we came opposite, they exchanged shouts in Gaelic. As our men resumed their oars again, we assisted in giving three cheers, which made the echoes of Benvenue ring again. Some one observed his dog, looking after us from a projecting rock, when he called out to him, "go home, you brute!" We asked him why he did not speak Gaelic also to his dog.

"Very few dogs, indeed," said he, "understand Gaelic, but they all understand English. And we therefore all use English when speaking to our dogs; indeed, I know some persons, who know nothing of English, that speak it to their dogs!"

They then sang, in a rude manner, a Gaelic song. The only word I could distinguish was Inch Caillach, the burying place of Clan Alpine. They told us it was the answer of a Highland girl to a foreign lord, who wished to make her his bride. Perhaps, like the American Indian, she would not leave the graves of her fathers. As we drew near the eastern end of the lake, the scenery became far more beautiful. The Trosachs opened before us. Ben Ledi looked down over the "forehead bare" of Ben An, and, as we turned a rocky point, Ellen's Isle rose up in front. It is a beautiful little turquoise in the silver setting of Loch Katrine. The northern side alone is accessible, all the others being rocky and perpendicular, and thickly grown with trees. We rounded the island to the little bay, bordered by the silver strand, above which is the rock from which Fitz-James wound his horn, and shot under an ancient oak which flung its long grey arms over the water; we here found a flight of rocky steps, leading to the top, where stood the bower erected by Lady Willoughby D'Eresby, to correspond with Scott's description. Two or three blackened beams are all that remain of it, having been burned down some years ago, by the carelessness of a traveler.

The mountains stand all around, like giants, to "sentinel this enchanted land." On leaving the island, we saw the Goblin's Cave, in the side of Benvenue, called by the Gaels, "Coirnan-Uriskin." Near it is Beal-nam-bo, the pass of cattle, overhung with grey weeping birch trees. Here the boatmen stopped to let us hear the fine echo, and the names of "Rob Roy," and "Roderick Dhu," were sent back to us apparently as loud as they were given. The description of Scott is wonderfully exact, though the forest that feathered o'er the sides of Benvenue, has since been cut down and sold by the Duke of Montrose. When we reached the end of the lake it commenced raining, and we hastened on through the pass of Beal-an-Duine, scarcely taking time to glance at the scenery, till Loch Achray appeared through the trees, and on its banks the ivy-grown front of the inn of Ardcheancrochan, with its unpronounceable name.

# CHAPTER IV. — THE BURNS FESTIVAL.

We passed a glorious summer morning on the banks of Loch Katrine. The air was pure, fresh and balmy, and the warm sunshine glowed upon forest and lake, upon dark crag and purple mountain-top. The lake was a scene in fairy-land. Returning over the rugged battle-plain in the jaws of the Trosachs, we passed the wild, lonely valley of Glenfinlas and Lanric Mead, at the head of Loch Vennachar, rounding the foot of Ben Ledi to Coilantogle Ford. We saw the desolate hills of Uam-var over which the stag fled from his lair in Glenartney, and keeping on through Callander, stopped for the night at a little inn on the banks of the Teith. The next day we walked through Doune, over the lowlands to Stirling. Crossing Allan Water and the Forth, we climbed Stirling Castle and looked on the purple peaks of the Ochill Mountains, the far Grampians, and the battle-fields of Bannockburn and Sheriff Muir. Our German comrade, feeling little interest in the memory of the poet-ploughman, left in the steamboat for Edinburg; we mounted an English coach and rode to Falkirk, where we took the cars for Glasgow in order to attend the Burns Festival, on the 6th of August.

This was a great day for Scotland—the assembling of all classes to do honor to the memory of her peasant-bard. And right fitting was it, too, that such a meeting should be hold on the banks of the Doon, the stream of which he has sung so sweetly, within sight of the cot where he was born, the beautiful monument erected by his countrymen, and more than all, beside "Alloway's witch-haunted wall!" One would think old Albyn would rise up at the call, and that from the wild hunters of the northern hills to the shepherds of the Cheviots, half her honest yeomanry would be there, to render gratitude to the memory of the sweet bard who was one of them, and who gave their wants and their woes such eloquent utterance.

For months before had the proposition been made to hold a meeting on the Doon, similar to the Shakspeare Festival on the Avon, and the 10th of July was first appointed for the day, but owing to the necessity of further time for preparation, it was postponed until the 6th of August. The Earl of Eglintoun was chosen Chairman, and Professor Wilson Vice-Chairman; in addition to this, all the most eminent British authors were invited to attend. A pavilion, capable of containing two thousand persons, had been erected near the monument, in a large field, which was thrown open to the public. Other preparations were made and the meeting was expected to be of the most interesting character.

When we arose it was raining, and I feared that the weather might dampen somewhat the pleasures of the day, as it had done to the celebrated tournament at Eglintoun Castle. We reached the station in time for the first train, and sped in the face of the wind over the plains of Ayrshire, which, under such a gloomy sky, looked most desolate. We ran some distance along the coast, having a view of the Hills of Arran, and reached Ayr about nine o'clock. We came first to the New Bridge, which had a triumphal arch in the middle, and the lines, from the "Twa Brigs of Ayr:"

*"Will your poor narrow foot-path of a street,*

*Where twa wheel-barrows tremble when they meet,*

*Your ruin'd, formless bulk o' stane and lime,*

*Compare wi' bonnie brigs o' modern time?"*

While on the arch of the 'old brig' was the reply:

*"I'll be a brig when ye're a shapeless stane."*

As we advanced into the town, the decorations became more frequent. The streets were crowded with people carrying banners and wreaths, many of the houses were adorned with green boughs and the vessels in the harbor hung out all their flags. We saw the Wallace Tower, a high Gothic building, having in front a statue of Wallace leaning on his sword, by Thom, a native of Ayr, and on our way to the green, where the procession was to assemble, passed under the triumphal arch thrown across the street opposite the inn where Tarn O'Shanter caroused so long with Souter Johnny. Leaving the companies to form on the long meadow bordering the shore, we set out for

45

the Doon, three miles distant. Beggars were seated at regular distances along the road, uttering the most dolorous whinings. Both bridges were decorated in the same manner, with miserable looking objects, keeping up, during the whole day, a continual lamentation. Persons are prohibited from begging in England and Scotland, but I suppose, this being an extraordinary day, license was given them as a favor, to beg free. I noticed that the women, with their usual kindness of heart, bestowed nearly all the alms which these unfortunate objects received. The night before, as I was walking through the streets of Glasgow, a young man of the poorer class, very scantily dressed, stepped up to me and begged me to listen to him for a moment. He spoke hurriedly, and agitatedly, begging me, in God's name, to give him something, however little. I gave him what few pence I had with me, when he grasped my hand with a quick motion, saying: "Sir, you little think how much you have done for me." I was about to inquire more particularly into his situation, but he had disappeared among the crowd.

We passed the "cairn where hunters found the murdered bairn," along a pleasant road to the Burns cottage, where it was spanned by a magnificent triumphal arch of evergreens and flowers. To the disgrace of Scotland, this neat little thatched cot, where Burns passed the first seven years of his life, is now occupied by somebody, who has stuck up a sign over the door, "licensed to retail spirits, to be drunk on the premises;" and accordingly the rooms were crowded full of people, all drinking. There was a fine original portrait of Burns in one room, and in the old fashioned kitchen we saw the recess where he was born. The hostess looked towards us as if to inquire what we would drink, and I hastened away—there was profanity in the thought. But by this time, the bell of Old Alloway, which still hangs in its accustomed place, though the walls only are left, began tolling, and we obeyed the call. The attachment of the people for this bell, is so great, that a short time ago, when it was ordered to be removed, the inhabitants rose en masse, and prevented it. The ruin, which is close by the road, stands in the middle of the church-yard, and the first thing I saw, on going in the gate, was the tomb of the father of Burns. I looked in the old window, but the interior was filled with rank weeds, and overshadowed by a young tree, which had grown nearly to the eaves.

The crowd was now fast gathering in the large field, in the midst of which the pavilion was situated. We went down by the beautiful monument to Burns, to the "Auld Brig o' Doon," which was spanned by an arch of evergreens, containing a representation of Tam O'Shanter and his grey mare, pursued by the witches. It had been arranged that the procession was to pass over the old and new bridges, and from thence by a temporary bridge over the hedge into the field. At this latter place a stand was erected for the sons of Burns, the officers of the day, and distinguished guests. Here was a beautiful specimen of English exclusiveness. The space adjoining the pavilion was fenced around, and admittance denied at first to any, except those who had tickets for the dinner, which, the price being fifteen shillings, entirely prevented the humble laborers, who, more than all, should participate on the occasion, from witnessing the review of the procession by the sons of Burns, and hearing the eloquent speeches of Professor Wilson and Lord Eglintoun. Thus, of the many thousands who were in the field, but a few hundred who were crowded between the bridge and the railing around the pavilion, enjoyed the interesting spectacle. By good fortune, I obtained a stand, where I had an excellent view of the scene. The sons of Burns were in the middle of the platform, with Eglintoun on the right, and Wilson on their left. Mrs. Begg, sister of the Poet, with her daughters, stood by the Countess of Eglintoun. She was a plain, benevolent looking woman, dressed in black, and appearing still active and vigorous, though she is upwards of eighty years old. She bears some likeness, especially in the expression of her eye, to the Poet. Robert Burns, the oldest son, appeared to me to have a strong resemblance of his father, and it is said he is the only one who remembers his face. He has for a long time had an office under Government, in London. The others have but lately returned from a residence of twenty years in India. Professor Wilson appeared to enter into the spirit of the scene better than any of them. He shouted and waved his hat, and, with his fine, broad forehead, his long brown locks already mixed with gray, streaming over his shoulders, and that eagle eye glancing over the vast assemblage, seemed a real Christopher North, yet full of the fire and vigor of youth—"a gray-haired, happy boy!"

About half of the procession consisted of lodges of masons, all of whom turned out on the occasion, as Burns was one of the fraternity. I was most interested in several companies of shepherds, from the hills, with their crooks and plaids; a body of archers in Lincoln green, with a handsome chief at their head, and some Highlanders in their most picturesque of costumes. As one of the companies, which carried a mammoth thistle in a box, came near the platform, Wilson snatched a branch, regardless of its pricks, and placed it on his coat. After this pageant, which could not have been much less than three miles long, had passed, a band was stationed on the platform in the centre of the field, around which it formed in a circle, and the whole company sang, "Ye Banks and Braes o' Bonnie Doon." Just at this time, a person dressed to represent Tam O'Shanter, mounted on a gray mare, issued from a field near the Burns Monument and rode along towards Alloway Kirk, from which, when he approached it, a whole legion of witches sallied out and commenced a hot pursuit. They turned back, however, at the keystone of the bridge, the witch with the "cutty sark" holding up in triumph the abstracted tail of Maggie. Soon after this the company entered the pavilion, and the thousands outside were entertained, as an especial favor, by the band of the 87th Regiment, while from the many liquor booths around the field, they could enjoy themselves in another way.

We went up to the Monument, which was of more particular interest to us, from the relics within, but admission was denied to all. Many persons were collected around the gate, some of whom, having come from a great distance, were anxious to see it; but the keeper only said, such were the orders and he could not disobey them. Among the crowd, a grandson of the original Tam O'Shanter was shown to us. He was a raw-looking boy of nineteen or twenty, wearing a shepherd's cap and jacket, and muttered his disapprobation very decidedly, at not being able to visit the Monument.

There were one or two showers during the day, and the sky, all the time, was dark and lowering, which was unfavorable for the celebration; but all were glad enough that the rain kept aloof till the ceremonies were nearly over. The speeches delivered at the dinner, which appeared in the papers next morning, are undoubtedly very eloquent. I noticed in the remarks of Robert Burns, in reply to Professor Wilson, an acknowledgment which the other speakers forgot. He said, "The Sons of Burns have grateful hearts, and to the last hour of their existence, they will remember the honor that has been paid them this day, by the noble, the lovely and the talented, of their native land—by men of genius and kindred spirit from our sister land—and lastly, they owe their thanks to the inhabitants of the far distant west, a country of a great, free, and kindred people! (loud cheers.)" In connexion with this subject, I saw an anecdote of the Poet, yesterday, which is not generally known. During his connexion with the Excise, he was one day at a party, where the health of Pitt, then minister, was proposed, as "his master and theirs." He immediately turned down his glass and said, "I will give you the health of a far greater and better man—GEORGE WASHINGTON!"

We left the field early and went back through the muddy streets of Ayr. The street before the railway office was crowded, and there was so dense a mass of people on the steps, that it seemed almost impossible to get near. Seeing no other chance, I managed to take my stand on the lowest steps, where the pressure of the crowd behind and the working of the throng on the steps, raised me off my feet, and in about a quarter of an hour carried me, compressed into the smallest possible space, up the steps to the door, where the crowd burst in by fits, like water rushing out of a bottle. We esteemed ourselves fortunate in getting room to stand in an open car, where, after a two hours' ride through the wind and pelting rain, we arrived at Glasgow.

# CHAPTER V. — WALK FROM EDINBURG OVER THE BORDER AND ARRIVAL AT LONDON.

We left Glasgow on the morning after returning from the Burns Festival, taking passage in the open cars for Edinburg, for six shillings. On leaving the depot, we plunged into the heart of the hill on which Glasgow Cathedral stands and were whisked through darkness and sulphury smoke to daylight again. The cars bore us past a spur of the Highlands, through a beautiful country where women were at work in the fields, to Linlithgow, the birth-place of Queen Mary. The majestic ruins of its once-proud palace, stand on a green meadow behind the town. In another hour we were walking through Edinburg, admiring its palace-like edifices, and stopping every few minutes to gaze up at some lofty monument. Really, thought I, we call Baltimore the "Monumental City" for its two marble columns, and here is Edinburg with one at every street-corner! These, too, not in the midst of glaring red buildings, where they seem to have been accidentally dropped, but framed in by lofty granite mansions, whose long vistas make an appropriate background to the picture.

We looked from Calton Hill on Salisbury Crags and over the Firth of Forth, then descended to dark old Holyrood, where the memory of lovely Mary lingers like a stray sunbeam in her cold halls, and the fair, boyish face of Rizzio looks down from the canvass on the armor of his murderer. We threaded the Canongate and climbed to the Castle; and finally, after a day and a half's sojourn, buckled on our knapsacks and marched out of the Northern Athens. In a short time the tall spire of Dalkeith appeared above the green wood, and we saw to the right, perched on the steep banks of the Esk, the picturesque cottage of Hawthornden, where Drummond once lived in poetic solitude. We made haste to cross the dreary waste of the Muirfoot Hills before nightfall, from the highest summit of which we took a last view of Edinburg Castle and the Salisbury Crags, then blue in the distance. Far to the east were the hills of Lammermuir and the country of Mid-Lothian lay before us. It was all Scott-land. The inn of Torsonce, beside the Gala Water, was our resting-place for the night. As we approached Galashiels the next morning, where the bed of the silver Gala is nearly emptied by a number of dingy manufactories, the hills opened, disclosing the sweet vale of the Tweed, guarded by the triple peak of the Eildon, at whose base lay nestled the village of Melrose.

I stopped at a bookstore to purchase a view of the Abbey; to my surprise nearly half the works were by American authors. There wore Bryant, Longfellow, Channing, Emerson, Dana, Ware and many others. The bookseller told me he had sold more of Ware's Letters than any other book in his store, "and also," to use his own words, "an immense number of the great Dr. Channing." I have seen English editions of Percival, Willis, Whittier and Mrs. Sigourney, but Bancroft and Prescott are classed among the "standard British historians."

Crossing the Gala we ascended a hill on the road to Selkirk, and behold! the Tweed ran below, and opposite, in the midst of embowering trees planted by the hand of Scott, rose the grey halls of Abbotsford. We went down a lane to the banks of the swift stream, but finding no ferry, B—— and I, as it looked very shallow, thought we might save a long walk by wading across. F—— preferred hunting for a boat; we two set out together, with our knapsacks on our backs, and our boots in our hands. The current was ice-cold and very swift, and as the bed was covered with loose stones, it required the greatest care to stand upright. Looking at the bottom, through the rapid water, made my head so giddy, I was forced to stop and shut my eyes; my friend, who had firmer nerves, went plunging on to a deeper and swifter part, where the strength of the current made him stagger very unpleasantly. I called to him to return; the next thing I saw, he gave a plunge and went down to the shoulder in the cold flood. While he was struggling with a frightened expression of face to recover his footing, I leaned on my staff and laughed till I was on the point of falling also. To crown our mortification, F—— had found a ferry a few yards higher up and was on the opposite shore, watching us wade back again, my friend with dripping clothes and boots full of water. I could not forgive the pretty Scotch damsel who rowed us across, the mischievous lurking smile which told that she too had witnessed the adventure.

We found a foot-path on the other side, which led through a young forest to Abbotsford. Rude pieces of sculpture, taken from Melrose Abbey, were scattered around the gate, some half buried in the earth and overgrown with weeds. The niches in the walls were filled with pieces of sculpture, and an antique marble greyhound reposed in the middle of the court yard. We rang the bell in an outer vestibule, ornamented with several pairs of antlers, when a lady appeared, who, from her appearance, I have no doubt was Mrs. Ormand, the "Duenna of Abbotsford," so humorously described by D'Arlincourt, in his "Three Kingdoms." She ushered us into the entrance hall, which has a magnificent ceiling of carved oak and is lighted by lofty stained windows. An effigy of a knight in armor stood at either end, one holding a huge two-handed sword found on Bosworth Field; the walls were covered with helmets and breastplates of the olden time.

Among the curiosities in the Armory are Napoleon's pistols, the blunderbuss of Hofer, Rob Roy's purse and gun, and the offering box of Queen Mary. Through the folding doors between the dining-room, drawing-room and library, is a fine vista, terminated by a niche, in which stands Chantrey's bust of Scott. The ceilings are of carved Scottish oak and the doors of American cedar. Adjoining the library is his study, the walls of which are covered with books; the doors and windows are double, to render it quiet and undisturbed. His books and inkstand are on the table and his writing-chair stands before it, as if he had left them but a moment before. In a little closet adjoining, where he kept his private manuscripts, are the clothes he last wore, his cane and belt, to which a hammer and small axe are attached, and his sword. A narrow staircase led from the study to his sleeping room above, by which he could come down at night and work while his family slept. The silence about the place is solemn and breathless, as if it waited to be broken by his returning footstep. I felt an awe in treading these lonely halls, like that which impressed me before the grave of Washington—a feeling that hallowed the spot, as if there yet lingered a low vibration of the lyre, though the minstrel had departed forever!

Plucking a wild rose that grew near the walls, I left Abbotsford, embosomed among the trees, and turned into a green lane that led down to Melrose. We went immediately to the Abbey, in the lower part of the village, near the Tweed. As I approached the gate, the porteress came out, and having scrutinized me rather sharply, asked my name. I told her;—"well," she added, "there is a prospect here for you." Thinking she alluded to the ruin, I replied: "Yes, the view is certainly very fine." "Oh! I don't mean that," she replied, "a young gentleman left a prospect here for you!"—whereupon she brought out a spy-glass, which I recognized us one that our German comrade had given to me. He had gone on, and hoped to meet us at Jedburgh.

Melrose is the finest remaining specimen of Gothic architecture in Scotland. Some of the sculptured flowers in the cloister arches are remarkably beautiful and delicate, and the two windows—the south and east oriels—are of a lightness and grace of execution really surprising. We saw the tomb of Michael Scott, of King Alexander II, and that of the Douglas, marked with a sword. The heart of Bruce is supposed to have been buried beneath the high altar. The chancel is all open to the sky, and rooks build their nests among the wild ivy that climbs over the crumbling arches. One of these came tamely down and perched upon the hand of our fair guide. By a winding stair in one of the towers we mounted to the top of the arch and looked down on the grassy floor. I sat on the broken pillar, which Scott always used for a seat when he visited the Abbey, and read the disinterring of the magic book, in the "Lay of the Last Minstrel." I never comprehended its full beauty till then: the memory of Melrose will give it a thrilling interest, in the future. When we left, I was willing to say, with the Minstrel:

*"Was never scene so sad and fair!"*

After seeing the home and favorite haunt of Scott, we felt a wish to stand by his grave, but we had Ancrum Moor to pass before night, and the Tweed was between us and Dryburgh Abbey. We did not wish to try another watery adventure, and therefore walked on to the village of Ancrum, where a gate-keeper on the road gave us lodging and good fare, for a moderate price. Many of this class practise this double employment, and the economical traveller, who looks more to comfort than luxury, will not fail to patronize them.

Next morning we took a foot-path over the hills to Jedburgh. From the summit there was a lovely view of the valley of the Teviot, with the blue

Cheviots in the distance. I thought of Pringle's beautiful farewell:

*"Our native land, our native vale,*

*A long, a last adieu,*

*farewell to bonny Teviot-dale,*

*And Cheviot's mountains blue!"*

The poet was born in the valley below, and one that looks upon its beauty cannot wonder how his heart clung to the scenes he was leaving. We saw Jedburgh and its majestic old Abbey, and ascended the valley of the Jed towards the Cheviots. The hills, covered with woods of a richness and even gorgeous beauty of foliage, shut out this lovely glen completely from the world. I found myself continually coveting the lonely dwellings that were perched on the rocky heights, or nestled, like a fairy pavilion, in the lap of a grove. These forests formerly furnished the wood for the celebrated Jedwood axe, used in the Border forays.

As we continued ascending, the prospect behind us widened, till we reached the summit of the Carter Fell, whence there is a view of great extent and beauty. The Eildon Hills, though twenty-five miles distant, seemed in the foreground of the picture. With a glass, Edinburgh Castle might be seen over the dim outline of the Muirfoot Hills. After crossing the border, we passed the scene of the encounter between Percy and Douglass, celebrated in "Chevy Chase," and at the lonely inn of Whitelee, in the valley below, took up our quarters for the night.

Travellers have described the Cheviots as being bleak and uninteresting. Although they are bare and brown, to me the scenery was of a character of beauty entirely original. They are not rugged and broken like the Highlands, but lift their round backs gracefully from the plain, while the more distant ranges are clad in many an airy hue. Willis quaintly and truly remarks, that travellers only tell you the picture produced in their own brain by what they see, otherwise the world would be like a pawnbroker's shop, where each traveller wears the cast-off clothes of others. Therefore let no one, of a gloomy temperament, journeying over the Cheviots in dull November, arraign me for having falsely praised their beauty.

I was somewhat amused with seeing a splendid carriage with footmen and outriders, crossing the mountain, the glorious landscape full in view, containing a richly dressed lady, fast asleep! It is no uncommon thing to meet carriages in the Highlands, in which the occupants are comfortably reading, while being whirled through the finest scenery. And apropos of this subject, my German friend related to me an incident. His brother was travelling on the Rhine, and when in the midst of the grandest scenes, met a carriage containing an English gentleman and lady, both asleep, while on the seat behind was stationed an artist, sketching away with all his might. He asked the latter the reason of his industry, when he answered, "Oh! my lord wishes to see every night what he has passed during the day, and so I sketch as we go along!"

The hills, particularly on the English side, are covered with flocks of sheep, and lazy shepherds lay basking in the sun, among the purple heather, with their shaggy black dogs beside them. On many of the hills are landmarks, by which, when the snow has covered all the trucks, they can direct their way. After walking many miles through green valleys, down which flowed the Red Water, its very name telling of the conflicts which had crimsoned its tide, we came to the moors, and ten miles of blacker, drearier waste I never saw. Before entering them we passed the pretty little village of Otterburn, near the scene of the battle. I brought away a wild flower that grew on soil enriched by the blood of the Percys. On the village inn, is their ancient coat of arms, a lion rampant, on a field of gold, with the motto, "Esperance en Dieu." Scarcely a house or a tree enlivened the black waste, and even the road was marked on each side by high poles, to direct the traveller in winter. We were glad when at length the green fields came again in sight, and the little village of Whelpington Knowes, with its old ivy-grown church tower, welcomed us after the lonely walk.

As one specimen of the intelligence of this part of England, we saw a board conspicuously posted at the commencement of a private road, declaring that "all persons travelling this way will be persecuted." As it led to a church, however, there may have been a design in the expression.

On the fifth day after leaving Edinburgh, we reached a hill, overlooking the valley of the Tyne and the German Ocean, as sunset was reddening in the west. A cloud of coal-smoke made us aware of the vicinity of Newcastle. On the summit of the hill a large cattle fair was being held, and crowds of people were gathered in and around a camp of gaudily decorated tents. Fires were kindled here and there, and drinking, carousing and horse-racing were flourishing in full vigor.

We set out one morning to hunt the Roman Wall. Passing the fine buildings in the centre of the city and the lofty monument to Earl Grey, we went towards the western gate and soon came to the ruins of a building, about whose origin there could be no doubt. It stood there, blackened by the rust of ages, a remnant of power passed away. There was no mistaking the massive round tower, with its projecting ornaments, such as are often seen in the ruder works of the Romans. On each side a fragment of wall remained standing, and there appeared to be a chamber in the interior, which was choked up with rubbish. There is another tower, much higher, in a public square in another part of the city, a portion of which is fitted up as a dwelling for the family which takes care of it; but there was such a ridiculous contrast between the ivy-grown top, and the handsome modern windows and doors of the lower story, that it did not impress me half as much as the other, with all its neglect. These are the farthest limits of that power whose mighty works I hope hereafter to view at the seat of her grandeur and glory.

I witnessed a scene at Newcastle that cannot soon be forgotten; as it showed more plainly than I had before an opportunity of observing, the state to which the laboring classes of England are reduced. Hearing singing in the street, under my window, one morning, I looked out and saw a body of men, apparently of the lower class, but decent and sober looking, who were singing in a rude and plaintive strain some ballad, the purport of which I could not understand. On making inquiry, I discovered it was part of a body of miners, who, about eighteen weeks before, in consequence of not being able to support their families with the small pittance allowed them, had "struck" for higher wages. This their employers refused to give them, and sent to Wales, where they obtained workmen at the former price. The houses these laborers had occupied were all taken from them, and for eighteen weeks they had no other means of subsistence than the casual charity given them for singing the story of their wrongs. It made my blood boil to hear those tones, wrung from the heart of poverty by the hand of tyranny. The ignorance, permitted by the government, causes an unheard amount of misery and degradation. We heard afterwards in the streets, another company who played on musical instruments. Beneath the proud swell of England's martial airs, there sounded to my ears a tone whose gathering murmur will make itself heard ere long by the dull cars of Power.

At last at the appointed time, we found ourselves on board the "London Merchant," in the muddy Tyne, waiting for the tide to rise high enough to permit us to descend the river. There is great competition among the steamboats this summer, and the price of passage to London is reduced to five and ten shillings. The second cabin, however, is a place of tolerable comfort, and as the steward had promised to keep berths for us, we engaged passage. Following the windings of the narrow river, we passed Sunderland and Tynemouth, where it expands into the German Ocean. The water was barely stirred by a gentle wind, and little resembled the stormy sea I expected to find it. We glided over the smooth surface, watching the blue line of the distant shore till dark, when I went below expecting to enjoy a few hours' oblivion. But the faithless steward had given up the promised berth to another, and it was only with difficulty that I secured a seat by the cabin table, where I dozed half the night with my head on my arms. It grew at last too close and wearisome; I went up on deck and lay down on the windlass, taking care to balance myself well before going to sleep. The earliest light of dawn awoke me to a consciousness of damp clothes and bruised limbs. We were in sight of the low shore the whole day, sometimes seeing the dim outline of a church, or group of trees over the downs or flat beds of sand, which border the eastern coast of England. About dark, the red light of the Nore was seen, and we hoped before many hours to be in London. The lights of Gravesend were passed, but about ten o'clock, as we entered the narrow channel of the Thames, we struck another steamboat in the darkness, and were obliged to cast anchor for some time. When I went on deck in the gray light of morning again, we were gliding up a narrow, muddy river, between rows of gloomy buildings, with many vessels lying at anchor. It grew lighter, till, as we turned a point, right before, me lay a vast crowd of vessels, and in the distance, above the wilderness of buildings, stood a dim, gigantic dome in the sky; what a bound my heart gave at the sight! And the tall pillar that stood near it—I did not need a second glance to recognize the Monument. I knew the majestic bridge that spanned the river above; but on the right bank stood a cluster of massive buildings, crowned with many a turret, that attracted my eye. A crowd of old associations pressed bewilderingly upon the mind, to see standing there, grim and dark with many a bloody page of England's history—the Tower of London! The morning sky was as yet but faintly obscured by the coal-smoke, and in the misty light of coming sunrise, all objects seemed grander than their wont. In spite of the thrilling interest of the scene, I could not help thinking of Byron's ludicrous but most expressive description:

"A mighty mass of brick and smoke and shipping,

Dirty and dusky, but as wide as eye

Can reach; with here and there a sail just skipping

In sight, then lost amidst the forestry

Of masts; a wilderness of steeples peeping

On tiptoe through their sea-coal canopy;

A huge dun cupola, like a fool's-cap crown

On a fool's head,—and there is London town."

# CHAPTER VI. — SOME OF THE "SIGHTS" OF LONDON.

In the course of time we came to anchor in the stream; skiffs from the shore pulled alongside, and after some little quarrelling, we were safely deposited in one, with a party who desired to be landed at the Tower Stairs. The dark walls frowned above us as we mounted from the water and passed into an open square on the outside of the moat. The laborers were about commencing work, the fashionable day having just closed, but there was still noise and bustle enough in the streets, particularly when we reached Whitechapel, part of the great thoroughfare, extending through the heart of London to Westminster Abbey and the Parliament buildings. Further on, through Leadenhall street and Fleet street—what a world! Here come the ever-thronging, ever-rolling waves of life, pressing and whirling on in their tumultuous career. Here day and night pours the stream of human beings, seeming amid the roar and din and clatter of the passing vehicles, like the tide of some great combat. How lonely it makes one to stand still and feel that of all the mighty throng which divides itself around him, not a being knows or cares for him! What knows he too of the thousands who pass him by? How many who bear the impress of godlike virtue, or hide beneath a goodly countenance a heart black with crime? How many fiery spirits, all glowing with hope for the yet unclouded future, or brooding over a darkened and desolate past in the agony of despair? There is a sublimity in this human Niagara that makes one look on his own race with something of awe.

We walked down the Thames, through the narrow streets of Wapping, Over the mouth of the Tunnel is a large circular building, with a dome to light the entrance below. Paying the fee of a penny, we descended by a winding staircase to the bottom, which is seventy-three feet below the surface. The carriage-way, still unfinished, will extend further into the city. From the bottom the view of the two arches of the Tunnel, brilliantly lighted with gas, is very fine; it has a much less heavy and gloomy appearance than I expected. As we walked along under the bed of the river, two or three girls at one end began playing on the French horn and bugle, and the echoes, when not too deep to confuse the melody, were remarkably beautiful. Between the arches of the division separating the two passages, are shops, occupied by venders of fancy articles, views of the Tunnel, engravings, &c. In the middle is a small printing press, where, a sheet containing a description of the whole work is printed for those who desire it. As I was no stranger to this art, I requested the boy to let me print one myself, but he had such a bad roller I did not succeed in getting a good impression. The air within is somewhat damp, but fresh and agreeably cool, and one can scarcely realize in walking along the light passage, that a river is rolling above his head. The immense solidity and compactness of the structure precludes the danger of accident, each of the sides being arched outwards, so that the heaviest pressure only strengthens the whole. It will long remain a noble monument of human daring and ingenuity.

St. Paul's is on a scale of grandeur excelling every thing I have yet seen. The dome seems to stand in the sky, as you look up to it; the distance from which you view it, combined with the atmosphere of London, give it a dim, shadowy appearance, that perfectly startles one with its immensity. The roof from which the dome springs is itself as high as the spires of most other churches—blackened for two hundred years with the coal-smoke of London, it stands like a relic of the giant architecture of the early world. The interior is what one would expect to behold, after viewing the outside. A maze of grand arches on every side, encompasses the dome, which you gaze up at, as at the sky; and from every pillar and wall look down the marble forms of the dead. There is scarcely a vacant niche left in all this mighty hall, so many are the statues that meet one on every side. With the exceptions of John Howard, Sir Astley Cooper and Wren, whose monument is the church itself, they are all to military men. I thought if they had all been removed except Howard's, it would better have suited such a temple, and the great soul it commemorated.

I never was more impressed with the grandeur of human invention, than when ascending the dome. I could with difficulty conceive the means by which such a mighty edifice had been lifted into the air. That small frame of Sir Christopher Wren must have contained a mind capable of vast conceptions. The dome is like the summit of a mountain; so wide is the prospect, and so great the pile upon which you stand. London lay beneath us, like an ant-hill, with the black insects swarming to and fro in their long avenues, the sound of their employments coming up like the roar of the sea. A cloud of coal-smoke hung over it, through which many a pointed spire was thrust up; sometimes the wind would blow it aside for a moment, and the thousands of red roofs would shine out clearer. The bridged Thames, covered with craft of all sizes, wound beneath us like a ringed and spotted serpent. The scene was like an immense circular picture in the blue frame of the hills around.

Continuing our way up Fleet street, which, notwithstanding the gaiety of its shops and its constant bustle, has an antique appearance, we came to the Temple Bar, the western boundary of the ancient city. In the inside of the middle arch, the old gates are still standing. From this point we entered the new portion of the city, which wore an air of increasing splendor as we advanced. The appearance of the Strand and Trafalgar Square is truly magnificent. Fancy every house in Broadway a store, all built of light granite, the Park stripped of all its trees and paved with granite, and a lofty column in the centre, double the crowd and the tumult of business, and you will have some idea of the view.

It was a relief to get into St. James's Park, among the trees and flowers again. Here, beautiful winding walks led around little lakes, in which were hundreds of water-fowl, swimming. Groups of merry children were sporting on the green lawn, enjoying their privilege of roaming every where at will, while the older bipeds were confined to the regular walks. At the western end stood Buckingham Palace, looking over the trees towards St. Paul's; through the grove on the eminence above, the towers of St. James's could be seen. But there was a dim building, with two lofty square towers, decorated with a profusion of pointed Gothic pinnacles, that I looked at with more interest than these appendages of royalty. I could not linger long in its vicinity, but going back again by the Horse Guards, took the road to Westminster Abbey.

We approached by the general entrance, Poet's Corner. I hardly stopped to look at the elaborate exterior of Henry VIIth's Chapel, but passed on to the door. On entering, the first thing that met my eyes were the words, "OH RARE BEN JONSON," under his bust. Near by stood the monuments of Spenser and Gay, and a few paces further looked down the sublime

61

countenance of Milton. Never was a spot so full of intense interest. The light was just dim enough to give it a solemn, religious appearance, making the marble forms of poets and philosophers so shadowy and impressive, that I felt as if standing in their living presence. Every step called up some mind linked with the associations of my childhood. There was the gentle feminine countenance of Thompson, and the majestic head of Dryden; Addison with his classic features, and Gray, full of the fire of lofty thought. In another chamber, I paused long before the ashes of Shakspeare; and while looking at the monument of Garrick, started to find that I stood upon his grave. What a glorious galaxy of genius is here collected—what a constellation of stars whose light is immortal! The mind is completely fettered by their spirit. Everything is forgotten but the mighty dead, who still "rule us from their urns."

The Chapel of Henry VII., which we next entered, is one of the most elaborate specimens of Gothic workmanship in the world. If the first idea of the Gothic arch sprung from observing the forms of trees, this chapel must resemble the first conceptions of that order, for the fluted columns rise up like tall trees, branching out at the top into spreading capitals covered with leaves, and supporting arches of the ceiling resembling a leafy roof.

The side-chapels are filled with tombs of knightly families, the husband and wife lying on their backs on the tombs, with their hands clasped, while their children, about the size of dolls, are kneeling around. Numberless are the Barons and Earls and Dukes, whose grim effigies stare from their tombs. In opposite chapels are the tombs of Mary and Elizabeth, and near the former that of Darnley. After having visited many of the scenes of her life, it was with no ordinary emotion that I stood by the sepulchre of Mary. How differently one looks upon it and upon that of the proud Elizabeth!

We descended to the Chapel of Edward the Confessor, within the splendid shrine of which repose his ashes. Here we were shown the chair on which the English monarchs have been crowned for several hundred years, Under the seat is the stone, brought from the Abbey of Scone, whereon the Kings of Scotland were crowned. The chair is of oak, carved and hacked over with names, and on the bottom some one has recorded his name with the fact that, he once slept in it. We sat down and rested in it without ceremony.

Passing along an aisle leading to the grand hall, we saw the tomb of Aymer de Valence, a knight of the Crusades. Near here is the hall where the Knights of the order of Bath met. Over each seat their dusty banners are still hanging, each with its crest, and their armor is rusting upon the wall. It seemed like a banqueting hall of the olden time, where the knights had left their seats for a moment vacant. Entering the nave, we were lost in the wilderness of sculpture. Here stood the forms of Pitt, Fox, Burke, Sheridan and Watts, from the chisels of Chantry, Bacon and Westmacott. Further down were Sir Isaac Newton and Sir Godfrey Kneller—opposite Andre, and Paoli, the Italian, who died here in exile. How can I convey an idea of the scene? Notwithstanding all the descriptions I had read, I was totally unprepared for the reality, nor could I have anticipated the hushed and breathless interest with which I paced the dim aisles, gazing, at every step, on the last resting place of some great and familiar name. A place so sacred to all who inherit the English tongue, is worthy of a special pilgrimage across the deep. To those who are unable to visit it, a description may be interesting; but so far does it fall short of the scene itself, that if I thought it would induce a few of our wealthy idlers, or even those who, like myself, must travel with toil and privation to come hither, I would write till the pen dropped from my hand.

More than twenty grand halls of the British Museum are devoted to antiquities, and include the Elgin Marbles—the spoils of the Parthenon—the Fellows Marbles, brought from the ancient city of Xanthus, and Sir William Hamilton's collection of Italian antiquities. It was painful to see the friezes of the Parthenon, broken and defaced as they are, in such a place. Rather let them moulder to dust on the ruin from which they were torn, shining through the blue veil of the Grecian atmosphere, from the summit of the Acropolis!

The National Gallery, on Trafalgar Square, is open four days in the week, to the public. The "Raising of Lazarus," by Sebastian del Piombo, is considered the gem of the collection, but my unschooled eyes could not view it as such. It is also remarkable for having been transferred from wood to canvass, without injury. This delicate operation was accomplished by gluing the panel on which it was painted, flat on a smooth table, and planing the wood gradually away till the coat of hardened paint alone remained. A proper canvass was then prepared, covered with a strong cement, and laid on the back of the picture, which adhered firmly to it. The owner's nerves must have had a severe trial, if he had courage to watch the operation. I was enraptured with Murillo's pictures of St. John and the Holy Family. St. John is represented as a boy in the woods, fondling a lamb. It is a glorious head. The dark curls cluster around his fair brow, and his eyes seem already glowing with the fire of future inspiration. There is an innocence, a childish sweetness of expression in the countenance, which makes one love to gaze upon it. Both of these paintings wore constantly surrounded by ladies, and they certainly deserved the preference. In the rooms devoted to English artists, there are many of the finest works of West, Reynolds, Hogarth and Wilkie.

We spent a day in visiting the lungs of London, as the two grand parks have been called. From the Strand through the Regent Circus, the centre of the fashionable part of the city, we passed to Piccadilly, culling on our way to see our old friends, the Iowas. They were at the Egyptian Hall, in connexion with Catlin's Indian collection. The old braves knew us at once, particularly Blister Feet, who used often to walk a linweon deck with me, at sea. Further along Piccadilly is Wellington's mansion of Apsley House, and nearly opposite it, in the corner of Hyde Park, stands the colossal statue of Achilles, cast from cannon taken at Salamanca and Vittoria. The Park resembles an open common, with here and there a grove of trees, intersected by carriage roads, it is like getting into the country again to be out on its broad, green field, with the city seen dimly around through the smoky atmosphere. We walked for a mile or two along the shady avenues and over the lawns, having a view of the princely terraces and gardens on one hand, and the gentle outline of Primrose Hill on the other. Regent's Park itself covers a space of nearly four hundred acres!

But if London is unsurpassed in splendor, it has also its corresponding share of crime. Notwithstanding the large and efficient body of police, who do much towards the control of vice, one sees enough of degradation and brutality in a short time, to make his heart sick. Even the public thorough fares are thronged at night with characters of the lowest description, and it is not expedient to go through many of the narrow bye-haunts of the old city in the day-time. The police, who are ever on the watch, immediately seize and carry off any offender, but from the statements of persons who have had an opportunity of observing, as well as from my own slight experience, I am convinced that there is an untold amount of misery and crime. London is one of the wonders of the world, but there is reason to believe it is one of the curses of the world also; though, in fact, nothing but an active and unceasing philanthropy can prevent any city from becoming so.

Aug. 22.—I have now been six days in London, and by making good use of my feet and eyes, have managed to become familiar with almost every object of interest within its precincts. Having a plan mapped out for the day, I started from my humble lodgings at the Aldgate Coffee House, where I slept off fatigue for a shilling a night, and walked up Cheapside or down Whitechapel, as the case might be, hunting out my way to churches, halls and theatres. In this way, at a trifling expense, I have perhaps seen as much as many who spend here double the time and ten times the money. Our whole tour from Liverpool hither, by way of Ireland and Scotland, cost us but twenty-five dollars each! although, except in one or two cases, we denied ourselves no necessary comfort. This shows that the glorious privilege of looking on the scenes of the old world need not be confined to people of wealth and leisure. It may be enjoyed by all who can occasionally forego a little bodily comfort for the sake of mental and spiritual gain. We leave this afternoon for Dover. Tomorrow I shall dine in Belgium!

## CHAPTER VII. — FLIGHT THROUGH BELGIUM.

Bruges.—On the Continent at last! How strangely look the century-old towers, antique monuments, and quaint, narrow streets of the Flemish cities! It is an agreeable and yet a painful sense of novelty to stand for the first time in the midst of a people whose language and manners are different from one's own. The old buildings around, linked with many a stirring association of past history, gratify the glowing anticipations with which one has looked forward to seeing them, and the fancy is busy at work reconciling the real scene with the ideal; but the want of a communication with the living world about, walls one up with a sense of loneliness he could not before have conceived. I envy the children in the streets of Bruges their childish language.

Yesterday afternoon we came from London through the green wooded lawns and vales of England, to Dover, which we reached at sunset, passing by a long tunnel through the lofty Shakspeare Cliff. We had barely time before it grew dark to ascend the cliff. The glorious coast view looked still wilder in the gathering twilight, which soon hid from our sight the dim hills of France. On the cliff opposite frowned the massive battlements of the Castle, guarding the town, which lay in a nook of the rocks below. As the Ostend boat was to leave at four in the morning, my cousin aroused us at three, and we felt our way down stairs in the dark. But the landlord was reluctant to part with us; we stamped and shouted and rang bells, till the whole house was in an uproar, for the door was double-locked, and the steamboat bell began to sound. At last he could stand it no longer; we gave a quick utterance to our overflowing wrath, and rushed down to the boat but a second or two before it left.

The water of the Channel was smooth as glass and as the sun rose, the far chalky cliffs gleamed along the horizon, a belt of fire. I waved a good-bye to Old England and then turned to see the spires of Dunkirk, which were visible in the distance before us. On the low Belgian coast we could see trees and steeples, resembling a mirage over the level surface of the sea; at length, about ten o'clock, the square tower of Ostend came in sight. The boat passed into a long muddy basin, in which many unwieldy, red-sailed Dutch craft were lying, and stopped beside a high pier. Here amid the confusion of three languages, an officer came on board and took charge of our passports and luggage. As we could not get the former for two or three hours, we did not hurry the passing of the latter, and went on shore quite unincumbered, for a stroll about the city, disregarding the cries of the hackney-coachmen on the pier, "Hotel d'Angleterre," "Hotel des Bains!" and another who called out in English, "I recommend you to the Royal Hotel, sir!"

There is little to be seen in Ostend. We wandered through long rows of plain yellow houses, trying to read the French and low Dutch signs, and at last came out on the wall near the sea. A soldier motioned us back as we attempted to ascend it, and muttering some unintelligible words, pointed to a narrow street near. Following this out of curiosity, we crossed the moat and found ourselves on the great bathing beach. To get out of the hands of the servants who immediately surrounded us, we jumped into one of the little wagons and were driven out into the surf.

To be certain of fulfilling the railroad regulations, we took our seats quarter of an hour before the time. The dark walls of Ostend soon vanished and we were whirled rapidly over a country perfectly level, but highly fertile and well cultivated. Occasionally there was a ditch or row of trees, but otherwise there was no division between the fields, and the plain stretched unbroken away into the distance. The twenty miles to Bruges we made in forty minutes. The streets of this antique city are narrow and crooked, and the pointed, ornamented gables of the houses, produce a novel impression on one who has been accustomed to the green American forests. Then there was the endless sound of wooden shoes clattering over the rough pavements, and people talking in that most unmusical of all languages, low Dutch. Walking at random through the streets, we came by chance upon the Cathedral of Notre Dame. I shall long remember my first impression of the scene within. The lofty gothic ceiling arched far above my head and through the stained windows the light came but dimly—it was all still, solemn and religious. A few worshippers were kneeling in silence before some of the shrines and the echo of my tread seemed like a profaning sound. On every side were pictures, saints gilded shrines. A few steps removed one from the bustle and din of the crowd to the stillness and solemnity of the holy retreat.

We learned from the guide, whom we had engaged because he spoke a few words of English, that there was still a treckshuyt line on the canals, and that one boat leaves to-night at ten o'clock for Ghent. Wishing to try this old Dutch method of travelling, he took us about half a mile along the Ghent road to the canal, where a moderate sized boat was lying. Our baggage deposited in the plainly furnished cabin, I ran back to Bruges, although it was beginning to grow dark, to get a sight of the belfry; for Longfellow's lines had been running through my head all day:

"In the market place of Bruges, stands the belfry old and brown, Thrice consumed and thrice rebuilded, still it watches o'er the town."

And having found the square, brown tower in one corner of the open market square, we waited to hear the chimes, which are said to be the finest in Europe. They rang out at last with a clear silvery tone, most beautifully musical indeed. We then returned to the boat in the twilight. We were to leave in about an hour, according to the arrangement, but as yet there was no sound to be heard, and we were the only tenants. However, trusting to Dutch regularity, we went to sleep in the full confidence of awakening in Ghent.

I awoke once in the night and saw the dark branches of trees passing before the window, but there was no perceptible sound nor motion; the boat glided along like a dream, and we were awakened next morning by its striking against the pier at Ghent. After paying three francs for the whole night journey, the captain gave us a guide to the railroad station, and as we had nearly an hour before the train left, I went to see the Cathedral of St. Bavon. After leaving Ghent, the road passes through a beautiful country, cultivated like a garden. The Dutch passion for flowers is displayed in the gardens around the cottages; even every vacant foot of ground along the railway is planted with roses and dahlias. At Ghent, the morning being fair, we took seats in the open cars. About noon it commenced raining and our situation was soon anything but comfortable. My cousin had fortunately a water-proof Indian blanket with him, which he had purchased in the "Far West," and by wrapping this around all three of us, we kept partly dry. I was much amused at the plight of a party of young Englishmen, who were in the same car; one of them held a little parasol which just covered his hat, and sent the water in streams down on his back and shoulders.

We had a misty view of Liege, through the torrents of rain, and then dashed away into the wild, mountain scenery of the Meuse. Steep, rocky hills, covered with pine and crowned with ruined towers, hemmed in the winding and swollen river, and the wet, cloudy sky seemed to rest like a canopy on their summits. Instead of threading their mazy defiles, we plunged directly into the mountain's heart, flew over the narrow valley on lofty and light-sprung arches, and went again into the darkness. At Verviers, our baggage was weighed, examined and transferred, with ourselves, to a Prussian train. There was a great deal of disputing on the occasion. A lady, who had a dog in a large willow basket, was not allowed to retain it, nor would they take it as baggage. The matter was finally compromised by their sending the basket, obliging her to carry the dog, which was none of the smallest, in her arms! The next station bore the sign of the black eagle, and here our passports were obliged to be given up. Advancing through long ranges of wooded hills, we saw at length, in the dull twilight of a rainy day, the old kingly city of Aix la Chapelle on a plain below us. After a scene at the custom-house, where our baggage was reclaimed with tickets given at Verviers, we drove to the Hotel du Rhin, and while warming our shivering limbs and drying our damp garments, felt tempted to exclaim with the old Italian author: "O! holy and miraculous tavern!"

The Cathedral with its lofty Gothic tower, was built by the emperor Otho in the tenth century. It seems at present to be undergoing repairs, for a large scaffold shut out the dome. The long hall was dim with incense smoke as we entered, and the organ sounded through the high arches with an effect that startled me. The windows glowed with the forms of kings and saints, and the dusty and mouldering shrines which rose around were colored with the light that came through. The music pealed out like a triumphal march, sinking at times into a mournful strain, as if it celebrated and lamented the heroes who slept below. In the stone pavement nearly under my feet was a

69

large square marble slab, with words "CAROLO MAGNO." It was like a dream, to stand there on the tomb of the mighty warrior, with the lofty arches of the Cathedral above, filled with the sound of the divine anthem. I mused above his ashes till the music ceased and then left the Cathedral, that nothing might break the romantic spell associated with that crumbling pile and the dead it covered. I have always revered the memory of Charlemagne. He lived in a stern age, but he was in mind and heart a man, and like Napoleon, who placed the iron crown which had lain with him centuries in the tomb, upon his own brow, he had an Alpine grandeur of mind, which the world was forced to acknowledge.

At noon we took the chars-à-banc, or second-class carriages, for fear of rain, and continued our journey over a plain dotted with villages and old chateaux. Two or three miles from Cologne we saw the spires of the different churches, conspicuous among which were the unfinished towers of the Cathedral, with the enormous crane standing as it did when they left off building, two hundred years ago or more. On arriving, we drove to the Bonn railway, where finding the last train did not leave for four hours, we left our baggage and set out for the Cathedral. Of all Gothic buildings, the plan of this is certainly the most stupendous; even ruin as it is, it cannot fail to excite surprise and admiration. The King of Prussia has undertaken to complete it according to the original plan, which was lately found in the possession of a poor man, of whom it was purchased for 40,000 florins, but he has not yet finished repairing what is already built. The legend concerning this plan may not be known to every one. It is related of the inventor of it, that in despair of finding any sufficiently great, he was walking one day by the river, sketching with his stick upon the sand, when he finally hit upon one which pleased him so much that he exclaimed: "This shall be the plan!" "I will show you a better one than that!" said a voice suddenly behind him, and a certain black gentleman who figures in all German legends stood by him, and pulled from his pocket a roll containing the present plan of the Cathedral. The architect, amazed at its grandeur, asked an explanation of every part. As he knew his soul was to be the price of it, he occupied himself while the devil was explaining, in committing its proportions carefully to memory. Having done this, he remarked that it did not please him and he would not take it.

The devil, seeing through the cheat, exclaimed in his rage: "You may build your Cathedral according to this plan, but you shall never finish it!" This prediction seems likely to be verified, for though it was commenced in 1248, and built for 250 years, only the choir and nave and one tower to half its original height, are finished.

We visited the chapel of the eleven thousand virgins, the walls of which are full of curious grated cells, containing their bones, and then threaded the narrow streets of Cologne, which are quite dirty enough to justify Coleridge's lines:

> "The river Rhine, it is well known
>
> Doth wash the city of Cologne;
>
> But tell me nymphs, what power divine
>
> Shall henceforth wash the river Rhine!"

# CHAPTER VIII. — THE RHINE TO HEIDELBERG.

HEIDELBERG, August 30. Here at last! and a most glorious place it is. This is our first morning in our new rooms, and the sun streams warmly in the eastern windows, as I write, while the old castle rises through the blue vapor on the side of the Kaiser-stuhl. The Neckar rushes on below; and the Odenwald, before, me, rejoices with its vineyards in the morning light. The bells of the old chapel near us are sounding most musically, and a confused sound of voices and the rolling of vehicles comes up from the street. It is a place to live in!

I must go back five or six days and take up the record of our journeyings at Bonn. We had been looking over Murray's infallible "Handbook," and observed that he recommended the "Star" hotel in that city, as "the most moderate in its prices of any on the Rhine;" so when the train from Cologne arrived and we were surrounded, in the darkness and confusion, by porters and valets, I sung out: "Hotel de l'Etoile d'or!" our baggage and ourselves were transferred to a stylish omnibus, and in five minutes we stopped under a brilliantly-lighted archway, where Mr. Joseph Schmidt received us with the usual number of smiles and bows bestowed upon untitled guests. We were furnished with neat rooms in the summit of the house, and then descended to the salle à manger. I found a folded note by my plate, which I opened—it contained an engraving of the front of the hotel, a plan of the city and catalogue of its lions, together with a list of the titled personages who have, from time to time, honored the "Golden Star" with their custom. Among this number were "Their Royal Highnesses the Duke and Duchess of Cambridge, Prince Albert," etc. Had it not been for fatigue, I should have spent an uneasy night, thinking of the heavy bill which was to be presented on the morrow. We escaped, however, for seven francs apiece, three of which were undoubtedly for the honor of breathing an aristocratic atmosphere.

I was glad when we were really in motion on the swift Rhine, the next morning, and nearing the chain of mountains that rose up before us. We passed Godesberg on the right, while on our left was the group of the seven mountains which extend back from the Drachenfels to the Wolkenberg, or Castle of the Clouds. Here we begin to enter the enchanted land. The Rhine sweeps around the foot of the Drachenfels, while opposite the precipitous rock of Rolandseek, crowned with the castle of the faithful knight, looks down upon the beautiful Island of Nonnenwerth, the white walls of the convent still gleaming through the trees, as they did when the warrior's weary eyes looked upon them for the last time. I shall never forget the enthusiasm with which I saw this scene in the bright, warm sunlight, the rough crags softened in the haze which filled the atmosphere, and the wild mountains springing up in the midst of vineyards, and crowned with crumbling towers, filled with the memories of a thousand years.

After passing Andernach, we saw in the distance the highlands of the middle Rhine, which rise above Coblentz, guarding the entrance to its wild scenery, and the mountains of the Moselle. They parted as we approached; from the foot shot up the spires of Coblentz, and the battlements of Ehrenbreitstein crowning the mountain opposite, grew larger and broader. The air was slightly hazy, and the clouds seemed laboring among the distant mountains to raise a storm. As we came opposite the mouth of the Moselle and under the shadow of the mighty fortress, I gazed up with awe at its massive walls. Apart from its magnitude and almost impregnable situation on a perpendicular rock, it is filled with the recollections of history and hallowed by the voice of poetry. The scene went past like a panorama, the bridge of boats opened, the city glided behind us and we entered the highlands again.

Above Coblentz almost every mountain has a ruin and a legend. One feels everywhere the spirit of the past, and its stirring recollections come back upon the mind with irresistible force. I sat upon the deck the whole afternoon, as mountains, towns and castles passed by on either side, watching them with a feeling of the most enthusiastic enjoyment. Every place was familiar to me in memory, and they seemed like friends I had long communed with in spirit and now met face to face. The English tourists, with whom the deck was covered, seemed interested too, but in a different manner. With Murray's Handbook open in their hands, they sat and read about the very towns and towers they were passing, scarcely lifting their eyes to the real scenes, except now and then, to observe that it was "very nice."

As we passed Boppart, I sought out the Inn of the "Star," mentioned in "Hyperion"; there was a maiden sitting on the steps who might have been Paul Flemming's fair boat-woman. The clouds which had here gathered among the hills, now came over the river, and the rain cleared the deck of its crowd of admiring tourists. As we were approaching Lurlei Berg, I did not go below, and so enjoyed some of the finest scenery on the Rhine alone. The mountains approach each other at this point, and the Lurlei Rock rises up for six hundred feet from the water. This is the haunt of the water nymph, Lurlei, whose song charmed the ear of the boatman while his barque was dashed to pieces on the rocks below. It is also celebrated for its remarkable echo. As we passed between the rocks, a guard, who has a little house built on the road-side, blew a flourish on his bugle, which was instantly answered by a blast from the rocky battlements of Lurlei. The German students have a witty trick with this echo: they call out, "Who is the Burgomaster of Oberwesel?" a town just above. The echo answers with the last syllable "Esel!" which is the German for ass.

The sun came out of the cloud as we passed Oberwesel, with its tall round tower, and the light shining through the ruined arches of Schonberg castle, made broad bars of light and shade in the still misty air. A rainbow sprang up out of the Rhine, and lay brightly on the mountain side, coloring vineyard and crag, in the most singular beauty, while its second reflection faintly arched like a glory above the high summits. In the bed of the river were the seven countesses of Schonberg, turned into seven rocks for their cruelty and hard-heartedness towards the knights whom their beauty had made captive. In front, at a little distance was the castle of Pfalz, in the middle of the river, and from the heights above Caub frowned the crumbling citadel of Gutenfels. Imagine all this, and tell me if it is not a picture whose memory should last a life-time!

We came at last to Bingen, the southern gate of the Highlands. Here, on an island in the middle of the stream, is the old Mouse tower where Bishop Hatto of Mayence was eaten up by the rats for his wicked deeds.

Passing Rudesheim and Geissenheim, celebrated for their wines, at sunset, we watched the varied shore in the growing darkness, till like a line of stars across the water, we saw before us the bridge of Mayence.

The next morning I parted from my friends, who were going to Heidelberg by way of Mannheim, and set out alone for Frankfort. The cars passed through Hochheim, whose wines are celebrated all over the world; there is little to interest the traveler till he arrives at Frankfort, whose spires are seen rising from groves of trees as he approaches. I left the cars, unchallenged for my passport, greatly to my surprise, as it had cost me a long walk and five shillings in London, to get the signature of the Frankfort Consul. I learned afterwards it was not at all necessary. Before leaving America, N.P. Willis had kindly given me a letter to his brother, Richard S. Willis, who is now cultivating a naturally fine taste for music in Frankfort, and my first care was to find the American Consul, in order to learn his residence. I discovered at last, from a gentleman who spoke a little French, that the Consul's office was in the street Bellevue, which street I not only looked for through the city, but crossed over the bridge to the suburb of Sachsenhausen, and traversed its narrow, dirty alleys three several times, but in vain. I was about giving up the search, when I stumbled upon the office accidentally. The name of the street had been given to me in French and very naturally it was not to be found. Willis received me very kindly and introduced me to the amiable German family with whom he resides.

After spending a delightful evening with my newly-found friends, I left the next morning in the omnibus for Heidelberg. We passed through Sachsenhausen and ascended a long hill to the watch-tower, whence there is a beautiful view of the Main valley. Four hours' driving over the monotonous plain, brought me to Darmstadt. The city wore a gay look, left by the recent fêtes. The monument of the old Duke Ludwig had just been erected in the centre of the great square, and the festival attendant upon the unveiling of it, which lasted three days, had just closed. The city was hung with garlands, and the square filled with the pavilions of the royal family and the musicians, of whom there were a thousand present, while everywhere were seen red and white flags—the colors of Darmstadt. We met wagons decorated with

garlands, full of pleasant girls, in the odd dress which they have worn for three
hundred years.

After leaving Darmstadt we entered upon the Bergstrasse, or Mountain-
way, leading along the foot of the mountain chain which extends all the way to
Heidelberg on the left, while on the right stretches far away the Rhine-plain,
across which we saw the dim outline of the Donnersberg, in France. The hills
are crowned with castles and their sides loaded with vines; along the road the
rich green foliage of the walnut trees arched and nearly met above us. The sun
shone warm and bright, and every body appeared busy and contented and
happy. All we met had smiling countenances. In some places we saw whole
families sitting under the trees shelling the nuts they had beaten down, while
others were returning from the vineyards, laden with baskets of purple and
white grapes. The scene seemed to realize all I had read of the happiness of the
German peasantry, and the pastoral beauty of the German plains.

With the passengers in the omnibus I could hold little conversation.
One, who knew about as much French as I did, asked me where I came
from, and I shall not soon forget his expression of incredulity, as I mentioned
America. "Why," said he, "you are white—the Americans are all black!"

We passed the ruined castles of Auerback and Starkenburg, and Burg
Windeck, on the summit of a mountain near Weinheim, formerly one of
the royal residences of Charlemagne, and finally came to the Heiligenberg
or Holy Mountain, guarding the entrance into the Odenwald by the valley
of the Neckar. As we wound around its base to the river, the Kaiserstuhl rose
before us, with the mighty castle hanging upon its side and Heidelberg at its
feet. It was a most strikingly beautiful scene, and for a moment I felt inclined
to assent to the remark of my bad-French acquaintance—"America is not
beautiful—Heidelberg is beautiful!" The sun had just set as we turned the
corner of the Holy Mountain and drove up the bank of the Neckar; all the
chimes of Heidelberg began suddenly to ring and a cannon by the riverside
was fired off every minute—the sound echoing five times distinctly from
mountain back to mountain, and finally crashing far off, along the distant
hills of the Odenwald. It was the birthday of the Grand Duke of Baden, and
these rejoicings were for the closing fête.

# CHAPTER IX. — SCENES IN AND AROUND HEIDELBERG.

Sept. 30.—There is so much to be seen around this beautiful place, that I scarcely know where to begin a description of it. I have been wandering among the wild paths that lead up and down the mountain side, or away into the forests and lonely meadows in the lap of the Odenwald. My mind is filled with images of the romantic German scenery, whose real beauty is beginning to displace the imaginary picture which I had painted with the enthusiastic words of Howitt. I seem to stand now upon the Kaiser-stuhl, which rises above Heidelberg, with that magnificent landscape around me, from the Black Forest and Strasburg to Mainz, and from the Vosges in France to the hills of Spessart in Bavaria. What a glorious panorama! and not less rich in associations than in its natural beauty. Below me had moved the barbarian hordes of old, the triumphant followers of Arminius, and the Cohorts of Rome; and later, full many a warlike host bearing the banners of the red cross to the Holy Land,—many a knight returning with his vassals from the field, to lay at the feet of his lady-love the scarf he had worn in a hundred battles and claim the reward of his constancy and devotion. But brighter spirits had also toiled below. That plain had witnessed the presence of Luther, and a host who strove with him to free the world from the chains of a corrupt and oppressive religion. There had also trodden the master spirits of German song—the giant twain, with their scarcely less harmonious brethren: they, too, had gathered inspiration from those scenes—more fervent worship of nature and a deeper love for their beautiful fatherland! Oh! what waves of crime and bloodshed have swept like the waves of a deluge down the valley of the Rhine! War has laid his mailed hand on those desolate towers and ruthlessly torn down what time has spared, yet he could not mar the beauty of the shore, nor could Time himself hurl down the mountains that guard it. And what if I feel a new inspiration on beholding the scene? Now that those ages have swept by, like the red waves of a tide of blood, we see not the darkened earth, but the golden sands which the flood has left behind. Besides, I have come from a new world, where the spirit of man is untrammeled by the mouldering shackles of the past, but in its youthful and joyous freedom, goes on to make itself a noble memory for the ages that are to come!

Then there is the Wolfsbrunnen, which one reaches by a beautiful walk up the bank of the Neckar, to a quiet dell in the side of the mountain. Through this the roads lead up by rustic mills, always in motion, and orchards laden with ripening fruit, to the commencement of the forest, where a quaint stone fountain stands, commemorating the abode of a sorceress of the olden time, who was torn in pieces by a wolf. There is a handsome rustic inn here, where every Sunday afternoon a band plays in the portico, while hundreds of people are scattered around in the cool shadow of the trees, or feeding the splendid trout in the basin formed by the little stream. They generally return to the city by another walk leading along the mountain side, to the eastern terrace of the castle, where they have fine views of the great Rhine plain, terminated by the Alsatian hills, stretching along the western horizon like the long crested swells on the ocean. We can even see these from the windows of our room on the bank of the Neckar; and I often look with interest on one sharp peak, for on its side stands the Castle of Trifels, where Coeur de Lion was imprisoned by the Duke of Austria, and where Blondel, his faithful minstrel, sang the ballad which discovered the retreat of the noble captive.

The people of Heidelberg are rich in places of pleasure and amusement. From the Carl Platz, an open square at the upper end of the city, two paths lead directly up to the castle. By the first walk we ascend a flight of steps to the western gate, passing through which, we enter a delightful garden, between the outer walls of the Castle, and the huge moat which surrounds it. Great linden, oak and beech trees shadow the walk, and in secluded nooks, little mountain streams spring from the side of the wall into stone basins. There is a tower over the moat on the south side, next the mountain, where the portcullis still hangs with its sharp teeth as it was last drawn up; on each side stand two grim knights guarding the entrance. In one of the wooded walks is an old tree brought from America in the year 1618. It is of the kind called arbor vitæ, and uncommonly tall and slender for one of this species; yet it does not seem to thrive well in a foreign soil. I noticed that persons had cut many slips off the lower branches, and I would have been tempted to do the

78

same myself if there had been any I could reach. In the curve of the mountain is a handsome pavilion, surrounded with beds of flowers and fountains; here all classes meet together in the afternoon to sit with their refreshments in the shade, while frequently a fine band of music gives them their invariable recreation. All this, with the scenery around them, leaves nothing unfinished to their present enjoyment. The Germans enjoy life under all circumstances, and in this way they make themselves much happier than we, who have far greater means of being so.

At the end of the terrace built for the princess Elizabeth, of England, is one of the round towers, which was split in twain by the French. Half has fallen entirely away, and the other semicircular shell which joins the terrace and part of the Castle buildings, clings firmly together, although part of its foundation is gone, so that its outer ends actually hang in the air. Some idea of the strength of the castle may be obtained when I state that the walls of this tower are twenty-two feet thick, and that a staircase has been made through them to the top, where one can sit under the lindens growing upon it, or look down from the end on the city below with the pleasant consciousness that the great mass upon which he stands is only prevented from crashing down with him by the solidity of its masonry. On one side, joining the garden, the statue of the Archduke Louis, in his breastplate and flowing beard, looks out from among the ivy.

There is little to be seen about the Castle except the walls themselves. The guide conducted us through passages, in which were heaped many of the enormous cannon balls which it had received in sieges, to some chambers in the foundation. This was the oldest part of the Castle, built in the thirteenth century. We also visited the chapel, which is in a tolerable state of preservation. A kind of narrow bridge crosses it, over which we walked, looking down on the empty pulpit and deserted shrines. We then went into the cellar to see the celebrated Tun. In a large vault are kept several enormous hogsheads, one of which is three hundred years old, but they are nothing in comparison with the tun, which itself fills a whole vault. It is as high as a common two story house; on the top is a platform upon which the people used to dance after it was filled, to which one ascends by two flights of steps. I forgot exactly how many casks it holds, but I believe eight hundred. It has been empty for fifty years.

We are very pleasantly situated here. My friends, who arrived a day before me, hired three rooms (with the assistance of a courier) in a large house on the banks of the Neckar. We pay for them, with attendance, thirty florins—about twelve dollars—a month, and Frau Dr. Grosch, our polite and talkative landlady, gives us a student's breakfast—coffee and biscuit—for about seven cents apiece. We are often much amused to hear her endeavors to make us understand. As if to convey her meaning plainer, she raises both thumbs and forefingers to her mouth and pulls out the words like a long string; her tongue goes so fast that it keeps my mind always on a painful stretch to comprehend an idea here and there. Dr. S——, from whom we take lessons in German, has kindly consented to our dining with his family for the sake of practice in speaking. We have taken several long walks with them along the banks of the Neckar, but I should be puzzled to repeat any of the conversations that took place. The language, however, is fast growing more familiar, since women are the principal teachers.

Opposite my window rises the Heiligenberg, on the other side of the Neckar. The lower part of it is rich with vineyards, and many cottages stand embosomed in shrubbery among them. Sometimes we see groups of maidens standing under the grape arbors, and every morning the peasant women go toiling up the steep paths with baskets on their heads, to labor among the vines. On the Neckar below us, the fishermen glide about in their boats, sink their square nets fastened to a long pole, and haul them up with the glittering fish, of which the stream is full. I often lean out of the window late at night, when the mountains above are wrapped in dusky obscurity, and listen to the low, musical ripple of the river. It tells to my excited fancy a knightly legend of the old German time. Then comes the bell, rung for closing the inns, breaking the spell with its deep clang, which vibrates far away on the night air, till it has roused all the echoes of the Odenwald. I then shut the window, turn into the narrow box which the Germans call a bed, and in a few minutes am wandering in America. Half way up the Heiligenberg runs a beautiful walk, dividing the vineyards from the forest above. This is called the

Philosopher's Way, because it was the favorite ramble of the old Professors of the University. It can be reached by a toilsome, winding path among the vines, called the Snake-way, and when one has ascended to it he is well rewarded by the lovely view. In the evening, when the sun has got behind the mountain, it is delightful to sit on the stone steps and watch the golden light creeping up the side of the Kaiser-stuhl, till at last twilight begins to darken in the valley and a mantle of mist gathers above the Neckar.

We ascended the mountain a few days ago. There is a path which leads up through the forest, but we took the shortest way, directly up the side, though it was at an angle of nearly fifty degrees. It was hard enough work, scrambling through the thick broom and heather, and over stumps and stones. In one of the stone-heaps I dislodged a large orange-colored salamander, seven or eight inches long. They are sometimes found on these mountains, as well as a very large kind of lizard, called the eidechse, which the Germans say is perfectly harmless, and if one whistles or plays a pipe, will come and play around him. The view from the top reminded me of that from Catskill Mountain House, but is on a smaller scale. The mountains stretch off sideways, confining the view to but half the horizon, and in the middle of the picture the Hudson is well represented by the lengthened windings of the "abounding Rhine." Nestled at the base below us, was the little village of Handschuhheim, one of the oldest in this part of Germany. The castle of its former lords has nearly all fallen down, but the massive solidity of the walls which yet stand, proves its antiquity. A few years ago, a part of the outer walls which was remarked to have a hollow sound, was taken down, when there fell from a deep niche built therein, a skeleton, clad in a suit of the old German armor. We followed a road through the woods to the peak on which stand the ruins of St. Michael's chapel, which was built in the tenth century and inhabited for a long time by a sect of white monks. There is now but a single tower remaining, and all around is grown over with tall bushes and weeds. It had a wild and romantic look, and I sat on a rock and sketched at it, till it grew dark, when we got down the mountain the best way we could.

We lately visited the great University Library. You walk through one hall after another, filled with books of all kinds, from the monkish manuscript of the middle ages, to the most elegant print of the present day. There is something to me more impressive in a library like this than a solemn Cathedral. I think involuntarily of the hundreds of mighty spirits who speak from these three hundred thousand volumes—of the toils and privations with which genius has ever struggled, and of his glorious reward. As in a church, one feels as it were, the presence of God; not because the place has been hallowed by his worship, but because all around stand the inspirations of his spirit, breathed through the mind of genius, to men. And if the mortal remains of saints and heroes do not repose within its walls, the great and good of the whole earth are there, speaking their counsels to the searcher for truth, with voices whose last reverberation will die away only when the globe falls into ruin.

A few nights ago there was a wedding of peasants across the river. In order to celebrate it particularly, the guests went to the house where it was given, by torchlight. The night was quite dark, and the bright red torches glowed on the surface of the Neckar, as the two couriers galloped along the banks to the bridegroom's house. Here, after much shouting and confusion, the procession was arranged, the two riders started back again with their torches, and the wagons containing the guests followed after with their flickering lights glancing on the water, till they disappeared around the foot of the mountain. The choosing of Conscripts also took place lately. The law requires one person out of every hundred to become a soldier, and this, in the city of Heidelberg, amounts to nearly 150. It was a sad spectacle. The young men, or rather boys, who were chosen, went about the city with cockades fastened on their hats, shouting and singing, many of them quite intoxicated. I could not help pitying them because of the dismal, mechanical life they are doomed to follow. Many were rough, ignorant peasants, to whom nearly any kind of life would be agreeable; but there were some whose countenances spoke otherwise, and I thought involuntarily, that their drunken gaiety was only affected to conceal their real feelings with regard to the lot which had fallen upon them.

We are gradually becoming accustomed to the German style of living, which is very different from our own. Their cookery is new to us, but is, nevertheless, good. We have every day a different kind of soup, so I have supposed they keep a regular list of three hundred and sixty-five, one for every day in the year! Then we have potatoes "done up" in oil and vinegar, veal flavored with orange peel, barley pudding, and all sorts of pancakes, boiled artichokes, and always rye bread, in loaves a yard long! Nevertheless, we thrive on such diet, and I have rarely enjoyed more sound and refreshing sleep than in their narrow and coffin-like beds, uncomfortable as they seem. Many of the German customs are amusing. We never see oxen working here, but always cows, sometimes a single one in a cart, and sometimes two fastened together by a yoke across their horns. The women labor constantly in the fields; from our window we can hear the nut-brown maidens singing their cheerful songs among the vineyards on the mountain side. Their costume, too, is odd enough. Below the light-fitting vest they wear such a number of short skirts, one above another, that it reminds one of an animated hogshead, with a head and shoulders starting out from the top. I have heard it gravely asserted that the wealth of a German damsel may be known by counting the number of her "kirtles." An acquaintance of mine remarked, that it would be an excellent costume for falling down a precipice!

We have just returned from a second visit to Frankfort, where the great annual fair filled the streets with noise and bustle. On our way back, we stopped at the village of Zwingenberg, which lies at the foot of the Melibochus, for the purpose of visiting some of the scenery of the Odenwald. Passing the night at the inn there, we slept with one bed under and two above, and started early in the morning to climb up the side of the Melibochus. After a long walk through the forests, which were beginning to change their summer foliage for a brighter garment, we reached the summit and ascended the stone tower which stands upon it. This view gives one a better idea of the Odenwald, than that from the Kaiser-stuhl at Heidelberg. In the soft autumn atmosphere it looked even more beautiful. After an hour in that heaven of uplifted thought, into which we step from the mountain-top, our minds went with the path downward to earth, and we descended the eastern side into the wild region which contains the Felsenmeer, or Sea of Rocks.

We met on the way a student from Fulda—a fine specimen of that free-spirited class, and a man whose smothered aspiration was betrayed in the

83

flashing of his eye, as he spoke of the present painful and oppressed condition of Germany. We talked so busily together that without noticing the path, which had been bringing us on, up hill and down, through forest and over rock, we came at last to a halt in a valley among the mountains. Making inquiries there, we found we had gone wrong, and must ascend by a different path the mountain we had just come down. Near the summit of this, in a wild pine wood, was the Felsenmeer—a great collection of rocks heaped together like pebbles on the sea shore, and worn and rounded as if by the action of water: so much do they resemble waves, that one standing at the bottom and looking up, cannot resist the idea, that they will flow down upon him. It must have been a mighty tide whose receding waves left these masses piled up together! The same formation continues at intervals, to the foot, of the mountains. It reminded me of a glacier of rocks instead of ice. A little higher up, lies a massive block of granite called the "Giant's Column." It is thirty-two feet long and three to four feet in diameter, and still bears the mark of the chisel. When or by whom it was made, remains a mystery. Some have supposed it was intended to be erected for the worship of the Sun, by the wild Teutonic tribes who inhabited this forest; it is more probably the work of the Romans. A project was once started, to erect it as a monument on the battle-field of Leipsic, but it was found too difficult to carry into execution.

After dining at the little village of Reichelsdorf in the valley below, where the merry landlord charged my friend two kreutzers less than myself because he was not so tall, we visited the Castle of Schönberg, and joined the Bergstrasse again. We walked the rest of the way here; long before we arrived, the moon shone down on us over the mountains, and when we turned around the foot of the Heiligenberg, the mist descending in the valley of the Neckar, rested like a light cloud on the church spires.

# CHAPTER X. – A WALK THROUGH THE ODENWALD.

B—— and I are now comfortably settled in Frankfort, having, with Mr. Willis's kind assistance, obtained lodgings with the amiable family, with whom he has resided for more than two years. My cousin remains in Heidelberg to attend the winter course of lectures at the University.

Having forwarded our baggage by the omnibus, we came hither on foot, through the heart of the Odenwald, a region full of interest, yet little visited by travellers. Dr. S—— and his family walked with us three or four miles of the way, and on a hill above Ziegelhausen, with a splendid view behind us, through the mountain-door, out of which the Neckar enters on the Rhine-plain, we parted. This was a first, and I must confess, a somewhat embarrassing experience in German leave-taking. After bidding adieu three or four times, we started to go up the mountain and they down it, but at every second step we had to turn around to acknowledge the waving of hands and handkerchiefs, which continued so long that I was glad when we were out of sight of each other. We descended on the other side into a wild and romantic valley, whose meadows were of the brightest green; a little brook which wound through them, put now and then its "silvery shoulder" to the wheel of a rustic mill. By the road-side two or three wild-looking gipsies sat around a fire, with some goats feeding near them.

Passing through this valley and the little village of Schönau, we commenced ascending one of the loftiest ranges of the Odenwald. The side of the mountain was covered with a thick pine forest. There was no wind to wake its solemn anthem; all was calm and majestic, and even awful. The trees rose all around like the pillars of a vast Cathedral, whose long arched aisles vanished far below in the deepening gloom.

> *"Nature with folded hands seemed there,*
>
> *Kneeling at her evening prayer,"*

for twilight had already begun to gather. We went on and up and ever higher, like the youth in "Excelsior;" the beech and dwarf oak took the place of the pine, and at last we arrived at a cleared summit whose long brown grass waved desolately in the dim light of evening. A faint glow still lingered over the forest-hills, but down in the valley the dusky shades hid every vestige of life, though its sounds came up softened through the long space. When we reached the top a bright planet stood like a diamond over the brow of the eastern hill, and the sound of a twilight bell came up clearly and sonorously on the cool damp air. The white veil of mist slowly descended down the mountain side, but the peaks rose above it like the wrecks of a world, floating in space. We made our way in the dusk down the long path, to the rude little dorf of Elsbach. I asked at the first inn for lodging, where we were ushered into a great room, in which a number of girls who had been at work in the fields, were assembled. They were all dressed in men's jackets, and short gowns, and some had their hair streaming down their back. The landlord's daughter, however, was a beautiful girl, whose modest, delicate features contrasted greatly with the coarse faces of the others. I thought of Uhland's beautiful little poem of "The Landlady's Daughter," as I looked on her. In the room hung two or three pair of antlers, and they told us deer were still plenty in the forests.

When we left the village the next morning, we again commenced ascending. Over the whole valley and halfway up the mountain, lay a thick white frost, almost like snow, which contrasted with the green trees and bushes scattered over the meadows, produced the most singular effect. We plucked blackberries ready iced from the bushes by the road-side, and went on in the cold, for the sun shone only on the top of the opposite mountain, into another valley, down which rushed the rapid Ulver. At a little village which bears the beautiful name Anteschönmattenwag, we took a foot-path directly over a steep mountain to the village of Finkenbach. Near the top I found two wild-looking children, cutting grass with knives, both of whom I prevailed upon for a few kreutzers to stand and let me sketch them. From the summit the view on the other side was very striking. The hills were nearly every one covered with wood, and not a dwelling in sight. It reminded me of our forest scenery at home. The principal difference is, that our trees are two or three times the size of theirs.

At length, after scaling another mountain, we reached a wide, elevated plain, in the middle of which stood the old dorf of Beerfelden. It was then crowded with people, on account of a great cattle-fair being held there. All the farmers of the neighborhood were assembled, clad in the ancient country costume—broad cocked hats and blue frocks. An orchard near the town was filled with cattle and horses, and near by, in the shade, a number of pedlars had arranged their wares. The cheerful looking country people touched their hats to us as we passed. This custom of greeting travellers, universal in Germany, is very expressive of their social, friendly manners. Among the mountains, we frequently met groups of children, who sang together their simple ballads as we passed by.

From Beerfelden we passed down the valley of the Mimling to Erbach, the principal city in the Odenwald, and there stopped a short time to view the Rittersaal in the old family castle of the Counts of Erbach. An officer, who stood at the gates, conducted us to the door, where we were received by a noble-looking, gray-headed steward. He took us into the Rittersaal at once, which was like stepping back three hundred years. The stained windows of the lofty Gothic hall, let in a subdued light which fell on the forms of kings and knights, clad in the armor they wore during life. On the left as we entered, were mail-covered figures of John and Cosmo do Medici; further on stood the Emperor Maximilian, and by his side the celebrated dwarf who was served up in a pie at one of the imperial feasts. His armor was most delicate and beautiful, but small as it was, General Thumb would have had room in it. Gustavus Adolphus and Wallenstein looked down from the neighboring pedestals, while at the other end stood Goetz von Berlichingen and Albert of Brunswick. Guarding the door were Hans, the robber-knight of Nuremberg, and another from the Thüringian forest. The steward told me that the iron hand of Goetz was in possession of the family, but not shown to strangers; he pointed out, however, the buckles on the armor, by which it was fastened. Adjoining the hall is an antique chapel, filled with rude old tombs, and containing the sarcophagus of Count Eginhard of Denmark, who lived about the tenth century. There were also monkish garments five hundred years old hanging up in it.

The collection of antiquities is large and interesting; but it is said that the old Count obtained some of them in rather a questionable manner. Among other incidents, they say that when in Rome he visited the Pope, taking with him an old servant who accompanied him in all his travels, and was the accomplice in most of his antiquarian thefts. In one of the outer halls, among the curiosities, was an antique shield of great value. The servant was left in this hall while the Count had his audience, and in a short time this shield was missed. The servant who wore a long cloak, was missed also; orders were given to close the gates and search every body, but it was too late—the thief was gone.

Leaving Erbach we found out the direction of Snellert, the Castle of the Wild Huntsman, and took a road that led us for two or three hours along the top of a mountain ridge. Through the openings in the pine and larch forests, we had glimpses of the hills of Spessart, beyond the Main. When we finally left the by-road we had chosen it was quite dark, and we missed the way altogether among the lanes and meadows. We came at last to a full stop at the house of a farmer, who guided us by a foot path over the fields to a small village. On entering the only inn, kept by the Burgomaster, the people finding we were Americans, regarded us with a curiosity quite uncomfortable. They crowded around the door, watching every motion, and gazed in through the windows. The wild huntsman himself could scarcely have made a greater sensation. The news of our arrival seemed to have spread very fast, for the next morning when we stopped at a prune orchard some distance from the village to buy some fruit, the farmer cried out from a tree, "they are the Americans; give them as many as they want for nothing!"

With the Burgomaster's little son for a guide, we went back a mile or two of our route to Snellert, which we had passed the night before, and after losing ourselves two or three times in the woods, arrived at last at the top of the mountain, where the ruins of the castle stand. The walls are nearly level with the ground. The interest of a visit rests entirely on the romantic legend, and the wild view over the hills around, particularly that in front, where on the opposite mountain are the ruins of Rodenstein, to which the wild Huntsman was wont to ride at midnight—where he now rides no more. The echoes of Rodenstein are no longer awakened by the sound of his bugle, and the hoofs of his demon steed clanging on the battlements. But the hills around are wild enough, and the roar of the pine forests deep enough to have inspired the simple peasants with the romantic tradition.

Stopping for dinner at the town of Rheinheim, we met an old man, who, on learning we were Americans, walked with us as far as the next village. He had a daughter in America and was highly gratified to meet any one from the country of her adoption. He made me promise to visit her, if I ever should go to St. Louis, and say that I had walked with her father from Rheinheim to Zwangenburg. To satisfy his fears that I might forget it, I took down his name and that of his daughter. He shook me warmly by the hand at parting, and was evidently made happier for that day.

We reached Darmstadt just in time to take a seat in the omnibus for Frankfort. Among the passengers were a Bavarian family, on their way to Bremen, to ship from thence to Texas. I endeavored to discourage the man from choosing such a country as his home, by telling him of its heats and pestilences, but he was too full of hope to be shaken in his purpose. I would have added that it was a slave-land, but I thought on our own country's curse, and was silent. The wife was not so sanguine; she seemed to mourn in secret at leaving her beautiful fatherland. It was saddening to think how lonely they would feel in that far home, and how they would long, with true German devotion, to look again on the green vintage-hills of their forsaken country. As night drew on, the little girl crept over to her father for his accustomed evening kiss, and then sank back to sleep in a corner of the wagon. The boy, in the artless confidence of childhood, laid his head on my breast, weary with the day's travel, and soon slept also. Thus we drove on in the dark, till at length the lights of Frankfort glimmered on the breast of the rapid Main, as we passed over the bridge, and when we stopped near the Cathedral, I delivered up my little charge and sent my sympathy with the wanderers on their lonely way.

# CHAPTER XI. — SCENES IN FRANKFORT—AN AMERICAN COMPOSER— THE POET FREILIGRATH.

Dec. 4.—This is a genuine old German city. Founded by Charlemagne, afterwards a rallying point of the Crusaders, and for a long time the capital of the German empire, it has no lack of interesting historical recollections, and notwithstanding it is fast becoming modernized, one is every where reminded of the Past. The Cathedral, old as the days of Peter the Hermit, the grotesque street of the Jews, the many quaint, antiquated dwellings and the mouldering watch-towers on the hills around, give it a more interesting character than any German city I have yet seen. The house we dwell in, on the Markt Platz, is more than two hundred years old; directly opposite is a great castellated building, gloomy with the weight of six centuries, and a few steps to the left brings me to the square of the Roemerberg, where the Emperors were crowned, in a corner of which is a curiously ornamented house, formerly the residence of Luther. There are legends innumerable connected with all these buildings, and even yet discoveries are frequently made in old houses, of secret chambers and staircases. When you add to all this, the German love of ghost stories, and, indeed, their general belief in spirits, the lover of romance could not desire a more agreeable residence.

I often look out on the singular scene below my window. On both sides of the street, leaving barely room to enter the houses, sit the market women, with their baskets of vegetables and fruit. The middle of the street is filled with women buying, and every cart or carriage that comes along, has to force its way through the crowd, sometimes rolling against and overturning the baskets on the side, when for a few minutes there is a Babel of unintelligible sounds. The country women in their jackets and short gowns go backwards and forwards with great loads on their heads, sometimes nearly as high as themselves. It is a most singular scene, and so varied that one never tires of looking upon it. These women sit here from sunrise till sunset, day after day, for years. They have little furnaces for cooking and for warmth in winter, and when it rains they sit in large wooden boxes. One or two policemen are generally on the ground in the morning to prevent disputing about their places, which often gives rise to interesting scenes. Perhaps this kind of life in the open air is conducive to longevity; for certainly there is no country on earth that has as many old women. Many of them look like walking machines made of leather; and to judge from what I see in the streets here, I should think they work till they die.

On the 21st of October a most interesting fete took place. The magnificent monument of Goethe, modelled by the sculptor Schwanthaler, at Munich, and cast in bronze, was unveiled. It arrived a few days before, and was received with much ceremony and erected in the destined spot, an open square in the western part of the city, planted with acacia trees. I went there at ten o'clock, and found the square already full of people. Seats had been erected around the monument for ladies, the singers and musicians. A company of soldiers was stationed to keep an entrance for the procession, which at length arrived with music and banners, and entered the enclosure. A song for the occasion was sung by the choir; it swelled up gradually, and with such perfect harmony and unity, that it seemed like some glorious instrument touched by a single hand. Then a poetical address was delivered; after which four young men took their stand at the corners of the monument; the drums and trumpets gave a flourish, and the mantle fell. The noble figure seemed to rise out of the earth, and thus amid shoutings and the triumphal peal of the band, the form of Goethe greeted the city of his birth. He is represented as leaning on the trunk of a tree, holding in his right hand a roll of parchment, and in his left a wreath. The pedestal, which is also of bronze, contains bas reliefs, representing scenes from Faust, Wilhelm Meister and Egmont. In the evening Goethe's house, in a street near, was illuminated by arches of lamps between the windows, and hung with wreaths of flowers. Four pillars of colored lamps lighted the statue. At nine o'clock the choir of singers came again in a procession, with colored lanterns, on poles, and after singing two or three songs, the statue was exhibited in the red glare of the Bengal light. The trees and houses around the square were covered with the glow, which streamed in broad sheets up against the dark sky.

Within the walls the greater part of Frankfort is built in the old German style—the houses six or seven stones high, and every story projecting out over the other, so that those living in the upper part can nearly shake hands out of the windows. At the corners figures of men are often seen, holding up the story above on their shoulders and making horrible faces at the weight. When I state that in all these narrow streets which constitute the greater part of the city, there are no sidewalks, the windows of the lower stories with an iron grating extending a foot or so into the street, which is only wide enough for one cart to pass along, you can have some idea of the facility of walking through them, to say nothing of the piles of wood, and market-women with baskets of vegetables which one is continually stumbling over. Even in the wider streets, I have always to look before and behind to keep out of the way of the fiacres; the people here get so accustomed to it, that they leave barely room for them to pass, and the carriages go dashing by at a nearness which sometimes makes me shudder.

As I walked across the Main, and looked down at the swift stream on its way from the distant Thuringian forest to join the Rhine, I thought of the time when Schiller stood there in the days of his early struggles, an exile from his native land, and looking over the bridge, said in the loneliness of his heart, "That water flows not so deep as my sufferings!" In the middle, on an iron ornament, stands the golden cock at which Goethe used to marvel when a boy. Perhaps you have not heard the legend connected with this. The bridge was built several hundred years ago, with such strength and solidity that it will stand many hundred yet. The architect had contracted to build it within a certain time, but as it drew near, without any prospect of fulfilment, the devil appeared to him and promised to finish it, on condition of having the first soul that passed over it. This was agreed upon end the devil performed his part of the bargain. The artist, however, on the day appointed, drove a cook across before he suffered any one to pass over it. His majesty stationed himself under the middle arch of the bridge, awaiting his prey; but enraged at the cheat, he tore the unfortunate fowl in pieces and broke two holes in the arch, saying they should never be built up again. The golden cock was erected on the bridge as a token of the event, but the devil has perhaps lost some of his power in these latter days, for the holes were filled up about thirty years ago.

From the hills on the Darmstadt road, I had a view of the country around—the fields were white and bare, and the dark Tannus, with the broad patches of snow on his sides, looked grim and shadowy through the dim atmosphere. It was like the landscape of a dream—dark, strange and silent. The whole of last month we saw the sun but two or three days, the sky being almost continually covered with a gloomy fog. England and Germany seem to have exchanged climates this year, for in the former country we had delightfully clear weather.

I have seen the banker Rothschild several times driving about the city. This one—Anselmo, the most celebrated of the brothers—holds a mortgage on the city of Jerusalem. He rides about in style, with officers attending his carriage. He is a little bald-headed man, with marked Jewish features, and is said not to deceive his looks. At any rate, his reputation is none of the best, either with Jews or Christians. A caricature was published some time ago, in which he is represented as giving a beggar woman by the way-side, a kreutzer—the smallest German coin. She is made to exclaim, "God reward you, a thousand fold!" He immediately replies, after reckoning up in his head: "How much have I then?—sixteen florins and forty kreutzers!"

I have lately heard one of the most perfectly beautiful creations that ever emanated from the soul of genius—the opera of Fidelio. I have caught faint glimpses of that rich world of fancy and feeling, to which music is the golden door. Surrendering myself to the grasp of Beethoven's powerful conception, I read in sounds far more expressive than words, the almost despairing agony of the strong-hearted, but still tender and womanly Fidelio—the ecstatic joy of the wasted prisoner, when he rose from his hard couch in the dungeon, seeming to fuel, in his maniac brain, the presentiment of a bright being who would come to unbind his chains—and. the sobbing and wailing, almost-human, which came from the orchestra, when they dug his grave, by the dim lantern's light. When it was done, the murderer stole into the dungeon, to gloat on the agonies of his victim, ere he gave the death-blow. Then, while the prisoner is waked to reason by that sight, and Fidelio throws herself before the uplifted dagger, rescuing her husband with the courage which love gives to a woman's heart, the storm of feeling which has been gathering in the music, swells to a height beyond which it seemed impossible for the soul to pass.

My nerves were thrilled till I could bear no more. A mist seemed to come before my eyes and I scarcely knew what followed, till the rescued kneeled together and poured forth in the closing hymn the painful fullness of their joy. I dreaded the sound of voices after the close, and the walk home amid the harsh rattling of vehicles on the rough streets. For days afterwards my brain was filled with a mingled and confused sense of melody, like the half-remembered music of a dream.

Why should such magnificent creations of art be denied the new world? There is certainly enthusiasm and refinement of feeling enough at home to appreciate them, were the proper direction given to the popular taste. What country possesses more advantages to foster the growth of such an art, than ours? Why should not the composer gain mighty conceptions from the grandeur of our mountain scenery, from the howling of the storm through our giant forests, from the eternal thunder of Niagara? All these collateral influences, which more or less tend to the development and expansion of genius, are characteristics of our country; and a taste for musical compositions of a refined and lofty character, would soon give birth to creators.

Fortunately for our country, this missing star in the crown of her growing glory, will probably soon be replaced. Richard S. Willis, with whom we have lived in delightful companionship, since coming here, has been for more than two years studying and preparing himself for the higher branches of composition. The musical talent he displayed while at college, and the success following the publication of a set of beautiful waltzes he there composed, led him to choose this most difficult but lofty path; the result justifies his early promise and gives the most sanguine anticipations for the future. He studied the first two years here under Schnyder von Wartensee, a distinguished Swiss composer; and his exercises have met with the warmest approval from Mendelsohn, at present the first German composer, and Rinck, the celebrated organist. The enormous labor and application required to go through the preparatory studies alone, would make it seem almost impossible for one with the restless energy of the American character, to undertake it; but as this very energy gives genius its greatest power, we may now trust with confidence that Willis, since he has nearly completed his studies, will win himself and his country honor in the difficult path he has chosen.

One evening, after sunset, we took a stroll around the promenades. The swans were still floating on the little lake, and the American poplar beside it, was in its full autumn livery. As we made the circuit of the walks, guns were firing far and near, celebrating the opening of the vintage the next day, and rockets went glittering and sparkling up into the dark air. Notwithstanding the late hour and lowering sky, the walks were full of people and we strolled about with them till it grew quite dark, watching the fire-works which arose from the gardens around.

The next day, we went into the Frankfort wood. Willis and his brother-in-law, Charles F. Dennett, of Boston, Dr. Dix and another young gentleman from the same city, formed the party—six Americans in all; we walked over the Main and through the dirty suburbs of Sachsenhausen, where we met many peasants laden with the first day's vintage, and crowds of people coming down from the vineyards. As we ascended the hill, the sound of firing was heard in every direction, and from many vineyards arose the smoke of fires where groups of merry children were collecting and burning the rubbish. We became lost among the winding paths of the pine forest, so that by the time we came out upon the eminence overlooking the valley of the Main, it was quite dark. From every side, far and near, rockets of all sizes and colors darted high up into the sky. Sometimes a flight of the most brilliant crimson and gold lights rushed up together, then again by some farm-house in the meadow, the vintagers would burn a Roman candle, throwing its powerful white light on the gardens and fields around. We stopped under a garden wall, by which a laughing company were assembled in the smoke and red blaze, and watched several comets go hissing and glancing far above us. The cracking of ammunition still continued, and when we came again upon the bridge, the city opposite was lighted as if illuminated. The full moon had just risen, softening and mellowing the beautiful scene, while beyond, over the tower of Frankfort, rose and fell the meteors that heralded the vintage.

Since I have been in Frankfort, an event has occurred, which shows very distinctly the principles at work in Germany, and gives us some foreboding of the future. Ferdinand Freiligrath, the first living poet with the exception of Uhland, has within a few weeks published a volume of poems entitled, "My Confession of Faith, or Poems for the Times." It contains some thrilling appeals to the free spirit of the German people, setting forth the injustice under which they labor, in simple but powerful language, and with the most forcible illustrations, adapted to the comprehension of everyone. Viewed as a work of genius alone, it is strikingly powerful and original: but when we consider the effect it is producing among the people—the strength it will add to the rising tide of opposition to every form of tyranny, it has a still higher interest. Freiligrath had three or four years before, received a pension of three hundred thalers from the King of Prussia, soon after his accession to the throne: he ceased to draw this about a year ago, stating in the preface to his volume that it was accepted in the belief the King would adhere to his promise of giving the people a new constitution, but that now since free spirit which characterises these men, who come from among the people, shows plainly the tendency of the times; and it is only the great strength with which tyranny here has environed himself, and the almost lethargic slowness of the Germans, which has prevented a change ere this.

In this volume of Freiligrath's, among other things, is a translation of Bryant's magnificent poem "The Winds," and Burns's "A man's a man for a' that;" and I have translated one of his, as a specimen of the spirit in which they are written:

*FREEDOM AND RIGHT.*

*Oh! think not she rests in the grave's chilly slumber*

*Nor sheds o'er the present her glorious light,*

*Since Tyranny's shackles the free soul incumber*

*And traitors accusing, deny to us Right!*

*No: whether to exile the sworn ones are wending,*

*Or weary of power that crushed them unending,*

*In dungeons have perished, their veins madly rending, [*]*

*Yet Freedom still liveth, and with her, the Right!*

*Freedom and Right!*

*A single defeat can confuse us no longer:*

*It adds to the combat's last gathering might,*

*It bids us but doubly to struggle, and stronger*

*To raise up our battle-cry—"Freedom and Right!"*

*For the Twain know a union forever abiding,*

*Together in Truth and in majesty striding;*

*Where Right is, already the free are residing*

*And ever, where dwell the free, governeth Right!*

*Freedom and Right!*

*And this is a trust: never made, us at present,*

*The glad pair from battle to battle their flight;*

*Never breathed through the soul of the down-trodden peasant,*

*Their spirit so deeply its promptings of light!*

*They sweep o'er the earth with a tempest-like token;*

*From strand unto strand words of thunder are spoken:*

*Already the serf finds his manacles broken,*

*And those of the negro are falling from sight*

*Freedom and Right!*

*Yes, every where wide is their war-banner waving.*

*On the armies of Wrong their revenge to requite;*

*The strength of Oppression they boldly are braving*

*And at last they will conquer, resistless in might!*

*Oh, God! what a glorious wreath then appearing*

*Will blend every leaf in the banner they're bearing—The*

*olive of Greece and the shamrock of Erin,*

*And the oak-bough of Germany, greenest in light!*

*Freedom and Right!*

*And many who suffered, are now calmly sleeping,*

*The slumber of freemen, borne down by the fight;*

*While the Twain o'er their graves still a bright watch are keeping,*

*Whom we bless for their memories—Freedom and Right!*

*Meanwhile lift your glasses! to those who have striven!*

*And striving with bold hearts, to misery were driven!*

*Who fought for the Right and but Wrong then were given!*

*To Right, the immortal—to Freedom through Right!*

*Freedom through Right!*

* [ This allusion is to Weidig, who, imprisoned for years at Darmstadt on account of his political principles, finally committed suicide by cutting his throat with the glass of his prison-window.]

# CHAPTER XII. — A WEEK AMONG THE STUDENTS.

Receiving a letter from my cousin one bright December morning, the idea of visiting him struck me, and so, within an hour, B—— and I were on our way to Heidelberg. It was delightful weather; the air was mild as the early days of spring, the pine forests around wore a softer green, and though the sun was but a hand's breadth high, even at noon, it was quite warm on the open road. We stopped for the night at Bensheim; the next morning was as dark as a cloudy day in the north can be, wearing a heavy gloom I never saw elsewhere. The wind blew the snow down from the summits upon us, but being warm from walking, we did not heed it. The mountains looked higher than in summer, and the old castles more grim and frowning. From the hard roads and freezing wind, my feet became very sore, and after limping along in excruciating pain for a league or two, I filled my boots with brandy, which deadened the wounds so much, that I was enabled to go on in a kind of trot, which I kept up, only stopping ten minutes to dinner, till we reached Heidelberg.

The same evening there was to be a general commers, or meeting of the societies among the students, and I determined not to omit witnessing one of the most interesting and characteristic features of student-life. So borrowing a cap and coat, I looked the student well enough to pass for one of them, though the former article was somewhat of the Philister form. Baader, a young poet of some note, and president of the "Palatia" Society, having promised to take us there, we met at eight o'clock at an inn frequented by the students, and went to the rendezvous, near the Markt Platz.

A confused sound of voices came from the inn, as we drew near; groups of students were standing around the door. In the entry we saw the Red Fisherman, one of the most conspicuous characters about the University. He is a small, stout man, with bare neck and breast, red hair, whence his name, and a strange mixture of roughness and benevolence in his countenance. He has saved many persons at the risk of his own life, from drowning in the

Neckar, and on that account is leniently dealt with by the faculty whenever he is arrested for assisting the students in any of their unlawful proceedings. Entering the room I could scarcely see at first, on account of the smoke that ascended from a hundred pipes. All was noise and confusion. Near the door sat some half dozen musicians who were getting their instruments ready for action, and the long room was filled with tables, all of which seemed to be full and the students were still pressing in. The tables were covered with great stone jugs and long beer glasses; the students were talking and shouting and drinking.—One who appeared to have the arrangement of the meeting, found seats for us together, and having made a slight acquaintance with those sitting next us, we felt more at liberty to witness their proceedings. They were all talking in a sociable, friendly way, and I saw no one who appeared to be intoxicated. The beer was a weak mixture, which I should think would make one fall over from its weight before it would intoxicate him. Those sitting near me drank but little, and that principally to make or return compliments. One or two at the other end of the table were more boisterous, and more than one glass was overturned on the legs below it. Leaves containing the songs for the evening lay at each seat, and at the head, where the President sat, were two swords crossed, with which he occasionally struck upon the table to preserve order. Our President was a fine, romantic-looking young man, dressed in the old German costume, which is far handsomer than the modern. I never saw in any company of young men, so many handsome, manly countenances. If their faces were any index of their characters, there were many noble, free souls among them. Nearly opposite to me sat a young poet, whose dark eyes flashed with feeling as he spoke to those near him. After some time passed in talking and drinking together, varied by an occasional air from the musicians, the President beat order with the sword, and the whole company joined in one of their glorious songs, to a melody at the same time joyous and solemn. Swelled by so many manly voices it rose up like a hymn of triumph—all other sounds were stilled. Three times during the singing all rose up, clashed their glasses together around the tables and drank to their Fatherland, a health and blessing to the patriot, and honor to those who struggle in the cause of freedom, at the close thundering out their motto:

*"Fearless in strife, to the banner still true!"*

After this song the same order as before was continued, except that students from the different societies made short speeches, accompanied by some toast or sentiment. One spoke of Germany—predicting that all her dissensions would be overcome, and she would rise up at last, like a phoenix among the nations of Europe; and at the close gave 'strong, united, regenerated Germany!' Instantly all sprang to their feet, and clashing the glasses together, gave a thundering "hoch!" This enthusiasm for their country is one of the strongest characteristics of the German students; they have ever been first in the field for her freedom, and on them mainly depends her future redemption.

Cloths were passed around, the tables wiped off, and preparations made to sing the "Landsfather" or consecration song. This is one of the most important and solemn of their ceremonies, since by performing it the new students are made burschen, and the bands of brotherhood continually kept fresh and sacred. All became still a moment, then they commenced the lofty song:

> "Silent bending, each one lending
>
> To the solemn tones his ear,
>
> Hark, the song of songs is sounding—
>
> Back from joyful choir resounding,
>
> Hear it, German brothers, hear!

> "German proudly, raise it loudly,
>
> Singing of your fatherland—
>
> Fatherland! thou land of story,
>
> To the altars of thy glory
>
> Consecrate us, sword in hand!

> "Take the beaker, pleasure seeker,
>
> With thy country's drink brimmed o'er!

*In thy left the sword is blinking.*

*Pierce it through the cap, while drinking*

*To thy Fatherland once more!"*

With the first line of the last stanza, the Presidents sitting at the head of the table, take their glasses in their right hands, and at the third line, the sword in their left, at the end striking their glasses together and drinking.

*"In left hand gleaming, thou art beaming,*

*Sword from all dishonour free!*

*Thus I pierce the cap, while swearing,*

*It in honor ever wearing,*

*I a valiant Bursch will be!"*

They clash their swords together till the third line is sung, when each takes his cap, and piercing the point of the sword through the crown, draws it down to the guard. Leaving their caps on the swords, the Presidents stand behind the two next students, who go through the same ceremony, receiving the swords at the appropriate time, and giving it back loaded with their caps also. This ceremony is going on at every table at the same time. These two stanzas are repeated for every pair of students, till all have gone through with it, and the Presidents have arrived at the bottom of the table, with their swords strung full of caps. Here they exchange swords, while all sing:

*"Come thou bright sword, now made holy,*

*Of free men the weapon free;*

*Bring it solemnly and slowly,*

*Heavy with pierced caps, to me!*

*From its burden now divest it;*

*Brothers be ye covered all,*

*And till our next festival,*

*Hallowed and unspotted rest it!*

*"Up, ye feast companions! ever*

*Honor ye our holy band!*

*And with heart and soul endeavor*

*E'er as high-souled men to stand!*

*Up to feast, ye men united!*

*Worthy be your fathers' fame,*

*And the sword may no one claim,*

*Who to honor is not plighted!"*

Then each President, taking a cap of his sword, reached it to the student opposite, and they crossed their swords, the ends resting on the two students' heads, while they sang the next stanza:

*"So take it back; thy head I now will cover*

*And stretch the bright sword over.*

*Live also then this Bursche, hoch!*

*Wherever we may meet him,*

*Will we, as Brother greet him—*

*Live also this, our Brother, hoch!"*

This ceremony was repeated till all the caps were given back, and they then concluded with the following:

*"Rest, the Bursehen-feast is over,*

*Hallowed sword and thou art free!*

*Each one strive a valiant lover*

*Of his fatherland to be!*

*Hail to him, who, glory-haunted,*

*Follows still his fathers bold;*

*And the sword may no one hold*

*But the noble and undaunted!"*

The Landsfather being over, the students were less orderly; the smoking and drinking began again and we left, as it was already eleven o'clock, glad to breathe the pure cold air.

In the University I heard Gervinus, who was formerly professor in Göttingen, but was obliged to leave on account of his liberal principles. He is much liked by the students and his lectures are very well attended. They had this winter a torchlight procession in honor of him. He is a stout, round-faced man, speaks very fast, and makes them laugh continually with his witty remarks. In the room I saw a son of Rückert, the poet, with a face strikingly like his father's. The next evening I went to hear Schlosser, the great historian. Among his pupils are the two princes of Baden, who are now at the University. He came hurriedly in, threw down his portfolio and began instantly to speak. He is an old, gray-headed man, but still active and full of energy. The Germans find him exceedingly difficult to understand, as he is said to use the English construction almost entirely; for this reason, perhaps, I understood him quite easily. He lectures on the French Revolution, but is engaged in writing a Universal History, the first numbers of which are published.

Two or three days after, we heard that a duel was to take place at Neuenheim, on the opposite side of the Neckur, where the students have a house hired for that purpose. In order to witness the spectacle, we started immediately with two or three students. Along the road were stationed old women, at intervals, as guards, to give notice of the approach of the police, and from these we learned that one duel had already been fought, and they were preparing for the other. The Red Fisherman was busy in an outer room grinding the swords, which are made as sharp as razors. In the large room some forty or fifty students were walking about, while the parties were preparing. This was done by taking off the coat and vest and binding a great thick leather garment on, which reached from the breast to the knees, completely protecting the body. They then put on a leather glove reaching nearly to the shoulder, tied a thick cravat around the throat, and drew on a cap with a large vizor. This done, they were walked about the room a short time, the seconds holding out their arms to strengthen them; their faces all this time betrayed considerable anxiety.

All being ready, the seconds took their stations immediately behind them, each armed with a sword, and gave the words: "ready—bind your weapons—loose!" They instantly sprang at each other, exchanged two or three blows, when the seconds cried "halt!" and struck their swords up. Twenty-four rounds of this kind ended the duel, without either being hurt, though the cap of one of them was cut through and his forehead grazed. All their duels do not end so fortunately, however, as the frightful scars on the faces of many of those present, testified. It is a gratification to know that but a small portion of the students keep up this barbarous custom. The great body is opposed to it; in Heidelberg, four societies, comprising more than one half the students, have been formed against it. A strong desire for such a reform seems to prevail, and the custom will probably be totally discontinued in a short time.

This view of the student-life was very interesting to me; it appeared in a much better light than I had been accustomed to view it. Their peculiar customs, except duelling and drinking, of course, may be the better tolerated when we consider their effect on the liberty of Germany. It is principally through them that a free spirit is kept alive; they have ever been foremost to rise up for their Fatherland, and bravest in its defence. And though many of their customs have so often been held up to ridicule, among no other class can one find warmer, truer or braver hearts.

# CHAPTER XIII. – CHRISTMAS AND NEW YEAR IN GERMANY.

Jan. 2, 1845.—I have lately been computing how much my travels have cost me up to the present time, and how long I can remain abroad to continue the pilgrimage, with my present expectations. The result has been most encouraging to my plan. Before leaving home, I wrote to several gentlemen who had visited Europe, requesting the probable expense of travel and residence abroad. They sent different accounts; E. Joy Morris said I must calculate to spend at least $1500 a year; another suggested $1000, and the most moderate of all, said that it was impossible to live in Europe a year on less than $500. Now, six months have elapsed since I left home—six months of greater pleasure and profit than any year of my former life—and my expenses, in full, amount to $130! This, however, nearly exhausts the limited sum with which I started, but through the kindness of the editorial friends who have been publishing my sketches of travel, I trust to receive a remittance shortly. Printing is a business attended with so little profit here, as there are already so many workmen, that it is almost useless for a stranger to apply. Besides, after a tough grapple, I am just beginning to master the language, and it seems so necessary to devote every minute to study, that I would rather undergo some privation, than neglect turning these fleeting hours into gold, for the miser Memory to stow away in the treasure-vaults of the mind.

We have lately witnessed the most beautiful and interesting of all German festivals—Christmas. This is here peculiarly celebrated. About the commencement of December, the Christmarkt or fair, was opened in the Roemerberg, and has continued to the present time. The booths, decorated with green boughs, were filled with toys of various kinds, among which during the first days the figure of St. Nicholas was conspicuous. There were bunches of wax candles to illuminate the Christmas tree, gingerbread with printed mottos in poetry, beautiful little earthenware, basket-work, and a wilderness of playthings. The 5th of December, being Nicholas evening, the booths were lighted up, and the square was filled with boys, running from one stand to another, all shouting and talking together in the most joyous confusion. Nurses were going around, carrying the smaller children in their arms, and parents bought presents decorated with sprigs of pine and carried them away. Some of the shops had beautiful toys, as for instance, a whole grocery store in miniature, with barrels, boxes and drawers, all filled with sweetmeats, a kitchen with a stove and all suitable utensils, which could really be used, and sets of dishes of the most diminutive patterns. All was a scene of activity and joyous feeling.

Many of the tables had bundles of rods with gilded bands, which were to be used that evening by the persons who represented St. Nicholas. In the family with whom we reside, one of our German friends dressed himself very comically, with a mask, fur robe and long tapering cap. He came in with a bunch of rods and a sack, and a broom for a sceptre. After we all had received our share of the beating, he threw the contents of his bag on the table, and while we were scrambling for the nuts and apples, gave us many smart raps over the fingers. In many families the children are made to say, "I thank you, Herr Nicolaus," and the rods are hung up in the room till Christmas to keep them in good behavior. This was only a forerunner of the Christ-kindchen's coming. The Nicolaus is the punishing spirit, the Christ-kindchen the rewarding one.

When this time was over, we all began preparing secretly our presents for Christmas. Every day there were consultations about the things which should be obtained. It was so arranged that all should interchange presents, but nobody must know beforehand what he would receive. What pleasure there was in all these secret purchases and preparations! Scarcely anything was thought or spoken of but Christmas, and every day the consultations became more numerous and secret. The trees were bought sometime beforehand, but as we were to witness the festival for the first time, we were not allowed to see them prepared, in order that the effect might be as great as possible. The market in the Roeinerberg Square grew constantly larger and more brilliant. Every night it was lit up with lamps and thronged with people. Quite a forest sprang up in the street before our door. The old stone house opposite, with the traces of so many centuries on its dark face, seemed to stand in the midst of a garden. It was a pleasure to go out every evening and see the children rushing

to and fro, shouting and seeking out toys from the booths, and talking all the
time of the Christmas that was so near. The poor people went by with their
little presents hid under their cloaks, lest their children might see them; every
heart was glad and every countenance wore a smile of secret pleasure.

Finally the day before Christmas arrived. The streets were so full I could
scarce make my way through, and the sale of trees went on more rapidly
than ever. These wore commonly branches of pine or fir, set upright in a
little miniature garden of moss. When the lamps were lighted at night, our
street had the appearance of an illuminated garden. We were prohibited from
entering the rooms up stairs in which the grand ceremony was to take place,
being obliged to take our seats in those arranged for the guests, and wait with
impatience the hour when Christ-kindchen should call. Several relations of
the family came, and what was more agreeable, they brought with them five
or six children. I was anxious to see how they would view the ceremony.
Finally, in the middle of an interesting conversation, we heard the bell ringing
up stairs. We all started up, and made for the door. I ran up the steps with
the children at my heels, and at the top met a blaze of light coming from
the open door, that dazzled me. In each room stood a great table, on which
the presents were arranged, amid flowers and wreaths. From the centre, rose
the beautiful Christmas tree covered with wax tapers to the very top, which
made it nearly as light as day, while every bough was hung with sweetmeats
and gilded nuts. The children ran shouting around the table, hunting their
presents, while the older persons had theirs pointed out to them. I had qui'e a
little library of German authors as my share; and many of the others received
quite valuable gifts.

But how beautiful was the heart-felt joy that shone on every countenance!
As each one discovered he embraced the givers, and all was a scene of the
purest feelings. It is a glorious feast, this Christmas time! What a chorus from
happy hearts went up on that evening to Heaven! Full of poetry and feeling
and glad associations, it is here anticipated with joy, and leaves a pleasant
memory behind it. We may laugh at such simple festivals at home, and prefer
to shake ourselves loose from every shackle that bears the rust of the Past, but
we would certainly be happier if some of these beautiful old customs were

better honored. They renew the bond of feeling between families and friends, and strengthen their kindly sympathy; even life-long friends require occasions of this kind to freshen the wreath that binds them together.

New Year's Eve is also favored with a peculiar celebration in Germany. Every body remains up and makes himself merry till midnight. The Christmas trees are again lighted, and while the tapers are burning down, the family play for articles which they have purchased and hung on the boughs. It is so arranged that each one shall win as much as he gives, which change of articles makes much amusement. One of the ladies rejoiced in the possession of a red silk handkerchief and a cake of soap, while a cup and saucer and a pair of scissors fell to my lot! As midnight drew near, it was louder in the streets, and companies of people, some of them singing in chorus, passed by on their way to the Zeil. Finally three-quarters struck, the windows were opened and every one waited anxiously for the clock to strike. At the first sound, such a cry arose as one may imagine, when thirty or forty thousand persons all set their lungs going at once. Every body in the house, in the street, over the whole city, shouted, "Prosst Neu Jahr?" In families, all the members embrace each other, with wishes of happiness for the new year. Then the windows are thrown open, and they cry to their neighbors or those passing by.

After we had exchanged congratulations, Dennett, B—— and I set out for the Zeil. The streets were full of people, shouting to one another and to those standing at the open windows. We failed not to cry, "Prosst Neu Jahr!" wherever we saw a damsel at the window, and the words came back to us more musically than we sent them. Along the Zeil the spectacle was most singular. The great wide street was filled with companies of men, marching up and down, while from the mass rang up one deafening, unending shout, that seemed to pierce the black sky above. The whole scene looked stranger and wilder from the flickering light of the swinging lamps, and I could not help thinking it must resemble a night in Paris during the French Revolution. We joined the crowd and used our lungs as well as any of them. For some time after we returned home, companies passed by, singing "with us 'tis ever so!" but at three o'clock all was again silent.

# CHAPTER XIV. — WINTER IN FRANKFORT—A FAIR, AN INUNDATION AND A FIRE.

After New Year, the Main, just above the city, and the lakes in the promenades, were frozen over. The ice was tried by the police, and having been found of sufficient thickness, to the great joy of the schoolboys, permission was given to skate. The lakes were soon covered with merry skaters, and every afternoon the banks were crowded with spectators. It was a lively sight to see two or three hundred persons darting about, turning and crossing like a flock of crows, while, by means of arm-chairs mounted on runners, the ladies were enabled to join in the sport, and whirl around among them. Some of the broad meadows near the city, which were covered with water, were the resort of the schools. I went there often in my walks, and always found two or three schools, with the teachers, all skating together, and playing their winter games on the ice. I have often seen them on the meadows along the Main; the teachers generally made quite as much noise as the scholars in their sports.

In the Art Institute I saw the picture of "Huss before the Council of Constance," by the painter Lessing. It contains upwards of twenty figures. The artist has shown the greatest skill in the expression and grouping of these. Bishops and Cardinals in their splendid robes are seated around a table, covered with parchment folios, and before them stands Huss alone. His face, pale and thin with long imprisonment, he has lain one hand on his breast, while with the other he has grasped one of the volumes on the table; there is an air of majesty, of heavenly serenity on his lofty forehead and calm eye. One feels instinctively that he has truth on his side. There can be no deception, no falsehood in those noble features. The three Italian cardinals before him appear to be full of passionate rage; the bishop in front, who holds the imperial pass given to Huss, looks on with an expression of scorn, and the priests around have an air of mingled curiosity and hatred. There is one, however, in whose mild features and tearful eye is expressed sympathy and pity for the prisoner. It is said this picture has had a great effect upon Catholics who have seen it, in softening the bigotry with which they regarded the early reformers; and if so, it is a triumphant proof how much art can effect in the cause of truth and humanity. I was much interested in a cast of the statue of St. George, by the old Italian sculptor Donatello. It is a figure full of youth and energy, with a countenance that seems to breathe. Donatello was the teacher of Michael Angelo, and when the young sculptor was about setting off for Rome, he showed him the statue, his favorite work. Michael gazed at it long and intensely, and at length, on parting, said to Donatello, "It wants but one thing." The artist pondered long over this expression, for he could not imagine in what could fail the matchless figure. At length, after many years, Michael Angelo, in the noon of his renown, visited the death-bed of his old master. Donatello begged to know, before he died, what was wanting to his St. George. Angelo answered, "the gift of speech!" and a smile of triumph lighted the old man's face, as he closed his eyes forever.

The Eschernheim Tower, at the entrance of one of the city gates, is universally admired by strangers, on account of its picturesque appearance, overgrown with ivy and terminated by the little pointed turrets, which one sees so often in Germany, on buildings three or four centuries old. There are five other watch towers of similar form, which stand on different sides of the city, at the distance of a mile or two, and generally upon an eminence overlooking the country. They were erected several centuries ago, to discern from afar the approach of an enemy, and protect the caravans of merchants, which at that time travelled from city to city, from the attacks of robbers. The Eschernheim Tower is interesting from another circumstance, which, whether true or not, is universally believed. When Frankfort was under the sway of a prince, a Swiss hunter, for some civil offence, was condemned to die. He begged his life from the prince, who granted it only on condition that he should fire the figure 9 with his rifle through the vane of this tower. He agreed, and did it; and at the present lime, one can distinguish a rude 9 on the vane, as if cut with bullets, while two or three marks at the side appear to be from shots that failed.

The promise of spring which lately visited us, was not destined for fulfilment. Shortly afterwards it grew cold again, with a succession of snows and sharp northerly winds. Such weather at the commencement of spring is not uncommon at home; but here they say there has not been such a winter known for 150 years. In the north of Prussia many persons have been starved to death on account of provisions becoming scarce. Among the Hartz also, the suffering is very great. We saw something of the misery even here. It was painful to walk through the streets and see so many faces bearing plainly the marks of want, so many pale, hollow-eyed creatures, with suffering written on every feature. We were assailed with petitions for help which could not be relieved, though it pained and saddened the heart to deny. The women, too, labor like brutes, day after day. Many of them appear cheerful and contented, and are no doubt, tolerably happy, for the Germans have all true, warm hearts, and are faithful to one another, as far as poverty will permit; but one cannot see old, gray-headed women, carrying loads on their heads as heavy as themselves, exposed to all kinds of weather and working from morning till night, without pity and indignation.

So unusually severe has been the weather, that the deer and hares in the mountains near, came nearly starved and tamed down by hunger, into the villages to hunt food. The people fed them everyday, and also carried grain into the fields for the partridges and pheasants, who flew up to them like domestic fowls. The poor ravens made me really sorry; some lay dead in the fields and many came into the city perfectly tame, flying along the Main with wings hardly strong enough to boar up their skeleton bodies. The storks came at the usual time, but went back again. I hope the year's blessing has not departed with them, according to the old German superstition.

March 26.—We have hopes of spring at last. Three days ago the rain began and has continued with little intermission till now. The air is warm, the snow goes fast, and every thing seems to announce that the long winter is breaking up. The Main rises fast, and goes by the city like an arrow, whirling large masses of ice upon the banks. The hills around are coming out from under the snow, and the lilac-buds in the promenades begin to expand for the second time.

The Fair has now commenced in earnest, and it is a most singular and interesting sight. The open squares are filled with booths, leaving narrow streets between them, across which canvas is spread. Every booth is open and filled with a dazzling display of wares of all kinds. Merchants assemble from all parts of Europe. The Bohemians come with their gorgeous crystal ware; the Nuremborgers with their toys, quaint and fanciful as the old city itself; men from the Thuringian forest, with minerals and canes, and traders from Berlin, Vienna, Paris and Switzerland, with dry goods and wares of all kinds. Near the Exchange are two or three companies of Tyrolese, who attract much of my attention. Their costume is exceedingly picturesque. The men have all splendid manly figures, and honor and bravery are written on their countenances. One of the girls is a really handsome mountain maiden, and with her pointed, broad-brimmed black hat, as romantic looking as one could desire. The musicians have arrived, and we are entertained the whole day long by wandering bands, some of whom play finely. The best, which is also the favorite company, is from Saxony, called "The Mountain Boys." They are now playing in our street, and while I write, one of the beautiful choruses from Norma comes up through the din of the crowd. In fact, music is heard over the whole city, and the throngs that fill every street with all sorts of faces and dresses, somewhat relieve the monotony that was beginning to make Frankfort tiresome.

We have an ever-varied and interesting scene from our window. Besides the motley crowd of passers-by, there are booths and tables stationed thick below. One man in particular is busily engaged in selling his store of blacking in the auction style, in a manner that would do credit to a real Down-caster. He has flaming certificates exhibited, and prefaces his calls to buy with a high-sounding description of his wonderful qualities. He has a bench in front, where he tests on the shoes of his customers, or if none of those are disposed to try it, he rubs it on his own, which shine like mirrors. So he rattles on with amazing fluency in French, German and Italian, and this, with his black beard and moustache and his polite, graceful manner, keeps a crowd of customers around him, so that the wonderful blacking goes off as fast as he can supply it.

April 6.—Old Winter's gales are shut close behind us, and the sun looks down with his summer countenance. The air, after the long cold rain, is like that of Paradise. All things are gay and bright, and everybody is in motion.

113

Spring commenced with yesterday in earnest, and lo! before night the roads were all dry and fine as if there had been no rain for a month; and the gardeners dug and planted in ground which, eight days before, was covered with snow!

After having lived through the longest winter here, for one hundred and fifty years, we were destined to witness the greatest flood for sixty, and little lower than any within the last three hundred years. On the 28th of March, the river overflooded the high pier along the Main, and rising higher and higher, began to come into the gates and alleys. Before night the whole bank was covered and the water intruded into some of the booths in the Römerberg. When I went there the next morning, it was a sorrowful sight. Persons were inside the gate with boats; so rapidly had it risen, that many of the merchants had no time to move their wares, and must suffer great damage. They were busy rescuing what property could bo seized in the haste, and constructing passages into the houses which were surrounded. No one seemed to think of buying or selling, but only on the best method to escape the danger. Along the Main it was still worse. From the measure, it had risen seventeen feet above its usual level, and the arches of the bridge were filled nearly to the top. At the Upper-Main gate, every thing was flooded—houses, gardens, workshops, &c.; the water had even overrun the meadows above and attacked the city from behind, so that a part of the beautiful promenades lay deep under water. On the other side, we could see houses standing in it up to the roof. It came up through the sewers into the middle of Frankfort; a large body of men were kept at work constructing slight bridges to walk on, and transporting boats to places where they were needed. This was all done at the expense of the city; the greatest readiness was everywhere manifested to render all possible assistance. In the Fischergasse, I saw them taking provisions to the people in boats; one man even fastened a loaf of bread to the end of a broomstick and reached it across the narrow street from an upper story window, to the neighbor opposite. News came that Hausen, a village towards the Taunus, about two miles distant, was quite under water, and that the people clung to the roofs and cried for help; but it was fortunately false. About noon, cannon shots were heard, and twenty boats were sent out from the city.

In the afternoon I ascended the tower of the Cathedral, which commands a wide view of the valley, up and down. Just above the city the whole plain was like a small lake—between two and three miles wide. A row of new-built houses stretched into it like a long promontory, and in the middle, like an island, stood a country-seat with large out-buildings. The river sent a long arm out below, that reached up through the meadows behind the city, as if to clasp it all and bear it away together. A heavy storm was raging along the whole extent of the Taunus; but a rainbow stood in the eastern sky. I thought of its promise, and hoped, for the sake of the hundreds of poor people who were suffering by the waters, that it might herald their fall.

We afterwards went over to Sachsenhausen, which was, if possible, in a still more unfortunate condition. The water had penetrated the passages and sewers, and from these leaped and rushed up into the streets, as out of a fountain. The houses next to the Main, which were first filled, poured torrents out of the doors and windows into the street below. These people were nearly all poor, and could ill afford the loss of time and damage of property it occasioned them. The stream was filled with wood and boards, and even whole roofs, with the tiles on, went floating down. The bridge was crowded with people; one saw everywhere mournful countenances, and heard lamentations over the catastrophe. After sunset, a great cloud, filling half the sky, hung above; the reflection of its glowing crimson tint, joined to the brown hue of the water, made it seem like a river of fire.

What a difference a little sunshine makes! I could have forgotten the season the next day, but for the bare trees and swelling Main, as I threaded my way through the hundreds of people who thronged its banks. It was that soft warmth that comes with the first spring days, relaxing the body and casting a dreamy hue over the mind. I leaned over the bridge in the full enjoyment of it, and listening to the roaring of the water under the arches, forgot every thing else for a time. It was amusing to walk up and down the pier and look at the countenances passing by, while the phantasy was ever ready, weaving a tale for all. My favorite Tyrolese were there, and I saw a Greek leaning over the stone balustrade, wearing the red cap and white frock, and with the long dark hair and fiery eye of the Orient. I could not but wonder, as he looked at the dim hills of the Odenwald, along the eastern horizon, whether they called up in his mind the purple isles of his native Archipelago.

The general character of a nation is plainly stamped on the countenances of its people. One who notices the faces in the streets, can soon distinguish, by the glance he gives in going by, the Englishman or the Frenchman from the German, and the Christian from the Jew. Not less striking is the difference of expression between the Germans themselves; and in places where all classes of people are drawn together, it is interesting to observe how accurately these distinctions are drawn. The boys have generally handsome, intelligent faces, and like all boys, they are full of life and spirit, for they know nothing of the laws by which their country is chained down, and would not care for them, if they did. But with the exception of the students, who talk, at least, of Liberty and Right, the young men lose this spirit and at last settle down into the calm, cautious, lethargic citizen. One distinguishes an Englishman and I should think an American, also, in this respect, very easily; the former, moreover, by a certain cold stateliness and reserve. There is something, however, about a Jew, whether English or German, which marks him from all others. However different their faces, there is a family character which runs through the whole of them. It lays principally in their high cheek-bones, prominent nose and thin, compressed lips; which, especially in elderly men, gives a peculiar miserly expression that is unmistakeable. I regret to say, one looks almost in vain, in Germany, for a handsome female countenance. Here and there, perhaps, is a woman with regular features, but that intellectual expression, which gives such a charm to the most common face, is wanting. I have seen more beautiful women in one night, in a public assembly in America, than during the seven months I have been on the Continent. Some of the young Jewesses, in Frankfort, are considered handsome, but their features soon become too strongly marked. In a public walk the number of positively ugly faces is really astonishing.

About ten o'clock that night, I heard a noise of persons running in the street, and going to the Römerberg, found the water had risen, all at once, much higher, and was still rapidly increasing. People were setting up torches and lengthening the rafts, which had been already formed. The lower part of the city was a real Venice—the streets were full of boats and people could even row about in their own houses; though it was not quite so bad as the flood in Georgia, where they went up stairs to bed in boats! I went to the bridge. Persons were calling around—"The water! the water! it rises continually!" The river rushed through the arches, foaming and dashing with a noise like thunder, and the red light of the torches along the shore cost a flickering glare on the troubled waves. It was then twenty-one feet above its usual level. Men were busy all around, carrying boats and ladders to the places most threatened, or emptying cellars into which it was penetrating. The sudden swelling was occasioned by the coming down of the floods from the mountains of Spessart.

Part of the upper quay cracked next morning and threatened to fall in, and one of the projecting piers of the bridge sunk away from the main body three or four inches. In Sachsenhausen the desolation occasioned by the flood is absolutely frightful; several houses have fallen into total ruin. All business was stopped for the day; the Exchange was even shut up. As the city depends almost entirely on pumps for its supply of water, and these were filled with the flood, we have been drinking the muddy current of the Main ever since. The damage to goods is very great. The fair was stopped at once, and the loss in this respect alone, must be several millions of florins. The water began to fall on the 1st, and has now sunk about ten feet, so that most of the houses are again released, though in a bad condition.

Yesterday afternoon, as I was sitting in my room, writing, I heard all at once an explosion like a cannon in the street, followed by loud and continued screams. Looking out the window, I saw the people rushing by with goods in their arms, some wringing their hands and crying, others running in all directions. Imagining that it was nothing less than the tumbling down of one of the old houses, we ran down and saw a store a few doors distant in flames. The windows were bursting and flying out, and the mingled mass of smoke and red flame reached half way across the street. We learned afterwards it was occasioned by the explosion of a jar of naphtha, which instantly enveloped the whole room in fire, the people barely escaping in time. The persons who had booths near were standing still in despair, while the flames were beginning to touch their property. A few butchers who first came up, did almost everything. A fire engine arrived soon, but it was ten minutes before it began to play, and by that time the flames were coming out of the upper stories. Then the supply of water soon failed, and though another engine came up shortly after, it was sometime before it could be put in order, so that by the time they got fairly to work, the fire had made its way nearly through the house. The water was first brought in barrels drawn by horses, till some officer came and opened the fire plug. The police were busy at work seizing those who came by and setting them to work; and as the alarm had drawn a great many together, they at last began to effect something. All the military are obliged to bo out, and the officers appeared eager to use their authority while they could, for every one was ordering and commanding, till all was a scene of perfect confusion and uproar. I could not help laughing heartily, so ludicrous did the scene appear. There were little, miserable engines, not much bigger than a hand-cart, and looking as if they had not been used for half a century, the horses running backwards and forwards, dragging barrels which were emptied into tubs, after which the water was finally dipped up in buckets, and emptied into the engines! These machines can only play into the second or third story, after which the hose was taken up in the houses on the opposite side of the street, and made to play across. After four hours the fire was overcome, the house being thoroughly burnt out; it happened to have double fire walls, which prevented those adjoining from catching easily.

# CHAPTER XV. — THE DEAD AND THE DEAF—MENDELSSOHN THE COMPOSER.

It is now a luxury to breathe. These spring days are the perfection of delightful weather. Imagine the delicious temperature of our Indian summer joined to the life and freshness of spring, add to this a sky of the purest azure, and a breeze filled with the odor of violets,—the most exquisite of all perfumes—and you have some idea of it. The meadows are beginning to bloom, and I have already heard the larks singing high up in the sky. Those sacred birds, the storks, have returned and taken possession of their old nests on the chimney-tops; they are sometimes seen walking about in the fields, with a very grave and serious air, as if conscious of the estimation in which they are held. Everybody is out in the open air; the woods, although they still look wintry, are filled with people, and the boatmen on the Main are busy ferrying gay parties across. The spring has been so long in coming, that all are determined to enjoy it well, while it lasts.

We visited the cemetery a few days ago. The dead-house, where corpses are placed in the hope of resuscitation, is an appendage to cemeteries found only in Germany. We were shown into a narrow chamber, on each side of which were six cells, into which one could distinctly see, by means of a large plate of glass. In each of these is a bier for the body, directly above which hangs a cord, having on the end ten thimbles, which are put upon the fingers of the corpse, so that the slightest motion strikes a bell in the watchman's room. Lamps are lighted at night, and in winter the rooms are warmed. In the watchman's chamber stands a clock with a dial-plate of twenty-four hours, and opposite every hour is a little plate, which can only be moved two minutes before it strikes. If then the watchman has slept or neglected his duty at that time, he cannot move it afterwards, and his neglect, is seen by the superintendent. In such a case, he is severely lined, and for the second or third offence, dismissed. There are other rooms adjoining, containing beds, baths, galvanic battery, &c. Nevertheless, they say there has been no resuscitation during the fifteen years it has been established.

We afterwards went to the end of the cemetery to see the bas-reliefs of Thorwaldsen, in the vault of the Bethmann family. They are three in number, representing the death of a son of the present banker, Moritz von Bethmann, who was drowned in the Arno about fourteen years ago. The middle one represents the young man drooping in his chair, the beautiful Greek Angel of Death standing at his back, with one arm over his shoulder, while his younger brother is sustaining him, and receiving the wreath that drops from his sinking hand. The young woman who showed us these, told us of Thorwaldsen's visit to Frankfort, about three years ago. She described him as a beautiful and venerable old man, with long white locks hanging over his shoulders, still vigorous and active for his years. There seems to have been much resemblance between him and Dannecker—not only in personal appearance and character, but, in the simple and classical beauty of their works.

The cemetery contains many other monuments; with the exception of one or two by Launitz, and an exquisite Death Angel in sandstone, from a young Frankfort sculptor, they are not remarkable. The common tombstone is a white wooden cross; opposite the entrance is a perfect forest of them, involuntarily reminding one of a company of ghosts, with outstretched arms. These contain the names of the deceased with mottoes, some of which are beautiful and touching, as for instance: "Through darkness unto light;" "Weep not for her; she is not dead, but sleepeth" "Slumber sweet!" etc. The graves are neatly bordered with grass, and planted with flowers, and many of the crosses have withered wreathes hanging upon them. In summer it is a beautiful place; in fact, the very name of cemetery in German—Friedhuf or Court of Peace—takes away the idea of death; the beautiful figure of the youth, with his inverted torch, makes one think of the grave only us a place of repose.

On our way back we stopped at the Institute for the Deaf; for by the new method of teaching they are no longer dumb. It is a handsome building in the gardens skirting the city. We applied, and on learning we were strangers, they gave us permission to enter. On finding we were Americans, the instructress immediately spoke of Dr. Howe, who had visited the Institute a year or two before, and was much pleased to find that Mr. Dennett was acquainted with him. She took us into a room where about fifteen small children were assembled, and addressing one of the girls, said in a distinct tone: "These gentlemen are from America; the deaf children there speak with their fingers—canst thou speak so?" To which the child answered distinctly, but with some effort: "No, we speak with our mouths." She then spoke to several others with the same success; one of the boys in particular, articulated with astonishing success. It was interesting to watch their countenances, which were alive with eager attention, and to see the apparent efforts they made to utter the words. They spoke in a monotonous tone, slowly and deliberately, but their voices had a strange, sepulchral sound, which was at first unpleasant to the ear. I put one or two questions to a little boy, which he answered quite readily; as I was a foreigner, this was the best test that could be given of the success of the method. We conversed afterwards with the director, who received us kindly, and appointed a day for us to come and witness the system more fully. He spoke of Dr. Howe and Horace Mann, of Boston, and seemed to take a great interest in the introduction of his system in America.

We went again at the appointed time, and as their drawing teacher was there, we had an opportunity of looking over their sketches, which were excellent. The director showed us the manner of teaching them, with a looking-glass, in which they were shown the different positions of the organs of the mouth, and afterwards made to feel the vibrations of the throat and breast, produced by the sound. He took one of the youngest scholars, covered her eyes, and placing her hand upon his throat, articulated the second sound of A. She followed him, making the sound softer or louder as he did. All the consonants were made distinctly, by placing her hand before his mouth. Their exercises in reading, speaking with one another, and writing from dictation, succeeded perfectly. He treated them all like his own children, and sought by jesting and playing, to make the exercise appear as sport. They call him father and appear to be much attached to him.

One of the pupils, about fourteen years old, interested me through his history. lie and his sister were found in Sachsenhausen, by a Frankfort merchant, in a horrible condition. Their mother had died about two years and a half before, and during all that time their father had neglected them till they were near dead through privation and filth. The boy was placed in this Institute, and the girl in that of the Orphans. He soon began to show a talent for modelling figures, and for some time he has been taking lessons of the sculptor Launitz. I saw a beautiful copy of a bas-relief of Thorwaldsen which he made, as well as an original, very interesting, from its illustration of his history. It was in two parts; the first represented himself and his sister, kneeling in misery before a ruined family altar, by which an angel was standing, who took him by one hand, while with the other he pointed to his benefactor, standing near. The other represented the two kneeling in gratitude before a restored altar, on which was the anchor of Hope. From above streamed down a light, where two angels were rejoicing over their happiness. For a boy of fourteen, deprived of one of the most valuable senses, and taken from such a horrible condition of life, it is a surprising work and gives brilliant hopes for his future.

We went lately into the Roemerberg, to see the Kaisersaal and the other rooms formerly used by the old Emperors of Germany, and their Senates. The former is now in the process of restoration. The ceiling is in the gorgeous illuminated style of the middle ages; along each side arc rows of niches for the portraits of the Emperors, which have been painted by the best artists in Berlin, Dresden, Vienna and Munich. It is remarkable that the number of the old niches in the hall should exactly correspond with the number of the German Emperors, so that the portrait of the Emperor Francis of Austria, who was the last, will close the long rank coming down from Charlemagne. The pictures, or at least such of them as are already finished, are kept in another room; they give one a good idea of the changing styles of royal costumes, from the steel shirt and helmet to the jewelled diadem and velvet robe. I looked with interest on a painting of Frederic Barbarossa, by Leasing, and mused over the popular tradition that he sits with his paladins in a mountain cave under the Castle of Kyffhäuser, ready to come forth and assist his Fatherland in the hour of need. There was the sturdy form of Maximilian; the martial Conrad; and Ottos, Siegfrieds and Sigismunds in plenty—many of whom moved a nation in their day, but are now dust and forgotten.

I yesterday visited Mendelssohn, the celebrated composer. Having heard rame of his music this winter, particularly that magnificent creation, the "Walpurgisnacht," I wished to obtain his autograph before leaving, and sent a note for that purpose. He sent a kind note in answer, adding a chorus out of the Walpurgisnacht from his own hand. After this, I could not repress the desire of speaking with him. lie received me with true German cordiality, and on learning I was an American, spoke of having been invited to attend a musical festival in New York. He invited me to call on him if he happened to bo in Leipsic or Dresden when we should pass through, and spoke particularly of the fine music there. I have rarely seen a man whose countenance bears so plainly the stamp of genius. He has a glorious dark eye, and Byron's expression of a "dome of thought," could never be more appropriately applied than to his lofty and intellectual forehead, the marble whiteness and polish of which arc heightened by the raven hue of his hair. He is about forty years of age, in the noon of his fame and the full maturity of his genius. Already as a boy of fourteen he composed an opera, which was played with much success at Berlin; he is now the first living composer of Germany. Moses Mendelssohn, the celebrated Jewish philosopher, was his grandfather; and his father, now living, is accustomed to say that in his youth he was spoken of as the son of the great Mendelssohn; now he is known as the father of the great Mendelssohn!

# CHAPTER XVI. — JOURNEY ON FOOT FROM FRANKFORT TO CASSEL.

The day for leaving Frankfort came at last, and I bade adieu to the gloomy, antique, but still quaint and pleasant city. I felt like leaving a second home, so much had the memories of many delightful hours spent there attached me to it: I shall long retain the recollection of its dark old streets, its massive, devil-haunted bridge and the ponderous cathedral, telling of the times of the Crusaders. I toiled up the long hill on the road to Friedberg, and from the tower at the top took a last look at the distant city, with a heart heavier than the knapsack whose unaccustomed weight rested uneasily on my shoulders. Being alone—starting out into the wide world, where us yet I know no one,—I felt much deeper what it was to find friends in a strange land. But such is the wanderer's lot.

We had determined on making the complete tour of Germany on foot, and in order to vary it somewhat, my friend and I proposed taking different routes from Frankfort to Leipsic. He choose a circuitous course, by way of Nuremberg and the Thuringian forests; while I, whose fancy had been running wild with Goethe's witches, preferred looking on the gloom and grandeur of the rugged Hartz. We both left Frankfort on the 23d of April, each bearing a letter of introduction to the same person in Leipsic, where we agreed to meet in fourteen days. As we were obliged to travel as cheaply as possible, I started with but seventynine florins, (a florin is forty cents American) well knowing that if I took more, I should, in all probability, spend proportionally more also. Thus, armed with my passport, properly viséd, a knapsack weighing fifteen pounds and a cane from the Kentucky Mammoth Cave, I began my lonely walk through Northern Germany. The warm weather of the week before had brought out the foliage of the willows and other early trees—violets and cowslips were springing up in the meadows. Keeping along the foot of the Taunus, I passed over great, broad hills, which were brown with the spring ploughing, and by sunset reached Friedberg—a, largo city, on the summit of a hill. The next morning, after sketching its old, baronial castle, I crossed the meadows to Nauheim, to see the salt springs there. They are fifteen in number; the water, which is very warm, rushes up with such force as to leap several feet above the earth. The buildings made for evaporation are nearly two miles in length; a walk along the top gives a delightful view of the surrounding valleys. After reaching the chaussée again, I was hailed by a wandering journeyman, or handwerker, as they are called, who wanted company. As I had concluded to accept all offers of this kind, we trudged along together very pleasantly, He was from Holstein, on the borders of Denmark and was just returning home, after an absence of six years, having escaped from Switzerland after the late battle of Luzerne, which he had witnessed. He had his knapsack and tools fastened on two wheels, which he drew after him quite conveniently. I could not help laughing at the adroit manner in which he begged his way along, through every village. He would ask me to go on and wait for him at the other end; after a few minutes he followed, with a handful of small copper money, which he said he had fought for,—the handworker's term for begged.

We passed over long ranges of hills, with an occasional view of the Vogelsgebirge, or Bird's Mountains, far to the cast. I knew at length, by the pointed summits of the hills, that we were approaching Giessen and the valley of the Lahn. Finally, two sharp peaks appeared in the distance, each crowned with a picturesque fortress, while the spires of Giessen rose from the valley below. Parting from my companion, I passed through the city without stopping, for it was the time of the university vacation, and Dr. Liebeg, the world-renowned chemist, whom I desired to see, was absent.

Crossing a hill or two, I came down into the valley of the Lahn, which flows through meadows of the brightest green, with redroofed cottages nestled among gardens and orchards upon its banks. The women here wear a remarkable costume, consisting of a red boddice with white sleeves, and a dozen skirts, one above another, reaching only to the knees. I slept again at a little village among the hills, and started early for Marburg. The meadows were of the purest emerald, through which the stream wound its way, with even borders, covered to the water's edge with grass so smooth and velvety, that a fairy might have danced along on it for miles without stumbling over an uneven tuft. This valley is one of the finest districts in Germany. I thought, as I saw the peaceful inhabitants at work in their fields, I had most probably, on the battle-field of Brandywine, walked over the bones of some of their ancestors, whom a despotic prince had torn from their happy homes, to die in a distant land, fighting against the cause of freedom.

I now entered directly into the heart of Hesse Cassel. The country resembled a collection of hills thrown together in confusion—sometimes a wide plain left between them, sometimes a clustre of wooded peaks, and here and there a single pointed summit rising above the rest. The vallies were green as ever, the hill-sides freshly ploughed and the forests beginning to be colored by the tender foliage of the larch and birch. I walked two or three hours at a "stretch," and then, when I could find a dry, shady bank, I would rest for half an hour and finish some hastily sketched landscape, or lay at full length, with my head on my knapsack, and peruse the countenances of those passing by. The observation which every traveller excites, soon ceases to be embarrassing. It was at first extremely unpleasant; but I am now so hardened, that the strange, magnetic influence of the human eye, which we cannot avoid feeling, passes by me as harmlessly as if turned aside by invisible mail.

During the day several showers came by, but as none of them penetrated further than my blouse, I kept on, and reached about sunset a little village in the valley. I chose a small inn, which had an air of neatness about it, and on going in, the tidy landlady's "be you welcome," as she brought a pair of slippers for my swollen feet, made me feel quite at home. After being furnished with eggs, milk, butter and bread, for supper, which I ate while listening to an animated discussion between the village schoolmaster and some farmers, I was ushered into a clean, sanded bedroom, and soon forgot all fatigue. For this, with breakfast in the morning, the bill was six and a half groschen—about sixteen cents! Tin air was freshened by the rain and I journeyed over the hills at a rapid rate. Stopping for dinner at the large village of Wabern, a boy at the inn asked me if I was going to America? I said no, I came from there. He then asked me many silly questions, after which he ran out and told the people of the village. When I set out again, the children pointed at me and cried: "see there! he is from America!" and the men took off their hats and bowed!

The sky was stormy, which added to the gloom of the hills around, though some of the distant ranges lay in mingled light and shade—the softest alternation of purple and brown. There were many isolated, rocky hills, two of which interested me, through their attendant legends. One is said to have been the scene of a battle between the Romans and Germans, where, after a long conflict the rock opened and swallowed up the former. The other, which is crowned with a rocky wall, so like a ruined fortress, as at a distance to be universally mistaken for one, tradition says is the death-place of Charlemagne, who still walks around its summit every night, clad in complete armor. On ascending a hill late in the afternoon, I saw at a great distance the statue of Hercules, which stands on the Wilhelmshöhe, near Cassel. Night set in with a dreary rain, and I stopped at an inn about five miles short of the city. While tea was preparing a company of students came in and asked for a separate room. Seeing I was alone, they invited me up with them. They seemed much interested in America, and leaving the table gradually, formed a ring around me, where I had enough to do to talk with them all at once. When the omnibus came along, the most of them went with it to Cassel; but five remained and persuaded me to set out with them on foot. They insisted on carrying my knapsack the whole way, through the rain and darkness, and when I had passed the city gate with them, unchallenged, conducted me to the comfortable hotel, "Zur Krone."

It is a pleasant thing to wake up in the morning in a strange city. Every thing is new; you walk around it for the first time in the full enjoyment of the novelty, or the not less agreeable feeling of surprise, if it is different from your anticipations. Two of my friends of the previous night called for me in the morning, to show me around the city, and the first impression, made in such agreeable company, prepossessed me very favorably. I shall not, however, take up time in describing its many sights, particularly the Frederick's Platz, where the statue of Frederick the Second, who sold ten thousand of his subjects to England, has been re-erected, after having lain for years in a stable where it was thrown by the French.

I was much interested in young Carl K——, one of my new acquaintances. His generous and unceasing kindness first won my esteem, and I found on nearer acquaintance, the qualities of his mind equal those of his heart. I saw many beautiful poems of his which were of remarkable merit, considering his youth, and thought I could read in his dark, dreamy eye, the unconscious presentiment of a power he does not yet possess. He seemed as one I had known for years.

He, with a brother student, accompanied me in the afternoon, to Wilhelmshöhe, the summer residence of the Prince, on the side of a range of mountains three miles west of the city. The road leads in a direct line to the summit of the mountain, which is thirteen hundred feet in height, surmounted by a great structure, called the Giant's Castle, on the summit of which is a pyramid ninety-six feet high, supporting a statue of Hercules, copied after the Farnese, and thirty-one feet in height. By a gradual ascent through beautiful woods, we reached the princely residence, a magnificent mansion standing on a natural terrace of the mountain. Near it is a little theatre built by Jerome Buonaparte, in which he himself used to play. We looked into the green house in passing, where the floral splendor of every zone was combined. There were lofty halls, with glass roofs, where the orange grew to a great tree, and one could sit in myrtle bowers, with the brilliant bloom of the tropics around him. It was the only thing there I was guilty of coveting.

The greatest curiosity is the water-works, which are perhaps unequalled in the world. The Giant's Castle on the summit contains an immense tank in which water is kept for the purpose; but unfortunately, at the time I was there, the pipes, which had been frozen through the winter, were not in condition to play. From the summit an inclined plane of masonry descends the mountain nine hundred feet, broken every one hundred and fifty feet by perpendicular descents. These are the Cascades, down which the water first rushes from the tank. After being again collected in a great basin at the bottom, it passes into an aqueduct, built like a Roman ruin, and goes over beautiful arches through the forest, where it falls in one sheet down a deep precipice. When it has descended several other beautiful falls, made in exact imitation of nature, it is finally collected and forms the great fountain, which rises twelve inches in diameter from the middle of a lake to the height of one hundred and ninety feet! We descended by lovely walks through the forest to the Löwenburg, built as the ruin of a knightly castle, and fitted out in every respect to correspond with descriptions of a fortress in the olden time, with moat, drawbridge, chapel and garden of pyramidal trees. Farther below, are a few small houses, inhabited by the descendants of the Hessians who fell in America, supported here at the Prince's expense!

# CHAPTER XVII. — ADVENTURES AMONG THE HARTZ.

On taking leave of Carl at the gate over the Göttingen road, I felt tempted to bestow a malediction upon traveling, from its merciless breaking of all links, as soon as formed. It was painful to think we should meet no more. The tears started into his eyes, and feeling a mist gathering over mine, I gave his hand a parting pressure, turned my back upon Cassel and started up the long mountain, at a desperate rate. On the summit I passed out of Hesse into Hanover, and began to descend the remaining six miles. The road went down by many windings, but I shortened the way considerably by a footpath through a mossy old forest. The hills bordering the Weser are covered with wood, through which I saw the little red-roofed city of Münden, at the bottom. I stopped there for the night, and next morning walked around the place. It is one of the old German cities that have not yet felt the effect of the changing spirit of the age. It is still walled, though the towers are falling to ruin. The streets are narrow, crooked, and full of ugly old houses, and to stand in the little square before the public buildings, one would think himself born in the sixteenth century. Just below the city the Werra and Fulda unito and form the Weser. The triangular point has been made into a public walk, and the little steamboat was lying at anchor near, waiting to start for Bremen.

In the afternoon I got into the omnibus for Göttingen. The ride over the wild, dreary, monotonous hills was not at all interesting. There were two other passengers inside, one of whom, a grave, elderly man, took a great interest in America, but the conversation was principally on his side, for I had been taken with a fever in Münden. I lay crouched up in the corner of the vehicle, trying to keep off the chills which constantly came over me, and wishing only for Göttingen, that I might obtain medicine and a bed. We reached it at last, and I got out with my knapsack and walked wearily through half a dozen streets till I saw an inn. But on entering, I found it so dark and dirty and unfriendly, that I immediately went out again and hired the first pleasant looking boy I met, to take me to a good hotel. He conducted me to the first one in the city. I felt a trepidation of pocket, but my throbbing head plead more powerfully, so I ordered a comfortable room and a physician. The host, Herr Wilhelm, sent for Professor Trefurt, of the University, who told me I had over-exerted myself in walking. He made a second call the next day, when, as he was retiring, I inquired the amount of his fee. He begged to be excused and politely bowed himself out. I inquired the meaning of this of Herr Wilhelm, who said it was customary for travellers to leave what they chose for the physician, as there was no regular fee. He added, moreover, that twenty groschen, or about sixty cents, was sufficient for the two visits!

I stayed in Göttingen two dull, dreary, miserable days, without getting much better. I took but one short walk through the city, in which I saw the outsides of a few old churches and got a hard fall on the pavement. Thinking that the cause of my illness might perhaps become its cure, I resolved to go on rather than remain in the melancholy—in spite of its black-eyed maidens, melancholy—Göttingen. On the afternoon of the second day, I took the post to Nordheim, about twelve miles distant. The Göttingen valley, down which we drove, is green and beautiful, and the trees seem to have come out all at once. we were not within sight of the Hartz, but the mountains along the Weser were visible on the left. The roads were extremely muddy from the late rains, so that I proceeded but slowly.

A blue range along the horizon told me of the Hartz, as I passed; although there were some fine side-glimpses through the hills, I did not see much of them till I reached Osterode, about twelve miles further. Here the country begins to assume a different aspect. The city lies in a narrow valley, and as the road goes down a steep hill towards it, one sees on each side many quarries of gypsum, and in front the gloomy pine mountains are piled one above another in real Alpine style. But alas! the city, though it looks exceedingly romantic from above, is one of the dirtiest I ever saw. I stopped at Herzberg, six miles farther, for the night. The scenery was very striking; and its effect was much heightened by a sky full of black clouds, which sent down a hail-storm as they passed over. The hills are covered with pine, fir and larch. The latter tree, in its first foliage, is most delicate and beautiful. Every bough is like a long ostrich plume, and when one of them stands among the dark pines, it seems so light and airy that the wind might carry it away. Just opposite Herzberg, the Hartz stands in its gloomy and mysterious grandeur, and I went to sleep with the pleasant thought that an hour's walk on the morrow would shut me up in its deep recesses.

The next morning I entered them. The road led up a narrow mountain valley, down which a stream was rushing—on all sides were magnificent forests of pine. It was glorious to look down their long aisles, dim and silent, with a floor of thick green moss. There was just room enough for the road and the wild stream which wound its way zigzag between the hills, affording the most beautiful mountain-view along the whole route. As I ascended, the mountains became rougher and wilder, and in the shady hollows were still drifts of snow. Enjoying every thing very much, I walked on without taking notice of the road, and on reaching a wild, rocky chasm called the "Schlucht," was obliged to turn aside and take a footpath over a high mountain to Andreasberg, a town built on a summit two thousand feet above the sea. It is inhabited almost entirely by the workmen in the mines.

The way from Andreasberg to the Brocken leads along the Rehberger Graben, which carry water about six miles for the oreworks. After going through a thick pine wood, I came out on the mountain-side, where rough crags overhung the way above, and through the tops of the trees I had glimpses into the gorge below. It was scenery of the wildest character. Directly opposite rose a mountain wall, dark and stern through the gloomy sky; far below the little stream of the Oder foamed over the rocks with a continual roar, and one or two white cloud-wreaths were curling up from the forests.

I followed the water-ditch around every projection of the mountain, still ascending higher amid the same wild scenery, till at length I reached the Oderteich, a great dam, in a kind of valley formed by some mountain peaks on the side of the Brocken. It has a breastwork of granite, very firm, and furnishes a continual supply of water for the works. It began to rain soon, and I took a foot-path which went winding up through the pine wood. The storm still increased, till everything was cloud and rain, so I was obliged to stop about five o'clock at Oderbruch, a toll-house and tavern on the side of the Brocken, on the boundary between Brunswick and Hanover—the second highest inhabited house in the Hartz. The Brocken was invisible through the storm and the weather forboded a difficult ascent. The night was cold, but by a warm fire I let the winds howl and the rain beat. When I awoke the next morning, we were in clouds. They were thick on every side, hiding what little view there was through the openings of the forest. After breakfast, however, they were somewhat thinner, and I concluded to start for the Brocken. It is not the usual way for travellers who ascend, being not only a bad road but difficult to find, as I soon discovered. The clouds gathered around again after I set out, and I was obliged to walk in a storm of mingled rain and snow. The snow lay several feet deep in the forests, and the path was, in many places, quite drifted over. The white cloud-masses were whirled past by the wind, continually enveloping me and shutting out every view. During the winter the path had become, in ninny places, the bed of a mountain torrent, so that I was obliged sometimes to wade kneedeep in snow, and sometimes to walk over the wet, spongy moss, crawling under the long, dripping branches of the stunted pines. After a long time of such dreary travelling, I came to two rocks called the Stag Horns, standing on a little peak. The storm, now all snow, blew more violently than ever, and the path became lost under the deep drifts.

Comforting myself with the assurance that if I could not find it, I could at least make my way back, I began searching, and after some time, came upon it again. Here the forest ceased; the way led on large stones over a marshy ascending plain, but what was above, or on either side, I could not see. It was solitude of the most awful kind. There was nothing but the storm, which had already wet me through, and the bleak gray waste of rocks. It grew sleeper and steeper; I could barely trace the path by the rocks which were worn, and the snow threatened soon to cover these. Added to this, although the walking and fresh mountain air had removed my illness, I was still weak from the effects of it, and the consequences of a much longer exposure to the storm were greatly to be feared. I was wondering if the wind increased at the same rate, how much longer it would be before I should be carried off, when suddenly something loomed up above me through the storm. A few steps more and I stood beside the Brocken House, on the very summit of the mountain! The mariner, who has been floating for days on a wreck at sea, could scarcely be more rejoiced at a friendly sail, than I was on entering the low building. Two large Alpine dogs in the passage, as I walked in, dripping with wet, gave notice to the inmates, and I was soon ushered into a warm room, where I changed my soaked garments for dry ones, and sat down by the fire with feelings of comfort not easily imagined. The old landlord was quite surprised, on hearing the path by which I came, that I found the way at all. The summit was wrapped in the thickest cloud, and he gave me no hope for several hours of any prospect at all, so I sat down and looked over the Stranger's Album.

I saw but two names from the United States—B.F. Atkins, of Boston, and C.A. Hay, from York, Pa. There were a great many long-winded German poems—among them, one by Schelling, the philosopher. Some of them spoke of having seen the "Spectre of the Brocken." I inquired of the landlord about the phenomenon; he says in winter it is frequently seen, in summer more seldom. The cause is very simple. It is always seen at sunrise, when the eastern side of the Brocken is free from clouds, and at the same time, the mist rises from the valley on the opposite side. The shadow of every thing on the Brocken is then thrown in grand proportions upon the mist, and is seen surrounded with a luminous halo. It is somewhat singular that such a spectacle can be seen upon the Brocken alone, but this is probably accounted for by the formation of the mountain, which collects the mist at just such a distance from the summit as to render the shadow visible.

Soon after dinner the storm subsided and the clouds separated a little. I could see down through the rifts on the plains of Brunswick, and sometimes, when they opened a little more, the mountains below us to the east and the adjoining plains, as far as Magdeburg. It was like looking on the earth from another planet, or from some point in the air which had no connection, with it; our station was completely surrounded by clouds, rolling in great masses around us, now and then giving glimpses through their openings of the blue plains, dotted with cities and villages, far below. At one time when they were tolerably well separated, I ascended the tower, fifty feet high, standing near the Brocken House. The view on three sides was quite clear, and I can easily imagine what a magnificent prospect it must be in fine weather. The Brocken is only about four thousand feet high, nearly the same as the loftiest peak of the Catskill, but being the highest mountain in Northern Germany, it commands a more extensive prospect. Imagine a circle described with a radius of a hundred miles, comprising thirty cities, two or three hundred villages and one whole mountain district! We could see Brunswick and Magdeburg, and beyond them the great plain which extends to the North Sea in one direction and to Berlin in the other, while directly below us lay the dark mountains of the Hartz, with little villages in their sequestered valleys. It was but a few moments I could look on this scene—in an instant the clouds swept together again and completely hid it. In accordance with a custom of the mountain, one of the girls made me a "Brocken nosegay," of heather, lichens and moss. I gave her a few pfennings and stowed it away carefully in a corner of my knapsack.

I now began descending the east side, by a good road over fields of bare rock and through large forests of pine. Two or three bare brown peaks rose opposite with an air of the wildest sublimity, and in many places through the forest towered lofty crags. This is the way by which Goethe brings Faust up the Brocken, and the scenery is graphically described in that part of the poem. At the foot of the mountain is the little village of Schiercke, the highest in the Hartz. Here I took a narrow path through the woods, and after following a tediously long road over the hills, reached Elbingerode, where I spent the night, and left the next morning for Blankenburg. I happened to take the wrong road, however, and went through Rubeland, a little village in the valley of the Bode. There are many iron works here, and two celebrated caves, called "Baumann's Höhle," and "Biel's Höhle." I kept on through the gray, rocky hills to Huttenrode, where I inquired the way to the Rosstrappe, but was directed wrong, and after walking nearly two hours in a heavy rain, arrived at Ludwigshütte, on the Bode, in one of the wildest and loneliest corners of the Hartz. I dried my wet clothes at a little inn, ate a dinner of bread and milk, and learning that I was just as far from the Rosstrappe as ever, and that the way was impossible to find alone, I hunted up a guide.

We went over the mountains through a fine old forest, for about two hours, and came out on the brow of a hill near the end of the Hartz, with a beautiful view of the country below and around. Passing the little inn, the path led through thick bushes along the summit, over a narrow ledge of rocks that seemed to stretch out into the air, for on either side the foot of the precipice vanished in the depth below.

Arrived at last at the end, I looked around me. What a spectacle! I was standing on the end of a line of precipice which ran out from the mountain like a wall for several hundred feet—the hills around rising up perpendicularly from the gorge below, where the Bode pressed into a narrow channel foamed its way through. Sharp masses of gray rock rose up in many places from the main body like pillars, with trees clinging to the clefts, and although the defile was near seven hundred feet deep, the summits, in one place, were very near to one another. Near the point at which I stood, which was secured by a railing, was an impression in the rock like the hoof of a giant horse, from which the place takes its name. It is very distinct and perfect, and nearly two feet in length.

I went back to the little inn and sat down to rest and chat awhile with the talkative landlady. Notwithstanding her horrible Prussian dialect, I was much amused with the budget of wonders, which she keeps for the information of travelers. Among other things, she related to me the legend of the Rosstrappe, which I give in her own words: "A great many hundred years ago, when there were plenty of giants through the world, there was a certain beautiful princess, who was very much loved by one of them. Now, although the parents of this princess were afraid of the giant, and wanted her to marry him, she herself hated him, because she was in love with a brave knight. But, you see, the brave knight could do nothing against the great giant, and so a day was appointed for the wedding of the princess. When they were married, the giant had a great feast and he and all his servants got drunk. So the princess mounted his black horse and rode away over the mountains, till she reached this valley. She stood on that square rock which you see there opposite to us, and when she saw her knight on this side, where we are, she danced for joy, and the rock is called the Tanzplatz, to this very day. But when the giant found she had gone, he followed her as fast as he might; then a holy bishop, who saw the princess, blessed the feet of her horse, and she jumped on it across to this side, where his fore feet made two marks in the rock, though there is only one left now. You should not laugh at this, for if there were giants then, there must have been very big horses too, as one can see from the hoofmark, and the valley was narrower then than it is now. My dear man, who is very old now, (you see him through the bushes, there, digging,) says it was so when he was a child, and that the old people living then, told him there were once four just such hoof-tracks, on the Tanzplatz, where the horse stood before he jumped over. And we cannot doubt the words of the good old people, for there were many strange things then, we all know, which the dear Lord does not let happen now. But I must tell you, lieber Herr, that the giant tried to jump after her and fell away down into the valley, where they say he lives yet in the shape of a big black dog, guarding the crown of the princess, which fell off as she was going over. But this part of the story is perhaps not true, as nobody, that I ever heard of, has seen either the black dog or the crown!"

After listening to similar gossip for a while, I descended the mountain-side, a short distance to the Bülowshöhe. This is a rocky shaft that shoots, upward from the mountain, having from its top a glorious view through the door which the Bode makes in passing out of the Hartz. I could see at a great distance the towers of Magdeburg, and further, the vast plain stretching away like a sea towards Berlin. From Thale, the village below, where the air was warmer than in the Hartz and the fruit-trees already in blossom, it was four hours' walk to Halberstadt, by a most tiresome road over long ranges of hills, all ploughed and planted, and extending as far as the eye could reach, without a single fence or hedge. It is pleasant to look over scenes where nature is so free and unshackled; but the people, alas! wear the fetters. The setting sun, which lighted up the old Brocken and his snowy top, showed me also Halberstadt, the end of my Hartz journey; but its deceitful towers fled as I approached, and I was half dead with fatigue on arriving there.

The ghostly, dark and echoing castle of an inn (the Black Eagle) where I stopped, was enough to inspire a lonely traveller, like myself, with unpleasant fancies. It looked heavy and massive enough to have been a stout baron's stronghold in some former century; the taciturn landlord and his wife, who, with a solemn servant girl, were the only tenants, had grown into perfect keeping with its gloomy character. When I groped my way under the heavy, arched portal into the guests' room—a large, lofty, cheerless hall—all was dark, and I could barely perceive, by the little light which came through two deep-set windows, the inmates of the house, sitting on opposite sides of the room. After some delay, the hostess brought a light. I entreated her to bring me something instantly for supper, and in half an hour she placed a mixture on the table, the like of which I never wish to taste again. She called it beer-soup! I found, on examination, it was beer, boiled with meat, and seasoned strongly with pepper and salt! My hunger disappeared, and pleading fatigue as an excuse for want of appetite, I left the table. When I was ready to retire, the landlady, who had been sitting silently in a dark corner, called the solemn servant girl, who took up a dim lamp, and bade me follow her to the "sleeping chamber." Taking up my knapsack and staff, I stumbled down the steps into the arched gateway; before me was a long, damp, deserted court-yard, across which the girl took her way. I followed her with some astonishment, imagining where the sleeping chamber could be, when she stopped at a small, one-story building, standing alone in the yard. Opening the door with a rusty key, she led me into a bare room, a few feet square, opening into another, equally bare, with the exception of a rough bed. "Certainly," said I, "I am not to sleep here!" "Yes," she answered, "this is the sleeping chamber," at the same time setting down the light and disappearing. I examined the place—it smelt mouldy, and the walls were cold and damp; there had been a window at the head of the bed, but it was walled up, and that at the foot was also closed to within a few inches of the top. The bed was course and dirty; and on turning down the ragged covers, I saw with horror, a dark brown stain near the pillow, like that of blood! For a moment I hesitated whether to steal out of the inn, and seek another lodging, late as it was; at last, overcoming my fears, I threw my clothes into a heap, and lay down, placing my heavy staff at the head of the bed. Persons passed up and down the courtyard several times, the light of their lamps streaming through the narrow aperture up against the ceiling, and I distinctly heard voices, which seemed to be near the door. Twice did I sit up in bed, breathless, with my hand on the cane, in the most intense anxiety; but fatigue finally overcame suspicion, and I sank into a deep sleep, from which I was gladly awakened by daylight. In reality, there may have been no cause for my fears—I may have wronged the lonely innkeepers by them; but certainly no place or circumstances ever seemed to me more appropriate to a deed of robbery or crime. I left immediately, and when a turn in the street hid the ill-omened front of the inn, I began to breathe with my usual freedom.

# CHAPTER XVIII. — NOTES IN LEIPSIC AND DRESDEN.

Leipsic, May 8.—I have now been nearly two days in this wide-famed city, and the more I see of it the better I like it. It is a pleasant, friendly town, old enough to be interesting, and new enough to be comfortable. There in much active business life, through which it is fast increasing in size and beauty. Its publishing establishments are the largest in the world, and its annual fairs attended by people from all parts of Europe. This is much for a city to accomplish, situated alone in the middle of a great plain, with no natural charms of scenery or treasures of art to attract strangers. The energy and enterprise of its merchants have accomplished all this, and it now stands, in importance, among the first cities of Europe.

The bad weather obliged me to take the railroad at Halberstadt, to keep the appointment with my friend, in this city. I left at six for Magdeburg, and after two hours' ride over a dull, tiresome plain, rode along under the mounds and fortifications by the side of the Elbe, and entered the old town. It was very cold, and the streets were muddy, so I contented myself with looking at the Broadway, (der breite Weg,) the Cathedral and one or two curious old churches, and in walking along the parapet leading to the fortress, which has a view of the winding Elbe. The Citadel was interesting from having been the prison in which Baron Trenck was confined, whose narrative I read years ago, when quite a child.

We were soon on the road to Leipsic. The way was over one great, uninterrupted plain—a more monotonous country, even, than Belgium. Two of the passengers in the car with me were much annoyed at being taken by the railway agents for Poles. Their movements were strictly watched by the gens d'arme at every station we passed, and they were not even allowed to sit together! At Kothen a branch track went off to Berlin. We passed by Halle without being able to see anything of it or its University, and arrived here in four hours after leaving Magdeburg.

On my first walk around the city, yesterday morning, I passed the

Augustus Platz—a broad green lawn, on which front the University and several other public buildings. A chain of beautiful promenades encircles the city, on the site of its old fortifications. Following their course through walks shaded by large trees and bordered with flowering shrubs, I passed a small but chaste monument to Sebastian Bach, the composer, which was erected almost entirely at the private cost of Mendelssohn, and stands opposite the building in which Bach once directed the choirs. As I was standing beside it, a glorious choral, swelled by a hundred voices, came through the open windows, like a tribute to the genius of the great master.

Having found my friend we went together to the Stern Warte, or Observatory, which gives a fine view of the country around the city, and in particular the battle field. The Castellan who is stationed there, is well acquainted with the localities, and pointed out the position of the hostile armies. It was one of the most bloody and hard-fought battles which history records. The army of Napoleon stretched like a semicircle around the southern and eastern sides of the city, and the plain beyond was occupied by the allies, whose forces met together here. Schwarzenberg, with his Austrians, came from Dresden; Blucher, from Halle, with the Emperor Alexander. Their forces amounted to three hundred thousand, while those of Napoleon ranked at one hundred and ninety-two thousand men. It must have been a terrific scene. Four days raged the battle, and the meeting of half a million of men in deadly conflict was accompanied by the thunder of sixteen hundred cannon. The small rivers which flow through Leipsic were swollen with blood, and the vast plain was strewed with more than fifty thousand dead. It is difficult to conceive of such slaughter, while looking at the quiet and tranquil landscape below. It seemed more like a legend of past ages, when ignorance and passion led men to murder and destroy, than an event which the last half century witnessed. For the sake of humanity it is to be hoped that the world will never see such another.

There are some lovely walks around Leipsic. We went yesterday afternoon with a few friends to the Rosenthal, a beautiful meadow, bordered by forests of the German oak, very few of whose Druid trunks have been left standing. There are Swiss cottages embowered in the foliage, where every afternoon the

140

social citizens assemble to drink their coffee enjoy a few hours' escape from the noisy and dusty streets, One can walk for miles along these lovely paths by the side of the velvet meadows, or the banks of some shaded stream. We visited the little village of Golis, a short distance off, where, in the second story of a little white house, hangs the sign: "Schiller's Room." Some of the Leipsic literati have built a stone arch over the entrance, with the inscription above: "Here dwelt Schiller in 1795, and wrote his Hymn to Joy." Every where through Germany the remembrances of Schiller are sacred. In every city where he lived, they show his dwelling. They know and reverence the mighty spirit who has been among them. The little room where he conceived that sublime poem is hallowed as if by the presence of unseen spirits.

I was anxious to see the spot where Poniatowsky fell. We returned over the plain to the city and passed in at the gate by which the Cossacks entered, pursuing the flying French. Crossing the lower part, we came to the little river Elster, in whose waves the gallant prince sank. The stone bridge by which we crossed was blown up by the French, to cut off pursuit. Napoleon had given orders that it should not be blown up till the Poles had all passed over, as the river, though narrow, is quite deep, and the banks are steep. Nevertheless, his officers did not wait, and the Poles, thus exposed to the fire of the enemy, were obliged to plunge into the stream to join the French army, which had begun the retreat towards Frankfort. Poniatowsky, severely wounded, made his way through a garden near and escaped on horseback into the water. He became entangled among the fugitives and sank. By walking a little distance along the road towards Frankfort, we could see the spot where his body was taken out of the river; it is now marked by a square stone, covered with the names of his countrymen who have visited it. We returned through the narrow arched way, by which Napoleon fled when the battle was lost.

Another interesting place in Leipsic is Auerback's Cellar, which, it is said, contains an old manuscript history of Faust, from which Goethe derived the first idea of his poem. He used to frequent this cellar, and one of his scenes in "Faust" is laid in it. We looked down the arched passage; not wishing to purchase any wine, we could find no pretence for entering. The streets are full of book stores and one half the business of the inhabitants appears to consist in printing, paper-making and binding. The publishers have a handsome Exchange of their own, and during the Fairs, the amount of business transacted is enormous. The establishment of Brockhaus is contained in an immense building, adjoining which stands his dwelling, in the midst of magnificent gardens. That of Tauchnitz is not less celebrated. His edition of the classics, in particular, are the best that have ever been made; and he has lately commenced publishing a number of English works, in a cheap form. Otto Wigand, who has also a large establishment, has begun to issue translations of American works. He has already published Prescott and Bancroft, and I believe intends giving out shortly, translations from some of our poets and novelists. I became acquainted at the Museum, with a young German author who had been some time in America, and was well versed in our literature. He is now engaged in translating American works, one of which—Hoffman's "Wild Scenes of the Forest and Prairie"—will soon appear. In no place in Germany have I found more knowledge of our country, her men and her institutions, than in Leipsic, and as yet I have seen few that would be preferable as a place of residence. Its attractions lie not in its scenery, but in the social and intellectual character of its inhabitants.

May 11.—At last in this "Florence of the Elbe," as the Saxons have christened it. Exclusive of its glorious galleries of art, which are scarcely surpassed by any in Europe, Dresden charms one by the natural beauty of its environs. It stands in a curve of the Elbe, in the midst of green meadows, gardens and fine old woods, with the hills of Saxony sweeping around like an amphitheatre, and the craggy peaks of the Highlands looking at it from afar. The domes and spires at a distance give it a rich Italian look, which is heightened by the white villas, embowered in trees, gleaming on the hills around. In the streets there is no bustle of business—nothing of the din and confusion of traffic which mark most cities; it seems like a place for study and quiet enjoyment.

The railroad brought us in three hours from Leipsic, over the eighty miles of plain that intervene. We came from the station through the Neustadt, passing the Japanese Palace and the equestrian statue of Augustus the Strong, The magnificent bridge over the Elbe was so much injured by the late inundation as to be impassable; we worn obliged to go some distance up the river bank and cross on a bridge of boats. Next morning my first search was for the picture gallery. We set off at random, and after passing the Church of Our Lady, with its lofty dome of solid stone, which withstood the heaviest bombs during the war with Frederick the Great, came to an open square, one side of which was occupied by an old, brown, red-roofed building, which I at once recognized, from pictures, as the object of our search.

I have just taken a last look at the gallery this morning, and left it with real regret; for, during the two visits, Raphael's heavenly picture of the Madonna and child had so grown into my love and admiration, that it was painful to think I should never see it again. There are many more which clung so strongly to my imagination, gratifying in the highest degree the love for the Beautiful, that I left them with sadness, and the thought that I would now only have the memory. I can see the inspired eye and god-like brow of the Jesus-child, as if I were still standing before the picture, and the sweet, holy countenance of the Madonna still looks upon me. Yet, though this picture is a miracle of art, the first glance filled me with disappointment. It has somewhat faded, during the three hundred years that have rolled away since the hand of Raphael worked on the canvass, and the glass with which it is covered for better preservation, injures the effect. After I had gazed on it awhile, every thought of this vanished. The figure of the virgin seemed to soar in the air, and it was difficult to think the clouds were not in motion. An aerial lightness clothes her form, and it is perfectly natural for such a figure to stand among the clouds. Two divine cherubs look up from below, and in her arms sits the sacred child. Those two faces beam from the picture like those of angels. The wild, prophetic eye and lofty brow of the young Jesus chains one like a spell. There is something more than mortal in its expression—something in the infant face which indicates a power mightier than the proudest manhood. There is no glory around the head; but the spirit which shines from those features, marks his divinity. In the sweet face of the mother there speaks a sorrowful foreboding mixed with its tenderness, as if she knew the world into which the Saviour was born, and foresaw the path in which he was to tread. It is a picture which one can scarce look upon without tears.

There are in the same room six pictures by Correggio, which are said to be among his best works; one of them his celebrated Magdalen. There is also Correggio's "Holy Night," or the virgin with the shepherds in the manger, in which all the light comes from the body of the child. The surprise of the shepherds is most beautifully expressed. In one of the halls there is a picture by Van der Werff, in which the touching story of Hagar is told more feelingly than words could do it. The young Ishmael is represented full of grief at parting with Isaac, who, in childish unconsciousness of what has taken place, draws in sport the corner of his mother's mantle around him, and smiles at the tears of his lost playmate. Nothing can come nearer real flesh and blood than the two portraits of Raphael Mengs, painted by himself when quite young. You almost think the artist has in sport crept behind the frame, and wishes to make you believe he is a picture. It would be impossible to speak of half the gems of art contained in this unrivalled collection. There are twelve large halls, containing in all nearly two thousand pictures.

The plain, south of Dresden, was the scene of the hard-fought battle between Napoleon and the allied armies, in 1813. On the heights above the little village of Räcknitz, Moreau was shot on the second day of the battle. We took a foot-path through the meadows, shaded by cherry trees in bloom, and reached the spot after an hour's walk. The monument is simple—a square block of granite, surmounted by a helmet and sword, with the inscription: "The hero Moreau fell here by the side of Alexander, August 17th, 1813." I gathered, as a memorial, a few leaves of the oak which shades it.

By applying an hour before the appointed time, we obtained admission to the Royal Library. It contains three hundred thousand volumes—among them the most complete collection of historical works in existence. Each hall is devoted to a history of a separate country, and one large room is filled with that of Saxony alone. There is a large number of rare and curious manuscripts, among which are old Greek works of the seventh and eighth centuries; a Koran which once belonged to the Sultan Bajazet; the handwriting of Luther and Melancthon; a manuscript volume with pen and ink sketches, by Albert Durer, and the earliest works after the invention of printing. Among these latter was a book published by Faust and Schaeffer, at Mayence, in 1457. There were also Mexican manuscripts, written on the Aloe leaf, and many illuminated monkish volumes of the middle ages.

We were fortunate in seeing the Grüne Gewölbe, or Green Gallery, a collection of jewels and costly articles, unsurpassed in Europe. The entrance is only granted to six persons at a time, who pay a fee of two thalers. The customary way is to employ a Lohnbedienter, who goes around from one hotel to another, till he has collected the number, when he brings them together and conducts them to the person in the palace, who has charge of the treasures. As our visit happened to be during the Pentecost holidays, when every body in Dresden goes to the mountains, there was some difficulty in effecting this, but after two mornings spent in hunting up curious travelers, the servant finally conducted us in triumph to the palace. The first hall into which we were ushered, contained works in bronze. They were all small, and chosen with regard to their artistical value. Some by John of Bologna were exceedingly fine, as was also a group in iron, cut out of a single block; perhaps the only successful attempt in this branch. The next room contained statues, and vases covered with reliefs, in ivory. The most remarkable work was the fall of Lucifer and his angels, containing ninety-two figures in all, carved out of a single piece of ivory sixteen inches high! It was the work of an Italian monk, and cost him many years of hard labor. There were two tables of mosaic-work, that would not be out of place in the fabled halls of the eastern genii, so much did they exceed my former ideas of human skill. The tops were of jasper, and each had a border of fruit and flowers, in which every color was represented by some precious stone, all with the utmost delicacy and truth to nature! It is impossible to conceive the splendid effect it produced. Besides some fine pictures on gold by Raphael Mengs, there was a Madonna, the largest specimen of enamel painting in existence.

However costly the contents of these halls, they were only an introduction to those which followed. Each one exceeded the other in splendor and costliness. The walls were covered to the ceiling with rows of goblets, vases, &c., of polished jasper, agate and lapiz lazuli. Splendid mosaic tables stood around, with caskets of the most exquisite silver and gold work upon them, and vessels of solid silver, some of them weighing six hundred pounds were placed at the foot of the columns. We were shown two goblets, each prized at six thousand thalers, made of gold and precious stones; also the great pearl called the Spanish Dwarf, nearly as large as a pullet's egg; globes and vases cut entirely out of the mountain crystal; magnificent Nuremberg watches and clocks, and a great number of figures, made ingeniously of rough pearls and diamonds. The officer showed us a hen's egg of silver. There was apparently nothing remarkable about it, but by unscrewing, it came apart, and disclosed the yelk of gold. This again opened and a golden chicken was seen; by touching a spring, a little diamond crown came from the inside, and the crown being again taken apart, out dropped a valuable diamond ring! The seventh hall contains the coronation robes of Augustus II., of Poland, and many costly specimens of carving in wood, A cherry stone is shown in a glass case, which has one hundred and twenty-five faces, all perfectly finished, carved upon it! The next room we entered sent back a glare of splendor that perfectly dazzled us. It was all gold, diamond, ruby and sapphire! Every case sent out such a glow and glitter that it seemed like a cage of imprisoned lightnings. Wherever the eye turned it was met by a blaze of broken rainbows. They were there by hundreds, and every gem was a fortune. Whole cases of swords, with hilts and scabbards of solid gold, studded with gems; the great two-handed coronation sword of the German emperors; daggers covered with brilliants and rubies; diamond buttons, chains and orders, necklaces and bracelets of pearl and emerald, and the order of the Golden Fleece made in gems of every kind. We were also shown the largest known onyx, nearly seven inches long and four inches broad! One of the most remarkable works is the throne and court of Aurungzebe, the Indian king, by Dinglinger, a celebrated goldsmith of the last century. It contains one hundred and thirty-two figures, all of enamelled gold, and each one most perfectly and elaborately finished. It was purchased by Prince Augustus for fifty-eight thousand thalers,[**] which was not a high sum, considering that the making of it occupied Dinglinger and thirteen workmen for seven years!

It is almost impossible to estimate the value of the treasures these halls contain. That of the gold and jewels alone must bo many millions of dollars, and the amount of labor expended on these toys of royalty is incredible. As monuments of patient and untiring toil, they are interesting: but it is sad to think how much labor and skill and energy have been wasted, in producing things which are useless to the world, and only of secondary importance as works of art. Perhaps, however, if men could be diverted by such play-things from more dangerous games, it would be all the better.

** [ A Prussian or Saxon thaler is about 70 cts.]

# CHAPTER XIX. — RAMBLES IN THE SAXON SWITZERLAND.

After four days' sojourn in Dresden we shouldered our knapsacks, not to be laid down again till we reached Prague. We were elated with the prospect of getting among the hills again, and we heeded not the frequent showers which had dampened the enjoyment of the Pentecost holidays, to the good citizens of Dresden, and might spoil our own. So we trudged gaily along the road to Pillnitz and waved an adieu to the domes behind us as the forest shut them out from view. After two hours' walk the road led down to the Elbe, where we crossed in a ferry-boat to Pillnitz, the seat of a handsome palace and gardens, belonging to the King of Saxony. He happened to be there at the time, on an afternoon excursion from Dresden; as we had seen him before, in the latter place, we passed directly on, only pausing to admire the flower-beds in the palace court. The King is a tall, benevolent looking man, and is apparently much liked by his people. As far as I have yet seen, Saxony is a prosperous and happy country. The people are noted all over Germany for their honest, social character, which is written on their cheerful, open countenances. On our entrance into the Saxon Switzerland, at Pillnitz, we were delighted with the neatness and home-like appearance of every thing. Every body greeted us; if we asked for information, they gave it cheerfully. The villages were all pleasant and clean and the meadows fresh and blooming. I felt half tempted to say, in the words of an old ballad, which I believe Longfellow has translated:

"*The fairest kingdom on this earth,*

*It is the Saxon land!*"

Going along the left bank of the Elbe, we passed over meadows purple with the tri-colored violet, which we have at home in gardens, and every little bank was bright with cowslips. At length the path led down into a cleft or ravine filled with trees, whose tops were on a level with the country around. This is a peculiar feature of Saxon scenery. The country contains many of these clefts, some of which are several hundred feet deep, having walls of perpendicular rock, in whose crevices the mountain pine roots itself and grows to a tolerable height without any apparent soil to keep it alive. We descended by a foot-path into this ravine, called the Liebethaler Grund. It is wider than many of the others, having room enough for a considerable stream and several mills. The sides are of sandstone rock, quite perpendicular. As we proceeded, it grew narrower and deeper, while the trees covering its sides and edges nearly shut out the sky. An hour's walk brought us to the end, where we ascended gradually to the upper level again.

After passing the night at the little village of Uttewalde, a short distance further, we set out early in the morning for the Bastei, a lofty precipice on the Elbe. The way led us directly through the Uttewalder Grund, the most remarkable of all these chasms. We went down by steps into its depths, which in the early morning were very cold. Water dripped from the rocks, which but a few feet apart, rose far above us, and a little rill made its way along the bottom, into which the sun has never shone. Heavy masses of rock, which had tumbled down from the sides lay in the way, and tall pine trees sprung from every cleft. In one place the defile is only four feet wide, and a large mass of rock, fallen from above, has lodged near the bottom, making an arch across, under which the traveller has to creep. After going under two or three arches of this kind, the defile widened and an arrow cut upon a rock directed us to a side path, which branched off from this into a mountain. Here the stone masses immediately assumed another form. They projected out like shelves sometimes as much as twenty feet from the straight side, and hung over the way, looking as if they might break off every moment. I felt glad when we had passed under them. Then as we ascended higher, we saw pillars of rock separated entirely from the side and rising a hundred feet in height, with trees growing on their summits. They stood there gray and limeworn, like the ruins of a Titan temple.

The path finally led us out into the forest and through the clustering pine trees, to the summit of the Bastei. An inn has been erected in the woods and an iron balustrade placed around the rock. Protected by this, we advanced to the end of the precipice and looked down to the swift Elbe, more than seven hundred feet below! Opposite through the blue mists of morning, rose Königstein, crowned with an impregnable fortress, and the

149

crags of Lilienstein, with a fine forest around their base, frowned from the left bank. On both sides were horrible precipices of gray rock, with rugged trees hanging from the crevices. A hill rising up from one side of the Bastei, terminates suddenly a short distance from it, in on abrupt precipice. In the intervening space stand three or four of those rock-columns, several hundred feet high, with their tops nearly on a level with the Bastei. A wooden bridge has been made across from one to the other, over which the traveller passes, looking on the trees and rocks far below him, to the mountain, where a steep zigzag path takes him to the Elbe below.

We crossed the Elbe for the fourth time at the foot of the Bastei, and walked along its right bank towards Königstein. The injury caused by the inundation was everywhere apparent. The receding flood had left a deposit of sand, in many places several feet deep on the rich meadows, so that the labor of years will be requisite to remove it and restore the land to an arable condition. Even the farm-houses on the hillside, some distance from the river, had been reached, and the long grass hung in the highest branches of the fruit trees. The people wore at work trying to repair their injuries, but it will fall heavily upon the poorer classes.

The mountain of Königstein is twelve hundred feet high. A precipice, varying from one to three hundred feet in height, runs entirely around the summit, which is flat, and a mile and a half in circumference. This has been turned into a fortress, whose natural advantages make it entirely impregnable. During the Thirty Years' War and the late war with Napoleon, it was the only place in Saxony unoccupied by the enemy. Hence is it used as a depository for the archives and royal treasures, in times of danger. By giving up our passports at the door, we received permission to enter; the officer called a guide to take us around the battlements. There is quite a little village on the summit, with gardens, fields, and a wood of considerable size. The only entrance is by a road cut through the rock, which is strongly guarded. A well seven hundred feet deep supplies the fortress with water, and there are storehouses sufficient to hold supplies for many years. The view from the ramparts is glorious—it takes in the whole of the Saxon Highlands, as far as the lofty Schneeberg in Bohemia. On the other side the eye follows the windings of the Elbe, as far as the spires of Dresden. Lilienstein, a mountain of exactly similar formation, but somewhat higher, stands directly opposite. On walking around, the guide pointed out a little square tower standing on the brink of a precipice, with a ledge, about two feet wide, running around it, just below the windows. He said during the reign of Augustus the Strong, a baron attached to his court, rose in his sleep after a night of revelry, and stepping out the window, stretched himself at full length along the ledge. A guard fortunately observed his situation and informed Augustus of it, who had him bound and secured with cords, and then awakened by music. It was a good lesson, and one which no doubt sobered him for the future.

Passing through the little city of Königstein, we walked on to Schandau, the capital of the Saxon Switzerland, situated on the left bank. It had sustained great damage from the flood, the whole place having been literally under water. Here we turned up a narrow valley which led to the Kuhstall, some eight miles distant. The sides, as usual, were of steep gray rock, but wide enough apart to give room to some lovely meadows, with here and there a rustic cottage. The mountain maidens, in their bright red dresses, with a fanciful scarf bound around the head, made a romantic addition to the scene. There were some quiet secluded nooks, where the light of day stole in dimly through the thick foliage above and the wild stream rushed less boisterously over the rocks. We sat down to rest in one of these cool retreats, and made the glen ring with a cheer for America. The echoes repeated the name as if they had heard it for the first time, and I gave them a strict injunction to give it back to the next countryman who should pass by.

As we advanced further into the hills the way became darker and wilder. We heard the sound of falling water in a little dell on one side, and going nearer, saw a picturesque fall of about fifteen feet. Great masses of black rock were piled together, over which the mountain-stream fell in a snowy sheet. The pines above and around grew so thick and close, that not a sunbeam could enter, and a kind of mysterious twilight pervaded the spot. In Greece it would have been chosen for an oracle. I have seen, somewhere, a picture of the Spirit of Poetry, sitting beside just such a cataract, and truly the nymph could choose no more appropriate dwelling. But alas for sentiment! while we were admiring its picturesque beauty, we did not notice a man who came from a hut near by and went up behind the rocks. All at once there was a roar of water, and a real torrent came pouring down. I looked up, and lo! there he stood, with a gate in his hand which had held the water imprisoned, looking down at us to observe the effect, I motioned him to shut it up again, and he ran down to us, lest he should lose his fee for the "sight!"

Our road now left the valley and ascended through a forest to the Kuhstall, which we came upon at once. It is a remarkable natural arch, through a rocky wall or rampart, one hundred and fifty feet thick. Going through, we came at the other end to the edge of a very deep precipice, while the rock towered precipitously far above. Below lay a deep circular valley, two miles in diameter, and surrounded on every side by ranges of crags, such as we saw on the Bastei. It was entirely covered with a pine forest, and there only appeared to be two or three narrow defiles which gave it a communication with the world. The top of the Kuhstall can be reached by a path which runs up through a split in the rock, directly to the summit. It is just wide enough for one person to squeeze himself through; pieces of wood have been fastened in as steps, and the rocks in many places close completely above. The place derives its name from having been used by the mountaineers as a hiding-place for their cattle in time of war.

Next morning we descended by another crevice in the rock to the lonely valley, which we crossed, and climbed the Little Winterberg on the opposite side. There is a wide and rugged view from a little tower on a precipitous rock near the summit, erected to commemorate the escape of Prince Augustus of Saxony, who, being pursued by a mad stag, rescued himself on the very brink, by a lucky blow. Among the many wild valleys that lay between the hills, we saw scarcely one without the peculiar rocky formation which gives to Saxon scenery its most interesting character. They resemble the remains of some mighty work of art, rather than one of the thousand varied forms in which Nature delights to clothe herself.

The Great Winterberg, which is reached by another hour's walk along an elevated ridge, is the highest of the mountains, celebrated for the grand view from its summit. We found the handsome Swiss hotel recently built there, full of tourists who had come to enjoy the scene, but the morning clouds hid every thing. We ascended the tower, and looking between them as they rolled by, caught glimpses of the broad landscape below. The Giant's Mountains in Silesia were hidden by the mist, but sometimes when the wind freshened, we could see beyond the Elbe into Bohemian Switzerland, where the long Schneeberg rose conspicuous above the smaller mountains. Leaving the other travellers to wait at their leisure for clearer weather, we set off for the Prebisehthor, in company with two or three students from the Polytechnic School in Dresden. An hour's walk over high hills, whose forest clothing had been swept off by fire a few years before, brought us to it.

The Prebisehthor is a natural arch, ninety feet high, in a wall of rock which projects at right angles from the precipitous side of the mountain. A narrow path leads over the top of the arch to the end of the rock, where, protected by a railing, the traveller seems to hang in the air. The valley is far below him—mountains rise up on either side—and only the narrow bridge connects him with the earth. We descended by a wooden staircase to the bottom of the arch, near which a rustic inn is built against the rock, and thence into the valley below, which we followed through rude lonely scenery, to Hirnischkretschen (!) on the Elbe.

Crossing the river again for the sixth and last time, we followed the right bank to Neidergrund, the first Austrian village. Here our passports were viséd for Prague, and we were allowed to proceed without any examination of baggage. I noticed a manifest change in our fellow travelers the moment we crossed the border. They appeared anxious and careful; if we happened to speak of the state of the country, they always looked around to see if anybody was near, and if we even passed a workman on the road, quickly changed to some other subject. They spoke much of the jealous strictness of the government, and from what I heard from Austrians themselves, there may have been ground for their cautiousness.

We walked seven or eight miles along the bank of the Elbe, to Tetschen, there left our companions and took the road to Teplitz. The scenery was very picturesque; it must be delightful to float down the swift current in a boat, as we saw several merry companies do. The river is just small enough and the banks near enough together, to render such a mode of travelling delightful, and the strength of the current would carry one to Dresden in a day.

I was pleasantly disappointed on entering Bohemia. Instead of a dull, uninteresting country, as I expected, it is a land full of the most lovely scenery. There is every thing which can gratify the eye—high blue mountains, valleys of the sweetest pastoral look and romantic old ruins. The very name of Bohemia is associated with wild and wonderful legends, of the rude barbaric ages. Even the chivalric tales of the feudal times of Germany grow tame beside these earlier and darker histories. The fallen fortresses of the Rhine, or the robber-castles of the Odenwald had not for me so exciting an interest as the shapeless ruins cumbering these lonely mountains. The civilized Saxon race was left behind; I saw around me the features and heard the language of one of those rude Sclavonic tribes, whose original home was on the vast steppes of Central Asia. I have rarely enjoyed traveling more than our first two days' journey towards Prague. The range of the Erzgebirge ran along on our right; the snow still lay in patches upon it, but the valleys between, with their little clusters of white cottages, were green and beautiful. About six miles before reaching Teplitz, we passed Kulm, the great battle-field, which in a measure decided the fate of Napoleon. He sent Vandamme with 40,000 men to attack the allies before they could unite their forces, and thus effect their complete destruction. Only the almost despairing bravery of the Russian guards under Ostermann, who held him in check till the allied troops united, prevented Napoleon's design. At the junction of the roads, where the fighting was hottest, the Austrians have erected a monument to one of their generals. Not far from it is that of Prussia, simple and tasteful. A woody hill near, with the little village of Kulm at its foot, was the station occupied by Vandamme at the commencement of the battle. There is now a beautiful chapel on its summit, which can be seen far and wide. A little distance further, the Emperor of Russia has erected a third monument to the memory of the Russians who fell. Four lions rest on the base of the pedestal, and on the top of the shaft, forty-five feet high, Victory is represented as engraving the date, "Aug. 30, 1813," on a shield. The dark, pine-covered mountains on the right, overlook the whole field and the valley of Teplitz; Napoleon rode along their crests several days after the battle, to witness the scene of his defeat.

154

Teplitz lies in a lovely valley, several miles wide, bounded by the Bohemian mountains on one side, and the Erzgebirge on the other. One straggling peak near is crowned with a picturesque ruin, at whose foot the spacious bath-buildings lie half hidden in foliage. As we went down the principal street, I noticed nearly every house was a hotel; we learned afterwards that in summer the usual average of visitors is five thousand. The waters resemble those of the celebrated Carlsbad; they are warm and particularly efficacious in rheumatism and diseases of like character. After leaving Teplitz, the road turned to the east, towards a lofty mountain, which we had seen the morning before. The peasants as they passed by, saluted us with "Christ greet you!"

We stopped for the night at the foot of the peak called the Milleschauer, and must have ascended nearly 2,000 feet, for we had a wide view the next morning, although the mists and clouds hid the half of it. The weather being so unfavorable, we concluded not to ascend, and taking leave of the Jena student who came there for that purpose, descended through green fields and orchards snowy with blossoms, to Lobositz, on the Elbe. Here we reached the plains again, where every thing wore the luxuriance of summer; it was a pleasant change from the dark and rough scenery we left. The road passed through Theresienstadt, the fortress of Northern Bohemia. The little city is surrounded by a double wall and moat, which can be filled with water, rendering it almost impossible to be taken. In the morning we were ferried over the Moldau, and after journeying nearly all day across barren, elevated plains, saw late in the afternoon the sixty-seven spires of Prague below us! The dark clouds which hung over the hills, gave us little time to look upon the singular scene; and we were soon comfortably settled in the half-barbaric, half-Asiatic city, with a pleasant prospect of seeing its wonders on the morrow.

# CHAPTER XX. – SCENES IN PRAGUE.

Prague.—I feel as if out of the world, in this strange, fantastic, yet beautiful old city. We have been rambling all morning through its winding streets, stopping sometimes at a church to see the dusty tombs and shrines, or to hear the fine music which accompanies the morning mass. I have seen no city yet that so forcibly reminds one of the past, and makes him forget everything but the associations connected with the scenes around him. The language adds to the illusion. Three-fourths of the people in the streets speak Bohemian and many of the signs are written in the same tongue, which is not at all like German. The palace of the Bohemian kings still looks down on the city from the western heights, and their tombs stand in the Cathedral of the holy Johannes. When one has climbed up the stone steps lending to the fortress, there is a glorious prospect before him. Prague, with its spires and towers, lies in the valley below, through which curves the Moldau with its green islands, disappearing among the hills which enclose the city on every side. The fantastic Byzantine architecture of many of the churches and towers, gives the city a peculiar oriental appearance; it seems to have been transported from the hills of Syria. Its streets are full of palaces, fallen and dwelt in now by the poorer classes. Its famous University, which once boasted forty thousand students, has long since ceased to exist. In a word, it is, like Venice, a fallen city; though as in Venice, the improving spirit of the age is beginning to give it a little life, and to send a quicker stream through its narrow and winding arteries. The railroad, which, joining that to Brünn, shall bring it in connection with Vienna, will be finished this year; in anticipation of the increased business which will arise from this, speculators are building enormous hotels in the suburbs and tearing down the old buildings to give place to more splendid edifices. These operations, and the chain bridge which spans the Moldau towards the southern end of the city, are the only things which look modern—every thing else is old, strange and solemn.

Having found out first a few of the locations, we hunted our way with difficulty through its labyrinths, seeking out every place of note or interest.

Reaching the bridge at last, we concluded to cross over and ascend to the Hradschin—the palace of the Bohemian kings. The bridge was commenced in 1357, and was one hundred and fifty years in building. That was the way the old Germans did their work, and they made a structure which will last a thousand years longer. Every pier is surmounted with groups of saints and martyrs, all so worn and time-beaten, that there is little left of their beauty, if they ever had any. The most important of them, at least to Bohemians, is that of the holy "Johannes of Nepomuck," now considered as the patron-saint of the land. He was a priest many centuries ago, whom one of the kings threw from the bridge into the Moldau, because he refused to reveal to him what the queen confessed. The legend says the body swam for some time on the river, with five stars around its head. The 16th of May, the day before we arrived, was that set apart for his particular honor; the statue on the bridge was covered with an arch of green boughs and flowers, and the shrine lighted with burning tapers. A railing was erected around it, near which numbers of the believers were kneeling, and a priest stood in the inside. The bridge was covered with passers-by, who all took their hats off till they had passed. Had it been a place of public worship, the act would have been natural and appropriate, but to uncover before a statue seemed to us too much like idolatry, and we ventured over without doing it. A few years ago it might have been dangerous, but now we only met with scowling looks. There are many such shrines and statues through the city, and I noticed that the people always took off their hats and crossed themselves in passing. On the hill above the western end of the city, stands a chapel on the spot where the Bavarians put an end to Protestantism in Bohemia by the sword, and the deluded peasantry of the land make pilgrimages to this spot, as if it were rendered holy by an act over which Religion weeps!

Ascending the broad flight of steps to the Hradschin, I paused a moment to look at the scene below. A slight blue haze hung over the clustering towers, and the city looked dim through it, like a city seen in a dream. It was well that it should so appear, for not less dim and misty are the memories that haunt its walls. There was no need of a magician's wand to bid that light cloud shadow forth the forms of other times. They came uncalled for, even by fancy. Far, far back in the past, I saw the warrior-princess who founded the kingly city—the renowned Libussa, whose prowess and talent inspired the women of Bohemia to rise at her death and storm the land that their sex might rule where it obeyed before. On the mountain opposite once stood the palace of the bloody Wlaska, who reigned with her Amazon band for seven years over half Bohemia. Those streets below had echoed with the fiery words of Huss, and the castle of his follower—the blind Ziska, who met and defeated the armies of the German Empire—moulders on the mountain above. Many a year of war and tempest has passed over the scene. The hills around have borne the armies of Wallenstein and Frederic the Great; the war-cry of Bavaria, Sweden and Poland has echoed in the valley, and the red glare of the midnight cannon or the flames of burning palaces have often gleamed along the "blood-dyed waters" of the Moldau!

But this was a day-dream. The throng of people coming up the steps waked me out of it. We turned and followed them through several spacious courts, till we arrived at the Cathedral, which is magnificent in the extreme. The dark Gothic pillars, whose arches unite high above, are surrounded with gilded monuments and shrines, and the side chapels are rich in elaborate decorations. A priest was speaking from a pulpit in the centre, in the Bohemian language, which not being the most intelligible, I went to the other end to see the shrine of the holy Johannes of Nepomuck. It stands at the end of one of the side aisles and is composed of a mass of gorgeous silver ornaments. At a little distance, on each side, hang four massive lamps of silver, constantly burning. The pyramid of statues, of the same precious metal, has at each corner a richly carved urn, three feet high, with a crimson lamp burning at the top. Above, four silver angels, the size of life, are suspended in the air, holding up the corners of a splendid drapery of crimson and gold. If these figures were melted down and distributed among the poor and miserable people who inhabit Bohemia, they would then be angels indeed, bringing happiness and blessing to many a ruined home- altar. In the same chapel is the splendid burial-place of the Bohemian kings, of gilded marble and alabaster. Numberless tombs, covered with elaborate ornamental work, fill the edifice. It gives one a singular feeling to stand at one end and look down the lofty hall, dim with incense smoke and dark with the weight of many centuries.

158

On the way down again, we stepped into the St. Nicholas Church, which was built by the Jesuits. The interior has a rich effect, being all of brown and gold. The massive pillars are made to resemble reddish-brown marble, with gilded capitals, and the statues at the base are profusely ornamented in the same style. The music chained me there a long time. There was a grand organ, assisted by a full orchestra and large choir of singers. It was placed above, and at every sound of the priest's bell, the flourish of trumpets and deep roll of the drums filled the dome with a burst of quivering sound, while the giant pipes of the organ breathed out their full harmony and the very air shook under the peal. It was like a triumphal strain; the soul became filled with thoughts of power and glory—every sense was changed into one dim, indistinct emotion of rapture, which held the spirit as if spell-bound. I could almost forgive the Jesuits the superstition and bigotry they have planted in the minds of men, for the indescribable enjoyment that music gave. When it ceased, we went out to the world again, and the recollection of it seems now like a dream—but a dream whose influence will last longer than many a more palpable reality.

Not far from this place is the palace of Wallenstein, in the same condition as when he inhabited it, and still in the possession of his descendants. It is a plain, large building, having beautiful gardens attached to it, which are open to the public. We went through the courtyard, threaded a passage with a roof of rough stalactitic rock, and entered the garden where a revolving fountain was casting up its glittering arches. Among the flowers at the other end of the garden there is a remarkable fountain. It is but a single jet of water which rises from the middle of a broad basin of woven wire, but by some means it sustains a hollow gilded ball, sometimes for many minutes at a time. When the ball drops, the sloping sides of the basin convey it directly to the fountain again, and it is carried up to dance a while longer on the top of the jet. I watched it once, thus supported on the water, for full fifteen minutes.

There is another part of Prague which is not less interesting, though much less poetical—the Jews' City. In our rambles we got into it before we were aware, but hurried immediately out of it again, perfectly satisfied with one visit. We came first into a dark, narrow street, whose sides were lined with booths of old clothes and second-hand articles. A sharp featured old woman thrust a coat before my face, exclaiming, "Herr, buy a fine coat!" Instantly a man assailed me on the other side, "Here are vests! pantaloons! shirts!" I broke loose from them and ran on, but it only became worse. One seized me by the arm, crying, "Lieber Herr, buy some stockings!" and another grasped my coat: "Hats, Herr! hats! buy something, or sell me something!" I rushed desperately on, shouting "no! no!" with all my might, and finally got safe through. My friend having escaped their clutches also, we hunted the way to the old Jewish cemetery. This stands in the middle of the city, and has not been used for a hundred years. We could find no entrance, but by climbing upon the ruins of an old house near, I could look over the wall. A cold shudder crept over me, to think that warm, joyous Life, as I then felt it, should grow chill and pass back to clay in such a foul charnel-house. Large mounds of earth, covered with black, decaying grave-stones, which were almost hidden under the weeds and rank grass, filled the inclosure. A few dark, crooked alder-trees grew among the crumbling tombs, and gave the scene an air of gloom and desolation, almost fearful. The dust of many a generation lies under these mouldering stones; they now scarcely occupy a thought in the minds of the living; and yet the present race toils and seeks for wealth alone, that it may pass away and leave nothing behind—not even a memory for that which will follow it!

# CHAPTER XXI. – JOURNEY THROUGH EASTERN BOHEMIA AND MORAVIA TO THE DANUBE.

Our road the first two days after leaving Prague led across broad, elevated plains, across which a cold wind came direct from the summits of the Riesengebirge, far to our left. Were it not for the pleasant view we had of the rich valley of the Upper Elbe, which afforded a delightful relief to the monotony of the hills around us, the journey would have been exceedingly tiresome. The snow still glistened on the distant mountains; but when the sun shone out, the broad valley below, clad in the luxuriance of summer, and extending for at least fifty miles with its woods, meadows and white villages, looked like a real Paradise. The long ridges over which we travelled extend for nearly a hundred and fifty miles—from the Elbe almost to the Danube. The soil is not fertile, the inhabitants are exceedingly poor, and from our own experience, the climate must be unhealthy. In winter the country is exposed to the full sweep of the northern winds, and in summer the sun shines down on it with unbroken force. There are few streams running through it, and the highest part, which divides the waters of the Baltic from those of the Black Sea is filled for a long distance with marshes and standing pools, whose exhalations must inevitably subject the inhabitants to disease. This was perceptible in their sallow, sickly countenances; many of the women are afflicted with the goitre, or swelling of the throat; I noticed that towards evening they always carefully muffled up their faces. According to their own statements, the people suffer much from the cold in winter, as the few forests the country affords are in possession of the noblemen to whom the land belongs, and they are not willing to let them be cut down. The dominions of these petty despots are marked along the road with as much precision as the boundaries of an empire; we saw sometimes their stalely castles at a distance, forming quite a contrast to the poor scattering villages of the peasants.

At Kollin, the road, which had been running eastward in the direction of Olmutz, turned to the south, and we took leave of the Elbe, after tracing back his course from Magdeburg nearly to his home in the mountains of

Silesia. The country was barren and monotonous, but a bright sunshine made it look somewhat cheerful. We passed, every few paces, some shrine or statue by the roadside. This had struck me, immediately on crossing the border, in the Saxon Switzerland—it seemed as if the boundary of Saxony was that of Protestantism. But here in the heart of Bohemia, the extent to which this image worship is carried, exceeds anything I had imagined. There is something pleasing as well as poetical in the idea of a shrine by the wayside, where the weary traveller can rest, and raise his heart in thankfulness to the Power that protects him; it was no doubt a pious spirit that placed them there; but the people appear to pay the reverence to the picture which they should give to its spiritual image, and the pictures themselves are so shocking and ghastly, they seem better calculated to excite horror than reverence. It was really repulsive to look on images of the Saviour covered with blood, and generally with swords sticking in different parts of the body. The Almighty is represented as an old man, wearing a Bishop's mitre, and the image of the Virgin is always drest in a gay silk robe, with beads and other ornaments. From the miserable painting, the faces often had an expression that would have been exceedingly ludicrous, if the shock given to our feelings of reverence were not predominant. The poor, degraded peasants always uncovered or crossed themselves when passing by these shrines, but it appeared to be rather the effect of habit than any good impulse, for the Bohemians are noted all over Germany for their dishonesty; we learned by experience they deserve it. It is not to be wondered at either; for a people so poor and miserable and oppressed will soon learn to take advantage of all who appear better off than themselves. They had one custom which was touching and beautiful. At the sound of the church bell, as it rung the morning, noon and evening chimes, every one uncovered, and repeated to himself a prayer. Often, as we rested at noon on a bank by the roadside, that voice spoke out from the house of worship and every one heeded its tone. Would that to this innate spirit of reverence were added the light of Knowledge, which a tyrannical government denies them!

The third night of our journey we stopped at the little village of Stecken, and the next morning, after three hours' walk over the ridgy heights, reached the old Moravian city of Iglau, built on a hill. It happened to be Corpus

Christi day, and the peasants of the neighborhood were hastening there in their gayest dresses. The young women wore a crimson scarf around the head, with long fringed and embroidered ends hanging over the shoulders, or falling in one smooth fold from the back of the head. They were attired in black velvet vests, with full white sleeves and skirts of some gay color, which were short enough to show to advantage their red stockings and polished shoe-buckles. Many of them were not deficient in personal beauty—there was a gipsy-like wildness in their eyes, that combined with their rich hair and graceful costume, reminded me of the Italian maidens. The towns too, with their open squares and arched passages, have quite a southern look; but the damp, gloomy weather was enough to dispel any illusion of this kind.

In the neighborhood of Iglau, and, in fact, through the whole of Bohemia, we saw some of the strangest teams that could well be imagined. I thought the Frankfort milkwomen with their donkeys and hearse-like carts, were comical objects enough, but they bear no comparison with these Bohemian turn-outs. Dogs—for economy's sake, perhaps—generally supply the place of oxen or horses, and it is no uncommon thing to see three large mastiffs abreast, harnessed to a country-cart. A donkey and a cow together, are sometimes met with, and one man, going to the festival at Iglau, had his wife and children in a little wagon, drawn by a dog and a donkey. These two, however, did not work well together; the dog would bite his lazy companion, and the man's time was constantly employed in whipping him off the donkey, and in whipping the donkey away from the side of the road. Once I saw a wagon drawn by a dog, with a woman pushing behind, while a man, doubtless her lord and master, sat comfortably within, smoking his pipe with the greatest complacency! The very climax of all was a woman and a dog harnessed together, taking a load of country produce to market! I hope, for the honor of the country, it was not emblematic of woman's condition there. But as we saw hundreds of them breaking stone along the road, and occupied at other laborious and not less menial labor, there is too much reason to fear that it is so.

As we approached Iglau, we heard cannon firing; the crowd increased, and following the road, we came to an open square, where a large number were already assembled; shrines were erected around it, hung with pictures and pine boughs, and a long procession of children was passing down the side as we entered. We went towards the middle, where Neptune and his Tritons poured the water from their urns into two fountains, and stopped to observe the scene. The procession came on, headed by a large body of priests, in white robes, with banners and crosses. They stopped before the principal shrine, in front of the Rathhaus, and began a solemn religious ceremony. The whole crowd of not less than ten thousand persons, stood silent and uncovered, and the deep voice of the officiating priest was heard over the whole square. At times the multitude sang responses, and I could mark the sound, swelling and rolling up like a mighty wave, till it broke and slowly sank down again to the deepest stillness. The effect was marred by the rough voice of the officers commanding the soldiery, and the volleys of musquetry which were occasionally discharged. It degraded the solemnity of the pageant to the level of a military parade.

In the afternoon we were overtaken by a travelling handwerker, on his way to Vienna, who joined company with us. We walked several miles together, talking on various matters, without his having the least suspicion we were not Germans. He had been at Trieste, and at length began speaking of the great beauty of the American vessels there. "Yes," said I, "our vessels are admired all over the world." He stared at me without comprehending;—"your vessels?" "Our country's," I replied; "we are Americans!" I can see still his look of incredulous astonishment and hear the amazed tone with which he cried: "You Americans—it is impossible!" We convinced him nevertheless, to his great joy, for all through Germany there is a curiosity to see our countrymen and a kindly feeling towards them. "I shall write down in my book," said he, "so that I shall never forget it, that I once travelled with two Americans!" We stopped together for the night at the only inn in a large, beggarly village, where we obtained a frugal supper with difficulty, for a regiment of Polish lancers was quartered there for the night, and the pretty Kellnerin was so busy in waiting on the officers that she had no eye for wandering journeymen, as she took us to be. She even told us the beds were all occupied and we must sleep on the floor. Just then the landlord came by. "Is it possible, Herr Landlord," asked our new companion, "that there is no bed here for us? Have the goodness to look again, for we are not in the habit of sleeping on the floor, like dogs!" This speech had its effect, for the Kellnerin was commanded to find us beds. She came back unwillingly after a time and reported that two, only, were vacant. As a German bed is only a yard wide, we pushed these two together, but they were still too small for three persons, and I had a severe cold in the morning, from sleeping crouched up against the damp wall.

The next day we passed the dividing ridge which separates the waters of the Elbe from the Danube, and in the evening arrived at Znaim, the capital of Moravia. It is built on a steep hill looking down on the valley of the Thaya, whose waters mingle with the Danube near Pressburg. The old castle on the height near, was formerly the residence of the Moravian monarchs, and traces of the ancient walls and battlements of the city are still to be seen. The handwerker took us to the inn frequented by his craft—the leather-curriers— and we conversed together till bed-time. While telling me of the oppressive laws of Austria, the degrading vassalage of the peasants and the horrors of the conscription system, he paused as in deep thought, and looking at me with a suppressed sigh, said: "Is it not true, America is free?" I told him of our country and her institutions, adding that though we were not yet as free as we hoped and wished to be, we enjoyed far more liberty than any country in the world. "Ah!" said he, "it is hard to leave one's fatherland oppressed as it is, but I wish I could go to America!"

We left next morning at eight o'clock, after having done full justice to the beds of the "Golden Stag," and taken leave of Florian Francke, the honest and hearty old landlord. Znaim appears to great advantage from the Vienna road; the wind which blew with fury against our backs, would not permit us to look long at it, but pushed us on towards the Austrian border. In the course of three hours we were obliged to stop at a little village; it blew a perfect hurricane and the rain began to soak through our garments. Here we stayed three hours among the wagoners who stopped on account of the weather. One miserable, drunken wretch, whom one would not wish to look at more than once, distinguished himself by insulting those around him, and devouring like a beast, large quantities of food. When the reckoning was given him, he declared he had already paid, and the waiter denying it, he said, "Stop, I will show you something!" pulled out his passport and pointed

to the name—"Baron von Reitzenstein." It availed nothing; he had fallen
so low that his title inspired no respect, and when we left the inn they were
still endeavoring to get their money and threatening him with a summary
proceeding if the demand was not complied with.

Next morning the sky was clear and a glorious day opened before us. The
country became more beautiful as we approached the Danube; the hills were
covered with vineyards, just in the tender green of their first leaves, and the
rich valleys lay in Sabbath stillness in the warm sunshine. Sometimes from an
eminence we could see far and wide over the garden-like slopes, where little
white villages shone among the blossoming fruit-trees. A chain of blue hills
rose in front, which I knew almost instinctively stood by the Danube; when
we climbed to the last height and began to descend to the valley, where the
river was still hidden by luxuriant groves, I saw far to the southwest, a range of
faint, silvery summits, rising through the dim ether like an airy vision. There
was no mistaking those snowy mountains. My heart bounded with a sudden
thrill of rapturous excitement at this first view of the Alps! They were at a
great distance, and their outline was almost blended with the blue drapery
of air which clothed them. I gazed till my vision became dim and I could no
longer trace their airy lines. They called up images blended with the grandest
events in the world's history. I thought of the glorious spirits who have looked
upon them and trodden their rugged sides—of the storms in which they veil
their countenances, and the avalanches they hurl thundering to the valleys—
of the voices of great deeds, which have echoed from their crags over the wide
earth—and of the ages which have broken, like the waves of a mighty sea,
upon their everlasting summits!

As we descended, the hills and forests shut out this sublime vision, and I
looked to the wood-clothed mountains opposite and tried to catch a glimpse
of the current that rolled at their feet. We here entered upon a rich plain,
about ten miles in diameter, which lay between a backward sweep of the hills
and a curve of the Danube. It was covered with the richest grain; every thing
wore the luxuriance of summer, and we seemed to have changed seasons since
leaving the dreary hills of Bohemia. Continuing over the plain, we had on our
left the fields of Wagram and Essling, the scene of two of Napoleon's blood-

166

bought victories. The outposts of the Carpathians skirted the horizon—that great mountain range which stretches through Hungary to the borders of Russia.

At length the road came to the river's side, and we crossed on wooden bridges over two or three arms of the Danube, all of which together were little wider than the Schuylkill at Philadelphia. When we crossed the last bridge, we came to a kind of island covered with groves of the silver ash. Crowds of people filled the cool walks; booths of refreshment stood by the roadside, and music was everywhere heard. The road finally terminated in a circle, where beautiful alleys radiated into the groves; from the opposite side a broad street lined with stately buildings extended into the heart of the city, and through this avenue, filled with crowds of carriages and people on their way to those delightful walks, we entered Vienna!

# CHAPTER XXII. — VIENNA.

May 31.—I have at last seen the thousand wonders of this great capital—this German Paris—this connecting link between the civilization of Europe and the barbaric magnificence of the East. It looks familiar to be in a city again, whose streets are thronged with people, and resound with the din and bustle of business. It reminds me of the never-ending crowds of London, or the life and tumult of our scarcely less active New York. Although the end may be sordid for which so many are laboring, yet the very sight of so much activity is gratifying. It is peculiarly so to an American. After residing in a foreign land for some time, the peculiarities of our nation are more easily noticed; I find in my countrymen abroad a vein of restless energy—a love for exciting action—which to many of our good German friends is perfectly incomprehensible. It might have been this which gave at once a favorable impression of Vienna.

The morning of our arrival we sallied out from our lodgings in the Leopoldstadt, to explore the world before us. Entering the broad Praterstrasse, we passed down to the little arm of the Danube, which separates this part of the new city from the old. A row of magnificent coffee-houses occupy the bank, and numbers of persons were taking their breakfasts in the shady porticoes. The Ferdinand's Bridge, which crosses the stream, was filled with people; in the motley crowd we saw the dark-eyed Greek, and Turks in their turbans and flowing robes. Little brown Hungarian boys were going around, selling bunches of lilies, and Italians with baskets of oranges stood by the side-walk. The throng became greater as we penetrated into the old city. The streets were filled with carts and carriages, and as there are no side-pavements, it required constant attention to keep out of their way. Splendid shops, fitted up with great taste, occupied the whole of the lower stories, and goods of all kinds hung beneath the canvass awnings in front of them. Almost every store or shop was dedicated to some particular person or place, which was represented on a large panel by the door. The number of these paintings added much to the splendor of the scene; I was gratified to find, among the images of kings and dukes, one dedicated "to the American," with an Indian chief in full costume.

The Altstadt, or old city, which contains about sixty thousand inhabitants, is completely separated from the suburbs, whose population, taking the whole extent within the outer barrier, numbers nearly half a million. It is situated on a small arm of the Danube, and encompassed by a series of public promenades, gardens and walks, varying from a quarter to half a mile in length, called the Glacis. This formerly belonged to the fortifications of the city, but as the suburbs grew up so rapidly on all sides, it was changed appropriately to a public walk. The city is still surrounded with a massive wall and a deep wide moat; but since it was taken by Napoleon in 1809, the moat has been changed into a garden, with a beautiful carriage road along the bottom, around the whole city. It is a beautiful sight, to stand on the summit of the wall and look over the broad Glacis, with its shady roads branching in every direction, and filled with inexhaustible streams of people. The Vorstaedte, or new cities, stretch in a circle around, beyond this; all the finest buildings front on the Glacis, among which the splendid Vienna Theatre and the church of San Carlo Borromeo are conspicuous. The mountains of the Vienna Forest bound the view, with here and there a stately castle on their woody summits. I was reminded of London as seen from Regent's Park, and truly this part of Vienna can well compare with it. On penetrating into the suburbs, the resemblance is at an end. Many of the public thoroughfares are still unpaved, and in dry weather one is almost choked by the clouds of fine dust. A furious wind blows from the mountains, sweeping the streets almost constantly and filling the eyes and ears with it, making the city an unhealthy residence for strangers.

There is no lack of places for pleasure or amusement. Beside the numberless walks of the Glacis, there are the Imperial Gardens, with their cool shades and flowers and fountains; the Augarten, laid out and opened to the public by the Emperor Joseph: and the Prater, the largest and most beautiful of all. It lies on an island formed by the arms of the Danube, and is between two and three miles square. From the circle at the end of the Praterstrasse, broad carriage-ways extend through its forests of oak and silver ash, and over its verdant lawns to the principal stream, which bounds it on the north. These roads are lined with stately horse chesnuts, whose branches unite and form a dense canopy, completely shutting out the sun. Every afternoon the beauty and nobility of Vienna whirl through the cool groves in their gay equipages, while the sidewalks are thronged with pedestrians, and the numberless tables and seats with which every house of refreshment is surrounded, are filled with merry guests. Here, on Sundays and holidays, the people repair in thousands. The woods are full of tame deer, which run perfectly free over the whole Prater. I saw several in one of the lawns, lying down in the grass, with a number of children playing around or sitting beside them. It is delightful to walk there in the cool of the evening, when the paths are crowded, and everybody is enjoying the release from the dusty city. It is this free, social life which renders Vienna so attractive to foreigners and draws yearly thousands of visitors from all parts of Europe.

St. Stephen's Cathedral, in the centre of the old city, is one of the finest specimens of Gothic architecture in Germany. Its unrivalled tower, which rises to the height of four hundred and twenty-eight feet, is visible from every part of Vienna. It is entirely of stone, most elaborately ornamented, and is supposed to be the strongest in Europe. If the tower was finished, it might rival any church in Europe in richness and brilliancy of appearance. The inside is solemn and grand; but the effect is injured by the number of small chapels and shrines. In one of these rests, the remains of Prince Eugene of Savoy, "der edle Ritter," known in a ballad to every man, woman and child in Germany.

The Belvidere Gallery fills thirty-five halls, and contains three thousand pictures! It is absolutely bewildering to walk through such vast collections; you can do no more than glance at each painting, and hurry by face after face, and figure after figure, on which you would willingly gaze for hours and inhale the atmosphere of beauty that surrounds them. Then after you leave, the brain is filled with their forms—radiant spirit-faces look upon you, and you see constantly, in fancy, the calm brow of a Madonna, the sweet young face of a child, or the blending of divine with mortal beauty in an angel's countenance. I endeavor, if possible, always to make several visits—to study those pictures which cling first to the memory, and pass over those which make little or no impression. It is better to have a few images fresh and enduring, than a confused and indistinct memory of many.

From the number of Madonnas in every European gallery, it would almost seem that the old artists painted nothing else. The subject is one which requires the highest genius to do it justice, and it is therefore unpleasant to see so many still, inexpressive faces of the virgin and child, particularly by the Dutch artists, who clothe their figures sometimes in the stiff costume of their own time. Raphael and Murillo appear to me to be almost the only painters who have expressed what, perhaps, was above the power of other masters— the combined love and reverence of the mother, and the divine expression in the face of the child, prophetic of his mission and godlike power.

There were many glorious old paintings in the second story, which is entirely taken up with pictures; two or three of the halls were devoted to selected works from modern artists. Two of these I would give every thing I have to possess. One of them is a winter scene, representing the portico of an old Gothic church. At the base of one of the pillars a woman is seated in the snow, half-benumbed, clasping an infant to her breast, while immediately in front stands a boy of perhaps seven or eight years, his little hands folded in prayer, while the chill wind tosses the long curls from his forehead. There is something so pure and holy in the expression of his childish countenance, so much feeling in the lip and sorrowful eye, that it moves one almost to tears to look upon it. I turned back half a dozen times from the other pictures to view it again, and blessed the artist in my heart for the lesson he gave. The other is by a young Italian painter, whose name I have forgotten, but who, if he never painted anything else, is worthy a high place among the artists of his country. It represents some scene from the history of Venice. On an open piazza, a noble prisoner, wasted and pale from long confinement, has just had an interview with his children. He reaches his arm toward them as if for the last time, while a savage keeper drags him away. A lovely little girl kneels at the feet of the Doge, but there is no compassion in his stern features, and it is easy to see that her father is doomed.

The Lower Belvidere, separated from the Upper by a large garden, laid out in the style of that at Versailles, contains the celebrated Ambraser

Sammlung, a collection of armor. In the first hall I noticed the complete armor of the Emperor Maximilian, for man and horse—the armor of Charles V., and Prince Moritz of Saxony, while the walls were filled with figures of German nobles and knights, in the suits they wore in life. There is also the armor of the great "Baver of Trient," trabant of the Archduke Ferdinand. He was nearly nine feet in stature, and his spear, though not equal to Satan's, in Paradise Lost, would still make a tree of tolerable dimensions.

In the second hall we saw weapons taken from the Turkish army who besieged Vienna, with the horse-tail standards of the Grand Vizier, Kara Mustapha. The most interesting article was the battle-axe of the unfortunate Montezuma, which was probably given to the Emperor Charles V., by Cortez. It is a plain instrument of dark colored stone, about three feet long.

We also visited the Bürgerliche Zeughaus, a collection of arms and weapons, belonging to the citizens of Vienna. It contains sixteen thousand weapons and suits of armor, including those plundered from the Turks, when John Sobieski conquered them and relieved Vienna from the siege. Besides a great number of sabres, lances and horsetails, there is the blood-red banner of the Grand Vizier, as well as his skull and shroud, which is covered with sentences from the Koran. On his return to Belgrade, after the defeat at Vienna, the Sultan sent him a bow-string, and he was accordingly strangled. The Austrians having taken Belgrade some time after, they opened his grave and carried off his skull and shroud, as well as the bow-string, as relics. Another large and richly embroidered banner, which hung in a broad sheet from the ceiling, was far more interesting to me. It had once waved from the vessels of the Knights of Malta, and had, perhaps, on the prow of the Grand Master's ship, led that romantic band to battle against the Infidel.

A large number of peasants and common soldiers were admitted to view the armory at the same time. The grave custode who showed us the curiosities, explaining every thing in phrases known by heart for years and making the same starts of admiration whenever he came to any thing peculiarly remarkable, singled us out as the two persons most worthy of attention. Accordingly his remarks were directed entirely to us, and his humble countrymen might as well have been invisible, for the notice he took of them. On passing out, we gave him a coin worth about fifteen cents, which happened to be so much more than the others gave him, that, bowing graciously, he invited us to write our names in the album for strangers. While we were doing this, a poor handwerker lingered behind, apparently for the same object, whom he scornfully dismissed, shaking the fifteen cent piece in his hand, and saying: "The album is not for such as you—it is for noble gentlemen!"

On our way through the city, we often noticed a house on the southern side of St. Stephen's Platz, dedicated to "the Iron Stick." In a niche by the window, stood what appeared to be the limb of a tree, completely filled with nails, which were driven in so thick that no part of the original wood is visible. We learned afterwards the legend concerning it. The Vienna Forest is said to have extended, several hundred years ago, to this place. A locksmith's apprentice was enabled, by the devil's help, to make the iron bars and padlock which confine the limb in its place; every locksmith's apprentice who came to Vienna after that, drove a nail into it, till finally there was room for no more. It is a singular legend, and whoever may have placed the limb there originally, there it has remained for two or three hundred years at least.

We spent two or three hours delightfully one evening in listening to Strauss's band. We went about sunset to the Odeon, a new building in the Leopoldstadt. It has a refreshment hall nearly five hundred feet long, with a handsome fresco ceiling and glass doors opening into a garden walk of the same length. Both the hall and garden were filled with tables, where the people seated themselves as they came, and conversed sociably over their coffee and wine. The orchestra was placed in a little ornamental temple in the garden, in front of which I stationed myself, for I was anxious to see the world's waltz-king, whose magic tones can set the heels of half Christendom in motion. After the band had finished tuning their instruments, a middle-sized, handsome man stepped forward with long strides, with a violin in one hand and bow in the other, and began waving the latter up and down, like a magician summoning his spirits. As if he had waved the sound out of his bow, the tones leaped forth from the instruments, and guided by his eye and hand, fell into a merry measure. The accuracy with which every instrument performed its part, was truly marvellous. He could not have struck the measure or the harmony more certainly from the keys of his own piano, than from that large band. The sounds struggled forth, so perfect and distinct, that one almost expected to see them embodied, whirling in wild dance around him. Sometimes the air was so exquisitely light and bounding, the feet could scarcely keep on the earth; then it sank into a mournful lament, with a sobbing tremulousness, and died away in a long-breathed sigh. Strauss seemed to feel the music in every limb. He would wave his fiddle-bow awhile, then commence playing with desperate energy, moving his whole body to the measure, till the sweat rolled from his brow. A book was lying on the stand before him, but he made no use of it. He often glanced around with a kind of half-triumphant smile at the restless crowd, whose feet could scarcely be restrained from bounding to the magic measure. It was the horn of Oberon realized. The composition of the music displayed great talent, but its charm consisted more in the exquisite combination of the different instruments, and the perfect, the wonderful exactness with which each performed its part—a piece of art of the most elaborate and refined character.

The company, which consisted of several hundred, appeared to be full of enjoyment. They sat under the trees in the calm, cool twilight, with the stars twinkling above, and talked and laughed sociably together between the pauses of the music, or strolled up and down the lighted alleys. We walked up and down with them, and thought how much we should enjoy such a scene at home, where the faces around us would be those of friends, and the language our mother tongue!

We went a long way through the suburbs one bright afternoon, to a little cemetery about a mile from the city, to find the grave of Beethoven. On ringing at the gate a girl admitted us into the grounds, in which are many monuments of noble families who have vaults there. I passed up the narrow walk, reading the inscriptions, till I came to the tomb of Franz Clement, a young composer, who died two or three years ago. On turning again, my eye fell instantly on the word "BEETHOVEN," in golden letters, on a tombstone of gray marble. A simple gilded lyre decorated the pedestal, above which was a serpent encircling a butterfly—the emblem of resurrection to eternal life. Here then, mouldered the remains of that restless spirit, who seemed to have strayed to earth from another clime, from such a height did he draw his glorious conceptions. The perfection he sought for here in vain, he has now attained in a world where the soul is freed from the bars which bind it in this. There were no flowers planted around the tomb by those who revered his genius; only one wreath, withered and dead, lay among the grass, as if left long ago by some solitary pilgrim, and a few wild buttercups hung with their bright blossoms over the slab. It might have been wrong, but I could not resist the temptation to steal one or two, while the old grave-digger was busy preparing a new tenement. I thought that other buds would open in a few days, but those I took would be treasured many a year as sacred relics. A few paces off is the grave of Schubert, the composer, whose beautiful songs are heard all over Germany.

It would employ one a week to visit all the rich collections of art in Vienna. They are all open to the public on certain days of the week, and we have been kept constantly in motion, running from one part of the city to another, in order to arrive at some gallery at the appointed time. Tickets, which have to be procured often in quite different parts of the city, are necessary for admittance to many; on applying after much trouble and search, we frequently found we came at the wrong hour, and must leave without effecting our object. We employed no guide, but preferred finding every thing ourselves. We made a list every morning, of the collections open during the day, and employed the rest of the time in visiting the churches and public gardens, or rambling through the suburbs.

We visited the Imperial Library a day or two ago. The hall is 245 feet long, with a magnificent dome in the centre, under which stands the statue of Charles V., of Carrara marble, surrounded by twelve other monarchs of the house of Hapsburg. The walls are of variegated marble, richly ornamented with gold, and the ceiling and dome are covered with brilliant fresco paintings. The library numbers 300,000 volumes, and 16,000 manuscripts, which are kept in walnut cases, gilded and adorned with medallions. The rich and harmonious effect of the whole cannot easily be imagined. It is exceedingly appropriate that a hall of such splendor, should be used to hold a library. The pomp of a palace may seem hollow and vain, for it is but the dwelling of a man; but no building can be too magnificent for the hundreds of great and immortal spirits to dwell in, who have visited earth during thirty centuries.

Among other curiosities preserved in the collection, we were shown a brass plate, containing one of the records of the Roman Senate, made 180 years before Christ, Greek manuscripts of the fifth and sixth centuries, and a volume of Psalms, printed on parchment, in the year 1457, by Faust and Schaeffer, the inventors of printing. There were also Mexican manuscripts, presented by Cortez; the prayer-book of Hildegard, wife of Charlemagne, in letters of gold; the signature of San Carlo Borromeo, and a Greek testament of the thirteenth century, which had been used by Erasmus in making his translation and contains notes in his own hand. The most interesting article was the "Jerusalem Delivered" of Tasso, in the poet's own hand, with his erasions and corrections.

We also visited the Cabinet of Natural History, which is open twice a week "to all respectably dressed persons," as the notice at the door says. But Heaven forbid that I should attempt to describe what we saw there. The Mineral Cabinet had a greater interest to me, inasmuch as it called up the recollections of many a school-boy ramble over the hills and into all kinds of quarries, far and near. It is said to be the most perfect collection in existence. I was pleased to find many old acquaintances there, from the mines of Pennsylvania; Massachusetts and New York were also very well represented. I had no idea before, that the mineral wealth of Austria was so great. Besides the iron and lead mines among the hills of Styria and the quicksilver of Idria, there is no small amount of gold and silver found, and the Carpathian mountains are rich in jasper, opal and lapiz lazuli. The largest opal ever found, was in this collection. It weighs thirty-four ounces and looks like a condensed rainbow.

In passing the palace, we saw several persons entering the basement story under the Library, and had the curiosity to follow them. By so doing, we saw the splendid equipages of the house of Austria. There must have been near a hundred carriages and sleds, of every shape and style, from the heavy, square vehicle of the last century to the most light and elegant conveyance of the present day. One clumsy, but magnificent machine, of crimson and

176

gold, was pointed out as being a hundred and fifty years old. The misery we witnessed in starving Bohemia, formed a striking contrast to all this splendor.

Beside the Imperial Picture Gallery, there are several belonging to princes and noblemen in Vienna, which are scarcely less valuable. The most important of these is that of Prince Liechtenstein, which we visited yesterday. We applied to the porter's lodge for admittance to the gallery, but he refused to open it for two persons; as we did not wish a long walk for nothing, we concluded to wait for other visitors. Presently a gentleman and lady came and inquired if the gallery was open. We told him it would probably be opened now, although the porter required a larger number, and he went to ask. After a short time he returned, saying: "He will come immediately; I thought best to put the number a little higher, and so I told him there were six of us!" Having little artistic knowledge of paintings, I judge of them according to the effect they produce upon me—in proportion as they gratify the innate love for the beautiful and the true. I have been therefore disappointed in some painters whose names are widely known, and surprised again to find works of great beauty by others of smaller fame. Judging by such a standard, I should say that "Cupid sleeping in the lap of Venus," by Correggio, is the glory of this collection. The beautiful limbs of the boy-god droop in the repose of slumber, as his head rests on his mother's knee, and there is a smile lingering around his half-parted lips, as if he was dreaming new triumphs. The face is not that of the wicked, mischief-loving child, but rather a sweet cherub, bringing a blessing to all he visits. The figure of the goddess is exquisite. Her countenance, unearthly in its loveliness, expresses the tenderness of a young mother, as she sits with one finger pressed on her rosy lip, watching his slumber. It is a picture which "stings the brain with beauty."

The chapel of St. Augustine contains one of the best works of Canova— the monument of the Grand Duchess, Maria Christina, of Sachsen-Teschen. It is a pyramid of gray marble, twenty-eight feet high, with an opening in the side, representing the entrance to a sepulchre. A female figure personating Virtue bears in an urn to the grave, the ashes of the departed, attended by two children with torches. The figure of Compassion follows, leading an aged beggar to the tomb of his benefactor, and a little child with its hands folded.

On the lower step rests a mourning Genius beside a sleeping lion, and a bas-relief on the pyramid above represents an angel carrying Christina's image, surrounded with the emblem of eternity, to Heaven. A spirit of deep sorrow, which is touchingly portrayed in the countenance of the old man, pervades the whole group. While we looked at it, the organ breathed out a slow, mournful strain, which harmonized so fully with the expression of the figures, that we seemed to be listening to the requiem of the one they mourned. The combined effect of music and sculpture, thus united in their deep pathos, was such, that I could have sat down and wept. It was not from sadness at the death of a benevolent though unknown individual,—but the feeling of grief, of perfect, unmingled sorrow, so powerfully represented, came to the heart like an echo of its own emotion, and carried it away with irresistible influence. Travellers have described the same feeling while listening to the Miserere in the Sistine Chapel, at Rome. Canova could not have chiseled the monument without tears.

One of the most interesting objects in Vienna, is the Imperial Armory. We were admitted through tickets previously procured from the Armory Direction; as there was already one large company within, we were told to wait in the court till our turn came. Around the wall on the inside, is suspended the enormous chain which the Turks stretched across the Danube at Buda, in the year 1529, to obstruct the navigation. It has eight thousand links and is nearly a mile in length. The court is filled with cannon of all shapes and sizes, many of which were conquered from other nations. I saw a great many which were cast during the French Revolution, with the words "Liberté! Egalité!" upon them, and a number of others bearing the simple letter "N."

Finally the first company came down and the forty or fifty persons who had collected during the interval, were admitted. The Armory runs around a hollow square, and must be at least a quarter of a mile in length. We were all taken into a circular hall, made entirely of weapons, to represent the four quarters of the globe. Here the crusty old guide who admitted us, rapped with his stick on the shield of an old knight who stood near, to keep silence, and then addressed us: "When I speak every one must be silent. No one can write or draw anything. No one shall touch anything, or go to look at anything

178

else, before I have done speaking. Otherwise, they shall be taken immediately into the street again!" Thus in every hall he rapped and scolded, driving the women to one side with his stick and the men to the other, till we were nearly through, when the thought of the coming fee made him a little more polite. He had a regular set of descriptions by heart, which he went through with a great flourish, pointing particularly to the common military caps of the late Emperors of Prussia and Austria, as "treasures beyond all price to the nation!" Whereupon, the crowd of common people gazed reverently on the shabby beavers, and I verily believe, would have devoutly kissed them, had the glass covering been removed. I happened to be next to a tall, dignified young man, who looked on all this with a displeasure almost amounting to contempt. Seeing I was a foreigner, he spoke, in a low tone, bitterly of the Austrian government. "You are not then an Austrian?" I asked. "No, thank God!" was the reply: "but I have seen enough of Austrian tyranny. I am a Pole!"

The first wing contains banners used in the French Revolution, and liberty trees with the red cap; the armor of Rudolph of Hapsburg, Maximilian I., the Emperor Charles V., and the hat, sword and order of Marshal Schwarzenberg. Some of the halls represent a fortification, with walls, ditches and embankments, made of muskets and swords. A long room in the second wing contains an encampment, in which twelve or fifteen large tents are formed in like manner. Along the sides are grouped old Austrian banners, standards taken from the French, and horsetails and flags captured from the Turks. "They make a great boast," said the Pole, "of a half dozen French colors, but let them go to the Hospital des Invalides, in Paris, and they will find hundreds of the best banners of Austria!" They also exhibited the armor of a dwarf king of Bohemia and Hungary, who died, a gray-headed old man, in his twentieth year; the sword of Marlborough; the coat of Gustavus Adolphus, pierced in the breast and back with the bullet which killed him at Lützen; the armor of the old Bohemian princess Libussa, and that of the amazon Wlaska, with a steel visor made to fit the features of her face. The last wing was the most remarkable. Here we saw the helm and breastplate of Attila, king of the Huns, which once glanced at the head of his myriads of wild hordes, before the walls of Rome; the armor of Count Stahremberg, who commanded Vienna during the Turkish siege in 1529, and the holy banner of

Mahomet, taken at that time from the Grand Vizier, together with the steel harness of John Sobieski of Poland, who rescued Vienna from the Turkish troops under Kara Mustapha; the hat, sword and breastplate of Godfrey of Bouillon, the Crusader-king of Jerusalem, with the banners of the cross the Crusaders had borne to Palestine, and the standard they captured from the Turks on the walls of the Holy City! I felt all my boyish enthusiasm for the romantic age of the Crusaders revive, as I looked on the torn and mouldering banners which once waved on the hills of Judea, or perhaps followed the sword of the Lion Heart through the fight on the field of Ascalon! What tales could they not tell, those old standards, cut and shivered by spear and lance! What brave hands have carried them through the storm of battle, what dying eyes have looked upwards to the cross on their folds, as the last prayer was breathed for the rescue of the Holy Sepulchre!

I must now close the catalogue. This morning we shall look upon Vienna for the last time. Our knapsacks are repacked, and the passports (precious documents!) visèd for Munich. The getting of this visè, however, caused a comical scene at the Police Office, yesterday. We entered the Inspector's Hall and took our stand quietly among the crowd of persons who were gathered around a railing which separated them from the main office. One of the clerks came up, scowling at us, and asked in a rough tone, "What do you want here?" We handed him our tickets of sojourn (for when a traveler spends more than twenty-four hours in a German city, he must take out a permission and pay for it) with the request that he would give us our passports. He glanced over the tickets, came back and with constrained politeness asked us to step within the railing. Here we were introduced to the Chief Inspector. "Desire Herr—— to come here," said he to a servant; then turning to us, "I am happy to see the gentlemen in Vienna." An officer immediately came up, who addressed us in fluent English. "You may speak in your native tongue," said the Inspector:—"excuse our neglect; from the facility with which you speak German, we supposed you were natives of Austria!" Our passports were signed at once and given us with a gracious bow, accompanied by the hope that we would visit Vienna again before long. All this, of course, was perfectly unintelligible to the wondering crowd outside the railing. Seeing however, the honors we were receiving, they crowded back and respectfully made room for us to pass out. I kept a grave face till we reached the bottom of the stairs, when I gave way to restrained laughter in a manner that shocked the dignity of the guard, who looked savagely at me over his forest of moustache. I would nevertheless have felt grateful for the attention we received as Americans, were it not for our uncourteous reception as suspected Austrians.

We have just been exercising the risible muscles again, though from a very different cause, and one which, according to common custom, ought to draw forth symptoms of a lachrymose nature. This morning B—— suggested an examination of our funds, for we had neglected keeping a strict account, and what with being cheated in Bohemia and tempted by the amusements of Vienna, there was an apparent dwindling away. So we emptied our pockets and purses, counted up the contents, and found we had just ten florins, or four dollars apiece. The thought of our situation, away in the heart of Austria, five hundred miles from our Frankfort home, seems irresistibly laughable. By allowing twenty days for the journey, we shall have half a florin a day, to travel on. This is a homoeopathic allowance, indeed, but we have concluded to try it. So now adieu, Vienna! In two hours we shall be among the hills again.

# CHAPTER XXIII. — UP THE DANUBE.

We passed out of Vienna in the face of one of the strongest winds it was ever my lot to encounter. It swept across the plain with such force that it was almost impossible to advance till we got under the lee of a range of hills. About two miles from the barrier we passed Schoenbrunn, the Austrian Versailles. It was built by the Empress Maria Theresa, and was the residence of Napoleon in 1809, when Vienna was in the hands of the French. Later, in 1832, the Duke of Reichstadt died in the same room which his father once occupied. Behind the palace is a magnificent garden, at the foot of a hill covered with rich forests and crowned with an open pillared hall, 300 feet long, called the Gloriette. The colossal eagle which surmounts it, can be seen a great distance.

The lovely valley in which Schoenbrunn lies, follows the course of the little river Vienna into the heart of that mountain region lying between the Styrian Alps and the Danube, and called the Vienna Forest. Into this our road led, between hills covered with wood, with here and there a lovely green meadow, where herds of cattle were grazing. The third day we came to the Danube again at Melk, a little city built under the edge of a steep hill, on whose summit stands the palace-like abbey of the Benedictine Monks. The old friars must have had a merry life of it, for the wine-cellar of the abbey furnished the French army 50,000 measures for several days in succession. The shores of the Danube here are extremely beautiful. The valley where it spreads out, is filled with groves, but where the hills approach the stream, its banks are rocky and precipitous, like the Rhine. Although not so picturesque as the latter river, the scenery of the Danube is on a grander scale. On the south side the mountains bend down to it with a majestic sweep, and there must be delightful glances into the valleys that lie between, in passing down the current.

But we soon left the river, and journeyed on through the enchanting inland vales. To give an idea of the glorious enjoyment of traveling through such scenes, let me copy a leaf out of my journal, written as we rested at noon on the top of a lofty hill:—"Here, while the delightful mountain breeze that comes fresh from the Alps cools my forehead, and the pines around are sighing their eternal anthem, I seize a few moments to tell what a paradise is around me. I have felt an elevation of mind and spirit, a perfect rapture from morning till night, since we left Vienna. It is the brightest and balmiest June weather; an ever fresh breeze sings through the trees and waves the ripening grain on the verdant meadows and hill-slopes. The air is filled with bird-music. The larks sing above us out of sight, the bullfinch wakes his notes in the grove, and at eve the nightingale pours forth her thrilling strain. The meadows are literally covered with flowers—beautiful purple salvias, pinks such as we have at home in our gardens and glowing buttercups, color the banks of every stream. I never saw richer or more luxuriant foliage. Magnificent forests clothe the hills, and the villages are imbedded in fruit trees, shrubbery and flowers. Sometimes we go for miles through some enchanting valley, lying like a paradise between the mountains, while the distant, white Alps look on it from afar; sometimes over swelling ranges of hills, where we can see to the right the valley of the Danube, threaded by his silver current and dotted with white cottages and glittering spires, and farther beyond, the blue mountains of the Bohemian Forest. To the left, the range of the Styrian Alps stretches along the sky, summit above summit, the farther ones robed in perpetual snow. I could never tire gazing on those glorious hills. They fill the soul with a conception of sublimity, such as one feels when listening to triumphal music. They seem like the marble domes of a mighty range of temples, where earth worships her Maker with an organ-anthem of storms!

"There is a luxury in traveling here. We walk all day through such scenes, resting often in the shade of the fruit trees which line the road, or on a mossy bank by the side of some cool forest. Sometimes for enjoyment as well as variety, we make our dining-place by a clear spring instead of within a smoky tavern; and our simple meals have a relish an epicure could never attain. Away with your railroads and steamboats and mail-coaches, or keep them for those who have no eye but for the sordid interests of life! With my knapsack and pilgrim-staff, I ask not their aid. If a mind and soul full of rapture with beauty, a frame in glowing and vigorous health, and slumbers unbroken even by dreams, are blessings any one would attain, let him pedestrianize it through Lower Austria!"

I have never been so strongly and constantly reminded of America, as during this journey. Perhaps the balmy season, the same in which I last looked upon the dear scenes of home, may have its effect; but there is besides a richness in the forests and waving fields of grain, a wild luxuriance over every landscape, which I have seen nowhere else in Europe. The large farm houses, buried in orchards, scattered over the valleys, add to the effect. Everything seems to speak of happiness and prosperity.

We were met one morning by a band of wandering Bohemian gipsies— the first of the kind I ever saw. A young woman with a small child in her arms came directly up to me, and looking full in my face with her wild black eyes, said, without any preface: "Yes, he too has met with sorrow and trouble already, and will still have more. But he is not false—he is true and sincere, and will also meet with good luck!" She said she could tell me three numbers with which I should buy a lottery ticket and win a great prize. I told her I would have nothing to do with the lottery, and would buy no ticket, but she persisted, saying: "Has he a twenty kreutzer piece?—will he give it? Lay it in his hand and make a cross over it, and I will reveal the numbers!" On my refusal, she became angry, and left me, saying: "Let him take care—the third day something will happen to him!" An old, wrinkled hag made the same proposition to my companion with no better success. They reminded me strikingly of our Indians; their complexion is a dark brown, and their eyes and hair are black as night. These belonged to a small tribe who wander through the forests of Bohemia, and support themselves by cheating and stealing.

We stopped the fourth night at Enns, a small city on the river of the same name, which divides Upper from Lower Austria. After leaving the beautiful little village where we passed the night before, the road ascended one of those long ranges of hills, which stretch off from the Danube towards the Alps. We walked for miles over the broad and uneven summit, enjoying the enchanting view which opened on both sides. If we looked to the right, we could trace the windings of the Danube for twenty miles, his current filled with green, wooded islands; white cities lie at the foot of the hills, which, covered to the summit with grain fields and vineyards, extended back one behind another, till the farthest were lost in the distance. I was glad we had taken the way from Vienna to Linz by land, for from the heights we had a view of the whole course of the Danube, enjoying besides, the beauty of the inland vales and the far-off Styrian Alps. From the hills we passed over we could see the snowy range as far as the Alps of Salzburg—some of them seemed robed to the very base in their white mantles. In the morning the glaciers on their summit glittered like stars; it was the first time I saw the sun reflected at a hundred miles' distance!

On descending we came into a garden-like plain, over which rose the towers of Enns, built by the ransom money paid to Austria for the deliverance of the Lion-hearted Richard. The country legends say that St. Florian was thrown into the river by the Romans in the third century, with a millstone around his neck, which, however, held him above the water like cork, until he had finished preaching them a sermon. In the villages we often saw his imago painted on the houses, in the act of pouring a pail of water on a burning building, with the inscription beneath—"Oh, holy Florian, pray for us!" This was supposed to be a charm against fire. In Upper Austria, it is customary to erect a shrine on the road, wherever an accident has happened, with a painting and description of it, and an admonition to all passers-by to pray for the soul of the unfortunate person. On one of them, for instance, was a cart with a wild ox, which a man was holding by the horns; a woman kneeling by the wheels appeared to be drawing a little girl by the feet from under it, and the inscription stated: "By calling on Jesus, Mary and Joseph, the girl was happily rescued." Many of the shrines had images which the people no doubt, in their ignorance and simplicity, considered holy, but they were to us impious and almost blasphemous.

From Enns a morning's walk brought us to Linz. The peasant girls in their broad straw hats were weeding the young wheat, looking as cheerful and contented as the larks that sung above them. A mile or two from Linz we passed one or two of the round towers belonging to the new fortifications of the city. As walls have grown out of fashion, Duke Maximilian substituted an invention of his own. The city is surrounded by thirty two towers, one to three miles distant from it, and so placed that they form a complete line of communication and defence. They are sunk in the earth, surrounded with a ditch and embankments, and each is capable of containing ten cannon and three hundred men. The pointed roofs of these towers are seen on all the hills around. We were obliged to give up our passports at the barrier, the officer telling us to call for them in three hours at the City Police Office; we spent the intervening time very agreeably in rambling through this gay, cheerful-looking town. With its gilded spires and ornamented houses, with their green lattice blinds, it reminds one strongly of Italy, or at least, of what Italy is said to be. It has now quite an active and business-like aspect, occasioned by the steamboat and railroad lines which connect it with Vienna, Prague, Ratisbon and Salzburg. Although we had not exceeded our daily allowance by more than a few kreutzers, we found that twenty days would be hardly sufficient to accomplish the journey, and our funds must therefore be replenished. Accordingly I wrote from Linz to Frankfort, directing a small sum to be forwarded to Munich, which city we hoped to reach in eight days.

We took the horse cars at Linz for Lambach, seventeen miles on the way towards Gmunden. The mountains were covered with clouds as we approached them, and the storms they had been brewing for two or three days began to march down on the plain. They had nearly reached us, when we crossed the Traun and arrived at Lambach, a small city built upon a hill. We left the next day at noon, and on ascending the hill after crossing the Traun, had an opportunity of seeing the portrait on the Traunstein, of which the old landlord told us. I saw it at the first glance—certainly it is a most remarkable freak of nature. The rough back of the mountain forms the exact profile of the human countenance, as if regularly hewn out of the rock. What is still more singular, it is said to be a correct portrait of the unfortunate Louis XVI. The landlord said it was immediately recognized by all Frenchmen. The road followed the course of the Traun, whose green waters roared at the bottom of the glen below us; we walked for several miles through a fine forest, through whose openings we caught glimpses of the mountains we longed to reach.

The river roared at last somewhat louder, and on looking down the bank, I saw rocks and rapids, and a few houses built on the edge of the stream.

186

Thinking it must be near the fall, we went down the path, and lo! on crossing a little wooden bridge, the whole affair burst in sight! Judge of our surprise at finding a fall of fifteen feet, after we had been led to expect a tremendous leap of forty or fifty, with all the accompaniment of rocks and precipices. Of course the whole descent of the river at the place was much greater, and there were some romantic cascades over the rocks which blocked its course. Its greatest beauty consisted in the color of the water—the brilliant green of the waves being broken into foam of the most dazzling white—and the great force with which it is thrown below.

The Traunstein grew higher as we approached, presenting the same profile till we had nearly reached Gmunden. From the green upland meadows above the town, the view of the mountain range was glorious, and I could easily conceive the effect of the Unknown Student's appeal to the people to fight for those free hills. I think it is Howitt who relates the incident—one of the most romantic in German history. Count Pappenheim led his forces here in the year 1626, to suppress a revolution of the people of the whole Salzburg region, who had risen against an invasion of their rights by the Austrian government. The battle which took place on these meadows was about being decided in favor of the oppressors, when a young man, clad as a student, suddenly appeared and addressed the people, pointing to the Alps above them and the sweet lake below, and asking if that land should not be free. The effect was electrical; they returned to the charge and drove back the troops of Pappenheim, who were about taking to flight, when the unknown leader fell, mortally wounded. This struck a sudden panic through his followers, and the Austrians turning again, gained a complete victory. But the name of the brave student is unknown, his deed unsung by his country's bards, and almost forgotten.

## CHAPTER XXIV. — THE UNKNOWN STUDENT.

*Ha! spears on Gmunden's meadows green,*

*And banners on the wood-crowned height!*

*Rank after rank, their helmets' sheen*

*Sends back the morning light!*

*Where late the mountain maiden sang,*

*The battle-trumpet's brazen clang*

*Vibrates along the air;*

*And wild dragoons wheel o'er the plain.*

*Trampling to earth the yellow grain,*

*From which no more the merry swain*

*His harvest sheaves shall bear.*

*The eagle, in his sweep at morn,*

*To meet the monarch-sun on high,*

*Heard the unwonted warrior's horn*

*Peal faintly up the sky!*

*He saw the foemen, moving slow*

*In serried legions, far below,*

*Against that peasant-band,*

*Who dared to break the tyrant's thrall*

*And by the sword of Austria fall,*

Or keep the ancient Right of all,
  Held by their mountain-land;

They came to meet that mail-clad host
  From glen and wood and ripening field;
A brave, stout arm, each man could boast—
  A soul, unused to yield!
They met: a shout, prolonged and loud,
Went hovering upward with the cloud
  That closed around them dun;
Blade upon blade unceasing clashed,
Spears in the onset shivering crashed,
And the red glare of cannon flashed
  Athwart the smoky sun!

The mountain warriors wavered back,
  Borne down by myriads of the foe,
Like pines before the torrent's track
  When spring has warmed the snow.
Shall Faith and Freedom vainly call,
And Gmunden's warrior-herdsmen fall
  On the red field in vain?
No! from the throng that back retired,
A student boy sprang forth inspired,
And while his words their bosoms fired,

*Led on the charge again!*

*"And thus your free arms would ye give*

*So tamely to a tyrant's band,*

*And with the hearts of vassals live*

*In this, your chainless land?*

*The emerald lake is spread below,*

*And tower above, the hills of snow—*

*Here, field and forest lie;*

*This land, so glorious and so free—*

*Say, shall it crushed and trodden be?*

*Say, would ye rather bend the knee*

*Than for its freedom die?*

*"Look! yonder stand in mid-day's glare*

*The everlasting Alps of snow,*

*And from their peaks a purer air*

*Breathes o'er the vales below!*

*The Traun his brow is bent in pride—*

*He brooks no craven on his side—*

*Would ye be fettered then?*

*There lifts the Sonnenstein his head,*

*There chafes the Traun his rocky bed*

*And Aurach's lovely vale is spread—*

*Look on them and be men!*

*"Let, like a trumpet's sound of fire,*

*These stir your souls to manhood's part—*

*The glory of the Alps inspire*

*Each yet unconquered heart!*

*For, through their unpolluted air*

*Soars fresher up the grateful prayer*

*From freemen, unto God;—*

*A blessing on those mountains old!*

*On to the combat, brethren bold!*

*Strike, that ye free the valleys hold,*

*Where free your fathers trod!"*

*And like a mighty storm that tears*

*The icy avalanche from its bed,*

*They rushed against th' opposing spears—*

*The student at their head!*

*The bands of Austria fought in vain;*

*A bloodier harvest heaped the plain*

*At every charge they made;*

*Each herdsman was a hero then—*

*The mountain hunters stood like men,*

*And echoed from the farthest glen*

*The clash of blade on blade!*

*The banner in the student's hand*

Waved triumph from the fight before;

What terror seized the conq'ring band?—

It fell, to rise no more!

And with it died the lofty flame,

That from his lips in lightning came

And burned upon their own;

Dread Pappenheim led back the foe,

The mountain peasants yielded slow,

And plain above and lake below

Were red when evening shone!


Now many a year has passed away

Since battle's blast rolled o'er the plain,

The Alps are bright in morning's ray—

The Traunstein smiles again.

But underneath the flowery sod,

By happy peasant children trod,

A hero's ashes lay.

O'er him no grateful nation wept,

Fame, of his deed no record kept,

And dull Forgetfulness hath swept

His very name away!


In many a grave, by poets sung,

There falls to dust a lofty brow,

*But he alone, the brave and young,*

  *Sleeps there forgotten now.*

*The Alps upon that field look down,*

*Which won his bright and brief renown,*

  *Beside the lake's green shore;*

*Still wears the land a tyrant's chain—*

*Still bondmen tread the battle-plain,*

*Culled by his glorious soul in vain*

  *To win their rights of yore.*

# CHAPTER XXV. — THE AUSTRIAN ALPS.

It was nearly dark when we came to the end of the plain and looked on the city at our feet and the lovely lake that lost itself in the mountains before us. We were early on board the steamboat next morning, with a cloudless sky above us and a snow-crested Alp beckoning on from the end of the lake. The water was of the most beautiful green hue, the morning light colored the peaks around with purple, and a misty veil rolled up the rocks of the Traunstein. We stood on the prow and enjoyed to the fullest extent the enchanting scenery. The white houses of Gmunden sank down to the water's edge like a flock of ducks; halfway we passed castle Ort, on a rock in the lake, whose summit is covered with trees.

As we neared the other extremity, the mountains became steeper and loftier; there was no path along their wild sides, nor even a fisher's hut nestled at their feet, and the snow filled the ravines more than half-way from the summit. An hour and a quarter brought us to Ebensee, at the head of the lake, where we landed and plodded on towards Ischl, following the Traun up a narrow valley, whose mountain walls shut out more than half the sky. They are covered with forests, and the country is inhabited entirely by the woodmen who fell the mountain pines and float the timber rafts down to the Danube. The steeps are marked with white lines, where the trees have been rolled, or rather thrown from the summit. Often they descend several miles over rooks and precipices, where the least deviation from the track would dash them in a thousand pieces. This generally takes place in the winter when the sides are covered with snow and ice. It must be a dangerous business, for there are many crosses by the way-side where the pictures represent persons accidentally killed by the trees; an additional painting represents them as burning in the flames of purgatory, and the pious traveler is requested to pray an Ave or a Paternoster for the repose of their souls.

On we went, up the valley of the Traun, between mountains five and six thousand feet high, through scenes constantly changing and constantly grand, for three or four hours. Finally the hills opened, disclosing a little triangular valley, whose base was formed by a mighty mountain covered with clouds. Through the two side angles came the Traun and his tributary the Ischl, while the little town of Ischl lay in the centre. Within a few years this has become a very fashionable bathing place, and the influx of rich visitors, which in the summer sometimes amounts to two thousand, has entirely destroyed the primitive simplicity the inhabitants originally possessed. From Ischl we took a road through the forests to St. Wolfgang, on the lake of the same name. The last part of the way led along the banks of the lake, disclosing some delicious views. These Alpine lakes surpass any scenery I have yet seen. The water is of the most beautiful green, like a sheet of molten beryl, and the cloud-piercing mountains that encompass them shut out the sun for nearly half the day. St. Wolfgang is a lovely village in a cool and quiet nook at the foot of the Schafberg. The houses tire built in the picturesque Swiss style, with flat, projecting roofs and ornamented balconies, and the people are the very picture of neatness and cheerfulness.

We started next morning to ascend the Schafberg, which is called the Righi of the Austrian Switzerland. It is somewhat higher than its Swiss namesake, and commands a prospect scarcely less extensive or grand. We followed a footpath through the thick forest by the side of a roaring torrent. The morning mist still covered the lake, but the white summits of the Salzburg and Noric Alps opposite us, rose above it and stood pure and bright in the upper air. We passed a little mill and one or two cottages, and then wound round one of the lesser heights into a deep ravine, down in whose dark shadow we sometimes heard the axe and saw of the mountain woodmen. Finally the path disappeared altogether under a mass of logs and rocks, which appeared to have been whirled together by a sudden flood. We deliberated what to do; the summit rose several thousand feet above us, almost precipitously steep, but we did not like to turn back, and there was still a hope of meeting with the path again. Clambering over the ruins and rubbish we pulled ourselves by the limbs of trees up a steep ascent and descended again to the stream. We here saw the ravine was closed by a wall of rock and our only chance was to cross to the west side of the mountain, where the ascent seemed somewhat easier. A couple of mountain maidens whom we fortunately met, carrying home grass for their goats, told us the mountain could be ascended on that side, by one who could climb well—laying a strong emphasis on the word. The very doubt implied in this expression was enough to decide us; so we began the work. And work it was, too! The side was very steep, the trees all leaned downwards, and we slipped at every step on the dry leaves and grass. After making a short distance this way with the greatest labor, we came to the track of an avalanche, which had swept away the trees and earth. Here the rock had been worn rough by torrents, but by using both hands and feet, we clomb directly up the side of the mountain, sometimes dragging ourselves up by the branches of trees where the rocks were smooth. After half an hour of such work we came above the forests, on the bare side of the mountain. The summit was far above us and so steep that our limbs involuntarily shrunk from the task of climbing. The side ran up at an angle of nearly sixty degrees, and the least slip threw us flat on our faces. We had to use both hand and foot, and were obliged to rest every few minutes to recover breath. Crimson-flowered moss and bright blue gentians covered the rocks, and I filled my books with blossoms for friends at home.

Up and up, for what seemed an age, we clambered. So steep was it, that the least rocky projection hid my friend from sight, as he was coming up below me. I let stones roll sometimes, which went down, down, almost like a cannonball, till I could see them no more. At length we reached the region of dwarf pines, which was even more difficult to pass through. Although the mountain was not so steep, this forest, centuries old, reached no higher than our breasts, and the trees leaned downwards, so that we were obliged to take hold of the tops of those above us, and drag ourselves up through the others. Here and there lay large patches of snow; we sat down in the glowing June sun, and bathed our hands and faces in it. Finally the sky became bluer and broader, the clouds seemed nearer, and a few more steps through the bushes brought us to the summit of the mountain, on the edge of a precipice a thousand feet deep, whose bottom stood in a vast field of snow!

We lay down on the heather, exhausted by five hours' incessant toil, and drank in like a refreshing draught, the sublimity of the scene, The green lakes of the Salzburg Alps lay far below us, and the whole southern horizon was

196

filled with the mighty range of the Styrian and Noric Alps, their summits of never-melting snow mingling and blending with the clouds. On the other side the mountains of Salzburg lifted their ridgy backs from the plains of Bavaria and the Chiem lake lay spread out in the blue distance. A line of mist far to the north betrayed the path of the Danube, and beyond it we could barely trace the outline of the Bohemian mountains. With a glass the spires of Munich, one hundred and twenty miles distant, can be seen. It was a view whose grandeur I can never forget. In that dome of the cloud we seemed to breathe a purer air than that of earth.

After an hour or two, we began to think of descending, as the path was yet to be found. The summit, which was a mile or more in length, extended farther westward, and by climbing over the dwarf pines for some time, we saw a little wooden house above us. It stood near the highest part of the peak, and two or three men were engaged in repairing it, as a shelter for travelers. They pointed out the path which went down on the side toward St. Gilgen, and we began descending. The mountain on this side is much less steep, but the descent is fatiguing enough. The path led along the side of a glen where mountain goats were grazing, and further down we saw cattle feeding on the little spots of verdure which lay in the forest. My knees became so weak from this continued descent, that they would scarcely support me; but we were three hours, partly walking and partly running down, before we reached the bottom. Half an hour's walk around the head of the St. Wolfgang See, brought us to the little village of St. Gilgen.

The valley of St. Gilgen lies like a little paradise between the mountains. Lovely green fields and woods slope gradually from the mountain behind, to the still greener lake spread out before it, in whose bosom the white Alps are mirrored. Its picturesque cottages cluster around the neat church with its lofty spire, and the simple inhabitants have countenances as bright and cheerful as the blue sky above them. We breathed an air of poetry. The Arcadian simplicity of the people, the pastoral beauty of the fields around and the grandeur of the mountains which shut it out from the world, realized my ideas of a dwelling place, where, with a few kindred spirits, the bliss of Eden might almost be restored.

We stopped there two or three hours to relieve our hunger and fatigue. My boots had suffered severely in our mountain adventure, and I called at a shoemaker's cottage to get them repaired. I sat down and talked for half an hour with the family. The man and his wife spoke of the delightful scenery around them, and expressed themselves with correctness and even elegance. They were much pleased that I admired their village so greatly, and related every thing which they supposed could interest me. As I rose to go, my head nearly touched the ceiling, which was very low. The man exclaimed: "Ach Gott! how tall!" I told him the people were all tall in our country; he then asked where I came from, and I had no sooner said America, than he threw up his hands and uttered an ejaculation of the greatest surprise. His wife observed that "it was wonderful how far man was permitted to travel." They wished me a prosperous journey and a safe return home.

St. Gilgen was also interesting to me from that beautiful chapter in "Hyperion"—"Footsteps of Angels,"—and on passing the church on my way back to the inn, I entered the graveyard mentioned in it. The green turf grows thickly over the rows of mounds, with here and there a rose planted by the hand of affection, and the white crosses were hung with wreaths, some of which had been freshly laid on. Behind the church, under the shade of a tree, stood a small chapel,—I opened the unfastened door, and entered. The afternoon sun shone through the side window, and all was still around. A little shrine, adorned with flowers, stood at the other end, and there were two tablets on the wall, to persons who slumbered beneath, I approached these and read on one of them with feelings not easily described: "Look not mournfully into the past—it comes not again; wisely improve the present—it is thine; and go forward to meet the shadowy future, without fear, and with a manly heart!" This then was the spot where Paul Flemming came in loneliness and sorrow to muse over what he had lost, and these were the words whose truth and eloquence strengthened and consoled him, "as if the unknown tenant of the grave had opened his lips of dust and spoken those words of consolation his soul needed." I sat down and mused a long time, for there was something in the silent holiness of the spot, that impressed me more than I could well describe.

We reached a little village on the Fuschel See, the same evening, and set

198

off the next morning for Salzburg. The day was hot and we walked slowly, so that it was not till two o'clock that we saw the castellated rocks on the side of the Gaissberg, guarding the entrance to the valley of Salzburg. A short distance further, the whole glorious panorama was spread out below us. From the height on which we stood, we looked directly on the summit of the Capuchin Mountain, which hid part of the city from sight; the double peak of the Staufen rose opposite, and a heavy storm was raging along the Alpine heights around it, while the lovely valley lay in sunshine below, threaded by the bright current of the Salza. As we descended and passed around the foot of the hill, the Untersberg came in sight, whose broad summits lift themselves seven thousand feet above the plain. The legend says that Charlemagne and his warriors sit in its subterraneous caverns in complete armor, and that they will arise and come forth again, when Germany recovers her former power and glory.

I wish I could convey in words some idea of the elevation of spirit experienced while looking on these eternal mountains. They fill the soul with a sensation of power and grandeur which frees it awhile from the cramps and fetters of common life. It rises and expands to the level of their sublimity, till its thoughts stand solemnly aloft, like their summits, piercing the free heaven. Their dazzling and imperishable beauty is to the mind an image of its own enduring existence. When I stand upon some snowy summit—the invisible apex of that mighty pyramid—there seems a majesty in my weak will which might defy the elements. This sense of power, inspired by a silent sympathy with the forms of nature, is beautifully described—as shown in the free, unconscious instincts of childhood—by the poet Uhland, in his ballad of the "Mountain Boy." I have attempted a translation.

*THE MOUNTAIN BOY.*

*A herd-boy on the mountain's brow,*

*I see the castles all below.*

*The sunbeam here is earliest cast*

*And by my side it lingers last—*

*I am the boy of the mountain!*

*The mother-house of streams is here—*

*I drink them in their cradles clear;*

*From out the rock they foam below,*

*I spring to catch them as they go!*

*I am the boy of the mountain!*

*To me belongs the mountain's bound,*

*Where gathering tempests march around;*

*But though from north and south they shout,*

*Above them still my song rings out—*

*"I am the boy of the mountain!"*

*Below me clouds and thunders move;*

*I stand amid the blue above.*

*I shout to them with fearless breast:*

*"Go, leave my father's house in rest!"*

*I am the boy of the mountain!*

*And when the loud bell shakes the spires*

*And flame aloft the signal-fires,*

*I go below and join the throng*

*And swing my sword and sing my song:*

*"I am the boy of the mountain!"*

Salzburg lies on both sides of the Salza, hemmed in on either hand by precipitous mountains. A large fortress overlooks it on the south, from the summit of a perpendicular rock, against which the houses in that part of the city arc built. The streets are narrow and crooked, but the newer part contains many open squares, adorned with handsome fountains. The variety of costume among the people, is very interesting. The inhabitants of the salt district have a peculiar dress; the women wear round fur caps, with little wings of gauze at the side. I saw other women with headdresses of gold or silver filagree, something in shape like a Roman helmet, with a projection at the back of the head, a foot long. The most interesting objects in Salzburg to us, were the house of Mozart, in which the composer was born, and the monument lately erected to him. The St. Peter's Church, near by, contains the tomb of Haydn, the great composer, and the Church of St. Sebastian, that of the renowned Paracelsus, who was also a native of Salzburg.

Two or three hours sufficed to see every thing of interest in the city. We had intended to go further through the Alps, to the beautiful vales of the Tyrol, but our time was getting short, our boots, which are the pedestrian's sole dependence, began to show symptoms of wearing out, and our expenses among the lakes and mountains of Upper Austria, left us but two florins apiece, so we reluctantly turned our backs upon the snowy hills and set out for Munich, ninety miles distant. After passing the night at Saalbruck, on the banks of the stream which separates the two kingdoms, we entered Bavaria next morning. I could not help feeling glad to leave Austria, although within her bounds I had passed scones whose beauty will long haunt me, and met with many honest friendly hearts among her people. We noticed a change as soon as we had crossed the border. The roads were neater and handsomer, and the country people greeted us in going by, with a friendly cheerfulness that made us feel half at home. The houses are built in the picturesque Swiss fashion, their balconies often ornamented with curious figures, carved in wood. Many of them, where they are situated remote from a church, have a little bell on the roof which they ring for morning and evening prayers; we often heard these simple monitors sounding from the cottages as we passed by.

The next night we stopped at the little village of Stein, famous in former

times for its robber-knight, Hans von Stein. The ruins of his castle stand on
the rock above, and the caverns hewn in the sides of the precipice, where he
used to confine his prisoners, are still visible. Walking on through a pleasant,
well-cultivated country, we came to Wasserburg, on the Inn. The situation
of the city is peculiar. The Inn has gradually worn his channel deeper in the
sandy soil, so that he now flows at the bottom of a glen, a hundred feet below
the plains around. Wasserburg lies in a basin, formed by the change of the
current, which flows around it like a horseshoe, leaving only a narrow neck of
land which connects it with the country above.

We left the little village where we were quartered for the night and took
a foot path which led across the country to the field of Hohenlinden, about
six miles distant. The name had been familiar to me from childhood, and
my love for Campbell, with the recollection of the school-exhibitions where
"On Linden when the sun was low" had been so often declaimed, induced
me to make the excursion to it. We traversed a large forest, belonging to
the King of Bavaria, and came out on a plain covered with grain fields and
bounded on the right by a semi-circle of low hills. Over the fields, about two
miles distant, a tall, minaret-like spire rose from a small cluster of houses,
and this was Hohenlinden! To tell the truth, I had been expecting something
more. The "hills of blood-stained snow" are very small hills indeed, and the
"Isar, rolling rapidly," is several miles off; it was the spot, however, and we
recited Campbell's poem, of course, and brought away a few wild flowers as
memorials. There is no monument or any other token of the battle, and the
people seem to endeavor to forget the scene of Moreau's victory and their
defeat.

From a hill twelve miles off we had our first view of the spires of Munich,
looking like distant ships over the sea-like plain. They kept in sight till we
arrived at eight o'clock in the evening, after a walk of more than thirty miles.
We crossed the rapid Isar on three bridges, entered the magnificent Isar Gate,
and were soon comfortably quartered in the heart of Munich.

Entering the city without knowing a single soul within it, we made
within a few minutes an agreeable acquaintance. After we passed the Isar
Gate, we began looking for a decent inn, for the day's walk was very fatiguing.

Presently a young man, who had been watching us for some time, came up and said, if we would allow him, he would conduct us to a good lodging-place. Finding we were strangers, he expressed the greatest regret that he had not time to go with us every day around the city. Our surprise and delight at the splendor of Munich, he said, would more than repay him for the trouble. In his anxiety to show us something, he took us some distance out of the way, (although it was growing dark and we were very tired,) to see the Palace and the Theatre, with its front of rich frescoes.

### END OF PART I. —

# PART II.

## CHAPTER XXVI. – MUNICH.

June 14.—I thought I had seen every thing in Vienna that could excite admiration or gratify fancy; here I have my former sensations to live over again, in an augmented degree. It is well I was at first somewhat prepared by our previous travel, otherwise the glare and splendor of wealth and art in this German Athens might blind me to the beauties of the cities we shall yet visit. I have been walking in a dream where the fairy tales of boyhood were realized, and the golden and jeweled halls of the Eastern genii rose glittering around me—"a vision of the brain no more." All I had conceived of oriental magnificence, all descriptions of the splendor of kingly halls and palaces, fall far short of what I here see. Where shall I begin to describe the crowd of splendid edifices that line its streets, or how give an idea of the profusion of paintings and statues—of marble, jasper and gold?

Art has done every thing for Munich. It lies on a large, flat plain, sixteen hundred feet above the sea, and continually exposed to the cold winds from the Alps. At the beginning of the present century it was but a third-rate city, and was rarely visited by foreigners. Since that time its population and limits have been doubled, and magnificent edifices in every style of architecture erected, rendering it scarcely secondary in this respect to any capital in Europe. Every art that wealth or taste could devise, seems to have been spent in its decoration. Broad, spacious streets and squares have been laid out, churches, halls and colleges erected, and schools of painting and sculpture established, which draw artists from all parts of the world. All this was principally brought about by the taste of the present king, Ludwig I., who began twenty or thirty years ago, when he was Crown Prince, to collect the best German artists around him and form plans for the execution of his grand design. He can boast of having done more for the arts than any other living monarch, and if he had accomplished it all without oppressing his people, he would deserve an immortality of fame.

Now, if you have nothing else to do, let us take a stroll down the Ludwigstrasse. As we pass the Theatiner Church, with its dome and towers, the broad street opens before us, stretching away to the north, between rows of magnificent buildings. Just at this southern end, is the Schlusshalle, an open temple of white marble terminating the avenue. To the right of us extend the arcades, with the trees of the Royal Garden peeping above them; on the left is the spacious concert building of the Odeon, and the palace of the Duke of Leuchtenberg, son of Eugene Beauharnois. Passing through a row of palace-like private buildings, we come to the Army Department, on the right—a neat and tasteful building of white sandstone. Beside it stands the Library, which possesses the first special claim on our admiration. With its splendid front of five hundred and eighteen feet, the yellowish brown cement with which the body is covered, making an agreeable contrast with the dark red window-arches and cornices, and the statues of Homer, Hippocrates, Thucydides and Aristotle guarding the portal, is it not a worthy receptacle for the treasures of ancient and modern lore which its halls contain?

Nearly opposite stands the Institute for the Blind, a plain but large building of dark red brick, covered with cement, and further, the Ludwig's Kirche, or Church of St. Louis. How lightly the two square towers of gray marble lift their network of sculpture! And what a novel and beautiful effect is produced by uniting the Byzantine style of architecture to the form of the Latin cross! Over the arched portal stand marble statues by Schwanthaler, and the roof of brilliant tiles worked into mosaic, looks like a rich Turkey carpet covering the whole. We must enter to get an idea of the splendor of this church. Instead of the pointed arch which one would expect to see meeting above his head, the lofty pillars on each side bear an unbroken semicircular vault, which is painted a brilliant blue, and spangled with silver stars. These pillars, and the little arches above, which spring from them, are painted in an arabesque style with gold and brilliant colors, and each side-chapel is a perfect casket of richness and elegance. The windows are of silvered glass, through which the light glimmers softly on the splendor within. The whole end of the church behind the high altar, is taken up with Cornelius's celebrated fresco painting of the "Last Judgment,"—the largest painting in the world—and the circular dome in the centre of the cross contains groups of martyrs, prophets, saints and kings, painted in fresco on a ground of gold. The work of Cornelius has been greatly praised for sublimity of design and beauty of execution, by many acknowledged judges; I was disappointed in it, but the fault lay most probably in me and not in the painting. The richness and elegance of the church took me all "aback;" it was so entirely different from anything I had seen, that it was difficult to decide whether I was most charmed by its novelty or its beauty. Still, as a building designed to excite feelings of worship, it seems to me inappropriate. A vast, dim Cathedral would be far preferable; the devout, humble heart cannot feel at home amid such glare and brightness.

As we leave the church and walk further on, the street expands suddenly into a broad square. One side is formed by the new University building and the other by the Royal Seminary, both displaying in their architecture new forms of the graceful Byzantine school, which the architects of Munich have adapted in a striking manner to so many varied purposes. On each side stands a splendid colossal fountain of bronze, throwing up a great mass of water, which falls in a triple cataract to the marble basin below. A short distance beyond this square the Ludwigstrasse terminates. It is said the end will be closed by a magnificent gate, on a style to correspond with the unequalled avenue to which it will give entrance. To one standing at the southern end, it would form a proper termination to the grand vista. Before we leave, turn around and glance back, down this street, which extends for half a mile between such buildings as we have just viewed, and tell me if it is not something of which a city and a king may boast, to have created all this within less than twenty years!

We went one morning to see the collection of paintings formerly belonging to Eugene Beauharnois, who was brother-in-law to the present king of Bavaria, in the palace of his son, the Duke of Leuchtenberg. The first hall contains works principally by French artists, among which are two by Gerard—a beautiful portrait of Josephine, and the blind Belisarius carrying his dead companion. The boy's head lies on the old man's shoulder; but for the livid paleness of his limbs, he would seem to be only asleep, while a deep and settled sorrow marks the venerable features of the unfortunate Emperor. In the middle of the room are six pieces of statuary, among which Canova's world-renowned group of the Graces at once attracts the eye. There is also a kneeling Magdalen, lovely in her woe, by the same sculptor, and a very touching work of Schadow, representing a shepherd boy tenderly binding his sash around a lamb which he has accidentally wounded with his arrow.

We have since seen in the St. Michael's Church, the monument to Eugene Beauharnois, from the chisel of Thorwaldsen. The noble, manly figure of the son of Josephine is represented in the Roman mantle, with his helmet and sword lying on the ground by him. On one side sits History, writing on a tablet; on the other, stand the two brother-angels, Death and Immortality. They lean lovingly together, with arms around each other, but the sweet countenance of Death has a cast of sorrow, as he stands with inverted torch and a wreath of poppies among his clustering locks. Immortality, crowned with never-fading flowers, looks upwards with a smile of triumph, and holds in one hand his blazing torch. It is a beautiful idea, and Thorwaldsen has made the marble eloquent with feeling.

The inside of the square formed by the Arcades and the New Residence, is filled with noble old trees, which in summer make a leafy roof over the pleasant walks. In the middle, stands a grotto, ornamented with rough pebbles and shells, and only needing a fountain to make it a perfect hall of Neptune. Passing through the northern Arcade, one comes into the magnificent park, called the English Garden, which extends more than four miles along the bank of the Isar, several branches of whose milky current wander through it, and form one or two pretty cascades. It is a beautiful alternation of forest and meadow, and has all the richness and garden-like luxuriance of English scenery. Winding walks lead along the Isar, or through the wood of venerable oaks, and sometimes a lawn of half a mile in length, with a picturesque temple at its further end, comes in sight through the trees. I was better pleased with this park than with the Prater in Vienna. Its paths are always filled with persons enjoying the change from the dusty streets to its quiet and cool retirement.

The New Residence is not only one of the wonders of Munich, but of the world. Although commenced in 1826 and carried on constantly since that time by a number of architects, sculptors and painters, it is not yet finished; if art were not inexhaustible it would be difficult to imagine what more could be added. The north side of the Max Joseph Platz is taken up by its front of four hundred and thirty feet, which was nine years in building, under the direction of the architect Klenze. The exterior is copied after the Palazzo Pitti, in Florence. The building is of light brown sandstone, and combines an elegance and even splendor, with the most chaste and classic style. The northern front, which faces on the Royal Garden, is now nearly finished. It has the enormous length of eight hundred feet; in the middle is a portico of ten Ionic columns; instead of supporting a triangular facade, each pillar stands separate and bears a marble statue from the chisel of Schwanthaler.

The interior of the building does not disappoint the promise of the outside. It is open every afternoon in the absence of the king, for the inspection of visitors; fortunately for us, his majesty is at present on a journey through his provinces on the Rhine. We went early to the waiting hall, where several travelers were already assembled, and at four o'clock, were admitted into the newer part of the palace, containing the throne hall, ballroom, etc. On entering the first hall, designed for the lackeys and royal servants, we were all obliged to thrust our feet into cloth slippers to walk over the polished mosaic floor. The walls are of scagliola marble and the ceilings ornamented brilliantly in fresco. The second hall, also for servants, gives tokens of increasing splendor in the richer decorations of the walls and the more elaborate mosaic of the floor. We next entered the receiving saloon, in which the Court Marshal receives the guests. The ceiling is of arabesque sculpture, profusely painted and gilded. Passing through a little cabinet, we entered the great dancing saloon. Its floor is the richest mosaic of wood of different colors, the sides are of polished scagliola marble, and the ceiling a dazzling mixture of sculpture, painting and gold. At one end is a gallery for the orchestra, supported by six columns of variegated marble, above which are six dancing nymphs, painted so beautifully that they appear like living creatures. Every decoration which could be devised has been used to heighten its splendor, and the artists appear to have made free use of the Arabian Nights in forming the plan.

We entered next two smaller rooms containing the portraits of beautiful women, principally from the German nobility. I gave the preference to the daughter of Marco Bozzaris, now maid of honor to the Queen of Greece. She had a wild dark eye, a beautiful proud lip, and her rich black hair rolled in glossy waves down her neck from under the red Grecian cap stuck jauntily on the side of her head. She wore a scarf and close-fitting vest embroidered with gold, and there was a free, lofty spirit in her countenance worthy the name she bore. These pictures form a gallery of beauty, whose equal cannot easily be found.

Returning to the dancing hall, we entered the dining saloon, also called the Hall of Charlemagne. Each wall has two magnificent fresco paintings of very large size, representing some event in the life of the great emperor, beginning with his anointing at St. Deny's as a boy of twelve years, and ending with his coronation by Leo III. A second dining saloon, the Hall of Barbarossa, adjoins the first. It has also eight frescoes as the former, representing the principal events in the life of Frederic Barbarossa. Then comes a third, called the Hapsburg Hall, with four grand paintings from the life of Rudolph of Hapsburg, and a triumphal procession along the frieze, showing the improvement in the arts and sciences which was accomplished under his reign. The drawing, composition and rich tone of coloring of these glorious frescoes, are scarcely excelled by any in existence.

Finally we entered the Hall of the Throne. Here the encaustic decoration, so plentifully employed in the other rooms, is dropped, and an effect even more brilliant obtained by the united use of marble and gold. Picture a long hall with a floor of polished marble, on each side twelve columns of white marble with gilded capitals, between which stand colossal statues of gold. At the other end is the throne of gold and crimson, with gorgeous hangings of crimson velvet. The twelve statues in the hall are called the "Wittlesbach Ancestors," and represent renowned members of the house of Wittlesbach from which the present family of Bavaria is descended. They were cast in bronze by Stiglmaier, after the models of Schwanthaler, and then completely covered with a coating of gold, so that they resemble solid golden statues. The value of the precious metal on each one is about $3,000, as they are nine feet in height! What would the politicians who made such an outcry about the new papering of the President's House, say to such a palace as this?

Going back to the starting point, we went to the other wing of the edifice and joined the party who came to visit the apartments of the king. Here we were led through two or three rooms, appropriated to the servants, with all the splendor of marble doors, floors of mosaic, and frescoed ceilings. From these we entered the king's dwelling. The entrance halls are decorated with paintings of the Argonauts and illustrations of the Hymns of Hesiod, after drawings by Schwanthaler. Then came the Service Hall, containing frescoes illustrating Homer, by Schnorr, and the Throne Hall, with Schwanthaler's bas-reliefs of the songs of Pindar, on a ground of gold. The throne stands under a splendid crimson canopy. The Dining Room with its floor of polished wood is filled with illustrations of the songs of Anacreon. To these follow the Dressing Room, with twenty-seven illustrations of the Comedies of Aristophanes, and the sleeping chamber with frescoes after the poems of Theocritus, and two beautiful bas-reliefs representing angels bearing children to Heaven. It is no wonder the King writes poetry, when he breathes, eats, and even sleeps in an atmosphere of it.

We were shown the rooms for the private parties of the Court, the school-room, with scenes from the life of the Ancient Greeks, and then conducted down the marble staircases to the lower story, which is to contain Schnorr's magnificent frescoes of the Nibelungen Lied—the old German Iliad. Two halls are at present finished; the first has the figure of the author, Heinrich von Ofterdingen, and those of Chriemhilde, Brunhilde, Siegfried and the other personages of the poem; and the second, called the Marriage Hall, contains the marriage of Chriemhilde and Siegfried, and the triumphal entry of Siegfried into Worms.

Adjoining the new residence on the east, is the Royal Chapel, lately finished in the Byzantine style, under the direction of Klenze. To enter it, is like stepping into a casket of jewels. The sides are formed by a double range of arches, the windows being so far back as to be almost out of sight, so that the eye falls on nothing but painting and gold. The lower row of arches is of alternate green and purple marble, beautifully polished; but the upper, as well as the small chancel behind the high altar, is entirely covered with fresco paintings on a ground of gold! The richness and splendor of the whole church is absolutely incredible. Even after one has seen the Ludwig's Kirche and the Residence itself, it excites astonishment. I was surprised, however, to find at this age, a painting on the wall behind the altar, representing the Almighty. It seems as if man's presumption has no end. The simple altar of Athens, with its inscription "to the Unknown God," was more truly reverent than this. As I sat down awhile under one of the arches, a poor woman came in, carrying a heavy basket, and going to the steps which led up to the altar, knelt down and prayed, spreading her arms out in the form of a cross. Then, after stooping and kissing the first step, she dragged herself with her knees upon it, and commenced praying again with outspread arms. This she continued till she had climbed them all, which occupied some time; then, as if she had fulfilled a vow she turned and departed. She was undoubtedly sincere in her piety, but it made me sad to look upon such deluded superstition.

We visited yesterday morning the Glyptothek, the finest collection of ancient sculpture except that in the British Museum, I have yet seen, and perhaps elsewhere unsurpassed, north of the Alps. The building which was finished by Klenze, in 1830, has an Ionic portico of white marble, with a group of allegorical figures, representing Sculpture and the kindred arts. On each side of the portico, there are three niches in the front, containing on one side, Pericles, Phidias and Vulcan; on the other, Hadrian, Prometheus and Dædalus. The whole building forms a hollow square, and is lighted entirely from the inner side. There are in all twelve halls, each containing the remains of a particular era in the art, and arranged according to time, so that, beginning with the clumsy productions of the ancient Egyptians, one passes through the different stages of Grecian art, afterwards that of Rome, and finally ends with the works of our own times—the almost Grecian perfection of Thorwaldsen and Canova. These halls are worthy to hold such treasures, and what more could be said of them? The floors are of marble mosaic, the sides of green or purple scagliola, and the vaulted ceilings covered with raised ornaments on a ground of gold. No two are alike in color and decoration, and yet there is a unity of taste and design in the whole, which renders the variety delightful.

From the Egyptian Hall, we enter one containing the oldest remains of Grecian sculpture, before the artists won power to mould the marble to their conceptions. Then follow the celebrated Egina marbles, from the temple of Jupiter Panhellenius, on the island of Egina. They formerly stood in the two porticoes, the one group representing the fight for the body of Laomedon, the other the struggle for the dead Patroclus. The parts wanting have been admirably restored by Thorwaldsen. They form almost the only existing specimens of the Eginetan school. Passing through the Apollo Hall, we enter the large hall of Bacchus, in which the progress of the art is distinctly apparent. A satyr, lying asleep on a goat-skin which he has thrown over a rock, is believed to be the work of Praxiteles. The relaxation of the figure and perfect repose of every limb, is wonderful. The countenance has traits of individuality which led me to think it might have been a portrait, perhaps of some rude country swain.

In the Hall of Niobe, which follows, is one of the most perfect works that ever grew into life under a sculptor's chisel. Mutilated as it is, without head and arms, I never saw a more expressive figure. Ilioneus, the son of Niobe, is represented as kneeling, apparently in the moment in which Apollo raises his arrow, and there is an imploring supplication in his attitude which is touching in the highest degree. His beautiful young limbs seem to shrink involuntarily from the deadly shaft; there is an expression of prayer, almost of agony, in the position of his body. It should be left untouched. No head could be added, which would equal that one pictures to himself, while gazing upon it.

The Pinacothek is a magnificent building of yellow sandstone, five hundred and thirty feet long, containing thirteen hundred pictures, selected with great care from the whole private collection of the king, which amounts to nine thousand. Above the cornice on the southern side, stand twenty-five colossal statues of celebrated painters, by Schwanthaler. As we approached, the tall bronze door was opened by a servant in the Bavarian livery, whose size harmonized so well with the giant proportions of the building, that, until I stood beside him and could mark the contrast, I did not notice his enormous frame. I saw then that he must be near eight feet high, and stout in proportion. He reminded me of the great "Baver of Trient," in Vienna. The Pinacothek contains the most complete collection of works by old German artists, anywhere to be found. There are in the hall of the Spanish masters, half a dozen of Murillo's inimitable beggar groups. It was a relief, after looking upon the distressingly stiff figures of the old German school, to view these fresh, natural countenances. One little black-eyed boy has just cut a slice out of a melon and turns with a full mouth to his companion, who is busy eating a bunch of grapes. The simple, contented expression on the faces of the beggars is admirable. I thought I detected in a beautiful child, with dark curly locks, the original of his celebrated Infant St. John. I was much interested in two small juvenile works of Raphael and his own portrait. The latter was taken most probably after he became known as a painter. The calm, serious smile which we see on his portrait as a boy, had vanished, and the thin features and sunken eye told of intense mental labor.

One of the most remarkable buildings now in the course of erection is the Basilica, or Church of St. Bonifacius. It represents another form of the Byzantine style, a kind of double edifice, a little like a North River steamboat, with a two story cabin on deck. The inside is not yet finished, although the artists have been at work on it for six years, but we heard many accounts of its splendor, which is said to exceed anything that has been yet done in Munich. We visited to-day the atelier of Sohwanthaler, which is always open to strangers. The sculptor himself was not there, but five or six of his scholars were at work in the rooms, building up clay statues after his models and working out bas-reliefs in frames. We saw here the original models of the statues on the Pinacothek, and the "Wittelsbach Ancestors" in the Throne Hall of the palace. I was glad also to find a miniature copy in plaster, of the Herrmannsschlacht, or combat of the old German hero, Herrmann, with the Romans, from the frieze of the Walhalla, at Ratisbon. It is one of Schwanthaler's best works. Herrmann, as the middle figure, is represented in fight with the Roman general; behind him the warriors are rushing on, and an old bard is striking the chords of his harp to inspire them, while women bind up the wounds of the fallen. The Roman soldiers on the other side are about turning in confusion to fly. It is a lofty and appropriate subject for the portico of a building containing the figures of the men who have labored for the glory and elevation of their Fatherland.

Our new-found friend came to visit us last evening and learn our impressions of Munich. In the course of conversation we surprised him by revealing the name of our country. His countenance brightened up and he asked us many questions about the state of society in America. In return, he told us something more about himself—his story was simple, but it interested me. His father was a merchant, who, having been ruined by unlucky transactions, died, leaving a numerous family without the means of support. His children were obliged to commence life alone and unaided, which, in a country where labor is so cheap, is difficult and disheartening. Our friend chose the profession of a machinist, which, after encountering great obstacles, he succeeded in learning, and now supports himself as a common laborer. But his position in this respect prevents him from occupying that station in society for which he is intellectually fitted. His own words, uttered with a simple pathos which I can never forget, will best describe how painful this must be to a sensitive spirit. "I tell you thus frankly my feelings," said he, "because I know you will understand me. I could not say this to any of my associates, for they would not comprehend it, and they would say I am proud, because I cannot bring my soul down to their level. I am poor and have but little to subsist upon; but the spirit has needs as well as the body, and I feel it a duty and a desire to satisfy them also. When I am with any of my common fellow-laborers, what do I gain from them? Their leisure hours are spent in drinking and idle amusement, and I cannot join them, for I have no sympathy with such things. To mingle with those above me, would be impossible. Therefore I am alone—I have no associate!"

I have gone into minute, and it may be, tiresome detail, in describing some of the edifices of Munich, because it seemed the only way in which I could give an idea of their wonderful beauty. It is true that in copying after the manner of the daguerreotype, there is danger of imitating its dullness also, but I trust to the glitter of gold and rich paintings, for a little brightness in the picture. We leave to-morrow morning, having received the sum written for, which, to our surprise, will be barely sufficient to enable us to reach Heidelberg.

# CHAPTER XXVII. — THROUGH WURTEMBERG TO HEIDELBERG.

We left Munich in the morning train for Augsburg. Between the two cities extends a vast unbroken plain, exceedingly barren and monotonous. Here and there is a little scrubby woodland, and sometimes we passed over a muddy stream which came down from the Alps. The land is not more than half-cultivated, and the villages are small and poor. We saw many of the peasants at their stations, in their gay Sunday dresses; the women wore short gowns with laced boddices, of gay colors, and little caps on the top of their heads, with streamers of ribbons three feet long. After two hours' ride, we saw the tall towers of Augsburg, and alighted on the outside of the wall. The deep moat which surrounds the city, is all grown over with velvet turf, the towers and bastions are empty and desolate, and we passed unchallenged under the gloomy archway. Immediately on entering the city, signs of its ancient splendor are apparent. The houses are old, many of them with quaint, elaborately carved ornaments, and often covered with fresco paintings. These generally represent some scene from the Bible history, encircled with arabesque borders, and pious maxims in illuminated scrolls. We went into the old Rathhaus, whose golden hall still speaks of the days of Augsburg's pride. I saw in the basement a bronze eagle, weighing sixteen tons, with an inscription on the pedestal stating that it was cast in 1606, and formerly stood on the top of an old public building, since torn down. In front of the Rathhaus is a fine bronze fountain, with a number of figures of angels and tritons.

The same afternoon, we left Augsburg for Ulm. Long, low ranges of hills, running from the Danube, stretched far across the country, and between them lay many rich, green valleys. We passed, occasionally, large villages, perhaps as old as the times of the crusaders, and looking quite pastoral and romantic from the outside; but we were always glad when we had gone through them and into the clean country again. The afternoon of the second day we came in sight of the fertile plain of the Danube; far, far to the right lay the field of Blenheim, where Marlborough and the Prince Eugene conquered the united French and Bavarian forces and decided the war of the Spanish succession.

We determined to reach Ulm the same evening, although a heavy storm was raging along the distant hills of Wurtemberg. The dark mass of the mighty Cathedral rose in the distance through the twilight, a perfect mountain in comparison with the little houses clustered around its base. We reached New Ulm, finally, and passed over the heavy wooden bridge into Wurtemberg, unchallenged for passport or baggage. I thought I could feel a difference in the atmosphere when I reached the other side—it breathed of the freer spirit that ruled through the land. The Danube is here a little muddy stream, hardly as large as my native Brandywine, and a traveler who sees it at Ulm for the first time would most probably be disappointed. It is not until below Vienna, where it receives the Drave and Save, that it becomes a river of more than ordinary magnitude.

We entered Ulm, as I have already said. It was after nine o'clock, nearly dark, and beginning to rain; we had walked thirty-three miles, and being of course tired, we entered the first inn we saw. But, to our consternation, it was impossible to get a place—the fair had just commenced, and the inn was full to the roof. We must needs hunt another, and then another, and yet another, with like fate at each. It grew quite dark, the rain increased, and we were unacquainted with the city. I grew desperate, and at last, when we had stopped at the eighth inn in vain, I told the people we must have lodgings, for it was impossible we should walk around in the rain all night. Some of the guests interfering in our favor, the hostess finally sent a servant with us to the first hotel in the city. I told him on the way we were Americans, strangers in Ulm, and not accustomed to sleeping in the streets. "Well," said he, "I will go before, and recommend you to the landlord of the Golden Wheel." I knew not what magic he used, but in half an hour our weary limbs were stretched in delightful repose and we thanked Heaven more gratefully than ever before, for the blessing of a good bed.

Next morning we ran about through the booths of the fair, and gazed up from all sides at the vast Cathedral. The style is the simplest and grandest Gothic; but the tower, which, to harmonize, with the body of the church, should be 520 feet high, was left unfinished at the height of 234 feet. I could not enough admire the grandeur of proportion in the great building. It seemed singular that the little race of animals who swarmed around its base, should have the power to conceive or execute such a gigantic work.

There is an immense fortification now in progress of erection behind Ulm. It leans on the side of the hill which rises from the Danube, and must be nearly a mile in length. Hundreds of laborers are at work, and from the appearance of the foundations, many years will be required to finish it. The lofty mountain-plain which we afterwards passed over, for eight or ten miles, divides the waters of the Danube from the Rhine. From the heights above Ulm, we bade adieu to the far, misty Alps, till we shall see them again in Switzerland. Late in the afternoon, we came to a lovely green valley, sunk as it were in the earth. Around us, on all sides, stretched the bare, lofty plains; but the valley lay below, its steep sides covered with the richest forest. At the bottom flowed the Fils. Our road led directly down the side; the glen spread out broader as we advanced, and smiling villages stood beside the stream. A short distance before reaching Esslingen, we came upon the banks of the Neckar, whom we hailed as an old acquaintance, although much smaller here in his mountain home than when he sweeps the walls of Heidelberg.

Delightful Wurtemberg! Shall I ever forget thy lovely green vales, watered by the classic current of the Neckar, or thy lofty hills covered with vineyards and waving forests, and crowned with heavy ruins, that tell many a tale of Barbarossa and Duke Ulric and Goetz with the Iron Hand! No—were even the Suabian hills less beautiful—were the Suabian people less faithful and kind and true, still I would love the land for the great spirits it has produced; still would the birth-place of Frederick Schiller, of Uhland and Hauff, be sacred. I do not wonder Wurtemberg can boast such glorious poets. Its lovely landscapes seem to have been made expressly for the cradle of genius; amid no other scenes could his infant mind catch a more benign inspiration. Even the common people are deeply imbued with a poetic feeling. We saw it in their friendly greetings and open, expressive countenances; it is shown in their love for their beautiful homes and the rapture and reverence with which they speak of their country's bards. No river in the world, equal to the Neckar in size, flows for its whole course through more delightful scenery, or among kinder and happier people.

After leaving Esslingen, we followed its banks for some time, at the foot of an amphitheatre of hills, covered to the very summit, as far as the eye could reach, with vineyards. The morning was cloudy, and white mist-wreaths hung along the sides. We took a road that led over the top of a range, and on arriving at the summit, saw all at once the city of Stuttgard, lying beneath our feet. It lay in a basin encircled by mountains, with a narrow valley opening to the south-east, and running off between the hills to the Neckar. The situation of the city is one of wonderful beauty, and even after seeing Salzburg, I could not but be charmed with it.

We descended the mountain and entered it. I inquired immediately for the monument of Schiller, for there was little else in the city I cared to see. We had become tired of running about cities, hunting this or that old church or palace, which perhaps was nothing when found. Stuttgard has neither galleries, ruins, nor splendid buildings, to interest the traveler; but it has Thorwaldsen's statue of Schiller, calling up at the same time its shame and its glory. For the poet in his youth was obliged to fly from this very same city—from home and friends, to escape the persecution of the government on account of the free sentiments expressed in his early works. We found the statue, without much difficulty. It stands in the Schloss Platz, at the southern end of the city, in an unfavorable situation, surrounded by dark old buildings. It should rather be placed aloft on a mountain summit, in the pure, free air of heaven, braving the storm and the tempest. The figure is fourteen feet high and stands on a pedestal of bronze, with bas reliefs on the four sides. The head, crowned with a laurel wreath, is inclined as if in deep thought, and all the earnest soul is seen in the countenance. Thorwaldsen has copied so truly the expression of poetic reverie, that I waited, half-expecting he would raise his head and look around him.

As we passed out the eastern gate, the workmen were busy near the city, making an embankment for the new railroad to Heilbroun, and we were obliged to wade through half a mile of mud. Finally the road turned to the left over a mountain, and we walked on in the rain, regardless of the touching entreaties of an omnibus-driver, who felt a great concern for our health, especially as he had two empty seats. There is a peculiarly agreeable sensation in walking in a storm, when the winds sweep by and the rain-drops rattle through the trees, and the dark clouds roll past just above one's head. It gives a dash of sublimity to the most common scene. If the rain did not finally soak through the boots, and if one did not lose every romantic feeling in wet garments, I would prefer storm to sunshine, for visiting some kinds of scenery. You remember, we saw the North Coast of Ireland and the Giant's Causeway in stormy weather, at the expense of being completely drenched, it is true; but our recollections of that wild day's journey are as vivid as any event of our lives—and the name of the Giant's Causeway calls up a series of pictures as terribly sublime as any we would wish to behold.

The rain at last did come down a little too hard for comfort, and we were quite willing to take shelter when we reached Ludwigsburg. This is here called a new city, having been laid out with broad streets and spacious squares, about a century ago, and is now about the size of our five-year old city of Milwaukie! It is the chief military station of Wurtemberg, and has a splendid castle and gardens, belonging to the king. A few miles to the eastward is the little village where Schiller was born. It is said the house where his parents lived is still standing.

It was not the weather alone, which prevented our making a pilgrimage to it, nor was it alone a peculiar fondness for rain which induced us to persist in walking in the storm. Our feeble pockets, if they could have raised an audible jingle, would have told another tale. Our scanty allowance was dwindling rapidly away, in spite of a desperate system of economy. We left Ulm with a florin and a half apiece—about sixty cents—to walk to Heidelberg, a distance of 110 miles. It was the evening of the third day, and this was almost exhausted. As soon therefore as the rain slackened a little, we started again, although the roads were very bad. At Betigheim, where we passed the night, the people told us of a much nearer and more beautiful road, passing through the Zabergau, a region fumed for its fertility and pastoral beauty. At the inn we were charged higher than usual for a bed, so that we had but thirteen kreutzers to start with in the morning. Our fare that day was a little bread and water; we walked steadily on, but owing to the wet roads, made only thirty miles.

A more delightful region than the Zabergau I have seldom passed through. The fields were full of rich, heavy grain, and the trees had a luxuriance of foliage that reminded me of the vale of the Jed, in Scotland. Without a single hedge or fence, stood the long sweep of hills, covered with waving fields of grain, except where they were steep and rocky, and the vineyard terraces rose one above another. Sometimes a fine old forest grew along the summit, like a mane waving back from the curved neck of a steed, and white villages lay coiled in the valleys between. A line of blue mountains always closed the vista, on looking down one of these long valleys; occasionally a ruined castle with donjon tower, was seen on a mountain at the side, making the picture complete. As we lay sometimes on the hillside and looked on one of those sweet vales, we were astonished at its Arcadian beauty. The meadows were as smooth as a mirror, and there seemed to be scarcely a grass-blade out of place. The streams wound through ("snaked themselves through," is the German expression,) with a subdued ripple, as if they feared to displace a pebble, and the great ash trees which stood here and there, had lined each of their leaves as carefully with silver and turned them as gracefully to the wind, us if they were making their toilettes for the gala-day of nature.

That evening brought us into the dominions of Baden, within five hours' walk of Heidelberg. At the humblest inn in an humble village, we found a bed which we could barely pay for, leaving a kreutzer or two for breakfast. Soon after starting the next morning, the distant Kaiserstuhl suddenly emerged from the mist, with the high tower on its summit, where nearly ten months before, we sat and looked at the summits of the Vosges in France, with all the excitement one feels on entering a foreign land. Now, the scenery around that same Kaiserstuhl was nearly as familiar to us as that of our own homes. Entering the hills again, we knew by the blue mountains of the Odenwald, that we were approaching the Neckar. At length we reached the last height. The town of Neckargemünd lay before us on the steep hillside, and the mountains on either side were scarred with quarries of the rich red sandstone, so much used in building. The blocks are hewn out, high up on the mountain side, and then sent rolling and sliding down to the river, where they are laden in boats and floated down with the current to the distant cities of the Rhine.

We were rejoiced on turning around the corner of a mountain, to see on the opposite side of the river, the road winding up through the forests, where last fall our Heidelberg friends accompanied us, as we set out to walk to Frankfort, through the Odenwald. Many causes combined to render it a glad scene to us. We were going to meet our comrade again, after a separation of months; we were bringing an eventful journey to its close; and finally, we were weak and worn out from fasting and the labor of walking in the rain. A little further we saw Kloster Neuburg, formerly an old convent, and remembered how we used to look at it every day from the windows of our room on the Neckar; but we shouted aloud, when we saw at last the well-known bridge spanning the river, and the glorious old castle lifting its shattered towers from the side of the mountain above us. I always felt a strong attachment to this matchless ruin, and as I beheld it again, with the warm sunshine falling through each broken arch, the wild ivy draping its desolate chambers, it seemed to smile on me like the face of a friend, and I confessed I had seen many a grander scene, but few that would cling to the memory so familiarly.

While we were in Heidelberg, a student was buried by torch-light. This is done when particular honor is shown to the memory of the departed brother. They assembled at dark in the University Square, each with a blazing pine torch three feet long, and formed into a double line. Between the files walked at short distances an officer, who, with his sword, broad lace collar, and the black and white plumes in his cap, looked like a cavalier of the olden time. Persons with torches walked on each side of the hearse, and the band played a lament so deeply mournful, that the scene, notwithstanding its singularity, was very sad and touching. The thick smoke from the torches filled the air, and a lurid, red light was cast over the hushed crowds in the streets and streamed into the dark alleys. The Hauptstrasse was filled with two lines of flame, as the procession passed down it; when they reached the extremity of the city, the hearse went on, attended with torch-bearers, to the Cemetery, some distance further, and the students turned back, running and whirling their torches in mingled confusion. The music struck up a merry march, and in the smoke and red glare, they looked like a company of mad demons. The presence of death awed them to silence for awhile, but as soon as it had left them, they turned relieved to revel again and thought no more of the lesson. It gave me a painful feeling to see them rushing so wildly and disorderly back. They assembled again in the square, and tossing their torches up into the air cast them blazing into a pile; while the flame and black smoke rose in a column into the air, they sang in solemn chorus, the song "Gaudeamus igitur," with which they close all public assemblies.

I shall neglect telling how we left Heidelberg, and walked along the Bergstrasse again, for the sixth time; how we passed the old Melibochus and through the quiet city of Darmstadt; how we watched the blue summits of the Taunus rising higher and higher over the plain, as a new land rises from the sea, and finally, how we reached at last the old watch-tower and looked down on the valley of the Main, clothed in the bloom and verdure of summer, with the houses and spires of Frankfort in the middle of the well-known panorama. We again took possession of our old rooms, and having to wait for a remittance from America, as well as a more suitable season for visiting Italy, we sat down to a month's rest and study.

## CHAPTER XXVIII. – FREIBURG AND THE BLACK FOREST.

Frankfort, July 29, 1845.—It would be ingratitude towards the old city in which I have passed so many pleasant and profitable hours, to leave it, perhaps forever, without a few words of farewell. How often will the old bridge, with its view up the Main, over the houses of Oberrad to the far mountains of the Odenwald, rise freshly and distinctly in memory, when I shall have been long absent from them! How often will I hear in fancy as I now do in reality, the heavy tread of passers-by on the rough pavement below, and the deep bell of the Cathedral, chiming the swift hours, with a hollow tone that seems to warn me, rightly to employ them! Even this old room, with its bare walls, little table and chairs, which I have thought and studied in so long, that it seems difficult to think and study anywhere else, will crowd out of memory images of many a loftier scene. May I but preserve for the future the hope and trust which have cheered and sustained me here, through the sorrow of absence and the anxiety of uncertain toil! It is growing towards midnight and I think of many a night when I sat here at this hour, answering the spirit-greeting which friends sent me at sunset over the sea. All this has now an end. I must begin a new wandering, and perhaps in ten days more I shall have a better place for thought, among the mountain-chambers of the everlasting Alps. I look forward to the journey with romantic, enthusiastic anticipation, for afar in the silvery distance, stand the Coliseum and St. Peter's, Vesuvius and the lovely Naples. Farewell, friends who have so long given us a home!

Aug. 9.—The airy, basket-work tower of the Freiburg Minster rises before me over the black roofs of the houses, and behind stand the gloomy, pine-covered mountains of the Black Forest. Of our walk to Heidelberg over the oft-trodden Bergstrasse, I shall say nothing, nor how we climbed the Kaiserstuhl again, and danced around on the top of the tower for one hour, amid cloud and mist, while there was sunshine below in the valley of the Neckar. I left Heidelberg yesterday morning in the stehwagen for Carlsruhe. The engine whistled, the train started, and although I kept my eyes steadily fixed on the spire of the Hauptkirche, three minutes hid it, and all the rest of the city from sight. Carlsruhe, the capital of Baden, which we reached in an hour and a half, is unanimously pronounced by travelers to be a most dull and tiresome city. From a glance I had through one of the gates, I should think its reputation was not undeserved. Even its name, in German, signifies a place of repose.

I stopped at Kork, on the branch road leading to Strasbourg, to meet a German-American about to return to my home in Pennsylvania, where he had lived for some time. I inquired according to the direction he had sent me to Frankfort, but he was not there; however, an old man, finding who I was, said Herr Otto had directed him to go with me to Hesselhurst, a village four or five miles off, where he would meet me. So we set off immediately over the plain, and reached the village at dusk.

At the little inn, were several of the farmers of the neighborhood, who seemed to consider it as something extraordinary to see a real, live, native-born American. They overwhelmed me with questions about the state of our country, its government, etc. The hostess brought me a supper of fried eggs and wurst, while they gathered around the table and began a real category in the dialect of the country, which is difficult to understand. I gave them the best information I could about our mode of farming, the different kinds of produce raised, and the prices paid to laborers; one honest old man cried out, on my saying I had worked on a farm, "Ah! little brother, give me your hand!" which he shook most heartily. I told them also something about our government, and the militia system, so different from the conscription of Europe, when a farmer becoming quite warm in our favor, said to the others with an air of the greatest decision: "One American is better than twenty Germans!" What particularly amused me, was, that although I spoke German with them, they seemed to think I did not understand what they said among one another, and therefore commented very freely over my appearance. I suppose they had the idea that we were a rude, savage race, for I overheard one say: "One sees, nevertheless, that he has been educated!" Their honest, unsophisticated mode of expression was very interesting to me, and we talked together till a late hour.

My friend arrived at three o'clock the next morning, and after two or three hours' talk about home, and the friends whom he expected to see so much sooner than I, a young farmer drove me in his wagon to Offenburg, a small city at the foot of the Black Forest, where I took the cars for Freiburg. The scenery between the two places is grand. The broad mountains of the Black Forest rear their fronts on the east, and the blue lines of the French Vosges meet the clouds on the west. The night before, in walking over the plain, I saw distinctly the whole of the Strasbourg Minster, whose spire is the highest in Europe, being four hundred and ninety feet, or but twenty-five feet lower than the Pyramid of Cheops.

I visited the Minster of Freiburg yesterday morning. It is a grand, gloomy old pile, dating from the eleventh century—one of the few Gothic churches in Germany that have ever been completed. The tower of beautiful fretwork, rises to the height of three hundred and ninety-five feet, and the body of the church including the choir, is of the same length. The interior is solemn and majestic. Windows stained in colors that burn, let in a "dim, religious light" which accords very well with the dark old pillars and antique shrines. In two of the chapels there are some fine altar-pieces by Holbein and one of his scholars; and a very large crucifix of silver and ebony, which is kept with great care, is said to have been carried with the Crusaders to the Holy Land. This morning was the great market-day, and the peasantry of the Black Forest came down from the mountains to dispose of their produce. The square around the Minster was filled with them, and the singular costume of the women gave the scene quite a strange appearance. Many of them wore bright red head-dresses and shawls, others had high-crowned hats of yellow oil-cloth; the young girls wore their hair in long plaits, reaching nearly to their feet. They brought grain, butter and cheese and a great deal of fine fruit to sell—I bought some of the wild, aromatic plums of the country, at the rate of thirty for a cent.

The railroad has only been open to Freiburg within a few days, and is consequently an object of great curiosity to the peasants, many of whom never saw the like before. They throng around the station at the departure of the train and watch with great interest the operations of getting up the steam and starting. One of the scenes that grated most harshly on my feelings, was seeing yesterday a company of women employed on the unfinished part of the road. They were digging and shoveling away in the rain, nearly up to their knees in mud and clay!

I called at the Institute for the Blind, under the direction of Mr. Müller. He showed me some beautiful basket and woven work by his pupils; the accuracy and skill with which everything was made astonished me. They read with amazing facility from the raised type, and by means of frames are taught to write with ease and distinctness. In music, that great solace of the blind, they most excelled. They sang with an expression so true and touching, that it was a delight to listen. The system of instruction adopted appears to be most excellent, and gives to the blind nearly every advantage which their more fortunate brethren enjoy.

I am indebted to Mr. Müller, to whom I was introduced by an acquaintance with his friend, Dr. Rivinus, of West Chester, Pa., for many kind attentions. He went with us this afternoon to the Jägerhaus, on a mountain near, where we had a very fine view of the city and its great black Minster, with the plain of the Briesgau, broken only by the Kaiserstuhl, a long mountain near the Rhine, whose golden stream glittered in the distance. On climbing the Schlossberg, an eminence near the city, we met the Grand Duchess Stephanie, a natural daughter of Napoleon, as I have heard, and now generally believed to be the mother of Caspar Hauser. Through a work lately published, which has since been suppressed, the whole history has come to light. Caspar Hauser was the lineal descendant of the house of Baden, and heir to the throne. The guilt of his imprisonment and murder rests, therefore, upon the present reigning family.

A chapel on the Schönberg, the mountain opposite, was pointed out as the spot where Louis XV., if I mistake not, usually stood while his army besieged Freiburg. A German officer having sent a ball to this chapel which struck the wall just above the king's head, the latter sent word that if they did not cease firing he would point his cannons at the Minster. The citizens thought it best to spare the monarch and save the cathedral.

We attended a meeting of the Walhalla, or society of the students who

226

visit the Freiburg University. They pleased me better than the enthusiastic but somewhat unrestrained Burschenschaft of Heidelberg. Here, they have abolished duelling; the greatest friendship prevails among the students, and they have not that contempt for every thing philister, or unconnected with their studies, which prevails in other universities. Many respectable citizens attend their meetings; to-night there was a member of the Chamber of Deputies at Carlsruhe present, who delivered two speeches, in which every third word was "freedom!" An address was delivered also by a merchant of the city, in which he made a play upon the word spear, which signifies also in a cant sense, citizen, find seemed to indicate that both would do their work in the good cause. He was loudly applauded. Their song of union was by Charles Follen, and the students were much pleased when I told them how he was honored and esteemed in America.

After two days, delightfully spent, we shouldered our knapsacks and left Freiburg. The beautiful valley, at the mouth of which the city lies, runs like an avenue for seven miles directly into the mountains, and presents in its loveliness such a contrast to the horrid defile which follows, that it almost deserves the name which has been given to a little inn at its head—the "Kingdom of Heaven." The mountains of the Black Forest enclose it on each side like walls, covered to the summit with luxuriant woods, and in some places with those forests of gloomy pine which give this region its name. After traversing its whole length, just before plunging into the mountain-depths, the traveler rarely meets with a finer picture than that which, on looking back, he sees framed between the hills at the other end. Freiburg looks around the foot of one of the heights, with the spire of her cathedral peeping above the top, while the French Vosges grew dim in the far perspective.

The road now enters a wild, narrow valley, which grows smaller as we proceed. From Himmelreich, a large rude inn by the side of the green meadows, we enter the Höllenthal—that is, from the "Kingdom of Heaven" to the "Valley of Hell!" The latter place better deserves its appellation than the former. The road winds between precipices of black rock, above which the thick foliage shuts out the brightness of day and gives a sombre hue to the scene. A torrent foams down the chasm, and in one place two mighty pillars interpose to prevent all passage. The stream, however, has worn its way through, and the road is hewn in the rock by its side. This cleft is the only entrance to a valley three or four miles long, which lies in the very heart of the mountains. It is inhabited by a few woodmen and their families, and but for the road which passes through, would be as perfect a solitude as the Happy Valley of Rasselas. At the farther end, a winding road called "The Ascent," leads up the steep mountain to an elevated region of country, thinly settled and covered with herds of cattle. The cherries which, in the Rhine-plain below, had long gone, were just ripe here. The people spoke a most barbarous dialect; they were social and friendly, for everybody greeted us, and sometimes, as we sat on a bank by the roadside, those who passed by would say "Rest thee!" or "Thrice rest!"

Passing by the Titi Lake, a small body of water which was spread out among the hills like a sheet of ink, so deep was its Stygian hue, we commenced ascending a mountain. The highest peak of the Schwarzwald, the Feldberg, rose not far off, and on arriving at the top of this mountain, we saw that a half hour's walk would bring us to its summit. This was too great a temptation for my love of climbing heights; so with a look at the descending sun to calculate how much time we could spare, we set out. There was no path, but we pressed directly up the steep side, through bushes and long grass, and in a short time reached the top, breathless from such exertion in the thin atmosphere. The pine woods shut out the view to the north and east, which is said to be magnificent, as the mountain is about five thousand feet high. The wild, black peaks of the Black Forest were spread below us, and the sun sank through golden mist towards the Alsatian hills. Afar to the south, through cloud and storm, we could just trace the white outline of the Swiss Alps. The wind swept through the pines around, and bent the long yellow grass among which we sat, with a strange, mournful sound, well suiting the gloomy and mysterious region. It soon grew cold, the golden clouds settled down towards us, and we made haste to descend to the village of Lenzkirch before dark.

Next morning we set out early, without waiting to see the trial of archery which was to take place among the mountain youths. Their booths and targets, gay with banners, stood on a green meadow beside the town. We walked through the Black Forest the whole forenoon. It might be owing to the many wild stories whose scenes are laid among these hills, but with me there was a peculiar feeling of solemnity pervading the whole region. The great pine woods are of the very darkest hue of green, and down their hoary, moss-floored aisles, daylight seems never to have shone. The air was pure and clear, and the sunshine bright, but it imparted no gaiety to the scenery: except the little meadows of living emerald which lay occasionally in the lap of a dell, the landscape wore a solemn and serious air. In a storm, it must be sublime.

About noon, from the top of the last range of hills, we had a glorious view. The line of the distant Alps could be faintly traced high in the clouds, and all the heights between were plainly visible, from the Lake of Constance to the misty Jura, which flanked the Vosges of the west. From our lofty station we overlooked half Switzerland, and had the air been a little clearer, we could have seen Mont Blanc and the mountains of Savoy. I could not help envying the feelings of the Swiss, who, after long absence from their native land, first see the Alps from this road. If to the emotions with which I then looked on them were added the passionate love of home and country which a long absence creates, such excess of rapture would be almost too great to be borne.

In the afternoon we crossed the border, and took leave of Germany with regret, after near a year's residence within its bounds. Still it was pleasant to know we were in a republic once more: the first step we took made us aware of the change. There was no policeman to call for our passports or search our baggage. It was just dark when we reached the hill overlooking the Rhine, on whose steep banks is perched the antique town of Schaffhausen. It is still walled in, with towers at regular intervals; the streets are wide and spacious, and the houses rendered extremely picturesque by the quaint projecting windows. The buildings are nearly all old, as we learned by the dates above the doors. At the inn, I met with one of the free troopers who marched against Luzerne. He was full of spirit, and ready to undertake another such journey. Indeed it is the universal opinion that the present condition of things cannot last much longer.

We took a walk before breakfast to the Falls of the Rhine, about a mile and a half from Schaffhausen. I confess I was somewhat disappointed in them, after the glowing descriptions of travelers. The river at this place is little more than thirty yards wide, and the body of water, although issuing from the Lake of Constance, is not remarkably strong. For some distance above, the fall of the water is very rapid, and as it finally reaches the spot where, narrowed between rocks, it makes the grand plunge, it has acquired a great velocity. Three rocks stand in the middle of the current, which thunders against and around their bases, but cannot shake them down. These and the rocks in the bed of the stream, break the force of the fall, so that it descends to the bottom, about fifty feet below, not in one sheet, but shivered into a hundred leaps of snowy foam. The precipitous shores, and the tasteful little castle which is perched upon the steep just over the boiling spray, add much to its beauty, taken as a picture. As a specimen of the picturesque, the whole scene is perfect. I should think Trenton Falls, in New York, must excel these in wild, startling effect; but there is such a scarcity of waterfalls in this land, that the Germans go into raptures about them, and will hardly believe that Niagara itself possesses more sublimity.

# CHAPTER XXIX. — PEOPLE AND PLACES IN EASTERN SWITZERLAND.

We left Schaffhausen for Zurich, in mist and rain, and walked for some time along the north bank of the Rhine. We could have enjoyed the scenery much better, had it not been for the rain, which not only hid the mountains from sight, but kept us constantly half soaked. We crossed the rapid Rhine at Eglisau, a curious antique village, and then continued our way through the forests of Canton Zurich, to Bülach, with its groves of lindens—"those tall and stately trees, with velvet down upon their shining leaves, and rustic benches placed beneath their overhanging eaves."

When we left the little village where the rain obliged us to stop for the night, it was clear and delightful. The farmers were out, busy at work, their long, straight scythes glancing through the wet grass, while the thick pines sparkled with thousands of dewy diamonds. The country was so beautiful and cheerful, that we half felt like being in America. The farm-houses were scattered over the country in real American style, and the glorious valley of the Limmat, bordered on the west by a range of woody hills, reminded me of some scenes in my native Pennsylvania. The houses were neatly and tastefully built, with little gardens around them—and the countenances of the people spoke of intelligence and independence. There was the same air of peace and prosperity which delighted us in the valleys of Upper Austria, with a look of freedom which those had not. The faces of a people are the best index to their condition. I could read on their brows a lofty self-respect, a consciousness of the liberties they enjoy, which the Germans of the laboring class never show. It could not be imagination, for the recent occurrences in Switzerland, with the many statements I heard in Germany, had prejudiced me somewhat against the land; and these marks of prosperity and freedom were as surprising as they were delightful.

As we approached Zurich, the noise of employment from mills, furnaces and factories, came to us like familiar sounds, reminding us of the bustle of our home cities. The situation of the city is lovely. It lies at the head of the lake, and on both sides of the little river Limmat, whose clear green waters carry the collected meltings of the Alps to the Rhine. Around the lake rise lofty green hills, which, sloping gently back, bear on their sides hundreds of pleasant country-houses and farms, and the snowy Alpine range extends along the southern sky. The Limmat is spanned by a number of bridges, and its swift waters turn many mills which are built above them. From these bridges one can look out over the blue lake and down the thronged streets of the city on each side, whose bright, cheerful houses remind him of Italy.

Zurich can boast of finer promenades than any other city in Switzerland. The old battlements are planted with trees and transformed into pleasant walks, which being elevated above the city, command views of its beautiful environs. A favorite place of resort is the Lindenhof, an elevated court-yard, shaded by immense trees. The fountains of water under them are always surrounded by washerwomen, and in the morning groups of merry school children may be seen tumbling over the grass. The teachers take them there in a body for exercise and recreation. The Swiss children are beautiful, bright-eyed creatures; there is scarcely one who does not exhibit the dawning of an active, energetic spirit. It may be partly attributed to the fresh, healthy climate of Switzerland, but I am partial enough to republics to believe that the influence of the Government under which they live, has also its share in producing the effect.

There is a handsome promenade on an elevated bastion which overlooks the city and lakes. While enjoying the cool morning breeze and listening to the stir of the streets below us, we were also made aware of the social and friendly politeness of the people. Those who passed by, on their walk around the rampart, greeted us, almost with the familiarity of an acquaintance. Simple as was the act, we felt grateful, for it had at least the seeming of a friendly interest and a sympathy with the loneliness which the stranger sometimes feels. A school-teacher leading her troop of merry children on their morning walk around the bastion, nodded to us pleasantly and forthwith the whole company of chubby-cheeked rogues, looking up at us with a pleasant archness, lisped a "guten morgen" that made the hearts glad within us. I know of nothing that has given me a more sweet and tender delight than

232

the greeting of a little child, who, leaving his noisy playmates, ran across the street to me, and taking my hand, which he could barely clasp in both his soft little ones, looked up in my face with an expression so winning and affectionate, that I loved him at once. The happy, honest farmers, too, spoke to us cheerfully everywhere. We learned a lesson from all this—we felt that not a word of kindness is ever wasted, that a simple friendly glance may cheer the spirit and warm the lonely heart, and that the slightest deed, prompted by generous sympathy, becomes a living joy in the memory of the receiver, which blesses unceasingly him who bestowed it.

We left Zurich the same afternoon, to walk to Stafa, where we were told the poet Freiligrath resided. The road led along the bank of the lake, whose shores sloped gently up from the water, covered with gardens and farm-houses, which, with the bolder mountains that rose behind them, made a combination of the lovely and grand, on which the eye rested with rapture and delight. The sweetest cottages were embowered among the orchards, and the whole country bloomed like a garden. The waters of the lake are of a pale, transparent green, and so clear that we could see its bottom of white pebbles, for some distance. Here and there floated a quiet boat on its surface. The opposite hills were covered with a soft blue haze, and white villages sat along the shore, "like swans among the reeds." Behind, we saw the woody range of the Brunig Alp. The people bade us a pleasant good evening; there was a universal air of cheerfulness and content on their countenances.

Towards evening, the clouds which hung in the south the whole day, dispersed a little and we could see the Dodiberg and the Alps of Glarus. As sunset drew on, the broad summits of snow and the clouds which were rolled around them, assumed a soft rosy hue, which increased in brilliancy as the light of day faded. The rough, icy crags and snowy steeps were fused in the warm light and half blended with the bright clouds. This blaze, as it were, of the mountains at sunset, is called the Alp-glow, and exceeds all one's highest conceptions of Alpine grandeur. We watched the fading glory till it quite died away, and the summits wore a livid, ashy hue, like the mountains of a world wherein there was no life. In a few minutes more the dusk of twilight spread over the scene, the boatmen glided home over the still lake and the herdsmen drove their cattle back from pasture on the slopes and meadows.

On inquiring for Freiligrath at Stafa, we found he had removed to Rapperschwyl, some distance further. As it was already late, we waited for the steamboat which leaves Zurich every evening. It came along about eight o'clock, and a little boat carried us out through rain and darkness to meet it, as it came like a fiery-eyed monster over the water. We stepped on board the "Republican," and in half an hour were brought to the wharf at Rapperschwyl.

There are two small islands in the lake, one of which, with a little chapel rising from among its green trees, is Ufnau, the grave of Ulrich von Hutten, one of the fathers of the German Reformation. His fiery poems have been the source from which many a German bard has derived his inspiration, and Freiligrath who now lives in sight of his tomb, has published an indignant poem, because an inn with gaming tables has been established in the ruins of the castle near Creuznach, where Hutten found refuge from his enemies with Franz von Sickingen, brother-in-law of "Goetz with the iron Hand." The monks of Einsiedeln, to whom Ufnau belongs, have carefully obliterated all traces of his grave, so that the exact spot is not known, in order that even a tombstone might be denied him who once strove to overturn their order. It matters little to that bold spirit whose motto was: "The die is cast—I have dared it!"—the whole island is his monument, if he need one.

I spent the whole of the morning with Freiligrath, the poet, who was lately banished from Germany on account of the liberal principles his last volume contains. He lives in a pleasant country-house on the Meyerberg, an eminence near Rapperschwyl, overlooking a glorious prospect. On leaving Frankfort, R.S. Willis gave me a letter to him, and I was glad to meet with a man personally whom I admired so much through his writings, and whose boldness in speaking out against the tyranny which his country suffers, forms such a noble contrast to the cautious slowness of his countrymen. He received me kindly and conversed much upon American literature. He is a warm admirer of Bryant and Longfellow, and has translated many of their poems into German. He said he had received a warm invitation from a colony of Germans in Wisconsin, to join them and enjoy that freedom which his native land denies, but that his circumstances would not allow it at present. He is perhaps thirty-five years of age. His brow is high and noble, and his eyes, which are large and of a clear gray, beam with serious, saddened thought. His long chesnut hair, uniting with a handsome beard and moustache, gives a lion-like dignity to his energetic countenance. His talented wife, Ida Freiligrath, who shares his literary labors, and an amiable sister, are with him in exile, and he is happier in their faithfulness than when he enjoyed the favors of a corrupt king.

We crossed the long bridge from Rapperschwyl, and took the road over the mountain opposite, ascending for nearly two hours along the side, with glorious views of the Lake of Zurich and the mountains which enclose it. The upper and lower ends of the lake were completely hid by the storms, which, to our regret, veiled the Alps, but the part below lay spread out dim and grand, like a vast picture. It rained almost constantly, and we were obliged occasionally to take shelter in the pine forests, whenever a heavier cloud passed over. The road was lined with beggars, who dropped on their knees in the rain before us, or placed bars across the way, and then took them down again, for which they demanded money.

At length we reached the top of the pass. Many pilgrims to Einsiedeln had stopped at a little inn there, some of whom came a long distance to pay their vows, especially as the next day was the Ascension day of the Virgin, whose image there is noted for performing many miracles. Passing on, we crossed a wild torrent by an arch called the "Devil's Bridge." The lofty, elevated plains were covered with scanty patches of grain and potatoes, and the boys tended their goats on the grassy slopes, sometimes trilling or yodling an Alpine melody. An hour's walk brought us to Einsiedeln, a small town, whose only attraction is the Abbey—after Loretto, in Italy, the most celebrated resort for pilgrims in Europe.

We entered immediately into the great church. The gorgeous vaulted roof and long aisles were dim with the early evening; hundreds of worshippers sat around the sides, or kneeled in groups on the broad stone pavements, chanting over their Paternosters and Ave Marias in a shrill, monotonous tone, while the holy image near the entrance was surrounded by persons, many of whom came in the hope of being healed of some disorder under which they suffered. I could not distinctly make out the image, for it was placed back within the grating, and a strong crimson lamp behind it was made to throw the light around, in the form of a glory. Many of the pilgrims came a long distance. I saw some in the costume of the Black Forest, and others who appeared to be natives of the Italian Cantons; and a group of young women wearing conical fur caps, from the forests of Bregenz, on the Lake of Constance.

I was astonished at the splendor of this church, situated in a lonely and unproductive Alpine valley. The lofty arches of the ceiling, which are covered with superb fresco paintings, rest on enormous pillars of granite, and every image and shrine is richly ornamented with gold. Some of the chapels were filled with the remains of martyrs, and these were always surrounded with throngs of believers. The choir was closed by a tall iron grating; a single lamp, which swung from the roof, enabled me to see through the darkness, that though much more rich in ornaments than the body of the church, it was less grand and impressive. The frescoes which cover the ceiling, are said to be the finest paintings of the kind in Switzerland.

In the morning our starting was delayed by the rain, and we took advantage of it to hear mass in the Abbey and enjoy the heavenly music. The latter was of the loftiest kind; there was one voice among the singers I shall not soon forget. It was like the warble of a bird who sings out of very wantonness. On and on it sounded, making its clear, radiant sweetness heard above the chant of the choir and the thunder of the orchestra. Such a rich, varied and untiring strain of melody I have rarely listened to.

When the service ceased, we took a small road leading to Schwytz. We had now fairly entered the Alpine region, and our first task was to cross a mountain. This having been done, we kept along the back of the ridge which bounds the lake of Zug on the south, terminating in the well known Rossberg. The scenery became wilder with every step. The luxuriant fields of herbage on the mountains were spotted with the picturesque chalets of the hunters and Alp-herds; cattle and goats were browsing along the declivities, their bells tinkling most musically, and the little streams fell in foam down the steeps. We here began to realize our anticipations of Swiss scenery. Just on

236

the other side of the range, along which we traveled, lay the little lake of Egeri and valley of Morgarten, where Tell and his followers overcame the army of the German Emperor; near the lake of Lowertz, we found a chapel by the roadside, built on the spot where the house of Werner Stauffacher, one of the "three men of Grütli," formerly stood. It bears a poetical inscription in old German, and a rude painting of the Battle of Morgarten.

As we wound around the lake of Lowertz, we saw the valley lying between the Rossberg and the Righi, which latter mountain stood full in view. To our regret, and that of all other travelers, the clouds hung low upon it, as they had done for a week at least, and there was no prospect of a change. The Rossberg, from which we descended, is about four thousand feet in height; a dark brown stripe from its very summit to the valley below, shows the track of the avalanche which, in 1806, overwhelmed Goldau, and laid waste the beautiful vale of Lowertz. We could trace the masses of rock and earth as far as the foot of the Righi. Four hundred and fifty persons perished by this catastrophe, which was so sudden that in five minutes the whole lovely valley was transformed into a desolate wilderness. The shock was so great that the lake of Lowertz overflowed its banks, and part of the village of Steinen at the upper end was destroyed by the waters.

An hour's walk through a blooming Alpine vale brought us to the little town of Schwytz, the capital of the Canton. It stands at the foot of a rock-mountain, in shape not unlike Gibraltar, but double its height. The bare and rugged summits seem to hang directly over the town, but the people dwell below without fear, although the warning ruins of Goldau are full in sight. A narrow blue line at the end of the valley which stretches westward, marks the lake of the Four Cantons. Down this valley we hurried, that we might not miss the boat which plies daily, from Luzerne to Fluelen. I regretted not being able to visit Luzerne, as I had a letter to the distinguished Swiss composer, Schnyder von Wartensee, who resides there at present. The place is said to present a most desolate appearance, being avoided by travelers, and even by artisans, so that business of all kinds has almost entirely ceased.

At the little town of Brunnen, on the lake, we awaited the coming of the steamboat. The scenery around it is exceedingly grand. Looking down towards Luzerne, we could see the dark mass of Mount Pilatus on one side, and on the other the graceful outline of the Righi, still wearing his hood of clouds. We put off in a skiff to meet the boat, with two Capuchin friars in long brown mantles and cowls, carrying rosaries at their girdles.

Nearly opposite Brunnen is the meadow of Grütli, where the union of the Swiss patriots took place, and the bond was sealed that enabled them to cast off their chains. It is a little green slope on the side of the mountain, between the two Cantons of Uri and Unterwalden, surrounded on all sides by precipices. A little crystal spring in the centre is believed by the common people to have gushed up on the spot where the three "linked the hands that made them free." It is also a popular belief that they slumber in a rocky cavern near the spot, and that they will arise and come forth when the liberties of Switzerland are in danger. She stands at present greatly in need of a new triad to restore the ancient harmony.

We passed this glorious scene, almost the only green spot on the bleak mountain-side, and swept around the base of the Axenberg, at whose foot, in a rocky cave, stands the chapel of William Tell. This is built on the spot where he leaped from Gessler's boat during the storm. It sits at the base of the rock, on the water's edge, and can be seen far over the waves. The Alps, whose eternal snows are lifted dazzling to the sky, complete the grandeur of a scene so hallowed by the footsteps of freedom. The grand and lonely solemnity of the landscape impressed me with an awe, like that one feels when standing in a mighty cathedral, when the aisles are dim with twilight. And how full of interest to a citizen of young and free America is a shrine where the votaries of Liberty have turned to gather strength and courage, through the storms and convulsions of five hundred years!

We stopped at the village of Fluelen, at the head of the lake, and walked on to Altorf, a distance of half a league. Here, in the market-place, is a tower said to be built on the spot where the linden tree stood, under which the child of Tell was placed, while, about a hundred yards distant, is a fountain with Tell's statue, on the spot from whence he shot the apple. If these localities are correct, he must indeed have been master of the cross-bow. The tower is covered with rude paintings of the principal events in the history of Swiss

238

liberty. I viewed these scenes with double interest from having read Schiller's "Wilhelm Tell," one of the most splendid tragedies ever written. The beautiful reply of his boy, when he described to him the condition of the "land where there are no mountains," was sounding in my ears during the whole day's journey:

*"Father, I'd feel oppressed in that broad land,*

*I'd rather dwell beneath the avalanche!"*

The little village of Burglen, whose spire we saw above the forest, in a glen near by, was the birth-place of Tell, and the place where his dwelling stood, is now marked by a small chapel. In the Schachen, a noisy mountain stream that comes down to join the Reuss, he was drowned, when an old man, in attempting to rescue a child who had fallen in—a death worthy of the hero! We bestowed a blessing on his memory in passing, and then followed the banks of the rapid Reuss. Twilight was gathering in the deep Alpine glen, and the mountains on each side, half-seen through the mist, looked like vast, awful phantoms. Soon they darkened to black, indistinct masses; all was silent except the deepened roar of the falling floods; dark clouds brooded above us like the outspread wings of night, and we were glad, when the little village of Amstegg was reached, and the parlor of the inn opened to us a more cheerful, if not so romantic scene.

# CHAPTER XXX. – PASSAGE OF THE ST. GOTHARD AND DESCENT INTO ITALY.

Leaving Amstegg, I passed the whole day among snowy, sky-piercing Alps, torrents, chasms and clouds! The clouds appeared to be breaking up as we set out, and the white top of the Reassberg was now and then visible in the sky. Just above the village are the remains of Zwing Uri, the castle begun by the tyrant Gessler, for the complete subjugation of the canton. Following the Reuss up through a narrow valley, we passed the Bristenstock, which lifts its jagged crags nine thousand feet in the air, while on the other side stand the snowy summits which lean towards the Rhone Glacier and St. Gothard. From the deep glen where the Reuss foamed down towards the Lake of the Forest Cantons, the mountains rose with a majestic sweep so far into the sky that the brain grew almost dizzy in following their outlines. Woods, chalets and slopes of herbage covered their bases, where the mountain cattle and goats were browsing, while the herd-boys sang their native melodies or woke the ringing echoes with the loud, sweet sounds of their wooden horns; higher up, the sides were broken into crags and covered with stunted pines; then succeeded a belt of bare rock with a little snow lying in the crevices, and the summits of dazzling white looked out from the clouds nearly three-fourths the height of the zenith. Sometimes when the vale was filled with clouds, it was startling to see them parting around a solitary summit, apparently isolated in the air at an immense height, for the mountain to which it belonged was hidden to the very base!

The road passed from one side of the valley to the other, crossing the Reuss on bridges sometimes ninety feet high. After three or four hours walking, we reached a frightful pass called the Schollenen. So narrow is the defile that before reaching it, the road seemed to enter directly into the mountain. Precipices a thousand feet high tower above, and the stream roars and boils in the black depth below. The road is a wonder of art; it winds around the edge of horrible chasms or is carried on lofty arches across, with sometimes a hold apparently so frail that one involuntarily shudders. At a place called the Devil's Bridge, the Reuss leaps about seventy feet in three or four cascades, sending up continually a cloud of spray, while a wind created by the fall, blows and whirls around, with a force that nearly lifts one from his feet. Wordsworth has described the scene in the following lines:

*"Plunge with the Reuss embrowned by terror's breath,*

*Where danger roofs the narrow walks of Death;*

*By floods that, thundering from their dizzy height,*

*Swell more gigantic on the steadfast sight,*

*Black, drizzling crags, that, beaten by the din,*

*Vibrate, us if a voice complained within,*

*Loose hanging rocks, the Day's blessed eye that hide,*

*And crosses reared to Death on every side!"*

Beyond the Devil's Bridge, the mountains which nearly touched before, interlock into each other, and a tunnel three hundred and seventy-five feet long leads through the rock into the vale of Urseren, surrounded by the Upper Alps. The little town of Andermatt lies in the middle of this valley, which with the peaks around is covered with short, yellowish-brown grass. We met near Amstegg a little Italian boy walking home, from Germany, quite alone and without money, for we saw him give his last kreutzer to a blind beggar along the road. We therefore took him with us, as he was afraid to cross the St. Gothard alone.

After refreshing ourselves at Andermatt, we started, five in number, including a German student, for the St. Gothard. Behind the village of Hospiz, which stands at the bottom of the valley leading to Realp and the Furca pass, the way commences, winding backwards and forwards, higher and higher, through a valley covered with rocks, with the mighty summits of the Alps around, untenanted save by the chamois and mountain eagle. Not a tree was to be seen. The sides of the mountains were covered with loose rocks waiting for the next torrent to wash them down, and the tops were robed in eternal snow. A thick cloud rolled down over us as we went on, following the diminishing brooks to their snowy source in the peak of St. Gothard. We cut off the bends of the road by footpaths up the rocks, which we ascended in single file, one of the Americans going ahead and little Pietro with his staff and bundle bringing up the rear. The rarefied air we breathed, seven thousand feet above the sea, was like exhilarating gas. We felt no fatigue, but ran and shouted and threw snowballs, in the middle of August!

After three hours' walk we reached the two clear and silent lakes which send their waters to the Adriatic and the North Sea. Here, as we looked down the Italian side, the sky became clear; we saw the top of St. Gothard many thousand feet above, and stretching to the south, the summits of the mountains which guard the vales of the Ticino and the Adda. The former monastery has been turned into an inn; there is, however, a kind of church attached, attended by a single monk. It was so cold that although late, we determined to descend to the first village. The Italian side is very steep, and the road, called the Via Trimola, is like a thread dropped down and constantly doubling back upon itself. The deep chasms were filled with snow, although exposed to the full force of the sun, and for a long distance there was scarcely a sign of vegetation.

We thought as we went down, that every step was bringing us nearer to a sunnier land—that the glories of Italy, which had so long lain in the airy background of the future, would soon spread themselves before us in their real or imagined beauty. Reaching at dusk the last height above the vale of the Ticino, we saw the little village of Airolo with its musical name, lying in a hollow of the mountains. A few minutes of leaping, sliding and rolling, took us down the grassy declivity, and we found we had descended from the top in an hour and a half, although the distance by the road is nine miles! I need not say how glad we were to relieve our trembling knees and exhausted limbs.

I have endeavored several times to give some idea of the sublimity of the Alps, but words seem almost powerless to measure these mighty mountains. No effort of the imagination could possibly equal their real grandeur. I wish also to describe the feelings inspired by being among them,—feelings which can best be expressed through the warmer medium of poetry.

*SONG OF THE ALP.*

*I. —      I sit aloft on my thunder throne,*

*And my voice of dread the nations own*

*    As I speak in storm below!*

*The valleys quake with a breathless fear,*

*When I hurl in wrath my icy spear*

*    And shake my locks of snow!*

*When the avalanche forth like a tiger leaps,*

*    How the vassal-mountains quiver!*

*And the storm that sweeps through the airy deeps*

*    Makes the hoary pine-wood shiver!*

*Above them all, in a brighter air,*

*I lift my forehead proud and bare,*

*And the lengthened sweep of my forest-robe*

*Trails down to the low and captured globe,*

*Till its borders touch the dark green wave*

*In whose soundless depths my feet I lave.*

*The winds, unprisoned, around me blow,*

*And terrible tempests whirl the snow;*

*Rocks from their caverned beds are torn,*

*And the blasted forest to heaven is borne;*

*High through the din of the stormy band,*

*Like misty giants the mountains stand,*

*And their thunder-revel o'er-sounds the woe,*

*That cries from the desolate vales below!*

*I part the clouds with my lifted crown,*

*Till the sun-ray slants on the glaciers down,*

*And trembling men, in the valleys pale,*

*Rejoice at the gleam of my icy mail!*

*II. —    I wear a crown of the sunbeam's gold,*

*With glacier-gems en my forehead old—*

   *A monarch crowned by God!*

*What son of the servile earth may dare*

*Such signs of a regal power to wear,*

   *While chained to her darkened sod?*

*I know of a nobler and grander lore*

   *Than Time records on his crumbling pages,*

*And the soul of my solitude teaches more*

   *Than the gathered deeds of perished ages!*

*For I have ruled since Time began*

*And wear no fetter made by man.*

*I scorn the coward and craven race*

*Who dwell around my mighty base,*

*For they leave the lessons I grandly gave*

*And bend to the yoke of the crouching slave.*

*I shout aloud to the chainless skies;*

The stream through its falling foam replies,

And my voice, like the sound of the surging sea,

To the nations thunders: "I am free!"

I spoke to Tell when a tyrant's hand

Lay heavy and hard on his native land,

And the spirit whose glory from mine he won

Blessed the Alpine dwellers with Freedom's sun!

The student-boy on the Gmunden-plain

Heard my solemn voice, but he fought in vain;

I called from the crags of the Passeir-glen,

When the despot stood in my realm again,

And Hofer sprang at the proud command

And roused the men of the Tyrol land!

III. —    I struggle up to the dim blue heaven,

From the world, far down in whose breast are driven

   The props of my pillared throne;

And the rosy fires of morning glow

Like a glorious thought, on my brow of snow,

   While the vales are dark and lone!

Ere twilight summons the first faint star,

I seem to the nations who dwell afar

Like a shadowy cloud, whose every fold

The sunset dyes with its purest gold,

*And the soul mounts up through that gateway fair*

*To try its wings in a loftier air!*

*The finger of God on my brow is pressed—*

*His spirit beats in my giant breast,*

*And I breathe, as the endless ages roll,*

*His silent words to the eager soul!*

*I prompt the thoughts of the mighty mind,*

*Who leaves his century far behind*

*And speaks from the Future's sun-lit snow*

*To the Present, that sleeps in its gloom below!*

*I stand, unchanged, in creation's youth—*

*A glorious type of Eternal Truth,*

*That, free and pure, from its native skies*

*Shines through Oppression's veil of lies,*

*And lights the world's long-fettered sod*

*With thoughts of Freedom and of God!*

When, at night, I looked out of my chamber-window, the silver moon of Italy, (for we fancied that her light was softer and that the skies were already bluer) hung trembling above the fields of snow that stretched in their wintry brilliance along the mountains around. I heard the roar of the Ticino and the deepened sound of falling cascades, and thought, if I were to take those waters for my guide, to what glorious places they would lead me!

We left Airolo early the next morning, to continue our journey down the valley of the Ticino. The mists and clouds of Switzerland were exchanged for a sky of the purest blue, and we felt, for the first time in ten days, uncomfortably warm. The mountains which flank the Alps on this side, are still giants—lofty and bare, and covered with snow in many places. The limit of the German dialect is on the summit of St. Gothard, and the peasants saluted us with a "buon giorno" as they passed. This, with the clearness of the skies and the warmth of the air, made us feel that Italy was growing nearer.

The mountains are covered with forests of dark pine, and many beautiful cascades come tumbling over the rocks in their haste to join the Ticino. One of these was so strangely beautiful, that I cannot pass it without a particular description. We saw it soon after leaving Airolo, on the opposite side of the valley. A stream of considerable size comes down the mountain, leaping from crag to crag till within forty or fifty feet of the bottom, where it is caught in a hollow rock, and flung upwards into the air, forming a beautiful arch as it falls out into the valley. As it is whirled up thus, feathery curls of spray are constantly driven off and seem to wave round it like the fibres on an ostrich plume. The sun shining through, gave it a sparry brilliance which was perfectly magnificent. If I were an artist, I would give much for such a new form of beauty.

On our first day's journey we passed through two terrific mountain gorges, almost equalling in grandeur the defile of the "Devil's Bridge." The Ticino, in its course to Lago Maggiore has to make a descent of nearly three thousand feet, passing through three valleys, which lie like terraces, one below the other. In its course from one to the other, it has to force its way down in twenty cataracts through a cleft in the mountains. The road, constructed with the utmost labor, threads these dark chasms, sometimes carried in a tunnel through the rock, sometimes passing on arches above the boiling flood. The precipices of bare rock rise far above and render the way difficult and dangerous. I here noticed another very beautiful effect of the water, perhaps attributable to some mineral substance it contained. The spray and foam thrown up in the dashing of the vexed current, was of a light, delicate pink, although the stream itself was a soft blue; and the contrast of these two colors was very remarkable.

As we kept on, however, there was a very perceptible change in the scenery. The gloomy pines disappeared and the mountains were covered, in their stead, with picturesque chestnut trees, with leaves of a shining green. The grass and vegetation was much more luxuriant than on the other side of the Alps, and fields of maize and mulberry orchards covered the valley. We saw the people busy at work reeling silk in the villages. Every mile we advanced made a sensible change in the vegetation. The chesnuts were larger, the maize higher, the few straggling grape-vines increased into bowers and vineyards, while the gardens were filled with plum, pear and fig-trees, and the stands of delicious fruit which we saw in the villages, gave us promise of the luxuriance that was to come.

The vineyards are much more beautiful than the German fields of stakes. The vines are not trimmed, but grow from year to year over a frame higher than the head, supported through the whole field on stone pillars. They interlace and form a complete leafy screen, while the clusters hang below. The light came dimly through the green, transparent leaves, and nothing was wanting to make them real bowers of Arcadia. Although we were still in Switzerland, the people began to have that lazy, indolent look which characterizes the Italians; most of the occupations were carried on in the open air, and brown-robed, sandalled friars were going about from house to house, collecting money and provisions for their support.

We passed Faidò and Giornico, near which last village are the remains of an old castle, supposed to have been built by the ancient Gauls, and stopped for the night at Cresciano, which being entirely Italian, we had an opportunity to put in practice the few words we had picked up from Pietro. The little fellow parted from us with regret a few hours before, at Biasco, where he had relations. The rustic landlord at Cresciano was an honest young fellow, who tried to serve us as well as he could, but we made some ludicrous mistakes through our ignorance of the language.

Three hours' walk brought us to Bellinzona, the capital of the canton. Before reaching it, our road joined that of the Splügen which comes down through the valley of Bernardino. From the bridge where the junction takes place we had a triple view, whose grandeur took me by surprise, even after coming from Switzerland. We stood at the union of three valleys—that leading to St. Gothard, terminated by the glaciers of the Bernese Oberland, that running off obliquely to the Splügen, and finally the broad vale of the

Ticino, extending to Lago Maggiore, whose purple mountains closed the vista. Each valley was perhaps two miles broad and from twenty to thirty long, and the mountains that enclosed them from five to seven thousand feet in height, so you may perhaps form some idea what a view down three such avenues in this Alpine temple would be. Bellinzona is romantically situated, on a slight eminence, with three castles to defend it, with those square turreted towers and battlements, which remind one involuntarily of the days of the Goths and Vandals.

We left Bellinzona at noon, and saw, soon after, from an eminence, the blue line of Lago Maggiore stretched across the bottom of the valley. We saw sunset fade away over the lake, but it was clouded, and did not realize my ideal of such a scene in Italy. A band of wild Italians paraded up and down the village, drawing one of their number in a hand-cart. They made a great noise with a drum and trumpet, and were received everywhere with shouts of laughter. A great jug of wine was not wanting, and the whole seemed to me a very characteristic scene.

We were early awakened at Magadino, at the head of Lago Maggiore, and after swallowing a hasty breakfast, went on board the steamboat "San Carlo," for Sesto Calende. We got under way at six o'clock, and were soon in motion over the crystal mirror. The water is of the most lovely green hue, and so transparent that we seemed to bo floating in mid-air. Another heaven arched far below us; other chains of mountains joined their bases to those which surrounded the lake, and the mirrored cascades leaped upward to meet their originals at the surface. It may be because I have seen it more recently, that the water of Lago Maggiore appears to be the most beautiful in the world. I was delighted with the Scotch lakes, and enraptured with the Traunsee and "Zurich's waters," but this last exceeds them both. I am now incapable of any stronger feeling, until I see the Egean from the Grecian Isles.

The morning was cloudy, and the white wreaths hung low on the mountains, whose rocky sides were covered every where with the rank and luxuriant growth of this climate. As we advanced further over this glorious mirror, the houses became more Italian-like; the lower stories rested on arched passages, and the windows were open, without glass, while in the gardens stood the solemn, graceful cypress, and vines, heavy with ripening grapes, hung from bough to bough through the mulberry orchards. Half-way down, in a broad bay, which receives the waters of a stream that comes down with the Simplon, are the celebrated Borromean Islands. They are four in number, and seem to float like fairy creations on the water, while the lofty hills form a background whose grandeur enhances by contrast their exquisite beauty. There was something in the scene that reminded me of Claude Melnotte's description of his home, by Bulwer, and like the lady of Lyons, I answer readily, "I like the picture."

On passing by Isola Madre, we could see the roses in its terraced gardens and the broad-leaved aloes clinging to the rocks. Isola Bella, the loveliest of them all, as its name denotes, was farther off; it rose like a pyramid from the water, terrace above terrace to the summit, and its gardens of never fading foliage, with the glorious panorama around, might make it a paradise, if life were to be dreamed away. On the northern side of the bay lies a large town (I forget its name,) with a lofty Romanesque tower, and noble mountains sweep around as if to shut out the world from such a scene. The sea was perfectly calm, and groves and gardens slept mirrored in the dark green wave, while the Alps rose afar through the dim, cloudy air. Towards the other end the hills sink lower, and slope off into the plains of Lombardy. Near Arona, on the western side, is a large monastery, overlooking the lower part of the lake. Beside it, on a hill, is a colossal statue of San Carlo Borromeo, who gave his name to the lovely islands above.

After a seven hours' passage, we ran into Sesto Calende, at the foot of the lake. Here, passengers and baggage were tumbled promiscuously on shore, the latter gathered into the office to be examined, and the former left at liberty to ramble about an hour until their passports could be signed. We employed the time in trying the flavor of the grapes and peaches of Lombardy, and looking at the groups of travelers who had come down from the Alps with the annual avalanche at this season. The custom house officers were extremely civil and obliging, as they did not think necessary to examine our knapsacks, and our passports being soon signed, we were at liberty to enter again into the dominions of His Majesty of Austria. Our companion, the German, whose feet could carry him no further, took a seat on the top of a diligence for Milan; we left Sesto Calende on foot, and plunged into the cloud of dust which was whirling towards the capital of Northern Italy.

Being now really in the "sunny land," we looked on the scenery with a deep interest. The first thing that struck me was a resemblance to America in the fields of Indian corn, and the rank growth of weeds by the roadside. The mulberry trees and hedges, too, looked quite familiar, coming as we did, from fenceless and hedgeless Germany. But here the resemblance ceased. The people were coarse, ignorant and savage-looking, the villages remarkable for nothing except the contrast between splendid churches and miserable, dirty houses, while the luxurious palaces and grounds of the rich noblemen formed a still greater contrast to the poverty of the people. I noticed also that if the latter are as lazy as they are said to be, they make their horses work for them, as in a walk of a few hours yesterday after noon, we saw two horses drawing heavy loads, drop down apparently dead, and several others seemed nearly ready to do the same.

We spent the night at the little village of Casina, about sixteen miles from Milan, and here made our first experience in the honesty of Italian inns. We had taken the precaution to inquire beforehand the price of a bed; but it seemed unnecessary and unpleasant, as well as evincing a mistrustful spirit, to do the same with every article we asked for, so we concluded to leave it to the host's conscience not to overcharge us. Imagine our astonishment, however, when at starting, a bill was presented to us, in which the smallest articles were set down at three or four times their value. We remonstrated, hut to little purpose; the fellow knew scarcely any French, and we as little Italian, so rather than lose time or temper, we paid what he demanded and went on, leaving him to laugh at the successful imposition. The experience was of value to us, however, and it may serve as a warning to some future traveler.

About noon, the road turned into a broad and beautiful avenue of poplars, down which we saw, at a distance, the triumphal arch terminating the Simplon road, which we had followed from Sesto Calende. Beyond it rose the slight and airy pinnacle of the Duomo. We passed by the exquisite structure, gave up our passports at the gates, traversed the broad Piazza d'Armi, and found ourselves at liberty to choose one of the dozen streets that led into the heart of the city.

# CHAPTER XXXI. — MILAN.

Aug. 21.—While finding our way at random to the "Pension Suisse," whither we had been directed by a German gentleman, we were agreeably impressed with the gaiety and bustle of Milan. The shops and stores are all open to the street, so that the city resembles a great bazaar. It has an odd look to see blacksmiths, tailors and shoemakers working unconcernedly in the open air, with crowds continually passing before them. The streets are filled with venders of fruit, who call out the names with a long, distressing cry, like that of a person in great agony. Organ-grinders parade constantly about and snatches of songs are heard among the gay crowd, on every side.

In this lively, noisy Italian city, nearly all there is to see may be comprised in four things: the Duomo, the triumphal arch over the Simplon, La Scala and the Picture Gallery. The first alone is more interesting than many an entire city. We went there yesterday afternoon soon after reaching here. It stands in an irregular open place, closely hemmed in by houses on two sides, so that it can be seen to advantage from only one point. It is a mixture of the Gothic and Romanesque styles; the body of the structure is entirely covered with statues and richly wrought sculpture, with needle-like spires of white marble rising up from every corner. But of the exquisite, airy look of the whole mass, although so solid and vast, it is impossible to convey an idea. It appears like some fabric of frost-work which winter traces on the window-panes. There is a unity of beauty about the whole, which the eye takes in with a feeling of perfect and satisfied delight.

Ascending the marble steps which lead to the front, I lifted the folds of the heavy curtain and entered. What a glorious aisle! The mighty pillars support a magnificent arched ceiling, painted to resemble fretwork, and the little light that falls through the small windows above, enters tinged with a dim golden hue. A feeling of solemn awe comes over one as he steps with a hushed tread along the colored marble floor, and measures the massive columns till they blend with the gorgeous arches above. There are four rows of these, nearly fifty in all, and when I state that they are eight feet in diameter, and sixty or seventy in height, some idea may be formed of the grandeur of the building. Imagine the Girard College, at Philadelphia, turned into one great hall, with four rows of pillars, equal in size to those around it, reaching to its roof, and you will have a rough sketch of the interior of the Duomo.

In the centre of the cross is a light and beautiful dome; he who will stand under this, and look down the broad middle aisle to the entrance, has one of the sublimest vistas to be found in the world. The choir has three enormous windows, covered with dazzling paintings, and the ceiling is of marble and silver. There are gratings under the high altar, by looking into which, I could see a dark, lonely chamber below, where one or two feeble lamps showed a circle of praying-places. It was probably a funeral vault, which persons visited to pray for the repose of their friends' souls. The Duomo is not yet entirely finished, the workmen being still employed in various parts, but it is said, that when completed there will be four thousand statues on the different parts of it.

The design of the Duomo is said to be taken from Monte Rosa, one of the loftiest peaks of the Alps. Its hundreds of sculptured pinnacles, rising from every part of the body of the church, certainly bear a striking resemblance to the splintered ice-crags of Savoy. Thus we see how Art, mighty and endless in her forms though she be, is in every thing but the child of Nature. Her most divine conceptions are but copies of objects which we behold every day. The faultless beauty of the Corinthian capital—the springing and intermingling arches of the Gothic aisle—the pillared portico or the massive and sky-piercing pyramid—are but attempts at reproducing, by the studied regularity of Art, the ever-varied and ever-beautiful forms of mountain, rock and forest. But there is oftentimes a more thrilling sensation of enjoyment produced by the creations of man's hand and intellect than the grander effects of Nature, existing constantly before our eyes. It would seem as if man marvelled more at his own work than at the work of the Power which created him.

The streets of Milan abound with priests in their cocked hats and long black robes. They all have the same solemn air, and seem to go about like beings shut out from all communion with pleasure. No sight lately has saddened me so much as to see a bright, beautiful boy, of twelve or thirteen years, in those gloomy garments. Poor child! he little knows now what he may have to endure. A lonely, cheerless life, where every affection must be crushed as unholy, and every pleasure denied as a crime! And I knew by his fair brow and tender lip, that he had a warm and loving heart. I could not help regarding this class as victims to a mistaken idea of religious duty, and if I am not mistaken, I read on more than one countenance the traces of passions that burned within. It is mournful to see a people oppressed in the name of religion. The holiest aspirations of man's nature, instead of lifting him up to a nearer view of Christian perfection, are changed into clouds and shut out the light of heaven. Immense treasures, wrung drop by drop from the credulity of the poor and ignorant, are made use of to pamper the luxury of those who profess to be mediators between man and the Deity. The poor wretch may perish of starvation on a floor of precious mosaic, which perhaps his own pittance has helped to form, while ceilings and shrines of inlaid gold mock his dying eye with their useless splendor. Such a system of oppression, disguised under the holiest name, can only be sustained by the continuance of ignorance and blind superstition. Knowledge—Truth—Reason—these are the ramparts which Liberty throws up to guard her dominions from the usurpations of oppression and wrong.

We were last night in La Scala. Rossini's opera of William Tell was advertised, and as we had visited so lately the scene where that glorious historical drama was enacted, we went to see it represented in sound. It is a grand subject, which in the hands of a powerful composer, might be made very effective, but I must confess I was disappointed in the present case. The overture is, however, very beautiful. It begins low and mournful, like the lament of the Swiss over their fallen liberties. Occasionally a low drum is heard, as if to rouse them to action, and meanwhile the lament swells to a cry of despair. The drums now wake the land; the horn of Uri is heard pealing forth its summoning strain, and the echoes seem to come back from the distant Alps. The sound then changes for the roar of battle—the clang of trumpets, drums and cymbals. The whole orchestra did their best to represent this combat in music, which after lasting a short time, changed into the loud, victorious march of the conquerors. But the body of the opera, although it

254

had several fine passages, was to me devoid of interest; in fact, unworthy the reputation of Rossini.

The theatre is perhaps the largest in the world. The singers are all good; in Italy it could not be otherwise, where everybody sings. As I write, a party of Italians in the house opposite have been amusing themselves with going through the whole opera of "La fille du Regiment," with the accompaniment of the piano, and they show the greatest readiness and correctness in their performance. They have now become somewhat boisterous, and appear to be improvising. One young gentleman executes trills with amazing skill, and another appears to have taken the part of a despairing lover, but the lady has a very pretty voice, and warbles on and on, like a nightingale. Occasionally a group of listeners in the street below clap them applause, for as the windows are always open, the whole neighborhood can enjoy the performance.

This forenoon I was in the Picture Gallery. It occupies a part of the Library Building, in the Palazzo Cabrera. It is not large, and many of the pictures are of no value to anybody but antiquarians; still there are some excellent paintings, which render it well worthy a visit. Among these, a marriage, by Raphael, is still in a very good state of preservation, and there are some fine pictures by Paul Veronese and the Caracci. The most admired painting, is "Abraham sending away Hagar," by Guercino. I never saw a more touching expression of grief than in the face of Hagar. Her eyes are red with weeping, and as she listens in an agony of tears to the patriarch's command, she still seems doubting the reality of her doom. The countenance of Abraham is venerable and calm, and expresses little emotion; but one can read in that of Sarah, as she turns away, a feeling of pity for her unfortunate rival.

Next to the Duomo, the most beautiful specimen of architecture in Milan is the ARCH OF PEACE, on the north side of the city, at the commencement of the Simplon Road. It was the intention of Napoleon to carry the road under this arch, across the Piazza d'Armi, and to cut a way for it directly into the heart of the city, but the fall of his dynasty prevented the execution of this magnificent design, as well as the completion of the arch itself. This has been done by the Austrian government, according to the original plan; they have inscribed upon it the name of Francis I., and changed

255

the bas-reliefs of Lodi and Marengo into those of a few fields where their forces had gained the victory. It is even said that in many parts which were already finished, they altered the splendid Roman profile of Napoleon into the haggard and repulsive features of Francis of Austria.

The bronze statues on the top were made by an artist of Bologna, by Napoleon's order, and are said to be the finest works of modern times. In the centre is the goddess of Peace, in a triumphal car, drawn by six horses, while on the corners four angels, mounted, are starting off to convey the tidings to the four quarters of the globe. The artist has caught the spirit of motion and chained it in these moveless figures. One would hardly feel surprised if the goddess, chariot, horses and all, were to start off and roll away through the air.

With the rapidity usual to Americans we have already finished seeing Milan, and shall start to-morrow morning on a walk to Genoa.

# CHAPTER XXXII. — WALK FROM MILAN TO GENOA.

It was finally decided we should leave Milan, so the next morning we arose at five o'clock for the first time since leaving Frankfort. The Italians had commenced operations at this early hour, but we made our way through the streets without attracting quite so much attention as on our arrival. Near the gate on the road to Pavia, we passed a long colonnade which was certainly as old as the times of the Romans. The pillars of marble were quite brown with age, and bound together with iron to keep them from falling to pieces. It was a striking contrast to see this relic of the past standing in the middle of a crowded thoroughfare and surrounded by all the brilliance and display of modern trade.

Once fairly out of the city we took the road to Pavia, along the banks of the canal, just as the rising sun gilded the marble spire of the Duomo. The country was a perfect level, and the canal, which was in many places higher than the land through which it passed, served also as a means of irrigation for the many rice-fields. The sky grew cloudy and dark, and before we reached Pavia gathered to a heavy storm. Torrents of rain poured down, accompanied with heavy thunder; we crept under an old gateway for shelter, as no house was near. Finally, as it cleared away, the square brown towers of the old city rose above the trees, and we entered the gate through a fine shaded avenue. Our passports were of course demanded, but we were only detained a minute or two. The only thing of interest is the University, formerly so celebrated; it has at present about eight hundred students.

We have reason to remember the city from another circumstance—the singular attention we excited. I doubt if Columbus was an object of greater curiosity to the simple natives of the new world, than we three Americans were to the good people of Pavia. I know not what part of our dress or appearance could have caused it, but we were watched like wild animals. If we happened to pause and look at anything in the street, there was soon a crowd of attentive observers, and as we passed on, every door and window was full of heads. We stopped in the marketplace to purchase some bread and fruit for dinner, which increased, if possible, the sensation. We saw eyes staring and fingers pointing at us from every door and alley. I am generally willing to contribute as much as possible to the amusement or entertainment of others, but such attention was absolutely embarrassing. There was nothing to do but to appear unconscious of it, and we went along with as much nonchalance as if the whole town belonged to us.

We crossed the Ticino, on whose banks near Pavia, was fought the first great battle between Hannibal and the Romans. On the other side our passports were demanded at the Sardinian frontier and our knapsacks searched, which having proved satisfactory, we were allowed to enter the kingdom. Late in the afternoon we reached the Po, which in winter must be quarter of a mile wide, but the summer heats had dried it up to a small stream, so that the bridge of boats rested nearly its whole length in sand. We sat on the bank in the shade, and looked at the chain of hills which rose in the south, following the course of the Po, crowned with castles and villages and shining towers. It was here that I first began to realize Italian scenery. Although the hills were bare, they lay so warm and glowing in the sunshine, and the deep blue sky spread so calmly above, that it recalled all my dreams of the fair clime we had entered.

We stopped for the night at the little village of Casteggio, which lies at the foot of the hills, and next morning resumed our pilgrimage. Here a new delight awaited us. The sky was of a heavenly blue, without even the shadow of a cloud, and full and fair in the morning sunshine we could see the whole range of the Alps, from the blue hills of Friuli, which sweep down to Venice and the Adriatic, to the lofty peaks which stretch away to Nice and Marseilles! Like a summer cloud, except that they were far more dazzling and glorious, lay to the north of us the glaciers and untrodden snow-fields of the Bernese Oberland; a little to the right we saw the double peak of St. Gothard, where six days before we shivered in the region of eternal winter, while far to the north-west rose the giant dome of Mount Blanc. Monte Rosa stood near him, not far from the Great St. Bernard, and further to the south Mont Cenis guarded the entrance from Piedmont into France. I leave you to conceive the majesty of such a scene, and you may perhaps imagine, for I cannot describe the feelings with which I gazed upon it.

At Tortona, the next post, a great market was being held; the town was filled with country people selling their produce, and with venders of wares of all kinds. Fruit was very abundant—grapes, ripe figs, peaches and melons were abundant, and for a trifle one could purchase a sumptuous banquet. On inquiring the road to Novi, the people made us understand, after much difficulty, that there was a nearer way across the country, which came into the post-road again, and we concluded to take it. After two or three hours' walking in a burning sun, where our only relief was the sight of the Alps and a view of the battle-field of Marengo, which lay just on our right, we came to a stand—the road terminated at a large stream, where workmen were busily engaged in making a bridge across. We pulled off our boots and waded through, took a refreshing bath in the clear waters, and walked on through by-lanes. The sides were lined with luxuriant vines, bending under the ripening vintage, and we often cooled our thirst with some of the rich bunches.

The large branch of the Po we crossed, came down from the mountains, which we were approaching. As we reached the post-road again, they were glowing in the last rays of the sun, and the evening vapors that settled over the plain concealed the distant Alps, although the snowy top of the Jungfrau and her companions the Wetterhorn and Schreckhorn, rose above it like the hills of another world. A castle or church of brilliant white marble glittered on the summit of one of the mountains near us, and as the sun went down without a cloud, the distant summits changed in hue to a glowing purple, amounting almost to crimson, which afterwards darkened into a deep violet. The western half of the sky was of a pale orange, and the eastern a dark red, which blended together in the blue of the zenith, that deepened as twilight came on. I know not if it was a fair specimen of an Italian sunset, but I must say, without wishing to be partial, that though certainly very soft and beautiful, there is no comparison with the splendor of such a scene in America. The day-sky of Italy better deserves its reputation. Although no clearer than our own, it is of a far brighter blue, arching above us like a dome of sapphire and seeming to sparkle all over with a kind of crystal transparency.

We stopped the second night at Arquato, a little village among the mountains, and after having bargained with the merry landlord for our lodgings, in broken Italian, took a last look at the plains of Piedmont and the Swiss Alps, in the growing twilight. We gazed out on the darkening scene till the sky was studded with stars, and went to rest with the exciting thought of seeing Genoa and the Mediterranean on the morrow. Next morning we started early, and after walking some distance made our breakfast in a grove of chesnuts, on the cool mountain side, beside a fresh stream of water. The sky shone like a polished gem, and the glossy leaves of the chesnuts gleamed in the morning sun. Here and there, on a rocky height, stood the remains of some knightly castle, telling of the Goths and Normans who descended through these mountain passes to plunder Rome.

As the sun grew high, the heat and dust became intolerable, and this, in connection with the attention we raised everywhere, made us somewhat tired of foot-traveling in Italy. I verily believe the people took us for pilgrims on account of our long white blouses, and had I a scallop shell I would certainly have stuck it into my hat to complete the appearance. We stopped once to ask a priest the road; when he had told us, he shook hands with us and gave us a parting benediction. At the common inns, where we stopped, we always met with civil treatment, though, indeed, as we only slept in them, there was little chance of practising imposition. We bought our simple meals at the baker's and grocer's, and ate them in the shade of the grape-bowers, whose rich clusters added to the repast. In this manner, we enjoyed Italy at the expense of a franc, daily. About noon, after winding about through the narrow defiles, the road began ascending. The reflected heat from the hills on each side made it like an oven; there was not a breath of air stirring; but we all felt, although no one said it, that from the summit we could see the Mediterranean, and we pushed on as if life or death depended on it. Finally, the highest point came in sight—we redoubled our exertions, and a few minutes more brought us to the top, breathless with fatigue and expectation. I glanced down the other side—there lay a real sea of mountains, all around; the farthest peaks rose up afar and dim, crowned with white towers, and between two of them which

260

stood apart like the pillars of a gateway, we saw the broad expanse of water stretching away to the horizon—

To where the blue of heaven on bluer waves shut down!"

It would have been a thrilling sight to see any ocean, when one has rambled thousands of miles among the mountains and vales of the inland, but to behold this sea, of all others, was glorious indeed! This sea, whose waves wash the feet of Naples, Constantinople and Alexandria, and break on the hoary shores where Troy and Tyre and Carthage have mouldered away!—whose breast has been furrowed by the keels of a hundred nations through more than forty centuries—from the first rude voyage of Jason and his Argonauts, to the thunders of Navarino that heralded the second birth of Greece! You cannot wonder we grew romantic; but short space was left for sentiment in the burning sun, with Genoa to be reached before night. The mountain we crossed is called the Bochetta, one of the loftiest of the sea-Alps (or Apennines)—the road winds steeply down towards the sea, following a broad mountain rivulet, now perfectly dried up, as nearly every stream among the mountains is. It was a long way to us; the mountains seemed as if they would never unfold and let us out on the shore, and our weary limbs did penance enough for a multitude of sins. The dusk was beginning to deepen over the bay and the purple hues of sunset were dying away from its amphitheatre of hills, as we came in sight of the gorgeous city. Half the population were out to celebrate a festival, and we made our entry in the triumphal procession of some saint.

# CHAPTER XXXIII. — SCENES IN GENOA, LEGHORN AND PISA.

Have you ever seen some grand painting of a city, rising with its domes and towers and palaces from the edge of a glorious bay, shut in by mountains—the whole scene clad in those deep, delicious, sunny hues which you admire so much in the picture, although they appear unrealized in Nature? If so, you can figure to yourself Genoa, as she looked to us at sunset, from the battlements west of the city. When we had passed through the gloomy gate of the fortress that guards the western promontory, the whole scene opened at once on us in all its majesty. It looked to me less like a real landscape than a mighty panoramic painting. The battlements where we were standing, and the blue mirror of the Mediterranean just below, with a few vessels moored near the shore, made up the foreground; just in front lay the queenly city, stretching out to the eastern point of the bay, like a great meteor—-this point, crowned with the towers and dome of a cathedral representing the nucleus, while the tail gradually widened out and was lost among the numberless villas that reached to the top of the mountains behind. A mole runs nearly across the mouth of the harbor, with a tall light-house at its extremity, leaving only a narrow passage for vessels. As we gazed, a purple glow lay on the bosom of the sea, while far beyond the city, the eastern half of the mountain crescent around the gulf was tinted with the loveliest hue of orange. The impressions which one derives from looking on remarkable scenery, depend, for much of their effect, on the time and weather. I have been very fortunate in this respect in two instances, and shall carry with me through life, two glorious pictures of a very different character—the wild sublimity of the Brocken in cloud and storm, and the splendor of Genoa in an Italian sunset.

Genoa has been called the "city of palaces." and it well deserves the appellation. Row above row of magnificent structures rise amid gardens along the side of the hills, and many of the streets, though narrow and crooked, are lined entirely with the splendid dwellings of the Genoese nobles. All these speak of the republic in its days of wealth and power, when it could cope successfully with Venice, and Doria could threaten to bridle the horses of St.

Mark. At present its condition is far different; although not so fallen as its rival, it is but a shadow of its former self—the life and energy it possessed as a republic, has withered away under the grasp of tyranny.

We entered Genoa, as I have already said, in a religious procession. On passing the gate we saw from the concourse of people and the many banners hanging from the windows or floating across the streets, that it was the day of a festa. Before entering the city we reached the procession itself, which was one of unusual solemnity. As it was impossible in the dense crowd, to pass it, we struggled through till we reached a good point for seeing the whole, and slowly moved on with it through the city. First went a company of boys in white robes; then followed a body of friars, dressed in long black cassocks, and with shaven crowns; then a company of soldiers with a band of music; then a body of nuns, wrapped from head to foot in blue robes, leaving only a small place to see out of—in the dusk they looked very solemn and ghost-like, and their low chant had to me something awful and sepulchral in it; then followed another company of friars, and after that a great number of priests in white and black robes, bearing the statue of the saint, with a pyramid of flowers, crosses and blazing wax tapers, while companies of soldiery, monks and music brought up the rear. Armed guards walked at intervals on each side of the procession, to keep the way clear and prevent disturbance; two or three bands played solemn airs, alternating with the deep monotonous chanting of the friars. The whole scene, dimly lighted by the wax tapers, produced in me a feeling nearly akin to fear, as if I were witnessing some ghostly, unearthly spectacle. To rites like these, however, which occur every few weeks, the people must be well accustomed.

Among the most interesting objects in Genoa, is the Doria palace, fit in its splendor for a monarch's residence. It stands in the Strada Nova, one of the three principal streets, and I believe is still in the possession of the family. There are many others through the city, scarcely less magnificent, among which that of the Durazzo family may be pointed out. The American consulate is in one of these old edifices, with a fine court-yard and ceilings covered with frescoes. Mr. Moro, the Vice Consul, did us a great kindness, which I feel bound to acknowledge, although it will require the disclosure of some private, and

263

perhaps uninteresting circumstances. On leaving Frankfort, we converted—
for the sake of convenience—the greater part of our funds into a draft on a
Saxon merchant in Leghorn, reserving just enough, as we supposed, to take us
thither. As in our former case, in Germany, the sum was too small, which we
found to our dismay on reaching Milan. Notwithstanding we had traveled the
whole ninety miles from that city to Genoa for three francs each, in the hope
of having enough, left to enable one at least to visit Leghorn, the expenses for
a passport in Genoa (more than twenty francs) prevented this plan. I went
therefore to the Vice Consul to ascertain whether the merchant on whom
the draft was drawn, had any correspondents there, who might advance a
portion of it. His secretary made many inquiries, but without effect; Mr.
Moro then generously offered to furnish me with means to reach Leghorn,
whence I could easily remit a sufficient sum to my two comrades. This put an
end to our anxiety, (for I must confess we could not help feeling some), and I
therefore prepared to leave that evening in the "Virgilio."

The feelings with which I look on this lovely land, are fast changing.
What with the dust and heat, and cheating landlords, and the dull plains of
Lombardy, my first experience was not very prepossessing. But the joyous and
romantic anticipation with which I looked forward to realizing the dream
of my earliest boyhood, is now beginning to be surpassed by the exciting
reality. Every breath I drew in the city of Columbus and Doria, was deeply
tinctured with the magic of history and romance. It was like entering on a
new existence, to look on scenes so lovely by nature and so filled with the
inspiring memories of old.

> *"Italia too, Italia! looking on thee,*
>
> *Full flashes on the soul the light of ages,*
>
> *Since the fierce Carthagenian almost won thee,*
>
> *To the last halo of the chiefs and sages*
>
> *Who glorify thy consecrated pages!*
>
> *Thou wert the throne and grave of empires."*

The Virgilio was advertised to leave at six o'clock, and I accordingly went out to her in a little boat half an hour beforehand; but we were delayed much longer, and I saw sunset again fade over the glorious amphitheatre of palaces and mountains, with the same orange glow—the same purple and crimson flush, deepening into twilight—as before. An old blind man in a skiff, floated around under the bows of the boat on the glassy water, singing to the violin a plaintive air that appeared to be an evening hymn to the virgin. There was something very touching in his venerable countenance, with the sightless eyes turned upward to the sunset heaven whose glory he could never more behold.

The lamps were lit on the tower at the end of the mole as we glided out on the open sea; I stood on deck and watched the receding lights of the city, till they and the mountains above them, were blended with the darkened sky. The sea-breeze was fresh and cool, and the stars glittered with a frosty clearness, which would have made the night delicious had not a slight rolling of the waves obliged me to go below. Here, besides being half seasick, I was placed at the mercy of many voracious fleas, who obstinately stayed, persisting in keeping me company. This was the first time I had suffered from these cannibals, and such were my torments, I almost wished some blood-thirsty Italian would come and put an end to them with his stiletto.

The first ray of dawn that stole into the cabin sent me on deck. The hills of Tuscany lay in front, sharply outlined on the reddening sky; near us was the steep and rocky isle of Gorgona; and far to the south-west, like a low mist along the water, ran the shores of Corsica—the birth place of Columbus and Napoleon![***] As the dawn brightened we saw on the southern horizon a cloud-like island, also imperishably connected with the name of the latter—the prison-kingdom of Elba! North of us extended the rugged mountains of Carrara—that renowned range whence has sprung many a form of almost breathing beauty, and where yet slumber, perhaps, in the unhewn marble, the god-like shapes of an age of art, more glorious than any the world has ever yet beheld!

*** [ By recent registers found in Corsica, it has been determined that this island also gave birth to the discoverer of the new world.]

The sun rose from behind the Apennines and masts and towers became visible through the golden haze, as we approached the shore. On a flat space between the sea and the hills, not far from the foot of Montenero, stands Leghorn. The harbor is protected by a mole, leaving a narrow passage, through which we entered, and after waiting two hours for the visit of the health and police officers, we were permitted to go on shore. The first thing that struck me, was the fine broad streets; the second, the motley character of the population. People were hurrying about noisy and bustling—Greeks in their red caps and capotes; grave turbaned and bearded Turks; dark Moors; the Corsair-looking natives of Tripoli and Tunis, and seamen of nearly every nation. At the hotel where I stayed, we had a singular mixture of nations at dinner:—two French, two Swiss, one Genoese, one Roman, one American and one Turk—and we were waited on by a Tuscan and an Arab! We conversed together in four languages, all at once.

To the merchant, Leghorn is of more importance than to the traveler. Its extensive trade, not only in the manufactures of Tuscany, but also in the productions of the Levant, makes it important to the former, while the latter seeks in vain for fine buildings, galleries of art, or in interesting historical reminiscences. Through the kind attention of the Saxon Consul, to whom I had letters, two or three days went by delightfully.

The only place of amusement here in summer is a drive along the sea shore, called the Ardenza, which is frequented every evening by all who can raise a vehicle. I visited it twice with a German friend. We met one evening the Princess Corsini, wife of the Governor of Leghorn, on horseback—a young, but not pretty woman. The road leads out along the Mediterranean, past an old fortress, to a large establishment for the sea bathers, where it ends in a large ring, around which the carriages pass and re-pass, until sunset has gone out over the sea, when they return to the city in a mad gallop, or as fast as the lean horses can draw them.

In driving around, we met two or three carriages of Turks, in one of which I saw a woman of Tunis, with a curious gilded head-dress, eighteen inches in height.

I saw one night a Turkish funeral. It passed me in one of the outer streets, on its way to the Turkish burying ground. Those following the coffin, which was covered with a heavy black pall, wore white turbans and long white robes—the mourning color of the Turks. Torches were borne by attendants, and the whole company passed on at a quick pace. Seen thus by night, it had a strange and spectral appearance.

There is another spectacle here which was exceedingly revolting to me. The condemned criminals, chained two and two, are kept at work through the city, cleaning the streets. They are dressed in coarse garments of a dirty red color, with the name of the crime for which they were convicted, painted on the back. I shuddered to see so many marked with the words—"omicidio premeditato." All day they are thus engaged, exposed to the scorn and contumely of the crowd, and at night dragged away to be incarcerated in damp, unwholesome dungeons, excavated under the public thoroughfares.

The employment of criminals in this way is common in Italy. Two days after crossing St. Gothard, we saw a company of abject-looking creatures, eating their dinner by the road-side, near Bellinzona. One of them had a small basket of articles of cotton and linen, and as he rose up to offer them to us, I was startled by the clank of fetters. They were all employed to labor on the road.

On going down to the wharf in Leghorn, in the morning, two or three days ago, I found F—— and B—— just stepping on shore from the steamboat, tired enough of the discomforts of the voyage, yet anxious to set out for Florence as soon as possible. After we had shaken off the crowd of porters, pedlars and vetturini, and taken a hasty breakfast at the Cafe Americano, we went to the Police Office to get our passports, and had the satisfaction of paying two francs for permission to proceed to Florence. The weather had changed since the preceding day, and the sirocco-wind which blows over from the coast of Africa, filled the streets with clouds of dust, which made walking very unpleasant. The clear blue sky had vanished, and a leaden cloud hung low on the Mediterranean, hiding the shores of Corsica and the rooky isles of Gorgona and Capraja.

The country between Leghorn and Pisa, is a flat marsh, intersected in several places by canals to carry off the stagnant water which renders this district so unhealthy. It is said that the entire plain between the mountains of Carrara and the hills back of Leghorn has been gradually formed by the deposits of the Arno and the receding of the Mediterranean, which is so shallow along the whole coast, that large vessels have to anchor several miles out. As we approached Pisa over the level marsh, I could see the dome of the Cathedral and the Leaning Tower rising above the gardens and groves which surround it.

Our baggage underwent another examination at the gate, where we were again assailed by the vetturini, one of whom hung on us like a leech till we reached a hotel, and there was finally no way of shaking him off except by engaging him to take us to Florence. The bargain having been concluded, we had still a few hours left and set off to hunt the Cathedral. We found it on an open square near the outer wall, and quite remote from the main part of the town. Emerging from the narrow and winding street, one takes in et a glance the Baptistery, the Campo Santo, the noble Cathedral and the Leaning Tower—forming altogether a view rarely surpassed in Europe for architectural effect. But the square is melancholy and deserted, and rank, untrampled grass fills the crevices of its marble pavement.

I was surprised at the beauty of the Leaning Tower. Instead of all old, black, crumbling fabric, as I always supposed, it is a light, airy, elegant structure, of white marble, and its declension, which is interesting as a work of art (or accident,) is at the same time pleasing from its novelty. There have been many conjectures as to the cause of this deviation, which is upwards of fourteen feet from the perpendicular; it is now generally believed that the earth having sunk when the building was half finished, it was continued by the architects in the same angle. The upper gallery, which is smaller than the others, shows a very perceptible inclination back towards the perpendicular, as if in some degree to counterbalance the deviation of the other part. There are eight galleries in all, supported by marble pillars, but the inside of the Tower is hollow to the very top.

We ascended by the same stairs which were trodden so often by Galileo in going up to make his astronomical observations; in climbing spirally around the hollow cylinder in the dark, it was easy to tell on which side of the Tower we were, from the proportionate steepness of the staircase. There is a fine view from the top, embracing the whole plain as far as Leghorn on one side, with its gardens and grain fields spread out like a vast map. In a valley of the Carrarrese Mountains to the north, we could see the little town of Lucca, much frequented at this season on account of its baths; the blue summits of the Appenines shut in the view to the east. In walking through the city I noticed two other towers, which had nearly as great a deviation from the perpendicular. We met a person who had the key of the Baptistery, which he opened for us. Two ancient columns covered with rich sculpture form the doorway, and the dome is supported by massive pillars of the red marble of Elba. The baptismal font is of the purest Parian marble. The most remarkable thing was the celebrated musical echo. Our cicerone stationed himself at the side of the font and sang a few notes. After a moment's pause they were repeated aloft in the dome, but with a sound of divine sweetness—as clear and pure as the clang of a crystal bell. Another pause—and we heard them again, higher, fainter and sweeter, followed by a dying note, as if they were fading far away into heaven. It seemed as if an angel lingered in the temple, echoing with his melodious lips the common harmonies of earth. Even thus does the music of good deeds, hardly noted in our grosser atmosphere, awake a divine echo in the far world of spirit.

The Campo Santo, on the north side of the Cathedral, was, until lately, the cemetery of the city; the space enclosed within its marble galleries is filled to the depth of eight or ten feet, with earth from the Holy Land. The vessels which carried the knights of Tuscany to Palestine were filled at Joppa, on returning, with this earth as ballast, and on arriving at Pisa it was deposited in the Cemetery. It has the peculiar property of decomposing all human bodies, in the space of two days. A colonnade of marble encloses it, with windows of the most exquisite sculpture opening on the inside. They reminded me of the beautiful Gothic oriels of Melrose. At each end are two fine, green cypresses, which thrive remarkably in the soil of Palestine. The dust of a German emperor, among others, rests in this consecrated ground. There are other fine churches in Pisa, but the four buildings I have mentioned, are the principal objects of interest. The tower where Count Ugolino and his sons were starved to death by the citizens of Pisa, who locked them up and threw the keys into the Arno, has lately been destroyed.

An Italian gentleman having made a bargain in the meantime with our vetturino, we found every thing ready on returning to the hotel. On the outside of the town we mounted into the vehicle, a rickety-looking concern, and as it commenced raining, I was afraid we would have a bad night of it. After a great deal of bargaining, the vetturino agreed to take us to Florence that night for five francs a piece, provided one person would sit on the outside with the driver. I accordingly mounted on front, protected by a blouse and umbrella, for it was beginning to rain dismally. The miserable, bare-boned horses were fastened with rope-traces, and the vetturino having taken the rope-lines in his hand, gave a flourish with his whip; one old horse tumbled nearly to the ground, but he jerked him up again and we rattled off.

After riding ten miles in this way, it became so wet and dreary, that I was fain to give the driver two francs extra, for the privilege of an inside seat. Our Italian companion was agreeable and talkative, but as we were still ignorant of the language, I managed to hold a scanty conversation with him in French. He seemed delighted to learn that we were from America; his polite reserve gave place to a friendly familiarity and he was loud in his praises of the Americans. I asked him why it was that he and the Italians generally, were so friendly towards us. "I hardly know," he answered; "you are so different from any other nation; and then, too, you have so much sincerity!"

The Appenines were wreathed and hidden in thick mist, and the prospect over the flat cornfields bordering the road was not particularly interesting. We had made about one-third of the way as night set in, when on ascending a hill soon after dark, F—— happened to look out, and saw one of the axles bent and nearly broken off. we were obliged to get out and walk through the mud to the next village, when after two hours' delay, the vetturino came along with another carriage. Of the rest of the way to Florence, I cannot say much. Cramped up in the narrow vehicle, we jolted along in the dark, rumbling now and then through some silent village, where lamps were burning before the solitary shrines. Sometimes a blinding light crossed the road, where we saw the tile-makers sitting in the red glare of their kilns, and often the black

270

boughs of trees were painted momentarily on the cloudy sky. If the jolting carriage had even permitted sleep, the horrid cries of the vetturino, urging on his horses, would have prevented it; and I decided, while trying to relieve my aching limbs, that three days' walking in sun and sand was preferable to one night of such travel.

Finally about four o'clock in the morning the carriage stopped; my Italian friend awoke and demanded the cause. "Signor," said the vetturino, "we are in Florence!" I blessed the man, and the city too. The good-humored officer looked at our passports and passed our baggage without examination; we gave the gatekeeper a paul and he admitted us. The carriage rolled through the dark, silent streets—passed a public square—came out on the Arno—crossed and entered the city again—and finally stopped at a hotel. The master of the "Lione Bianco" came down in an undress to receive us, and we shut the growing dawn out of our rooms to steal that repose from the day which the night had not given.

# CHAPTER XXXIV. – FLORENCE AND ITS GALLERIES.

Sept. 11.—Our situation here is as agreeable as we could well desire. We have three large and handsomely furnished rooms, in the centre of the city, for which we pay Signor Lazzeri, a wealthy goldsmith, ten scudo per month—a scudo being a trifle more than an American dollar. We live at the Cafès and Trattone very conveniently for twenty-five cents a day, enjoying moreover, at our dinner in the Trattoria del Cacciatore, the company of several American artists with whom we have become acquainted. The day after our arrival we met at the table d'hote of the "Lione Bianco," Dr. Boardman of New York, through whose assistance we obtained our present lodgings. There are at present ten or twelve American artists in Florence, and we promise ourselves much pleasure and profit from their acquaintance. B—— and I are so charmed with the place and the beautiful Tuscan dialect, that we shall endeavor to spend three or four months here. F—— returns to Germany in two weeks, to attend the winter term of the University at his favorite Heidelberg.

Our first walk in Florence was to the Royal Gallery—we wished to see the "goddess living in stone" without delay. Crossing the neighboring Piazza del Granduca, we passed Michael Angelo's colossal statue of David, and an open gallery containing, besides some antiques, the master-piece of John of Bologna. The palace of the Uffizii, fronting on the Arno, extends along both sides of an avenue running back to the Palazzo Vecchio. We entered the portico which passes around under the great building, and after ascending three or four flights of steps, came into a long hall, filled with paintings and ancient statuary. Towards the end of this, a door opened into the Tribune— that celebrated room, unsurpassed by any in the world for the number and value of the gems it contains. I pushed aside a crimson curtain and stood in the presence of the Venus.

It may be considered heresy, but I confess I did not at first go into raptures, nor perceive any traces of superhuman beauty. The predominant feeling, if I may so express it, was satisfaction; the eye dwells on its faultless outline with a gratified sense, that nothing is wanting to render it perfect. It is the ideal of a woman's form—a faultless standard by which all beauty may be measured, but without striking expression, except in the modest and graceful position of the limbs. The face, though regular, is not handsome, and the body appears small, being but five feet in height, which, I think, is a little below the average stature of women. On each side, as if to heighten its elegance by contrast with rude and unrefined nature, are the statues of the Wrestlers, and the slave listening to the conspiracy of Catiline, called also The Whetter.

As if to correspond with the value of the works it holds, the Tribune is paved with precious marbles and the ceiling studded with polished mother-of-pearl. A dim and subdued light fills the hall, which throws over the mind that half-dreamy tone necessary to the full enjoyment of such objects. On each side of the Venus de Medici hangs a Venus by Titian, the size of life, and painted in that rich and gorgeous style of coloring which has been so often and vainly attempted since his time.

Here are six of Raphael's best preserved paintings. I prefer the "St. John in the Desert" to any other picture in the Tribune. His glorious form, in the fair proportions of ripening boyhood—the grace of his attitude, with the arm lifted eloquently on high—the divine inspiration which illumines his young features—chain the step irresistibly before it. It is one of those triumphs of the pencil which few but Raphael have accomplished—the painting of spirit in its loftiest and purest form. Near it hangs the Fornarina, which he seems to have painted in as deep a love as he entertained for the original. The face is modest and beautiful, and filled with an expression of ardent and tender attachment. I never tire looking upon either of these two.

Let me not forget, while we are in this peerless hall, to point out Guercino's Samian Sybil. It is a glorious work. With her hands clasped over her volume, she is looking up with a face full of deep and expressive sadness. A picturesque turban is twined around her head, and bands of pearls gleam amidst her rich, dark brown tresses. Her face bears the softness of dawning womanhood, and nearly answers my ideal of female beauty. The same artist has another fine picture here—a sleeping Endymion. The mantle has fallen from his shoulders, as he reclines asleep, with his head on his hand, and his crook beside him. The silver crescent of Dian looks over his shoulder from the sky behind, and no wonder if she should become enamored, for a lovelier shepherd has not been seen since that of King Admetus went back to drive his chariot in the heavens.

The "Drunken Bacchus" of Michael Angelo is greatly admired, and indeed it might pass for a relic of the palmiest times of Grecian art. The face, amidst its half-vacant, sensual expression, shows traces of its immortal origin, and there is still an air of dignity preserved in the swagger of his beautiful form. It is, in a word, the ancient idea of a drunken god. It may be doubted whether the artist's talents might not have been employed better than in ennobling intoxication. If he had represented Bacchus as he really is—degraded even below the level of humanity—it might be more beneficial to the mind, though less beautiful to the eye. However, this is a question on which artists and moralists cannot agree. Perhaps, too, the rich blood of the Falernian grape produced a more godlike delirium than the vulgar brandy which oversets the moderns!

At one end of the gallery is a fine copy in marble of the Laocoon, by Bandinelli, one of the rivals of Michael Angelo. When it was finished, the former boasted it was better than the original, to which Michael made the apt reply: "It is foolish for those who walk in the footsteps of others, to say they go before them!"

Let us enter the hall of Niobe. One starts back on seeing the many figures in the attitude of flight, for they seem at first about to spring from their pedestals. At the head of the room stands the afflicted mother, bending over the youngest daughter who clings to her knees, with an upturned countenance of deep and imploring agony. In vain! the shafts of Apollo fall thick, and she will soon be childless. No wonder the strength of that woe depicted on her countenance should change her into stone. One of her sons—a beautiful, boyish form,—is lying on his back, just expiring, with the chill langour of death creeping over his limbs. We seem to hear the quick whistling of the arrows, and look involuntarily into the air to see the hovering figure of the avenging god. In a chamber near is kept the head of a faun, made by Michael Angelo, at the age of fourteen, in the garden of Lorenzo de Medici, from a piece of marble given him by the workmen.

The portraits of the painters are more than usually interesting. Every countenance is full of character. There is the pale, enthusiastic face of Raphael, the stern vigor of Titian, the majesty and dignity of Leonardo da Vinci, and the fresh beauty of Angelica Kauffmann. I liked best the romantic head of Raphael Mengs. In one of the rooms there is a portrait of Alfieri, with an autograph sonnet of his own on the back of it. The house in which he lived and died, is on the north bank of the Arno, near the Ponte Caraja, and his ashes rest in Santa Croce.

Italy still remains the home of art, and it is but just she should keep these treasures, though the age that brought them forth has passed away. They are her only support now; her people are dependent for their subsistence on the glory of the past. The spirits of the old painters, living still on their canvass, earn from year to year the bread of an indigent and oppressed people. This ought to silence those utilitarians at home, who oppose the cultivation of the fine arts, on the ground of their being useless luxuries. Let them look to Italy, where a picture by Raphael or Correggio is a rich legacy for a whole city. Nothing is useless that gratifies that perception of beauty, which is at once the most delicate and the most intense of our mental sensations, binding us by an unconscious link nearer to nature and to Him, whose every thought is born of Beauty, Truth and Love. I envy not the one who looks with a cold and indifferent spirit on these immortal creations of the old masters—these poems written in marble and on the canvass. They who oppose every thing which can refine and spiritualize the nature of man, by binding him down to the cares of the work-day world alone, cheat life of half its glory.

The eighth of this month was the anniversary of the birth of the Virgin, and the celebration, if such it might be called, commenced the evening before, It is the custom, and Heaven only knows how it originated, for the people of the lower class to go through the streets in a company, blowing little penny whistles. We were walking that night in the direction of the Duomo, when we met a band of these men, blowing with all their might on the shrill whistles, so that the whole neighborhood resounded with one continual, piercing, ear-splitting shriek. They marched in a kind of quick trot through the streets, followed by a crowd of boys, and varying the noise occasionally by shouts and howls of the most horrible character. They paraded through all the principal streets of the city, which for an hour sent up such an agonizing scream that you might have fancied it an enormous monster, expiring in great torment. The people seemed to take the whole thing as a matter of course, but it was to us a novel manner of ushering in a religious festival.

The sky was clear and blue, as it always is in this Italian paradise, when we left Florence a few days ago for Fiesole. In spite of many virtuous efforts to rise early, it was nine o'clock before we left the Porta San Gallo, with its triumphal arch to the Emperor Francis, striding the road to Bologna. We passed through the public walk at this end of the city, and followed the road to Fiesole along the dried-up bed of a mountain torrent. The dwellings of the Florentine nobility occupy the whole slope, surrounded with rich and lovely gardens. The mountain and plain are both covered with luxuriant olive orchards, whose foliage of silver gray gives the scene the look of a moonlight landscape.

At the base of the mountain of Fiesole we passed one of the summer palaces of Lorenzo the Magnificent, and a little distance beyond, took a foot-path overshadowed by magnificent cypresses, between whose dark trunks we looked down on the lovely Val d'Arno. But I will reserve all description of the view till we arrive at the summit.

The modern village of Fiesole occupies the site of an ancient city, generally supposed to be of Etrurian origin. Just above, on one of the peaks of the mountain, stands the Acropolis, formerly used as a fortress, but now untenanted save by a few monks. From the side of its walls, beneath the shade of a few cypresses, there is a magnificent view of the whole of Val d'Arno, with Florence—the gem of Italy—in the centre. Stand with me a moment on the height, and let us gaze on this grand panorama, around which the Apennines stretch with a majestic sweep, wrapped in a robe of purple air, through which shimmer the villas and villages on their sides! The lovely vale lies below us in its garb of olive groves, among which beautiful villas are

276

sprinkled as plentifully as white anemones in the woods of May. Florence lies in front of us, the magnificent cupola of the Duomo crowning its clustered palaces. We see the airy tower of the Palazzo Vecchio—the new spire of Santa Croce—and the long front of the Palazzo Pitti, with the dark foliage of the Boboli Gardens behind. Beyond, far to the south, are the summits of the mountains near Siena. We can trace the sandy bed of the Arno down the valley till it disappears at the foot of the Lower Apennines, which mingle in the distance with the mountains of Carrara.

Galileo was wont to make observations "at evening from the top of Fiesole," and the square tower of the old church is still pointed out as the spot. Many a night did he ascend to its projecting terrace, and watch the stars as they rolled around through the clearest heaven to which a philosopher ever looked up.

We passed through an orchard of fig trees, and vines laden with beautiful purple and golden clusters, and in a few minutes reached the remains of an amphitheatre, in a little nook on the mountain side. This was a work of Roman construction, as its form indicates. Three or four ranges of seats alone, are laid bare, and these have only been discovered within a few years. A few steps further we came to a sort of cavern, overhung with wild fig-trees. After creeping in at the entrance, we found ourselves in an oval chamber, tall enough to admit of our standing upright, and rudely but very strongly built. This was one of the dens in which the wild beasts were kept; they were fed by a hole in the top, now closed up. This cell communicates with four or five others, by apertures broken in the walls. I stepped into one, and could see in the dim light, that it was exactly similar to the first, and opened into another beyond.

Further down the mountain we found the ancient wall of the city, without doubt of Etrurian origin. It is of immense blocks of stone, and extends more or less dilapidated around the whole brow of the mountain. In one place there stands a solitary gateway, of large stones, which looks as if it might have been one of the first attempts at using the principle of the arch. These ruins are all gray and ivied, and it startles one to think what a history Earth has lived through since their foundations were laid!

We sat all the afternoon under the cypress trees and looked down on the lovely valley, practising Italian sometimes with two young Florentines who came up to enjoy the "bell'aria" of Fiesole. Descending as sunset drew on, we reached the Porta San Gallo, as the people of Florence were issuing forth to their evening promenade.

One of my first visits was to the church of Santa Croce. This is one of the oldest in Florence, venerated alike by foreigners and citizens, for the illustrious dead whose remains it holds. It is a plain, gloomy pile, the front of which is still unfinished, though at the base, one sees that it was originally designed to be covered with black marble. On entering the door we first saw the tomb of Michael Angelo. Around the marble sarcophagus which contains his ashes are three mourning figures, representing Sculpture, Painting and Architecture, and his bust stands above—a rough, stern countenance, like a man of vast but unrefined mind. Further on are the tombs of Alfieri and Machiavelli and the colossal cenotaph lately erected to Dante. Opposite reposes Galileo. What a world of renown in these few names! It makes one venerate the majesty of his race, to stand beside the dust of such lofty spirits.

Dante's monument may be said to be only erected to his memory; he sleeps at the place of his exile,

*"Like Scipio, buried by the upbraiding shore!"*

It is the work of Ricci, a Florentine artist, and has been placed there within a few years. The colossal figure of Poetry weeping over the empty urn, might better express the regret of Florence in being deprived of his ashes. The figure of Dante himself, seated above, is grand and majestic; his head is inclined as if in meditation, and his features bear the expression of sublime thought. Were this figure placed there alone, on a simple and massive pedestal, it would be more in keeping with his fame than the lumbering heaviness of the present monument.

Machiavelli's tomb is adorned with a female figure representing History, bearing his portrait. The inscription, which seems to be somewhat exaggerated, is: tanto nomini nullum par elogium. Near lies Alfieri, the "prince of tragedy," as he is called by the Italians. In his life he was fond of wandering among the

278

tombs of Santa Croce, and it is said that there the first desire and presentiment of his future glory stirred within his breast. Now he slumbers among them, not the least honored name of that immortal company.

Galileo's tomb is adorned with his bust. His face is calm and dignified, and he holds appropriately in his hands, a globe and telescope. Aretino, the historian, lies on his tomb with a copy of his works clasped to his breast; above that of Lanzi, the historian of painting, there is a beautiful fresco of the angel of fame; and opposite to him is the scholar Lamio. The most beautiful monument in the church is that of a Polish princess, in the transept. She is lying on the bier, her features settled in the repose of death, and her thin, pale hands clasped across her breast. The countenance wears that half-smile, "so coldly sweet and sadly fair," which so often throws a beauty over the face of the dead, and the light pall reveals the fixed yet graceful outline of the form.

In that part of the city, which lies on the south bank of the Arno, is the palace of the Grand Duke, known by the name of the Palazzo Pitti, from a Florentine noble of that name, by whom it was first built. It is a very large, imposing pile, preserving an air of lightness in spite of the rough, heavy stones of which it is built. It is another example of a magnificent failure. The Marquis Strozzi, having built a palace which was universally admired for its beauty, (which stands yet, a model of chaste and massive elegance,) his rival, the Marquis Pitti, made the proud boast that he would build a palace, in the court-yard of which could bo placed that of Strozzi. These are actually the dimensions of the court-yard; but in building the palace, although he was liberally assisted by the Florentine people, he ruined himself, and his magnificent residence passed into other hands, while that of Strozzi is inhabited by his descendants to this very day.

The gallery of the Palazzo Pitti is one of the finest in Europe. It contains six or seven hundred paintings, selected from the best works of the Italian masters. By the praiseworthy liberality of the Duke, they are open to the public, six hours every day, and the rooms are thronged with artists of all nations.

Among Titian's works, there is his celebrated "Bella," a half-length figure of a young woman. It is a masterpiece of warm and brilliant coloring, without any decided expression. The countenance is that of vague, undefined thought, as of one who knew as yet nothing of the realities of life. In another room is his Magdalen, a large, voluptuous form, with her brown hair falling like a veil over her shoulders and breast, but in her upturned countenance one can sooner read a prayer for an absent lover than repentance for sins she has committed.

What could excel in beauty the Madonna della Sedia of Raphael? It is another of those works of that divine artist, on which we gaze and gaze with a never-tiring enjoyment of its angelic beauty. To my eye it is faultless; I could not wish a single outline of form, a single shade of color changed. Like his unrivalled Madonna in the Dresden Gallery, its beauty is spiritual as well as earthly; and while gazing on the glorious countenance of the Jesus-child, I feel an impulse I can scarcely explain—a longing to tear it from the canvas as if it were a breathing form, and clasp it to my heart in a glow of passionate love. What a sublime inspiration Raphael must have felt when he painted it! Judging from its effect on the beholder, I can conceive of no higher mental excitement than that required to create it.

Here are also some of the finest and best preserved pictures of Salvator Rosa, and his portrait—a wild head, full of spirit and genius. Besides several landscapes in his savage and stormy style, there are two large sea-views, in which the atmosphere is of a deep and exquisite softness, without impairing the strength and boldness of the composition. "A Battle Scene," is terrible. Hundreds of combatants are met in the shock and struggle of conflict. Horses, mailed knights, vassals are mixed together in wild confusion; banners are waving and lances flashing amid the dust and smoke, while the wounded and dying are trodden under foot in darkness and blood. I now first begin to comprehend the power and sublimity of his genius. From the wildness and gloom of his pictures, he might almost be called the Byron of painters.

There is a small group of the "Fates," by Michael Angelo, which is one of the best of the few pictures which remain of him. As is well known, he disliked the art, saying it was only fit for women. This picture shows, however, how much higher he might have gone, had he been so inclined. The three weird sisters are ghostly and awful—the one who stands behind, holding the distaff, almost frightful. She who stands ready to cut the thread as it is spun out, has a slight trace of pity on her fixed and unearthly lineaments. It is a faithful embodiment of the old Greek idea of the Fates. I have wondered why some artist has not attempted the subject in a different way. In the Northern Mythology they are represented as wild maidens, armed with swords and mounted on fiery coursers. Why might they not also be pictured as angels, with countenances of a sublime and mysterious beauty—one all radiant with hope and promise of glory, and one with the token of a better future mingled with the sadness with which it severs the links of life?

There are many, many other splendid works in this collection, but it is unnecessary to mention them. I have only endeavored, by taking a few of the best known, to give some idea of them as they appear to me. There are hundreds of pictures here, which, though gems in themselves, are by masters who are rarely heard of in America, and it would be of little interest to go through the Gallery, describing it in guide-book fashion. Indeed, to describe galleries, however rich and renowned they may be, is in general a work of so much difficulty, that I know not whether the writer or the reader is made most tired thereby.

This collection possesses also the celebrated statue of Venus, by Canova. She stands in the centre of a little apartment, filled with the most delicate and graceful works of painting. Although undoubtedly a figure of great beauty, it by no means struck me as possessing that exquisite and classic perfection which has been ascribed to it. The Venus de Medici far surpasses it. The head is larger in proportion to the size of the body, than that of the latter, but has not the same modest, virgin expression. The arm wrapped in the robe which she is pressing to her breast, is finely executed, but the fingers of the other hand are bad—looking, as my friend said, as if the ends were whittled off! The body is, however, of fine proportions, though, taken as a whole, the statue is inferior to many other of Canova's works.

Occupying all the hill back of the Pitti Palace, are the Boboli Gardens, three times a week the great resort of the Florentines. They are said to be the most beautiful gardens in Italy. Numberless paths, diverging from a magnificent amphitheatre in the old Roman style, opposite the court-yard, lend either in long flights of steps and terraces, or gentle windings among beds sweet with roses, to the summit. Long avenues, entirely arched and interwoven with the thick foliage of the laurel, which here grows to a tree, stretch along the slopes or wind in the woods through thickets of the fragrant bay. Parterres, rich with flowers and shrubbery, alternate with delightful groves of the Italian pine, acacia and laurel-leaved oak, and along the hillside, gleaming among the foliage, are placed statues of marble, some of which are from the chisels of Michael Angelo and Bandinelli. In one part there is a little sheet of water, with an island of orange-trees in the centre, from which a broad avenue of cypresses and statues leads to the very summit of the hill.

We often go there to watch the sun set over Florence and the vale of the Arno. The palace lies directly below, and a clump of pine-trees on the hillside, that stand out in bold relief on the glowing sky, makes the foreground to one of the loveliest pictures this side of the Atlantic. I saw one afternoon the Grand Duke and his family get into their carriage to drive out. One of the little dukes, who seemed a mischievous imp, ran out on a projection of the portico, where considerable persuasion had to be used to induce him to jump into the arms of his royal papa. I turned from these titled infants to watch a group of beautiful American children playing, for my attention was drawn to them by the sound of familiar words, and I learned afterwards they were the children of the sculptor Powers. I contrasted involuntarily the destinies of each;—one to the enjoyment and proud energy of freedom, and one to the confining and vitiating atmosphere of a court. The merry voices of the latter, as they played on the grass, came to my ears most gratefully. There is nothing so sweet as to hear one's native tongue in a foreign land from the lips of children!

# CHAPTER XXXV. — A PILGRIMAGE TO VALLOMBROSA.

A pilgrimage to Vallombrosa!—in sooth it has a romantic sound. The phrase calls up images of rosaries, and crosses, and shaven-headed friars. Had we lived in the olden days, such things might verily have accompanied our journey to that holy monastery. We might then have gone barefoot, saying prayers as we toiled along the banks of the Arno and up the steep Appenines, as did Benevenuto Cellini, before he poured the melted bronze into the mould of his immortal Perseus. But we are pilgrims to the shrines of Art and Genius; the dwelling-places of great minds are our sanctuaries. The mean dwelling, in which a poet has battled down poverty with the ecstacy of his mighty conceptions, and the dungeon in which a persecuted philosopher has languished, are to us sacred; we turn aside from the palaces of kings and the battle-fields of conquerors, to visit them. The famed miracles of San Giovanni Gualberto added little, in our eyes, to the interest of Vallombrosa, but there were reverence and inspiration in the names of Dante, Milton, and Ariosto.

We left Florence early, taking the way that leads from the Porta della Croce, up the north bank of the Arno. It was a bright morning, but there was a shade of vapor on the hills, which a practised eye might have taken as a prognostic of the rain that too soon came on. Fiesole, with its tower and Acropolis, stood out brightly from the blue background, and the hill of San Miniato lay with its cypress groves in the softest morning light. The Contadini were driving into the city in their basket wagons, and there were some fair young faces among them, that made us think Italian beauty was not altogether in the imagination.

After walking three or four miles, we entered the Appenines, keeping along the side of the Arno, whose bed is more than half dried up from the long summer heats. The mountain sides were covered with vineyards, glowing with their wealth of white and purple grapes, but the summits were naked and barren. We passed through the little town of Ponte Sieve, at the entrance of a romantic valley, where our view of the Arno was made more interesting by the lofty range of the Appenines, amid whose forests we could see the white front of the monastery of Vallombrosa. But the clouds sank low and hid it from sight, and the rain came on so hard that we were obliged to take shelter occasionally in the cottages by the wayside. In one of these we made a dinner of the hard, black bread of the country, rendered palatable by the addition of mountain cheese and some chips of an antique Bologna sausage. We were much amused in conversing with the simple hosts and their shy, gipsy-like children, one of whom, a dark-eyed, curly-haired boy, bore the name of Raphael. We also became acquainted with a shoemaker and his family, who owned a little olive orchard and vineyard, which they said produced enough to support them. Wishing to know much a family of six consumed in a year, we inquired the yield of their property. They answered, twenty small barrels of wine, and ten of oil. It was nearly sunset when we reached Pellago, and the wet walk and coarse fare we were obliged to take on the road, well qualified us to enjoy the excellent supper the pleasant landlady gave us.

This little town is among the Appenines, at the foot of the magnificent mountain of Vallombrosa. What a blessing it was for Milton, that he saw its loveliness before his eyes closed on this beautiful earth, and gained from it another hue in which to dip his pencil, when he painted the bliss of Eden! I watched the hills all day as we approached them, and thought how often his eyes had rested on their outlines, and how he had carried their forms in his memory for many a sunless year. The banished Dante, too, had trodden them, flying from his ungrateful country; and many another, whose genius has made him a beacon in the dark sea of the world's history. It is one of those places where the enjoyment is all romance, and the blood thrills as we gaze upon it.

We started early next morning, crossed the ravine, and took the well-paved way to the monastery along the mountain side. The stones are worn smooth by the sleds in which ladies and provisions are conveyed up, drawn by the beautiful white Tuscan oxen. The hills are covered with luxuriant chesnut and oak trees, of those picturesque forms which they only wear in Italy: one wild dell in particular is much resorted to by painters for the ready-made foregrounds it supplies. Further on, we passed the Paterno, a rich farm belonging to the Monks. The vines which hung from tree to tree, were almost breaking beneath clusters as heavy and rich as those which the children of Israel bore on staves from the Promised Land. Of their flavor, we can say, from experience, they were worthy to have grown in Paradise. We then entered a deep dell of the mountain, where little shepherd girls were sitting on the rocks tending their sheep and spinning with their fingers from a distaff, in the same manner, doubtless, as the Roman shepherdesses two thousand years ago. Gnarled, gray olive trees, centuries old, grew upon the bare soil, and a little rill fell in many a tiny cataract down the glen. By a mill, in one of the coolest and wildest nooks I ever saw, two of us acted the part of water-spirits under one of these, to the great astonishment of four peasants, who watched us from a distance.

Beyond, our road led through forests of chestnut and oak, and a broad view of mountain and vale lay below us. We asked a peasant boy we met, how much land the Monks of Vallombrosa possessed. "All that you see!" was the reply. The dominion of the good fathers reached once even to the gates of Florence. At length, about noon, we emerged from the woods into a broad avenue leading across a lawn, at whose extremity stood the massivs buildings of the monastery. On a rock that towered above it, was the Paradisino, beyond which rose the mountain, covered with forests—

*"Shade above shade, a woody theatre.*

*Of stateliest view"*—

as Milton describes it. We were met at the entrance by a young monk in cowl and cassock, to whom we applied for permission to stay till the next day, which was immediately given. Brother Placido (for that was his name) then asked us if we would not have dinner. We replied that our appetites were none the worse for climbing the mountain; and in half an hour sat down to a dinner, the like of which we had not seen for a long time. Verily, thought I, it must be a pleasant thing to be a monk, after all!—that is, a monk of Vallombrosa.

In the afternoon we walked through a grand pine forest to the western brow of the mountain, where a view opened which it would require a wonderful

power of the imagination for you to see in fancy, as I did in reality. From the
height where we stood, the view was uninterrupted to the Mediterranean,
a distance of more than seventy miles; a valley watered by a brunch of the
Arno swept far to the east, to the mountains near the Luke of Thrasymene;
northwestwards the hills of Carrara bordered the horizon; the space between
these wide points was filled with mountains and valleys, all steeped in that
soft blue mist which makes Italian landscapes more like heavenly visions than
realities. Florence was visible afar off, and the current of the Arno flashed in
the sun. A cool and almost chilling wind blew constantly over the mountain,
although the country below basked in summer heat. We lay on the rocks,
and let our souls luxuriate in the lovely scene till near sunset. Brother Placido
brought us supper in the evening, with his ever-smiling countenance, and
we soon after went to our beds in the neat, plain chambers, to get rid of the
unpleasant coldness.

Next morning it was damp and misty, and thick clouds rolled down the
forests towards the convent. I set out for the "Little Paradise," taking in my
way the pretty cascade which falls some fifty feet down the rocks. The building
is not now as it was when Milton lived here, having been rebuilt within a
short time. I found no one there, and satisfied my curiosity by climbing over
the wall and looking in at the windows. A little chapel stands in a cleft of the
rock below, to mark the miraculous escape of St. John Gualberto, founder
of the monastery. Being one day very closely pursued by the Devil, he took
shelter under the rock, which immediately became soft and admitted him
into it, while the fiend, unable to stop, was precipitated over the steep. All
this is related in a Latin inscription, and we saw a large hollow in the rock
near, which must have been intended for the imprint left by his sacred person.

One of the monks told us another legend, concerning a little chapel
which stands alone on a wild part of the mountain, above a rough pile of
crags, called the "Peak of the Devil." "In the time of San Giovanni Gualberto,
the holy founder of our order," said he, "there was a young man, of a noble
family in Florence, who was so moved by the words of the saintly father, that
he forsook the world, wherein he had lived with great luxury and dissipation,
and became monk. But, after a time, being young and tempted again by the

pleasures he had renounced, he put off the sacred garments. The holy San Giovanni warned him of the terrible danger in which he stood, and at length the wicked young man returned. It was not a great while, however, before he became dissatisfied, and in spite all holy counsel, did the same thing again. But behold what happened! As he was walking along the peak where the chapel stands, thinking nothing of his great crime, the devil sprang suddenly from behind a rock, and catching the young man in his arms, before he could escape, carried him with a dreadful noise and a great red flame and smoke over the precipice, so that he was never afterwards seen."

The church attached to the monastery is small, but very solemn and venerable. I went several times to muse in its still, gloomy aisle, and hear the murmuring chant of the Monks, who went through their exercises in some of the chapels. At one time I saw them all, in long black cassocks, march in solemn order to the chapel of St. John Gualberto, where they sang a deep chant, which to me had something awful and sepulchral in it. Behind the high altar I saw their black, carved chairs of polished oak, with ponderous gilded foliants lying on the rails before them. The attendant opened one of these, that we might see the manuscript notes, three or four centuries old, from which they sung.

We were much amused in looking through two or three Italian books, which were lying in the traveler's room. One of these which our friend Mr. Tandy, of Kentucky, read, described the miracles of the patron saint with an air of the most ridiculous solemnity. The other was a description of the Monastery, its foundation, history, etc. In mentioning its great and far-spread renown, the author stated then even an English poet, by the name of Milton, had mentioned it in the following lines, which I copied verbatim from the book:

> *"Thick as autumnal scaves that strow she brooks*
>
> *In vallombrosa, whereth Etruian Jades*
>
> *Stigh over orch d'embrover!"*

In looking over the stranger's book, I found among the names of my countrymen, that of S. V. Clevenger, the talented and lamented sculptor who died at sea on his passage home. There were also the names of Mrs. Shelley and the Princess Potemkin, and I saw written on the wall, the autograph of Jean Reboul, the celebrated modern French poet. We were so delighted with the place we would have stayed another day, but for fear of trepassing too much on the lavish and unceasing hospitality of the good fathers.

So in the afternoon we shook hands with Brother Placido, and turned our backs regretfully upon one of the loneliest and loveliest spots of which earth can boast. The sky became gradually clear as we descended, and the mist raised itself from the distant mountains. We ran down through the same chesnut groves, diverging a little to go through the village of Tosi, which is very picturesque when seen from a distance, but extremely dirty to one passing through. I stopped in the ravine below to take a sketch of the mill and bridge, and as we sat, the line of golden sunlight rose higher on the mountains above. On walking down the shady side of this glen, we were enraptured with the scenery. A brilliant yet mellow glow lay over the whole opposing height, lighting up the houses of Tosi and the white cottages half seen among the olives, while the mountain of Vallombrosa stretched far heavenward like a sunny painting, with only a misty wreath floating and waving around its summit. The glossy foliage of the chesnuts was made still brighter by the warm light, and the old olives softened down into a silvery gray, whose contrast gave the landscape a character of the mellowest beauty. As we wound out of the deep glen, the broad valleys and ranges of the Appenines lay before us, forests, castles and villages steeped in the soft, vapory blue of the Italian atmosphere, and the current of the Arno flashing like a golden belt through the middle of the picture.

The sun was nearly down, and the mountains just below him were of a deep purple hue, while those that ran out to the eastward wore the most aerial shade of blue. A few scattered clouds, floating above, soon put on the sunset robe of orange and a band of the same soft color encircled the western horizon. It did not reach half way to the zenith, however; the sky above was blue, of such a depth and transparency, that to gaze upward was like looking into eternity. Then how softly and soothingly the twilight came on! How deep a hush sank on the chesnut glades, broken only by the song of the cicada, chirping its "good-night carol!" The mountains, too, how majestic they stood in their deep purple outlines! Sweet, sweet Italy! I can feel now how the soul may cling to thee, since thou canst thus gratify its insatiable thirst for the Beautiful. Even thy plainest scene is clothed in hues that seem borrowed of heaven! In the twilight, more radiant than light, and the stillness, more eloquent than music, which sink down over the sunny beauty of thy shores, there is a silent, intense poetry that stirs the soul through all its impassioned depths. With warm, blissful tears filling the eyes and a heart overflowing with its own bright fancies, I wander in the solitude and calm of such a time, and love thee as if I were a child of thy soil!

# CHAPTER XXXVI. — WALK TO SIENA AND PRATOLINO—INCIDENTS IN FLORENCE.

October 16.—My cousin, being anxious to visit Rome, and reach Heidelberg before the commencement of the winter semestre, set out towards the end of September, on foot. We accompanied him as far as Siena, forty miles distant. As I shall most probably take another road to the Eternal City, the present is a good opportunity to say something of that romantic old town, so famous throughout Italy for the honesty of its inhabitants.

We dined the first day, seventeen miles from Florence, at Tavenella, where, for a meagre dinner the hostess had the assurance to ask us seven pauls. We told her we would give but four and a half, and by assuming a decided manner, with a plentiful use of the word "Signora" she was persuaded to be fully satisfied with the latter sum. From a height near, we could see the mountains coasting the Mediterranean, and shortly after, on descending a long hill, the little town of Poggibonsi lay in the warm afternoon light, on an eminence before us. It was soon passed with its dusky towers, then Stagia looking desolate in its ruined and ivied walls, and following the advice of a peasant, we stopped for the night at the inn of Querciola. As we knew something of Italian by this time, we thought it best to inquire the price of lodging, before entering. The padrone asked if we meant to take supper also. We answered in the affirmative; "then," said he, "you will pay half a paul (about five emits) apiece for a bed." We passed under the swinging bunch of boughs, which in Italy is the universal sign of an inn for the common people, and entered the bare, smoky room appropriated to travelers. A long table, with well-worn benches, were the only furniture; we threw our knapsacks on one end of it and sat down, amusing ourselves while supper was preparing, in looking at a number of grotesque charcoal drawings on the wall, which the flaring light of our tall iron lamp revealed to us. At length the hostess, a kindly-looking woman, with a white handkerchief folded gracefully around her head, brought us a dish of fried eggs, which, with the coarse black bread of the peasants and a basket full of rich grapes, made us an excellent supper.

We slept on mattresses stuffed with corn husks, placed on square iron frames, which are the bedsteads most used in Italy. A brightly-painted caricature of some saint or a rough crucifix, trimmed with bay leaves, hung at the head of each bed, and under their devout protection we enjoyed a safe and unbroken slumber.

Next morning we set out early to complete the remaining ten miles to Siena. The only thing of interest on the road, is the ruined wall and battlements of Castiglione, circling a high hill and looking as old as the days of Etruria. The towers of Siena are seen at some distance, but approaching it from this side, the traveler does not perceive its romantic situation until he arrives. It stands on a double hill, which is very steep on some sides; the hollow between the two peaks is occupied by the great public square, ten or fifteen feet lower than the rest of the city. We left our knapsacks at a cafè and sought the celebrated Cathedral, which stands in the highest part of the town, forming with its flat dome and lofty marble tower, an apex to the pyramidal mass of buildings.

The interior is rich and elegantly perfect. Every part is of black and white marble, in what I should call the striped style, which has a singular but agreeable effect. The inside of the dome and the vaulted ceilings of the chapels, are of blue, with golden stars; the pavement in the centre is so precious a work that it is kept covered with boards and only shown once a year. There are some pictures of great value in this Cathedral; one of "The Descent of the Dove," is worthy of the best days of Italian art. In an adjoining chamber, with frescoed walls, and a beautiful tesselated pavement, is the library, consisting of a few huge old volumes, which with their brown covers and brazen clasps, look as much like a collection of flat leather trunks as any thing else. In the centre of the room stands the mutilated group of the Grecian Graces, found in digging the foundation of the Cathedral. The figures are still beautiful and graceful, with that exquisite curve of outline which is such a charm in the antique statues. Canova has only perfected the idea in his celebrated group, which is nearly a copy of this.

We strolled through the square and then accompanied our friend to the Roman gate, where we took leave of him for six months at least. He felt lonely at the thought of walking in Italy without a companion, but was cheered by the anticipation of soon reaching Rome. We watched him awhile, walking rapidly over the hot plain towards Radicofani, and then, turning our faces with much pleasure towards Florence, we commenced the return walk. I must not forget to mention the delicious grapes which we bought, begged and stole on the way. The whole country is like one vineyard—and the people live, in a great measure, on the fruit, during this part of the year. Would you not think it highly romantic and agreeable to sit in the shade of a cypress grove, beside some old weather-beaten statues, looking out over the vales of the Appenines, with a pile of white and purple grapes beside you, the like of which can scarcely be had in America for love or money, and which had been given you by a dark-eyed peasant girl? If so, you may envy us, for such was exactly our situation on the morning before reaching Florence.

Being in the Duomo, two or three days ago, I met a German traveler, who has walked through Italy thus far, and intends continuing his journey to Rome and Naples. His name is Von Raumer. He was well acquainted with the present state of America, and I derived much pleasure from his intelligent conversation. We concluded to ascend the cupola in company. Two black-robed boys led the way; after climbing an infinite number of steps, we reached the gallery around the foot of the dome. The glorious view of that paradise, the vale of the Arno, shut in on all sides by mountains, some bare and desolate, some covered with villas, gardens, and groves, lay in soft, hazy light, with the shadows of a few light clouds moving slowly across it. They next took us to a gallery on the inside of the dome, where we first saw the immensity of its structure. Only from a distant view, or in ascending it, can one really measure its grandeur. The frescoes, which from below appear the size of life, are found to be rough and monstrous daubs; each figure being nearly as many fathoms in length as a man is feet. Continuing our ascent, we mounted between the inside and outside shells of the dome. It was indeed a bold idea for Brunelleschi to raise such a mass in air. The dome of Saint Peter's, which is scarcely as large, was not made until a century after, and this was, therefore, the first attempt at raising one on so grand a scale. It seems still as solid as if just built.

There was a small door in one of the projections of the lantern, which the sacristan told us to enter and ascend still higher. Supposing there was a fine view to be gained, two priests, who had just come up, entered it; the German followed, and I after him. After crawling in at the low door, we found ourselves in a hollow pillar, little wider than our bodies. Looking up, I saw the German's legs just above my head, while the other two were above him, ascending by means of little iron bars fastened in the marble. The priests were very much amused, and the German said:—"This is the first time I ever learned chimney-sweeping!" We emerged at length into a hollow cone, hot and dark, with a rickety ladder going up somewhere; we could not see where. The old priest, not wishing to trust himself to it, sent his younger brother up, and we shouted after him:—"What kind of a view have you?" He climbed up till the cone got so narrow he could go no further, and answered back in the darkness:—"I see nothing at all!" Shortly after he came down, covered with dust and cobwebs, and we all descended the chimney quicker than we went up. The old priest considered it a good joke, and laughed till his fat sides shook. We asked the sacristan why he sent us up, and he answered:—"To see the construction of the Church!"

I attended service in the Cathedral one dark, rainy morning, and was never before so deeply impressed with the majesty and grandeur of the mighty edifice. The thick, cloudy atmosphere darkened still more the light which came through the stained windows, and a solemn twilight reigned in the long aisles. The mighty dome sprang far aloft, as if it enclosed a part of heaven, for the light that struggled through the windows around its base, lay in broad bars on the blue, hazy air. I would not have been surprised at seeing a cloud float along within it. The lofty burst of the organ, that seemed like the pantings of a monster, boomed echoing away through dome and nave, with a chiming, metallic vibration, that shook the massive pillars which it would defy an earthquake to rend. All was wrapped in dusky obscurity, except where, in the side-chapels, crowns of tapers were burning around the images. One knows not which most to admire, the genius which could conceive, or the perseverance which could accomplish such a work, On one side of the square, the colossal statue of the architect, glorious old Brunelleschi, is most appropriately placed, looking up with pride at his performance.

The sunshine and genial airs of Italy have gone, leaving instead a cold, gloomy sky and chilling winds. The autumnal season has fairly commenced, and I suppose I must bid adieu to the brightness which made me in love with the land. The change has been no less sudden than unpleasant, and if, as they say, it will continue all winter with little variation, I shall have to seek a clearer climate. In the cold of these European winters, there is, as I observed last year in Germany, a dull, damp chill, quite different from the bracing, exhilarating frosts of America. It stagnates the vital principle and leaves the limbs dull and heavy, with a lifeless feeling which can scarcely be overcome by vigorous action. At least, such has been my experience.

We lately made an excursion to Pratolino, on the Appenines, to see the vintage and the celebrated colossus, by John of Bologna. Leaving Florence in the morning, with a cool, fresh wind blowing down from the mountains, we began ascending by the road to Bologna. We passed Fiesole with its tower and acropolis on the right, ascending slowly, with the bold peak of one of the loftiest Appenines on our left. The abundant fruit of the olive was beginning to turn brown, and the grapes were all gathered in from the vineyards, but we learned from a peasant boy that the vintage was not finished at Pratolino.

We finally arrived at an avenue shaded with sycamores, leading to the royal park. The vintagers were busy in the fields around, unloading the vines of their purple tribute, and many a laugh and jest among the merry peasants enlivened the toil. We assisted them in disposing of some fine clusters, and then sought the "Colossus of the Appenines." He stands above a little lake, at the head of a long mountain-slope, broken with clumps of magnificent trees. This remarkable figure, the work of John of Bologna, impresses one like a relic of the Titans. He is represented as half-kneeling, supporting himself with one hand, while the other is pressed upon the head of a dolphin, from which a little stream falls into the lake. The height of the figure when erect, would amount to more than sixty feet! We measured one of the feet, which is a single piece of rock, about eight feet long; from the ground to the top of one knee is nearly twenty feet. The limbs are formed of pieces of stone, joined together, and the body of stone and brick. His rough hair and eyebrows, and the beard, which reached nearly to the ground, are formed of stalactites, taken from caves, and fastened together in a dripping and crusted mass. These hung also from his limbs and body, and gave him the appearance of Winter in his

294

mail of icicles. By climbing up the rocks at his back, we entered his body, which contains a small-sized room; it was even possible to ascend through his neck and look out at his ear! The face is in keeping with the figure—stern and grand, and the architect (one can hardly say sculptor) has given to it the majestic air and sublimity of the Appenines. But who can build up an image of the Alp?

We visited the factory on the estate, where wine and oil are made. The men had just brought in a cart load of large wooden vessels, filled with grapes, which they were mashing with heavy wooden pestles. When the grapes were pretty well reduced to pulp and juice, they emptied them into an enormous tub, which they told us would be covered air-tight, and left for three or four weeks, after which the wine would be drawn off at the bottom. They showed us also a great stone mill for grinding olives; this estate of the Grand Duke produces five hundred barrels of wine and a hundred and fifty of oil, every year. The former article is the universal beverage of the laboring classes in Italy, or I might say of all classes; it is, however, the pure blood of the grape, and although used in such quantities, one sees little drunkenness—far less than in our own land.

Tuscany enjoys at present a more liberal government than any other part of Italy, and the people are, in many respects, prosperous and happy. The Grand Duke, although enjoying almost absolute privileges, is disposed to encourage every measure which may promote the welfare of his subjects. The people are, indeed, very heavily taxed, but this is less severely felt by them, than it would be by the inhabitants of colder climes. The soil produces with little labor all that is necessary for their support; though kept constantly in a state of comparative poverty, they appear satisfied with their lot, and rarely look further than the necessities of the present. In love with the delightful climate, they cherish their country, fallen as she is, and are rarely induced to leave her. Even the wealthier classes of the Italians travel very little; they can learn the manners and habits of foreigners nearly as well in their own country as elsewhere, and they prefer their own hills of olive and vine to the icy grandeur of the Alps or the rich and garden-like beauty of England.

But, although this sweet climate, with its wealth of sunlight and balmy airs, may enchant the traveler for awhile and make him wish at times that his whole life might be spent amid such scenes, it exercises a most enervating influence on those who are born to its enjoyment. It relaxes mental and physical energy, and disposes body and mind to dreamy inactivity. The Italians, as a race, are indolent and effeminate. Of the moral dignity of man they have little conception. Those classes who are engaged in active occupation seem even destitute of common honesty, practising all kinds of deceits in the most open manner and apparently without the least shame. The state of morals is lower than in any other country of Europe; what little virtue exists is found among the peasants. Many of the most sacred obligations of society are universally violated, and as a natural consequence, the people are almost entire strangers to that domestic happiness, which constitutes the true enjoyment of life.

This dark shadow in the moral atmosphere of Italy hangs like a curse on her beautiful soil, weakening the sympathies of citizens of freer lands with her fallen condition. I often feel vividly the sentiment which Percival puts into the mouth of a Greek in slavery:

> *"The spring may here with autumn twine*
>
> *And both combined may rule the year,*
>
> *And fresh-blown flowers and racy wine*
>
> *In frosted clusters still be near—*
>
> *Dearer the wild and snowy hills*
>
> *Where hale and ruddy Freedom smiles."*

No people can ever become truly great or free, who are not virtuous. If the soul aspires for liberty—pure and perfect liberty—it also aspires for everything that is noble in Truth, everything that is holy in Virtue. It is greatly to be feared that all those nervous and impatient efforts which have been made and are still being made by the Italian people to better their condition, will be of little avail, until they set up a better standard of principle and make their private actions more conformable with their ideas of political independence.

Oct. 22.—I attended to-day the fall races at the Cascine. This is a dairy farm of the Grand Duke on the Arno, below the city; part of it, shaded with magnificent trees, has been made into a public promenade and drive, which extends for three miles down the river. Towards the lower end, on a smooth green lawn, is the race-course. To-day was the last of the season, for which the best trials had been reserved; on passing out the gate at noon, we found a number of carriages and pedestrians going the same way. It was the very perfection of autumn temperature, and I do not remember to have ever seen so blue hills, so green meadows, so fresh air and so bright sunshine combined in one scene before. All that gloom and coldness of which I lately complained has vanished.

Traveling increases very much one's capacity for admiration. Every beautiful scene appears as beautiful as if it had been the first; and although I may have seen a hundred times as lovely a combination of sky and landscape, the pleasure which it awakens is never diminished. This is one of the greatest blessings we enjoy—the freshness and glory which Nature wears to our eyes forever. It shows that the soul never grows old—that the eye of age can take in the impression of beauty with the same enthusiastic joy that leaped through the heart of childhood.

We found the crowd around the race-course but thin; half the people there, and all the horses, appeared to be English. It was a good place to observe the beauty of Florence, which however, may be done in a short time, as there is not much of it. There is beauty in Italy, undoubtedly, but it is either among the peasants or the higher class of nobility. I will tell our American women confidentially, for I know they have too much sense to be vain of it, that they surpass the rest of the world as much in beauty as they do in intelligence and virtue. I saw in one of the carriages the wife of Alexander Dumas, the French author. She is a large, fair complexioned woman, and is now, from what cause I know not, living apart from her husband.

The jockeys paced up and down the fields, preparing their beautiful animals for the approaching heat, and as the hour drew nigh the mounted dragoons busied themselves in clearing the space. It was a one-mile course, to the end of the lawn and back. At last the bugle sounded, and off went three steeds like arrows let fly. They passed us, their light limbs bounding over the turf, a beautiful dark-brown taking the lead. We leaned over the railing and watched them eagerly. The bell rang—they reached the other end—we saw them turn and come dashing back, nearer, nearer; the crowd began to shout, and in a few seconds the brown one had won it by four or five lengths. The fortunate horse was led around in triumph, and I saw an English lady, remarkable for her betting propensities, come out from the crowd and kiss it in apparent delight.

After an interval, three others took the field—all graceful, spirited creatures. This was a more exciting race than the first; they flew past us nearly abreast, and the crowd looked after them in anxiety. They cleared the course like wild deer, and in a minute or two came back, the racer of an English nobleman a short distance ahead. The jockey threw up his hand in token of triumph as he approached the goal, and the people cheered him. It was a beautiful sight to see those noble animals stretching to the utmost of their speed, as they dashed down the grassy lawn. The lucky one always showed by his proud and erect carriage, his consciousness of success.

Florence is fast becoming modernized. The introduction of gas, and the construction of the railroad to Pisa, which is nearly completed, will make sad havoc with the air of poetry which still lingers in its silent streets. There is scarcely a bridge, a tower, or a street, which is not connected with some stirring association. In the Via San Felice, Raphael used to paint when a boy; near the Ponte Santa Trinita stands Michael Angelo's house, with his pictures, clothes, and painting implements, just as he left it three centuries ago; on the south side of the Arno is the house of Galileo, and that of Machiavelli stands in an avenue near the Ducal Palace. While threading my way through some dark, crooked streets in an unfrequented part of the city, I noticed an old, untenanted house, bearing a marble tablet above the door. I drew near and read:—"In this house of the Alighieri was born the Divine Poet!" It was the birth-place of Dante!

Nov. 1.—Yesterday morning we were apprised of the safe arrival of a new scion of the royal family in the world by the ringing of the city bells. To-day, to celebrate the event, the shops were closed, and the people made a holiday of it. Merry chimes pealed out from every tower, and discharges of cannon thundered up from the fortress. In the evening the dome of the Cathedral was illuminated, and the lines of cupola, lantern, and cross were traced in flame on the dark sky, like a crown of burning stars dropped from Heaven on the holy pile. I went in and walked down the aisle, listening for awhile to the grand choral, while the clustered tapers under the dome quivered and trembled, as if shaken by the waves of music which burst continually within its lofty concave.

A few days ago Prince Corsini, Prime Minister of Tuscany, died at an advanced age. I saw his body brought in solemn procession by night, with torches and tapers, to the church of Santa Trinita. Soldiers followed with reversed arms and muffled drums, the band playing a funeral march. I forced myself through the crowd into the church, which was hung with black and gold, and listened to the long drawn chanting of the priests around the bier.

We lately visited the Florentine Museum. Besides the usual collection of objects of natural history, there is an anatomical cabinet, very celebrated for its preparations in wax. All parts of the human frame are represented so wonderfully exact, that students of medicine pursue their studies here in summer with the same facility as from real "subjects." Every bone, muscle, and nerve in the body is perfectly counterfeited, the whole forming a collection as curious as it is useful. One chamber is occupied with representations of the plague of Rome, Milan, and Florence. They are executed with horrible truth to nature, but I regretted afterwards having seen them. There are enough forms of beauty and delight in the world on which to employ the eye, without making it familiar with scenes which can only be remembered with a shudder.

We derive much pleasure from the society of the American artists who are now residing in Florence. At the houses of Powers, and Brown, the painter, we spend many delightful evenings in the company of our gifted countrymen. They are drawn together by a kindred, social feeling as well as by their mutual aims, and form among themselves a society so unrestrained, American-like, that the traveler who meets them forgets his absence for a time. These noble representatives of our country, all of whom possess the true, inborn spirit of republicanism, have made the American name known and respected in Florence. Powers, especially, who is intimate with many of the principal Italian families, is universally esteemed. The Grand Duke has more than once visited his studio and expressed the highest admiration of his talents.

# CHAPTER XXXVII. — AMERICAN ART IN FLORENCE.

I have seen Ibrahim Pacha, the son of old Mehemet Ali, driving in his carriage through the streets. He is hero on a visit from Lucca, where he has been spending some time on account of his health. He is a man of apparently fifty years of age; his countenance wears a stern and almost savage look, very consistent with the character he bears and the political part he has played. He is rather portly in person, the pale olive of his complexion contrasting strongly with a beard perfectly white. In common with all his attendants, he wears the high red cap, picturesque blue tunic and narrow trowsers of the Egyptians. There is scarcely a man of them whose face with its wild, oriental beauty, does not show to advantage among us civilized and prosaic Christians.

In Florence, and indeed through all Italy, there is much reason for our country to be proud of the high stand her artists are taking. The sons of our rude western clime, brought up without other resources than their own genius and energy, now fairly rival those, who from their cradle upwards have drawn inspiration and ambition from the glorious masterpieces of the old painters and sculptors. Wherever our artists are known, they never fail to create a respect for American talent, and to dissipate the false notions respecting our cultivation and refinement, which prevail in Europe. There are now eight or ten of our painters and sculptors in Florence, some of whom, I do not hesitate to say, take the very first rank among living artists.

I have been highly gratified in visiting the studio of Mr. G.L. Brown, who, as a landscape painter, is destined to take a stand second to few, since the days of Claude Lorraine. He is now without a rival in Florence, or perhaps in Italy, and has youth, genius and a plentiful stock of the true poetic enthusiasm for his art, to work for him far greater triumphs. His Italian landscapes have that golden mellowness and transparency of atmosphere which give such a charm to the real scenes, and one would think he used on his pallette, in addition to the more substantial colors, condensed air and sunlight and the liquid crystal of streams. He has wooed Nature like a lover, and she has not withheld her sympathy. She has taught him how to raise and curve her trees, load their boughs with foliage, and spread underneath them the broad, cool shadows—to pile up the shattered crag, and steep the long mountain range in the haze of alluring distance.

He has now nearly finished, a large painting of "Christ Preaching in the Wilderness," which is of surprising beauty. You look upon one of the fairest scenes of Judea. In front, the rude multitude are grouped on one side, in the edge of a magnificent forest; on the other side, towers up a rough wall of rock and foliage that stretches back into the distance, where some grand blue mountains are piled against the sky, and a beautiful stream, winding through the middle of the picture, slides away out of the foreground. Just emerging from the shade of one of the cliffs, is the benign figure of the Saviour, with the warm light which breaks from behind the trees, falling around him as he advances. There is a smaller picture of the "Shipwreck of St. Paul," in which he shows equal skill in painting a troubled sea and breaking storm. He is one of the young artists from whom we have most to hope.

I have been extremely interested in looking over a great number of sketches made by Mr. Kellogg, of Cincinnati, during a tour through Egypt, Arabia Petræa and Palestine. He visited many places out of the general route of travelers, and beside the great number of landscape views, brought away many sketches of the characters and costumes of the Orient. From some of these he has commenced paintings, which, as his genius is equal to his practice, will be of no ordinary value. Indeed, some of these must give him at once an established reputation in America. In Constantinople, where he resided several months, he enjoyed peculiar advantges for the exercise of his art, through the favor and influence of Mr. Carr, the American, and Sir Stratford Canning, the British Minister. I saw a splendid diamond cup, presented to him by Riza Pacha, the late Grand Vizier. The sketches he brought from thence and from the valleys of Phrygia and the mountain solitudes of old Olympus, are of great interest and value. Among his later paintings, I might mention an angel, whose countenance beams with a rapt and glorious beauty. A divine light shines through all the features and heightens the glow of adoration to an expression all spiritual and immortal. If Mr. Kellogg will give us a few more

302

of these heavenly conceptions, we will place him on a pedestal, little lower than that of Guido.

Greenough, who has been sometime in Germany, returned lately to Florence, where he has a colossal group in progress for the portico of the Capitol. I have seen part of it, which is nearly finished in the marble. It shows a backwoodsman just triumphing in the struggle with an Indian; another group to be added, will represent the wife and child of the former. The colossal size of the statues gives a grandeur to the action, as if it were a combat of Titans; there is a consciousness of power, an expression of lofty disdain in the expansion of the hunter's nostril and the proud curve of his lip, that might become a god. The spirit of action, of breathing, life-like exertion, so much more difficult to infuse into the marble than that of repose, is perfectly attained. I will not enter into a more particular description, as it will probably be sent to the United States in a year or two. It is a magnificent work; the best, unquestionably, that Greenough has yet made. The subject, and the grandeur he has given it in the execution, will ensure it a much more favorable reception than a false taste gave to his Washington.

Mr. C.B. Ives, a young sculptor from Connecticut, has not disappointed the high promise he gave before leaving home. I was struck with some of his busts in Philadelphia, particularly those of Mrs. Sigourney and Joseph R. Chandler, and it has been no common pleasure to visit his studio here in Florence, and look on some of his ideal works. He has lately made two models, which, when finished in marble, will be works of great beauty. They will contribute greatly to his reputation here and in America. One of these represents a child of four or five years of age, holding in his hand a dead bird, on which he is gazing, with childish grief and wonder, that it is so still and drooping. It is a beautiful thought; the boy is leaning forward as he sits, holding the lifeless playmate close in his hands, his sadness touched with a vague expression, as if he could not yet comprehend the idea of death.

The other is of equal excellence, in a different style; it is a bust of "Jephthah's daughter," when the consciousness of her doom first flashes upon her. The face and bust are beautiful with the bloom of perfect girlhood. A simple robe covers her breast, and her rich hair is gathered up behind, and bound with a slender fillet. Her head, of the pure classical mould, is bent forward, as if weighed down by the shock, and there is a heavy drooping in the mouth and eyelids, that denotes a sudden and sickening agony. It is not a violent, passionate grief, but a deep and almost paralyzing emotion—a shock from which the soul will finally rebound, strengthened to make the sacrifice.

Would it not be better for some scores of our rich merchants to lay out their money on statues and pictures, instead of balls and spendthrift sons? A few such expenditures, properly directed, would do much for the advancement of the fine arts. An occasional golden blessing, bestowed on genius, might be returned on the giver, in the fame he had assisted in creating. There seems, however, to be at present a rapid increase in refined taste, and a better appreciation of artistic talent, in our country. And as an American, nothing has made me feel prouder than this, and the steadily increasing reputation of our artists.

Of these, no one has done more within the last few years, than Powers. With a tireless and persevering energy, such as could have belonged to few but Americans, he has already gained a name in his art, that posterity will pronounce in the same breath with Phidias, Michael Angelo and Thorwaldsen. I cannot describe the enjoyment I have derived from looking at his matchless works. I should hesitate in giving my own imperfect judgment of their excellence, if I had not found it to coincide with that of many others who are better versed in the rules of art. The sensation which his "Greek Slave" produced in England, has doubtless ere this been breezed across the Atlantic, and I see by the late American papers that they are growing familiar with his fame. When I read a notice seven or eight years ago, of the young sculptor of Cincinnati, whose busts exhibited so much evidence of genius, I little dreamed I should meet him in Florence, with the experience of years of toil added to his early enthusiasm, and every day increasing his renown.

You would like to hear of his statue of Eve, which men of taste pronounce one of the finest works of modern times. A more perfect figure never filled my eye. I have seen the masterpieces of Thorwaldsen, Dannecker and Canova, and the Venus de Medici, but I have seen nothing yet that can exceed the beauty of this glorious statue. So completely did the first view excite my surprise and delight, and thrill every feeling that awakes at the sight of the Beautiful, that my mind dwelt intensely on it for days afterwards. This is the Eve of Scripture—the Eve of Milton—mother of mankind and fairest of all her race. With the full and majestic beauty of ripened womanhood, she wears the purity of a world as yet unknown to sin. With the hearing of a queen, there is in her countenance the softness and grace of a tender, loving woman;

*"God-like erect, with native honor clad*

*In naked majesty."*

She holds the fatal fruit extended in her hand, and her face expresses the struggle between conscience, dread and desire. The serpent, whose coiled length under the leaves and flowers entirely surrounds her, thus forming a beautiful allegorical symbol, is watching her decision from an ivied trunk at her side. Her form is said to be fully as perfect as the Venus de Medici, and from its greater size, has an air of conscious and ennobling dignity. The head is far superior in beauty, and soul speaks from every feature of the countenance. I add a few stanzas which the contemplation of this statue called forth. Though unworthy the subject, they may perhaps faintly shadow the sentiment which Powers has so eloquently embodied in marble:

*THE "EVE" OF POWERS.*

*A faultless being from the marble sprung,*

   *She stands in beauty there!*

*As when the grace of Eden 'round her clung—*

   *Fairest, where all was fair!*

*Pure, as when first from God's creating hand*

   *She came, on man to shine;*

*So seems she now, in living stone to stand—*

   *A mortal, yet divine!*

*The spark the Grecian from Olympus caught,*

    *Left not a loftier trace;*

*The daring of the sculptor's hand has wrought*

    *A soul in that sweet face!*

*He won as well the sacred fire from heaven.*

    *God-sent, not stolen down,*

*And no Promethean doom for him is given,*

    *But ages of renown!*

*The soul of beauty breathes around that form*

    *A more enchanting spell;*

*There blooms each virgin grace, ere yet the storm*

    *On blighted Eden fell!*

*The first desire upon her lovely brow,*

    *Raised by an evil power;*

*Doubt, longing, dread, are in her features now—*

    *It is the trial-hour!*

*How every thought that strives within her breast,*

    *In that one glance is shown!*

*Say, can that heart of marble be at rest,*

    *Since spirit warms the stone?*

*Will not those limbs, of so divine a mould,*

    *Move, when her thought is o'er—*

*When she has yielded to the tempter's hold*

*And Eden blooms no more?*

*Art, like a Phoenix, springs from dust again—*

   *She cannot pass away!*

*Bound down in gloom, she breaks apart the chain*

   *And struggles up today!*

*The flame, first kindled in the ages gone,*

   *Has never ceased to burn,*

*And westward now, appears the kindling dawn,*

   *Which marks the day's return!*

The "Greek Slave" is now in the possession of Mr. Grant, of London, and I only saw the clay model. Like the Eve, it is a form that one's eye tells him is perfect, unsurpassed; but it is the budding loveliness of a girl, instead of the perfected beauty of a woman. In England it has been pronounced superior to Canova's works, and indeed I have seen nothing of his, that could be placed beside it.

Powers has now nearly finished a most exquisite figure of a fisher-boy, standing on the shore, with his net and rudder in one hand, while with the other he holds a shell to his ear and listens if it murmur to him of a gathering storm. His slight, boyish limbs are full of grace and delicacy—you feel that the youthful frame could grow up into nothing less than an Apollo. Then the head—how beautiful! Slightly bent on one side, with the rim of the shell thrust under his locks, lips gently parted, and the face wrought up to the most hushed and breathless expression, he listens whether the sound be deeper than its wont. It makes you hold your breath and listen, to look at it. Mrs. Jameson somewhere remarks that repose or suspended motion, should be always chosen for a statue that shall present a perfect, unbroken impression to the mind. If this be true, the enjoyment must be much more complete where not only the motion, but almost breath and thought are suspended, and all the faculties wrought into one hushed and intense sensation. In gazing on this exquisite conception, I feel my admiration filled to the utmost, without that painful, aching impression, so often left by beautiful works. It glides into my vision like a form long missed from the gallery of beauty I am forming in my mind, and I gaze on it with an ever new and increasing delight.

Now I come to the last and fairest of all—the divine Proserpine. Not the form, for it is but a bust rising from a capital of acanthus leaves, which curve around the breast and arms and turn gracefully outward, but the face, whose modest maiden beauty can find no peer among goddesses or mortals. So looked she on the field of Ennæ—that "fairer flower," so soon to be gathered by "gloomy Dis." A slender crown of green wheatblades, showing alike her descent from Ceres and her virgin years, circles her head. Truly, if Pygmalion stole his fire to warm such a form as this, Jove should have pardoned him. Of Powers' busts it is unnecessary for me to speak. He has lately finished a very beautiful one of the Princess Demidoff, daughter of Jerome Bonaparte.

We will soon, I hope, have the "Eve" in America. Powers has generously refused many advantageous offers for it, that he might finally send it home; and his country, therefore, will possess this statue, his first ideal work. She may well be proud of the genius and native energy of her young artist, and she should repay them by a just and liberal encouragement.

## CHAPTER XXXVIII. – AN ADVENTURE ON THE GREAT ST. BERNARD– WALKS AROUND FLORENCE.

Nov. 9.—A few days ago I received a letter from my cousin at Heidelberg, describing his solitary walk from Genoa over the Alps, and through the western part of Switzerland. The news of his safe arrival dissipated the anxiety we were beginning to feel, on account of his long silence, while it proved that our fears concerning the danger of such a journey were not altogether groundless. He met with a startling adventure on the Great St. Bernard, which will be best described by an extract from his own letter:

"Such were my impressions of Rome. But leaving the 'Eternal City,' I must hasten on to give you a description of an adventure I met with in crossing the Alps, omitting for the present an account of the trip from Rome to Genoa, and my lonely walk through Sardinia. When I had crossed the mountain range north of Genoa, the plains of Piedmont stretched out before me. I could see the snowy sides and summits of the Alps more than one hundred miles distant, looking like white, fleecy clouds on a summer day. It was a magnificent prospect, and I wonder not that the heart of the Swiss soldier, after years of absence in foreign service, beats with joy when he again looks on his native mountains.

"As I approached nearer, the weather changed, and dark, gloomy clouds enveloped them, so that they seemed to present an impassible barrier to the lands beyond them. At Ivrea, I entered the interesting valley of Aosta. The whole valley, fifty miles in length, is inhabited by miserable looking people, nearly one half of them being afflicted with goitre and cretinism. They looked more idiotic and disgusting than any I have ever seen, and it was really painful to behold such miserable specimens of humanity dwelling amid the grandest scenes of nature. Immediately after arriving in the town of Aosta, situated at the upper end of the valley, I began, alone, the ascent of the Great St. Bernard. It was just noon, and the clouds on the mountains indicated rain. The distance from Aosta to the monastery or hospice of St. Bernard, is about twenty English miles.

"At one o'clock it commenced raining vary hard, and to gain shelter I went into a rude hut; but it was filled with so many of those idiotic cretins, lying down on the earthy floor with the dogs and other animals, that I was glad to leave them as soon as the storm had abated in some degree. I walked rapidly for three hours, when I met a traveler and his guide descending the mountain. I asked him in Italian the distance to the hospice, and he undertook to answer me in French, but the words did not seem to flow very fluently, so I said quickly, observing then that he was an Englishman: 'Try some other language, if you please, sir!' He replied instantly in his vernacular: 'You have a d——d long walk before you, and you'll have to hurry to get to the top before night!' Thanking him, we shook hands and hurried on, he downward and I upward. About eight miles from the summit, I was directed into the wrong path by an ignorant boy who was tending sheep, and went a mile out of the course, towards Mont Blanc, before I discovered my mistake. I hurried back into the right path again, and soon overtook another boy ascending the mountain, who asked me if he might accompany me as he was alone, to which I of course answered, yes; but when we began to enter the thick clouds that covered the mountains, he became alarmed, and said he would go no farther. I tried to encourage him by saying we had only five miles more to climb, but, turning quickly, he ran down the path and was soon out of sight.

"After a long and most toilsome ascent, spurred on as I was by the storm and the approach of night, I saw at last through the clouds a little house, which I supposed might be a part of the monastery, but it turned out to be only a house of refuge, erected by the monks to take in travelers in extreme cases or extraordinary danger. The man who was staying there, told me the monastery was a mile and a half further, and thinking therefore that I could soon reach it, I started out again, although darkness was approaching. In a short time the storm began in good earnest, and the cold winds blew with the greatest fury. It grew dark very suddenly and I lost sight of the poles which are placed along the path to guide the traveler. I then ran on still higher, hoping to find them again, but without success. The rain and snow fell thick, and although I think I am tolerably courageous, I began to be alarmed, for it was

310

impossible to know in what direction I was going. I could hear the waterfalls dashing and roaring down the mountain hollows on each side of me; in the gloom, the foam and leaping waters resembled streaming fires. I thought of turning back to find the little house of refuge again, but it seemed quite as dangerous and uncertain as to go forward. After the fatigue I had undergone since noon, it would have been dangerous to be obliged to stay, out all night in the driving storm, which was every minute increasing in coldness and intensity.

"I stopped and shouted aloud, hoping I might be somewhere near the monastery, but no answer came—no noise except the storm and the roar of the waterfalls. I climbed up the rocks nearly a quarter of a mile higher, and shouted again. I listened with anxiety for two or three minutes, but hearing no response, I concluded to find a shelter for the night under a ledge of rocks. While looking around me, I fancied I heard in the distance a noise like the trampling of hoofs over the rocks, and thinking travelers might be near, I called aloud for the third time. After wailing a moment, a voice came ringing on my ears through the clouds, like one from Heaven in response to my own. My heart beat quickly; I hurried in the direction from which the sound came, and to my joy found two men—servants of the monastery— who were driving their mules into shelter. Never in my whole life was I more glad to hear the voice of man. These men conducted me to the monastery, one-fourth of a mile higher, built by the side of a lake at the summit of the pass, while on each side, the mountains, forever covered with snow, tower some thousands of feet higher.

"Two or three of the noble St. Bernard dogs barked a welcome as we approached, which brought a young monk to the door. I addressed him in German, but to my surprise he answered in broken English. He took me into a warm room and gave me a suit of clothes, such as are worn by the monks, for my dress, as well as my package of papers, were completely saturated with rain. I sat down to supper in company with till the monks of the Hospice, I in my monkish robe looking like one of the holy order. You would have laughed to have seen me in their costume. Indeed, I felt almost satisfied to turn monk, as everything seemed so comfortable in the warm supper room, with its blazing wood fire, while outside raged the storm still more violently. But when I thought of their voluntary banishment from the world, up in that high pass of the Alps, and that the affection of woman never gladdened their hearts, I was ready to renounce my monkish dress next morning, without reluctance.

"In the address book of the monastery, I found Longfellow's 'Excelsior' written on a piece of paper and signed 'America.' You remember the stanza:

*At break of clay, as heavenward,*

*The pious monks of St. Bernard*

*Uttered the oft-repeated prayer,*

*A voice cried through the startled air:*

*Excelsior!*

It seemed to add a tenfold interest to the poem, to read it on old St. Bernard. In the morning I visited the house where are kept the bodies of the travelers, who perish in crossing the mountain. It is filled with corpses, ranged in rows, and looking like mummies, for the cold is so intense that they will keep for years without decaying, and are often recognized and removed by their friends.

"Of my descent to Martigny, my walk down the Rhone, and along the shores of Lake Leman, my visit to the prison of Chilian and other wanderings across Switzerland, my pleasure in seeing the old river Rhine again, and my return to Heidelberg at night, with the bright moon shining on the Neckar and the old ruined castle, I can now say no more, nor is it necessary, for are not all these things 'written in my book of Chronicles,' to be seen by you when we meet again in Paris?

Ever yours, FRANK."

Dec. 16.—I took a walk lately to the tower of Galileo. In company with three friends, I left Florence by the Porta Romana, and ascended the Poggie Imperiale. This beautiful avenue, a mile and a quarter in length, leading up a gradual ascent to a villa of the Grand Duke, is bordered with splendid cypresses and evergreen oaks, and the grass banks are always fresh and green, so that even in winter it calls up a remembrance of summer. In fact, winter does not wear the scowl here that he has at home; he is robed rather in a threadbare garment of autumn, and it is only high up on the mountain tops, out of the reach of his enemy, the sun, that he dares to throw it off, and bluster about with his storms and scatter down his snow-flakes. The roses still bud and bloom in the hedges, the emerald of the meadows is not a whit paler, the sun looks down lovingly as yet, and there are only the white helmets of some of the Appenines, with the leafless mulberries and vines, to tell us that we have changed seasons.

A quarter of an hour's walk, part of it by a path through an olive orchard, brought us to the top of a hill, which was surmounted by a square, broken, ivied tower, forming part of a storehouse for the produce of the estate. We entered, saluted by a dog, and passing through a court-yard, in which stood two or three carts full of brown olives, found our way to the rickety staircase. I spared my sentiment in going up, thinking the steps might have been renewed since Galileo's time, but the glorious landscape which opened around us when we reached the top, time could not change, and I gazed upon it with interest and emotion, as my eye took in those forms which had once been mirrored in the philosopher's. Let me endeavor to describe the features of the scene.

Fancy yourself lifted to the summit of a high hill, whose base slopes down to the valley of the Arno, and looking northward. Behind you is a confusion of hill and valley, growing gradually dimmer away to the horizon. Before and below you is a vale, with Florence and her great domes and towers in its lap, and across its breadth of five miles the mountain of Fiesole. To the west it stretches away unbroken for twenty miles, covered thickly with white villas—like a meadow of daisies, magnified. A few miles to the east the plain is rounded with mountains, between whose interlocking bases we can see the brown current of the Arno. Some of their peaks, as well as the mountain of Vallombrosa, along the eastern sky, are tipped with snow. Imagine the air filled with a thick blue mist, like a semi-transparent veil, which softens every thing into dreamy indistinctness, the sunshine falling slantingly through this

313

in spots, touching the landscape here and there as with a sudden blaze of fire, and you will complete the picture. Does it not repay your mental flight across the Atlantic.

One evening, on coming out of the cafè, the moon was shining so brightly and clearly, that I involuntarily bent my steps towards the river; I walked along the Lung'Arno, enjoying the heavenly moonlight—"the night of cloudless climes and starry skies!" A purer silver light never kissed the brow of Endymion. The brown Arno took into his breast "the redundant glory," and rolled down his pebbly bed with a more musical ripple; opposite stretched the long mass of buildings—the deep arches that rose from the water were filled with black shadow, and the irregular fronts of the houses touched with a mellow glow. The arches of the upper bridge were in shadow, cutting their dark outline on the silvery sweep of the Appenines, far up the stream. A veil of luminous gray covered the hill of San Miniato, with its towers and cypress groves, and there was a crystal depth in the atmosphere, as if it shone with its own light. The whole scene affected me as something too glorious to be real—painful from the very intensity of its beauty. Three moons ago, at the foot of Vallombrosa, I saw the Appenines flooded with the same silvery gush, and thought also, then, that I had seen the same moon amid far dearer scenes, but never before the same dreamy and sublime glory showered down from her pale orb. Some solitary lights were burning along the river, and occasionally a few Italians passed by, wrapped in their mantles. I went home to the Piazza del Granduca as the light, pouring into the square from behind the old palace, fell over the fountain of Neptune and sheathed in silver the back of the colossal god.

Whoever looks on the valley of the Arno from San Miniato, and observes the Appenine range, of which Fiesole is one, bounding it on the north, will immediately notice to the northwest a double peak rising high above all the others. The bare, brown forehead of this, known by the name of Monte Morello, seemed so provokingly to challenge an ascent, that we determined to try it. So we started early, the day before yesterday, from the Porta San Gallo, with nothing but the frosty grass and fresh air to remind us of the middle of December. Leaving the Prato road, at the base of the mountain, we passed

314

Careggi, a favorite farm of Lorenzo the Magnificent, and entered a narrow glen where a little brook was brawling down its rocky channel. Here and there stood a rustic mill, near which women were busy spreading their washed clothes on the grass. Following the footpath, we ascended a long eminence to a chapel where some boys were amusing themselves with a common country game. They have a small wheel, around which they wind a rope, and, running a little distance to increase the velocity, let it off with a sudden jerk. On a level road it can be thrown upwards of a quarter of a mile.

From the chapel, a gradual ascent along the ridge of a hill brought us to the foot of the peak, which rose high before us, covered with bare rocks and stunted oaks. The wind blew coldly from a snowy range to the north, as we commenced ascending with a good will. A few shepherds were leading their flocks along the sides, to browse on the grass and withered bushes, and we started up a large hare occasionally from his leafy covert. The ascent was very toilsome; I was obliged to stop frequently on account of the painful throbbing of my heart, which made it difficult to breathe. When the summit was gained, we lay down awhile on the leeward side to recover ourselves.

We looked on the great valley of the Arno, perhaps twenty-five miles long, and five or six broad, lying like a long elliptical basin sunk among the hills. I can liken it to nothing but a vast sea; for a dense, blue mist covered the level surface, through which the domes of Florence rose up like a craggy island, while the thousands of scattered villas resembled ships, with spread sails, afloat on its surface. The sharp, cutting wind soon drove us down, with a few hundred bounds, to the path again. Three more hungry mortals did not dine at the Cacciatore that day.

The chapel of the Medici, which we visited, is of wonderful beauty. The walls are entirely encrusted with pietra dura and the most precious kinds of marble. The ceiling is covered with gorgeous frescoes by Benevenuto, a modern painter. Around the sides, in magnificent sarcophagi of marble and jasper, repose the ashes of a few Cosmos and Ferdinands. I asked the sacristan for the tomb of Lorenzo the Magnificent. "Oh!" said he, "he lived during the republic—he has no tomb; these are only for Dukes!" I could not repress a sigh at the lavish waste of labor and treasure on this one princely chapel. They might have slumbered unnoted, like Lorenzo, if they had done as much for their country and Italy.

December 19.—It is with a heavy heart, that I sit down tonight to make my closing note in this lovely city and in the journal which has recorded my thoughts and impressions since leaving America. I should find it difficult to analyze my emotions, but I know that they oppress me painfully. So much rushes at once over the mind and heart—memories of what has passed through both, since I made the first note in its pages—alternations of hope and anxiety and aspiration, but never despondency—that it resembles in a manner, the closing of a life. I seem almost to have lived through the common term of a life in this short period. Much spiritual and mental experience has crowded into a short time the sensations of years. Painful though some of it has been, it was still welcome. Difficulty and toil give the soul strength to crush, in a loftier region, the passions which draw strength only from the earth. So long as we listen to the purer promptings within us, there is a Power invisible, though not unfelt, who protects us—amid the toil and tumult and soiling struggle, there is ever an eye that watches, ever a heart that overflows with Infinite and Almighty Love! Let us trust then in that Eternal Spirit, who pours out on us his warm and boundless blessings, through the channels of so many kindred human hearts!

# CHAPTER XXXIX. — WINTER TRAVELING AMONG THE APPENINES.

Valley of the Arno, Dec 22.—It is a glorious morning after our two days' walk, through rain and mud, among these stormy Appenines. The range of high peaks, among which is the celebrated monastery of Camaldoli, lie just before us, their summits dazzling with the new fallen snow. The clouds are breaking away, and a few rosy flushes announce the approach of the sun. It has rained during the night, and the fields are as green and fresh as on a morning in spring.

We left Florence on the 20th, while citizens and strangers were vainly striving to catch a glimpse of the Emperor of Russia. He is, from some cause, very shy of being seen, in his journeys from place to place, using the greatest art and diligence to prevent the time of his departure and arrival from being known. On taking leave of Powers, I found him expecting the Autocrat, as he had signified his intention of visiting his studio; it was a cause of patriotic pride to find that crowned heads know and appreciate the genius of our sculptor. The sky did not promise much, as we set out; when we had entered the Appenines and taken a last look of the lovely valley behind us, and the great dome of the city where we had spent four delightful months, it began to rain heavily. Determined to conquer the weather at the beginning, we kept on, although before many miles were passed, it became too penetrating to be agreeable. The mountains grew nearly black under the shadow of the clouds, and the storms swept drearily down their passes and defiles, till the scenery looked more like the Hartz than Italy. We were obliged to stop at Ponte Sieve and dry our saturated garments: when, as the rain slackened somewhat, we rounded the foot of the mountain of Vallombrosa, above the swollen and noisy Arno, to the little village of Cucina.

We entered the only inn in the place, followed by a crowd of wondering boys, for two such travelers had probably never been seen there. They made a blazing fire for us in the broad chimney, and after the police of the place satisfied themselves that we were not dangerous characters, they asked many questions about our country. I excited the sympathy of the women greatly in our behalf by telling them we had three thousand miles of sea between us and our homes. They exclaimed in the most sympathising tones: "Poverini! so far to go!—three thousand miles of water!"

The next morning we followed the right bank of the Arno. At Incisa, a large town on the river, the narrow pass broadens into a large and fertile plain, bordered on the north by the mountains. The snow storms were sweeping around their summits the whole day, and I thought of the desolate situation of the good monks who had so hospitably entertained us three months before. It was weary traveling; but at Levane our fatigues were soon forgotten. Two or three peasants were sitting last night beside the blazing fire, and we were amused to hear them talking about us. I overheard one asking another to converse with us awhile. "Why should I speak to them?" said he; "they are not of our profession—we are swineherds, and they do not care to talk with us." However, his curiosity prevailed at last, and we had a long conversation together. It seemed difficult for them to comprehend how there could be so much water to cross, without any land, before reaching our country. Finding we were going to Rome, I overheard one remark we were pilgrims, which seemed to be the general supposition, as there are few foot-travelers in Italy. The people said to one another as we passed along the road:—"They are making a journey of penance!" Those peasants expressed themselves very well for persons of their station, but they were remarkably ignorant of everything beyond their own olive orchards and vine fields.

Perugia, Dec. 24.—On leaving Levane, the morning gave a promise, and the sun winked at us once or twice through the broken clouds, with a watery eye; but our cup was not yet full. After crossing one or two shoulders of the range of hills, we descended to the great upland plain of Central Italy, watered by the sources of the Arno and the Tiber. The scenery is of a remarkable character. The hills appear to have been washed and swept by some mighty flood. They are worn into every shape—pyramids, castles, towers—standing desolate and brown, in long ranges, like the ruins of mountains. The plain is scarred with deep gulleys, adding to the look of decay which accords so well with the Cyclopean relics of the country.

A storm of hail which rolled away before us, disclosed the city of Arezzo, on a hill at the other end of the plain, its heavy cathedral crowning the pyramidal mass of buildings. Our first care was to find a good trattoria, for hunger spoke louder than sentiment, and then we sought the house where Petrarch was born. A young priest showed it to us on the summit of the hill. It has not been changed since he lived in it.

On leaving Florence, we determined to pursue the same plan as in Germany, of stopping at the inns frequented by the common people. They treated us here, as elsewhere, with great kindness and sympathy, and we were freed from the outrageous impositions practised at the greater hotels. They always built a large fire to dry us, after our day's walk in the rain, and placing chairs in the hearth, which was raised several feet above the floor, stationed us there, like the giants Gog and Magog, while the children, assembled below, gazed up in open-mouthed wonder at our elevated greatness. They even invited us to share their simple meals with them, and it was amusing to hear their goodhearted exclamations of pity at finding we were so far from home. We slept in the great beds (for the most of the Italian beds are calculated for a man, wife, and four children!) without fear of being assassinated, and only met with banditti in dreams.

This is a very unfavorable time of the year for foot-traveling. We were obliged to wait three or four weeks in Florence for a remittance from America, which not only prevented our leaving as soon as was desirable, but, by the additional expense of living, left us much smaller means than we required. However, through the kindness of a generous countryman, who unhesitatingly loaned us a considerable sum, we were enabled to start with thirty dollars each, which, with care and economy, will be quite sufficient to take us to Paris, by way of Rome and Naples, if these storms do not prevent us from walking. Greece and the Orient, which I so ardently hoped to visit, are now out of the question. We walked till noon to-day, over the Val di Chiana to Camuscia, the last post-station in the Tuscan dominions. On a mountain near it is the city of Cortona, still enclosed within its Cyclopean walls, built long before the foundation of Rome. Here our patience gave way, melted down by the unremitting rains, and while eating dinner we made a bargain for a vehicle to bring us to this city. We gave a little more than half of what the vetturino demanded, which was still an exorbitant price—two scudi each for a ride of thirty miles.

In a short time we were called to take our seats; I beheld with consternation a rickety, uncovered, two-wheeled vehicle, to which a single lean horse was attached. "What!" said I; "is that the carriage you promised?" "You bargained for a calesino," said he, "and there it is!" adding, moreover, that there was nothing else in the place. So we clambered up, thrust our feet among the hay, and the machine rolled off with a kind of saw-mill motion, at the rate of five miles an hour.

Soon after, in ascending the mountain of the Spelunca, a sheet of blue water was revealed below us—the Lake of Thrasymene! From the eminence around which we drove, we looked on the whole of its broad surface and the mountains which encompass it. It is a magnificent sheet of water, in size and shape somewhat like New York Bay, but the heights around it are far higher than the hills of Jersey or Staten Island. Three beautiful islands lie in it, near the eastern shore.

While our calesino was stopped at the papal custom-house, I gazed on the memorable field below us. A crescent plain, between the mountain and the lake, was the arena where two mighty empires met in combat. The place seems marked by nature for the scene of some great event. I experienced a thrilling emotion, such as no battle plain has excited, since, when a schoolboy, I rambled over the field of Brandywine. I looked through the long arcades of patriarchal olives, and tried to cover the field with the shadows of the Roman and Carthaginian myriads. I recalled the shock of meeting legions, the clash of swords and bucklers, and the waving standards amid the dust of battle, while stood on the mountain amphitheatre, trembling and invisible, the protecting deities of Rome.

*"Far other scene is Thrasymene now!"*

We rode over the plain, passed through the dark old town of Passignano, built on a rocky point by the lake, and dashed along the shore. A dark, stormy sky bent over us, and the roused waves broke in foam on the rocks. The winds

320

whistled among the bare oak boughs, and shook the olives till they twinkled all over. The vetturino whipped our old horse into a gallop, and we were borne on in unison with the scene, which would have answered for one of Hoffman's wildest stories.

Ascending a long hill, we took a last look in the dusk at Thrasymene, and continued our journey among the Appenines. The vetturino was to have changed horses at Magione, thirteen miles from Perugia, but there were none to be had, and our poor beast was obliged to perform the whole journey without rest or food. It grew very dark, and a storm, with thunder and lightning, swept among the hills. The clouds were of pitchy darkness, and we could see nothing beyond the road, except the lights of peasant-cottages trembling through the gloom. Now and then a flash of lightning revealed the black masses of the mountains, on which the solid sky seemed to rest. The wind and cold rain swept wailing past us, as if an evil spirit were abroad on the darkness. Three hours of such nocturnal travel brought us here, wet and chilly, as well as our driver, but I pitied the poor horse more than him.

When we looked out the window, on awaking, the clustered house-tops of the city, and the summits of the mountains near were covered with snow. But on walking to the battlements we saw that the valleys below were green and untouched. Perugia, for its "pride of place," must endure the storms, while the humbler villages below escape them. As the rain continues, we have taken seats in a country diligence for Foligno and shall depart in a few minutes.

Dec. 28.—We left Perugia in a close but covered vehicle, and descending the mountain, crossed the muddy and rapid Tiber in the valley below. All day we rode slowly among the hills; where the ascent was steep, two or four large oxen were hitched before the horses. I saw little of the scenery, for our Italian companions would not bear the windows open. Once, when we stopped, I got out and found we were in the region of snow, at the foot of a stormy peak, which towered sublimely above. At dusk, we entered Foligno, and were driven to the "Croce Bianca"—glad to be thirty miles further on our way to Rome.

After some discussion with a vetturino, who was to leave next morning, we made a contract with him for the remainder of the journey, for the rain, which fell in torrents, forbade all thought of pedestrianism. At five o'clock we rattled out of the gate, and drove by the waning moon and morning starlight, down the vale of the Clitumnus. As the dawn stole on, I watched eagerly the features of the scene. Instead of a narrow glen, as my fancy had pictured, we were in a valley, several miles broad, covered with rich orchards and fertile fields. A glorious range of mountains bordered it on the north, looking like Alps in their winter garments. A rosy flush stole over the snow, which kindled with the growing morn, till they shone like clouds that float in the sunrise. The Clitumnus, beside us, was the purest of streams. The heavy rains which had fallen, had not soiled in the least its limpid crystal.

When it grew light enough, I looked at our companions for the three days' journey. The two other inside seats were occupied by a tradesman of Trieste, with his wife and child; an old soldier, and a young dragoon going to visit his parents after seven years' absence, occupied the front part. Persons traveling together in a carriage are not long in becoming acquainted—close companionship soon breeds familiarity. Before night, I had made a fast friend of the young soldier, learned to bear the perverse humor of the child with as much patience as its father, and even drawn looks of grim kindness from the crusty old vetturino.

Our mid-day resting place was Spoleto. As there were two hours given us, we took a ramble through the city, visited the ruins of its Roman theatre and saw the gate erected to commemorate the victory gained here over Hannibal, which stopped his triumphal march towards Rome. A great part of the afternoon was spent in ascending among the defiles of Monte Somma, the highest pass on the road between Ancona and Rome. Assisted by two yoke of oxen we slowly toiled up through the snow, the mountains on both sides covered with thickets of box and evergreen oaks, among whose leafy screens the banditti hide themselves. It is not considered dangerous at present, but as the dragoons who used to patrol this pass have been sent off to Bologna, to keep down the rebellion, the robbers will probably return to their old haunts again. We saw many suspicious looking coverts, where they might have hidden.

322

We slept at Terni and did not see the falls—not exactly on Wordsworth's principle of leaving Yarrow "unvisited," but because under the circumstances, it was impossible. The vetturino did not arrive there till after dark; he was to leave before dawn; the distance was five miles, and the roads very bad. Besides, we had seen falls quite as grand, which needed only a Byron to make them as renowned—we had been told that those of Tivoli, which we shall see, were equally fine. The Velino, which we crossed near Terni, was not a large stream—in short, we hunted as many reasons as we could find, why the falls need not be seen.

Leaving Terni before day, we drove up the long vale towards Narni. The roads were frozen hard; the ascent becoming more difficult, the vetturino was obliged to stop at a farm-house and get another pair of horses, with which, and a handsome young contadino as postillion, we reached Narni in a short time. In climbing the hill, we had a view of the whole valley of Terni, shut in on all sides by snow-crested Appenines, and threaded by the Nar, whose waters flow "with many windings, through the vale!"

At Otricoli, while dinner was preparing, I walked around the crumbling battlements to look down into the valley and trace the far windings of the Tiber. In rambling through the crooked streets, we saw everywhere the remains of the splendor which this place boasted in the days of Rome. Fragments of fluted pillars stood here and there in the streets; large blocks of marble covered with sculpture and inscriptions were built into the houses, defaced statues used as door-ornaments, and the steppingstone to our rude inn, worn every day by the feet of grooms and vetturini, contained some letters of an inscription which may have recorded the glory of on emperor.

Traveling with a vetturino, is unquestionably the pleasantest way of seeing Italy. The easy rate of the journey allows time for becoming well acquainted with the country, and the tourist is freed from the annoyance of quarrelling with cheating landlords. A translation of our written contract, will best explain this mode of traveling:

*"CARRIAGE" FOR ROME.*

*"Our contract is, to be conducted to Rome for the sum of twenty*

*francs each, say 20f. and the buona mano, if we are well*

*served. We must have from the vetturino, Giuseppe Nerpiti, supper*

*each night, a free chamber with two beds, and fire, until we shall*

*arrive at Rome.*

"*I, Geronymo Sartarelli, steward of the Inn of the White Cross, at*

*Foligno, in testimony of the above contract.*"

Beyond Otricoli, we passed through some relics of an age anterior to
Rome. A few soiled masses of masonry, black with age, stood along the brow
of the mountain, on whose extremity were the ruins of a castle of the middle
ages. We crossed the Tiber on a bridge built by Augustus Cæsar, and reached
Borghetto as the sun was gilding with its last rays the ruined citadel above. As
the carriage with its four horses was toiling slowly up the hill, we got out and
walked before, to gaze on the green meadows of the Tiber.

On descending from Narni, I noticed a high, prominent mountain,
whose ridgy back, somewhat like the profile of a face, reminded me of the
Traunstein, in Upper Austria. As we approached, its form gradually changed,
until it stood on the Campagna

*"Like a long-swept wave about to break,*

*That on the curl hangs pausing"*—

and by that token of a great bard, I recognized Monte Soracte. The
dragoon took us by the arms, and away we scampered over the Campagna,
with one of the loveliest sunsets before us, that ever painted itself on my
retina. I cannot portray in words the glory that flooded the whole western
heaven. It was like a sea of melted ruby, amethyst and topaz—deep, dazzling
and of crystal transparency. The color changed in tone every few minutes, till
in half an hour it sank away before the twilight to a belt of deep orange along
the west.

We left Civita Castellana before daylight. The sky was red with dawn

324

as we approached Nepi, and we got out to walk, in the clear, frosty air. A magnificent Roman aqueduct, part of it a double row of arches, still supplies the town with water. There is a deep ravine, appearing as if rent in the ground by some convulsion, on the eastern side of the city. A clear stream that steals through the arches of the aqueduct, falls in a cascade of sixty feet down into the chasm, sending up constant wreaths of spray through the evergreen foliage that clothes the rocks. In walking over the desolate Campagna, we saw many deep chambers dug in the earth, used by the charcoal burners; the air was filled with sulphureous exhalations, very offensive to the smell, which rose from the ground in many places.

Miles and miles of the dreary waste, covered only with flocks of grazing sheep, were passed,—and about noon we reached Baccano, a small post station, twenty miles from Rome. A long hill rose before us, and we sprang out of the carriage and ran ahead, to see Rome from its summit. As we approached the top, the Campagna spread far before and around us, level and blue as an ocean. I climbed up a high bank by the roadside, and the whole scene came in view. Perhaps eighteen miles distant rose the dome of St. Peter's, near the horizon—a small spot on the vast plain. Beyond it and further east, were the mountains of Albano—on our left Soracte and the Appenines, and a blue line along the west betrayed the Mediterranean. There was nothing peculiarly beautiful or sublime in the landscape, but few other scenes on earth combine in one glance such a myriad of mighty associations, or bewilder the mind with such a crowd of confused emotions.

As we approached Rome, the dragoon, with whom we had been walking all day, became anxious and impatient. He had not heard from his parents for a long time, and knew not if they were living. His desire to be at the end of his journey finally became so great, that he hailed a peasant who was driving by in a light vehicle, left our slow carriage and went out of sight in a gallop.

As we descended to the Tiber in the dusk of evening, the domes and spires of Rome came gradually into view, St. Peter's standing like a mountain in the midst of them. Crossing the yellow river by the Ponte Molle, two miles of road, straight as an arrow, lay before us, with the light of the Porta del Popolo at the end. I felt strangely excited as the old vehicle rumbled

325

through the arch, and we entered a square with fountains and an obelisk of Egyptian granite in the centre. Delivering up our passports, we waited until the necessary examinations were made, and then went forward. Three streets branch out from the square, the middle one of which, leading directly to the Capitol, is the Corso, the Roman Broadway. Our vetturino chose that to the left, the Via della Scrofa, leading off towards the bridge of St. Angelo. I looked out the windows as we drove along, but saw nothing except butcher-shops, grocer-stores, etc.—horrible objects for a sentimental traveler!

Being emptied out on the pavement at last, our first care was to find rooms; after searching through many streets, with a coarse old Italian who spoke like an angel, we arrived at a square where the music of a fountain was heard through the dusk and an obelisk cut out some of the starlight. At the other end I saw a portico through the darkness, and my heart gave a breathless bound on recognizing the Pantheon—the matchless temple of Ancient Rome! And now while I am writing, I hear the gush of the fountain—and if I step to the window, I see the time-worn but still glorious edifice.

On returning for our baggage, we met the funeral procession of the Princess Altieri. Priests in white and gold carried flaming torches, and the coffin, covered with a magnificent golden pall, was borne in a splendid hearse, guarded by four priests. As we were settling our account with the vetturino, who demanded much more buona mano than we were willing to give, the young dragoon returned. He was greatly agitated. "I have been at home!" said he, in a voice trembling with emotion. I was about to ask him further concerning his family, but he kissed and embraced us warmly and hurriedly, saying he had only come to say "addio!" and to leave us. I stop writing to ramble through Rome. This city of all cities to me—this dream of my boyhood—giant, god-like, fallen Rome—is around me, and I revel in a glow of anticipation and exciting thought that seems to change my whole state of being.

# CHAPTER XL. ROME.

Dec. 29.—One day's walk through Rome—how shall I describe it? The Capitol, the Forum, St. Peter's, the Coliseum—what few hours' ramble ever took in places so hallowed by poetry, history and art? It was a golden leaf in my calendar of life. In thinking over it now, and drawing out the threads of recollection from the varied woof of thought I have woven to-day, I almost wonder how I dared so much at once; but within reach of them all, how was it possible to wait? Let me give a sketch of our day's ramble.

Hearing that it was better to visit the ruins by evening or moonlight, (alas! there is no moon now) we started out to hunt St. Peter's. Going in the direction of the Corso, we passed the ruined front of the magnificent Temple of Antoninus, now used as the Papal Custom House. We turned to the right on entering the Corso, expecting to have a view of the city from the hill at its southern end. It is a magnificent street, lined with palaces and splendid edifices of every kind, and always filled with crowds of carriages and people. On leaving it, however, we became bewildered among the narrow streets—passed through a market of vegetables, crowded with beggars and contadini—threaded many by-ways between dark old buildings—saw one or two antique fountains and many modern churches, and finally arrived at a hill.

We ascended many steps, and then descending a little towards the other side, saw suddenly below us the Roman Forum! I knew it at once—and those three Corinthian columns that stood near us—what could they be but the remains of the temple of Jupiter Stator? We stood on the Capitoline Hill; at the foot was the Arch of Septimus Severus, brown with age and shattered; near it stood the majestic front of the Temple of Fortune, its pillars of polished granite glistening in the sun, as if they had been erected yesterday, while on the left the rank grass was waving from the arches and mighty walls of the Palace of the Cæsars! In front, ruin upon ruin lined the way for half a mile, where the Coliseum towered grandly through the blue morning mist, at the base of the Esquiline Hill!

Good heavens, what a scene! Grandeur, such as the world never saw, once rose through that blue atmosphere; splendor inconceivable, the spoils of a world, the triumphs of a thousand armies had passed over that earth; minds which for ages moved the ancient world had thought there, and words of power and glory, from the lips of immortal men, had been syllabled on that hallowed air. To call back all this on the very spot, while the wreck of what once was, rose mouldering and desolate around, aroused a sublimity of thought and feeling too powerful for words.

Returning at hazard through the streets, we came suddenly upon the column of Trajan, standing in an excavated square below the level of the city, amid a number of broken granite columns, which formed part of the Forum dedicated to him by Rome, after the conquest of Dacia. The column is one hundred and thirty-two feet high, entirely covered with bas-reliefs representing his victories, winding about it in a spiral line to the top. The number of figures is computed at two thousand five hundred, and they were of such excellence that Raphael used many of them for his models. They are now much defaced, and the column is surmounted by a statue of some saint. The inscription on the pedestal has been erased, and the name of Sixtus V. substituted. Nothing can exceed the ridiculous vanity of the old popes in thus mutilating the finest monuments of ancient art. You cannot look upon any relic of antiquity in Rome, but your eyes are assailed by the words "PONTIFEX MAXIMUS," in staring modern letters. Even the magnificent bronzes of the Pantheon were stripped to make the baldachin under the dome of St. Peter's.

Finding our way back again, we took a fresh start, happily in the right direction, and after walking some time, came out on the Tiber, at the Bridge of St. Angelo. The river rolled below in his muddy glory, and in front, on the opposite bank, stood "the pile which Hadrian retired on high"—now, the Castle of St. Angelo. Knowing that St. Peter's was to he seen from this bridge, I looked about in search of it. There was only one dome in sight, large and of beautiful proportions. I said at once, "surely that cannot be St. Peter's!" On looking again, however, I saw the top of a massive range of building near it, which corresponded so nearly with the pictures of the Vatican, that I was unwillingly forced to believe the mighty dome was really before me. I recognized it as one of those we saw from the Capitol, but it appeared so much smaller when viewed from a greater distance, that I was quite deceived. On considering we were still three-fourths of a mile from it, and that we could see its minutest parts distinctly, the illusion was explained.

Going directly down the Borgo Vecchio, towards it, it seemed a long time before we arrived at the square of St. Peter's; when at length we stood in front with the majestic colonnade sweeping around—the fountains on each side sending up their showers of silvery spray—the mighty obelisk of Egyptian granite piercing the sky—and beyond, the great front and dome of the Cathedral, I confessed my unmingled admiration. It recalled to my mind the grandeur of ancient Rome, and mighty as her edifices must have been, I doubt if there were many views more overpowering than this. The façade of St. Peter's seemed close to us, but it was a third of a mile distant, and the people ascending the steps dwindled to pigmies.

I passed the obelisk, went up the long ascent, crossed the portico, pushed aside the heavy leathern curtain at the entrance, and stood in the great nave. I need not describe my feelings at the sight, but I will tell the dimensions, and you may then fancy what they were. Before me was a marble plain six hundred feet long, and under the cross four hundred and seventeen feet wide! One hundred and fifty feet above, sprang a glorious arch, dazzling with inlaid gold, and in the centre of the cross there were four hundred feet of air between me and the top of the dome! The sunbeam, stealing through the lofty window at one end of the transept, made a bar of light on the blue air, hazy with incense, one-tenth of a mile long, before it fell on the mosaics and gilded shrines of the other extremity. The grand cupola alone, including lantern and cross, is two hundred and eighty-five feet high, or sixty feet higher than the Bunker Hill Monument, and the four immense pillars on which it rests are each one hundred and thirty-seven feet in circumference! It seems as if human art had outdone itself in producing this temple—the grandest which the world ever erected for the worship of the Living God! The awe felt in looking up at the giant arch of marble and gold, did not humble me; on

329

the contrary, I felt exalted, ennobled—beings in the form I wore planned the
glorious edifice, and it seemed that in godlike power perseverance, they were
indeed but "a little lower than the angels!" I felt that, if fallen, my race was
still mighty and immortal.

The Vatican is only open twice a week, on days which are not festas; most
fortunately, to-day happened to be one of these, and we took a run through
its endless halls. The extent and magnificence of the gallery of sculpture is
perfectly amazing. The halls, which are filled to overflowing with the finest
works of ancient art, would, if placed side by side, make a row more than two
miles in length! You enter at once into a hall of marble, with a magnificent
arched ceiling, a third of a mile long; the sides are covered for a great distance
with inscriptions of every kind, divided into compartments according to the
era of the empire to which they refer. One which I examined, appeared to
be a kind of index of the roads in Italy, with the towns on them; and we
could decipher on that time-worn block, the very route I had followed from
Florence hither.

Then came the statues, and here I am bewildered, how to describe them.
Hundreds upon hundreds of figures—statues of citizens, generals, emperors
and gods—fauns, satyrs and nymphs—children, cupids and tritons—in fact,
it seemed inexhaustible. Many of them, too, were forms of matchless beauty;
there were Venuses and nymphs, born of the loftiest dreams of grace; fauns on
whose faces shone the very soul of humor, and heroes and divinities with an
air of majesty worthy the "land of lost gods and godlike men!"

I am lost in astonishment at the perfection of art attained by the Greeks
and Romans. There is scarcely a form of beauty, that has ever met my eye,
which is not to be found in this gallery. I should almost despair of such
another blaze of glory on the world, were it not my devout belief that what
has been done may be done again, and had I not faith that the dawn in
which we live will bring another day equally glorious. And why should not
America, with the experience and added wisdom which three thousand years
have slowly yielded to the old world, joined to the giant energy of her youth
and freedom, re-bestow on the world the divine creations of art? Let Powers
answer!

330

But let us step on to the hemicycle of the Belvidere, and view some works greater than any we have yet seen, or even imagined. The adjoining gallery is filled with masterpieces of sculpture, but we will keep our eyes unwearied and merely glance along the rows. At length we reach a circular court with a fountain flinging up its waters in the centre. Before us is an open cabinet; there is a beautiful, manly form within, but you would not for an instant take it for the Apollo. By the Gorgon head it holds aloft, we recognize Canova's Perseus—he has copied the form and attitude of the Apollo, but he could not breathe into it the same warming fire. It seemed to me particularly lifeless, and I greatly preferred his Boxers, who stand on either side of it. One, who has drawn back in the attitude of striking, looks as if he could fell an ox with a single blow of his powerful arm. The other is a more lithe and agile figure, and there is a quick fire in his countenance which might overbalance the massive strength of his opponent.

Another cabinet—this is the far-famed Antinous. A countenance of perfect Grecian beauty, with a form such as we would imagine for one of Homer's heroes. His features are in repose, and there is something in their calm, settled expression, strikingly like life.

Now we look on a scene of the deepest physical agony. Mark how every muscle of old Laocoon's body is distended to the utmost in the mighty struggle! What intensity of pain in the quivering, distorted, features! Every nerve, which despair can call into action, is excited in one giant effort, and a scream of anguish seems just to have quivered on those marble lips. The serpents have rolled their strangling coils around father and sons, but terror has taken away the strength of the latter, and they make but feeble resistance. After looking with indifference on the many casts of this group, I was the more moved by the magnificent original. It deserves all the admiration that has been heaped upon it.

I absolutely trembled on approaching the cabinet of the Apollo, I had built up in fancy a glorious ideal, drawn from all that bards have sung or artists have rhapsodized about its divine beauty. I feared disappointment—I dreaded to have my ideal displaced and my faith in the power of human genius overthrown by a form less than perfect. However, with a feeling of desperate excitement, I entered and looked upon it.

Now what shall I say of it? How make you comprehend its immortal beauty? To what shall I liken its glorious perfection of form, or the fire that imbues the cold marble with the soul of a god? Not with sculpture, for it stands alone and above all other works of art—nor with men, for it has a majesty more than human. I gazed on it, lost in wonder and joy—joy that I could, at last, take into my mind a faultless ideal of godlike, exalted manhood. The figure appears actually to possess a spirit, and I looked on it, not as on a piece of marble, but a being of loftier mould, and half expected to see him step forward when the arrow had reached its mark. I would give worlds to feel one moment the sculptor's mental triumph when his work was completed; that one exulting thrill must have repaid him for every ill he might have suffered on earth! With what divine inspiration has he wrought its faultless lines! There is a spirit in every limb which mere toil could not have given. It must have been caught in those lofty moments.

> *"When each conception was a heavenly guest—a*
>
> *ray of immortality—and stood*
>
> *star-like, around, until they gathered to a god?"*

We ran through a series of halls, roofed with golden stars on a deep blue, midnight sky, and filled with porphyry vases, black marble gods, and mummies. Some of the statues shone with the matchless polish they had received from a Theban artisan before Athens was founded, and are, apparently, as fresh and perfect as when looked upon by the vassals of Sesostris. Notwithstanding their stiff, rough-hewn limbs, there were some figures of great beauty, and they gave me a much higher idea of Egyptian sculpture. In an adjoining hall, containing colossal busts of the gods, is a vase forty-one feet in circumference, of one solid block of red porphyry.

The "Transfiguration" is truly called the first picture in the world. The same glow of inspiration which created the Belvidere, must have been required to paint the Saviour's aerial form. The three figures hover above the earth in a blaze of glory, seemingly independent of all material laws. The terrified

Apostles on the mount, and the wondering group below, correspond in the grandeur of their expression to the awe and majesty of the scene. The only blemish in the sublime perfection of the picture is the introduction of the two small figures on the left hand; who, by-the-bye, were Cardinals, inserted there by command. Some travelers say the color is all lost, but I was agreeably surprised to find it well preserved. It is, undoubtedly, somewhat imperfect in this respect, as Raphael died before it was entirely finished; but "take it all in all," you may search the world in vain to find its equal.

January 1, 1846.—New Year's Day in the Eternal City! It will be something to say in after years, that I have seen one year open in Rome— that, while my distant friends were making up for the winter without, with good cheer around the merry board, I have walked in sunshine by the ruins of the Coliseum, watched the orange groves gleaming with golden fruitage in the Farnese gardens, trodden the daisied meadow around the sepulchre of Caius Cestius, and mused by the graves of Shelley, Keats and Salvator Rosa! The Palace of the Cæsars looked even more mournful in the pale, slant sunshine, and the yellow Tiber, as he flowed through the "marble wilderness," seemed sullenly counting up the long centuries during which degenerate slaves have trodden his banks. A leaden-colored haze clothed the seven hills, and heavy silence reigned among the ruins, for all work was prohibited, and the people were gathered in their churches. Rome never appeared so desolate and melancholy as to-day.

In the morning I climbed the Quirinal Hill, now called Monte Cavallo, from the colossal statues of Castor and Pollux, with their steeds, supposed to be the work of Phidias and Praxiteles. They stand on each side of an obelisk of Egyptian granite, beside which a strong stream of water gushes up into a magnificent bronze basin, found in the old Forum. The statues, entirely browned by age, are considered masterpieces of Grecian art, and whether or not from the great masters, show in all their proportions, the conceptions of lofty genius.

We kept on our way between gardens filled with orange groves, whose glowing fruit reminded me of Mignon's beautiful reminiscence—"Im dunkeln Laub die Gold Orangen glühn!" Rome, although subject to cold winds from the Appenines, enjoys so mild a climate that oranges and palm trees grow in the open air, without protection. Daisies and violets bloom the whole winter, in the meadows of never-fading green. The basilic of the Lateran equals St. Peter's in splendor, though its size is much smaller. The walls are covered with gorgeous hangings of velvet embroidered with gold, and before the high altar, which glitters with precious stones, are four pillars of gilt bronze, said to be those which Augustus made of the spars of Egyptian vessels captured at the battle of Actium.

We descended the hill to the Coliseum, and passing under the Arch of Constantine, walked along the ancient triumphal way, at the foot of the Palatine Hill, which is entirely covered with the ruins of the Cæsars' Palace. A road, rounding its southern base towards the Tiber, brought us to the Temple of Vesta—a beautiful little relic which has been singularly spared by the devastations that have overthrown so many mightier fabrics. It is of circular form, surrounded by nineteen Corinthian columns, thirty-six feet in height; a clumsy tiled roof now takes the place of the elegant cornice which once gave the crowning charm to its perfect proportions. Close at hand are the remains of the temple of Fortuna Virilis, of which some Ionic pillars alone are left, and the house of Cola di Rienzi—the last Tribune of Rome.

As we approached the walls, the sepulchre of Caius Cestius came in sight—a single solid pyramid, one hundred feet in height. The walls are built against it, and the light apex rises far above the massive gate beside it, which was erected by Belisarius. But there were other tombs at hand, for which we had more sympathy than that of the forgotten Roman, and we turned away to look for the graves of Shelley and Keats.

They lie in the Protestant burying ground, on the side of a mound that slopes gently up to the old wall of Rome, beside the pyramid of Cestius. The meadow around is still verdant and sown thick with daisies, and the soft green of the Italian pine mingles with the dark cypress above the slumberers. Huge aloes grow in the shade, and the sweet bay and bushes of rosemary make the air fresh and fragrant. There is a solemn, mournful beauty about the place, green and lonely as it is, beside the tottering walls of ancient Rome, that takes away the gloomy associations of death, and makes one wish to lie there, too,

334

when his thread shall be spun to the end.

We found first the simple head-stone of Keats, alone, in the grassy meadow. Its inscription states that on his death-bed, in the bitterness of his heart, at the malice of his enemies, be desired these words to be written on his tombstone: "Here lies one whose name was written in water." Not far from him reposes the son of Shelley.

Shelley himself lies at the top of the shaded slope, in a lonely spot by the wall, surrounded by tall cypresses. A little hedge of rose and bay surrounds his grave, which bears the simple inscription—

"PERCY BYSSHE SHELLEY; Cor Cordium."

> "Nothing of him that doth fade,
>
> But doth suffer a sea-change
>
> Into something rich and strange."

Glorious, but misguided Shelley! He sleeps calmly now in that silent nook, and the air around his grave is filled with sighs from those who mourn that the bright, erratic star should have been blotted out ere it reached the zenith of its mounting fame. I plucked a leaf from the fragrant bay, as a token of his fame, and a sprig of cypress from the bough that bent lowest over his grave; and passing between tombs shaded with blooming roses or covered with unwithered garlands, left the lovely spot.

Amid the excitement of continually changing scenes, I have forgotten to mention our first visit to the Coliseum. The day after our arrival we set out with two English friends, to see it by sunset. Passing by the glorious fountain of Trevi, we made our way to the Forum, and from thence took the road to the Coliseum, lined on both sides with the remains of splendid edifices. The grass-grown ruins of the Palace of the Cæsars stretched along on our right; on our left we passed in succession the granite front of the Temple of Antoninus and Faustina, the three grand arches of the Temple of Peace and the ruins of the Temple of Venus and Rome. We went under the ruined triumphal arch of Titus, with broken friezes representing the taking of Jerusalem, and the

335

mighty walls of the Coliseum gradually rose before us. They grew in grandeur as we approached them, and when at length we stood in the centre, with the shattered arches and grassy walls rising above and beyond one another, far around us, the red light of sunset giving them a soft and melancholy beauty, I was fain to confess that another form of grandeur had entered my mind, of which I before knew not.

A majesty like that of nature clothes this wonderful edifice. Walls rise above walls, and arches above arches, from every side of the grand arena, like a sweep of craggy, pinnacled mountains around an oval lake. The two outer circles have almost entirely disappeared, torn away by the rapacious nobles of Rome, during the middle ages, to build their palaces. When entire, and filled with its hundred thousand spectators, it must have exceeded any pageant which the world can now produce. No wonder it was said—

*"While stands the Coliseum, Rome shall stand;*

*When falls the Coliseum, Rome shall fall;*

*And when Rome falls, the world!"*

—a prediction, which time has not verified. The world is now going forward, prouder than ever, and though we thank Rome for the legacy she has left us, we would not wish the dust of her ruin to cumber our path.

While standing in the arena, impressed with the spirit of the scene around me, which grew more spectral and melancholy as the dusk of evening began to fill up the broken arches, my eye was assailed by the shrines ranged around the space, doubtless to remove the pollution of paganism. In the middle stands also a cross, with an inscription, granting an absolution of forty days to all who kiss it. Now, although a simple cross in the centre might be very appropriate, both as a token of the heroic devotion of the martyr Telemachus and the triumph of a true religion over the barbarities of the Past, this congregation of shrines and bloody pictures mars very much the unity of association so necessary to the perfect enjoyment of any such scene.

We saw the flush of sunset fade behind the Capitoline Hill, and passed homeward by the Forum, as its shattered pillars were growing solemn and

336

spectral through the twilight. I intend to visit them often again, and "meditate amongst decay." I begin already to grow attached to their lonely grandeur. A spirit, almost human, speaks from the desolation, and there is something in the voiceless oracles it utters, that strikes an answering chord in my own breast.

In the Via de' Pontefici, not far distant from the Borghese Palace, we saw the Mausoleum of Augustus. It is a large circular structure somewhat after the plan of that of Hadrian, but on a much smaller scale. The interior has been cleared out, seats erected around the walls, and the whole is now a summer theatre, for the amusement of the peasantry and tradesmen. What a commentary on greatness! Harlequin playing his pranks in the tomb of an Emperor, and the spot which nations approached with reverence, resounding with the mirth of beggars and degraded vassals!

I visited lately the studio of a young Philadelphian, Mr. W. B. Chambers, who has been here two or three years. In studying the legacies of art which the old masters left to their country, he has caught some of the genuine poetic inspiration which warmed them. But he is modest as talented, and appears to undervalue his works, so long as they do not reach his own mental ideal. He chooses principally subjects from the Italian peasant-life, which abounds with picturesque and classic beauty. His pictures of the shepherd boy of the Albruzzi, and the brown maidens of the Campagna are fine illustrations of this class, and the fidelity with which he copies nature, is an earnest of his future success.

I was in the studio of Crawford, the sculptor; he has at present nothing finished in the marble. There were many casts of his former works, which, judging from their appearance in plaster, must be of no common excellence— for the sculptor can only be justly judged in marble. I saw some fine bas-reliefs of classical subjects, and an exquisite group of Mercury and Psyche, but his masterpiece is undoubtedly the Orpheus. There is a spirit in this figure which astonished me. The face is full of the inspiration of the poet, softened by the lover's tenderness, and the whole fervor of his soul is expressed in the eagerness with which he gazes forward, on stepping past the sleeping Cerberus. Crawford is now engaged on the statue of an Indian girl, pierced by an arrow, and dying. It is a simple and touching figure, and will, I think, be one of his best works.

We are often amused with the groups in the square of the Pantheon, which we can see from our chamber-window. Shoemakers and tinkers carry on their business along the sunny side, while the venders of oranges and roasted chesnuts form a circle around the Egyptian obelisk and fountain. Across the end of an opposite street we get a glimpse of the vegetable-market, and now and then the shrill voice of a pedlar makes its nasal solo audible above the confused chorus. As the beggars choose the Corso, St. Peter's, and the ruins for their principal haunts, we are now spared the hearing of their lamentations. Every time we go out we are assailed with them. "Maladetta sia la vostra testa!"—"Curses be upon your head!"—said one whom I passed without notice. The priests are, however, the greatest beggars. In every church are kept offering boxes, for the support of the church or some unknown institution; they even go from house to house, imploring support and assistance in the name of the Virgin and all the saints, while their bloated, sensual countenances and capacious frames tell of anything but fasts and privations. Once, as I was sitting among the ruins, I was suddenly startled by a loud, rattling sound; turning my head, I saw a figure clothed in white from head to foot, with only two small holes for the eyes. He held in his hand a money-box, on which was a figure of the Virgin, which he held close to my lips, that I might kiss it. This I declined doing, but dropped a baiocco into his box, when, making the sign of the cross, he silently disappeared.

Our present lodging (Trattoria del Sole) is a good specimen of an Italian inn for mechanics and common tradesmen. Passing through the front room, which is an eating-place for the common people—with a barrel of wine in the corner, and bladders of lard hanging among orange boughs in the window— we enter a dark court-yard filled with heavy carts, and noisy with the neighing of horses and singing of grooms, for the stables occupy part of the house. An open staircase, running all around this hollow square, leads to the second, third, and fourth stories,

On the second story is the dining-room for the better class of travelers, who receive the same provisions as those below for double the price, and

338

the additional privilege of giving the waiter two baiocchi. The sleeping apartments are in the fourth story, and are named according to the fancy of a former landlord, in mottos above each door. Thus, on arriving here, the Triester, with his wife and child, more fortunate than our first parents, took refuge in "Paradise," while we Americans were ushered into the "Chamber of Jove." We have occupied it ever since, and find a paul (ten cents) apiece cheap enough for a good bed and a window opening on the Pantheon.

Next to the Coliseum, the baths of Caracalla are the grandest remains of Rome. The building is a thousand feet square, and its massive walls look as if built by a race of giants. These Titan remains are covered with green shrubbery, and long, trailing vines sweep over the cornice, and wave down like tresses from architrave and arch. In some of its grand halls the mosaic pavement is yet entire. The excavations are still carried on; from the number of statues already found, this would seem to have been one of the most gorgeous edifices of the olden time.

I have been now several days loitering and sketching among the ruins, and I feel as if I could willingly wander for months beside these mournful relics, and draw inspiration from the lofty yet melancholy lore they teach. There is a spirit haunting them, real and undoubted. Every shattered column, every broken arch and mouldering wall, but calls up more vividly to mind the glory that has passed away. Each lonely pillar stands as proudly as if it still helped to bear up the front of a glorious temple, and the air seems scarcely to have ceased vibrating with the clarions that heralded a conqueror's triumph.

> "—the old majestic trees
>
> Stand ghost-like in the Cæsar's home,
>
> As if their conscious roots were set
>
> In the old graves of giant Rome,
>
> And drew their sap all kingly yet!"

> "There every mouldering stone beneath
>
> Is broken from some mighty thought,

*And sculptures in the dust still breathe*

*The fire with which their lines were wrought,*

*And sunder'd arch and plundered tomb*

*Still thunder back the echo—'Rome!'"*

In Rome there is no need that the imagination be excited to call up thrilling emotion or poetic reverie—they are forced on the mind by the sublime spirit of the scene. The roused bard might here pour forth his thoughts in the wildest climaces, and I could believe he felt it all. This is like the Italy of my dreams—that golden realm whose image has been nearly chased away by the earthly reality. I expected to find a land of light and beauty, where every step crushed a flower or displaced a sunbeam—whose very air was poetic inspiration, and whose every scene filled the soul with romantic feelings. Nothing is left of my picture but the far-off mountains, robed in the sapphire veil of the Ausonian air, and these ruins, amid whose fallen glory sits triumphant the spirit of ancient song.

I have seen the flush of morn and eve rest on the Coliseum; I have seen the noon-day sky framed in its broken loopholes, like plates of polished sapphire; and last night, as the moon has grown into the zenith, I went to view it with her. Around the Forum all was silent and spectral—a sentinel challenged us at the Arch of Titus, under which we passed and along the Cæsar's wall, which lay in black shadow. Dead stillness brooded around the Coliseum; the pale, silvery lustre streamed through its arches, and over the grassy walls, giving them a look of shadowy grandeur which day could not bestow. The scene will remain fresh in my memory forever.

# CHAPTER XLI. – TIVOLI AND THE ROMAN CAMPAGNA.

Jan. 9.—A few days ago we returned from an excursion to Tivoli, one of the loveliest spots in Italy. We left the Eternal City by the Gate of San Lorenzo, and twenty minutes walk brought us to the bare and bleak Campagna, which was spread around us for leagues in every direction. Here and there a shepherd-boy in his woolly coat, with his flock of browsing sheep, were the only objects that broke its desert-like monotony.

At the fourth mile we crossed the rapid Anio, the ancient Teverone, formerly the boundary between Latium and the Sabine dominions, and at the tenth, came upon some fragments of the old Tibertine way, formed of large irregular blocks of basaltic lava. A short distance further, we saw across the plain the ruins of the bath of Agrippa, built by the side of the Tartarean Lake. The wind, blowing from it, bore us an overpowering smell of sulphur; the waters of the little river Solfatara, which crosses the road, are of a milky blue color, and carry those of the lake into the Anio. A fragment of the old bridge over it still remains.

Finding the water quite warm, we determined to have a bath. So we ran down the plain, which was covered with a thick coat of sulphur, and sounded hollow to our tread, till we reached a convenient place, where we threw off our clothes, and plunged in. The warm wave was delightful to the skin, but extremely offensive to the smell, and when we came out, our mouths and throats were filled with the stifling gas.

It was growing dark as we mounted through the narrow streets of Tivoli, but we endeavored to gain some sight of the renowned beauties of the spot, before going to rest. From a platform on a brow of the hill, we looked down into the defile, at whose bottom the Anio was roaring, and caught a sideward glance of the Cascatelles, sending up their spray amid the evergreen bushes that fringe the rocks. Above the deep glen that curves into the mountain, stands the beautiful temple of the Sybil—a building of the most perfect and graceful proportion. It crests the "rocky brow" like a fairy dwelling, and looks all the lovelier for the wild caverns below. Gazing downward from the bridge, one sees the waters of the Anio tumbling into the picturesque grotto of the Sirens; around a rugged corner, a cloud of white spray whirls up continually, while the boom of a cataract rumbles down the glen. All these we marked in the deepening dusk, and then hunted an albergo.

The shrill-voiced hostess gave us a good supper and clean beds; in return we diverted the people very much by the relation of our sulphur bath. We were awakened in the night by the wind shaking the very soul out of our loose casement. I fancied I heard torrents of rain dashing against the panes, and groaned in bitterness of spirit on thinking of a walk back to Rome in such weather. When morning came, we found it was only a hurricane of wind which was strong enough to tear off pieces of the old roofs. I saw some capuchins nearly overturned in crossing the square, by the wind seizing their white robes.

I had my fingers frozen and my eyes filled with sand, in trying to draw the Sybil's temple, and therefore left it to join my companions, who had gone down into the glen to see the great cascade. The Anio bursts out of a cavern in the mountain-side, and like a prisoner giddy with recovered liberty, reels over the edge of a precipice more than two hundred feet deep. The bottom is hid in a cloud of boiling spray, that shifts from side to side, and driven by the wind, sweeps whistling down the narrow pass. It stuns the ear with a perpetual boom, giving a dash of grandeur to the enrapturing beauty of the scene. I tried a footpath that appeared to lead down to the Cascatelles, but after advancing some distance along the side of an almost perpendicular precipice, I came to a corner that looked so dangerous, especially as the wind was nearly strong enough to carry me off, that it seemed safest to return. We made another vain attempt to get down, by creeping along the bed of a torrent, filled with briars. The Cascatelles are formed by that part of the Anio, which is used in the iron works, made out of the ruins of Mecænas' villa. They gush out from under the ancient arches, and tumble more than a hundred feet down the precipice, their white waters gleaming out from the dark and feathery foliage. Not far distant are the remains of the villa of Horace.

We took the road to Frascati, and walked for miles among cane-swamps

342

and over plains covered with sheep. The people we saw, were most degraded and ferocious-looking, and there were many I would not willingly meet alone after nightfall. Indeed it is still considered quite unsafe to venture without the walls of Rome, after dark. The women, with their yellow complexions, and the bright red blankets they wear folded around the head and shoulders, resemble Indian Squaws.

I lately spent three hours in the Museum of the Capitol, on the summit of the sacred hill. In the hall of the Gladiator I noticed an exquisite statue of Diana. There is a pure, virgin grace in the classic outlines of the figure that keeps the eye long upon it. The face is full of cold, majestic dignity, but it is the ideal of a being to be worshipped, rather than loved. The Faun of Praxiteles, in the same room, is a glorious work; it is the perfect embodiment of that wild, merry race the Grecian poets dreamed of. One looks on the Gladiator with a hushed breath and an awed spirit. He is dying; the blood flows more slowly from the deep wound in his side; his head is sinking downwards, and the arm that supports his body becomes more and more nerveless. You feel that a dull mist is coming over his vision, and almost wait to see his relaxing limbs sink suddenly on his shield. That the rude, barbarian form has a soul, may be read in his touchingly expressive countenance. It warms the sympathies like reality to look upon it. Yet how many Romans may have gazed on this work, moved nearly to tears, who have seen hundreds perish in the arena without a pitying emotion! Why is it that Art has a voice frequently more powerful than Nature?

How cold it is here! I was forced to run home to-night, nearly at full speed, from the Café delle Belle Arti through the Corso and the Piazza Colonna, to keep warm. The clear, frosty moon threw the shadow of the column of Antoninus over me as I passed, and it made me shiver to look at the thin, falling sheet of the fountain. Winter is winter everywhere, and even the sun of Italy cannot always scorch his icy wings.

Two days ago we took a ramble outside the walls. Passing the Coliseum and Caracalla's Baths, we reached the tomb of Scipio, a small sepulchral vault, near the roadside. The ashes of the warrior were scattered to the winds long ago, and his mausoleum is fast falling to decay. The old arch over the Appian

way is still standing, near the modern Porta San Sebastiano through which
we entered on the far-famed road. Here and there it is quite entire, and we
walked over the stones once worn by the feet of Virgil and Horace and Cicero.
After passing the temple of Romulus—a shapeless and ivy-grown ruin—and
walking a mile or more beyond the walls, we reached the Circus of Caracalla,
whose long and shattered walls fill the hollow of one of the little dells of the
Campagna. The original structure must have been of great size and splendor,
but those twin Vandals—Time and Avarice—have stripped away everything
but the lofty brick masses, whose nakedness the pitying ivy strives to cover.

Further, on a gentle slope, is the tomb of "the wealthiest Roman's wife,"
familiar to every one through Childe Harold's musings. It is a round, massive
tower, faced with large blocks of marble, and still bearing the name of Cecilia
Metella. One side is much ruined, and the top is overgrown with grass and
wild bushes. The wall is about thirty feet thick, so that but a small round
space is left in the interior, which is open to the rain and filled will rubbish.
The echoes pronounced hollowly after us the name of the dead for whom it
was built, but they could tell us nothing of her life's history—

*"How lived, how loved, how died she?"*

I made a hurried drawing of it, and we then turned to the left, across the
Campagna, to seek the grotto of Egeria. Before us, across the brown plain,
extended the Sabine Mountains; in the clear air the houses of Tivoli, twenty
miles distant, were plainly visible. The giant aqueduct stretched in a long line
across the Campagna to the mountain of Albano, its broken and disjointed
arches resembling the vertebræ of some mighty monster. With the ruins of
temples and tombs strewing the plain for miles around it, it might be called
the spine to the skeleton of Rome.

We passed many ruins, made beautiful by the clinging ivy, and reached
a solemn grove of ever-green oak, overlooking a secluded valley. I was soon
in the meadow, leaping ditches, rustling through cane-brakes, and climbing
up to mossy arches to find out the fountain of Numa's nymph; while my
companion, who had less taste for the romantic, looked on complacently
from the leeward side of the hill. At length we found an arched vault in the

344

hill-side, overhung with wild vines, and shaded in summer by umbrageous trees that grow on the soil above. At the further end a stream of water gushed out from beneath a broken statue, and an aperture in the wall revealed a dark cavern behind. This, then, was "Egeria's grot." The ground was trampled by the feet of cattle, and the taste of the water was anything but pleasant. But it was not for Numa and his nymph alone, that I sought it so ardently. The sunbeam of another mind lingers on the spot. See how it gilds the ruined and neglected fount!

> "*The mosses of thy fountain still are sprinkled*
>
>   *With thine Elysian water-drops; the face*
>
> *Of thy cave-guarded spring, with years unwrinkled,*
>
>   *Reflects the meek-eyed genius of the place,*
>
> *Whose wild, green margin, now no more erase*
>
>   *Art's works; no more its sparkling waters sleep,*
>
> *Prisoned in marble; bubbling from the base*
>
>   *Of the cleft statue, with a gentle leap,*
>
> *The rill runs o'er, and 'round, fern, flowers and ivy creep,*
>
>   *Fantastically tangled.*"

I tried to creep into the grotto, but it was unpleasantly dark, and no nymph appeared to chase away the shadow with her lustrous eyes. The whole hill is pierced by subterranean chambers and passages.

I spent another Sunday morning in St. Peter's. High mass was being celebrated in one of the side Chapels, and a great number of the priesthood were present. The music was simple, solemn, and very impressive, and a fine effect was produced by the combination of the full, sonorous voices of the priests, and the divine sweetness of that band of mutilated unfortunates, who sing here. They sang with a full, clear tone, sweet as the first lispings of a child, but it was painful to hear that melody, purchased at the expense of manhood.

Near the dome is a bronze statue of St. Peter, which seems to have a peculiar atmosphere of sanctity. People say their prayers before it by hundreds, and then kiss its toe, which is nearly worn away by the application of so many thousand lips. I saw a crowd struggle most irreverently to pay their devotion to it. There was a great deal of jostling and confusion; some went so far as to thrust the faces of others against the toe as they were about to kiss it. What is more remarkable, it is an antique statue of Jupiter, taken, I believe, from the Pantheon. An English artist, showing it to a friend, just arrived in Rome, remarked very wittily that it was the statue of Jew-Peter.

I went afterwards to the Villa Borghese, outside the Porta del Popolo. The gardens occupy thirty or forty acres, and are always thronged in the afternoon with the carriages of the Roman and foreign nobility. In summer, it must be a heavenly place; even now, with its musical fountains, long avenues, and grassy slopes, crowned with the fan-like branches of the Italian pine, it reminds one of the fairy landscapes of Boccaccio. We threaded our way through the press of carriages on the Pincian hill, and saw the enormous bulk of St. Peter's loom up against the sunset sky. I counted forty domes and spires in that part of Rome that lay below us—but on what a marble glory looked that sun eighteen centuries ago! Modern Rome—it is in comparison, a den of filth, cheats and beggars!

Yesterday, while taking a random stroll through the city, I visited the church of St. Onofrio, where Tasso is buried. It is not far from St. Peter's, on the summit of a lonely hill. The building was closed, but an old monk admitted us on application. The interior is quite small, but very old, and the floor is covered with the tombs of princes and prelates of a past century. Near the end I found a small slab with the inscription:

*"TORQUATI TASSI*

*OSSA*

*HIC JACENT."*

That was all—but what more was needed? Who knows not the name and fame and sufferings of the glorious bard? The pomp of gold and marble are not needed to deck the slumber of genius. On the wall, above, hangs an old and authentic portrait of him, very similar to the engravings in circulation. A crown of laurel encircles the lofty brow, and the eye has that wild, mournful expression, which accords so well with the mysterious tale of his love and madness.

Owing to the mountain storms, which imposed on us the expense of a carriage-journey to Rome, we shall be prevented from going further. One great cause of this is the heavy fee required for passports in Italy. In most of the Italian cities, the cost of the different visès amounts to $4 or $5; a few such visits as these reduce our funds very materially. The American Consul's fee is $2, owing to the illiberal course of our government, in withholding all salary from her Consuls in Europe. Mr. Brown, however, in whose family we spent last evening very pleasantly, on our requesting that he would deduct something from the usual fee, kindly declined accepting anything. We felt this kindness the more, as from the character which some of our late Consuls bear in Italy, we had not anticipated it. We shall remember him with deeper gratitude than many would suppose, who have never known what it was to be a foreigner.

To-morrow, therefore, we leave Rome—here is, at last, the limit of our wanderings. We have spent much toil and privation to reach here, and now, after two weeks' rambling and musing among the mighty relics of past glory, we turn our faces homeward. The thrilling hope I cherished during the whole pilgrimage—to climb Parnassus and drink from Castaly, under the blue heaven of Greece (both far easier than the steep hill and hidden fount of poesy, I worship afar off)—to sigh for fallen art, beneath the broken friezes of the Parthenon, and look with a pilgrim's eye on the isles of Homer and of Sappho—must be given up, unwillingly and sorrowfully though it be. These glorious anticipations—among the brightest that blessed my boyhood—are slowly wrung from me by stern necessity. Even Naples, the lovely Parthenope, where the Mantuan bard sleeps on the sunny shore, by the bluest of summer seas, with the disinterred Pompeii beyond, and Pæstum amid its roses on the lonely Calabrian plain—even this, almost within sight of the cross of St. Peter's, is barred from me. Farewell then, clime of "fame and eld," since it must be! A pilgrim's blessing for the lore ye have taught him!

# CHAPTER XLII. —

Palo.—The sea is breaking in long swells below the window, and a glorious planet shines in the place of the sunset that has died away. This is our first resting-place since leaving Rome. We have been walking all day over the bare and dreary Campagna, and it is a relief to look at last on the broad, blue expanse of the Tyrrhene Sea.

When we emerged from the cool alleys of Rome, and began to climb up and down the long, barren swells, the sun beat down on us with an almost summer heat. On crossing a ridge near Castel Guido, we took our last look of Rome, and saw from the other side the sunshine lying like a dazzling belt on the far Mediterranean. The country is one of the most wretched that can be imagined. Miles and miles of uncultivated land, with scarcely a single habitation, extend on either side of the road, and the few shepherds who watch their flocks in the marshy hollows, look wild and savage enough for any kind of crime. It made me shudder to see every face bearing such a villainous stamp.

Civita Vecchia, Jan. 1.—We left Palo just after sunrise, and walked in the cool of the morning beside the blue Mediterranean. On the right, the low outposts of the Appenines rose, bleak and brown, the narrow plain between them and the shore resembling a desert, so destitute was it of the signs of civilized life. A low, white cloud that hung over the sea, afar off, showed us the locality of Sardinia, though the land was not visible. The sun shone down warmly, and with the blue sky and bluer sea we could easily have imagined a milder season. The barren scenery took a new interest in my eyes, when I remembered that I was spending amidst it that birth-day which removes me, in the eyes of the world, from dependant youth to responsible manhood.

In the afternoon we found a beautiful cove in a curve of the shore, and went to bathe in the cold surf. It was very refreshing, but not quite equal to the sulphur-bath on the road to Tivoli. The mountains now ran closer to the sea, and the road was bordered with thickets of myrtle. I stopped often to beat my staff into the bushes, and inhale the fragrance that arose from their crushed leaves. The hills were covered with this poetical shrub, and any acre of the ground would make the fortune of a florist at home.

The sun was sinking in a sky of orange and rose, as Civita Vecchia came in sight on a long headland before us. Beyond the sea stretched the dim hills of Corsica. We walked nearly an hour in the clear moonlight, by the sounding shore, before the gate of the city was reached. We have found a tolerable inn, and are now enjoying the pleasures of supper and rest.

Marseilles, Jan. 16.—At length we tread the shore of France—of sunny Provence—the last unvisited realm we have to roam through before returning home. It is with a feeling of more than common relief that we see around us the lively faces and hear the glib tongues of the French. It is like an earnest that the "roughing" we have undergone among Bohemian boors and Italian savages is well nigh finished, and that, henceforth, we shall find civilized sympathy and politeness, if nothing more, to make the way smoother. Perhaps the three woful days which terminated at half-past two yesterday afternoon, as we passed through the narrow strait into the beautiful harbor which Marseilles encloses in her sheltering heart, make it still pleasanter. Now, while there is time, I must describe those three days, for who could write on the wet deck of a steamboat, amid all the sights and smells which a sea voyage creates? Description does not flourish when the bones are sore with lying on planks, and the body shivering like an aspen leaf with cold.

About the old town of Civita Vecchia there is not much to be said, except that it has the same little harbor which Trajan dug for it, and is as dirty and disagreeable as a town can well be. We saw nothing except a little church, and the prison-yard, full of criminals, where the celebrated bandit, Gasparoni, has been now confined for eight years.

The Neapolitan Company's boat, Mongibello, was advertised to leave the 12th, so, after procuring our passports, we went to the office to take passage. The official, however, refused to give us tickets for the third place, because, forsooth, we were not servants or common laborers! and words were wasted in trying to convince him that it would make no difference. As the second cabin fare was nearly three times as high, and entirely too dear for us, we went to the office of the Tuscan Company, whose boat was to leave in two days. Through the influence of an Italian gentleman, secretary to Bartolini, the American Consul, whom we met, they agreed to take us for forty-five francs, on deck, the price of the Neapolitan boat being thirty.

Rather than stay two days longer in the dull town, we went again to the latter Company's office and offered them forty-five francs to go that day in their boat. This removed the former scruples, and tickets were immediately made out. After a plentiful dinner at the albergo, to prepare ourselves for the exposure, we filled our pockets with a supply of bread, cheese, and figs, for the voyage. We then engaged a boatman, who agreed to row us out to the steamer for two pauls, but after he had us on board and an oar's length from the quay, he said two pauls apiece was his bargain. I instantly refused, and, summoning the best Italian I could command, explained our agreement; but he still persisted in demanding double price. The dispute soon drew a number of persons to the quay, some of whom, being boatmen, sided with him. Finding he had us safe in his boat, his manner was exceedingly calm and polite. He contradicted me with a "pardon, Signore!" accompanying the words with a low bow and a graceful lift of his scarlet cap, and replied to my indignant accusations in the softest and most silvery-modulated Roman sentences. I found, at last, that if I was in the right, I cut the worse figure of the two, and, therefore, put an end to the dispute by desiring him to row on at his own price.

The hour of starting was two, but the boat lay quietly in the harbor till four, when we glided out on the open sea, and went northward, with the blue hills of Corsica far on our left. A gorgeous sunset faded away over the water, and the moon rose behind the low mountains of the Italian coast. Having found a warm and sheltered place near the chimney, I drew my beaver further over my eyes, to keep out the moonlight, and lay down on the deck with my knapsack under my head. It was a hard bed, indeed; and the first time I attempted to rise, I found myself glued to the floor by the pitch which was smeared along the seams of the boards! Our fellow-sufferers were a company of Swiss soldiers going home after a four years' service under the King of

350

Naples, but they took to their situation more easily than we.

Sleep was next to impossible, so I paced the deck occasionally, looking out on the moonlit sea and the dim shores on either side. A little after midnight we passed between Elba and Corsica. The dark crags of Elba rose on our right, and the bold headlands of Napoleon's isle stood opposite, at perhaps twenty miles' distance. There was something dreary and mysterious in the whole scene, viewed at such a time—the grandeur of his career, who was born on one and exiled to the other, gave it a strange and thrilling interest.

We made the light-house before the harbor of Leghorn at dawn, and by sunrise were anchored within the mole. I sat on the deck the whole day, watching the picturesque vessels that skimmed about with their lateen sails, and wondering how soon the sailors, on the deck of a Boston brig anchored near us, would see my distant country. Leaving at four o'clock, we dashed away, along the mountain coast of Carrara, at a rapid rate. The wind was strong and cold, but I lay down behind the boiler, and though the boards were as hard as ever, slept two or three hours. When I awoke at half-past two in the morning, after a short rest, Genoa was close at hand. We glided between the two revolving lights on the mole, into the harbor, with the amphitheatre on which the superb city sits, dark and silent around us. It began raining soon, the engine-fire sank down, and as there was no place of shelter, we were shortly wet to the skin.

How long those dreary hours seemed, till the dawn came! All was cold and rainy and dark, and we waited in a kind of torpid misery for daylight. The entire day, I passed sitting in a coil of rope under the stern of the cabin, and even the beauties of the glorious city scarce affected me. We lay opposite the Doria palace, and the constellation of villas and towers still glittered along the hills; but who, with his teeth chattering and limbs numb and damp, could feel pleasure in looking on Elysium itself?

We got under way again at three o'clock. The rain very soon hid the coast from view, and the waves pitched our boat about in a manner not at all pleasant. I soon experienced sea-sickness in all its horrors. We had accidentally made the acquaintance of one of the Neapolitan sailors, who had been in America. He was one of those rough, honest natures I like to meet with—their blunt kindness, is better than refined and oily-tongued suavity. As we were standing by the chimney, reflecting dolefully how we should pass the coming night, he came up and said; "I am in trouble about you, poor fellows! I don't think I shall sleep three hours to-night, to think of you. I shall tell all the cabin they shall give you beds, because they shall see you are gentlemen!" Whether he did so or the officers were moved by spontaneous commiseration, we knew not, but in half an hour a servant beckoned us into the cabin, and berths were given us.

I turned in with a feeling of relief not easily imagined, and forgave the fleas willingly, in the comfort of a shelter from the storm. When I awoke, it was broad day. A fresh breeze was drying the deck, and the sun was half-visible among breaking clouds. We had just passed the Isle of the Titan, one of the Isles des Hyères, and the bay of Toulon opened on our right. It was a rugged, rocky coast, but the hills of sunny Provence rose beyond. The sailor came up with a smile of satisfaction on his rough countenance, and said: "You did sleep better, I think; I did tell them all!" coupling his assertion with a round curse on the officers.

We ran along, beside the brown, bare crags till nearly noon, when we reached the eastern point of the Bay of Marseilles. A group of small islands, formed of bare rocks, rising in precipices three or four hundred feet high, guards the point; on turning into the Gulf, we saw on the left the rocky islands of Pomegues, and If, with the castle crowning the latter, in which Mirabeau was confined. The ranges of hills which rose around the great bay, were spotted and sprinkled over with thousands of the country cottages of the Marseilles merchants, called Bastides; the city itself was hidden from view. We saw apparently the whole bay, but there was no crowd of vessels, such as would befit a great sea-port; a few spires peeping over a hill, with some fortifications, were all that was visible. At length we turned suddenly aside and entered a narrow strait, between two forts. Immediately a broad harbor opened before us, locked in the very heart of the hills on which the city stands. It was covered with vessels of all nations; on leaving the boat, we rowed past the "Aristides," bearing the blue cross of Greece, and I searched eagerly and found, among the crowded masts, the starry banner of America.

I have rambled through all the principal parts of Marseilles, and am very favorably impressed with its appearance. Its cleanliness and the air of life and business which marks the streets, are the more pleasant after coming from the dirty and depopulated Italian cities. The broad avenues, lined with trees, which traverse its whole length, must be delightful in summer. I am often reminded, by its spacious and crowded thoroughfares, of our American cities. Although founded by the Phoceans, three thousand years ago, it has scarcely an edifice of greater antiquity than three or four centuries, and the tourist must content himself with wandering through the narrow streets of the old town, observing the Provençal costumes, or strolling among Turks and Moors on the Quai d'Orléans.

We have been detained here a day longer than was necessary, owing to some misunderstanding about the passports. This has not been favorable to our reduced circumstances, for we have, now but twenty francs each, left, to take us to Paris. Our boots, too, after serving us so long, begin to show signs of failing in this hour of adversity. Although we are somewhat accustomed to such circumstances, I cannot help shrinking when I think of the solitary napoleon and the five hundred miles to be passed. Perhaps, however, the coin will do as much as its great namesake, and achieve for us a Marengo in the war with fate.

# CHAPTER XLIII. — PILGRIMAGE TO VAUCLUSE AND JOURNEY UP THE RHONE.

We left Marseilles about nine o'clock, on a dull, rainy morning, for Avignon and the Rhone, intending to take in our way the glen of Vaucluse. The dirty faubourgs stretch out along the road for a great distance, and we trudged through them, past foundries, furnaces and manufactories, considerably disheartened with the prospect. We wound among the bleak stony hills, continually ascending, for nearly three hours. Great numbers of cabarets, frequented by the common people, lined the roads, and we met continually trains of heavy laden wagons, drawn by large mules. The country is very wild and barren, and would have been tiresome, except for the pine groves with their beautiful green foliage. We got something to eat with difficulty at an inn, for the people spoke nothing but the Provençal dialect, and the place was so cold and cheerless we were glad to go out again into the storm. It mattered little to us, that we heard the language in which the gay troubadours of king René sung their songs of love. We thought more of our dripping clothes and numb, cold limbs, and would have been glad to hear instead, the strong, hearty German tongue, full of warmth and kindly sympathy for the stranger. The wind swept drearily among the hills; black, gusty clouds covered the sky, and the incessant rain filled the road with muddy pools. We looked at the country chateaux, so comfortable in the midst of their sheltering poplars, with a sigh, and thought of homes afar off, whose doors were never closed to us.

This was all forgotten, when we reached Aix, and the hostess of the Café d'Afrique filled her little stove with fresh coal, and hung our wet garments around it, while her daughter, a pale-faced, crippled child, smiled kindly on us and tried to talk with us in French. Putting on our damp, heavy coats again, B—— and I rambled through the streets, while our frugal supper was preparing. We saw the statue of the Bon Roi René, who held at Aix his court of shepherds and troubadours—the dark Cathedral of St. Saveur—the ancient walls and battlements, and gazed down the valley at the dark, precipitous mass of Mont St. Victor, at whose base Marius obtained a splendid victory over the barbarians.

After leaving next morning, we saw at some distance to the south, the enormous aqueduct now being erected for the canal from the Rhone to Marseilles. The shallow, elevated valleys we passed in the forenoon's walk were stony and barren, but covered with large orchards of almond trees, the fruit of which forms a considerable article of export. This district borders on the desert of the Crau, a vast plain of stones, reaching to the mouth of the Rhone and almost entirely uninhabited. We caught occasional glimpses of its sea-like waste, between the summits of the hills. At length, after threading a high ascent, we saw the valley of the Durance suddenly below us. The sun, breaking through the clouds, shone on the mountain wall, which stood on the opposite side, touching with his glow the bare and rocky precipices that frowned far above the stream. Descending to the valley, we followed its course towards the Rhone, with the ruins of feudal bourgs crowning the crags above us.

It was dusk, when we reached the village of Senas, tired with the day's march. A landlord, standing in his door, on the lookout for customers, invited us to enter, in a manner so polite and pressing, we could not choose but do so. This is a universal custom with the country innkeepers. In a little village which we passed towards evening, there was a tavern, with the sign: "The Mother of Soldiers." A portly woman, whose face beamed with kindness and cheerfulness, stood in the door and invited us to stop there for the night. "No, mother!" I answered; "we must go much further to-day." "Go, then," said she, "with good luck, my children! a pleasant journey!" On entering the inn at Senas, two or three bronzed soldiers were sitting by the table. My French vocabulary happening to give out in the middle of a consultation about eggs and onion-soup, one of them came to my assistance and addressed me in German. He was from Fulda, in Hesse Cassel, and had served fifteen years in Africa. Two other young soldiers, from the western border of Germany, came during the evening, and one of them being partly intoxicated, created such a tumult, that a quarrel arose, which ended in his being beaten and turned out of the house.

We met, every day, large numbers of recruits in companies of one or two hundred, on their way to Marseilles to embark for Algiers. They were mostly youths, from sixteen to twenty years of age, and seemed little to forebode their probable fate. In looking on their fresh, healthy faces and bounding forms, I saw also a dim and ghastly vision of bones whitening on the desert, of men perishing with heat and fever, or stricken down by the aim of the savage Bedouin.

Leaving next morning at day-break, we walked on before breakfast to Orgon, a little village in a corner of the cliffs which border the Durance, and crossed the muddy river by a suspension bridge a short distance below, to Cavaillon, where the country people were holding a great market. From this place a road led across the meadow-land to L'Isle, six miles distant. This little town is so named, because it is situated on an island formed by the crystal Sorgues, which flows from the fountains of Vaucluse. It is a very picturesque and pretty place. Great mill-wheels, turning slowly and constantly, stand at intervals in the stream, whose grassy banks are now as green as in spring-time. We walked along the Sorgues, which is quite as beautiful and worthy to be sung as the Clitumnus, to the end of the village, to take the road to Vaucluse. Beside its banks stands a dirty, modern "Hotel de Petrarque et Laure." Alas, that the names of the most romantic and impassioned lovers of all history should be desecrated to a sign-post to allure gormandizing tourists!

The bare mountain in whose heart lies the poet's solitude, now rose before us, at the foot of the lofty Mont Ventoux, whose summit of snows extended beyond. We left the river, and walked over a barren plain, across which the wind blew most drearily. The sky was rainy and dark, and completed the desolateness of the scene, which in no wise heightened our anticipations of the renowned glen. At length we rejoined the Sorgues and entered a little green valley running up into the mountain. The narrowness of the entrance entirely shut out the wind, and except the rolling of the waters over their pebbly bed, all was still and lonely and beautiful. The sides of the dell were covered with olive trees, and a narrow strip of emerald meadow lay at the bottom. It grew more hidden and sequestered as we approached the little village of Vaucluse. Here, the mountain towers far above, and precipices of

356

grey rock, many hundred feet high, hang over the narrowing glen. On a crag over the village are the remains of a castle; the slope below this, now rugged and stony, was once graced by the cottage and garden of Petrarch. All traces of them have long since vanished, but a simple column, bearing the inscription; "À PETRARQUE," stands beside the Sorgues.

We ascended into the defile by a path among the rocks, overshadowed by olive and wild fig trees, to the celebrated fountains of Vaucluse. The glen seems as if struck into the mountain's depths by one blow of an enchanter's wand; and just at the end, where the rod might have rested in its downward sweep, is the fathomless well whose overbrimming fulness gives birth to the Sorgues. We climbed up over the mossy rocks and sat down in the grot, beside the dark, still pool. It was the most absolute solitude. The rocks towered above and over us, to the height of six hundred feet, and the gray walls of the wild glen below shut out all appearance of life. I leaned over the rock and drank of the blue crystal that grew gradually darker towards the centre, till it became a mirror, and gave back a perfect reflection of the crags above it. There was no bubbling—no gushing up from its deep bosom—but the wealth of sparkling waters continually welled over, as from a too-full goblet.

It was with actual sorrow that I turned away from the silent spot. I never visited a place to which the fancy clung more suddenly and fondly. There is something holy in its solitude, making one envy Petrarch the years of calm and unsullied enjoyment which blessed him there. As some persons, whom we pass as strangers, strike a hidden chord in our spirits, compelling a silent sympathy with them, so some landscapes have a character of beauty which harmonizes thrillingly with the mood in which we look upon them, till we forget admiration in the glow of spontaneous attachment. They seem like abodes of the Beautiful, which the soul in its wanderings long ago visited, and now recognizes and loves as the home of a forgotten dream. It was thus I felt by the fountains of Vaucluse; sadly and with weary steps I turned away, leaving its loneliness unbroken as before.

We returned over the plain in the wind, under the gloomy sky, passed L'Isle at dusk, and after walking an hour with a rain following close behind us, stopped at an auberge in Le Thor, where we rested our tired frames and broke our long day's fasting. We were greeted in the morning with a dismal rain and wet roads, as we began the march. After a time, however, it poured down in such torrents, that we were obliged to take shelter in a remise by the road, side, where a good woman, who addressed us in the unintelligible Provençal, kindled up a blazing fire. On climbing a long hill, when the storm had abated, we experienced a delightful surprise. Below us lay the broad valley of the Rhone, with its meadows looking fresh and spring-like after the rain. The clouds were breaking away; clear blue sky was visible over Avignon, and a belt of sunlight lay warmly along the mountains of Languedoc. Many villages, with their tall, picturesque towers, dotted the landscape, and the groves of green olive enlivened the barrenness of winter. Two or three hours' walk over the plain, by a road fringed with willows, brought us to the gates of Avignon.

We walked around its picturesque turreted wall, and rambled through its narrow streets, washed here and there by streams which turn the old mill-wheels lazily around. We climbed up to the massive palace, which overlooks the city from its craggy seat, attesting the splendor it enjoyed, when for thirty years the Papal Court was held there, and the gray, weather-beaten, irregular building, resembling a pile of precipitous rocks, echoed with the revels of licentious prelates. We could not enter to learn the terrible secrets of the Inquisition, here unveiled, but we looked up at the tower, from which the captive Rienzi was liberated at the intercession of Petrarch.

After leaving Avignon, we took the road up the Rhone for Lyons, turning our backs upon the rainy south. We reached the village of Sorgues by dusk, and accepted the invitation of an old dame to lodge at her inn, which proved to be a blacksmith's shop! It was nevertheless clean and comfortable, and we sat down in one corner, out of the reach of the showers of sparks, which flew hissing from a red-hot horseshoe, that the smith and his apprentice were hammering. A Piedmontese pedlar, who carried the "Song of the Holy St. Philomène" to sell among the peasants, came in directly, and bargained for a sleep on some hay, for two sous. For a bed in the loft over the shop, we were charged five sous each, which, with seven sous for supper, made our expenses for the night about eleven cents! Our circumstances demanded the greatest economy, and we began to fear whether even this spare allowance would enable us to reach Lyons. Owing to a day's delay in Marseilles, we had left that city with but fifteen francs each; the incessant storms of winter and the worn-out state of our shoes, which were no longer proof against water or mud, prolonged our journey considerably, so that by starting before dawn and walking till dark, we were only able to make thirty miles a day. We could always procure beds for five sous, and as in the country inns one is only charged for what he chooses to order, our frugal suppers cost us but little. We purchased bread and cheese in the villages, and made our breakfasts and dinners on a bank by the roadside, or climbed the rocks and sat down by the source of some trickling rill. This simple fare had an excellent relish, and although we walked in wet clothes from morning till night, often laying down on the damp, cold earth to rest, our health was never affected.

It is worth all the toil and privation we have as yet undergone, to gain, from actual experience, the blessed knowledge that man always retains a kindness and brotherly sympathy towards his fellow—that under all the weight of vice and misery which a grinding oppression of soul and body brings on the laborers of earth, there still remain many bright tokens of a better nature. Among the starving mountaineers of the Hartz—the degraded peasantry of Bohemia—the savage contadini of Central Italy, or the dwellers on the hills of Provence and beside the swift Rhone, we almost invariably found kind, honest hearts, and an aspiration for something better, betokening the consciousness that such brute-like, obedient existence was not their proper destiny. We found few so hardened as to be insensible to a kind look or a friendly word, and nothing made us forget we were among strangers so much as the many tokens of sympathy which met us when least looked for. A young Englishman, who had traveled on foot from Geneva to Rome, enduring many privations on account of his reduced circumstances, said to me, while speaking on this subject: "A single word of kindness from a stranger would make my heart warm and my spirits cheerful, for days afterwards." There is not so much evil in man as men would have us believe; and it is a happy comfort to know and feel this.

Leaving our little inn before day break next morning, we crossed the

Sorgues, grown muddy since its infancy at Vaucluse, like many a young soul, whose mountain purity goes out into the soiling world and becomes sullied forever. The road passed over broad, barren ranges of hills, and the landscape was destitute of all interest, till we approached Orange. This city is built at the foot of a rocky height, a great square projection of which seemed to stand in its midst. As we approached nearer, however, arches and lines of cornice could be discerned, and we recognized it as the celebrated amphitheatre, one of the grandest Roman relics in the south of France.

I stood at the foot of this great fabric, and gazed up at it in astonishment. The exterior wall, three hundred and thirty-four feet in length, and rising to the height of one hundred and twenty-one feet, is still in excellent, preservation, and through its rows of solid arches one looks on the broken ranges of seats within. On the crag above, and looking as if about to topple down on it, is a massive fragment of the fortress of the Princes of Orange, razed by Louis XIV. Passing through the city, we came to the beautiful Roman triumphal arch, which to my eye is a finer structure than that of Constantino at Rome. It is built of a rich yellow marble and highly ornamented with sculptured trophies. From the barbaric shields and the letters MARIO, still remaining, it has been supposed to commemorate the victory of Marius over the barbarians, near Aix. A frieze, running along the top, on each side, shows, although broken and much defaced by the weather, the life and action which once marked the struggling figures. These Roman ruins, scattered through Provence and Languedoc, though inferior in historical interest, equal in architectural beauty the greater part of those in the Eternal City itself.

The rest of the day the road was monotonous, though varied somewhat by the tall crags of Mornas and Mont-dragon, towering over the villages of the same name. Night came on as the rock of Pierrelatte, at whose foot we were to sleep, appeared in the distance, rising like a Gibraltar from the plain, and we only reached it in time to escape the rain that came down the valley of the Rhone.

Next day we passed several companies of soldiers on their way to Africa. One of them was accompanied by a young girl, apparently the wife of the recruit by whose side she was marching. She wore the tight blue jacket of the troop, and a red skirt, reaching to the knees, over her soldier pantaloons; while her pretty face showed to advantage beneath a small military cap. It was a "Fille du Regiment" in real life. Near Montelimart, we lost sight of Mont Ventoux, whose gleaming white crest had been visible all the way from Vaucluse, and passed along the base of a range of hills running near to the river. So went our march, without particular incident, till we bivouacked for the night among a company of soldiers in the little village of Loriol.

Leaving at six o'clock, wakened by the trumpets which called up the soldiery to their day's march, we reached the river Drome at dawn, and from the bridge over its rapid current, gazed at the dim, ash-colored masses of the Alps of Dauphiné, piled along the sky, far up the valley. The coming of morn threw a yellow glow along their snowy sides, and lighted up, here and there, a flashing glacier. The peasantry were already up and at work, and caravans of pack-wagons rumbled along in the morning twilight We trudged on with them, and by breakfast-time had made some distance of the way to Valence. The road, which does not approach the Rhone, is devoid of interest and tiresome, though under a summer sky, when the bare vine-hills are latticed over with green, and the fruit-trees covered with blossoms and foliage, it might be a scene of great beauty.

Valence, which we reached towards noon, is a commonplace city on the Rhone; and my only reasons for traversing its dirty streets in preference to taking the road, which passes without the walls, were—to get something for dinner, and because it might have been the birth-place of Aymer de Valence, the valorous Crusader, chronicled in "Ivanhoe," whose tomb I had seen in Westminster Abbey. One of the streets which was marked "Rue Bayard," shows that my valiant namesake—the knight without fear and reproach—is still remembered in his native province. The ruins of his chateau are still standing among the Alps near Grenoble.

In the afternoon we crossed the Isère, a swift, muddy river, which rises among the Alps of Dauphiné, We saw their icy range, among which is the desert solitude of the Grand Chartreuse, far up the valley; but the thick atmosphere hid the mighty Mont Blanc, whose cloudy outline, eighty miles distant in a "bee line," is visible in fair weather. At Tain, we came upon the

Rhone again, and walked along the base of the hills which contract its current. Here, I should call it beautiful. The scenery has a wildness that approaches to that of the Rhine. Rocky, castellated heights frown over the rushing waters, which have something of the majesty of their "exulting and abounding" rival. Winding around the curving hills, the scene is constantly varied, and the little willowed islets clasped in the embrace of the stream, mingle a trait of softened beauty with its sterner character.

After passing the night at a village on its banks, we left it again at St. Vallier, the next morning. At sunset, the spires of Vienne were visible, and the lofty Mont Pilas, the snows of whose riven summits feed the springs of the Loire on its western side, stretched majestically along the opposite bank of the Rhone. In a meadow, near Vienne, stands a curious Roman obelisk, seventy-six feet in height. The base is composed of four pillars, connected by arches, and the whole structure has a barbaric air, compared with the more elegant monuments of Orange and Nismes. Vienne, which is mentioned by several of the Roman historians under its present name, was the capital of the Allobroges, and I looked upon it with a new and strange interest, on calling to mind my school-boy days, when I had become familiar with that war-like race, in toiling over the pages of Cæsar. We walked in the mud and darkness for what seemed a great distance, and finally took shelter in a little inn at the northern end of the city. Two Belgian soldiers, coming from Africa, were already quartered there, and we listened to their tales of the Arab and the desert, while supper was preparing.

The morning of the 25th was dull and rainy; the road, very muddy and unpleasant, led over the hills, avoiding the westward curve of the Rhone, directly towards Lyons. About noon, we came in sight of the broad valley in which the Rhone first clasps his Burgundian bride—the Saone, and a cloud of impenetrable coal-smoke showed us the location of Lyons. A nearer approach revealed a large flat dome, and some ranges of tall buildings near the river. We soon entered the suburb of La Guillotière, which has sprung up on the eastern bank of the Rhone. Notwithstanding our clothes were like sponges, our boots entirely worn out, and our bodies somewhat thin with nine days exposure to the wintry storms in walking two hundred and forty miles, we

362

entered Lyons with suspense and anxiety. But one franc apiece remained out of the fifteen with which we left Marseilles. B—— wrote home some time ago, directing a remittance to be forwarded to a merchant at Paris, to whom he had a letter of introduction, and in the hope that this had arrived, he determined to enclose the letter in a note, stating our circumstances, and requesting him to forward a part of the remittance to Lyons. We had then to wait at least four days; people are suspicious and mistrustful in cities, and if no relief should come, what was to be done?

After wading through the mud of the suburbs, we chose a common-looking inn near the river, as the comfort of our stay depended wholly on the kindness of our hosts, and we hoped to find more sympathy among the laboring classes. We engaged lodgings for four or five days; after dinner the letter was dispatched, and we wandered about through the dark, dirty city until night. Our landlord, Monsieur Ferrand, was a rough, vigorous man, with a gloomy, discontented expression; his words were few and blunt; but a certain restlessness of manner, and a secret flashing of his cold, forbidding eye betrayed to me some strong hidden excitement. Madame Ferrand was kind and talkative, though passionate; but the appearance of the place gave me an unfavorable impression, which was heightened by the thought that it was now impossible to change our lodgings until relief should arrive. When bed-time came, a ladder was placed against a sort of high platform along one side of the kitchen; we mounted and found a bed, concealed from the view of those below by a dusty muslin curtain. We lay there, between heaven and earth—the dirty earth of the brick floor and the sooty heaven of the ceiling—listening until midnight to the boisterous songs, and loud, angry disputes in the room adjoining. Thus ended our first day in Lyons.

Five weary days, each of them containing a month of torturing suspense, have since passed. Our lodging-place grew so unpleasant that we preferred wandering all day through the misty, muddy, smoky streets, taking refuge in the covered bazaars when it rained heavily. The gloom of every thing around us, entirely smothered down the lightness of heart which made us laugh over our embarrassments at Vienna. When at evening, the dull, leaden hue of the clouds seemed to make the air dark and cold and heavy, we walked beside the swollen and turbid Rhone, under an avenue of leafless trees, the damp soil chilling our feet and striking a numbness through our frames, and then I knew what those must feel who have no hope in their destitution, and not a friend in all the great world, who is not wretched as themselves. I prize the lesson, though the price of it is hard.

"This morning," I said to B——, "will terminate our suspense." I felt cheerful in spite of myself; and this was like a presentiment of coming good luck. To pass the time till the mail arrived we climbed to the chapel of Fourvières, whose walls are covered with votive offerings to a miraculous picture of the Virgin. But at the precise hour we were at the Post Office. What an intensity of suspense can be felt in that minute, while the clerk is looking over the letters! And what a lightning-like shock of joy when it did come, and was opened with eager, trembling hands, revealing the relief we had almost despaired of! The city did not seem less gloomy, for that was impossible, but the faces of the crowd which had appeared cold and suspicious, were now kind and cheerful. we came home to our lodgings with changed feelings, and Madame Ferrand must have seen the joy in our faces, for she greeted us with an unusual smile.

We leave to-morrow morning for Chalons. I do not feel disposed to describe Lyons particularly, although I have become intimately acquainted with every part of it, from Presqu' isle Perrache to Croix Rousse. I know the contents of every shop in the Bazaar, and the passage of the Hotel Dieu—the title of every volume in the bookstores in the Place Belcour—and the countenance of every boot-block and apple-woman on the Quais on both sides of the river. I have walked up the Saone to Pierre Seise—down the Rhone to his muddy marriage—climbed the Heights of Fourvières, and promenaded in the Cours Napoleon! Why, men have been presented with the freedom of cities, when they have had far less cause for such an honor than this!

# CHAPTER XLIV. — TRAVELING IN BURGUNDY—THE MISERIES OF A COUNTRY DILIGENCE.

Paris, Feb. 6, 1840.—Every letter of the date is traced with an emotion of joy, for our dreary journey is over. There was a magic in the name that revived us during a long journey, and now the thought that it is all over—that these walls which enclose us, stand in the heart of the gay city—seems almost too joyful to be true. Yesterday I marked with the whitest chalk, on the blackest of all tablets to make the contrast greater, for I got out of the cramped diligence at the Barrière de Charenton, and saw before me in the morning twilight, the immense groy mass of Paris. I forgot my numbed and stiffened frame, and every other of the thousand disagreeable feelings of diligence traveling, in the pleasure which that sight afforded.

We arose in the dark at Lyons, and after bidding adieu to morose Monsieur Ferrand, traversed the silent city and found our way in the mist and gloom to the steamboat landing on the Saone. The waters were swollen much above their usual level, which was favorable for the boat, as long as there was room enough left to pass under the bridges. After a great deal of bustle we got under way, and were dashing out of Lyons, against the swift current, before day-break. We passed L'Isle Barbe, once a favorite residence of Charlemagne, and now the haunt of the Lyonnaise on summer holidays, and going under the suspension bridges with levelled chimneys, entered the picturesque hills above, which are covered with vineyards nearly to the top; the villages scattered over them have those square, pointed towers, which give such a quaintness to French country scenery.

The stream being very high, the meadows on both sides were deeply overflowed. To avoid the strong current in the centre, our boat ran along the banks, pushing aside the alder thickets and poplar shoots; in passing the bridges, the pipes were always brought down flat on the deck. A little after noon, we passed the large town of Macon, the birth-place of the poet Lamartine. The valley of the Saone, no longer enclosed among the hills, spread out to several miles in width. Along the west lay in sunshine the vine-mountains of Côte d'Or, and among the dark clouds in the eastern sky, we could barely distinguish the outline of the Jura. The waters were so much swollen as to cover the plain for two or three miles. We seemed to be sailing down a lake, with rows of trees springing up out of the water, and houses and villages lying like islands on its surface. A sunset that promised better weather tinged the broad brown flood, as Chalons came in sight, looking like a city built along the shore of a lake. We squeezed through the crowd of porters and diligence men, declining their kind offers, and hunted quarters to suit ourselves.

We left Chalons on the morning of the 1st, in high spirits at the thought that there were but little more than two hundred miles between us and Paris. In walking over the cold, muddy plain, we passed a family of strolling musicians, who were sitting on a heap of stones by the roadside. An ill-dressed, ill-natured man and woman, each carrying a violin, and a thin, squalid girl, with a tamborine, composed the group. Their faces bore that unfeeling stamp, which springs from depravity and degradation. When we had walked somewhat more than a mile, we overtook a little girl, who was crying bitterly. By her features, from which the fresh beauty of childhood had not been worn, and the steel triangle which was tied to her belt, we knew she belonged to the family we had passed. Her dress was thin and ragged and a pair of wooden shoes but ill protected her feet from the sharp cold. I stopped and asked her why she cried, but she did not at first answer. However, by questioning, I found her unfeeling parents had sent her on without food; she was sobbing with hunger and cold. Our pockets were full of bread and cheese which we had bought for breakfast, and we gave her half a loaf, which stopped her tears at once. She looked up and thanked us, smiling; and sitting down on a bank, began to eat as if half famished.

The physiognomy of this region is very singular. It appears as if the country had been originally a vast elevated plain, and some great power had scooped out, as with a hand, deep circular valleys all over its surface. In winding along the high ridges, we often looked down, on either side, into such hollows, several miles in diameter, and sometimes entirely covered with

366

vineyards. At La Rochepot, a quaint, antique village, lying in the bottom of one of these dells, we saw the finest ruin of the middle ages that I have met with in France. An American lady had spoken to me of it in Rome, and I believe Willis mentions it in his "Pencillings," but it is not described in the guide books, nor could we learn what feudal lord had ever dwelt in its halls. It covers the summit of a stately rock, at whose foot the village is crouched, and the green ivy climbs up to the very top of its gray towers.

As the road makes a wide curve around the side of the hill, we descended to the village by the nearer foot-path, and passed among its low, old houses, with their pointed gables and mossy roofs. The path led close along the foot of the rock, and we climbed up to the ruin, and stood in its grass-grown courtyard. Only the outer walls and the round towers at each corner are left remaining; the inner part has been razed to the ground, and where proud barons once marshalled their vassals, the villagers now play their holiday games. On one side, several Gothic windows are left standing, perfect, though of simple construction, and in the towers we saw many fire-places and door-ways of richly cut stone, which looked as fresh as if just erected.

We passed the night at Ivry (not the Ivry which gained Henri Quatre his kingdom) and then continued our march over roads which I can only compare to our country roads in America during the spring thaw. In addition to this, the rain commenced early in the morning and continued all day, so that we were completely wet the whole time. The plains, too high and cold to produce wine, were varied by forests of beech and oak, and the population was thinly scattered over them in small villages. Travelers generally complain very much of the monotony of this part of France, and, with such dreary weather, we could not disagree with them.

As the day wore on, the rain increased, and the sky put on that dull, gray cast, which denotes a lengthened storm. We were fain to stop at nightfall, but there was no inn near at hand—not even a hovel of a cabaret in which to shelter ourselves, and, on enquiring of the wagoners, we received the comforting assurance that there was yet a league and a half to the nearest stopping place. On, then, we went, with the pitiless storm beating in our faces and on our breasts, till there was not a dry spot left, except what our knapsacks covered. We could not have been more completely saturated if we had been dipped in the Yonne. At length, after two hours of slipping and sliding along in the mud and wet and darkness, we reached Saulieu, and, by the warm fire, thanked our stars that the day's dismal tramp was over.

By good or bad luck (I have not yet decided which) a vehicle was to start the next morning for Auxerre, distant sixty miles, and the fare being but five francs, we thought it wisest to take places. It was always with reluctance that we departed from our usual mode of traveling, but, in the present instance, the circumstances absolutely compelled it.

Next morning, at sunrise, we took our seats in a large, square vehicle on two wheels, calculated for six persons and a driver, with a single horse. But, as he was fat and round as an elephant, and started off at a brisk pace, and we were well protected from the rain, it was not so bad after all, barring the jolts and jarred vertebræ. We drove on, over the same dreary expanse of plain and forest, passing through two or three towns in the course of the day, and by evening had made somewhat more than half our journey. Owing to the slowness of our fresh horse, we were jolted about the whole night, and did not arrive at Auxerre until six o'clock in the morning. After waiting an hour in a hotel beside the rushing Yonne, a lumbering diligence was got ready, and we were given places to Paris for seven francs. As the distance is one hundred and ten miles, this would be considered cheap, but I should not want to travel it again and be paid for doing so. Twelve persons were packed into a box not large enough for a cow, and no cabinet-maker ever dove-tailed the corners of his bureaus tighter than we did our knees and nether extremities. It is my lot to be blessed with abundance of stature, and none but tall persons can appreciate the misery of sitting for hours with their joints in an immovable vice. The closeness of the atmosphere—for the passengers would not permit the windows to be opened for fear of taking cold—combined with loss of sleep, made me so drowsy that my head was continually falling on my next neighbor, who, being a heavy country lady, thrust it indignantly away. I would then try my best to keep it up awhile, but it would droop gradually, till the crash of a bonnet or a smart bump against some other head would recall me, for a moment, to consciousness.

We passed Joigny, on the Yonne, Sens, with its glorious old cathedral, and at dusk reached Montercau, on the Seine. This was the scene of one of Napoleon's best victories, on his return from Elba. In driving over the bridge, I looked down on the swift and swollen current, and hoped that its hue might never be darkened again so fearfully as the last sixty years have witnessed. No river in Europe has such an association connected with it. We think of the Danube, for its majesty, of the Rhine, for its wild beauty, but of the Seine— for its blood!

In coming thus to the last famed stream I shall visit in Europe, I might say, with Barry Cornwall:

> *"We've sailed through banks of green,*
>
> *Where the wild waves fret and quiver;*
>
> *And we've down the Danube been—*
>
> *The dark, deep, thundering river!*
>
> *We've thridded the Elbe and Rhone,*
>
> *The Tiber and blood dyed Seine,*
>
> *And we've been where the blue Garonne*
>
> *Goes laughing to meet the main!"*

All that night did we endure squeezing and suffocation, and no morn was ever more welcome than that which revealed to us Paris. With matted hair, wild, glaring eyes, and dusty and dishevelled habiliments, we entered the gay capital, and blessed every stone upon which we placed our feet, in the fulness of our joy.

In paying our fare at Auxerre, I was obliged to use a draft on the banker, Rougemont de Lowenberg. The ignorant conductor hesitated to change this, but permitted us to go, on condition of keeping it until we should arrive. Therefore, on getting out of the diligence, after forty-eight hours of sleepless and fasting misery, the facteur of the office went with me to get it paid, leaving B—— to wait for us. I knew nothing of Paris, and this merciless man kept me for three hours at his heels, following him on all his errands, before he did mine, in that time traversing the whole length of the city, in order to leave a chèvre-feuille at an aristocratic residence in the Faubourg St. Germain. Yet even combined weariness and hunger could not prevent me from looking with vivid interest down a long avenue, at the Column of the place Vendôme, in passing, and gazing up in wonder at the splendid portico of the Madeleine. But of anything else I have a very faint remembrance. "You can eat breakfast, now, I think," said he, when we returned, "we have walked more than four leagues!"

I know we will be excused, that, instead of hurrying away to Notre Dame or the Louvre, we sat down quietly to a most complete breakfast. Even the most romantic must be forced to confess that admiration does not sit well on an empty stomach. Our first walk was to a bath, and then, with complexions several shades lighter, and limbs that felt us if lifted by invisible wings, we hurried away to the Post Office. I seized the welcome missives from my far home, with a beating heart, and hastening back, read till the words became indistinct in the twilight.

# CHAPTER XLV. – POETICAL SCENES IN PARIS.

What a gay little world in miniature this is! I wonder not that the French, with their exuberant gaiety of spirit, should revel in its ceaseless tides of pleasure, as if it were an earthly Elysium. I feel already the influence of its cheerful atmosphere, and have rarely threaded the crowds of a stranger city, with so light a heart as I do now daily, on the thronged banks of the Seine. And yet it would be difficult to describe wherein consists this agreeable peculiarity. You can find streets as dark and crooked and dirty anywhere in Germany, and squares and gardens as gay and sunny beyond the Alps, and yet they would affect you far differently. You could not, as here, divest yourself of every particle of sad or serious thought and be content to gaze for hours on the showy scene, without an idea beyond the present moment. It must be that the spirit of the croud is magnetically contagious.

The evening of our arrival we walked out past the massive and stately Hotel de Ville, and took a promenade along the Quais. The shops facing the river presented a scene of great splendor. Several of the Quais on the north bank of the Seine are occupied almost entirely by jewellers, the windows of whose shops, arranged in a style of the greatest taste, make a dazzling display. Rows of gold watches and chains are arranged across the crystal panes, and heaped in pyramids on long glass slabs; cylindrical wheels of wire, hung with jewelled breastpins and earrings, turn slowly around by some invisible agency, displaying row after row of their glittering treasures.

From the centre of the Pont Neuf, we could see for a long distance up and down the river. The different bridges traced on either side a dozen starry lines through the dark air, and a continued blaze lighted the two shores in their whole length, revealing the outline of the Isle da la Cité. I recognized the Palaces of the Louvre and the Tuileries in the dusky mass beyond. Eastward, looming against the dark sky, I could faintly trace the black towers of Notre Dame, The rushing of the swift waters below mingled with the rattling of a thousand carts and carriages, and the confusion of a thousand voices, till it seemed like some grand nightly festival.

I first saw Notre Dame by moonlight. The shadow of its stupendous front was thrown directly towards me, hiding the innumerable lines of the ornamental sculpture which cover its tall, square towers. I walked forward until the interlacing, Moorish arches between them stood full against the moon, and the light, struggling through the quaint openings of the tracery, streamed in silver lines down into the shadow. The square before it was quite deserted, for it stands on a lonely part of the Isle de la Cité, and it looked thus far more majestic and solemn than in the glaring daylight.

The great quadrangle of the Tuileries encloses the Place du Carrousel, in the centre of which stands a triumphal arch, erected by Napoleon after his Italian victories. Standing in the middle of this arch, you look through the open passage in the central building of the palace, into the Gardens beyond. Further on, in a direct line, the middle avenue of the Gardens extends away to the Place de la Concorde, where the Obelisk of Luxor makes a perpendicular line through your vista; still further goes the broad avenue through the Elysian Fields, until afar off, the Arc de l'Etoile, two miles distant, closes this view through the palace doorway.

Let us go through it, and on, to the Place de la Concorde, reserving the Gardens for another time. What is there in Europe—nay, in the world,—equal to this? In the centre, the mighty obelisk of red granite pierces the sky,—on either hand showers of silver spray are thrown up from splendid bronze fountains—statues and pillars of gilded bronze sweep in a grand circle around the square, and on each side magnificent vistas lead the eye off, and combine the distant with the near, to complete this unparalleled view! Eastward, beyond the tall trees in the garden of the Tuileries, rises the long front of the Palace, with the tri-color floating above; westward, in front of us, is the Forest of the Elysian Fields, with the arch of triumph nearly a mile and a half distant, looking down from the end of the avenue, at the Barriere de Neuilly. To the right and left are the marble fronts of the Church of the Madeleine and the Chamber of Deputies, the latter on the other side of the Seine. Thus the groves and gardens of Paris—the palace of her kings— the proud monument of her sons' glory—and the masterpieces of modern

French architecture are all embraced in this one splendid coup d'oeil.

Following the motley multitude to the bridge, I crossed and made my way to the Hotel des Invalides. Along the esplanade, playful companies of children were running and tumbling in their sports over the green turf, which was as fresh as a meadow; while, not the least interesting feature of the scene, numbers of scarred and disabled veterans, in the livery of the Hospital, basked in the sunshine, watching with quiet satisfaction the gambols of the second generation they have seen arise. What tales could they not tell, those wrinkled and feeble old men! What visions of Marengo and Austerlitz and Borodino shift still with a fiery vividness through their fading memories! Some may have left a limb on the Lybian desert; and the sabre of the Cossack may have scarred the brows of others. They witnessed the rising and setting of that great meteor, which intoxicated France with such a blaze of power and glory, and now, when the recollection of that wonderful period seems almost like a stormy dream, they are left to guard the ashes of their ancient General, brought back from his exile to rest in the bosom of his own French people. It was to me a touching and exciting thing, to look on those whose eyes had witnessed the filling up of such a fated leaf in the world's history.

Entrance is denied to the tomb of Napoleon until it is finished, which will not be for three or four yours yet. I went, however, into the "Church of the Banners"—a large chapel, hung with two or three hundred flags taken by the armies of the Empire. The greater part of them were Austrian and Russian. It appeared to be empty when I entered, but on looking around, I saw an old gray-headed soldier kneeling at one side. His head was bowed over his hands, and he seemed perfectly absorbed in his thoughts. Perhaps the very tattered banners which hung down motionless above his head, he might have assisted in conquering. I looked a moment on those eloquent trophies, and then noiselessly withdrew.

There is at least one solemn spot near Paris; the laughing winds that come up from the merry city sink into sighs under the cypress boughs of Pere Lachaise. And yet it is not a gloomy place, but full of a serious beauty, fitting for a city of the dead. I shall never forget the sunny afternoon when I first entered its gate and walked slowly up the hill, between rows of tombs, gleaming white amid the heavy foliage, while the green turf around them was just beginning to be starred by the opening daisies, From the little chapel on its summit I looked back at the blue spires of the city, whose roar of life dwindled to a low murmur. Countless pyramids, obelisks and urns, rising far and wide above the cedars and cypresses, showed the extent of the splendid necropolis, which is inhabited by pale, shrouded emigrants from its living sister below. The only sad part of the view, was the slope of the hill alloted to the poor, where legions of plain black crosses are drawn up into solid squares on its side and stand alone gloomy—the advanced guard of the army of Death! I mused over the tombs of Molière and La Fontaine; Massena, Mortier and Lefebre; General Foy and Casimir Perier; and finally descended to the shrine where Abelard reposes by the side of his Heloise. The old sculptured tomb, brought away from the Paraclete, still covers their remains, and pious hands (of lovers, perhaps,) keep fresh the wreaths of immortelles above their marble effigies.

In the Theatre Français, I saw Rachel, the actress. She appeared in the character of "Virginia," in a tragedy of that name, by the poet Latour. Her appearance as she came upon the stage alone, convinced me she would not belie her renown. She is rather small in stature, with dark, piercing eyes and rich black hair; her lips are full, but delicately formed, and her features have a marked yet flexible outline, which conveys the minutest shades of expression. Her voice is clear, deep and thrilling, and like sonic grand strain of music, there is power and meaning in its slightest modulations. Her gestures embody the very spirit of the character; she has so perfectly attained that rare harmony of thought, sound and action, or rather, that unity of feeling which renders them harmonious, that her acting seems the unstudied, irrepressible impulse of her soul. With the first sentence she uttered, I forgot Rachel. I only saw the innocent Roman girl; I awaited in suspense and with a powerful sympathy, the developement of the oft-told tragedy. My blood grew warm with indignation when the words of Appius roused her to anger, and I could scarcely keep back my tears, when, with a voice broken by sobs, she bade farewell to the protecting gods of her father's hearth.

Among the bewildering variety of ancient ornaments and implements

374

in the Egyptian Gallery of the Louvre, I saw an object of startling interest. A fragment of the Iliad, written nearly three thousand years ago! One may even dare to conjecture that the torn and half-mouldered slip of papyrus, upon which he gazes, may have been taken down from the lips of the immortal Chiun. The eyes look on those faded characters, and across the great gulf of Time, the soul leaps into the Past, brought into shadowy nearness by a mirage of the mind. There, as in the desert, images start up, vivid, yet of a vague and dreamy beauty. We see the olive groves of Greece—white-robed youths and maidens sit in the shade of swaying boughs—and one of them reads aloud, in words that sound like the clashing of shields, the deeds of Achilles.

As we step out the western portal of the Tuileries, a beautiful scene greets us. We look on the palace garden, fragrant with flowers and classic with bronze copies of ancient sculpture. Beyond this, broad gravel walks divide the flower-bordered lawns and ranks of marble demigods and heroes look down on the joyous crowd. Children troll their hoops along the avenues or skip the rope under the clipped lindens, whose boughs are now tinged a pale yellow by the bursting buds. The swans glide about on a pond in the centre, begging bread of the bystanders, who watch a miniature ship which the soft breeze carries steadily across. Paris is unseen, but heard, on every side; only the Column of Luxor and the Arc de Triomphe rise blue and grand above the top of the forest. What with the sound of voices, the merry laughter of the children and a host of smiling faces, the scene touches a happy chord in one's heart, and he mingles with it, lost in pleasant reverie, till the sounds fade away with the fading light.

Just below the Baths of the Louvre, there are several floating barges belonging to the washer-women, anchored at the foot of the great stone staircase leading down to the water. They stand there day after day, beating their clothes upon flat boards and rinsing them in the Seine. One day there seemed to have been a wedding or some other cause of rejoicing among them, for a large number of the youngest were talking in great glee on one of the platforms of the staircase, while a handsome, German-looking youth stood near, with a guitar slung around his neck. He struck up a lively air, and the girls fell into a droll sort of a dance. They went at it heavily and roughly enough, but made up in good humor what they lacked in grace; the older members of the craft looked up from their work with satisfaction and many shouts of applause wore sent down to them from the spectators on the Quai and the Pont Neuf. Not content with this, they seized on some luckless men who were descending the steps, and clasping them with their powerful right arms, spun them around like so many tops and sent them whizzing off at a tangent. Loud bursts of laughter greeted this performance, and the stout river maidens returned to their dance with redoubled spirit.

Yesterday, the famous procession of the "boeuf gras" took place for the second time, with great splendor. The order of march had been duly announced beforehand, and by noon all the streets and squares through which it was to pass, were crowded with waiting spectators. Mounted gens d'armes rode constantly to and fro, to direct the passage of vehicles and keep an open thoroughfare. Thousands of country peasants poured into the city, the boys of whom were seen in all directions, blowing distressingly through hollow ox-horns. Altogether, the spirit of nonsense which animated the crowd, displayed itself very amusingly.

A few mounted guards led the procession, followed by a band of music. Then appeared Roman lictors and officers of sacrifice, leading Dagobert, the famous bull of Normandy, destined to the honor of being slaughtered as the Carnival beef. He trod rather tenderly, finding, no doubt, a difference between the meadows of Caen and the pavements of Paris, and I thought he would have been willing to forego his gilded horns and flowery crown, to get back there again. His weight was said to be four thousand pounds, and the bills pompously declared that he had no rival in France, except the elephant in the Jardin des Plantes.

After him came the farmer by whom he was raised, and M. Roland, the butcher of the carnival, followed by a hundred of the same craft, dressed as cavaliers of the different ages of France. They made a very showy appearance, although the faded velvet and soiled tinsel of their mantles were rather too apparent by daylight.

After all these had gone by, came an enormous triumphal car, very

376

profusely covered with gilding and ornamental flowers. A fellow with long woollen hair and beard, intended to represent Time, acted as driver. In the car, under a gilded canopy, reposed a number of persons, in blue silk smocks and yellow "fleshtights," said to be Venus, Apollo, the Graces, &c. but I endeavored in vain to distinguish one divinity from another. However, three children on the back seat, dressed in the same style, with the addition of long flaxy ringlets, made very passable Cupids. This closed the march; which passed onward towards the Place de la Concorde, accompanied by the sounds of music and the shouts of the mob. The broad, splendid line of Boulevards, which describe a semi-circle around the heart of the city, were crowded, and for the whole distance of three miles, it required no slight labor to make one's way. People in masks and fancy costumes were continually passing and re-passing, and I detected in more than one of the carriages, checks rather too fair to suit the slouched hunter's hats which shaded them. It seemed as if all Paris was taking a holiday, and resolved to make the most of it.

## CHAPTER XLVI. — A GLIMPSE OF NORMANDY.

After a residence of five weeks, which, in spite of some few troubles, passed away quickly and delightfully, I turned my back on Paris. It was not regret I experienced on taking my seat in the cars for Versailles, but that feeling of reluctance with which we leave places whose brightness and gaiety force the mind away from serious toil. Steam, however, cuts short all sentiment, and in much less time than it takes to bid farewell to a German, we had whizzed past the Place d'Europe, through the barrier, and were watching the spires start up from the receding city, on the way to St. Cloud.

At Versailles I spent three hours in a hasty walk through the palace, which allowed but a bare glance at the gorgeous paintings of Horace Vernet. His "Taking of Constantine" has the vivid look of reality. The white houses shine in the sun, and from the bleached earth to the blue and dazzling sky, there seems to hang a heavy, scorching atmosphere. The white smoke of the artillery curls almost visibly off the canvass, and the cracked and half-sprung walls look as if about to topple down on the besiegers. One series of halls is devoted to the illustration of the knightly chronicles of France, from the days of Charlemagne to those of Bayard and Gaston de Foix. Among these pictured legends, I looked with the deepest interest on that of the noble girl of Orleans. Her countenance—the same in all these pictures and in a beautiful statue of her, which stands in one of the corridors—is said to be copied from an old and well-authenticated portrait. United to the sweetness and purity of peasant beauty, she has the lofty brow and inspired expression of a prophetess. There is a soft light in her full blue eye that does not belong to earth. I wonder not the soldiery deemed her chosen by God to lead them to successful battle; had I lived in those times I could have followed her consecrated banner to the ends of the earth. In the statue, she stands musing, with her head drooping forward, as if the weight of the breastplate oppressed her woman's heart; the melancholy soul which shines through the marble seems to forebode the fearful winding-up of her eventful destiny.

The afternoon was somewhat advanced, by the time I had seen the palace and gardens. After a hurried dinner at a restaurant, I shouldered my knapsack and took the road to St. Germain. The day was gloomy and cheerless, and I should have felt very lonely but for the thought of soon reaching England. There is no time of the year more melancholy than a cold, cloudy day in March; whatever may be the beauties of pedestrian traveling in fairer seasons, my experience dictates that during winter storms and March glooms, it had better be dispensed with. However, I pushed on to St. Germain, threaded its long streets, looked down from the height over its magnificent tract of forest and turned westward down the Seine. Owing to the scantiness of villages, I was obliged to walk an hour and a half in the wind and darkness, before I reached a solitary inn. As I opened the door and asked for lodging, the landlady inquired if I had the necessary papers. I answered in the affirmative and was admitted. While I was eating supper, they prepared their meal on the other end of the small table and sat down together. They fell into the error, so common to ignorant persons, of thinking a foreigner could not understand them, and began talking quite unconcernedly about me. "Why don't he take the railroad?" said the old man: "he must have very little money—it would be bad for us if he had none." "Oh!" remarked his son, "if he had none, he would not be sitting there so quiet and unconcerned." I thought there was some knowledge of human nature in this remark. "And besides," added the landlady, "there is no danger for us, for we have his passport." Of course I enjoyed this in secret, and mentally pardoned their suspicions, when I reflected that the high roads between Paris and London are frequented by many imposters, which makes the people naturally mistrustful. I walked all the next day through a beautiful and richly cultivated country. The early fruit trees were bursting into bloom, and the farmers led out their cattle to pasturage in the fresh meadows. The scenery must be delightful in summer— worthy of all that has been said or sung about lovely Normandy. On the morning of the third day, before reaching Rouen, I saw at a distance the remains of Chateau Galliard, the favorite castle of Richard Coeur de Lion. Rouen breathes everywhere of the ancient times of Normandy. Nothing can be more picturesque than its quaint, irregular wooden houses, and the low, mossy mills, spanning the clear streams which rush through its streets. The Cathedral, with its four towers, rises from among the clustered cottages like a

379

giant rook, split by the lightning and worn by the rains of centuries is into a thousand fantastic shapes.

Resuming my walk in the afternoon, I climbed the heights west of the city, and after passing through a suburb four or five miles in length, entered the vale of the Cailly. This is one of the sweetest scenes in France. It lies among the woody hills like a Paradise, with its velvet meadows and villas and breathing gardens. The grass was starred with daisies and if I took a step into the oak and chesnut woods, I trampled on thousands of anemones and fragrant daffodils. The upland plain, stretching inward from the coast, wears a different character. As I ascended, towards evening, and walked over its monotonous swells, I felt almost homesick beneath its saddening influence. The sun, hazed over with dull clouds, gave out that cold and lifeless light which is more lonely than complete darkness. The wind, sweeping dismally over the fields, sent clouds of blinding dust down the road, and as it passed through the forests, the myriads of fine twigs sent up a sound as deep and grand as the roar of a roused ocean. Every chink of the Norman cottage where I slept, whistled most drearily, and as I looked out the little window of my room, the trees were swaying in the gloom, and long, black clouds scudded across the sky. Though my bed was poor and hard, it was a sublime sound that cradled me into slumber. Homer might have used it as the lullaby of Jove.

My last day on the continent came. I rose early and walked over the hills towards Dieppe. The scenery grew more bleak as I approached the sea, but the low and sheltered valleys preserved the pastoral look of the interior. In the afternoon, as I climbed a long, elevated ridge, over which a strong northwester was blowing, I was struck with a beautiful rustic church, in one of the dells below me. While admiring its neat tower I had gained unconsciously the summit of the hill, and on turning suddenly around, lo! there was the glorious old Atlantic stretching far before and around me! A shower was sweeping mistily along the horizon and I could trace the white line of the breakers that foamed at the foot of the cliffs. The scene came over me like a vivid electric shock, and I gave an involuntary shout, which might have been heard in all the valleys around. After a year and a half of wandering over the continent, that gray ocean was something to be revered and loved, for it clasped the shores of my native America.

I entered Dieppe in a heavy shower, and after finding an inn suited to my means and obtaining a permis d'embarquement from the police office, I went out to the battlements and looked again on the sea. The landlord promised to call me in time for the boat, but my anxiety waked me sooner, and mistaking the strokes of the cathedral bell, I shouldered my knapsack and went down to the wharf at one o'clock. No one was stirring on board the boat, and I was obliged to pace the silent, gloomy streets of the town for two hours. I watched the steamer glide out on the rainy channel, and turning into the topmost berth, drew the sliding curtain and strove to keep out cold and sea-sickness. But it was unavailing; a heavy storm of snow and rain rendered our passage so dreary that I did not stir until we were approaching the chain pier of Brighton.

I looked out on the foggy shores of England with a feeling of relief; my tongue would now be freed from the difficult bondage of foreign languages, and my ears be rejoiced with the music of my own. After two hours' delay at the Custom House, I took my seat in an open car for London. The day was dull and cold; the sun resembled a milky blotch in the midst of a leaden sky. I sat and shivered, as we flew onward, amid the rich, cultivated English scenery. At last the fog grew thicker; the road was carried over the tops of houses; the familiar dome of St. Paul's stood out above the spires; and I was again in London!

# CHAPTER XLVII. — LOCKHART, BERNARD BARTON AND CROLY— LONDON CHIMES AND GREENWICH FAIR.

My circumstances, on arriving at London, were again very reduced. A franc and a half constituted the whole of my funds. This, joined to the knowledge of London expenses, rendered instant exertion necessary, to prevent still greater embarrassment. I called on a printer the next morning, hoping to procure work, but found, as I had no documents with me to show I had served a regular apprenticeship, this would be extremely difficult, although workmen were in great demand. Mr. Putnam, however, on whom I had previously called, gave me employment for a time in his publishing establishment, and thus I was fortunately enabled to await the arrival of a remittance from home.

Mrs. Trollope, whom I met in Florence, kindly gave me a letter to Murray, the publisher, and I visited him soon after my arrival. In his library I saw the original portraits of Byron, Moore, Campbell and the other authors who were intimate with him and his father. A day or two afterwards I had the good fortune to breakfast with Lockhart and Bernard Barton, at the house of the former. Mr. Murray, through whom the invitation was given, accompanied me there. As it was late when we arrived at Regent's Park, we found them waiting, and sat down immediately to breakfast.

I was much pleased with Lockhart's appearance and manners. He has a noble, manly countenance—in fact, the handsomest English face I ever saw—a quick, dark eye and an ample forehead, shaded by locks which show, as yet, but few threads of gray. There is a peculiar charm in his rich, soft voice; especially when reciting poetry, it has a clear, organ-like vibration, which thrills deliciously on the ear. His daughter, who sat at the head of the table, is a most lovely and amiable girl.

Bernard Burton, who is now quite an old man, is a very lively and sociable Friend. His head is gray and almost bald, but there is still plenty of fire in his eyes and life in his limbs. His many kind and amiable qualities endear him to a large circle of literary friends. He still continues writing, and within the last year has brought out a volume of simple, touching "Household Verses." A picture of cheerful and contented old age has never been more briefly and beautifully drawn, than in the following lines, which he sent me, in answer to my desire to possess one of his poems in his own hand:

*STANZAS.*

*I feel that I am growing old,*
   *Nor wish to hide that truth;*
*Conscious my heart is not more cold*
   *Than in my by-gone youth.*

*I cannot roam the country round,*
   *As I was wont to do;*
*My feet a scantier circle bound,*
   *My eyes a narrower view.*

*But on my mental vision rise*
   *Bright scenes of beauty still:*
*Morn's splendor, evening's glowing skies,*
   *Valley, and grove, and hill.*

*Nor can infirmities o'erwhelm*
   *The purer pleasures brought*
*From the immortal spirit's realm*
   *Of feeling and of Thought!*

*My heart! let not dismay or doubt*

*In thee an entrance win!*

*Thou hast enjoyed thyself without—*

*Now seek thy joy within!*

During breakfast he related to us a pleasant anecdote of Scott. He once wrote to the poet in behalf of a young lady, who wished to have the description of Melrose, in the "Lay of the last Minstrel," in the poet's own writing. Scott sent it, but added these lines to the conclusion:

*"Then go, and muse with deepest awe*

*On what the writer never saw;*

*Who would not wander 'neath the moon*

*To see what he could see at noon!"*

We went afterwards into Lockhart's library, which was full of interesting objects. I saw the private diary of Scott, kept until within a short time of his death. It was melancholy to trace the gradual failing of all his energies in the very wavering of the autograph. In a large volume of his correspondence, containing letters from Campbell, Wordsworth, Byron, and all the distinguished characters of the age, I saw Campbell's "Battle of the Baltic" in his own hand. I was highly interested and gratified with the whole visit; the more so, as Mr. Lockhart had invited me voluntarily, without previous acquaintance. I have since heard him spoken of in the highest terms of esteem.

I went one Sunday to the Church of St. Stephen, to hear Croly, the poet. The service, read by a drowsy clerk, was long and monotonous; I sat in a side-aisle, looking up at the dome, and listening to the rain which dashed in torrents against the windowpanes. At last, a tall, gray-haired man came down the passage. He bowed with a sad smile, so full of benevolence and resignation, that it went into my heart at once, and I gave him an involuntary tribute of sympathy. He has a heavy affliction to bear—the death of his gallant son, one of the officers who were slain in the late battle of Ferozeshaw. His whole manner betrays the tokens of subdued but constant grief.

His sermon was peculiarly finished and appropriate; the language was clear and forcible, without that splendor of thought and dazzling vividness of imagery which mark "Salathiel." Yet I could not help noticing that he delighted to dwell on the spiritualities of religion, rather than its outward observances, which he seemed inclined to hurry over as lightly as possible. His mild, gray eye and lofty forehead are more like the benevolent divine than the poet. I thought of Salathiel, and looked at the dignified, sorrowful man before me. The picture of the accursed Judean vanished, and his own solemn lines rang on my ear:

> "*The mighty grave*
>
> *Wraps lord and slave,*
>
> *Nor pride, nor poverty dares come*
>
> *Within that prison-house, that tomb!*"

Whenever I hear them, or think of them again, I shall see, in memory, Croly's calm, pale countenance.

> "*The chimes, the chimes of Mother-land,*
>
> *Of England, green and old;*
>
> *That out from thane and ivied tower*
>
> *A thousand years have tolled!*"

I often thought of Coxe's beautiful ballad, when, after a day spent in Waterloo Place, I have listened, on my way homeward, to the chimes of Mary-le-bone Chapel, sounding sweetly and clearly above all the din of the Strand. There is something in their silvery vibration, which is far more expressive than the ordinary tones of a bell. The ear becomes weary of a continued toll—the sound of some bells seems to have nothing more in it than the ordinary clang of metal—but these simple notes, following one another so melodiously, fall on the ear, stunned by the ceaseless roar of carriages or the mingled cries of the mob, as gently and gratefully as drops of dew. Whether it be morning, and they ring out louder and deeper through the mist, or midnight, when the vast ocean of being beneath them surges less noisily than its wont, they

are alike full of melody and poetry. I have often paused, deep in the night, to
hear those clear tones, dropping down from the darkness, thrilling, with their
full, tremulous sweetness, the still air of the lighted Strand, and winding away
through dark, silent lanes and solitary courts, till the ear of the care-worn
watcher is scarcely stirred with their dying vibrations. They seemed like those
spirit-voices, which, at such times, speak almost audibly to the heart. How
delicious it must be, to those who dwell within the limits of their sound, to
wake from some happy dream and hear those chimes blending in with their
midnight fancies, like the musical echo of the promised bliss. I love these
eloquent bells, and I think there must be many, living out a life of misery
and suffering, to whom their tones come with an almost human consolation.
The natures of the very cockneys, who never go without the horizon of their
vibrations, is, to my mind, invested with one hue of poetry!

A few days ago, an American friend invited me to accompany him
to Greenwich Fair. We took a penny steamer from Hungerford Market to
London Bridge, and jumped into the cars, which go every live minutes.
Twelve minutes' ride above the chimneys of London and the vegetable-fields
of Rotherhithe and Deptford brought us to Greenwich, we followed the
stream of people which was flowing from all parts of the city into the Park.

Here began the merriment. We heard on every side the noise of the
"scratchers," or, as the venders of these articles denominated them—"the fun
of the fair." By this is meant a little notched wheel, with a piece of wood
fastened on it, like a miniature watchman's rattle. The "fun" consists in
drawing them down the back of any one you pass, when they make a sound
precisely like that of ripping cloth. The women take great delight in this,
and as it is only deemed politeness to return the compliment, we soon had
enough to do. Nobody seemed to take the diversion amiss, but it was so
irresistibly droll to see a large crowd engaged in this singular amusement, that
we both burst into hearty laughter.

As we began ascending Greenwich Hill, we were assailed with another
kind of game. The ground was covered with smashed oranges, with which the
people above and below were stoutly pelting each other. Half a dozen heavy
ones whizzed uncomfortably near my head as I went up, and I saw several

386

persons get the full benefit of a shot on their backs and breasts. The young country lads and lasses amused themselves by running at full spend down the steep side of a hill. This was, however, a feat attended with some risk; for I saw one luckless girl describe an arc of a circle, of which her feet was the centre and her body the radius. All was noise and nonsense. They ran to and fro under the long, hoary bough of the venerable oaks that crest the summit, and clattered down the magnificent forest-avenues, whose budding foliage gave them little shelter from the passing April showers.

The view from the top is splendid. The stately Thames curves through the plain below, which loses itself afar off in the mist; Greenwich, with its massive hospital, lies just at one's feet, and in a clear day the domes of London skirt the horizon. The wood of the Park is entirely oak—the majestic, dignified, English oak—which covers, in picturesque clumps, the sides and summits of the two billowy hills. It must be a sweet place in summer, when the dark, massive foliage is heavy on every mossy arm, and the smooth and curving sward shines with thousands of field-flowers.

Owing to the showers, the streets were coated with mud, of a consistence as soft and yielding as the most fleecy Persian carpet. Near the gate, boys were holding scores of donkeys, which they offered us at threepence for a ride of two miles. We walked down towards the river, and came at last to a group of tumblers, who with muddy hands and feet were throwing somersets in the open street. I recognized them as old acquaintances of the Rue St. Antoine and the Champs Elysées; but the little boy who cried before, because he did not want to bend his head and foot into a ring, like a hoop-snake, had learned his part better by this time, so that he went through it all without whimpering and came off with only a fiery red face. The exercises of the young gentlemen were of course very graceful and classic, and the effect of their poses of strength was very much heightened by the muddy foot-marks which they left on each other's orange-colored skins.

The avenue of booths was still more diverting. Here under sheets of leaky awning, were exposed for sale rows of gilded gingerbread kings and queens, and I cannot remember how many men and women held me fast by the arms, determined to force me into buying a pound of them. We paused at the sign: "SIGNOR URBANI'S GRAND MAGICAL DISPLAY." The title was attractive, so we paid the penny admission, and walked behind the dark, mysterious curtain. Two bare brick walls, three benches and a little boy appeared to us. A sheet hung before us upon which quivered the shadow of some terrible head. At my friend's command, the boy (also a spectator) put out the light, when the awful and grinning face of a black woman became visible. While we were admiring this striking production, thus mysteriously revealed, Signor Urbani came in, and seeing no hope of any more spectators, went behind the curtain and startled our sensitive nerves with six or seven skeleton and devil apparitions, winding up the wonderful entertainment with the same black head. We signified our entire approbation by due applause and then went out to seek further novelties.

The centre of the square was occupied by swings, where some eight or ten boat-loads of persons were flying topsy-turvy into the air, making one giddy to look at them, and constant fearful shrieks arose from the lady swingers, at finding themselves in a horizontal or inverted position, high above the ground. One of the machines was like a great wheel, with four cars attached, which mounted and descended with their motley freight. We got into the boat by way of experiment. The starting motion was pleasant, but very soon it flew with a swiftness and to a height rather alarming. I began to repent having chosen such a mode of amusement, but held on as well as I could, in my uneasy place. Presently we mounted till the long beam of our boat was horizontal; at one instant, I saw three young ladies below me, with their heads downward, like a shadow in the water—the next I was turned heels up, looking at thorn as a shadow does at its original. I was fast becoming sea-sick, when, after a few minutes of such giddy soaring, the ropes were slackened and we all got out, looking somewhat pale, and feeling nervous, if nothing else.

There were also many great tents, hung with boughs and lighted with innumerable colored lamps, where the people danced their country dances in a choking cloud of dry saw-dust. Conjurors and gymnastic performers were showing off on conspicuous platforms, and a continual sound of drums, cymbals and shrill trumpets called the attention of the crowd to some "Wonderful Exhibition"—some infant phenomenon, giant, or three-headed pig. A great part of the crowd belonged evidently to the very worst part of society, but the watchfulness of the police prevented any open disorder. We came away early and in a quarter of an hour were in busy London, leaving far behind us the revel and debauch, which was prolonged through the whole night.

London has the advantage of one of the most gloomy atmospheres in the world. During this opening spring weather, no light and scarcely any warmth can penetrate the dull, yellowish-gray mist, which incessantly hangs over the city. Sometimes at noon we have for an hour or two a sickly gleam of sunshine, but it is soon swallowed up by the smoke and drizzling fog. The people carry umbrellas at all times, for the rain seems to drop spontaneously out of the very air, without wailing for the usual preparation of a gathering cloud. Professor Espy's rules would be of little avail here.

A few days ago we had a real fog—a specimen of November weather, as the people said. If November wears such a mantle, London, during that sober month, must furnish a good idea of the gloom of Hades. The streets wore wrapped in a veil of dense mist, of a dirty yellow color, as if the air had suddenly grown thick and mouldy. The houses on the opposite sides of the street were invisible, and the gas lamps, lighted in the shops, burned with a white and ghastly flame. Carriages ran together in the streets, and I was kept constantly on the look-out, lest some one should come suddenly out of the cloud around me, and we should meet with a shock like that of two knights at a tournament. As I stood in the centre of Trafalgar Square, with every object invisible around me, it reminded me, (hoping the comparison will not be accepted in every particular) of Satan resting in the middle of Chaos. The weather sometimes continues thus for whole days together.

April 26.—An hour and a half of land are still allowed us, and then we shall set foot on the back of the oak-ribbed leviathan, which will be our home until a thousand leagues of blue ocean are crossed. I shall hear the old Aldgate clock strike for the last time—I shall take a last walk through the Minories and past the Tower yard, and as we glide down the Thames, St. Pauls, half-hidden in mist and coal-smoke, will probably be my last glimpse of London.

# CHAPTER XLVIII. – HOMEWARD BOUND——CONCLUSION.

We slid out of St. Katharine's Dock at noon on the appointed day, and with a pair of sooty steamboats hitched to our vessel, moved slowly down the Thames in mist and drizzling rain. I stayed on the wet deck all afternoon, that I might more forcibly and joyously feel we were again in motion on the waters and homeward bound! My attention was divided between the dreary views of Blackwall, Greenwich and Woolwich, and the motley throng of passengers who were to form our ocean society. An English family, going out to settle in Canada, were gathered together in great distress and anxiety, for the father had gone ashore in London at a late hour, and was left behind. When we anchored for the night at Gravesend, their fears were quieted by his arrival in a skiff from the shore, as he had immediately followed us by railroad.

My cousin and B—— had hastened on from Paris to join me, and a day before the sailing of the "Victoria," we took berths in the second cabin, for twelve pounds ten shillings each, which in the London line of packets, includes coarse but substantial fare for the whole voyage. Our funds were insufficient to pay even this; but Captain Morgan, less mistrustful than my Norman landlord, generously agreed that the remainder of the fare should be paid in America. B—— and I, with two young Englishmen, took possession of a State-room of rough boards, lighted by a bull's-eye, which in stormy weather leaked so much that our trunks swam in water. A narrow mattrass and blanket, with a knapsack for a pillow, formed a passable bed. A long entry between the rooms, lighted by a feeble swinging lamp, was filled with a board table, around which the thirty-two second cabin passengers met to discuss politics and salt pork, favorable winds and hard sea-biscuit.

We lay becalmed opposite Sheerness the whole of the second day. At dusk a sudden squall came up, which drove us foaming towards the North Foreland. When I went on deck in the morning, we had passed Dover and Brighton, and the Isle of Wight was rising dim ahead of us. The low English coast on our right was bordered by long reaches of dazzling chalky sand, which glittered along the calm blue water.

Gliding into the Bay of Portsmouth, we dropped anchor opposite the romantic town of Ryde, built on the sloping shore of the green Isle of Wight. Eight or nine vessels of the Experimental Squadron were anchored near us, and over the houses of Portsmouth, I saw the masts of the Victory—the flag-ship in the battle of Trafalgar, on board of which Nelson was killed. The wind was not strong enough to permit the passage of the Needles, so at midnight we succeeded in wearing back again into the channel, around the Isle of Wight. A head wind forced us to tack away towards the shore of France. We were twice in sight of the rocky coast of Brittany, near Cherbourg, but the misty promontory of Land's End was our last glimpse of the old world.

On one of our first days at sea, I caught a curlew, which came flying on weary wings towards us, and alighted on one of the boats. Two of his brethren, too much exhausted or too timid to do likewise, dropped flat on the waves and resigned themselves to their fate without a struggle. I slipped up and caught his long, lank legs, while he was resting with flagging wings and half-shut eyes. We fed him, though it was difficult to get anything down his reed-shaped bill; but he took kindly to our force-work, and when we let him loose on the deck, walked about with an air quite tame and familiar. He died, however, two days afterwards. A French pigeon, which was caught in the rigging, lived and throve during the whole of the passage.

A few days afterwards, a heavy storm came on, and we were all sleepless and sea-sick, as long as it lasted. Thanks, however, to a beautiful law of memory, the recollection of that dismal period soon lost its unpleasantness, while the grand forms of beauty the vexed ocean presented, will remain forever, as distinct and abiding images. I kept on deck as long as I could stand, watching the giant waves over which our vessel took her course. They rolled up towards us, thirty or forty feet in height—dark gray masses, changing to a beautiful vitriol tint, wherever the light struck through their countless and changing crests. It was a glorious thing to see our good ship mount slowly up the side of one of these watery lulls, till her prow was lifted high in air, then, rocking over its brow, plunge with a slight quiver downward, and plough up a briny cataract, as she struck the vale. I never before realized the terrible sublimity of the sea. And yet it was a pride to see how man—strong in his godlike will—could bid defiance to those whelming surges, and bravo their wrath unharmed.

We swung up and down on the billows, till we scarcely knew which way to stand. The most grave and sober personages suddenly found themselves reeling in a very undignified manner, and not a few measured their lengths on the slippery decks. Boxes and barrels were affected in like manner; everything danced around us. Trunks ran out from under the berths; packages leaped down from the shelves; chairs skipped across the rooms, and at table, knives, forks and mugs engaged in a general waltz and break down. One incident of this kind was rather laughable. One night, about midnight, the gale, which had been blowing violently, suddenly lulled, "as if," to use a sailor's phrase, "it had been chopped off!" Instantly the ship gave a tremendous lurch, which was the signal for a general breaking loose. Two or three others followed, so violent, that for a moment I imagined the vessel had been thrown on her beam ends. Trunks, crockery and barrels went banging down from one end of the ship to the other. The women in the steerage set up an awful scream, and the German emigrants, thinking we were in terrible danger, commenced praying with might and main. In the passage near our room stood several barrels, filled with broken dishes, which at every lurch went banging from side to side, jarring the board partition and making a horrible din. I shall not soon forget the Babel which kept our eyes open that night.

The 19th of May a calm came on. Our white wings flapped idly on the mast, and only the top-gallant sails were bent enough occasionally to lug us along at a mile an hour. A barque from Ceylon, making the most of the wind, with every rag of canvass set, passed us slowly on the way eastward. The sun went down unclouded, and a glorious starry night brooded over us. Its clearness and brightness were to me indications of America. I longed to be on shore. The forests about home were then clothed in the delicate green of their first leaves, and that bland weather embraced the sweet earth like a blessing of heaven. The gentle breath from out the west seemed made for the odor of violets, and as it came to me over the slightly-ruffled deep, I thought how much sweeter it were to feel it, while "wasting in wood-paths the voluptuous hours."

Soon afterwards a fresh wind sprung up, which increased rapidly, till every sail was bent to the full. Our vessel parted the brine with an arrowy glide, the ease and grace of which it is impossible to describe. The breeze held on steadily for two or three days, which brought us to the southern extremity of the Banks. Here the air felt so sharp and chilling, that I was afraid we might be under the lee of an iceberg, but in the evening the dull gray mass of clouds lifted themselves from the horizon, and the sun set in clear, American beauty away beyond Labrador. The next morning we were enveloped in a dense fog, and the wind which bore us onward was of a piercing coldness. A sharp look-out was kept on the bow, but as we could see but a short distance, it might have been dangerous had we met one of the Arctic squadron. At noon it cleared away again, and the bank of fog was visible a long time astern, piled along the horizon, reminding me of the Alps, as seen from the plains of Piedmont.

On the 31st, the fortunate wind which carried us from the Banks, failed us about thirty-five miles from Sandy Hook. We lay in the midst of the mackerel fishery, with small schooners anchored all around us. Fog, dense and impenetrable, weighed on the moveless ocean, like an atmosphere of wool. The only incident to break the horrid monotony of the day, was the arrival of a pilot, with one or two newspapers, detailing the account of the Mexican War. We heard in the afternoon the booming of the surf along the low beach of Long Island—hollow and faint, like the murmur of a shell. When the mist lifted a little, we saw the faint line of breakers along the shore. The Germans gathered on deck to sing their old, familiar songs, and their voices blended beautifully together in the stillness.

Next morning at sunrise we saw Sandy Hook; at nine o'clock we were telegraphed in New York by the station at Coney Island; at eleven the steamer "Hercules" met us outside the Hook; and at noon we were gliding up the Narrows, with the whole ship's company of four hundred persons on deck, gazing on the beautiful shores of Staten Island and agreeing almost universally, that it was the most delightful scene they had ever looked upon.

And now I close the story of my long wandering, as I began it—with a lay written on the deep.

### HOMEWARD BOUND.

*Farewell to Europe! Days have come and gone*

*Since misty England set behind the sea.*

*Our ship climbs onward o'er the lifted waves,*

*That gather up in ridges, mountain-high,*

*And like a sea-god, conscious in his power,*

*Buffets the surges. Storm-arousing winds*

*That sweep, unchecked, from frozen Labrador,*

*Make wintry music through the creaking shrouds.*

*Th' horizon's ring, that clasps the dreary view,*

*Lays mistily upon the gray Atlantic's breast.*

*Shut out, at times, by bulk of sparry blue,*

*That, rolling near us, heaves the swaying prow*

*High on its shoulders, to descend again*

*Ploughing a thousand cascades, and around*

*Spreading the frothy foam. These watery gulfs,*

*With storm, and winds far-sweeping, hem us in,*

*Alone upon the waters!*

*Days must pass—*

*Many and weary—between sea and sky.*

*Our eyes, that long e'en now for the fresh green*

*Of sprouting forests, and the far blue stretch*

Of regal mountains piled along the sky,

Must see, for many an eve, the level sun

Sheathe, with his latest gold, the heaving brine,

By thousand ripples shivered, or Night's pomp

Brooding in silence, ebon and profound,

Upon the murmuring darkness of the deep,

Broken by flashings, that the parted wave

Sends white and star-like throujch its bursting foam.

Yet not more dear the opening dawn of heaven

Poured on the earth in an Italian May,

When souls take wings upon the scented air

Of starry meadows, and the yearning heart

Pains with deep sweetness in the balmy time,

Than these gray morns, and days of misty blue,

And surges, never-ceasing;—for our prow

Points to the sunset like a morning ray,

And o'er the waves, and through the sweeping storms,

Through day and darkness, rushes ever on,

Westward and westward still! What joy can send

The spirit thrilling onward with the wind,

In untamed exultation, like the thought

That fills the Homeward Bound?

    Country and home!

*Ah! not the charm of silver-tongued romance,*

*Born of the feudal time, nor whatsoe'er*

*Of dying glory fills the golden realms*

*Of perished song, where heaven-descended Art*

*Still boasts her later triumphs, can compare*

*With that one thought of liberty inherited—*

*Of free life giv'n by fathers who were free,*

*And to be left to children freer still!*

*That pride and consciousness of manhood, caught*

*From boyish musings on the holy graves*

*Of hero-martyrs, and from every form*

*Which virgin Nature, mighty and unchained,*

*Takes in an empire not less proudly so—*

*Inspired in mountain airs, untainted yet*

*By thousand generations' breathing—felt*

*Like a near presence in the awful depths*

*Of unhewn forests, and upon the steep*

*Where giant rivers take their maddening plunge—*

*Has grown impatient of the stifling damps*

*Which hover close on Europe's shackled soil.*

*Content to tread awhile the holy steps*

*Of Art and Genius, sacred through all time,*

*The spirit breathed that dull, oppressive air—*

Which, freighted with its tyrant-clouds, o'erweighs

The upward throb of many a nation's soul—

Amid those olden memories, felt the thrall.

But kept the birth-right of its freer home,

Here, on the world's blue highway, comes again

The voice of Freedom, heard amid the roar

Of sundered billows, while above the wave

Rise visions of the forest and the stream.

Like trailing robes the morning mists uproll,

Torn by the mountain pines; the flashing rills

Shout downward through the hollows of the vales;

Down the great river's bosom shining sails

Glide with a gradual motion, while from all—

Hamlet, and bowered homestead, and proud town—

Voices of joy ring up into heaven!

Yet louder, winds! Urge on our keel, ye waves,

Swift as the spirit's yearnings! We would ride

With a loud stormy motion o'er your crests,

With tempests shouting like a sudden joy—

Interpreting our triumph! 'Tis your voice,

Ye unchained elements, alone can speak

The sympathetic feeling of the free—

The arrowy impulse of the Homeward Bound!

Although the narrative of my journey, "with knapsack and staff," is now strictly finished, a few more words of explanation seem necessary, to describe more fully the method of traveling which we adopted. I add them the more willingly, as it is my belief that many, whose circumstances are similar to mine, desire to undertake the same romantic journey. Some matter-of-fact statements may be to them useful as well as interesting.

We found the pedestrian style not only by far the best way to become acquainted with the people and scenery of a country, but the pleasantest mode of traveling. To be sure, the knapsack was, at first, rather heavy, our feet were often sore and our limbs weary, but a few days walking made a great difference, and after we had traveled two weeks, this disappeared altogether. Every morning we rose as fresh and strong as if it had been the first day—even after a walk of thirty miles, we felt but little fatigue. We enjoyed slumber in its fullest luxury, and our spirits were always light and joyous. We made it a rule to pay no regard to the weather, unless it was so bad as to render walking unhealthy. Often, during the day, we rested for half an hour on the grassy bank, or sometimes, if it was warm weather, lay at full length in the shade with our knapsacks under our heads. This is a pleasure which none but the pedestrian can comprehend.

We always accepted a companion, of whatever kind, while walking—from chimney-sweeps to barons. In a strange country one can learn something from every peasant, and we neglected no opportunity, not only to obtain information, but impart it. We found everywhere great curiosity respecting America, and we were always glad to tell them all they wished to know. In Germany, we were generally taken for Germans from some part of the country where the dialect was a little different, or, if they remarked our foreign peculiarities, they supposed we were either Poles, Russians, or Swiss. The greatest ignorance in relation to America, prevails among the common people. They imagine we are a savage race, without intelligence and almost without law. Persons of education, who had some slight knowledge of our history, showed a curiosity to know something of our political condition. They are taught by the German newspapers (which are under a strict censorship in this respect) to look only at the evil in our country, and they almost invariably began by adverting to Slavery and Repudiation. While we admitted, often with shame and mortification, the existence of things so inconsistent with true republicanism, we endeavored to make them comprehend the advantages enjoyed by the free citizen—the complete equality of birth—which places America, despite her sins, far above any other nation on earth. I could plainly see, by the kindling eye and half-suppressed sigh, that they appreciated a freedom so immeasurably greater than that which they enjoyed.

In large cities we always preferred to take the second or third-rate hotels, which are generally visited by merchants and persons who travel on business; for, with the same comforts as the first rank, they are nearly twice as cheap. A traveler, with a guide-book and a good pair of eyes, can also dispense with the services of a courier, whose duty it is to conduct strangers about the city, from one lion to another. We chose rather to find out and view the "sights" at our leisure. In small villages, where we were often obliged to stop, we chose the best hotels, which, particularly in Northern Germany and in Italy, are none too good. But if it was a post, that is, a town where the post-chaise stops to change horses, we usually avoided the post-hotel, where one must pay high for having curtains before his windows and a more elegant cover on his bed. In the less splendid country inns, we always found neat, comfortable lodging, and a pleasant, friendly reception from the people. They saluted us on entering, with "Be you welcome," and on leaving, wished us a pleasant journey and good fortune. The host, when he brought us supper or breakfast, lifted his cap, and wished us a good appetite—and when he lighted us to our chambers, left us with "May you sleep well!" We generally found honest, friendly people; they delighted in telling us about the country around; what ruins there were in the neighborhood—and what strange legends were connected with them. The only part of Europe where it is unpleasant to travel in this manner, is Bohemia. We could rarely find a comfortable inn; the people all spoke an unknown language, and were not particularly celebrated for their honesty. Beside this, travelers rarely go on foot in those regions; we were frequently taken for traveling handworker, and subjected to imposition.

With regard to passports, although they were vexatious and often expensive, we found little difficulty when we had acquainted ourselves with the regulations concerning them. In France and Germany they are comparatively little trouble; in Italy they are the traveler's greatest annoyance. Americans are treated with less strictness, in this respect, than citizens of other nations, and, owing to the absence of rank among us, we also enjoy greater advantages of acquaintance and intercourse.

The expenses of traveling in England, although much greater than in our own country, may, as we learned by experience, be brought, through economy, within the same compass. Indeed, it is my belief, from observation, that, with few exceptions, throughout Europe, where a traveler enjoys the same comfort and abundance as in America, he must pay the same prices. The principal difference is, that he only pays for what he gets, so that, if he be content with the necessities of life, without its luxuries, the expense is in proportion. I have given, at times, through the foregoing chapters, the cost of travel and residence in Europe, yet a connected estimate will better show the minimum expense of a two years' pilgrimage:

*Voyage to Liverpool, in the second cabin* . . . . . . . . . . . . . . . . $24.00

*Three weeks' travel in Ireland and Scotland* . . . . . . . . . . . . . . 25.00

*A week in London, at three shillings a day* . . . . . . . . . . . . . . 4.50

*From London to Heidelberg* . . . . . . . . . . . . . . . . . . . . . . . 15.00

*A month at Heidelberg, and trip to Frankfort* . . . . . . . . . . . . 20.00

*Seven months in Frankfort, at $10 per month* . . . . . . . . . . 70.00

*Fuel, passports, excursions and other expenses* . . . . . . . . . . . 30.00

*Tour through Cassel, the Hartz, Saxony, Austria, Bavaria, etc.* 40.00

*A month in Frankfort* . . . . . . . . . . . . . . . . . . . . . . . . . . . . 10.00

*From Frankfort through Switzerland, and over the Alps*

  *to Milan* . . . . . . . . . . . . . . . . . . . . . . . . . . . . . . . . . . . 15.00

*From Milan to Genoa* . . . . . . . . . . . . . . . . . . . . . . . . . 60

*Expenses from Genoa to Florence* . . . . . . . . . . . . . . . . . . . 14.00

*Four months in Florence* .......................... *50.00*

*Eight day's journey from Florence to Rome, two weeks in*

   *Rome, voyage to Marseilles and journey to Paris* ........ *40.00*

*Five weeks in Paris* ............................. *15.00*

*From Paris to London* ............................ *8.00*

*Six weeks in London, at three shillings a day* .......... *31.00*

*Passage home* .................................. *60.00*

——————

*$472.00*

The cost for places of amusement, guides' fees, and other small expenses, not included in this list, increase the sum total to $500, for which the tour may be made. Now, having, I hope, established this to the reader's satisfaction, I respectfully take leave of him.

**THE END.**

# BEAUTY AND THE BEAST
# AND TALES OF HOME

# BEAUTY AND THE BEAST.

## A STORY OF OLD RUSSIA.

### I.

We are about to relate a story of mingled fact and fancy. The facts are borrowed from the Russian author, Petjerski; the fancy is our own. Our task will chiefly be to soften the outlines of incidents almost too sharp and rugged for literary use, to supply them with the necessary coloring and sentiment, and to give a coherent and proportioned shape to the irregular fragments of an old chronicle. We know something, from other sources, of the customs described, something of the character of the people from personal observation, and may therefore the more freely take such liberties as we choose with the rude, vigorous sketches of the Russian original. One who happens to have read the work of Villebois can easily comprehend the existence of a state of society, on the banks of the Volga, a hundred years ago, which is now impossible, and will soon become incredible. What is strangest in our narrative has been declared to be true.

### II.

We are in Kinesma, a small town on the Volga, between Kostroma and Nijni-Novgorod. The time is about the middle of the last century, and the month October.

There was trouble one day, in the palace of Prince Alexis, of Kinesma. This edifice, with its massive white walls, and its pyramidal roofs of green copper, stood upon a gentle mound to the eastward of the town, overlooking it, a broad stretch of the Volga, and the opposite shore. On a similar hill, to the westward, stood the church, glittering with its dozen bulging, golden domes. These two establishments divided the sovereignty of Kinesma between them.

Prince Alexis owned the bodies of the inhabitants, (with the exception of a few merchants and tradesmen,) and the Archimandrite Sergius owned their souls. But the shadow of the former stretched also over other villages, far beyond the ring of the wooded horizon. The number of his serfs was ten thousand, and his rule over them was even less disputed than theirs over their domestic animals.

The inhabitants of the place had noticed with dismay that the slumber-flag had not been hoisted on the castle, although it was half an hour after the usual time. So rare a circumstance betokened sudden wrath or disaster, on the part of Prince Alexis. Long experience had prepared the people for anything that might happen, and they were consequently not astonished at the singular event which presently transpired.

The fact is, that in the first place, the dinner had been prolonged full ten minutes beyond its accustomed limit, owing to a discussion between the Prince, his wife, the Princess Martha, and their son Prince Boris. The last was to leave for St. Petersburg in a fortnight, and wished to have his departure preceded by a festival at the castle. The Princess Martha was always ready to second the desires of her only child. Between the two they had pressed some twenty or thirty thousand rubles out of the old Prince, for the winter diversions of the young one. The festival, to be sure, would have been a slight expenditure for a noble of such immense wealth as Prince Alexis; but he never liked his wife, and he took a stubborn pleasure in thwarting her wishes. It was no satisfaction that Boris resembled her in character. That weak successor to the sovereignty of Kinesma preferred a game of cards to a bear hunt, and could never drink more than a quart of vodki without becoming dizzy and sick.

"Ugh!" Prince Alexis would cry, with a shudder of disgust, "the whelp barks after the dam!"

A state dinner he might give; but a festival, with dances, dramatic representations, burning tar-barrels, and cannon,—no! He knitted his heavy brows and drank deeply, and his fiery gray eyes shot such incessant glances from side to side that Boris and the Princess Martha could not exchange a single wink of silent advice. The pet bear, Mishka, plied with strong wines, which Prince Alexis poured out for him into a golden basin, became at last comically drunk, and in endeavoring to execute a dance, lost his balance, and fell at full length on his back.

The Prince burst into a yelling, shrieking fit of laughter. Instantly the yellow-haired serfs in waiting, the Calmucks at the hall-door, and the half-witted dwarf who crawled around the table in his tow shirt, began laughing in chorus, as violently as they could. The Princess Martha and Prince Boris laughed also; and while the old man's eyes were dimmed with streaming tears of mirth, quickly exchanged nods. The sound extended all over the castle, and was heard outside of the walls.

"Father!" said Boris, "let us have the festival, and Mishka shall perform again. Prince Paul of Kostroma would strangle, if he could see him."

"Good, by St. Vladimir!" exclaimed Prince Alexis. "Thou shalt have it, my Borka! [1] Where's Simon Petrovitch? May the Devil scorch that vagabond, if he doesn't do better than the last time! Sasha!"

A broad-shouldered serf stepped forward and stood with bowed head.

"Lock up Simon Petrovitch in the southwestern tower. Send the tailor and the girls to him, to learn their parts. Search every one of them before they go in, and if any one dares to carry vodki to the beast, twenty-five lashes on the back!"

Sasha bowed again and departed. Simon Petrovitch was the court-poet of Kinesma. He had a mechanical knack of preparing allegorical diversions which suited the conventional taste of society at that time; but he had also a failing,—he was rarely sober enough to write. Prince Alexis, therefore, was in the habit of locking him up and placing a guard over him, until the inspiration had done its work. The most comely young serfs of both sexes were selected to perform the parts, and the court-tailor arranged for them the appropriate dresses. It depended very much upon accident—that is to say, the mood of Prince Alexis—whether Simon Petrovitch was rewarded with stripes or rubles.

The matter thus settled, the Prince rose from the table and walked out upon an overhanging balcony, where an immense reclining arm-chair of stuffed leather was ready for his siesta. He preferred this indulgence in the open air; and although the weather was rapidly growing cold, a pelisse of sables enabled him to slumber sweetly in the face of the north wind. An attendant stood with the pelisse outspread; another held the halyards to which was attached the great red slumber-flag, ready to run it up and announce to all Kinesma that the noises of the town must cease; a few seconds more, and all things would have been fixed in their regular daily courses. The Prince, in fact, was just straightening his shoulders to receive the sables; his eyelids were dropping, and his eyes, sinking mechanically with them, fell upon the river-road, at the foot of the hill. Along this road walked a man, wearing the long cloth caftan of a merchant.

Prince Alexis started, and all slumber vanished out of his eyes. He leaned forward for a moment, with a quick, eager expression; then a loud roar, like that of an enraged wild beast, burst from his mouth. He gave a stamp that shook the balcony.

"Dog!" he cried to the trembling attendant, "my cap! my whip!"

The sables fell upon the floor, the cap and whip appeared in a twinkling, and the red slumber-flag was folded up again for the first time in several years, as the Prince stormed out of the castle. The traveller below had heard the cry,—for it might have been heard half a mile. He seemed to have a presentiment of evil, for he had already set off towards the town at full speed.

To explain the occurrence, we must mention one of the Prince's many peculiar habits. This was, to invite strangers or merchants of the neighborhood to dine with him, and, after regaling them bountifully, to take his pay in subjecting them to all sorts of outrageous tricks, with the help of his band of willing domestics. Now this particular merchant had been invited, and had attended; but, being a very wide-awake, shrewd person, he saw what was coming, and dexterously slipped away from the banquet without being perceived. The Prince vowed vengeance, on discovering the escape, and he was not a man to forget his word.

Impelled by such opposite passions, both parties ran with astonishing speed. The merchant was the taller, but his long caftan, hastily ungirdled, swung behind him and dragged in the air.

408

The short, booted legs of the Prince beat quicker time, and he grasped his short, heavy, leathern whip more tightly as he saw the space diminishing. They dashed into the town of Kinesma a hundred yards apart. The merchant entered the main street, or bazaar, looking rapidly to right and left, as he ran, in the hope of espying some place of refuge. The terrible voice behind him cried,—

"Stop, scoundrel! I have a crow to pick with you!"

And the tradesmen in their shops looked on and laughed, as well they might, being unconcerned spectators of the fun. The fugitive, therefore, kept straight on, notwithstanding a pond of water glittered across the farther end of the street.

Although Prince Alexis had gained considerably in the race, such violent exercise, after a heavy dinner, deprived him of breath. He again cried,—

"Stop!"

"But the merchant answered,—

"No, Highness! You may come to me, but I will not go to you."

"Oh, the villian!" growled the Prince, in a hoarse whisper, for he had no more voice.

The pond cut of all further pursuit. Hastily kicking off his loose boots, the merchant plunged into the water, rather than encounter the princely whip, which already began to crack and snap in fierce anticipation. Prince Alexis kicked off his boots and followed; the pond gradually deepened, and in a minute the tall merchant stood up to his chin in the icy water, and his short pursuer likewise but out of striking distance. The latter coaxed and entreated, but the victim kept his ground.

"You lie, Highness!" he said, boldly. "If you want me, come to me."

"Ah-h-h!" roared the Prince, with chattering teeth, "what a stubborn rascal you are! Come here, and I give you my word that I will not hurt you. Nay,"—seeing that the man did not move,—"you shall dine with me as often as you please. You shall be my friend; by St. Vladimir, I like you!"

"Make the sign of the cross, and swear it by all the Saints," said the merchant, composedly.

With a grim smile on his face, the Prince stepped back and shiveringly obeyed. Both then waded out, sat down upon the ground and pulled on their boots; and presently the people of Kinesma beheld the dripping pair walking side by side up the street, conversing in the most cordial manner. The merchant dried his clothes FROM WITHIN, at the castle table; a fresh keg of old Cognac was opened; and although the slumber-flag was not unfurled that afternoon, it flew from the staff and hushed the town nearly all the next day.

## III.

The festival granted on behalf of Prince Boris was one of the grandest ever given at the castle. In character it was a singular cross between the old Muscovite revel and the French entertainments which were then introduced by the Empress Elizabeth.

All the nobility, for fifty versts around, including Prince Paul and the chief families of Kostroma, were invited. Simon Petrovitch had been so carefully guarded that his work was actually completed and the parts distributed; his superintendence of the performance, however, was still a matter of doubt, as it was necessary to release him from the tower, and after several days of forced abstinence he always manifested a raging appetite. Prince Alexis, in spite of this doubt, had been assured by Boris that the dramatic part of the entertainment would not be a failure. When he questioned Sasha, the poet's strong-shouldered guard, the latter winked familiarly and answered with a proverb,—

"I sit on the shore and wait for the wind,"—which was as much as to say that Sasha had little fear of the result.

The tables were spread in the great hall, where places for one hundred chosen guests were arranged on the floor, while the three or four hundred of minor importance were provided for in the galleries above. By noon the

410

whole party were assembled. The halls and passages of the castle were already permeated with rich and unctuous smells, and a delicate nose might have picked out and arranged, by their finer or coarser vapors, the dishes preparing for the upper and lower tables. One of the parasites of Prince Alexis, a dilapidated nobleman, officiated as Grand Marshal,—an office which more than compensated for the savage charity he received, for it was performed in continual fear and trembling. The Prince had felt the stick of the Great Peter upon his own back, and was ready enough to imitate any custom of the famous monarch.

An orchestra, composed principally of horns and brass instruments, occupied a separate gallery at one end of the dining-hall. The guests were assembled in the adjoining apartments, according to their rank; and when the first loud blast of the instruments announced the beginning of the banquet, two very differently attired and freighted processions of servants made their appearance at the same time. Those intended for the princely table numbered two hundred,—two for each guest. They were the handsomest young men among the ten thousand serfs, clothed in loose white trousers and shirts of pink or lilac silk; their soft golden hair, parted in the middle, fell upon their shoulders, and a band of gold-thread about the brow prevented it from sweeping the dishes they carried. They entered the reception-room, bearing huge trays of sculptured silver, upon which were anchovies, the finest Finnish caviar, sliced oranges, cheese, and crystal flagons of Cognac, rum, and kummel. There were fewer servants for the remaining guests, who were gathered in a separate chamber, and regaled with the common black caviar, onions, bread, and vodki. At the second blast of trumpets, the two companies set themselves in motion and entered the dining-hall at opposite ends. Our business, however, is only with the principal personages, so we will allow the common crowd quietly to mount to the galleries and satisfy their senses with the coarser viands, while their imagination is stimulated by the sight of the splendor and luxury below.

Prince Alexis entered first, with a pompous, mincing gait, leading the Princess Martha by the tips of her fingers. He wore a caftan of green velvet laced with gold, a huge vest of crimson brocade, and breeches of yellow

411

satin. A wig, resembling clouds boiling in the confluence of opposing winds, surged from his low, broad forehead, and flowed upon his shoulders. As his small, fiery eyes swept the hall, every servant trembled: he was as severe at the commencement as he was reckless at the close of a banquet. The Princess Martha wore a robe of pink satin embroidered with flowers made of small pearls, and a train and head-dress of crimson velvet.

Her emeralds were the finest outside of Moscow, and she wore them all. Her pale, weak, frightened face was quenched in the dazzle of the green fires which shot from her forehead, ears, and bosom, as she moved.

Prince Paul of Kostroma and the Princess Nadejda followed; but on reaching the table, the gentlemen took their seats at the head, while the ladies marched down to the foot. Their seats were determined by their relative rank, and woe to him who was so ignorant or so absent-minded as to make a mistake! The servants had been carefully trained in advance by the Grand Marshal; and whoever took a place above his rank or importance found, when he came to sit down, that his chair had miraculously disappeared, or, not noticing the fact, seated himself absurdly and violently upon the floor. The Prince at the head of the table, and the Princess at the foot, with their nearest guests of equal rank, ate from dishes of massive gold; the others from silver. As soon as the last of the company had entered the hall, a crowd of jugglers, tumblers, dwarfs, and Calmucks followed, crowding themselves into the corners under the galleries, where they awaited the conclusion of the banquet to display their tricks, and scolded and pummelled each other in the mean time.

On one side of Prince Alexis the bear Mishka took his station. By order of Prince Boris he had been kept from wine for several days, and his small eyes were keener and hungrier than usual. As he rose now and then, impatiently, and sat upon his hind legs, he formed a curious contrast to the Prince's other supporter, the idiot, who sat also in his tow-shirt, with a large pewter basin in his hand. It was difficult to say whether the beast was most man or the man most beast. They eyed each other and watched the motions of their lord with equal jealousy; and the dismal whine of the bear found an echo in the drawling, slavering laugh of the idiot. The Prince glanced form one to the other; they put him in a capital humor, which was not lessened as he

412

perceived an expression of envy pass over the face of Prince Paul.

The dinner commenced with a botvinia—something between a soup and a salad—of wonderful composition. It contained cucumbers, cherries, salt fish, melons, bread, salt, pepper, and wine. While it was being served, four huge fishermen, dressed to represent mermen of the Volga, naked to the waist, with hair crowned with reeds, legs finned with silver tissue from the knees downward, and preposterous scaly tails, which dragged helplessly upon the floor, entered the hall, bearing a broad, shallow tank of silver. In the tank flapped and swam four superb sterlets, their ridgy backs rising out of the water like those of alligators. Great applause welcomed this new and classical adaptation of the old custom of showing the LIVING fish, before cooking them, to the guests at the table. The invention was due to Simon Petrovitch, and was (if the truth must be confessed) the result of certain carefully measured supplies of brandy which Prince Boris himself had carried to the imprisoned poet.

After the sterlets had melted away to their backbones, and the roasted geese had shrunk into drumsticks and breastplates, and here and there a guest's ears began to redden with more rapid blood, Prince Alexis judged that the time for diversion had arrived. He first filled up the idiot's basin with fragments of all the dishes within his reach,—fish, stewed fruits, goose fat, bread, boiled cabbage, and beer,—the idiot grinning with delight all the while, and singing, "Ne uyesjai golubchik moi," (Don't go away, my little pigeon), between the handfuls which he crammed into his mouth. The guests roared with laughter, especially when a juggler or Calmuck stole out from under the gallery, and pretended to have designs upon the basin. Mishka, the bear, had also been well fed, and greedily drank ripe old Malaga from the golden dish. But, alas! he would not dance. Sitting up on his hind legs, with his fore paws hanging before him, he cast a drunken, languishing eye upon the company, lolled out his tongue, and whined with an almost human voice. The domestics, secretly incited by the Grand Marshal, exhausted their ingenuity in coaxing him, but in vain. Finally, one of them took a goblet of wine in one hand, and, embracing Mishka with the other, began to waltz. The bear stretched out his paw and clumsily followed the movements, whirling round and round after the enticing goblet. The orchestra struck up, and the spectacle, though not exactly what Prince Alexis wished, was comical enough to divert the company immensely.

But the close of the performance was not upon the programme. The impatient bear, getting no nearer his goblet, hugged the man violently with the other paw, striking his claws through the thin shirt. The dance-measure was lost; the legs of the two tangled, and they fell to the floor, the bear undermost. With a growl of rage and disappointment, he brought his teeth together through the man's arm, and it might have fared badly with the latter, had not the goblet been refilled by some one and held to the animal's nose.

Then, releasing his hold, he sat up again, drank another bottle, and staggered out of the hall.

Now the health of Prince Alexis was drunk,—by the guests on the floor of the hall in Champagne, by those in the galleries in kislischi and hydromel. The orchestra played; a choir of serfs sang an ode by Simon Petrovitch, in which the departure of Prince Boris was mentioned; the tumblers began to posture; the jugglers came forth and played their tricks; and the cannon on the ramparts announced to all Kinesma, and far up and down the Volga, that the company were rising from the table.

Half an hour later, the great red slumber-flag floated over the castle. All slept,—except the serf with the wounded arm, the nervous Grand Marshal, and Simon Petrovich with his band of dramatists, guarded by the indefatigable Sasha. All others slept,—and the curious crowd outside, listening to the music, stole silently away; down in Kinesma, the mothers ceased to scold their children, and the merchants whispered to each other in the bazaar; the captains of vessels floating on the Volga directed their men by gestures; the mechanics laid aside hammer and axe, and lighted their pipes. Great silence fell upon the land, and continued unbroken so long as Prince Alexis and his guests slept the sleep of the just and the tipsy.

By night, however, they were all awake and busily preparing for the diversions of the evening. The ball-room was illuminated by thousands of wax-lights, so connected with inflammable threads, that the wicks could

414

all be kindled in a moment. A pyramid of tar-barrels had been erected on each side of the castle-gate, and every hill or mound on the opposite bank of the Volga was similarly crowned. When, to a stately march,—the musicians blowing their loudest,—Prince Alexis and Princess Martha led the way to the ball-room, the signal was given: candles and tar-barrels burst into flame, and not only within the castle, but over the landscape for five or six versts, around everything was bright and clear in the fiery day. Then the noises of Kinesma were not only permitted, but encouraged. Mead and qvass flowed in the very streets, and the castle trumpets could not be heard for the sound of troikas and balalaikas.

After the Polonaise, and a few stately minuets, (copied from the court of Elizabeth), the company were ushered into the theatre. The hour of Simon Petrovitch had struck: with the inspiration smuggled to him by Prince Boris, he had arranged a performance which he felt to be his masterpiece. Anxiety as to its reception kept him sober. The overture had ceased, the spectators were all in their seats, and now the curtain rose. The background was a growth of enormous, sickly toad-stools, supposed to be clouds. On the stage stood a girl of eighteen, (the handsomest in Kinesma), in hoops and satin petticoat, powdered hair, patches, and high-heeled shoes. She held a fan in one hand, and a bunch of marigolds in the other. After a deep and graceful curtsy to the company, she came forward and said,—

"I am the goddess Venus. I have come to Olympus to ask some questions of Jupiter."

Thunder was heard, and a car rolled upon the stage. Jupiter sat therein, in a blue coat, yellow vest, ruffled shirt and three-cornered hat. One hand held a bunch of thunderbolts, which he occasionally lifted and shook; the other, a gold-headed cane.

"Here am, I Jupiter," said he; "what does Venus desire?"

A poetical dialogue then followed, to the effect that the favorite of the goddess, Prince Alexis of Kinesma, was about sending his son, Prince Boris, into the gay world, wherein himself had already displayed all the gifts of all the divinities of Olympus. He claimed from her, Venus, like favors for his

415

son: was it possible to grant them? Jupiter dropped his head and meditated. He could not answer the question at once: Apollo, the Graces, and the Muses must be consulted: there were few precedents where the son had succeeded in rivalling the father,—yet the father's pious wishes could not be overlooked. Venus said,—

"What I asked for Prince Alexis was for HIS sake: what I ask for the son is for the father's sake."

Jupiter shook his thunderbolt and called "Apollo!"

Instantly the stage was covered with explosive and coruscating fires,— red, blue, and golden,—and amid smoke, and glare, and fizzing noises, and strong chemical smells, Apollo dropped down from above. He was accustomed to heat and smoke, being the cook's assistant, and was sweated down to a weight capable of being supported by the invisible wires. He wore a yellow caftan, and wide blue silk trousers. His yellow hair was twisted around and glued fast to gilded sticks, which stood out from his head in a circle, and represented rays of light. He first bowed to Prince Alexis, then to the guests, then to Jupiter, then to Venus. The matter was explained to him.

He promised to do what he could towards favoring the world with a second generation of the beauty, grace, intellect, and nobility of character which had already won his regard. He thought, however, that their gifts were unnecessary, since the model was already in existence, and nothing more could be done than to IMITATE it.

(Here there was another meaning bow towards Prince Alexis,—a bow in which Jupiter and Venus joined. This was the great point of the evening, in the opinion of Simon Petrovitch. He peeped through a hole in one of the clouds, and, seeing the delight of Prince Alexis and the congratulations of his friends, immediately took a large glass of Cognac).

The Graces were then summoned, and after them the Muses—all in hoops, powder, and paint. Their songs had the same burden,—intense admiration of the father, and good-will for the son, underlaid with a delicate doubt. The close was a chorus of all the deities and semi-deities in praise of

416

the old Prince, with the accompaniment of fireworks. Apollo rose through the air like a frog, with his blue legs and yellow arms wide apart; Jupiter's chariot rolled off; Venus bowed herself back against a mouldy cloud; and the Muses came forward in a bunch, with a wreath of laurel, which they placed upon the venerated head.

Sasha was dispatched to bring the poet, that he might receive his well-earned praise and reward. But alas for Simon Petrovitch? His legs had already doubled under him. He was awarded fifty rubles and a new caftan, which he was not in a condition to accept until several days afterward.

The supper which followed resembled the dinner, except that there were fewer dishes and more bottles. When the closing course of sweatmeats had either been consumed or transferred to the pockets of the guests, the Princess Martha retired with the ladies. The guests of lower rank followed; and there remained only some fifteen or twenty, who were thereupon conducted by Prince Alexis to a smaller chamber, where he pulled off his coat, lit his pipe, and called for brandy. The others followed his example, and their revelry wore out the night.

Such was the festival which preceded the departure of Prince Boris for St. Petersburg.

## IV.

Before following the young Prince and his fortunes, in the capital, we must relate two incidents which somewhat disturbed the ordered course of life in the castle of Kinesma, during the first month or two after his departure.

It must be stated, as one favorable trait in the character of Prince Alexis, that, however brutally he treated his serfs, he allowed no other man to oppress them. All they had and were—their services, bodies, lives—belonged to him; hence injustice towards them was disrespect towards their lord. Under the fear which his barbarity inspired lurked a brute-like attachment, kept alive by the recognition of this quality.

One day it was reported to him that Gregor, a merchant in the bazaar at Kinesma, had cheated the wife of one of his serfs in the purchase of a piece of cloth. Mounting his horse, he rode at once to Gregor's booth, called for the cloth, and sent the entire piece to the woman, in the merchant's name, as a confessed act of reparation.

"Now, Gregor, my child," said he, as he turned his horse's head, "have a care in future, and play me no more dishonest tricks. Do you hear? I shall come and take your business in hand myself, if the like happens again."

Not ten days passed before the like—or something fully as bad—did happen. Gregor must have been a new comer in Kinesma, or he would not have tried the experiment. In an hour from the time it was announced, Prince Alexis appeared in the bazaar with a short whip under his arm.

He dismounted at the booth with an ironical smile on his face, which chilled the very marrow in the merchant's bones.

"Ah, Gregor, my child," he shouted, "you have already forgotten my commands. Holy St. Nicholas, what a bad memory the boy has! Why, he can't be trusted to do business: I must attend to the shop myself. Out of the way! march!"

He swung his terrible whip; and Gregor, with his two assistants, darted under the counter, and made their escape. The Prince then entered the booth, took up a yard-stick, and cried out in a voice which could be heard from one end of the town to the other,—"Ladies and gentlemen, have the kindness to come and examine our stock of goods! We have silks and satins, and all kinds of ladies' wear; also velvet, cloth, cotton, and linen for the gentlemen. Will your Lordships deign to choose? Here are stockings and handkerchiefs of the finest. We understand how to measure, your Lordships, and we sell cheap. We give no change, and take no small money. Whoever has no cash may have credit. Every thing sold below cost, on account of closing up the establishment. Ladies and gentlemen, give us a call?"

Everybody in Kinesma flocked to the booth, and for three hours Prince Alexis measured and sold, either for scant cash or long credit, until the last article had been disposed of and the shelves were empty. There was great rejoicing in the community over the bargains made that day. When all was

418

over, Gregor was summoned, and the cash received paid into his hands.

"It won't take you long to count it," said the Prince; "but here is a list of debts to be collected, which will furnish you with pleasant occupation, and enable you to exercise your memory. Would your Worship condescend to take dinner to-day with your humble assistant? He would esteem it a favor to be permitted to wait upon you with whatever his poor house can supply."

Gregor gave a glance at the whip under the Prince's arm, and begged to be excused. But the latter would take no denial, and carried out the comedy to the end by giving the merchant the place of honor at his table, and dismissing him with the present of a fine pup of his favorite breed. Perhaps the animal acted as a mnemonic symbol, for Gregor was never afterwards accused of forgetfulness.

If this trick put the Prince in a good humor, some thing presently occurred which carried him to the opposite extreme. While taking his customary siesta one afternoon, a wild young fellow—one of his noble poor relations, who "sponged" at the castle—happened to pass along a corridor outside of the very hall where his Highness was snoring. Two ladies in waiting looked down from an upper window. The young fellow perceived them, and made signs to attract their attention. Having succeeded in this, he attempted, by all sorts of antics and grimaces, to make them laugh or speak; but he failed, for the slumber-flag waved over them, and its fear was upon them. Then, in a freak of incredible rashness, he sang, in a loud voice, the first line of a popular ditty, and took to his heels.

No one had ever before dared to insult the sacred quiet. The Prince was on his feet in a moment, and rushed into the corridor, (dropping his mantle of sables by the way,) shouting.—

"Bring me the wretch who sang!"

The domestics scattered before him, for his face was terrible to look upon. Some of them had heard the voice, indeed, but not one of them had seen the culprit, who al ready lay upon a heap of hay in one of the stables, and appeared to be sunk in innocent sleep.

"Who was it? who was it?" yelled the Prince, foaming at the mouth with rage, as he rushed from chamber to chamber.

At last he halted at the top of the great flight of steps leading into the court-yard, and repeated his demand in a voice of thunder.

The servants, trembling, kept at a safe distance, and some of them ventured to state that the offender could not be discovered. The Prince turned and entered one of the state apartments, whence came the sound of porcelain smashed on the floor, and mirrors shivered on the walls. Whenever they heard that sound, the inmates of the castle knew that a hurricane was let loose.

They deliberated hurriedly and anxiously. What was to be done? In his fits of blind animal rage, there was nothing of which the Prince was not capable, and the fit could be allayed only by finding a victim. No one, however, was willing to be a Curtius for the others, and meanwhile the storm was increasing from minute to minute. Some of the more active and shrewd of the household pitched upon the leader of the band, a simple-minded, good-natured serf, named Waska. They entreated him to take upon himself the crime of having sung, offering to have his punishment mitigated in every possible way. He was proof against their tears, but not against the money which they finally offered, in order to avert the storm. The agreement was made, although Waska both scratched his head and shook it, as he reflected upon the probable result.

The Prince, after his work of destruction, again appeared upon the steps, and with hoarse voice and flashing eyes, began to announce that every soul in the castle should receive a hundred lashes, when a noise was heard in the court, and amid cries of "Here he is!" "We've got him, Highness!" the poor Waska, bound hand and foot, was brought forward. They placed him at the bottom of the steps. The Prince descended until the two stood face to face. The others looked on from courtyard, door, and window. A pause ensued, during which no one dared to breathe.

At last Prince Alexis spoke, in a loud and terrible voice—

"It was you who sang it?"

420

"Yes, your Highness, it was I," Waska replied, in a scarcely audible tone, dropping his head and mechanically drawing his shoulders together, as if shrinking from the coming blow.

It was full three minutes before the Prince again spoke. He still held the whip in his hand, his eyes fixed and the muscles of his face rigid. All at once the spell seemed to dissolve: his hand fell, and he said in his ordinary voice—

"You sing remarkably well. Go, now: you shall have ten rubles and an embroidered caftan for your singing."

But any one would have made a great mistake who dared to awaken Prince Alexis a second time in the same manner.

## V.

Prince Boris, in St. Petersburg, adopted the usual habits of his class. He dressed elegantly; he drove a dashing troika; he played, and lost more frequently than he won; he took no special pains to shun any form of fashionable dissipation. His money went fast, it is true; but twenty-five thousand rubles was a large sum in those days, and Boris did not inherit his father's expensive constitution. He was presented to the Empress; but his thin face, and mild, melancholy eyes did not make much impression upon that ponderous woman. He frequented the salons of the nobility, but saw no face so beautiful as that of Parashka, the serf-maiden who personated Venus for Simon Petrovitch. The fact is, he had a dim, undeveloped instinct of culture, and a crude, half-conscious worship of beauty,—both of which qualities found just enough nourishment in the life of the capital to tantalize and never satisfy his nature. He was excited by his new experience, but hardly happier.

Although but three-and-twenty, he would never know the rich, vital glow with which youth rushes to clasp all forms of sensation.

He had seen, almost daily, in his father's castle, excess in its most excessive development. It had grown to be repulsive, and he knew not how to fill the void in his life. With a single spark of genius, and a little more culture, he might have become a passable author or artist; but he was doomed to be one of those deaf and dumb natures that see the movements of the lips of others, yet have no conception of sound. No wonder his savage old father looked upon him with contempt, for even his vices were without strength or character.

The dark winter days passed by, one by one, and the first week of Lent had already arrived to subdue the glittering festivities of the court, when the only genuine adventure of the season happened to the young Prince. For adventures, in the conventional sense of the word, he was not distinguished; whatever came to him must come by its own force, or the force of destiny.

One raw, gloomy evening, as dusk was setting in, he saw a female figure in a droschky, which was about turning from the great Morskoi into the Gorokhovaya (Pea) Street. He noticed, listlessly, that the lady was dressed in black, closely veiled, and appeared to be urging the istvostchik (driver) to make better speed. The latter cut his horse sharply: it sprang forward, just at the turning, and the droschky, striking a lamp-post was instantly overturned. The lady, hurled with great force upon the solidly frozen snow, lay motionless, which the driver observing, he righted the sled and drove off at full speed, without looking behind him. It was not inhumanity, but fear of the knout that hurried him away.

Prince Boris looked up and down the Morskoi, but perceived no one near at hand. He then knelt upon the snow, lifted the lady's head to his knee, and threw back her veil. A face so lovely, in spite of its deadly pallor, he had never before seen. Never had he even imagined so perfect an oval, such a sweet, fair forehead, such delicately pencilled brows, so fine and straight a nose, such wonderful beauty of mouth and chin. It was fortunate that she was not very severely stunned, for Prince Boris was not only ignorant of the usual modes of restoration in such cases, but he totally forgot their necessity, in his rapt contemplation of the lady's face. Presently she opened her eyes, and they dwelt, expressionless, but bewildering in their darkness and depth, upon his own, while her consciousness of things slowly returned.

She strove to rise, and Boris gently lifted and supported her. She would have withdrawn from his helping arm, but was still too weak from the shock. He, also, was confused and (strange to say) embarrassed; but he had

422

self-possession enough to shout, "Davei!" (Here!) at random. The call was answered from the Admiralty Square; a sled dashed up the Gorokhovaya and halted beside him. Taking the single seat, he lifted her gently upon his lap and held her very tenderly in his arms.

"Where?" asked the istvostchik.

Boris was about to answer "Anywhere!" but the lady whispered in a voice of silver sweetness, the name of a remote street, near the Smolnoi Church.

As the Prince wrapped the ends of his sable pelisse about her, he noticed that her furs were of the common foxskin worn by the middle classes. They, with her heavy boots and the threadbare cloth of her garments, by no means justified his first suspicion,—that she was a grande dame, engaged in some romantic "adventure." She was not more than nineteen or twenty years of age, and he felt—without knowing what it was—the atmosphere of sweet, womanly purity and innocence which surrounded her. The shyness of a lost boyhood surprised him.

By the time they had reached the Litenie, she had fully recovered her consciousness and a portion of her strength. She drew away from him as much as the narrow sled would allow.

"You have been very kind, sir, and I thank you," she said; "but I am now able to go home without your further assistance."

"By no means, lady!" said the Prince. "The streets are rough, and here are no lamps. If a second accident were to happen, you would be helpless. Will you not allow me to protect you?"

She looked him in the face. In the dusky light, she saw not the peevish, weary features of the worldling, but only the imploring softness of his eyes, the full and perfect honesty of his present emotion. She made no further objection; perhaps she was glad that she could trust the elegant stranger.

Boris, never before at a loss for words, even in the presence of the Empress, was astonished to find how awkward were his attempts at conversation. She was presently the more self-possessed of the two, and nothing was ever so

423

sweet to his ears as the few commonplace remarks she uttered. In spite of the
darkness and the chilly air, the sled seemed to fly like lightning. Before he
supposed they had made half the way, she gave a sign to the istvostchik, and
they drew up before a plain house of squared logs.

The two lower windows were lighted, and the dark figure of an old man,
with a skull-cap upon his head, was framed in one of them. It vanished as the
sled stopped; the door was thrown open and the man came forth hurriedly,
followed by a Russian nurse with a lantern.

"Helena, my child, art thou come at last? What has befallen thee?"

He would evidently have said more, but the sight of Prince Boris caused
him to pause, while a quick shade of suspicion and alarm passed over his face.
The Prince stepped forward, instantly relieved of his unaccustomed timidity,
and rapidly described the accident. The old nurse Katinka, had meanwhile
assisted the lovely Helena into the house.

The old man turned to follow, shivering in the night-air. Suddenly
recollecting himself, he begged the Prince to enter and take some refreshments,
but with the air and tone of a man who hopes that his invitation will not be
accepted. If such was really his hope, he was disappointed; for Boris instantly
commanded the istvostchik to wait for him, and entered the humble dwelling.

The apartment into which he was ushered was spacious, and plainly, yet
not shabbily furnished. A violoncello and clavichord, with several portfolios
of music, and scattered sheets of ruled paper, proclaimed the profession or
the taste of the occupant. Having excused himself a moment to look after his
daughter's condition, the old man, on his return, found Boris turning over
the leaves of a musical work.

"You see my profession," he said. "I teach music?"

"Do you not compose?" asked the Prince.

"That was once my ambition. I was a pupil of Sebastian Bach. But—
circumstances—necessity—brought me here. Other lives changed the
direction of mine. It was right!"

"You mean your daughter's?" the Prince gently suggested.

"Hers and her mother's. Our story was well known in St. Petersburg twenty years ago, but I suppose no one recollects it now. My wife was the daughter of a Baron von Plauen, and loved music and myself better than her home and a titled bridegroom. She escaped, we united our lives, suffered and were happy together,—and she died. That is all."

Further conversation was interrupted by the entrance of Helena, with steaming glasses of tea. She was even lovelier than before. Her close-fitting dress revealed the symmetry of her form, and the quiet, unstudied grace of her movements. Although her garments were of well-worn material, the lace which covered her bosom was genuine point d'Alencon, of an old and rare pattern. Boris felt that her air and manner were thoroughly noble; he rose and saluted her with the profoundest respect.

In spite of the singular delight which her presence occasioned him, he was careful not to prolong his visit beyond the limits of strict etiquette. His name, Boris Alexeivitch, only revealed to his guests the name of his father, without his rank; and when he stated that he was employed in one of the Departments, (which was true in a measure, for he was a staff officer,) they could only look upon him as being, at best, a member of some family whose recent elevation to the nobility did not release them from the necessity of Government service. Of course he employed the usual pretext of wishing to study music, and either by that or some other stratagem managed to leave matters in such a shape that a second visit could not occasion surprise.

As the sled glided homewards over the crackling snow, he was obliged to confess the existence of a new and powerful excitement. Was it the chance of an adventure, such as certain of his comrades were continually seeking? He thought not; no, decidedly not. Was it—could it be—love? He really could not tell; he had not the slightset idea what love was like.

## VI.

It was something at least, that the plastic and not un-virtuous nature of the young man was directed towards a definite object. The elements out of which he was made, although somewhat diluted, were active enough to make him uncomfortable, so long as they remained in a confused state. He had very little power of introversion, but he was sensible that his temperament was changing,—that he grew more cheerful and contented with life,—that a chasm somewhere was filling up,—just in proportion as his acquaintance with the old music-master and his daughter became more familiar. His visits were made so brief, were so adroitly timed and accounted for by circumstances, that by the close of Lent he could feel justified in making the Easter call of a friend, and claim its attendant privileges, without fear of being repulsed.

That Easter call was an era in his life. At the risk of his wealth and rank being suspected, he dressed himself in new and rich garments, and hurried away towards the Smolnoi. The old nurse, Katinka, in her scarlet gown, opened the door for him, and was the first to say, "Christ is arisen!" What could he do but give her the usual kiss? Formerly he had kissed hundreds of serfs, men and women, on the sacred anniversary, with a passive good-will. But Katinka's kiss seemed bitter, and he secretly rubbed his mouth after it. The music-master came next: grisly though he might be, he was the St. Peter who stood at the gate of heaven. Then entered Helena, in white, like an angel. He took her hand, pronounced the Easter greeting, and scarcely waited for the answer, "Truly he has arisen!" before his lips found the way to hers. For a second they warmly trembled and glowed together; and in another second some new and sweet and subtle relation seemed to be established between their natures.

That night Prince Boris wrote a long letter to his "chere maman," in piquantly misspelt French, giving her the gossip of the court, and such family news as she usually craved. The purport of the letter, however, was only disclosed in the final paragraph, and then in so negative a way that it is doubtful whether the Princess Martha fully understood it.

"Poing de mariajes pour moix!" he wrote,—but we will drop the original,—"I don't think of such a thing yet. Pashkoff dropped a hint, the other day, but I kept my eyes shut. Perhaps you remember her?—fat, thick lips, and crooked teeth. Natalie D—— said to me, 'Have you ever been in love, Prince?" HAVE I, MAMAN? I did not know what answer to make. What is love? How does one feel, when one has it? They laugh at it here, and of course I should not wish to do what is laughable. Give me a hint: forewarned is forearmed, you know,'"—etc., etc.

Perhaps the Princess Martha DID suspect something; perhaps some word in her son's letter touched a secret spot far back in her memory, and renewed a dim, if not very intelligible, pain. She answered his question at length, in the style of the popular French romances of that day. She had much to say of dew and roses, turtledoves and the arrows of Cupid.

"Ask thyself," she wrote, "whether felicity comes with her presence, and distraction with her absence,—whether her eyes make the morning brighter for thee, and her tears fall upon thy heart like molten lava,—whether heaven would be black and dismal without her company, and the flames of hell turn into roses under her feet."

It was very evident that the good Princess Martha had never felt—nay, did not comprehend—a passion such as she described.

Prince Boris, however, whose veneration for his mother was unbounded, took her words literally, and applied the questions to himself. Although he found it difficult, in good faith and sincerity, to answer all of them affirmatively (he was puzzled, for instance, to know the sensation of molten lava falling upon the heart), yet the general conclusion was inevitable: Helena was necessary to his happiness.

Instead of returning to Kinesma for the summer, as had been arranged, he determined to remain in St. Petersburg, under the pretence of devoting himself to military studies. This change of plan occasioned more disappointment to the Princess Martha than vexation to Prince Alexis. The latter only growled at the prospect of being called upon to advance a further supply of rubles, slightly comforting himself with the muttered reflection,—

"Perhaps the brat will make a man of himself, after all."

It was not many weeks, in fact, before the expected petition came to hand. The Princess Martha had also foreseen it, and instructed her son how to attack his father's weak side. The latter was furiously jealous of certain other noblemen of nearly equal wealth, who were with him at the court of

Peter the Great, as their sons now were at that of Elizabeth. Boris compared the splendor of these young noblemen with his own moderate estate, fabled a few "adventures" and drinking-bouts, and announced his determination of doing honor to the name which Prince Alexis of Kinesma had left behind him in the capital.

There was cursing at the castle when the letter arrived. Many serfs felt the sting of the short whip, the slumber-flag was hoisted five minutes later than usual, and the consumption of Cognac was alarming; but no mirror was smashed, and when Prince Alexis read the letter to his poor relations, he even chuckled over some portions of it. Boris had boldly demanded twenty thousand rubles, in the desperate hope of receiving half that amount,—and he had calculated correctly.

Before midsummer he was Helena's accepted lover. Not, however, until then, when her father had given his consent to their marriage in the autumn, did he disclose his true rank. The old man's face lighted up with a glow of selfish satisfaction; but Helena quietly took her lover's hand, and said,—

"Whatever you are, Boris, I will be faithful to you."

## VII.

Leaving Boris to discover the exact form and substance of the passion of love, we will return for a time to the castle of Kinesma.

Whether the Princess Martha conjectured what had transpired in St. Petersburg, or was partially informed of it by her son, cannot now be ascertained. She was sufficiently weak, timid, and nervous, to be troubled with the knowledge of the stratagem in which she had assisted in order to procure money, and that the ever-present consciousness thereof would betray itself to the sharp eyes of her husband. Certain it is, that the demeanor of the latter towards her and his household began to change about the end of the summer. He seemed to have a haunting suspicion, that, in some way he had been, or was about to be, overreached. He grew peevish, suspicious, and more violent than ever in his excesses.

When Mishka, the dissipated bear already described, bit off one of the ears of Basil, a hunter belonging to the castle, and Basil drew his knife and plunged it into Mishka's heart, Prince Alexis punished the hunter by cutting off his other ear, and sending him away to a distant estate. A serf, detected in eating a few of the pickled cherries intended for the Prince's botvinia, was placed in a cask, and pickled cherries packed around him up to the chin. There he was kept until almost flayed by the acid. It was ordered that these two delinquents should never afterwards be called by any other names than "Crop-Ear" and "Cherry."

But the Prince's severest joke, which, strange to say, in no wise lessened his popularity among the serfs, occurred a month or two later. One of his leading passions was the chase,—especially the chase in his own forests, with from one to two hundred men, and no one to dispute his Lordship. On such occasions, a huge barrel of wine, mounted upon a sled, always accompanied the crowd, and the quantity which the hunters received depended upon the satisfaction of Prince Alexis with the game they collected.

Winter had set in early and suddenly, and one day, as the Prince and his retainers emerged from the forest with their forenoon's spoil, and found themselves on the bank of the Volga, the water was already covered with a thin sheet of ice. Fires were kindled, a score or two of hares and a brace of deer were skinned, and the flesh placed on sticks to broil; skins of mead foamed and hissed into the wooden bowls, and the cask of unbroached wine towered in the midst. Prince Alexis had a good appetite; the meal was after his heart; and by the time he had eaten a hare and half a flank of venison, followed by several bowls of fiery wine, he was in the humor for sport. He ordered a hole cut in the upper side of the barrel, as it lay; then, getting astride of it, like a grisly Bacchus, he dipped out the liquor with a ladle, and plied his thirsty serfs until they became as recklessly savage as he.

They were scattered over a slope gently falling from the dark, dense fir-forest towards the Volga, where it terminated in a rocky palisade, ten to fifteen feet in height. The fires blazed and crackled merrily in the frosty air; the yells and songs of the carousers were echoed back from the opposite shore of the river. The chill atmosphere, the lowering sky, and the approaching night could not touch the blood of that wild crowd. Their faces glowed and their eyes sparkled; they were ready for any deviltry which their lord might suggest.

Some began to amuse themselves by flinging the clean-picked bones of deer and hare along the glassy ice of the Volga. Prince Alexis, perceiving this diverson, cried out in ecstasy,—

"Oh, by St. Nicholas the Miracle-Worker, I'll give you better sport than that, ye knaves! Here's the very place for a reisak,—do you hear me children?—a reisak! Could there be better ice? and then the rocks to jump from! Come, children, come! Waska, Ivan, Daniel, you dogs, over with you!"

Now the reisak was a gymnastic performance peculiar to old Russia, and therefore needs to be described. It could become popular only among a people of strong physical qualities, and in a country where swift rivers freeze rapidly from sudden cold. Hence we are of the opinion that it will not be introduced into our own winter diversions. A spot is selected where the water is deep and the current tolerably strong; the ice must be about half an inch in thickness. The performer leaps head foremost from a rock or platform, bursts through the ice, is carried under by the current, comes up some distance below, and bursts through again. Both skill and strength are required to do the feat successfully.

Waska, Ivan, Daniel, and a number of others, sprang to the brink of the rocks and looked over. The wall was not quite perpendicular, some large fragments having fallen from above and lodged along the base. It would therefore require a bold leap to clear the rocks and strike the smooth ice. They hesitated,—and no wonder.

Prince Alexis howled with rage and disappointment.

"The Devil take you, for a pack of whimpering hounds!" he cried. "Holy Saints! they are afraid to make a reisak!"

Ivan crossed himself and sprang. He cleared the rocks, but, instead of bursting through the ice with his head, fell at full length upon his back.

"O knave!" yelled the Prince,—"not to know where his head is! Thinks it's his back! Give him fifteen stripes."

Which was instantly done.

The second attempt was partially successful. One of the hunters broke through the ice, head foremost, going down, but he failed to come up again; so the feat was only half performed.

The Prince became more furiously excited.

"This is the way I'm treated!" he cried. "He forgets all about finishing the reisak, and goes to chasing sterlet! May the carps eat him up for an ungrateful vagabond! Here, you beggars!" (addressing the poor relations,) "take your turn, and let me see whether you are men."

Only one of the frightened parasites had the courage to obey. On reaching the brink, he shut his eyes in mortal fear, and made a leap at random. The next moment he lay on the edge of the ice with one leg broken against a fragment of rock.

This capped the climax of the Prince's wrath. He fell into a state bordering on despair, tore his hair, gnashed his teeth, and wept bitterly.

"They will be the death of me!" was his lament. "Not a man among them! It wasn't so in the old times. Such beautiful reisaks as I have seen! But the people are becoming women,—hares,—chickens,—skunks! Villains, will you force me to kill you? You have dishonored and disgraced me; I am ashamed to look my neighbors in the face. Was ever a man so treated?"

The serfs hung down their heads, feeling somehow responsible for their master's misery. Some of them wept, out of a stupid sympathy with his tears.

All at once he sprang down from the cask, crying in a gay, triumphant tone,—

"I have it! Bring me Crop-Ear. He's the fellow for a reisak,—he can make three, one after another."

One of the boldest ventured to suggest that Crop-Ear had been sent away in disgrace to another of the Prince's estates.

431

"Bring him here, I say? Take horses, and don't draw rein going or coming. I will not stir from this spot until Crop-Ear comes."

With these words, he mounted the barrel, and recommenced ladling out the wine. Huge fires were made, for the night was falling, and the cold had become intense. Fresh game was skewered and set to broil, and the tragic interlude of the revel was soon forgotten.

Towards midnight the sound of hoofs was heard, and the messengers arrived with Crop-Ear. But, although the latter had lost his ears, he was not inclined to split his head. The ice, meanwhile, had become so strong that a cannon-ball would have made no impression upon it. Crop-Ear simply threw down a stone heavier than himself, and, as it bounced and slid along the solid floor, said to Prince Alexis,—

"Am I to go back, Highness, or stay here?"

"Here, my son. Thou'rt a man. Come hither to me."

Taking the serf's head in his hands, he kissed him on both cheeks. Then he rode homeward through the dark, iron woods, seated astride on the barrel, and steadying himself with his arms around Crop-Ear's and Waska's necks.

## VIII.

The health of the Princess Martha, always delicate, now began to fail rapidly. She was less and less able to endure her husband's savage humors, and lived almost exclusively in her own apartments. She never mentioned the name of Boris in his presence, for it was sure to throw him into a paroxysm of fury. Floating rumors in regard to the young Prince had reached him from the capital, and nothing would convince him that his wife was not cognizant of her son's doings. The poor Princess clung to her boy as to all that was left her of life, and tried to prop her failing strength with the hope of his speedy return. She was now too helpless to thwart his wishes in any way; but she dreaded, more than death, the terrible SOMETHING which would surely take place between father and son if her conjectures should prove to be true.

One day, in the early part of November, she received a letter from Boris, announcing his marriage. She had barely strength and presence of mind

432

enough to conceal the paper in her bosom before sinking in a swoon. By some means or other the young Prince had succeeded in overcoming all the obstacles to such a step: probably the favor of the Empress was courted, in order to obtain her consent. The money he had received, he wrote, would be sufficient to maintain them for a few months, though not in a style befitting their rank. He was proud and happy; the Princess Helena would be the reigning beauty of the court, when he should present her, but he desired the sanction of his parents to the marriage, before taking his place in society. He would write immediately to his father, and hoped, that, if the news brought a storm, Mishka might be on hand to divert its force, as on a former occasion.

Under the weight of this imminent secret, the Princess Martha could neither eat nor sleep. Her body wasted to a shadow; at every noise in the castle, she started and listened in terror, fearing that the news had arrived.

Prince Boris, no doubt, found his courage fail him when he set about writing the promised letter; for a fortnight elapsed before it made its appearance. Prince Alexis received it on his return from the chase. He read it hastily through, uttered a prolonged roar like that of a wounded bull, and rushed into the castle. The sound of breaking furniture, of crashing porcelain and shivered glass, came from the state apartments: the domestics fell on their knees and prayed; the Princess, who heard the noise and knew what it portended, became almost insensible from fright.

One of the upper servants entered a chamber as the Prince was in the act of demolishing a splendid malachite table, which had escaped all his previous attacks. He was immediately greeted with a cry of,—

"Send the Princess to me!"

"Her Highness is not able to leave her chamber," the man replied.

How it happened he could never afterwards describe but he found himself lying in a corner of the room. When he arose, there seemed to be a singular cavity in his mouth: his upper front teeth were wanting.

We will not narrate what took place in the chamber of the Princess.

The nerves of the unfortunate woman had been so wrought upon by her fears, that her husband's brutal rage, familiar to her from long experience, now possessed a new and alarming significance. His threats were terrible to hear; she fell into convulsions, and before morning her tormented life was at an end.

There was now something else to think of, and the smashing of porcelain and cracking of whips came to an end. The Archimandrite was summoned, and preparations, both religious and secular, were made for a funeral worthy the rank of the deceased. Thousands flocked to Kinesma; and when the immense procession moved away from the castle, although very few of the persons had ever known or cared in the least, for the Princess Martha, all, without exception, shed profuse tears. Yes, there was one exception,— one bare, dry rock, rising alone out of the universal deluge,—Prince Alexis himself, who walked behind the coffin, his eyes fixed and his features rigid as stone. They remarked that his face was haggard, and that the fiery tinge on his cheeks and nose had faded into livid purple. The only sign of emotion which he gave was a convulsive shudder, which from time to time passed over his whole body.

Three archimandrites (abbots) and one hundred priests headed the solemn funeral procession from the castle to the church on the opposite hill. There the mass for the dead was chanted, the responses being sung by a choir of silvery boyish voices. All the appointments were of the costliest character. Not only all those within the church, but the thousands outside, spared not their tears, but wept until the fountains were exhausted. Notice was given, at the close of the services, that "baked meats" would be furnished to the multitude, and that all beggars who came to Kinesma would be charitably fed for the space of six weeks. Thus, by her death, the amiable Princess Martha was enabled to dispense more charity than had been permitted to her life.

At the funeral banquet which followed, Prince Alexis placed the Abbot Sergius at his right hand, and conversed with him in the most edifying manner upon the necessity of leading a pure and godly life. His remarks upon the duty of a Christian, upon brotherly love, humility, and self-sacrifice, brought tears into the eyes of the listening priests. He expressed his conviction that the departed Princess, by the piety of her life, had attained unto salvation,—and added, that his own life had now no further value unless he should devote it to religious exercises.

"Can you not give me a place in your monastery?" he asked, turning to the Abbot. "I will endow it with a gift of forty thousand rubles, for the privilege of occupying a monk's cell."

"Pray, do not decide too hastily, Highness," the Abbot replied. "You have yet a son."

"What!" yelled Prince Alexis, with flashing eyes, every trace of humility and renunciation vanishing like smoke,—"what! Borka? The infamous wretch who has ruined me, killed his mother, and brought disgrace upon our name? Do you know that he has married a wench of no family and without a farthing,—who would be honored, if I should allow her to feed my hogs? Live for HIM? live for HIM? Ah-R-R-R!"

This outbreak terminated in a sound between a snarl and a bellow. The priests turned pale, but the Abbot devoutly remarked—

"Encompassed by sorrows, Prince, you should humbly submit to the will of the Lord."

"Submit to Borka?" the Prince scornfully laughed. "I know what I'll do. There's time enough yet for a wife and another child,—ay,—a dozen children! I can have my pick in the province; and if I couldn't I'd sooner take Masha, the goose-girl, than leave Borka the hope of stepping into my shoes. Beggars they shall be,—beggars!"

What further he might have said was interrupted by the priests rising to chant the Blajennon uspennie (blessed be the dead),—after which, the trisna, a drink composed of mead, wine, and rum, was emptied to the health of the departed soul. Every one stood during this ceremony, except Prince Alexis, who fell suddenly prostrate before the consecrated pictures, and sobbed so passionately that the tears of the guests flowed for the third time. There he lay until night; for whenever any one dared to touch him, he struck out furiously with fists and feet. Finally he fell asleep on the floor, and the servants then bore him to his sleeping apartment.

For several days afterward his grief continued to be so violent that the occupants of the castle were obliged to keep out of his way. The whip was never out of his hand, and he used it very recklessly, not always selecting the right person. The parasitic poor relations found their situation so uncomfortable, that they decided, one and all, to detach themselves from the tree upon which they fed and fattened, even at the risk of withering on a barren soil. Night and morning the serfs prayed upon their knees, with many tears and groans, that the Saints might send consolation, in any form, to their desperate lord.

The Saints graciously heard and answered the prayer. Word came that a huge bear had been seen in the forest stretching towards Juriewetz. The sorrowing Prince pricked up his ears, threw down his whip, and ordered a chase. Sasha, the broad-shouldered, the cunning, the ready, the untiring companion of his master, secretly ordered a cask of vodki to follow the crowd of hunters and serfs. There was a steel-bright sky, a low, yellow sun, and a brisk easterly wind from the heights of the Ural. As the crisp snow began to crunch under the Prince's sled, his followers saw the old expression come back to his face. With song and halloo and blast of horns, they swept away into the forest.

Saint John the Hunter must have been on guard over Russia that day.

The great bear was tracked, and after a long and exciting chase, fell by the hand of Prince Alexis himself. Halt was made in an open space in the forest, logs were piled together and kindled on the snow, and just at the right moment (which no one knew better than Sasha) the cask of vodki rolled into its place. When the serfs saw the Prince mount astride of it, with his ladle in his hand, they burst into shouts of extravagant joy. "Slava Bogu!" (Glory be to God!) came fervently from the bearded lips of those hard, rough, obedient children. They tumbled headlong over each other, in their efforts to drink first from the ladle, to clasp the knees or kiss the hands of the restored Prince. And the dawn was glimmering against the eastern stars, as they took the way to the castle, making the ghostly fir-woods ring with shout and choric song.

Nevertheless, Prince Alexis was no longer the same man; his giant strength and furious appetite were broken. He was ever ready, as formerly, for the chase and the drinking-bout; but his jovial mood no longer grew into a crisis which only utter physical exhaustion or the stupidity of drunkenness could overcome. Frequently, while astride the cask, his shouts of laughter would suddenly cease, the ladle would drop from his hand, and he would sit motionless, staring into vacancy for five minutes at a time. Then the serfs, too, became silent, and stood still, awaiting a change. The gloomy mood passed away as suddenly. He would start, look about him, and say, in a melancholy voice,—

"Have I frightened you, my children? It seems to me that I am getting old. Ah, yes, we must all die, one day. But we need not think about it, until the time comes. The Devil take me for putting it into my head! Why, how now? can't you sing, children?"

Then he would strike up some ditty which they all knew: a hundred voices joined in the strain, and the hills once more rang with revelry.

Since the day when the Princess Martha was buried, the Prince had not again spoken of marriage. No one, of course, dared to mention the name of Boris in his presence.

## IX.

The young Prince had, in reality, become the happy husband of Helena. His love for her had grown to be a shaping and organizing influence, without which his nature would have fallen into its former confusion. If a thought of a less honorable relation had ever entered his mind, it was presently banished by the respect which a nearer intimacy inspired; and thus Helena, magnetically drawing to the surface only his best qualities, loved, unconsciously to herself, her own work in him. Ere long, she saw that she might balance the advantages he had conferred upon her in their marriage by the support and encouragement which she was able to impart to him; and this knowledge, removing all painful sense of obligation, made her both happy and secure in her new position.

The Princess Martha, under some presentiment of her approaching death, had intrusted one of the ladies in attendance upon her with the secret of her son's marriage, in addition to a tender maternal message, and such presents of money and jewelry as she was able to procure without her husband's knowledge. These presents reached Boris very opportunely; for, although Helena developed a wonderful skill in regulating his expenses, the spring was approaching, and even the limited circle of society in which they had moved during the gay season had made heavy demands upon his purse. He became restless and abstracted, until his wife, who by this time clearly comprehended the nature of his trouble, had secretly decided how it must be met.

The slender hoard of the old music-master, with a few thousand rubles from Prince Boris, sufficed for his modest maintenance. Being now free from the charge of his daughter, he determined to visit Germany, and, if circumstances were propitious, to secure a refuge for his old age in his favorite Leipsic. Summer was at hand, and the court had already removed to Oranienbaum. In a few weeks the capital would be deserted.

"Shall we go to Germany with your father?" asked Boris, as he sat at a window with Helena, enjoying the long twilight.

"No, my Boris," she answered; "we will go to Kinesma."

"But—Helena,—golubchik, mon ange,—are you in earnest?"

"Yes, my Boris. The last letter from your—our cousin Nadejda convinces me that the step must be taken. Prince Alexis has grown much older since your mother's death; he is lonely and unhappy. He may not welcome us, but he will surely suffer us to come to him; and we must then begin the work of reconciliation. Reflect, my Boris, that you have keenly wounded him in the tenderest part,—his pride,—and you must therefore cast away your own pride, and humbly and respectfully, as becomes a son, solicit his pardon."

"Yes," said he, hesitatingly, "you are right. But I know his violence and recklessness, as you do not. For myself, alone, I am willing to meet him; yet I fear for your sake. Would you not tremble to encounter a maddened and brutal mujik?—then how much more to meet Alexis Pavlovitch of Kinesma!"

"I do not and shall not tremble," she replied. "It is not your marriage that has estranged your father, but your marriage with ME. Having been,

438

unconsciously, the cause of the trouble, I shall deliberately, and as a sacred duty, attempt to remove it. Let us go to Kinesma, as humble, penitent children, and cast ourselves upon your father's mercy. At the worst, he can but reject us; and you will have given me the consolation of knowing that I have tried, as your wife, to annul the sacrifice you have made for my sake."

"Be it so, then!" cried Boris, with a mingled feeling of relief and anxiety.

He was not unwilling that the attempt should be made, especially since it was his wife's desire; but he knew his father too well to anticipate immediate success. All threatening POSSIBILITIES suggested themselves to his mind; all forms of insult and outrage which he had seen perpetrated at Kinesma filled his memory. The suspense became at last worse than any probable reality. He wrote to his father, announcing a speedy visit from himself and his wife; and two days afterwards the pair left St. Petersburg in a large travelling kibitka.

## X.

When Prince Alexis received his son's letter, an expression of fierce, cruel delight crept over his face, and there remained, horribly illuminating its haggard features. The orders given for swimming horses in the Volga—one of his summer diversions—were immediately countermanded; he paced around the parapet of the castle-wall until near midnight, followed by Sasha with a stone jug of vodki. The latter had the useful habit, notwithstanding his stupid face, of picking up the fragments of soliloquy which the Prince dropped, and answering them as if talking to himself. Thus he improved upon and perfected many a hint of cruelty, and was too discreet ever to dispute his master's claim to the invention.

Sasha, we may be sure, was busy with his devil's work that night. The next morning the stewards and agents of Prince Alexis, in castle, village, and field, were summoned to his presence.

"Hark ye!" said he; "Borka and his trumpery wife send me word that they will be here to-morrow. See to it that every man, woman, and child, for ten versts out on the Moskovskoi road, knows of their coming. Let it be known that whoever uncovers his head before them shall uncover his back for a hundred lashes. Whomsoever they greet may bark like a dog, meeeouw like a

439

cat, or bray like an ass, as much as he chooses; but if he speaks a decent word, his tongue shall be silenced with stripes. Whoever shall insult them has my pardon in advance. Oh, let them come!—ay, let them come! Come they may: but how they go away again"——

The Prince Alexis suddenly stopped, shook his head, and walked up and down the hall, muttering to himself. His eyes were bloodshot, and sparkled with a strange light. What the stewards had heard was plain enough; but that something more terrible than insult was yet held in reserve they did not doubt. It was safe, therefore, not only to fulfil, but to exceed, the letter of their instructions. Before night the whole population were acquainted with their duties; and an unusual mood of expectancy, not unmixed with brutish glee, fell upon Kinesma.

By the middle of the next forenoon, Boris and his wife, seated in the open kibitka, drawn by post-horses, reached the boundaries of the estate, a few versts from the village. They were both silent and slightly pale at first, but now began to exchange mechanical remarks, to divert each other's thoughts from the coming reception.

"Here are the fields of Kinesma at last!" exclaimed Prince Boris. "We shall see the church and castle from the top of that hill in the distance. And there is Peter, my playmate, herding the cattle!

"Peter! Good-day, brotherkin!"

Peter looked, saw the carriage close upon him, and, after a moment of hesitation, let his arms drop stiffly by his sides, and began howling like a mastiff by moonlight. Helena laughed heartily at this singular response to the greeting; but Boris, after the first astonishment was over, looked terrified.

"That was done by order," said he, with a bitter smile. "The old bear stretches his claws out. Dare you try his hug?"

"I do not fear," she answered, her face was calm.

Every serf they passed obeyed the order of Prince Alexis according to his own idea of disrespect. One turned his back; another made contemptuous

440

grimaces and noises; another sang a vulgar song; another spat upon the ground or held his nostrils. Nowhere was a cap raised, or the stealthy welcome of a friendly glance given.

The Princess Helena met these insults with a calm, proud indifference. Boris felt them more keenly; for the fields and hills were prospectively his property, and so also were the brutish peasants. It was a form of chastisement which he had never before experienced, and knew not how to resist. The affront of an entire community was an offence against which he felt himself to be helpless.

As they approached the town, the demonstrations of insolence were redoubled. About two hundred boys, between the ages of ten and fourteen, awaited them on the hill below the church, forming themselves into files on either side of the road. These imps had been instructed to stick out their tongues in derision, and howl, as the carriage passed between them. At the entrance of the long main street of Kinesma, they were obliged to pass under a mock triumphal arch, hung with dead dogs and drowned cats; and from this point the reception assumed an outrageous character. Howls, hootings, and hisses were heard on all sides; bouquets of nettles and vile weeds were flung to them; even wreaths of spoiled fish dropped from the windows. The women were the most eager and uproarious in this carnival of insult: they beat their saucepans, threw pails of dirty water upon the horses, pelted the coachman with rotten cabbages, and filled the air with screeching and foul words.

It was impossible to pass through this ordeal with indifference. Boris, finding that his kindly greetings were thrown away,—that even his old acquaintances in the bazaar howled like the rest,—sat with head bowed and despair in his heart. The beautiful eyes of Helena were heavy with tears; but she no longer trembled, for she knew the crisis was yet to come.

As the kibitka slowly climbed the hill on its way to the castle-gate, Prince Alexis, who had heard and enjoyed the noises in the village from a balcony on the western tower, made his appearance on the head of the steps which led from the court-yard to the state apartments. The dreaded whip was in his hand; his eyes seemed about to start from their sockets, in their wild, eager, hungry gaze; the veins stood out like cords on his forehead; and his lips, twitching involuntarily, revealed the glare of his set teeth. A frightened hush filled the castle. Some of the domestics were on their knees; others watching, pale and breathless, from the windows: for all felt that a greater storm than they had ever experienced was about to burst. Sasha and the castle-steward had taken the wise precaution to summon a physician and a priest, provided with the utensils for extreme unction. Both of these persons had been smuggled in through a rear entrance, and were kept concealed until their services should be required.

The noise of wheels was heard outside the gate, which stood invitingly open. Prince Alexis clutched his whip with iron fingers, and unconsciously took the attitude of a wild beast about to spring from its ambush. Now the hard clatter of hoofs and the rumbling, of wheels echoed from the archway, and the kibitka rolled into the courtyard. It stopped near the foot of the grand staircase. Boris, who sat upon the farther side, rose to alight, in order to hand down his wife; but no sooner had he made a movement than Prince Alexis, with lifted whip and face flashing fire, rushed down the steps. Helena rose, threw back her veil, let her mantle (which Boris had grasped, in his anxiety to restrain her action,) fall behind her, and stepped upon the pavement.

Prince Alexis had already reached the last step, and but a few feet separated them. He stopped as if struck by lightning,—his body still retaining, in every limb, the impress of motion. The whip was in his uplifted fist; one foot was on the pavement of the court, and the other upon the edge of the last step; his head was bent forward, his mouth open, and his eyes fastened upon the Princess Helena's face.

She, too, stood motionless, a form of simple and perfect grace, and met his gaze with soft, imploring, yet courageous and trustful eyes. The women who watched the scene from the galleries above always declared that an invisible saint stood beside her in that moment, and surrounded her with a dazzling glory. The few moments during which the suspense of a hundred hearts hung upon those encountering eyes seemed an eternity.

Prince Alexis did not move, but he began to tremble from head to foot.

His fingers relaxed, and the whip fell ringing upon the pavement. The wild fire of his eyes changed from wrath into an ecstasy as intense, and a piercing cry of mingled wonder, admiration and delight burst from his throat. At that cry Boris rushed forward and knelt at his feet. Helena, clasping her fairest hands, sank beside her husband, with upturned face, as if seeking the old man's eyes, and perfect the miracle she had wrought.

The sight of that sweet face, so near his own, tamed the last lurking ferocity of the beast. His tears burst forth in a shower; he lifted and embraced the Princess, kissing her brow, her cheeks, her chin, and her hands, calling her his darling daughter, his little white dove, his lambkin.

"And, father, my Boris, too!" said she.

The pure liquid voice sent thrills of exquisite delight through his whole frame. He embraced and blessed Boris, and then, throwing an arm around each, held them to his breast, and wept passionately upon their heads. By this time the whole castle overflowed with weeping. Tears fell from every window and gallery; they hissed upon the hot saucepans of the cooks; they moistened the oats in the manger; they took the starch out of the ladies' ruffles, and weakened the wine in the goblets of the guests. Insult was changed into tenderness in a moment. Those who had barked or stuck out their tongues at Boris rushed up to kiss his boots; a thousand terms of endearment were showered upon him.

Still clasping his children to his breast, Prince Alexis mounted the steps with them. At the top he turned, cleared his throat, husky from sobbing, and shouted—

"A feast! a feast for all Kinesma! Let there be rivers of vodki, wine and hydromel! Proclaim it everywhere that my dear son Boris and my dear daughter Helena have arrived, and whoever fails to welcome them to Kinesma shall be punished with a hundred stripes! Off, ye scoundrels, ye vagabonds, and spread the news!"

It was not an hour before the whole sweep of the circling hills resounded with the clang of bells, the blare of horns, and the songs and shouts of the

443

rejoicing multitude. The triumphal arch of unsavory animals was whirled into the Volga; all signs of the recent reception vanished like magic; festive fir-boughs adorned the houses, and the gardens and window-pots were stripped of their choicest flowers to make wreaths of welcome. The two hundred boys, not old enough to comprehend this sudden bouleversement of sentiment, did not immediately desist from sticking out their tongues: whereupon they were dismissed with a box on the ear. By the middle of the afternoon all Kinesma was eating, drinking, and singing; and every song was sung, and every glass emptied in honor of the dear, good Prince Boris, and the dear, beautiful Princess Helena. By night all Kinesma was drunk.

## XI.

In the castle a superb banquet was improvised. Music, guests, and rare dishes were brought together with wonderful speed, and the choicest wines of the cellar were drawn upon. Prince Boris, bewildered by this sudden and incredible change in his fortunes, sat at his father's right hand, while the Princess filled, but with much more beauty and dignity, the ancient place of the Princess Martha. The golden dishes were set before her, and the famous family emeralds—in accordance with the command of Prince Alexis—gleamed among her dark hair and flashed around her milk-white throat. Her beauty was of a kind so rare in Russia that it silenced all question and bore down all rivalry. Every one acknowledged that so lovely a creature had never before been seen. "Faith, the boy has eyes!" the old Prince constantly repeated, as he turned away from a new stare of admiration, down the table.

The guests noticed a change in the character of the entertainment. The idiot, in his tow shirt, had been crammed to repletion in the kitchen, and was now asleep in the stable. Razboi, the new bear,—the successor of the slaughtered Mishka,—was chained up out of hearing. The jugglers, tumblers, and Calmucks still occupied their old place under the gallery, but their performances were of a highly decorous character. At the least-sign of a relapse into certain old tricks, more grotesque than refined, the brows of Prince Alexis would grow dark, and a sharp glance at Sasha was sufficient to correct the indiscretion. Every one found this natural enough; for they were equally impressed with the elegance and purity of the young wife. After the healths had been drunk and the slumber-flag was raised over the castle, Boris led her into the splendid apartments of his mother,—now her own,—and knelt at her feet.

"Have I done my part, my Boris?" she asked.

"You are an angel!" he cried. "It was a miracle! My life was not worth a copek, and I feared for yours. If it will only last!—if it will only last!"

"It WILL," said she. "You have taken me from poverty, and given me rank, wealth, and a proud place in the world: let it be my work to keep the peace which God has permitted me to establish between you and your father!"

The change in the old Prince, in fact, was more radical than any one who knew his former ways of life would have considered possible. He stormed and swore occasionally, flourished his whip to some purpose, and rode home from the chase, not outside of a brandy cask, as once, but with too much of its contents inside of him: but these mild excesses were comparative virtues. His accesses of blind rage seemed to be at an end. A powerful, unaccustomed feeling of content subdued his strong nature, and left its impress on his voice and features. He joked and sang with his "children," but not with the wild recklessness of the days of reisaks and indiscriminate floggings. Both his exactions and his favors diminished in quantity. Week after week passed by, and there was no sign of any return to his savage courses.

Nothing annoyed him so much as a reference to his former way of life, in the presence of the Princess Helena. If her gentle, questioning eyes happened to rest on him at such times, something very like a blush rose into his face, and the babbler was silenced with a terribly significant look. It was enough for her to say, when he threatened an act of cruelty and injustice, "Father, is that right?" He confusedly retracted his orders, rather than bear the sorrow of her face.

The promise of another event added to his happiness: Helena would soon become a mother. As the time drew near he stationed guards at the distance of a verst around the castle, that no clattering vehicles should pass, no dogs bark loudly, nor any other disturbance occur which might agitate the

Princess. The choicest sweetmeats and wines, flowers from Moscow and fruits from Astrakhan, were procured for her; and it was a wonder that the midwife performed her duty, for she had the fear of death before her eyes. When the important day at last arrived the slumber-flag was instantly hoisted, and no mouse dared to squeak in Kinesma until the cannon announced the advent of a new soul.

That night Prince Alexis lay down in the corridor, outside of Helena's door: he glared fiercely at the nurse as she entered with the birth-posset for the young mother. No one else was allowed to pass, that night, nor the next. Four days afterwards, Sasha, having a message to the Princess, and supposing the old man to be asleep, attempted to step noiselessly over his body. In a twinkle the Prince's teeth fastened themselves in the serf's leg, and held him with the tenacity of a bull-dog. Sasha did not dare to cry out: he stood, writhing with pain, until the strong jaws grew weary of their hold, and then crawled away to dress the bleeding wound. After that, no one tried to break the Prince's guard.

The christening was on a magnificent scale. Prince Paul of Kostroma was godfather, and gave the babe the name of Alexis. As the Prince had paid his respects to Helena just before the ceremony, it may be presumed that the name was not of his own inspiration. The father and mother were not allowed to be present, but they learned that the grandfather had comported himself throughout with great dignity and propriety. The Archimandrite Sergius obtained from the Metropolitan at Moscow a very minute fragment of the true cross, which was encased in a hollow bead of crystal, and hung around the infant's neck by a fine gold chain, as a precious amulet.

Prince Alexis was never tired of gazing at his grandson and namesake.

"He has more of his mother than of Boris," he would say. "So much the better! Strong dark eyes, like the Great Peter,—and what a goodly leg for a babe! Ha! he makes a tight little fist already,—fit to handle a whip,—or" (seeing the expression of Helena's face)—"or a sword. He'll be a proper Prince of Kinesma, my daughter, and we owe it to you."

Helena smiled, and gave him a grateful glance in return. She had had her secret fears as to the complete conversion of Prince Alexis; but now she saw in this babe a new spell whereby he might be bound. Slight as was her knowledge of men, she yet guessed the tyranny of long-continued habits; and only her faith, powerful in proportion as it was ignorant, gave her confidence in the result of the difficult work she had undertaken.

# XII.

Alas! the proud predictions of Prince Alexis, and the protection of the sacred amulet, were alike unavailing. The babe sickened, wasted away, and died in less than two months after its birth. There was great and genuine sorrow among the serfs of Kinesma. Each had received a shining ruble of silver at the christening; and, moreover, they were now beginning to appreciate the milder regime of their lord, which this blow might suddenly terminate. Sorrow, in such natures as his, exasperates instead of chastening: they knew him well enough to recognize the danger.

At first the old man's grief appeared to be of a stubborn, harmless nature. As soon as the funeral ceremonies were over he betook himself to his bed, and there lay for two days and nights, without eating a morsel of food. The poor Princess Helena, almost prostrated by the blow, mourned alone, or with Boris, in her own apartments. Her influence, no longer kept alive by her constant presence, as formerly, began to decline. When the old Prince aroused somewhat from his stupor, it was not meat that he demanded, but drink; and he drank to angry excess. Day after day the habit resumed its ancient sway, and the whip and the wild-beast yell returned with it. The serfs even began to tremble as they never had done, so long as his vices were simply those of a strong man; for now a fiendish element seemed to be slowly creeping in. He became horribly profane: they shuddered when he cursed the venerable Metropolitan of Moscow, declaring that the old sinner had deliberately killed his grandson, by sending to him, instead of the true cross of the Saviour, a piece of the tree to which the impenitent thief was nailed.

Boris would have spared his wife the knowledge of this miserable relapse, in her present sorrow, but the information soon reached her in other ways. She saw the necessity of regaining, by a powerful effort, what she had lost. She therefore took her accustomed place at the table, and resumed her inspection of household matters. Prince Alexis, as if determined to cast off the yoke which her beauty and gentleness had laid upon him, avoided looking at her face or speaking to her, as much as possible: when he did so, his manner was cold and unfriendly. During her few days of sad retirement he had brought back the bear Razboi and the idiot to his table, and vodki was habitually poured out to him and his favorite serfs in such a measure that the nights became hideous with drunken tumult.

The Princess Helena felt that her beauty no longer possessed the potency of its first surprise. It must now be a contest of nature with nature, spiritual with animal power. The struggle would be perilous, she foresaw, but she did not shrink; she rather sought the earliest occasion to provoke it.

That occasion came. Some slight disappointment brought on one of the old paroxysms of rage, and the ox-like bellow of Prince Alexis rang through the castle. Boris was absent, but Helena delayed not a moment to venture into his father's presence. She found him in a hall over-looking the court-yard, with his terrible whip in his hand, giving orders for the brutal punishment of some scores of serfs. The sight of her, coming thus unexpectedly upon him, did not seem to produce the least effect.

"Father!" she cried, in an earnest, piteous tone, "what is it you do?"

"Away, witch!" he yelled. "I am the master in Kinesma, not thou! Away, or—"

The fierceness with which he swung and cracked the whip was more threatening than any words. Perhaps she grew a shade paler, perhaps her hands were tightly clasped in order that they might not tremble; but she did not flinch from the encounter. She moved a step nearer, fixed her gaze upon his flashing eyes, and said, in a low, firm voice—

"It is true, father, you are master here. It is easy to rule over those poor, submissive slaves. But you are not master over yourself; you are lashed and trampled upon by evil passions, and as much a slave as any of these. Be not weak, my father, but strong!"

An expression of bewilderment came into his face. No such words had ever before been addressed to him, and he knew not how to reply to them.

The Princess Helena followed up the effect—she was not sure that it was an advantage—by an appeal to the simple, childish nature which she believed to exist under his ferocious exterior. For a minute it seemed as if she were about to re-establish her ascendancy: then the stubborn resistance of the beast returned.

Among the portraits in the hall was one of the deceased Princess Martha. Pointing to this, Helena cried—

"See, my father! here are the features of your sainted wife! Think that she looks down from her place among the blessed, sees you, listens to your words, prays that your hard heart may be softened! Remember her last farewell to you on earth, her hope of meeting you—"

A cry of savage wrath checked her. Stretching one huge, bony hand, as if to close her lips, trembling with rage and pain, livid and convulsed in every feature of his face, Prince Alexis reversed the whip in his right hand, and weighed its thick, heavy butt for one crashing, fatal blow. Life and death were evenly balanced. For an instant the Princess became deadly pale, and a sickening fear shot through her heart. She could not understand the effect of her words: her mind was paralyzed, and what followed came without her conscious volition.

Not retreating a step, not removing her eyes from the terrible picture before her, she suddenly opened her lips and sang. Her voice of exquisite purity, power, and sweetness, filled the old hall and overflowed it, throbbing in scarcely weakened vibrations through court-yard and castle. The melody was a prayer—the cry of a tortured heart for pardon and repose; and she sang it with almost supernatural expression. Every sound in the castle was hushed: the serfs outside knelt and uncovered their heads.

The Princess could never afterwards describe, or more than dimly recall, the exaltation of that moment. She sang in an inspired trance: from the utterance of the first note the horror of the imminent fate sank out of sight. Her eyes were fixed upon the convulsed face, but she beheld it not: all the concentrated forces of her life flowed into the music. She remembered, however, that Prince Alexis looked alternately from her face to the portrait of his wife; that he at last shuddered and grew pale; and that, when with the closing note her own strength suddenly dissolved, he groaned and fell upon the floor.

She sat down beside him, and took his head upon her lap. For a long time he was silent, only shivering as if in fever.

"Father!" she finally whispered, "let me take you away!"

He sat up on the floor and looked around; but as his eyes encountered the portrait, he gave a loud howl and covered his face with his hands.

"She turns her head!" he cried. "Take her away,—she follows me with her eyes! Paint her head black, and cover it up!"

With some difficulty he was borne to his bed, but he would not rest until assured that his orders had been obeyed, and the painting covered for the time with a coat of lamp-black. A low, prolonged attack of fever followed, during which the presence of Helena was indispensable to his comfort. She ventured to leave the room only while he slept. He was like a child in her hands; and when she commended his patience or his good resolutions, his face beamed with joy and gratitude. He determined (in good faith, this time) to enter a monastery and devote the rest of his life to pious works.

But, even after his recovery, he was still too weak and dependent on his children's attentions to carry out this resolution. He banished from the castle all those of his poor relations who were unable to drink vodki in moderation; he kept careful watch over his serfs, and those who became intoxicated (unless they concealed the fact in the stables and outhouses) were severely punished: all excess disappeared, and a reign of peace and gentleness descended upon Kinesma.

In another year another Alexis was born, and lived, and soon grew strong enough to give his grandfather the greatest satisfaction he had ever known in his life, by tugging at his gray locks, and digging the small fingers into his tamed and merry eyes. Many years after Prince Alexis was dead the serfs used to relate how they had seen him, in the bright summer afternoons, asleep in his armchair on the balcony, with the rosy babe asleep on his bosom, and the slumber-flag waving over both.

Legends of the Prince's hunts, reisaks, and brutal revels are still current along the Volga; but they are now linked to fairer and more gracious stories; and the free Russian farmers (no longer serfs) are never tired of relating incidents of the beauty, the courage, the benevolence, and the saintly piety of the Good Lady of Kinesma.

# TALES OF HOME.

## THE STRANGE FRIEND.

It would have required an intimate familiarity with the habitual demeanor of the people of Londongrove to detect in them an access of interest (we dare not say excitement), of whatever kind. Expression with them was pitched to so low a key that its changes might be compared to the slight variations in the drabs and grays in which they were clothed. Yet that there was a moderate, decorously subdued curiosity present in the minds of many of them on one of the First-days of the Ninth-month, in the year 1815, was as clearly apparent to a resident of the neighborhood as are the indications of a fire or a riot to the member of a city mob.

The agitations of the war which had so recently come to an end had hardly touched this quiet and peaceful community. They had stoutly "borne their testimony," and faced the question where it could not be evaded; and although the dashing Philadelphia militia had been stationed at Camp Bloomfield, within four miles of them, the previous year, these good people simply ignored the fact. If their sons ever listened to the trumpets at a distance, or stole nearer to have a peep at the uniforms, no report of what they had seen or heard was likely to be made at home. Peace brought to them a relief, like the awakening from an uncomfortable dream: their lives at once reverted to the calm which they had breathed for thirty years preceding the national disturbance. In their ways they had not materially changed for a hundred years. The surplus produce of their farms more than sufficed for the very few needs which those farms did not supply, and they seldom touched the world outside of their sect except in matters of business. They were satisfied with themselves and with their lot; they lived to a ripe and beautiful age, rarely "borrowed trouble," and were patient to endure that which came in the fixed course of things. If the spirit of curiosity, the yearning for an active, joyous grasp of life, sometimes pierced through this placid temper, and stirred the blood of the adolescent members, they were persuaded by grave voices, of almost prophetic authority, to turn their hearts towards "the Stillness and the Quietness."

It was the pleasant custom of the community to arrive at the meeting-house some fifteen or twenty minutes before the usual time of meeting, and exchange quiet and kindly greetings before taking their places on the plain benches inside. As most of the families had lived during the week on the solitude of their farms, they liked to see their neighbors' faces, and resolve, as it were, their sense of isolation into the common atmosphere, before yielding to the assumed abstraction of their worship. In this preliminary meeting, also, the sexes were divided, but rather from habit than any prescribed rule. They were already in the vestibule of the sanctuary; their voices were subdued and their manner touched with a kind of reverence.

If the Londongrove Friends gathered together a few minutes earlier on that September First-day; if the younger members looked more frequently towards one of the gates leading into the meeting-house yard than towards the other; and if Abraham Bradbury was the centre of a larger circle of neighbors than Simon Pennock (although both sat side by side on the highest seat of the gallery),—the cause of these slight deviations from the ordinary behavior of the gathering was generally known. Abraham's son had died the previous Sixth-month, leaving a widow incapable of taking charge of his farm on the Street Road, which was therefore offered for rent. It was not always easy to obtain a satisfactory tenant in those days, and Abraham was not more relieved than surprised on receiving an application from an unexpected quarter. A strange Friend, of stately appearance, called upon him, bearing a letter from William Warner, in Adams County, together with a certificate from a Monthly Meeting on Long Island. After inspecting the farm and making close inquiries in regard to the people of the neighborhood, he accepted the terms of rent, and had now, with his family, been three or four days in possession.

In this circumstance, it is true, there was nothing strange, and the interest of the people sprang from some other particulars which had transpired. The new-comer, Henry Donnelly by name, had offered, in place of the usual security, to pay the rent annually in advance; his speech and manner were not, in all respects, those of Friends, and he acknowledged that he was of Irish birth; and moreover, some who had passed the wagons bearing his household goods had been struck by the peculiar patterns of the furniture piled upon them. Abraham Bradbury had of course been present at the arrival, and the Friends upon the adjoining farms had kindly given their assistance, although it was a busy time of the year. While, therefore, no one suspected that the farmer could possibly accept a tenant of doubtful character, a general sentiment of curious expectancy went forth to meet the Donnelly family.

Even the venerable Simon Pennock, who lived in the opposite part of the township, was not wholly free from the prevalent feeling. "Abraham," he said, approaching his colleague, "I suppose thee has satisfied thyself that the strange Friend is of good repute."

Abraham was assuredly satisfied of one thing—that the three hundred silver dollars in his antiquated secretary at home were good and lawful coin. We will not say that this fact disposed him to charity, but will only testify that he answered thus:

"I don't think we have any right to question the certificate from Islip, Simon; and William Warner's word (whom thee knows by hearsay) is that of a good and honest man. Henry himself will stand ready to satisfy thee, if it is needful."

Here he turned to greet a tall, fresh-faced youth, who had quietly joined the group at the men's end of the meeting-house. He was nineteen, blue-eyed, and rosy, and a little embarrassed by the grave, scrutinizing, yet not unfriendly eyes fixed upon him.

"Simon, this is Henry's oldest son, De Courcy," said Abraham.

Simon took the youth's hand, saying, "Where did thee get thy outlandish name?"

The young man colored, hesitated, and then said, in a low, firm voice, "It was my grandfather's name."

One of the heavy carriages of the place and period, new and shiny, in spite of its sober colors, rolled into the yard. Abraham Bradbury and De Courcy Donnelly set forth side by side, to meet it.

Out of it descended a tall, broad-shouldered figure—a man in the prime of life, whose ripe, aggressive vitality gave his rigid Quaker garb the air of a military undress. His blue eyes seemed to laugh above the measured accents of his plain speech, and the close crop of his hair could not hide its tendency to curl. A bearing expressive of energy and the habit of command was not unusual in the sect, strengthening, but not changing, its habitual mask; yet in Henry Donnelly this bearing suggested—one could scarcely explain why—a different experience. Dress and speech, in him, expressed condescension rather than fraternal equality.

He carefully assisted his wife to alight, and De Courcy led the horse to the hitching-shed. Susan Donnelly was a still blooming woman of forty; her dress, of the plainest color, was yet of the richest texture; and her round, gentle, almost timid face looked forth like a girl's from the shadow of her scoop bonnet. While she was greeting Abraham Bradbury, the two daughters, Sylvia and Alice, who had been standing shyly by themselves on the edge of the group of women, came forward. The latter was a model of the demure Quaker maiden; but Abraham experienced as much surprise as was possible to his nature on observing Sylvia's costume. A light-blue dress, a dark-blue cloak, a hat with ribbons, and hair in curls—what Friend of good standing ever allowed his daughter thus to array herself in the fashion of the world?

Henry read the question in Abraham's face, and preferred not to answer it at that moment. Saying, "Thee must make me acquainted with the rest of our brethren," he led the way back to the men's end. When he had been presented to the older members, it was time for them to assemble in meeting.

The people were again quietly startled when Henry Donnelly deliberately mounted to the third and highest bench facing them, and sat down beside Abraham and Simon. These two retained, possibly with some little inward exertion, the composure of their faces, and the strange Friend became like unto them. His hands were clasped firmly in his lap; his full, decided lips were set together, and his eyes gazed into vacancy from under the broad brim. De

455

Courcy had removed his hat on entering the house, but, meeting his father's eyes, replaced it suddenly, with a slight blush.

When Simon Pennock and Ruth Treadwell had spoken the thoughts which had come to them in the stillness, the strange Friend arose. Slowly, with frequent pauses, as if waiting for the guidance of the Spirit, and with that inward voice which falls so naturally into the measure of a chant, he urged upon his hearers the necessity of seeking the Light and walking therein. He did not always employ the customary phrases, but neither did he seem to speak the lower language of logic and reason; while his tones were so full and mellow that they gave, with every slowly modulated sentence, a fresh satisfaction to the ear. Even his broad a's and the strong roll of his r's verified the rumor of his foreign birth, did not detract from the authority of his words. The doubts which had preceded him somehow melted away in his presence, and he came forth, after the meeting had been dissolved by the shaking of hands, an accepted tenant of the high seat.

That evening, the family were alone in their new home. The plain rush-bottomed chairs and sober carpet, in contrast with the dark, solid mahogany table, and the silver branched candle-stick which stood upon it, hinted of former wealth and present loss; and something of the same contrast was reflected in the habits of the inmates. While the father, seated in a stately arm-chair, read aloud to his wife and children, Sylvia's eyes rested on a guitar-case in the corner, and her fingers absently adjusted themselves to the imaginary frets. De Courcy twisted his neck as if the straight collar of his coat were a bad fit, and Henry, the youngest boy, nodded drowsily from time to time.

"There, my lads and lasses!" said Henry Donnelly, as he closed the book, "now we're plain farmers at last,—and the plainer the better, since it must be. There's only one thing wanting—"

He paused; and Sylvia, looking up with a bright, arch determination, answered: "It's too late now, father,—they have seen me as one of the world's people, as I meant they should. When it is once settled as something not to be helped, it will give us no trouble."

"Faith, Sylvia!" exclaimed De Courcy, "I almost wish I had kept you

456

company."

"Don't be impatient, my boy," said the mother, gently. "Think of the vexations we have had, and what a rest this life will be!"

"Think, also," the father added, "that I have the heaviest work to do, and that thou'lt reap the most of what may come of it. Don't carry the old life to a land where it's out of place. We must be what we seem to be, every one of us!"

"So we will!" said Sylvia, rising from her seat,—"I, as well as the rest. It was what I said in the beginning, you—no, THEE knows, father. Somebody must be interpreter when the time comes; somebody must remember while the rest of you are forgetting. Oh, I shall be talked about, and set upon, and called hard names; it won't be so easy. Stay where you are, De Courcy; that coat will fit sooner than you think."

Her brother lifted his shoulders and made a grimace. "I've an unlucky name, it seems," said he. "The old fellow—I mean Friend Simon—pronounced it outlandish. Couldn't I change it to Ezra or Adonijah?"

"Boy, boy—"

"Don't be alarmed, father. It will soon be as Sylvia says; thee's right, and mother is right. I'll let Sylvia keep my memory, and start fresh from here. We must into the field to-morrow, Hal and I. There's no need of a collar at the plough-tail."

They went to rest, and on the morrow not only the boys, but their father were in the field. Shrewd, quick, and strong, they made available what they knew of farming operations, and disguised much of their ignorance, while they learned. Henry Donnelly's first public appearance had made a strong public impression in his favor, which the voice of the older Friends soon stamped as a settled opinion. His sons did their share, by the amiable, yielding temper they exhibited, in accommodating themselves to the manners and ways of the people. The graces which came from a better education, possibly, more refined associations, gave them an attraction, which was none the less felt because it was not understood, to the simple-minded young men who worked with the hired hands in their fathers' fields. If the Donnelly family had not been accustomed, in former days, to sit at the same table with laborers in shirt-sleeves, and be addressed by the latter in fraternal phrase, no little awkwardnesses or hesitations betrayed the fact. They were anxious to make their naturalization complete, and it soon became so.

The "strange Friend" was now known in Londongrove by the familiar name of "Henry." He was a constant attendant at meeting, not only on First-days, but also on Fourth-days, and whenever he spoke his words were listened to with the reverence due to one who was truly led towards the Light. This respect kept at bay the curiosity that might still have lingered in some minds concerning his antecedent life. It was known that he answered Simon Pennock, who had ventured to approach him with a direct question, in these words:

"Thee knows, Friend Simon, that sometimes a seal is put upon our mouths for a wise purpose. I have learned not to value the outer life except in so far as it is made the manifestation of the inner life, and I only date my own from the time when I was brought to a knowledge of the truth. It is not pleasant to me to look upon what went before; but a season may come when it shall be lawful for me to declare all things—nay, when it shall be put upon me as a duty.

"Thee must suffer me to wait the call."

After this there was nothing more to be said. The family was on terms of quiet intimacy with the neighbors; and even Sylvia, in spite of her defiant eyes and worldly ways, became popular among the young men and maidens. She touched her beloved guitar with a skill which seemed marvellous to the latter; and when it was known that her refusal to enter the sect arose from her fondness for the prohibited instrument, she found many apologists among them. She was not set upon, and called hard names, as she had anticipated. It is true that her father, when appealed to by the elders, shook his head and said, "It is a cross to us!"—but he had been known to remain in the room while she sang "Full high in Kilbride," and the keen light which arose in his eyes was neither that of sorrow nor anger.

At the end of their first year of residence the farm presented evidences of much more orderly and intelligent management than at first, although the adjoining neighbors were of the opinion that the Donnellys had hardly made their living out of it. Friend Henry, nevertheless, was ready with the advance rent, and his bills were promptly paid. He was close at a bargain, which was considered rather a merit than otherwise,—and almost painfully exact in observing the strict letter of it, when made.

As time passed by, and the family became a permanent part and parcel of the remote community, wearing its peaceful color and breathing its untroubled atmosphere, nothing occurred to disturb the esteem and respect which its members enjoyed. From time to time the postmaster at the corner delivered to Henry Donnelly a letter from New York, always addressed in the same hand. The first which arrived had an "Esq." added to the name, but this "compliment" (as the Friends termed it) soon ceased. Perhaps the official may have vaguely wondered whether there was any connection between the occasional absence of Friend Henry—not at Yearly-Meeting time—and these letters. If he had been a visitor at the farm-house he might have noticed variations in the moods of its inmates, which must have arisen from some other cause than the price of stock or the condition of the crops. Outside of the family circle, however, they were serenely reticent.

In five or six years, when De Courcy had grown to be a hale, handsome man of twenty-four, and as capable of conducting a farm as any to the township born, certain aberrations from the strict line of discipline began to be rumored. He rode a gallant horse, dressed a little more elegantly than his membership prescribed, and his unusually high, straight collar took a knack of falling over. Moreover, he was frequently seen to ride up the Street Road, in the direction of Fagg's Manor, towards those valleys where the brick Presbyterian church displaces the whitewashed Quaker meeting-house.

Had Henry Donnelly not occupied so high a seat, and exercised such an acknowledged authority in the sect, he might sooner have received counsel, or proffers of sympathy, as the case might be; but he heard nothing until the rumors of De Courcy's excursions took a more definite form.

But one day, Abraham Bradbury, after discussing some Monthly-

Meeting matters, suddenly asked: "Is this true that I hear, Henry,—that thy son De Courcy keeps company with one of the Alison girls?"

"Who says that?" Henry asked, in a sharp voice.

"Why, it's the common talk! Surely, thee's heard of it before?"

"No!"

Henry set his lips together in a manner which Abraham understood. Considering that he had fully performed his duty, he said no more.

That evening, Sylvia, who had been gently thrumming to herself at the window, began singing "Bonnie Peggie Alison." Her father looked at De Courcy, who caught his glance, then lowered his eyes, and turned to leave the room.

"Stop, De Courcy," said the former; "I've heard a piece of news about thee to-day, which I want thee to make clear."

"Shall I go, father?" asked Sylvia.

"No; thee may stay to give De Courcy his memory. I think he is beginning to need it. I've learned which way he rides on Seventh-day evenings."

"Father, I am old enough to choose my way," said De Courcy.

"But no such ways NOW, boy! Has thee clean forgotten? This was among the things upon which we agreed, and you all promised to keep watch and guard over yourselves. I had my misgivings then, but for five years I've trusted you, and now, when the time of probation is so nearly over—"

He hesitated, and De Courcy, plucking up courage, spoke again. With a strong effort the young man threw off the yoke of a self-taught restraint, and asserted his true nature. "Has O'Neil written?" he asked.

"Not yet."

"Then, father," he continued, "I prefer the certainty of my present life to the uncertainty of the old. I will not dissolve my connection with the Friends by a shock which might give thee trouble; but I will slowly work away from them. Notice will be taken of my ways; there will be family visitations, warnings, and the usual routine of discipline, so that when I marry Margaret Alison, nobody will be surprised at my being read out of meeting. I shall soon be twenty-five, father, and this thing has gone on about as long as I can bear it. I must decide to be either a man or a milksop."

The color rose to Henry Donnelly's cheeks, and his eyes flashed, but he showed no signs of anger. He moved to De Courcy's side and laid his hand upon his shoulder.

"Patience, my boy!" he said. "It's the old blood, and I might have known it would proclaim itself. Suppose I were to shut my eyes to thy ridings, and thy merry-makings, and thy worldly company. So far I might go; but the girl is no mate for thee. If O'Neil is alive, we are sure to hear from him soon; and in three years, at the utmost, if the Lord favors us, the end will come. How far has it gone with thy courting? Surely, surely, not too far to withdraw, at least under the plea of my prohibition?"

De Courcy blushed, but firmly met his father's eyes. "I have spoken to her," he replied, "and it is not the custom of our family to break plighted faith."

"Thou art our cross, not Sylvia. Go thy ways now. I will endeavor to seek for guidance."

"Sylvia," said the father, when De Courcy had left the room, "what is to be the end of this?"

"Unless we hear from O'Neil, father, I am afraid it cannot be prevented. De Courcy has been changing for a year past; I am only surprised that you did not sooner notice it. What I said in jest has become serious truth; he has already half forgotten. We might have expected, in the beginning, that one of two things would happen: either he would become a plodding Quaker farmer or take to his present courses. Which would be worse, when this life is over,—if that time ever comes?"

Sylvia sighed, and there was a weariness in her voice which did not escape her father's ear. He walked up and down the room with a troubled air. She sat down, took the guitar upon her lap, and began to sing the verse, commencing, "Erin, my country, though sad and forsaken," when—perhaps opportunely—Susan Donnelly entered the room.

"Eh, lass!" said Henry, slipping his arm around his wife's waist, "art thou tired yet? Have I been trying thy patience, as I have that of the children? Have there been longings kept from me, little rebellions crushed, battles fought that I supposed were over?"

"Not by me, Henry," was her cheerful answer. "I have never have been happier than in these quiet ways with thee. I've been thinking, what if something has happened, and the letters cease to come? And it has seemed to me—now that the boys are as good farmers as any, and Alice is such a tidy housekeeper—that we could manage very well without help. Only for thy sake, Henry: I fear it would be a terrible disappointment to thee. Or is thee as accustomed to the high seat as I to my place on the women's side?"

"No!" he answered emphatically. "The talk with De Courcy has set my quiet Quaker blood in motion. The boy is more than half right; I am sure Sylvia thinks so too. What could I expect? He has no birthright, and didn't begin his task, as I did, after the bravery of youth was over. It took six generations to establish the serenity and content of our brethren here, and the dress we wear don't give us the nature. De Courcy is tired of the masquerade, and Sylvia is tired of seeing it. Thou, my little Susan, who wert so timid at first, puttest us all to shame now!"

"I think I was meant for it,—Alice, and Henry, and I," said she.

No outward change in Henry Donnelly's demeanor betrayed this or any other disturbance at home. There were repeated consultations between the father and son, but they led to no satisfactory conclusion. De Courcy was sincerely attached to the pretty Presbyterian maiden, and found livelier society in her brothers and cousins than among the grave, awkward Quaker youths of Londongrove.

With the occasional freedom from restraint there awoke in him a desire for independence—a thirst for the suppressed license of youth. His new acquaintances were accustomed to a rigid domestic regime, but of a different character, and they met on a common ground of rebellion. Their aberrations, it is true, were not of a very formidable character, and need not have been guarded but for the severe conventionalities of both sects. An occasional fox-chase, horse-race, or a "stag party" at some outlying tavern, formed the sum of their dissipation; they sang, danced reels, and sometimes ran into little excesses through the stimulating sense of the trespass they were committing.

By and by reports of certain of these performances were brought to the notice of the Londongrove Friends, and, with the consent of Henry Donnelly himself, De Courcy received a visit of warning and remonstrance. He had foreseen the probability of such a visit and was prepared. He denied none of the charges brought against him, and accepted the grave counsel offered, simply stating that his nature was not yet purified and chastened; he was aware he was not walking in the Light; he believed it to be a troubled season through which he must needs pass. His frankness, as he was shrewd enough to guess, was a source of perplexity to the elders; it prevented them from excommunicating him without further probation, while it left him free to indulge in further recreations.

Some months passed away, and the absence from which Henry Donnelly always returned with a good supply of ready money did not take place. The knowledge of farming which his sons had acquired now came into play. It was necessary to exercise both skill and thrift in order to keep up the liberal footing upon which the family had lived; for each member of it was too proud to allow the community to suspect the change in their circumstances. De Courcy, retained more than ever at home, and bound to steady labor, was man enough to subdue his impatient spirit for the time; but he secretly determined that with the first change for the better he would follow the fate he had chosen for himself.

Late in the fall came the opportunity for which he had longed. One evening he brought home a letter, in the well-known handwriting. His father opened and read it in silence.

"Well, father?" he said.

"A former letter was lost, it seems. This should have come in the spring; it is only the missing sum."

"Does O'Neil fix any time?"

"No; but he hopes to make a better report next year."

"Then, father," said De Courcy, "it is useless for me to wait longer; I am satisfied as it is. I should not have given up Margaret in any case; but now, since thee can live with Henry's help, I shall claim her."

"MUST it be, De Courcy?"

"It must."

But it was not to be. A day or two afterwards the young man, on his mettled horse, set off up the Street Road, feeling at last that the fortune and the freedom of his life were approaching. He had become, in habits and in feelings, one of the people, and the relinquishment of the hope in which his father still indulged brought him a firmer courage, a more settled content. His sweetheart's family was in good circumstances; but, had she been poor, he felt confident of his power to make and secure for her a farmer's home. To the past—whatever it might have been—he said farewell, and went carolling some cheerful ditty, to look upon the face of his future.

That night a country wagon slowly drove up to Henry Donnelly's door. The three men who accompanied it hesitated before they knocked, and, when the door was opened, looked at each other with pale, sad faces, before either spoke. No cries followed the few words that were said, but silently, swiftly, a room was made ready, while the men lifted from the straw and carried up stairs an unconscious figure, the arms of which hung down with a horrible significance as they moved. He was not dead, for the heart beat feebly and slowly; but all efforts to restore his consciousness were in vain. There was concussion of the brain the physician said. He had been thrown from his horse, probably alighting upon his head, as there were neither fractures nor external wounds. All that night and next day the tenderest, the most unwearied care was exerted to call back the flickering gleam of life. The shock had been too great; his deadly torpor deepened into death.

464

In their time of trial and sorrow the family received the fullest sympathy, the kindliest help, from the whole neighborhood. They had never before so fully appreciated the fraternal character of the society whereof they were members. The plain, plodding people living on the adjoining farms became virtually their relatives and fellow-mourners. All the external offices demanded by the sad occasion were performed for them, and other eyes than their own shed tears of honest grief over De Courcy's coffin. All came to the funeral, and even Simon Pennock, in the plain yet touching words which he spoke beside the grave, forgot the young man's wandering from the Light, in the recollection of his frank, generous, truthful nature.

If the Donnellys had sometimes found the practical equality of life in Londongrove a little repellent they were now gratefully moved by the delicate and refined ways in which the sympathy of the people sought to express itself. The better qualities of human nature always develop a temporary good-breeding. Wherever any of the family went, they saw the reflection of their own sorrow; and a new spirit informed to their eyes the quiet pastoral landscapes.

In their life at home there was little change. Abraham Bradbury had insisted on sending his favorite grandson, Joel, a youth of twenty-two, to take De Courcy's place for a few months. He was a shy quiet creature, with large brown eyes like a fawn's, and young Henry Donnelly and he became friends at once. It was believed that he would inherit the farm at his grandfather's death; but he was as subservient to Friend Donnelly's wishes in regard to the farming operations as if the latter held the fee of the property. His coming did not fill the terrible gap which De Courcy's death had made, but seemed to make it less constantly and painfully evident.

Susan Donnelly soon remarked a change, which she could neither clearly define nor explain to herself, both in her husband and in their daughter Sylvia. The former, although in public he preserved the same grave, stately face,—its lines, perhaps, a little more deeply marked,—seemed to be devoured by an internal unrest. His dreams were of the old times: words and names long unused came from his lips as he slept by her side. Although he bore his grief with more strength than she had hoped, he grew nervous and excitable,—sometimes unreasonably petulant, sometimes gay to a pitch which impressed her with pain. When the spring came around, and the mysterious correspondence again failed, as in the previous year, his uneasiness increased. He took his place on the high seat on First-days, as usual, but spoke no more.

Sylvia, on the other hand, seemed to have wholly lost her proud, impatient character. She went to meeting much more frequently than formerly, busied herself more actively about household matters, and ceased to speak of the uncertain contingency which had been so constantly present in her thoughts. In fact, she and her father had changed places. She was now the one who preached patience, who held before them all the bright side of their lot, who brought Margaret Alison to the house and justified her dead brother's heart to his father's, and who repeated to the latter, in his restless moods, "De Courcy foresaw the truth, and we must all in the end decide as he did."

"Can THEE do it, Sylvia?" her father would ask.

"I believe I have done it already," she said. "If it seems difficult, pray consider how much later I begin my work. I have had all your memories in charge, and now I must not only forget for myself, but for you as well."

Indeed, as the spring and summer months came and went, Sylvia evidently grew stronger in her determination. The fret of her idle force was allayed, and her content increased as she saw and performed the possible duties of her life. Perhaps her father might have caught something of her spirit, but for his anxiety in regard to the suspended correspondence. He wearied himself in guesses, which all ended in the simple fact that, to escape embarrassment, the rent must again be saved from the earnings of the farm.

The harvests that year were bountiful; wheat, barley, and oats stood thick and heavy in the fields. No one showed more careful thrift or more cheerful industry than young Joel Bradbury, and the family felt that much of the fortune of their harvest was owing to him.

On the first day after the crops had been securely housed, all went to meeting, except Sylvia. In the walled graveyard the sod was already green over

De Courcy's unmarked mound, but Alice had planted a little rose-tree at the head, and she and her mother always visited the spot before taking their seats on the women's side. The meeting-house was very full that day, as the busy season of the summer was over, and the horses of those who lived at a distance had no longer such need of rest.

It was a sultry forenoon, and the windows and doors of the building were open. The humming of insects was heard in the silence, and broken lights and shadows of the poplar-leaves were sprinkled upon the steps and sills. Outside there were glimpses of quiet groves and orchards, and blue fragments of sky,—no more semblance of life in the external landscape than there was in the silent meeting within. Some quarter of an hour before the shaking of hands took place, the hoofs of a horse were heard in the meeting-house yard—the noise of a smart trot on the turf, suddenly arrested.

The boys pricked up their ears at this unusual sound, and stole glances at each other when they imagined themselves unseen by the awful faces in the gallery. Presently those nearest the door saw a broader shadow fall over those flickering upon the stone. A red face appeared for a moment, and was then drawn back out of sight. The shadow advanced and receded, in a state of peculiar restlessness. Sometimes the end of a riding-whip was visible, sometimes the corner of a coarse gray coat. The boys who noticed these apparitions were burning with impatience, but they dared not leave their seats until Abraham Bradbury had reached his hand to Henry Donnelly.

Then they rushed out. The mysterious personage was still beside the door, leaning against the wall. He was a short, thick-set man of fifty, with red hair, round gray eyes, a broad pug nose, and projecting mouth. He wore a heavy gray coat, despite the heat, and a waistcoat with many brass buttons; also corduroy breeches and riding boots. When they appeared, he started forward with open mouth and eyes, and stared wildly in their faces. They gathered around the poplar-trunks, and waited with some uneasiness to see what would follow.

Slowly and gravely, with the half-broken ban of silence still hanging over them, the people issued from the house. The strange man stood, leaning forward, and seemed to devour each, in turn, with his eager eyes. After the young men came the fathers of families, and lastly the old men from the gallery seats. Last of these came Henry Donnelly. In the meantime, all had seen and wondered at the waiting figure; its attitude was too intense and self-forgetting to be misinterpreted. The greetings and remarks were suspended until the people had seen for whom the man waited, and why.

Henry Donnelly had no sooner set his foot upon the door-step than, with something between a shout and a howl, the stranger darted forward, seized his hand, and fell upon one knee, crying: "O my lord! my lord! Glory be to God that I've found ye at last!"

If these words burst like a bomb on the ears of the people, what was their consternation when Henry Donnelly exclaimed, "The Divel! Jack O'Neil, can that be you?"

"It's me, meself, my lord! When we heard the letters went wrong last year, I said 'I'll trust no such good news to their blasted mail-posts: I'll go meself and carry it to his lordship,—if it is t'other side o' the say. Him and my lady and all the children went, and sure I can go too. And as I was the one that went with you from Dunleigh Castle, I'll go back with you to that same, for it stands awaitin', and blessed be the day that sees you back in your ould place!"

"All clear, Jack? All mine again?"

"You may believe it, my lord! And money in the chest beside. But where's my lady, bless her sweet face! Among yon women, belike, and you'll help me to find her, for it's herself must have the news next, and then the young master—"

With that word Henry Donnelly awoke to a sense of time and place. He found himself within a ring of staring, wondering, scandalized eyes. He met them boldly, with a proud, though rather grim smile, took hold of O'Neil's arm and led him towards the women's end of the house, where the sight of Susan in her scoop bonnet so moved the servant's heart that he melted into tears. Both husband and wife were eager to get home and hear O'Neil's news in private; so they set out at once in their plain carriage, followed by the latter on horseback. As for the Friends, they went home in a state of bewilderment.

Alice Donnelly, with her brother Henry and Joel Bradbury, returned on foot. The two former remembered O'Neil, and, although they had not witnessed his first interview with their father, they knew enough of the family history to surmise his errand. Joel was silent and troubled.

"Alice, I hope it doesn't mean that we are going back, don't you?" said Henry.

"Yes," she answered, and said no more.

They took a foot-path across the fields, and reached the farm-house at the same time with the first party. As they opened the door Sylvia descended the staircase dressed in a rich shimmering brocade, with a necklace of amethysts around her throat. To their eyes, so long accustomed to the absence of positive color, she was completely dazzling. There was a new color on her cheeks, and her eyes seemed larger and brighter. She made a stately courtesy, and held open the parlor door.

"Welcome, Lord Henry Dunleigh, of Dunleigh Castle!" she cried; "welcome, Lady Dunleigh!"

Her father kissed her on the forehead. "Now give us back our memories, Sylvia!" he said, exultingly.

Susan Donnelly sank into a chair, overcome by the mixed emotions of the moment.

"Come in, my faithful Jack! Unpack thy portmanteau of news, for I see thou art bursting to show it; let us have every thing from the beginning. Wife, it's a little too much for thee, coming so unexpectedly. Set out the wine, Alice!"

The decanter was placed upon the table. O'Neil filled a tumbler to the brim, lifted it high, made two or three hoarse efforts to speak, and then walked away to the window, where he drank in silence. This little incident touched the family more than the announcement of their good fortune. Henry Donnelly's feverish exultation subsided: he sat down with a grave,

thoughtful face, while his wife wept quietly beside him. Sylvia stood waiting
with an abstracted air; Alice removed her mother's bonnet and shawl; and
Henry and Joel, seated together at the farther end of the room, looked on in
silent anticipation.

O'Neil's story was long, and frequently interrupted. He had been Lord
Dunleigh's steward in better days, as his father had been to the old lord,
and was bound to the family by the closest ties of interest and affection.
When the estates became so encumbered that either an immediate change or
a catastrophe was inevitable, he had been taken into his master's confidence
concerning the plan which had first been proposed in jest, and afterwards
adopted in earnest.

The family must leave Dunleigh Castle for a period of probably eight
or ten years, and seek some part of the world where their expenses could be
reduced to the lowest possible figure. In Germany or Italy there would be the
annoyance of a foreign race and language, of meeting of tourists belonging
to the circle in which they had moved, a dangerous idleness for their sons,
and embarrassing restrictions for their daughters. On the other hand, the
suggestion to emigrate to America and become Quakers during their exile
offered more advantages the more they considered it. It was original in
character; it offered them economy, seclusion, entire liberty of action inside
the limits of the sect, the best moral atmosphere for their children, and an
occupation which would not deteriorate what was best in their blood and
breeding.

How Lord Dunleigh obtained admission into the sect as plain Henry
Donnelly is a matter of conjecture with the Londongrove Friends. The
deception which had been practised upon them—although it was perhaps less
complete than they imagined—left a soreness of feeling behind it. The matter
was hushed up after the departure of the family, and one might now live for
years in the neighborhood without hearing the story. How the shrewd plan
was carried out by Lord Dunleigh and his family, we have already learned.
O'Neil, left on the estate, in the north of Ireland, did his part with equal
fidelity. He not only filled up the gaps made by his master's early profuseness,
but found means to move the sympathies of a cousin of the latter—a rich,

eccentric old bachelor, who had long been estranged by a family quarrel. To this cousin he finally confided the character of the exile, and at a lucky time; for the cousin's will was altered in Lord Dunleigh's favor, and he died before his mood of reconciliation passed away. Now, the estate was not only unencumbered, but there was a handsome surplus in the hands of the Dublin bankers. The family might return whenever they chose, and there would be a festival to welcome them, O'Neil said, such as Dunleigh Castle had never known since its foundations were laid.

"Let us go at once!" said Sylvia, when he had concluded his tale. "No more masquerading,—I never knew until to-day how much I have hated it! I will not say that your plan was not a sensible one, father; but I wish it might have been carried out with more honor to ourselves. Since De Courcy's death I have begun to appreciate our neighbors: I was resigned to become one of these people had our luck gone the other way. Will they give us any credit for goodness and truth, I wonder? Yes, in mother's case, and Alice's; and I believe both of them would give up Dunleigh Castle for this little farm."

"Then," her father exclaimed, "it IS time that we should return, and without delay. But thee wrongs us somewhat, Sylvia: it has not all been masquerading. We have become the servants, rather than the masters, of our own parts, and shall live a painful and divided life until we get back in our old place. I fear me it will always be divided for thee, wife, and Alice and Henry. If I am subdued by the element which I only meant to assume, how much more deeply must it have wrought in your natures! Yes, Sylvia is right, we must get away at once. To-morrow we must leave Londongrove forever!"

He had scarcely spoken, when a new surprise fell upon the family. Joel Bradbury arose and walked forward, as if thrust by an emotion so powerful that it transformed his whole being. He seemed to forget every thing but Alice Donnelly's presence. His soft brown eyes were fixed on her face with an expression of unutterable tenderness and longing. He caught her by the hands. "Alice, O, Alice!" burst from his lips; "you are not going to leave me?"

The flush in the girl's sweet face faded into a deadly paleness. A moan came from her lips; her head dropped, and she would have fallen, swooning,

471

from the chair had not Joel knelt at her feet and caught her upon his breast.

For a moment there was silence in the room.

Presently, Sylvia, all her haughtiness gone, knelt beside the young man, and took her sister from his arms. "Joel, my poor, dear friend," she said, "I am sorry that the last, worst mischief we have done must fall upon you."

Joel covered his face with his hands, and convulsively uttered the words, "MUST she go?"

Then Henry Donnelly—or, rather, Lord Dunleigh, as we must now call him—took the young man's hand. He was profoundly moved; his strong voice trembled, and his words came slowly. "I will not appeal to thy heart, Joel," he said, "for it would not hear me now.

"But thou hast heard all our story, and knowest that we must leave these parts, never to return. We belong to another station and another mode of life than yours, and it must come to us as a good fortune that our time of probation is at an end. Bethink thee, could we leave our darling Alice behind us, parted as if by the grave? Nay, could we rob her of the life to which she is born—of her share in our lives? On the other hand, could we take thee with us into relations where thee would always be a stranger, and in which a nature like thine has no place? This is a case where duty speaks clearly, though so hard, so very hard, to follow."

He spoke tenderly, but inflexibly, and Joel felt that his fate was pronounced. When Alice had somewhat revived, and was taken to another room, he stumbled blindly out of the house, made his way to the barn, and there flung himself upon the harvest-sheaves which, three days before, he had bound with such a timid, delicious hope working in his arm.

The day which brought such great fortune had thus a sad and troubled termination. It was proposed that the family should start for Philadelphia on the morrow, leaving O'Neil to pack up and remove such furniture as they wished to retain; but Susan, Lady Dunleigh, could not forsake the neighborhood without a parting visit to the good friends who had mourned with her over her firstborn; and Sylvia was with her in this wish. So two more

472

days elapsed, and then the Dunleighs passed down the Street Road, and the plain farm-house was gone from their eyes forever. Two grieved over the loss of their happy home; one was almost broken-hearted; and the remaining two felt that the trouble of the present clouded all their happiness in the return to rank and fortune.

They went, and they never came again. An account of the great festival at Dunleigh Castle reached Londongrove two years later, through an Irish laborer, who brought to Joel Bradbury a letter of recommendation signed "Dunleigh." Joel kept the man upon his farm, and the two preserved the memory of the family long after the neighborhood had ceased to speak of it. Joel never married; he still lives in the house where the great sorrow of his life befell.

His head is gray, and his face deeply wrinkled; but when he lifts the shy lids of his soft brown eyes, I fancy I can see in their tremulous depths the lingering memory of his love for Alice Dunleigh.

# JACOB FLINT'S JOURNEY.

If there ever was a man crushed out of all courage, all self-reliance, all comfort in life, it was Jacob Flint. Why this should have been, neither he nor any one else could have explained; but so it was. On the day that he first went to school, his shy, frightened face marked him as fair game for the rougher and stronger boys, and they subjected him to all those exquisite refinements of torture which boys seem to get by the direct inspiration of the Devil. There was no form of their bullying meanness or the cowardice of their brutal strength which he did not experience. He was born under a fading or falling star,—the inheritor of some anxious or unhappy mood of his parents, which gave its fast color to the threads out of which his innocent being was woven.

Even the good people of the neighborhood, never accustomed to look below the externals of appearance and manner, saw in his shrinking face and awkward motions only the signs of a cringing, abject soul.

"You'll be no more of a man than Jake Flint!" was the reproach which many a farmer addressed to his dilatory boy; and thus the parents, one and all, came to repeat the sins of the children.

If, therefore, at school and "before folks," Jacob's position was always uncomfortable and depressing, it was little more cheering at home. His parents, as all the neighbors believed, had been unhappily married, and, though the mother died in his early childhood, his father remained a moody, unsocial man, who rarely left his farm except on the 1st of April every year, when he went to the county town for the purpose of paying the interest upon a mortgage. The farm lay in a hollow between two hills, separated from the road by a thick wood, and the chimneys of the lonely old house looked in vain for a neighbor-smoke when they began to grow warm of a morning.

Beyond the barn and under the northern hill there was a log tenant-house, in which dwelt a negro couple, who, in the course of years had become fixtures on the place and almost partners in it. Harry, the man, was the medium by which Samuel Flint kept up his necessary intercourse with the world beyond the valley; he took the horses to the blacksmith, the grain to the mill, the turkeys to market, and through his hands passed all the incomings and outgoings of the farm, except the annual interest on the mortgage. Sally, his wife, took care of the household, which, indeed, was a light and comfortable task, since the table was well supplied for her own sake, and there was no sharp eye to criticise her sweeping, dusting, and bed-making. The place had a forlorn, tumble-down aspect, quite in keeping with its lonely situation; but perhaps this very circumstance flattered the mood of its silent, melancholy owner and his unhappy son.

In all the neighborhood there was but one person with whom Jacob felt completely at ease—but one who never joined in the general habit of making his name the butt of ridicule or contempt. This was Mrs. Ann Pardon, the hearty, active wife of Farmer Robert Pardon, who lived nearly a mile farther down the brook. Jacob had won her good-will by some neighborly services, something so trifling, indeed, that the thought of a favor conferred never entered his mind. Ann Pardon saw that it did not; she detected a streak of most unconscious goodness under his uncouth, embarrassed ways, and she determined to cultivate it. No little tact was required, however, to coax the wild, forlorn creature into so much confidence as she desired to establish; but tact is a native quality of the heart no less than a social acquirement, and so she did the very thing necessary without thinking much about it.

Robert Pardon discovered by and by that Jacob was a steady, faithful hand in the harvest-field at husking-time, or whenever any extra labor was required, and Jacob's father made no objection to his earning a penny in this way; and so he fell into the habit of spending his Saturday evenings at the Pardon farm-house, at first to talk over matters of work, and finally because it had become a welcome relief from his dreary life at home.

Now it happened that on a Saturday in the beginning of haying-time, the village tailor sent home by Harry a new suit of light summer clothes, for which Jacob had been measured a month before. After supper he tried them on, the day's work being over, and Sally's admiration was so loud and emphatic that he felt himself growing red even to the small of his back.

"Now, don't go for to take 'em off, Mr. Jake," said she. "I spec' you're gwine down to Pardon's, and so you jist keep 'em on to show 'em all how nice you KIN look."

The same thought had already entered Jacob's mind. Poor fellow! It was the highest form of pleasure of which he had ever allowed himself to conceive. If he had been called upon to pass through the village on first assuming the new clothes, every stitch would have pricked him as if the needle remained in it; but a quiet walk down the brookside, by the pleasant path through the thickets and over the fragrant meadows, with a consciousness of his own neatness and freshness at every step, and with kind Ann Pardon's commendation at the close, and the flattering curiosity of the children,—the only ones who never made fun of him,—all that was a delightful prospect. He could never, NEVER forget himself, as he had seen other young fellows do; but to remember himself agreeably was certainly the next best thing.

Jacob was already a well-grown man of twenty-three, and would have made a good enough appearance but for the stoop in his shoulders, and the drooping, uneasy way in which he carried his head. Many a time when he was alone in the fields or woods he had straightened himself, and looked courageously at the buts of the oak-trees or in the very eyes of the indifferent oxen; but, when a human face drew near, some spring in his neck seemed to snap, some buckle around his shoulders to be drawn three holes tighter, and he found himself in the old posture. The ever-present thought of this weakness was the only drop of bitterness in his cup, as he followed the lonely path through the thickets.

Some spirit in the sweet, delicious freshness of the air, some voice in the mellow babble of the stream, leaping in and out of sight between the alders, some smile of light, lingering on the rising corn-fields beyond the meadow and the melting purple of a distant hill, reached to the seclusion of his heart. He was soothed and cheered; his head lifted itself in the presentiment of a future less lonely than the past, and the everlasting trouble vanished from his eyes.

Suddenly, at a turn of the path, two mowers from the meadow, with their scythes upon their shoulders, came upon him. He had not heard their feet on the deep turf. His chest relaxed, and his head began to sink; then, with the most desperate effort in his life, he lifted it again, and, darting a rapid side glance at the men, hastened by. They could not understand the mixed defiance and supplication of his face; to them he only looked "queer."

"Been committin' a murder, have you?" asked one of them, grinning.

"Startin' off on his journey, I guess," said the other.

The next instant they were gone, and Jacob, with set teeth and clinched hands, smothered something that would have been a howl if he had given it voice. Sharp lines of pain were marked on his face, and, for the first time, the idea of resistance took fierce and bitter possession of his heart. But the mood was too unusual to last; presently he shook his head, and walked on towards Pardon's farm-house.

Ann wore a smart gingham dress, and her first exclamation was: "Why, Jake! how nice you look. And so you know all about it, too?"

"About what?"

"I see you don't," said she. "I was too fast; but it makes no difference. I know you are willing to lend me a helping hand."

"Oh, to be sure," Jacob answered.

"And not mind a little company?"

Jacob's face suddenly clouded; but he said, though with an effort: "No— not much—if I can be of any help."

"It's rather a joke, after all," Ann Pardon continued, speaking rapidly; "they meant a surprise, a few of the young people; but sister Becky found a way to send me word, or I might have been caught like Meribah Johnson last week, in the middle of my work; eight or ten, she said, but more may drop in: and it's moonlight and warm, so they'll be mostly under the trees; and Robert won't be home till late, and I DO want help in carrying chairs, and getting up some ice, and handing around; and, though I know you don't care for merry makings, you CAN help me out, you see—"

Here she paused. Jacob looked perplexed, but said nothing.

"Becky will help what she can, and while I'm in the kitchen she'll have an eye to things outside," she said.

Jacob's head was down again, and, moreover, turned on one side, but his ear betrayed the mounting blood. Finally he answered, in a quick, husky voice: "Well, I'll do what I can. What's first?"

Thereupon he began to carry some benches from the veranda to a grassy bank beside the sycamore-tree. Ann Pardon wisely said no more of the coming surprise-party, but kept him so employed that, as the visitors arrived by twos and threes, the merriment was in full play almost before he was aware of it. Moreover, the night was a protecting presence: the moonlight poured splendidly upon the open turf beyond the sycamore, but every lilac-bush or trellis of woodbine made a nook of shade, wherein he could pause a moment and take courage for his duties. Becky Morton, Ann Pardon's youngest sister, frightened him a little every time she came to consult about the arrangement of seats or the distribution of refreshments; but it was a delightful, fascinating fear, such as he had never felt before in his life. He knew Becky, but he had never seen her in white and pink, with floating tresses, until now. In fact, he had hardly looked at her fairly, but now, as she glided into the moonlight and he paused in the shadow, his eyes took note of her exceeding beauty. Some sweet, confusing influence, he knew not what, passed into his blood.

The young men had brought a fiddler from the village, and it was not long before most of the company were treading the measures of reels or cotillons on the grass. How merry and happy they all were! How freely and unembarrassedly they moved and talked! By and by all became involved in the dance, and Jacob, left alone and unnoticed, drew nearer and nearer to the gay and beautiful life from which he was expelled.

With a long-drawn scream of the fiddle the dance came to an end, and the dancers, laughing, chattering, panting, and fanning themselves, broke into groups and scattered over the enclosure before the house. Jacob was surrounded before he could escape. Becky, with two lively girls in her wake, came up to him and said: "Oh Mr. Flint, why don't you dance?"

If he had stopped to consider, he would no doubt have replied very differently. But a hundred questions, stirred by what he had seen, were clamoring for light, and they threw the desperate impulse to his lips.

"If I COULD dance, would you dance with me?"

The two lively girls heard the words, and looked at Becky with roguish faces.

"Oh yes, take him for your next partner!" cried one.

"I will," said Becky, "after he comes back from his journey."

Then all three laughed. Jacob leaned against the tree, his eyes fixed on the ground.

"Is it a bargain?" asked one of the girls.

"No," said he, and walked rapidly away.

He went to the house, and, finding that Robert had arrived, took his hat, and left by the rear door. There was a grassy alley between the orchard and garden, from which it was divided by a high hawthorn hedge. He had scarcely taken three paces on his way to the meadow, when the sound of the voice he had last heard, on the other side of the hedge, arrested his feet.

"Becky, I think you rather hurt Jake Flint," said the girl.

"Hardly," answered Becky; "he's used to that."

"Not if he likes you; and you might go further and fare worse."

"Well, I MUST say!" Becky exclaimed, with a laugh; "you'd like to see me stuck in that hollow, out of your way!"

"It's a good farm, I've heard," said the other.

"Yes, and covered with as much as it'll bear!"

Here the girls were called away to the dance. Jacob slowly walked up the dewy meadow, the sounds of fiddling, singing, and laughter growing fainter behind him.

"My journey!" he repeated to himself,—"my journey! why shouldn't I start on it now? Start off, and never come back?"

It was a very little thing, after all, which annoyed him, but the mention of it always touched a sore nerve of his nature. A dozen years before, when a boy at school, he had made a temporary friendship with another boy of his age, and had one day said to the latter, in the warmth of his first generous confidence: "When I am a little older, I shall make a great journey, and come back rich, and buy Whitney's place!"

Now, Whitney's place, with its stately old brick mansion, its avenue of silver firs, and its two hundred acres of clean, warm-lying land, was the finest, the most aristocratic property in all the neighborhood, and the boy-friend could not resist the temptation of repeating Jacob's grand design, for the endless amusement of the school. The betrayal hurt Jacob more keenly than the ridicule. It left a wound that never ceased to rankle; yet, with the inconceivable perversity of unthinking natures, precisely this joke (as the people supposed it to be) had been perpetuated, until "Jake Flint's Journey" was a synonyme for any absurd or extravagant expectation. Perhaps no one imagined how much pain he was keeping alive; for almost any other man than Jacob would have joined in the laugh against himself and thus good-naturedly buried the joke in time. "He's used to that," the people said, like Becky Morton, and they really supposed there was nothing unkind in the remark!

After Jacob had passed the thickets and entered the lonely hollow in which his father's house lay, his pace became slower and slower.

He looked at the shabby old building, just touched by the moonlight behind the swaying shadows of the weeping-willow, stopped, looked again, and finally seated himself on a stump beside the path.

"If I knew what to do!" he said to himself, rocking backwards and forwards, with his hands clasped over his knees,—"if I knew what to do!"

480

The spiritual tension of the evening reached its climax: he could bear no more. With a strong bodily shudder his tears burst forth, and the passion of his weeping filled him from head to foot. How long he wept he knew not; it seemed as if the hot fountains would never run dry. Suddenly and startlingly a hand fell upon his shoulder.

"Boy, what does this mean?"

It was his father who stood before him.

Jacob looked up like some shy animal brought to bay, his eyes full of a feeling mixed of fierceness and terror; but he said nothing.

His father seated himself on one of the roots of the old stump, laid one hand upon Jacob's knee, and said with an unusual gentleness of manner, "I'd like to know what it is that troubles you so much."

After a pause, Jacob suddenly burst forth with: "Is there any reason why I should tell you? Do you care any more for me than the rest of 'em?"

"I didn't know as you wanted me to care for you particularly," said the father, almost deprecatingly. "I always thought you had friends of your own age."

"Friends? Devils!" exclaimed Jacob. "Oh, what have I done—what is there so dreadful about me that I should always be laughed at, and despised, and trampled upon? You are a great deal older than I am, father: what do you see in me? Tell me what it is, and how to get over it!"

The eyes of the two men met. Jacob saw his father's face grow pale in the moonlight, while he pressed his hand involuntarily upon his heart, as if struggling with some physical pain. At last he spoke, but his words were strange and incoherent.

"I couldn't sleep," he said; "I got up again and came out o' doors. The white ox had broken down the fence at the corner, and would soon have been in the cornfield. I thought it was that, maybe, but still your—your mother would come into my head. I was coming down the edge of the wood when I saw you, and I don't know why it was that you seemed so different, all at

481

once—"

Here he paused, and was silent for a minute. Then he said, in a grave, commanding tone: "Just let me know the whole story. I have that much right yet."

Jacob related the history of the evening, somewhat awkwardly and confusedly, it is true; but his father's brief, pointed questions kept him to the narrative, and forced him to explain the full significance of the expressions he repeated. At the mention of "Whitney's place," a singular expression of malice touched the old man's face.

"Do you love Becky Morton?" he asked bluntly, when all had been told.

"I don't know," Jacob stammered; "I think not; because when I seem to like her most, I feel afraid of her."

"It's lucky that you're not sure of it!" exclaimed the old man with energy; "because you should never have her."

"No," said Jacob, with a mournful acquiescence, "I can never have her, or any other one."

"But you shall—and will I when I help you. It's true I've not seemed to care much about you, and I suppose you're free to think as you like; but this I say: I'll not stand by and see you spit upon! 'Covered with as much as it'll bear!' THAT'S a piece o' luck anyhow. If we're poor, your wife must take your poverty with you, or she don't come into MY doors. But first of all you must make your journey!"

"My journey!" repeated Jacob.

"Weren't you thinking of it this night, before you took your seat on that stump? A little more, and you'd have gone clean off, I reckon."

Jacob was silent, and hung his head.

"Never mind! I've no right to think hard of it. In a week we'll have finished our haying, and then it's a fortnight to wheat; but, for that matter, Harry and I can manage the wheat by ourselves. You may take a month, two months, if any thing comes of it. Under a month I don't mean that you shall come back. I'll give you twenty dollars for a start; if you want more you must earn it on the road, any way you please. And, mark you, Jacob! since you ARE poor, don't let anybody suppose you are rich. For my part, I shall not expect you to buy Whitney's place; all I ask is that you'll tell me, fair and square, just what things and what people you've got acquainted with. Get to bed now— the matter's settled; I will have it so."

They rose and walked across the meadow to the house. Jacob had quite forgotten the events of the evening in the new prospect suddenly opened to him, which filled him with a wonderful confusion of fear and desire. His father said nothing more. They entered the lonely house together at midnight, and went to their beds; but Jacob slept very little.

Six days afterwards he left home, on a sparkling June morning, with a small bundle tied in a yellow silk handkerchief under his arm. His father had furnished him with the promised money, but had positively refused to tell him what road he should take, or what plan of action he should adopt. The only stipulation was that his absence from home should not be less than a month.

After he had passed the wood and reached the highway which followed the course of the brook, he paused to consider which course to take. Southward the road led past Pardon's, and he longed to see his only friends once more before encountering untried hazards; but the village was beyond, and he had no courage to walk through its one long street with a bundle, denoting a journey, under his arm. Northward he would have to pass the mill and blacksmith's shop at the cross-roads. Then he remembered that he might easily wade the stream at a point where it was shallow, and keep in the shelter of the woods on the opposite hill until he struck the road farther on, and in that direction two or three miles would take him into a neighborhood where he was not known.

Once in the woods, an exquisite sense of freedom came upon him. There was nothing mocking in the soft, graceful stir of the expanded foliage, in the twittering of the unfrightened birds, or the scampering of the squirrels, over the rustling carpet of dead leaves. He lay down upon the moss under a spreading beech-tree and tried to think; but the thoughts would not come. He could not even clearly recall the keen troubles and mortifications he had endured: all things were so peaceful and beautiful that a portion of their peace and beauty fell upon men and invested them with a more kindly character.

Towards noon Jacob found himself beyond the limited geography of his life. The first man he encountered was a stranger, who greeted him with a hearty and respectful "How do you do, sir?"

"Perhaps," thought Jacob, "I am not so very different from other people, if I only thought so myself."

At noon, he stopped at a farm-house by the roadside to get a drink of water. A pleasant woman, who came from the door at that moment with a pitcher, allowed him to lower the bucket and haul it up dripping with precious coolness. She looked upon him with good-will, for he had allowed her to see his eyes, and something in their honest, appealing expression went to her heart.

"We're going to have dinner in five minutes," said she; "won't you stay and have something?"

Jacob stayed and brake bread with the plain, hospitable family. Their kindly attention to him during the meal gave him the lacking nerve; for a moment he resolved to offer his services to the farmer, but he presently saw that they were not really needed, and, besides, the place was still too near home.

Towards night he reached an old country tavern, lording it over an incipient village of six houses. The landlord and hostler were inspecting a drooping-looking horse in front of the stables. Now, if there was any thing which Jacob understood, to the extent of his limited experience, it was horse nature. He drew near, listened to the views of the two men, examined the animal with his eyes, and was ready to answer, "Yes, I guess so," when the landlord said, "Perhaps, sir, you can tell what is the matter with him."

His prompt detection of the ailment, and prescription of a remedy which in an hour showed its good effects, installed him in the landlord's best graces. The latter said, "Well, it shall cost you nothing to-night," as he led the way to the supper-room. When Jacob went to bed he was surprised on reflecting that he had not only been talking for a full hour in the bar-room, but had been looking people in the face.

Resisting an offer of good wages if he would stay and help look after the stables, he set forward the next morning with a new and most delightful confidence in himself. The knowledge that now nobody knew him as "Jake Flint" quite removed his tortured self-consciousness. When he met a person who was glum and ungracious of speech, he saw, nevertheless, that he was not its special object. He was sometimes asked questions, to be sure, which a little embarrassed him, but he soon hit upon answers which were sufficiently true without betraying his purpose.

Wandering sometimes to the right and sometimes to the left, he slowly made his way into the land, until, on the afternoon of the fourth day after leaving home, he found himself in a rougher region—a rocky, hilly tract, with small and not very flourishing farms in the valleys. Here the season appeared to be more backward than in the open country; the hay harvest was not yet over.

Jacob's taste for scenery was not particularly cultivated, but something in the loneliness and quiet of the farms reminded him of his own home; and he looked at one house after another, deliberating with himself whether it would not be a good place to spend the remainder of his month of probation. He seemed to be very far from home—about forty miles, in fact,—and was beginning to feel a little tired of wandering.

Finally the road climbed a low pass of the hills, and dropped into a valley on the opposite side. There was but one house in view—a two-story building of logs and plaster, with a garden and orchard on the hillside in the rear. A large meadow stretched in front, and when the whole of it lay clear before him, as the road issued from a wood, his eye was caught by an unusual harvest picture.

Directly before him, a woman, whose face was concealed by a huge, flapping sun-bonnet, was seated upon a mowing machine, guiding a span of horses around the great tract of thick grass which was still uncut. A little distance off, a boy and girl were raking the drier swaths together, and a hay-cart, drawn by oxen and driven by a man, was just entering the meadow from the side next the barn.

Jacob hung his bundle upon a stake, threw his coat and waistcoat over the rail, and, resting his chin on his shirted arms, leaned on the fence, and watched the hay-makers. As the woman came down the nearer side she appeared to notice him, for her head was turned from time to time in his direction. When she had made the round, she stopped the horses at the corner, sprang lightly from her seat and called to the man, who, leaving his team, met her half-way. They were nearly a furlong distant, but Jacob was quite sure that she pointed to him, and that the man looked in the same direction. Presently she set off across the meadow, directly towards him.

When within a few paces of the fence, she stopped, threw back the flaps of her sun-bonnet, and said, "Good day to you!" Jacob was so amazed to see a bright, fresh, girlish face, that he stared at her with all his eyes, forgetting to drop his head. Indeed, he could not have done so, for his chin was propped upon the top rail of the fence.

"You are a stranger, I see," she added.

"Yes, in these parts," he replied.

"Looking for work?"

He hardly knew what answer to make, so he said, at a venture, "That's as it happens." Then he colored a little, for the words seemed foolish to his ears.

"Time's precious," said the girl, "so I'll tell you at once we want help. Our hay MUST be got in while the fine weather lasts."

"I'll help you!" Jacob exclaimed, taking his arms from the rail, and looking as willing as he felt.

"I'm so glad! But I must tell you, at first, that we're not rich, and the hands are asking a great deal now. How much do you expect?"

486

"Whatever you please?" said he, climbing the fence.

"No, that's not our way of doing business. What do you say to a dollar a day, and found?"

"All right!" and with the words he was already at her side, taking long strides over the elastic turf.

"I will go on with my mowing," said she, when they reached the horses, "and you can rake and load with my father. What name shall I call you by?"

"Everybody calls me Jake."

"'Jake!' Jacob is better. Well, Jacob, I hope you'll give us all the help you can."

With a nod and a light laugh she sprang upon the machine. There was a sweet throb in Jacob's heart, which, if he could have expressed it, would have been a triumphant shout of "I'm not afraid of her! I'm not afraid of her!"

The farmer was a kindly, depressed man, with whose quiet ways Jacob instantly felt himself at home. They worked steadily until sunset, when the girl, detaching her horses from the machine, mounted one of them and led the other to the barn. At the supper-table, the farmer's wife said: "Susan, you must be very tired."

"Not now, mother!" she cheerily answered. "I was, I think, but after I picked up Jacob I felt sure we should get our hay in."

"It was a good thing," said the farmer; "Jacob don't need to be told how to work."

Poor Jacob! He was so happy he could have cried. He sat and listened, and blushed a little, with a smile on his face which it was a pleasure to see. The honest people did not seem to regard him in the least as a stranger; they discussed their family interests and troubles and hopes before him, and in a little while it seemed as if he had known them always.

How faithfully he worked! How glad and tired he felt when night came, and the hay-mow was filled, and the great stacks grew beside the barn! But ah!

the haying came to an end, and on the last evening, at supper, everybody was constrained and silent. Even Susan looked grave and thoughtful.

"Jacob," said the farmer, finally, "I wish we could keep you until wheat harvest; but you know we are poor, and can't afford it. Perhaps you could—"

He hesitated; but Jacob, catching at the chance and obeying his own unselfish impulse, cried: "Oh, yes, I can; I'll be satisfied with my board, till the wheat's ripe."

Susan looked at him quickly, with a bright, speaking face. "It's hardly fair to you," said the farmer.

"But I like to be here so much!" Jacob cried. "I like—all of you!"

"We DO seem to suit," said the farmer, "like as one family. And that reminds me, we've not heard your family name yet."

"Flint."

"Jacob FLINT!" exclaimed the farmer's wife, with sudden agitation.

Jacob was scared and troubled. They had heard of him, he thought, and who knew what ridiculous stories? Susan noticed an anxiety on his face which she could not understand, but she unknowingly came to his relief.

"Why, mother," she asked, "do you know Jacob's family?"

"No, I think not," said her mother, "only somebody of the name, long ago."

His offer, however, was gratefully accepted. The bright, hot summer days came and went, but no flower of July ever opened as rapidly and richly and warmly as his chilled, retarded nature. New thoughts and instincts came with every morning's sun, and new conclusions were reached with every evening's twilight. Yet as the wheat harvest drew towards the end, he felt that he must leave the place. The month of absence had gone by, he scarce knew how. He was free to return home, and, though he might offer to bridge over the gap between wheat and oats, as he had already done between hay and wheat, he imagined the family might hesitate to accept such an offer. Moreover, this life at Susan's side was fast growing to be a pain, unless he could assure himself that it would be so forever.

They were in the wheat-field, busy with the last sheaves; she raking and he binding. The farmer and younger children had gone to the barn with a load. Jacob was working silently and steadily, but when they had reached the end of a row, he stopped, wiped his wet brow, and suddenly said, "Susan, I suppose to-day finishes my work here."

"Yes," she answered very slowly.

"And yet I'm very sorry to go."

"I—WE don't want you to go, if we could help it."

Jacob appeared to struggle with himself. He attempted to speak. "If I could—" he brought out, and then paused. "Susan, would you be glad if I came back?"

His eyes implored her to read his meaning. No doubt she read it correctly, for her face flushed, her eyelids fell, and she barely murmured, "Yes, Jacob."

"Then I'll come!" he cried; "I'll come and help you with the oats. Don't talk of pay! Only tell me I'll be welcome! Susan, don't you believe I'll keep my word?"

"I do indeed," said she, looking him firmly in the face.

That was all that was said at the time; but the two understood each other tolerably well.

On the afternoon of the second day, Jacob saw again the lonely house of his father. His journey was made, yet, if any of the neighbors had seen him, they would never have believed that he had come back rich.

Samuel Flint turned away to hide a peculiar smile when he saw his son; but little was said until late that evening, after Harry and Sally had left. Then he required and received an exact account of Jacob's experience during his absence. After hearing the story to the end, he said, "And so you love this Susan Meadows?"

"I'd—I'd do any thing to be with her."

"Are you afraid of her?"

"No!" Jacob uttered the word so emphatically that it rang through the house.

"Ah, well!" said the old man, lifting his eyes, and speaking in the air, "all the harm may be mended yet. But there must be another test." Then he was silent for some time.

"I have it!" he finally exclaimed. "Jacob, you must go back for the oats harvest. You must ask Susan to be your wife, and ask her parents to let you have her. But,—pay attention to my words!—you must tell her that you are a poor, hired man on this place, and that she can be engaged as housekeeper. Don't speak of me as your father, but as the owner of the farm. Bring her here in that belief, and let me see how honest and willing she is. I can easily arrange matters with Harry and Sally while you are away; and I'll only ask you to keep up the appearance of the thing for a month or so."

"But, father,"—Jacob began.

"Not a word! Are you not willing to do that much for the sake of having her all your life, and this farm after me? Suppose it is covered with a mortgage, if she is all you say, you two can work it off. Not a word more! It is no lie, after all, that you will tell her."

"I am afraid," said Jacob, "that she could not leave her home now. She is too useful there, and the family is so poor."

"Tell them that both your wages, for the first year, shall go to them. It'll be my business to rake and scrape the money together somehow. Say, too, that the housekeeper's place can't be kept for her—must be filled at once. Push matters like a man, if you mean to be a complete one, and bring her here, if she carries no more with her than the clothes on her back!"

During the following days Jacob had time to familiarize his mind with this startling proposal. He knew his father's stubborn will too well to suppose that it could be changed; but the inevitable soon converted itself into the possible and desirable. The sweet face of Susan as she had stood before him in the wheat-field was continually present to his eyes, and ere long, he began to place her, in his thoughts, in the old rooms at home, in the garden, among the thickets by the brook, and in Ann Pardon's pleasant parlor. Enough; his father's plan became his own long before the time was out.

On his second journey everybody seemed to be an old acquaintance and an intimate friend. It was evening as he approached the Meadows farm, but the younger children recognized him in the dusk, and their cry of, "Oh, here's Jacob!" brought out the farmer and his wife and Susan, with the heartiest of welcomes. They had all missed him, they said—even the horses and oxen had looked for him, and they were wondering how they should get the oats harvested without him.

Jacob looked at Susan as the farmer said this, and her eyes seemed to answer, "I said nothing, but I knew you would come." Then, first, he felt sufficient courage for the task before him.

He rose the next morning, before any one was stirring, and waited until she should come down stairs. The sun had not risen when she appeared, with a milk-pail in each hand, walking unsuspectingly to the cow-yard. He waylaid her, took the pails in his hand and said in nervous haste, "Susan, will you be my wife?"

She stopped as if she had received a sudden blow; then a shy, sweet consent seemed to run through her heart. "O Jacob!" was all she could say.

"But you will, Susan?" he urged; and then (neither of them exactly knew how it happened) all at once his arms were around her, and they had kissed each other.

"Susan," he said, presently, "I am a poor man—only a farm hand, and must work for my living. You could look for a better husband."

"I could never find a better than you, Jacob."

"Would you work with me, too, at the same place?"

"You know I am not afraid of work," she answered, "and I could never want any other lot than yours."

Then he told her the story which his father had prompted. Her face grew bright and happy as she listened, and he saw how from her very heart she accepted the humble fortune. Only the thought of her parents threw a cloud over the new and astonishing vision. Jacob, however, grew bolder as he saw fulfilment of his hope so near. They took the pails and seated themselves beside neighbor cows, one raising objections or misgivings which the other manfully combated. Jacob's earnestness unconsciously ran into his hands, as he discovered when the impatient cow began to snort and kick.

The harvesting of the oats was not commenced that morning. The children were sent away, and there was a council of four persons held in the parlor. The result of mutual protestations and much weeping was, that the farmer and his wife agreed to receive Jacob as a son-in-law; the offer of the wages was four times refused by them, and then accepted; and the chance of their being able to live and labor together was finally decided to be too fortunate to let slip. When the shock and surprise was over all gradually became cheerful, and, as the matter was more calmly discussed, the first conjectured difficulties somehow resolved themselves into trifles.

It was the simplest and quietest wedding,—at home, on an August morning. Farmer Meadows then drove the bridal pair half-way on their journey, to the old country tavern, where a fresh conveyance had been engaged for them. The same evening they reached the farm-house in the valley, and Jacob's happy mood gave place to an anxious uncertainty as he remembered the period of deception upon which Susan was entering. He keenly watched his father's face when they arrived, and was a little relieved when he saw that his wife had made a good first impression.

"So, this is my new housekeeper," said the old man. "I hope you will suit me as well as your husband does."

"I'll do my best, sir," said she; "but you must have patience with me for a few days, until I know your ways and wishes."

"Mr. Flint," said Sally, "shall I get supper ready?" Susan looked up in astonishment at hearing the name.

"Yes," the old man remarked, "we both have the same name. The fact is, Jacob and I are a sort of relations."

Jacob, in spite of his new happiness, continued ill at ease, although he could not help seeing how his father brightened under Susan's genial influence, how satisfied he was with her quick, neat, exact ways and the cheerfulness with which she fulfilled her duties. At the end of a week, the old man counted out the wages agreed upon for both, and his delight culminated at the frank simplicity with which Susan took what she supposed she had fairly earned.

"Jacob," he whispered when she had left the room, "keep quiet one more week, and then I'll let her know."

He had scarcely spoken, when Susan burst into the room again, crying, "Jacob, they are coming, they have come!"

"Who?"

"Father and mother; and we didn't expect them, you know, for a week yet."

All three went to the door as the visitors made their appearance on the veranda. Two of the party stood as if thunderstruck, and two exclamations came together:

"Samuel Flint!"

"Lucy Wheeler!"

There was a moment's silence; then the farmer's wife, with a visible effort to compose herself, said, "Lucy Meadows, now."

The tears came into Samuel Flint's eyes. "Let us shake hands, Lucy," he said: "my son has married your daughter."

All but Jacob were freshly startled at these words. The two shook hands, and then Samuel, turning to Susan's father, said: "And this is your husband, Lucy. I am glad to make his acquaintance."

493

"Your father, Jacob!" Susan cried; "what does it all mean?"

Jacob's face grew red, and the old habit of hanging his head nearly came back upon him. He knew not what to say, and looked wistfully at his father.

"Come into the house and sit down," said the latter. "I think we shall all feel better when we have quietly and comfortably talked the matter over."

They went into the quaint, old-fashioned parlor, which had already been transformed by Susan's care, so that much of its shabbiness was hidden. When all were seated, and Samuel Flint perceived that none of the others knew what to say, he took a resolution which, for a man of his mood and habit of life, required some courage.

"Three of us here are old people," he began, "and the two young ones love each other. It was so long ago, Lucy, that it cannot be laid to my blame if I speak of it now. Your husband, I see, has an honest heart, and will not misunderstand either of us. The same thing often turns up in life; it is one of those secrets that everybody knows, and that everybody talks about except the persons concerned. When I was a young man, Lucy, I loved you truly, and I faithfully meant to make you my wife."

"I thought so too, for a while," said she, very calmly.

Farmer Meadows looked at his wife, and no face was ever more beautiful than his, with that expression of generous pity shining through it.

"You know how I acted," Samuel Flint continued, "but our children must also know that I broke off from you without giving any reason. A woman came between us and made all the mischief. I was considered rich then, and she wanted to secure my money for her daughter. I was an innocent and unsuspecting young man, who believed that everybody else was as good as myself; and the woman never rested until she had turned me from my first love, and fastened me for life to another. Little by little I discovered the truth; I kept the knowledge of the injury to myself; I quickly got rid of the money which had so cursed me, and brought my wife to this, the loneliest and dreariest place in the neighborhood, where I forced upon her a life of poverty. I thought it was a just revenge, but I was unjust. She really loved me:

494

she was, if not quite without blame in the matter, ignorant of the worst that had been done (I learned all that too late), and she never complained, though the change in me slowly wore out her life. I know now that I was cruel; but at the same time I punished myself, and was innocently punishing my son. But to HIM there was one way to make amends. 'I will help him to a wife,' I said, 'who will gladly take poverty with him and for his sake.' I forced him, against his will, to say that he was a hired hand on this place, and that Susan must be content to be a hired housekeeper. Now that I know Susan, I see that this proof might have been left out; but I guess it has done no harm. The place is not so heavily mortgaged as people think, and it will be Jacob's after I am gone. And now forgive me, all of you,—Lucy first, for she has most cause; Jacob next; and Susan,—that will be easier; and you, Friend Meadows, if what I have said has been hard for you to hear."

The farmer stood up like a man, took Samuel's hand and his wife's, and said, in a broken voice: "Lucy, I ask you, too, to forgive him, and I ask you both to be good friends to each other."

Susan, dissolved in tears, kissed all of them in turn; but the happiest heart there was Jacob's.

It was now easy for him to confide to his wife the complete story of his troubles, and to find his growing self-reliance strengthened by her quick, intelligent sympathy. The Pardons were better friends than ever, and the fact, which at first created great astonishment in the neighborhood, that Jacob Flint had really gone upon a journey and brought home a handsome wife, began to change the attitude of the people towards him. The old place was no longer so lonely; the nearest neighbors began to drop in and insist on return visits. Now that Jacob kept his head up, and they got a fair view of his face, they discovered that he was not lacking, after all, in sense or social qualities.

In October, the Whitney place, which had been leased for several years, was advertised to be sold at public sale. The owner had gone to the city and become a successful merchant, had outlived his local attachments, and now took advantage of a rise in real estate to disburden himself of a property which he could not profitably control.

Everybody from far and wide attended the sale, and, when Jacob Flint and his father arrived, everybody said to the former: "Of course you've come to buy, Jacob." But each man laughed at his own smartness, and considered the remark original with himself.

Jacob was no longer annoyed. He laughed, too, and answered: "I'm afraid I can't do that; but I've kept half my word, which is more than most men do."

"Jake's no fool, after all," was whispered behind him.

The bidding commenced, at first very spirited, and then gradually slacking off, as the price mounted above the means of the neighboring farmers. The chief aspirant was a stranger, a well-dressed man with a lawyer's air, whom nobody knew. After the usual long pauses and passionate exhortations, the hammer fell, and the auctioneer, turning to the stranger, asked, "What name?"

"Jacob Flint!"

There was a general cry of surprise. All looked at Jacob, whose eyes and mouth showed that he was as dumbfoundered as the rest.

The stranger walked coolly through the midst of the crowd to Samuel Flint, and said, "When shall I have the papers drawn up?"

"As soon as you can," the old man replied; then seizing Jacob by the arm, with the words, "Let's go home now!" he hurried him on.

The explanation soon leaked out. Samuel Flint had not thrown away his wealth, but had put it out of his own hands. It was given privately to trustees, to be held for his son, and returned when the latter should have married with his father's consent. There was more than enough to buy the Whitney place.

Jacob and Susan are happy in their stately home, and good as they are happy. If any person in the neighborhood ever makes use of the phrase "Jacob Flint's Journey," he intends thereby to symbolize the good fortune which sometimes follows honesty, reticence, and shrewdness.

# CAN A LIFE HIDE ITSELF?

I had been reading, as is my wont from time to time, one of the many volumes of "The New Pitaval," that singular record of human crime and human cunning, and also of the inevitable fatality which, in every case, leaves a gate open for detection. Were it not for the latter fact, indeed, one would turn with loathing from such endless chronicles of wickedness. Yet these may be safely contemplated, when one has discovered the incredible fatuity of crime, the certain weak mesh in a network of devilish texture; or is it rather the agency of a power outside of man, a subtile protecting principle, which allows the operation of the evil element only that the latter may finally betray itself? Whatever explanation we may choose, the fact is there, like a tonic medicine distilled from poisonous plants, to brace our faith in the ascendancy of Good in the government of the world.

Laying aside the book, I fell into a speculation concerning the mixture of the two elements in man's nature. The life of an individual is usually, it seemed to me, a series of RESULTS, the processes leading to which are not often visible, or observed when they are so. Each act is the precipitation of a number of mixed influences, more or less unconsciously felt; the qualities of good and evil are so blended therein that they defy the keenest moral analysis; and how shall we, then, pretend to judge of any one? Perhaps the surest indication of evil (I further reflected) is that it always tries to conceal itself, and the strongest incitement to good is that evil cannot be concealed. The crime, or the vice, or even the self-acknowledged weakness, becomes a part of the individual consciousness; it cannot be forgotten or outgrown. It follows a life through all experiences and to the uttermost ends of the earth, pressing towards the light with a terrible, demoniac power. There are noteless lives, of course—lives that accept obscurity, mechanically run their narrow round of circumstance, and are lost; but when a life endeavors to lose itself,— to hide some conscious guilt or failure,—can it succeed? Is it not thereby lifted above the level of common experience, compelling attention to itself by the very endeavor to escape it?

I turned these questions over in my mind, without approaching, or indeed expecting, any solution,—since I knew, from habit, the labyrinths into which they would certainly lead me,—when a visitor was announced. It was one of the directors of our county almshouse, who came on an errand to which he attached no great importance. I owed the visit, apparently, to the circumstance that my home lay in his way, and he could at once relieve his conscience of a very trifling pressure and his pocket of a small package, by calling upon me. His story was told in a few words; the package was placed upon my table, and I was again left to my meditations.

Two or three days before, a man who had the appearance of a "tramp" had been observed by the people of a small village in the neighborhood. He stopped and looked at the houses in a vacant way, walked back and forth once or twice as if uncertain which of the cross-roads to take, and presently went on without begging or even speaking to any one. Towards sunset a farmer, on his way to the village store, found him sitting at the roadside, his head resting against a fence-post. The man's face was so worn and exhausted that the farmer kindly stopped and addressed him; but he gave no other reply than a shake of the head.

The farmer thereupon lifted him into his light country-wagon, the man offering no resistance, and drove to the tavern, where, his exhaustion being so evident, a glass of whiskey was administered to him. He afterwards spoke a few words in German, which no one understood. At the almshouse, to which he was transported the same evening, he refused to answer the customary questions, although he appeared to understand them. The physician was obliged to use a slight degree of force in administering nourishment and medicine, but neither was of any avail. The man died within twenty-four hours after being received. His pockets were empty, but two small leathern wallets were found under his pillow; and these formed the package which the director left in my charge. They were full of papers in a foreign language, he said, and he supposed I might be able to ascertain the stranger's name and home from them.

I took up the wallets, which were worn and greasy from long service, opened them, and saw that they were filled with scraps, fragments, and folded pieces of paper, nearly every one of which had been carried for a long time loose in the pocket. Some were written in pen and ink, and some in pencil, but all were equally brown, worn, and unsavory in appearance. In turning them over, however, my eye was caught by some slips in the Russian character, and three or four notes in French; the rest were German. I laid aside "Pitaval" at once, emptied all the leathern pockets carefully, and set about examining the pile of material.

I first ran rapidly through the papers to ascertain the dead man's name, but it was nowhere to be found. There were half a dozen letters, written on sheets folded and addressed in the fashion which prevailed before envelopes were invented; but the name was cut out of the address in every case. There was an official permit to embark on board a Bremen steamer, mutilated in the same way; there was a card photograph, from which the face had been scratched by a penknife. There were Latin sentences; accounts of expenses; a list of New York addresses, covering eight pages; and a number of notes, written either in Warsaw or Breslau. A more incongruous collection I never saw, and I am sure that had it not been for the train of thought I was pursuing when the director called upon me, I should have returned the papers to him without troubling my head with any attempt to unravel the man's story.

The evidence, however, that he had endeavored to hide his life, had been revealed by my first superficial examination; and here, I reflected, was a singular opportunity to test both his degree of success and my own power of constructing a coherent history out of the detached fragments. Unpromising as is the matter, said I, let me see whether he can conceal his secret from even such unpractised eyes as mine.

I went through the papers again, read each one rapidly, and arranged them in separate files, according to the character of their contents. Then I rearranged these latter in the order of time, so far as it was indicated; and afterwards commenced the work of picking out and threading together whatever facts might be noted. The first thing I ascertained, or rather conjectured, was that the man's life might be divided into three very distinct phases, the first ending in Breslau, the second in Poland, and the third and final one in America. Thereupon I once again rearranged the material, and attacked that which related to the first phase.

It consisted of the following papers: Three letters, in a female hand, commencing "My dear brother," and terminating with "Thy loving sister, Elise;" part of a diploma from a gymnasium, or high school, certifying that [here the name was cut out] had successfully passed his examination, and was competent to teach,—and here again, whether by accident or design, the paper was torn off; a note, apparently to a jeweller, ordering a certain gold ring to be delivered to "Otto," and signed "B. V. H.;" a receipt from the package-post for a box forwarded to Warsaw, to the address of Count Ladislas Kasincsky; and finally a washing-list, at the bottom of which was written, in pencil, in a trembling hand: "May God protect thee! But do not stay away so very long."

In the second collection, relating to Poland, I found the following: Six orders in Russian and three in French, requesting somebody to send by "Jean" sums of money, varying from two to eight hundred rubles. These orders were in the same hand, and all signed "Y." A charming letter in French, addressed "cher ami," and declining, in the most delicate and tender way, an offer of marriage made to the sister of the writer, of whose signature only "Amelie de" remained, the family name having been torn off. A few memoranda of expenses, one of which was curious: "Dinner with Jean, 58 rubles;" and immediately after it: "Doctor, 10 rubles." There were, moreover, a leaf torn out of a journal, and half of a note which had been torn down the middle, both implicating "Jean" in some way with the fortunes of the dead man.

The papers belonging to the American phase, so far as they were to be identified by dates, or by some internal evidence, were fewer, but even more enigmatical in character. The principal one was a list of addresses in New York, divided into sections, the street boundaries of which were given. There were no names, but some of the addresses were marked +, and others?, and a few had been crossed out with a pencil. Then there were some leaves of a journal of diet and bodily symptoms, of a very singular character; three fragments of drafts of letters, in pencil, one of them commencing, "Dog and villain!" and a single note of "Began work, September 10th, 1865." This was about a year before his death.

The date of the diploma given by the gymnasium at Breslau was June 27, 1855, and the first date in Poland was May 3, 1861. Belonging to the time between these two periods there were only the order for the ring (1858), and a little memorandum in pencil, dated "Posen, Dec., 1859." The last date in Poland was March 18, 1863, and the permit to embark at Bremen was dated in October of that year. Here, at least, was a slight chronological framework. The physician who attended the county almshouse had estimated the man's age at thirty, which, supposing him to have been nineteen at the time of receiving the diploma, confirmed the dates to that extent.

I assumed, at the start, that the name which had been so carefully cut out of all the documents was the man's own. The "Elise" of the letters was therefore his sister. The first two letters related merely to "mother's health," and similar details, from which it was impossible to extract any thing, except that the sister was in some kind of service. The second letter closed with: "I have enough work to do, but I keep well. Forget thy disappointment so far as I am concerned, for I never expected any thing; I don't know why, but I never did."

Here was a disappointment, at least, to begin with. I made a note of it opposite the date, on my blank programme, and took up the next letter. It was written in November, 1861, and contained a passage which keenly excited my curiosity. It ran thus: "Do, pray, be more careful of thy money. It may be all as thou sayest, and inevitable, but I dare not mention the thing to mother, and five thalers is all I can spare out of my own wages. As for thy other request, I have granted it, as thou seest, but it makes me a little anxious. What is the joke? And how can it serve thee? That is what I do not understand, and I have plagued myself not a little to guess."

Among the Polish memoranda was this: "Sept. 1 to Dec. 1, 200 rubles," which I assumed to represent a salary. This would give him eight hundred a year, at least twelve times the amount which his sister—who must either have been cook or housekeeper, since she spoke of going to market for the family—could have received. His application to her for money, and the manner of her reference to it, indicated some imprudence or irregularity on his part. What the "other request" was, I could not guess; but as I was turning and twisting the worn leaf in some perplexity, I made a sudden discovery. One side of the bottom edge had been very slightly doubled over in folding, and as I smoothed it out, I noticed some diminutive letters in the crease. The paper had been worn nearly through, but I made out the words: "Write very soon, dear Otto!"

This was the name in the order for the gold ring, signed "B. V. H."—a link, indeed, but a fresh puzzle. Knowing the stubborn prejudices of caste in Germany, and above all in Eastern Prussia and Silesia, I should have been compelled to accept "Otto," whose sister was in service, as himself the servant of "B. V. H.," but for the tenderly respectful letter of "Amelie de——," declining the marriage offer for her sister. I re-read this letter very carefully, to determine whether it was really intended for "Otto." It ran thus:

> *"DEAR FRIEND,—I will not say that your letter was entirely*
>
> *unexpected, either to Helmine or myself. I should, perhaps, have*
>
> *less faith in the sincerity of your attachment if you had not*
>
> *already involuntarily betrayed it. When I say that although I*
>
> *detected the inclination of your heart some weeks ago, and that I*
>
> *also saw it was becoming evident to my sister, yet I refrained from*
>
> *mentioning the subject at all until she came to me last evening*
>
> *with your letter in her hand,—when I say this, you will understand*
>
> *that I have acted towards you with the respect and sympathy which*
>
> *I profoundly feel. Helmine fully shares this feeling, and her poor*
>
> *heart is too painfully moved to allow her to reply. Do I not say,*
>
> *in saying this, what her reply must be? But, though her heart*
>
> *cannot respond to your love, she hopes you will always believe her*
>
> *a friend to whom your proffered devotion was an honor, and will*
>
> *be—if you will subdue it to her deserts—a grateful thing to*

*remember. We shall remain in Warsaw a fortnight longer, as I think*

*yourself will agree that it is better we should not*

*immediately return to the castle. Jean, who must carry a fresh*

*order already, will bring you this, and we hope to have good news*

*of Henri. I send back the papers, which were unnecessary; we never*

*doubted you, and we shall of course keep your secret so long as you*

*choose to wear it.*

*"AMELIE DE——"*

The more light I seemed to obtain, the more inexplicable the circumstances became. The diploma and the note of salary were grounds for supposing that "Otto" occupied the position of tutor in a noble Polish family. There was the receipt for a box addressed to Count Ladislas Kasincsky, and I temporarily added his family name to the writer of the French letter, assuming her to be his wife. "Jean" appeared to be a servant, and "Henri" I set down as the son whom Otto was instructing in the castle or family seat in the country, while the parents were in warsaw. Plausible, so far; but the letter was not such a one as a countess would have written to her son's tutor, under similar circumstances. It was addressed to a social equal, apparently to a man younger than herself, and for whom—supposing him to have been a tutor, secretary, or something of the kind—she must have felt a special sympathy. Her mention of "the papers" and "your secret" must refer to circumstances which would explain the mystery. "So long as you choose to WEAR it," she had written: then it was certainly a secret connected with his personal history.

Further, it appeared that "Jean" was sent to him with "an order." What could this be, but one of the nine orders for money which lay before my eyes? I examined the dates of the latter, and lo! there was one written upon the same day as the lady's letter. The sums drawn by these orders amounted in all to four thousand two hundred rubles. But how should a tutor or secretary be in possession of his employer's money? Still, this might be accounted for; it would imply great trust on the part of the latter, but no more than one man frequently reposes in another. Yet, if it were so, one of the memoranda confronted me with a conflicting fact: "Dinner with Jean, 58 rubles." The unusual amount—nearly fifty dollars—indicated an act of the most reckless dissipation, and in company with a servant, if "Jean," as I could scarcely doubt, acted in that character. I finally decided to assume both these conjectures as true, and apply them to the remaining testimony.

I first took up the leaf which had been torn out of a small journal or pocket note-book, as was manifested by the red edge on three sides. It was scribbled over with brief notes in pencil, written at different times. Many of them were merely mnemonic signs; but the recurrence of the letters J and Y seemed to point to transactions with "Jean," and the drawer of the various sums of money. The letter Y reminded me that I had been too hasty in giving the name of Kasincsky to the noble family; indeed, the name upon the post-office receipt might have no connection with the matter I was trying to investigate.

Suddenly I noticed a "Ky" among the mnemonic signs, and the suspicion flashed across my mind that Count Kasincsky had signed the order with the last letter of his family name! To assume this, however, suggested a secret reason for doing so; and I began to think that I had already secrets enough on hand.

The leaf was much rubbed and worn, and it was not without considerable trouble that I deciphered the following (omitting the unintelligible signs):

"Oct. 30 (Nov. 12)—talk with Y; 20—Jean. Consider.

"Nov. 15—with J—H—hope.

"Dec. 1—Told the C. No knowledge of S—therefore safe. Uncertain of—— C to Warsaw. Met J. as agreed. Further and further.

"Dec. 27—All for naught! All for naught!

"Jan. 19, '63—Sick. What is to be the end? Threats. No tidings of Y. Walked the streets all day. At night as usual.

"March 1—News. The C. and H. left yesterday. No more to hope. Let it come, then!"

These broken words warmed my imagination powerfully. Looking at them in the light of my conjecture, I was satisfied that "Otto" was involved in some crime, or dangerous secret, of which "Jean" was either the instigator or the accomplice. "Y.," or Count Kasincsky,—and I was more than ever inclined to connect the two,—also had his mystery, which might, or might not, be identical with the first. By comparing dates, I found that the entry made December 27 was three days later than the date of the letter of "Amelie de——"; and the exclamation "All for naught!" certainly referred to the disappointment it contained. I now guessed the "H." in the second entry to mean "Helmine." The two last suggested a removal to Warsaw from the country. Here was a little more ground to stand on; but how should I ever get at the secret?

I took up the torn half of a note, which, after the first inspection, I had laid aside as a hopeless puzzle. A closer examination revealed several things which failed to impress me at the outset. It was written in a strong and rather awkward masculine hand; several words were underscored, two misspelled, and I felt—I scarcely knew why—that it was written in a spirit of mingled contempt and defiance. Let me give the fragment just as it lay before me:

"ARON!

*It is quite time*

*be done. Who knows*

*is not his home by this*

CONCERN FOR THE

*that they are well off,*

*sian officers are*

*cide at once, my*

*risau, or I must*

*t TEN DAYS DELAY*

*money can be divi-*

*tier, and you may*

*ever you please.*

*untess goes, and she*

*will know who you*

*time, unless you carry*

*friend or not*

*decide,*

*ann Helm."*

Here, I felt sure, was the clue to much of the mystery. The first thing that struck me was the appearance of a new name. I looked at it again, ran through in my mind all possible German names, and found that it could only be "Johann,"—and in the same instant I recalled the frequent habit of the Prussian and Polish nobility of calling their German valets by French names. This, then, was "Jean!" The address was certainly "Baron," and why thrice underscored, unless in contemptuous satire? Light began to break upon the matter at last. "Otto" had been playing the part, perhaps assuming the name, of a nobleman, seduced to the deception by his passion for the Countess' sister, Helmine. This explained the reference to "the papers," and "the secret," and would account for the respectful and sympathetic tone of the Countess' letter. But behind this there was certainly another secret, in which "Y." (whoever he might be) was concerned, and which related to money. The close of the note, which I filled out to read, "Your friend or not, as you may decide," conveyed a threat, and, to judge from the halves of lines immediately preceding it, the threat referred to the money, as well as to the betrayal of an assumed character.

Here, just as the story began to appear in faint outline, my discoveries stopped for a while. I ascertained the breadth of the original note by a part of the middle-crease which remained, filled out the torn part with blank paper, completed the divided words in the same character of manuscript, and endeavored to guess the remainder, but no clairvoyant power of divination came to my aid. I turned over the letters again, remarking the neatness with which the addresses had been cut off, and wondering why the man had not destroyed the letters and other memoranda entirely, if he wished to hide a possible crime. The fact that they were not destroyed showed the hold which his past life had had upon him even to his dying hour. Weak and vain, as I had already suspected him to be,—wanting in all manly fibre, and of the very material which a keen, energetic villain would mould to his needs,—I felt that his love for his sister and for "Helmine," and other associations connected with his life in Germany and Poland, had made him cling to these worn records.

I know not what gave me the suspicion that he had not even found the heart to destroy the exscinded names; perhaps the care with which they had been removed; perhaps, in two instances, the circumstance of their taking words out of the body of the letters with them. But the suspicion came, and led to a re-examination of the leathern wallets. I could scarcely believe my eyes, when feeling something rustle faintly as I pressed the thin lining of an inner pocket, I drew forth three or four small pellets of paper, and unrolling them, found the lost addresses! I fitted them to the vacant places, and found that the first letters of the sister in Breslau had been forwarded to "Otto Lindenschmidt," while the letter to Poland was addressed "Otto von Herisau."

I warmed with this success, which exactly tallied with the previous discoveries, and returned again to the Polish memoranda The words "[Rus]sian officers" in "Jean's" note led me to notice that it had been written towards the close of the last insurrection in Poland—a circumstance which I immediately coupled with some things in the note and on the leaf of the journal. "No tidings of Y" might indicate that Count Kasincsky had been concerned in the rebellion, and had fled, or been taken prisoner. Had he left a large amount of funds in the hands of the supposed Otto von Herisau, which were drawn from time to time by orders, the form of which had been previously agreed upon? Then, when he had disappeared, might it not have been the remaining funds which Jean urged Otto to divide with him, while the latter, misled and entangled in deception rather than naturally dishonest, held back from such a step? I could hardly doubt so much, and it now required but a slight effort of the imagination to complete the torn note.

The next letter of the sister was addressed to Bremen. After having established so many particulars, I found it easily intelligible. "I have done what I can," she wrote. "I put it in this letter; it is all I have. But do not ask me for money again; mother is ailing most of the time, and I have not yet dared to tell her all. I shall suffer great anxiety until I hear that the vessel has sailed. My mistress is very good; she has given me an advance on my wages, or I could not have sent thee any thing. Mother thinks thou art still in Leipzig: why didst thou stay there so long? but no difference; thy money would have gone anyhow."

It was nevertheless singular that Otto should be without money, so soon after the appropriation of Count Kasincsky's funds. If the "20" in the first memorandum on the leaf meant "twenty thousand rubles," as I conjectured, and but four thousand two hundred were drawn by the Count previous to his flight or imprisonment, Otto's half of the remainder would amount to nearly eight thousand rubles; and it was, therefore, not easy to account for his delay in Leipzig, and his destitute condition.

Before examining the fragments relating to the American phase of his life,—which illustrated his previous history only by occasional revelations of his moods and feelings,—I made one more effort to guess the cause of his having assumed the name of "Von Herisau." The initials signed to the order for the ring ("B. V. H.") certainly stood for the same family name; and the possession of papers belonging to one of the family was an additional evidence that Otto had either been in the service of, or was related to, some Von Herisau. Perhaps a sentence in one of the sister's letters—"Forget thy disappointment so far as I am concerned, for I never expected any thing"—referred to something of the kind. On the whole, service seemed more likely than kinship; but in that case the papers must have been stolen.

I had endeavored, from the start, to keep my sympathies out of the investigation, lest they should lead me to misinterpret the broken evidence, and thus defeat my object. It must have been the Countess' letter, and the brief, almost stenographic, signs of anxiety and unhappiness on the leaf of the journal, that first beguiled me into a commiseration, which the simple devotion and self-sacrifice of the poor, toiling sister failed to neutralize. However, I detected the feeling at this stage of the examination, and turned to the American records, in order to get rid of it.

The principal paper was the list of addresses of which I have spoken. I looked over it in vain, to find some indication of its purpose; yet it had been carefully made out and much used. There was no name of a person upon it,— only numbers and streets, one hundred and thirty-eight in all. Finally, I took these, one by one, to ascertain if any of the houses were known to me, and found three, out of the whole number, to be the residences of persons whom I knew. One was a German gentleman, and the other two were Americans who had visited Germany. The riddle was read! During a former residence in New York, I had for a time been quite overrun by destitute Germans,— men, apparently, of some culture, who represented themselves as theological students, political refugees, or unfortunate clerks and secretaries,—soliciting assistance. I found that, when I gave to one, a dozen others came within the next fortnight; when I refused, the persecution ceased for about the same length of time. I became convinced, at last, that these persons were members of an organized society of beggars, and the result proved it; for when I made it an inviolable rule to give to no one who could not bring me an indorsement of his need by some person whom I knew, the annoyance ceased altogether.

The meaning of the list of addresses was now plain. My nascent commiseration for the man was not only checked, but I was in danger of changing my role from that of culprit's counsel to that of prosecuting attorney.

When I took up again the fragment of the first draught of a letter commencing, "Dog and villain!" and applied it to the words "Jean" or "Johann Helm," the few lines which could be deciphered became full of meaning. "Don't think," it began, "that I have forgotten you, or the trick you played me! If I was drunk or drugged the last night, I know how it happened, for all that. I left, but I shall go back. And if you make use of" (here some words

were entirely obliterated).... "is true. He gave me the ring, and meant".... This
was all I could make out. The other papers showed only scattered memoranda,
of money, or appointments, or addresses, with the exception of the diary in
pencil.

I read the letter attentively, and at first with very little idea of its meaning.
Many of the words were abbreviated, and there were some arbitrary signs. It
ran over a period of about four months, terminating six weeks before the
man's death. He had been wandering about the country during this period,
sleeping in woods and barns, and living principally upon milk. The condition
of his pulse and other physical functions was scrupulously set down, with
an occasional remark of "good" or "bad." The conclusion was at last forced
upon me that he had been endeavoring to commit suicide by a slow course
of starvation and exposure. Either as the cause or the result of this attempt, I
read, in the final notes, signs of an aberration of mind. This also explained the
singular demeanor of the man when found, and his refusal to take medicine
or nourishment. He had selected a long way to accomplish his purpose, but
had reached the end at last.

The confused material had now taken shape; the dead man, despite his
will, had confessed to me his name and the chief events of his life. It now
remained—looking at each event as the result of a long chain of causes—
to deduce from them the elements of his individual character, and then fill
up the inevitable gaps in the story from the probabilities of the operation
of those elements. This was not so much a mere venture as the reader may
suppose, because the two actions of the mind test each other. If they cannot,
thus working towards a point and back again, actually discover what WAS,
they may at least fix upon a very probable MIGHT HAVE BEEN.

A person accustomed to detective work would have obtained my little
stock of facts with much less trouble, and would, almost instinctively, have
filled the blanks as he went along. Being an apprentice in such matters, I
had handled the materials awkwardly. I will not here retrace my own mental
zigzags between character and act, but simply repeat the story as I finally
settled and accepted it.

Otto Lindenschmidt was the child of poor parents in or near Breslau.

His father died when he was young; his mother earned a scanty subsistence as a washerwoman; his sister went into service. Being a bright, handsome boy, he attracted the attention of a Baron von Herisau, an old, childless, eccentric gentleman, who took him first as page or attendant, intending to make him a superior valet de chambre. Gradually, however, the Baron fancied that he detected in the boy a capacity for better things; his condescending feeling of protection had grown into an attachment for the handsome, amiable, grateful young fellow, and he placed him in the gymnasium at Breslau, perhaps with the idea, now, of educating him to be an intelligent companion.

The boy and his humble relatives, dazzled by this opportunity, began secretly to consider the favor as almost equivalent to his adoption as a son. (The Baron had once been married, but his wife and only child had long been dead.) The old man, of course, came to look upon the growing intelligence of the youth as his own work: vanity and affection became inextricably blended in his heart, and when the cursus was over, he took him home as the companion of his lonely life. After two or three years, during which the young man was acquiring habits of idleness and indulgence, supposing his future secure, the Baron died,—perhaps too suddenly to make full provision for him, perhaps after having kept up the appearance of wealth on a life-annuity, but, in any case, leaving very little, if any, property to Otto. In his disappointment, the latter retained certain family papers which the Baron had intrusted to his keeping. The ring was a gift, and he wore it in remembrance of his benefactor.

Wandering about, Micawber-like, in hopes that something might turn up, he reached Posen, and there either met or heard of the Polish Count, Ladislas Kasincsky, who was seeking a tutor for his only son. His accomplishments, and perhaps, also, a certain aristocratic grace of manner unconsciously caught from the Baron von Herisau, speedily won for him the favor of the Count and Countess Kasincsky, and emboldened him to hope for the hand of the Countess' sister, Helmine ——, to whom he was no doubt sincerely attached. Here Johann Helm, or "Jean," a confidential servant of the Count, who looked upon the new tutor as a rival, yet adroitly flattered his vanity for the purpose of misleading and displacing him, appears upon the stage. "Jean" first detected Otto's passion; "Jean," at an epicurean dinner, wormed out of Otto the secret of the Herisau documents, and perhaps suggested the part which the latter afterwards played.

This "Jean" seemed to me to have been the evil agency in the miserable history which followed. After Helmine's rejection of Otto's suit, and the flight or captivity of Count Kasincsky, leaving a large sum of money in Otto's hands, it would be easy for "Jean," by mingled persuasions and threats, to move the latter to flight, after dividing the money still remaining in his hands. After the theft, and the partition, which took place beyond the Polish frontier, "Jean" in turn, stole his accomplice's share, together with the Von Herisau documents.

Exile and a year's experience of organized mendicancy did the rest.

Otto Lindenschmidt was one of those natures which possess no moral elasticity—which have neither the power nor the comprehension of atonement. The first real, unmitigated guilt—whether great or small—breaks them down hopelessly. He expected no chance of self-redemption, and he found none. His life in America was so utterly dark and hopeless that the brightest moment in it must have been that which showed him the approach of death.

My task was done. I had tracked this weak, vain, erring, hunted soul to its last refuge, and the knowledge bequeathed to me but a single duty. His sins were balanced by his temptations; his vanity and weakness had revenged themselves; and there only remained to tell the simple, faithful sister that her sacrifices were no longer required. I burned the evidences of guilt, despair and suicide, and sent the other papers, with a letter relating the time and circumstances of Otto Lindenschmidt's death, to the civil authorities of Breslau, requesting that they might be placed in the hands of his sister Elise.

This, I supposed, was the end of the history, so far as my connection with it was concerned. But one cannot track a secret with impunity; the fatality connected with the act and the actor clings even to the knowledge of the act. I had opened my door a little, in order to look out upon the life of another, but in doing so a ghost had entered in, and was not to be dislodged until I had done its service.

In the summer of 1867 I was in Germany, and during a brief journey of idlesse and enjoyment came to the lovely little watering-place of Liebenstein, on the southern slope of the Thuringian Forest. I had no expectation or even desire of making new acquaintances among the gay company who took their afternoon coffee under the noble linden trees on the terrace; but, within the first hour of my after-dinner leisure, I was greeted by an old friend, an author, from Coburg, and carried away, in my own despite, to a group of his associates. My friend and his friends had already been at the place a fortnight, and knew the very tint and texture of its gossip. While I sipped my coffee, I listened to them with one ear, and to Wagner's overture to "Lohengrin" with the other; and I should soon have been wholly occupied with the fine orchestra had I not been caught and startled by an unexpected name.

"Have you noticed," some one asked, "how much attention the Baron von Herisau is paying her?"

I whirled round and exclaimed, in a breath, "The Baron von Herisau!"

"Yes," said my friend; "do you know him?"

I was glad that three crashing, tremendous chords came from the orchestra just then, giving me time to collect myself before I replied: "I am not sure whether it is the same person: I knew a Baron von Herisau long ago: how old is the gentleman here?"

"About thirty-five, I should think," my friend answered.

"Ah, then it can't be the same person," said I: "still, if he should happen to pass near us, will you point him out to me?"

It was an hour later, and we were all hotly discussing the question of Lessing's obligations to English literature, when one of the gentlemen at the table said: "There goes the Baron von Herisau: is it perhaps your friend, sir?"

I turned and saw a tall man, with prominent nose, opaque black eyes, and black mustache, walking beside a pretty, insipid girl. Behind the pair went an elderly couple, overdressed and snobbish in appearance. A carriage, with servants in livery, waited in the open space below the terrace, and having received the two couples, whirled swiftly away towards Altenstein.

Had I been more of a philosopher I should have wasted no second thought on the Baron von Herisau. But the Nemesis of the knowledge which I had throttled poor Otto Lindenschmidt's ghost to obtain had come upon me at last, and there was no rest for me until I had discovered who and what was the Baron. The list of guests which the landlord gave me whetted my curiosity to a painful degree; for on it I found the entry: "Aug. 15.—Otto V. Herisau, Rentier, East Prussia."

It was quite dark when the carriage returned. I watched the company into the supper-room, and then, whisking in behind them, secured a place at the nearest table. I had an hour of quiet, stealthy observation before my Coburg friend discovered me, and by that time I was glad of his company and had need of his confidence. But, before making use of him in the second capacity, I desired to make the acquaintance of the adjoining partie carree. He had bowed to them familiarly in passing, and when the old gentleman said, "Will you not join us, Herr ——?" I answered my friend's interrogative glance with a decided affirmative, and we moved to the other table.

My seat was beside the Baron von Herisau, with whom I exchanged the usual commonplaces after an introduction. His manner was cold and taciturn, I thought, and there was something forced in the smile which accompanied his replies to the remarks of the coarse old lady, who continually referred to the "Herr Baron" as authority upon every possible subject. I noticed, however, that he cast a sudden, sharp glance at me, when I was presented to the company as an American.

The man's neighborhood disturbed me. I was obliged to let the conversation run in the channels already selected, and stupid enough I found them. I was considering whether I should not give a signal to my friend and withdraw, when the Baron stretched his hand across the table for a bottle of Affenthaler, and I caught sight of a massive gold ring on his middle finger. Instantly I remembered the ring which "B. V. H." had given to Otto Lindenschmidt, and I said to myself, "That is it!" The inference followed like lightning that it was "Johann Helm" who sat beside me, and not a Baron von Herisau!

That evening my friend and I had a long, absorbing conversation in my room. I told him the whole story, which came back vividly to memory, and learned, in return, that the reputed Baron was supposed to be wealthy, that the old gentleman was a Bremen merchant or banker, known to be rich, that neither was considered by those who had met them to be particularly intelligent or refined, and that the wooing of the daughter had already become so marked as to be a general subject of gossip. My friend was inclined to think my conjecture correct, and willingly co-operated with me in a plan to test the matter. We had no considerable sympathy with the snobbish parents, whose servility to a title was so apparent; but the daughter seemed to be an innocent and amiable creature, however silly, and we determined to spare her the shame of an open scandal.

If our scheme should seem a little melodramatic, it must not be forgotten that my friend was an author. The next morning, as the Baron came up the terrace after his visit to the spring, I stepped forward and greeted him politely, after which I said: "I see by the strangers' list that you are from East Prussia, Baron; have you ever been in Poland?" At that moment, a voice behind him called out rather sharply, "Jean!" The Baron started, turned round and then back to me, and all his art could not prevent the blood from rushing to his face. I made, as if by accident, a gesture with my hand, indicating success, and went a step further.

"Because," said I, "I am thinking of making a visit to Cracow and Warsaw, and should be glad of any information—"

"Certainly!" he interrupted me, "and I should be very glad to give it, if I had ever visited Poland."

"At least," I continued, "you can advise me upon one point; but excuse me, shall we not sit down a moment yonder? As my question relates to money, I should not wish to be overheard."

I pointed out a retired spot, just before reaching which we were joined by my friend, who suddenly stepped out from behind a clump of lilacs. The Baron and he saluted each other.

"Now," said I to the former, "I can ask your advice, Mr. Johann Helm!"

He was not an adept, after all. His astonishment and confusion were brief, to be sure, but they betrayed him so completely that his after-impulse to assume a haughty, offensive air only made us smile.

"If I had a message to you from Otto Lindenschmidt, what then?" I asked.

He turned pale, and presently stammered out, "He—he is dead!"

"Now," said my friend, "it is quite time to drop the mask before us. You see we know you, and we know your history. Not from Otto Lindenschmidt alone; Count Ladislas Kasincsky—"

"What! Has he come back from Siberia?" exclaimed Johann Helm. His face expressed abject terror; I think he would have fallen upon his knees before us if he had not somehow felt, by a rascal's instinct, that we had no personal wrongs to redress in unmasking him.

Our object, however, was to ascertain through him the complete facts of Otto Lindenschmidt's history, and then to banish him from Liebenstein. We allowed him to suppose for awhile that we were acting under the authority of persons concerned, in order to make the best possible use of his demoralized mood, for we knew it would not last long.

My guesses were very nearly correct. Otto Lindenschmidt had been educated by an old Baron, Bernhard von Herisau, on account of his resemblance in person to a dead son, whose name had also been Otto.

He could not have adopted the plebeian youth, at least to the extent of giving him an old and haughty name, but this the latter nevertheless expected, up to the time of the Baron's death. He had inherited a little property from his benefactor, but soon ran through it. "He was a light-headed fellow," said Johann Helm, "but he knew how to get the confidence of the old Junkers. If he hadn't been so cowardly and fidgety, he might have made himself a career."

The Polish episode differed so little from my interpretation that I need not repeat Helm's version. He denied having stolen Otto's share of the money, but could not help admitting his possession of the Von Herisau papers, among which were the certificates of birth and baptism of the old Baron's son, Otto. It seems that he had been fearful of Lindenschmidt's return from America, for he managed to communicate with his sister in Breslau, and in this way learned the former's death. Not until then had he dared to assume his present disguise.

We let him go, after exacting a solemn pledge that he would betake himself at once to Hamburg, and there ship for Australia. (I judged that America was already amply supplied with individuals of his class.) The sudden departure of the Baron von Herisau was a two days' wonder at Liebenstein; but besides ourselves, only the Bremen banker knew the secret. He also left, two days afterwards, with his wife and daughter—their cases, it was reported, requiring Kissingen.

Otto Lindenschmidt's life, therefore, could not hide itself. Can any life?

# TWIN-LOVE.

When John Vincent, after waiting twelve years, married Phebe Etheridge, the whole neighborhood experienced that sense of relief and satisfaction which follows the triumph of the right. Not that the fact of a true love is ever generally recognized and respected when it is first discovered; for there is a perverse quality in American human nature which will not accept the existence of any fine, unselfish passion, until it has been tested and established beyond peradventure. There were two views of the case when John Vincent's love for Phebe, and old Reuben Etheridge's hard prohibition of the match, first became known to the community. The girls and boys, and some of the matrons, ranged themselves at once on the side of the lovers, but a large majority of the older men and a few of the younger supported the tyrannical father.

Reuben Etheridge was rich, and, in addition to what his daughter would naturally inherit from him, she already possessed more than her lover, at the time of their betrothal. This in the eyes of one class was a sufficient reason for the father's hostility. When low natures live (as they almost invariably do) wholly in the present, they neither take tenderness from the past nor warning from the possibilities of the future. It is the exceptional men and women who remember their youth. So, these lovers received a nearly equal amount of sympathy and condemnation; and only slowly, partly through their quiet fidelity and patience, and partly through the improvement in John Vincent's worldly circumstances, was the balance changed. Old Reuben remained an unflinching despot to the last: if any relenting softness touched his heart, he sternly concealed it; and such inference as could be drawn from the fact that he, certainly knowing what would follow his death, bequeathed his daughter her proper share of his goods, was all that could be taken for consent.

They were married: John, a grave man in middle age, weather-beaten and worn by years of hard work and self-denial, yet not beyond the restoration of a milder second youth; and Phebe a sad, weary woman, whose warmth of longing had been exhausted, from whom youth and its uncalculating surrenders of hope and feeling had gone forever. They began their wedded life under the shadow of the death out of which it grew; and when, after a ceremony in which neither bridesmaid nor groomsman stood by their side, they united their divided homes, it seemed to their neighbors that a separated husband and wife had come together again, not that the relation was new to either.

John Vincent loved his wife with the tenderness of an innocent man, but all his tenderness could not avail to lift the weight of settled melancholy which had gathered upon her. Disappointment, waiting, yearning, indulgence in long lament and self-pity, the morbid cultivation of unhappy fancies—all this had wrought its work upon her, and it was too late to effect a cure. In the night she awoke to weep at his side, because of the years when she had awakened to weep alone; by day she kept up her old habit of foreboding, although the evening steadily refuted the morning; and there were times when, without any apparent cause, she would fall into a dark, despairing mood which her husband's greatest care and cunning could only slowly dispel.

Two or three years passed, and new life came to the Vincent farm. One day, between midnight and dawn, the family pair was doubled; the cry of twin sons was heard in the hushed house. The father restrained his happy wonder in his concern for the imperilled life of the mother; he guessed that she had anticipated death, and she now hung by a thread so slight that her simple will might snap it. But her will, fortunately, was as faint as her consciousness; she gradually drifted out of danger, taking her returning strength with a passive acquiescence rather than with joy. She was hardly paler than her wont, but the lurking shadow seemed to have vanished from her eyes, and John Vincent felt that her features had assumed a new expression, the faintly perceptible stamp of some spiritual change.

It was a happy day for him when, propped against his breast and gently held by his warm, strong arm, the twin boys were first brought to be laid upon her lap. Two staring, dark-faced creatures, with restless fists and feet, they were alike in every least feature of their grotesque animality. Phebe placed a hand under the head of each, and looked at them for a long time in silence.

"Why is this?" she said, at last, taking hold of a narrow pink ribbon, which was tied around the wrist of one.

"He's the oldest, sure," the nurse answered. "Only by fifteen minutes or so, but it generally makes a difference when twins come to be named; and you may see with your own eyes that there's no telling of 'em apart otherways."

"Take off the ribbon, then," said Phebe quietly; "I know them."

"Why, ma'am, it's always done, where they're so like! And I'll never be able to tell which is which; for they sleep and wake and feed by the same clock. And you might mistake, after all, in giving 'em names—"

"There is no oldest or youngest, John; they are two and yet one: this is mine, and this is yours."

"I see no difference at all, Phebe," said John; "and how can we divide them?"

"We will not divide," she answered; "I only meant it as a sign."

She smiled, for the first time in many days. He was glad of heart, but did not understand her. "What shall we call them?" he asked. "Elias and Reuben, after our fathers?"

"No, John; their names must be David and Jonathan."

And so they were called. And they grew, not less, but more alike, in passing through the stages of babyhood. The ribbon of the older one had been removed, and the nurse would have been distracted, but for Phebe's almost miraculous instinct. The former comforted herself with the hope that teething would bring a variation to the two identical mouths; but no! they teethed as one child. John, after desperate attempts, which always failed in spite of the headaches they gave him, postponed the idea of distinguishing one from the other, until they should be old enough to develop some dissimilarity of speech, or gait, or habit. All trouble might have been avoided, had Phebe consented to the least variation in their dresses; but herein she was mildly immovable.

"Not yet," was her set reply to her husband; and one day, when he manifested a little annoyance at her persistence, she turned to him, holding a child on each knee, and said with a gravity which silenced him thenceforth: "John, can you not see that our burden has passed into them? Is there no meaning in this—that two children who are one in body and face and nature, should be given to us at our time of life, after such long disappointment and trouble? Our lives were held apart; theirs were united before they were born, and I dare not turn them in different directions. Perhaps I do not know all that the Lord intended to say to us, in sending them; but His hand is here!"

"I was only thinking of their good," John meekly answered. "If they are spared to grow up, there must be some way of knowing one from the other."

"THEY will not need it, and I, too, think only of them. They have taken the cross from my heart, and I will lay none on theirs. I am reconciled to my life through them, John; you have been very patient and good with me, and I will yield to you in all things but in this. I do not think I shall live to see them as men grown; yet, while we are together, I feel clearly what it is right to do. Can you not, just once, have a little faith without knowledge, John?"

"I'll try, Phebe," he said. "Any way, I'll grant that the boys belong to you more than to me."

Phebe Vincent's character had verily changed. Her attacks of semi-hysterical despondency never returned; her gloomy prophecies ceased. She was still grave, and the trouble of so many years never wholly vanished from her face; but she performed every duty of her life with at least a quiet willingness, and her home became the abode of peace; for passive content wears longer than demonstrative happiness.

David and Jonathan grew as one boy: the taste and temper of one was repeated in the other, even as the voice and features. Sleeping or waking, grieved or joyous, well or ill, they lived a single life, and it seemed so natural for one to answer to the other's name, that they probably would have themselves confused their own identities, but for their mother's unerring knowledge. Perhaps unconsciously guided by her, perhaps through the voluntary action of their own natures, each quietly took the other's place when called upon, even to the sharing of praise or blame at school, the friendships and quarrels of the playground. They were healthy and happy lads, and John Vincent was accustomed to say to his neighbors, "They're no more trouble than one would be; and yet they're four hands instead of two."

Phebe died when they were fourteen, saying to them, with almost her latest breath, "Be one, always!" Before her husband could decide whether to change her plan of domestic education, they were passing out of boyhood, changing in voice, stature, and character with a continued likeness which bewildered and almost terrified him. He procured garments of different colors, but they were accustomed to wear each article in common, and the result was only a mixture of tints for both. They were sent to different schools, to be returned the next day, equally pale, suffering, and incapable of study. Whatever device was employed, they evaded it by a mutual instinct which rendered all external measures unavailing. To John Vincent's mind their resemblance was an accidental misfortune, which had been confirmed through their mother's fancy. He felt that they were bound by some deep, mysterious tie, which, inasmuch as it might interfere with all practical aspects of life, ought to be gradually weakened. Two bodies, to him, implied two distinct men, and it was wrong to permit a mutual dependence which prevented either from exercising his own separate will and judgment.

But, while he was planning and pondering, the boys became young men, and he was an old man. Old, and prematurely broken; for he had worked much, borne much, and his large frame held only a moderate measure of vital force. A great weariness fell upon him, and his powers began to give way, at first slowly, but then with accelerated failure. He saw the end coming, long before his sons suspected it; his doubt, for their sakes, was the only thing which made it unwelcome. It was "upon his mind" (as his Quaker neighbors would say) to speak to them of the future, and at last the proper moment came.

It was a stormy November evening. Wind and rain whirled and drove among the trees outside, but the sitting-room of the old farm-house was bright and warm. David and Jonathan, at the table, with their arms over each other's backs and their brown locks mixed together, read from the same book: their father sat in the ancient rocking-chair before the fire, with his feet upon

522

a stool. The housekeeper and hired man had gone to bed, and all was still in the house.

John waited until he heard the volume closed, and then spoke.

"Boys," he said, "let me have a bit of talk with you. I don't seem to get over my ailments rightly,—never will, maybe. A man must think of things while there's time, and say them when they HAVE to be said. I don't know as there's any particular hurry in my case; only, we never can tell, from one day to another. When I die, every thing will belong to you two, share and share alike, either to buy another farm with the money out, or divide this: I won't tie you up in any way. But two of you will need two farms for two families; for you won't have to wait twelve years, like your mother and me."

"We don't want another farm, father!" said David and Jonathan together.

"I know you don't think so, now. A wife seemed far enough off from me when I was your age. You've always been satisfied to be with each other, but that can't last. It was partly your mother's notion; I remember her saying that our burden had passed into you. I never quite understood what she meant, but I suppose it must rather be the opposite of what WE had to bear."

The twins listened with breathless attention while their father, suddenly stirred by the past, told them the story of his long betrothal.

"And now," he exclaimed, in conclusion, "it may be putting wild ideas into your two heads, but I must say it! THAT was where I did wrong—wrong to her and to me,—in waiting! I had no right to spoil the best of our lives; I ought to have gone boldly, in broad day, to her father's house, taken her by the hand, and led her forth to be my wife. Boys, if either of you comes to love a woman truly, and she to love you, and there is no reason why God (I don't say man) should put you asunder, do as I ought to have done, not as I did! And, maybe, this advice is the best legacy I can leave you."

"But, father," said David, speaking for both, "we have never thought of marrying."

"Likely enough," their father answered; "we hardly ever think of what surely comes. But to me, looking back, it's plain. And this is the reason why I want you to make me a promise, and as solemn as if I was on my death-bed. Maybe I shall be, soon."

Tears gathered in the eyes of the twins. "What is it, father?" they both said.

"Nothing at all to any other two boys, but I don't know how YOU'll take it. What if I was to ask you to live apart for a while?"

"Oh father!" both cried. They leaned together, cheek pressing cheek, and hand clasping hand, growing white and trembling. John Vincent, gazing into the fire, did not see their faces, or his purpose might have been shaken.

"I don't say NOW," he went on. "After a while, when—well, when I'm dead. And I only mean a beginning, to help you toward what HAS to be. Only a month; I don't want to seem hard to you; but that's little, in all conscience. Give me your word: say, 'For mother's sake!'"

There was a long pause. Then David and Jonathan said, in low, faltering voices, "For mother's sake, I promise."

"Remember that you were only boys to her. She might have made all this seem easier, for women have reasons for things no man can answer. Mind, within a year after I'm gone!"

He rose and tottered out of the room.

The twins looked at each other: David said, "Must we?" and Jonathan, "How can we?" Then they both thought, "It may be a long while yet." Here was a present comfort, and each seemed to hold it firmly in holding the hand of the other, as they fell asleep side by side.

The trial was nearer than they imagined. Their father died before the winter was over; the farm and other property was theirs, and they might have allowed life to solve its mysteries as it rolled onwards, but for their promise to the dead. This must be fulfilled, and then—one thing was certain; they would never again separate.

"The sooner the better," said David. "It shall be the visit to our uncle and cousins in Indiana. You will come with me as far as Harrisburg; it may be easier to part there than here. And our new neighbors, the Bradleys, will want your help for a day or two, after getting home."

"It is less than death," Jonathan answered, "and why should it seem to be more? We must think of father and mother, and all those twelve years; now I know what the burden was."

"And we have never really borne any part of it! Father must have been right in forcing us to promise."

Every day the discussion was resumed, and always with the same termination. Familiarity with the inevitable step gave them increase of courage; yet, when the moment had come and gone, when, speeding on opposite trains, the hills and valleys multiplied between them with terrible velocity, a pang like death cut to the heart of each, and the divided life became a chill, oppressive dream.

During the separation no letters passed between them. When the neighbors asked Jonathan for news of his brother, he always replied, "He is well," and avoided further speech with such evidence of pain that they spared him. An hour before the month drew to an end, he walked forth alone, taking the road to the nearest railway station. A stranger who passed him at the entrance of a thick wood, three miles from home, was thunderstruck on meeting the same person shortly after, entering the wood from the other side; but the farmers in the near fields saw two figures issuing from the shade, hand in hand.

Each knew the other's month, before they slept, and the last thing Jonathan said, with his head on David's shoulder, was, "You must know our neighbors, the Bradleys, and especially Ruth." In the morning, as they dressed, taking each other's garments at random, as of old, Jonathan again said, "I have never seen a girl that I like so well as Ruth Bradley. Do you remember what father said about loving and marrying? It comes into my mind whenever I see Ruth; but she has no sister."

"But we need not both marry," David replied, "that might part us, and this will not. It is for always now."

"For always, David."

Two or three days later Jonathan said, as he started on an errand to the village: "I shall stop at the Bradleys this evening, so you must walk across and meet me there."

When David approached the house, a slender, girlish figure, with her back towards him, was stooping over a bush of great crimson roses, cautiously clipping a blossom here and there. At the click of the gate-latch she started and turned towards him. Her light gingham bonnet, falling back, disclosed a long oval face, fair and delicate, sweet brown eyes, and brown hair laid smoothly over the temples. A soft flush rose suddenly to her cheeks, and he felt that his own were burning.

"Oh Jonathan!" she exclaimed, transferring the roses to her left hand, and extending her right, as she came forward.

He was too accustomed to the name to recognize her mistake at once, and the word "Ruth!" came naturally to his lips.

"I should know your brother David has come," she then said; "even if I had not heard so. You look so bright. How glad I am!"

"Is he not here?" David asked.

"No; but there he is now, surely!" She turned towards the lane, where Jonathan was dismounting. "Why, it is yourself over again, Jonathan!"

As they approached, a glance passed between the twins, and a secret transfer of the riding-whip to David set their identity right with Ruth, whose manner toward the latter innocently became shy with all its friendliness, while her frank, familiar speech was given to Jonathan, as was fitting. But David also took the latter to himself, and when they left, Ruth had apparently forgotten that there was any difference in the length of their acquaintance.

On their way homewards David said: "Father was right. We must marry, like others, and Ruth is the wife for us,—I mean for you, Jonathan. Yes, we

526

must learn to say MINE and YOURS, after all, when we speak of her."

"Even she cannot separate us, it seems," Jonathan answered. "We must give her some sign, and that will also be a sign for others. It will seem strange to divide ourselves; we can never learn it properly; rather let us not think of marriage."

"We cannot help thinking of it; she stands in mother's place now, as we in father's."

Then both became silent and thoughtful. They felt that something threatened to disturb what seemed to be the only possible life for them, yet were unable to distinguish its features, and therefore powerless to resist it. The same instinct which had been born of their wonderful spiritual likeness told them that Ruth Bradley already loved Jonathan: the duty was established, and they must conform their lives to it. There was, however, this slight difference between their natures—that David was generally the first to utter the thought which came to the minds of both. So when he said, "We shall learn what to do when the need comes," it was a postponement of all foreboding. They drifted contentedly towards the coming change.

The days went by, and their visits to Ruth Bradley were continued. Sometimes Jonathan went alone, but they were usually together, and the tie which united the three became dearer and sweeter as it was more closely drawn. Ruth learned to distinguish between the two when they were before her: at least she said so, and they were willing to believe it. But she was hardly aware how nearly alike was the happy warmth in her bosom produced by either pair of dark gray eyes and the soft half-smile which played around either mouth. To them she seemed to be drawn within the mystic circle which separated them from others—she, alone; and they no longer imagined a life in which she should not share.

Then the inevitable step was taken. Jonathan declared his love, and was answered. Alas! he almost forgot David that late summer evening, as they sat in the moonlight, and over and over again assured each other how dear they had grown. He felt the trouble in David's heart when they met.

"Ruth is ours, and I bring her kiss to you," he said, pressing his lips to

527

David's; but the arms flung around him trembled, and David whispered, "Now the change begins."

"Oh, this cannot be our burden!" Jonathan cried, with all the rapture still warm in his heart.

"If it is, it will be light, or heavy, or none at all, as we shall bear it," David answered, with a smile of infinite tenderness.

For several days he allowed Jonathan to visit the Bradley farm alone, saying that it must be so on Ruth's account. Her love, he declared, must give her the fine instinct which only their mother had ever possessed, and he must allow it time to be confirmed. Jonathan, however, insisted that Ruth already possessed it; that she was beginning to wonder at his absence, and to fear that she would not be entirely welcome to the home which must always be equally his.

David yielded at once.

"You must go alone," said Jonathan, "to satisfy yourself that she knows us at last."

Ruth came forth from the house as he drew near. Her face beamed; she laid her hands upon his shoulders and kissed him. "Now you cannot doubt me, Ruth!" he said, gently.

"Doubt you, Jonathan!" she exclaimed with a fond reproach in her eyes. "But you look troubled; is any thing the matter?"

"I was thinking of my brother," said David, in a low tone.

"Tell me what it is," she said, drawing him into the little arbor of woodbine near the gate. They took seats side by side on the rustic bench. "He thinks I may come between you: is it not that?" she asked. Only one thing was clear to David's mind—that she would surely speak more frankly and freely of him to the supposed Jonathan than to his real self. This once he would permit the illusion.

"Not more than must be," he answered. "He knew all from the very

528

beginning. But we have been like one person in two bodies, and any change seems to divide us."

"I feel as you do," said Ruth. "I would never consent to be your wife, if I could really divide you. I love you both too well for that."

"Do you love me?" he asked, entirely forgetting his representative part.

Again the reproachful look, which faded away as she met his eyes. She fell upon his breast, and gave him kisses which were answered with equal tenderness. Suddenly he covered his face with his hands, and burst into a passion of tears.

"Jonathan! Oh Jonathan!" she cried, weeping with alarm and sympathetic pain.

It was long before he could speak; but at last, turning away his head, he faltered, "I am David!"

There was a long silence.

When he looked up she was sitting with her hands rigidly clasped in her lap: her face was very pale.

"There it is, Ruth," he said; "we are one heart and one soul. Could he love, and not I? You cannot decide between us, for one is the other. If I had known you first, Jonathan would be now in my place. What follows, then?"

"No marriage," she whispered.

"No!" he answered; "we brothers must learn to be two men instead of one. You will partly take my place with Jonathan; I must live with half my life, unless I can find, somewhere in the world, your other half."

"I cannot part you, David!"

"Something stronger than you or me parts us, Ruth. If it were death, we should bow to God's will: well, it can no more be got away from than death or judgment. Say no more: the pattern of all this was drawn long before we were born, and we cannot do any thing but work it out."

He rose and stood before her. "Remember this, Ruth," he said; "it is no blame in us to love each other. Jonathan will see the truth in my face when we meet, and I speak for him also. You will not see me again until your wedding-day, and then no more afterwards—but, yes! ONCE, in some far-off time, when you shall know me to be David, and still give me the kiss you gave to-day."

"Ah, after death!" she thought: "I have parted them forever." She was about to rise, but fell upon the seat again, fainting. At the same moment Jonathan appeared at David's side.

No word was said. They bore her forth and supported her between them until the fresh breeze had restored her to consciousness. Her first glance rested on the brother's hands, clasping; then, looking from one to the other, she saw that the cheeks of both were wet.

"Now, leave me," she said, "but come to-morrow, Jonathan!" Even then she turned from one to the other, with a painful, touching uncertainty, and stretched out both hands to them in farewell.

How that poor twin heart struggled with itself is only known to God. All human voices, and as they believed, also the Divine Voice, commanded the division of their interwoven life. Submission would have seemed easier, could they have taken up equal and similar burdens; but David was unable to deny that his pack was overweighted. For the first time, their thoughts began to diverge.

At last David said: "For mother's sake, Jonathan, as we promised. She always called you HER child. And for Ruth's sake, and father's last advice: they all tell me what I must do."

It was like the struggle between will and desire, in the same nature, and none the less fierce or prolonged because the softer quality foresaw its ultimate surrender. Long after he felt the step to be inevitable, Jonathan sought to postpone it, but he was borne by all combined influences nearer and nearer to the time.

And now the wedding-day came. David was to leave home the same evening, after the family dinner under his father's roof. In the morning he said to Jonathan: "I shall not write until I feel that I have become other than now, but I shall always be here, in you, as you will be in me, everywhere. Whenever you want me, I shall know it; and I think I shall know when to return."

The hearts of all the people went out towards them as they stood together in the little village church. Both were calm, but very pale and abstracted in their expression, yet their marvellous likeness was still unchanged. Ruth's eyes were cast down so they could not be seen; she trembled visibly, and her voice was scarcely audible when she spoke the vow. It was only known in the neighborhood that David was going to make another journey. The truth could hardly have been guessed by persons whose ideas follow the narrow round of their own experiences; had it been, there would probably have been more condemnation than sympathy. But in a vague way the presence of some deeper element was felt—the falling of a shadow, although the outstretched wing was unseen. Far above them, and above the shadow, watched the Infinite Pity, which was not denied to three hearts that day.

It was a long time, more than a year, and Ruth was lulling her first child on her bosom, before a letter came from David. He had wandered westwards, purchased some lands on the outer line of settlement, and appeared to be leading a wild and lonely life. "I know now," he wrote, "just how much there is to bear, and how to bear it. Strange men come between us, but you are not far off when I am alone on these plains. There is a place where I can always meet you, and I know that you have found it,—under the big ash-tree by the barn. I think I am nearly always there about sundown, and on moonshiny nights, because we are then nearest together; and I never sleep without leaving you half my blanket. When I first begin to wake I always feel your breath, so we are never really parted for long. I do not know that I can change much; it is not easy; it is like making up your mind to have different colored eyes and hair, and I can only get sunburnt and wear a full beard. But we are hardly as unhappy as we feared to be; mother came the other night, in a dream, and took us on her knees. Oh, come to me, Jonathan, but for one day! No, you will not find me; I am going across the Plains!"

And Jonathan and Ruth? They loved each other tenderly; no external trouble visited them; their home was peaceful and pure; and yet, every room and stairway and chair was haunted by a sorrowful ghost. As a neighbor said after visiting them, "There seemed to be something lost." Ruth saw how constantly and how unconsciously Jonathan turned to see his own every feeling reflected in the missing eyes; how his hand sought another, even while its fellow pressed hers; how half-spoken words, day and night, died upon his lips, because they could not reach the twin-ear. She knew not how it came, but her own nature took upon itself the same habit. She felt that she received a less measure of love than she gave—not from Jonathan, in whose whole, warm, transparent heart no other woman had ever looked, but something of her own passed beyond him and never returned. To both their life was like one of those conjurer's cups, seemingly filled with red wine, which is held from the lips by the false crystal hollow.

Neither spoke of this: neither dared to speak. The years dragged out their slow length, with rare and brief messages from David. Three children were in the house, and still peace and plenty laid their signs upon its lintels. But at last Ruth, who had been growing thinner and paler ever since the birth of her first boy, became seriously ill. Consumption was hers by inheritance, and it now manifested itself in a form which too surely foretold the result. After the physician had gone, leaving his fatal verdict behind him, she called to Jonathan, who, bewildered by his grief, sank down on his knees at her bedside and sobbed upon her breast.

"Don't grieve," she said; "this is my share of the burden. If I have taken too much from you and David, now comes the atonement. Many things have grown clear to me. David was right when he said that there was no blame. But my time is even less than the doctor thinks: where is David? Can you not bid him come?"

"I can only call him with my heart," he answered. "And will he hear me now, after nearly seven years?"

"Call, then!" she eagerly cried. "Call with all the strength of your love for him and for me, and I believe he will hear you!"

The sun was just setting. Jonathan went to the great ash-tree, behind the barn, fell upon his knees, and covered his face, and the sense of an exceeding bitter cry filled his heart. All the suppressed and baffled longing, the want, the hunger, the unremitting pain of years, came upon him and were crowded into the single prayer, "Come, David, or I die!" Before the twilight faded, while he was still kneeling, an arm came upon his shoulder, and the faint touch of another cheek upon his own. It was hardly for the space of a thought, but he knew the sign.

"David will come!" he said to Ruth.

From that day all was changed. The cloud of coming death which hung over the house was transmuted into fleecy gold. All the lost life came back to Jonathan's face, all the unrestful sweetness of Ruth's brightened into a serene beatitude. Months had passed since David had been heard from; they knew not how to reach him without many delays; yet neither dreamed of doubting his coming.

Two weeks passed, three, and there was neither word nor sign. Jonathan and Ruth thought, "He is near," and one day a singular unrest fell upon the former. Ruth saw it, but said nothing until night came, when she sent Jonathan from her bedside with the words, "Go and meet him?"

An hour afterwards she heard double steps on the stone walk in front of the house. They came slowly to the door; it opened; she heard them along the hall and ascending the stairs; then the chamber-lamp showed her the two faces, bright with a single, unutterable joy.

One brother paused at the foot of the bed; the other drew near and bent over her. She clasped her thin hands around his neck, kissed him fondly, and cried, "Dear, dear David!"

"Dear Ruth," he said, "I came as soon as I could. I was far away, among wild mountains, when I felt that Jonathan was calling me. I knew that I must return, never to leave you more, and there was still a little work to finish. Now we shall all live again!"

"Yes," said Jonathan, coming to her other side, "try to live, Ruth!"

Her voice came clear, strong, and full of authority. "I DO live, as never before. I shall take all my life with me when I go to wait for one soul, as I shall find it there! Our love unites, not divides, from this hour!"

The few weeks still left to her were a season of almost superhuman peace. She faded slowly and painlessly, taking the equal love of the twin-hearts, and giving an equal tenderness and gratitude. Then first she saw the mysterious need which united them, the fulness and joy wherewith each completed himself in the other. All the imperfect past was enlightened, and the end, even that now so near, was very good.

Every afternoon they carried her down to a cushioned chair on the veranda, where she could enjoy the quiet of the sunny landscape, the presence of the brothers seated at her feet, and the sports of her children on the grass. Thus, one day, while David and Jonathan held her hands and waited for her to wake from a happy sleep, she went before them, and, ere they guessed the truth, she was waiting for their one soul in the undiscovered land.

And Jonathan's children, now growing into manhood and girlhood, also call David "father." The marks left by their divided lives have long since vanished from their faces; the middle-aged men, whose hairs are turning gray, still walk hand in hand, still sleep upon the same pillow, still have their common wardrobe, as when they were boys. They talk of "our Ruth" with no sadness, for they believe that death will make them one, when, at the same moment, he summons both. And we who know them, to whom they have confided the touching mystery of their nature, believe so too.

# THE EXPERIENCES OF THE A. C.

"Bridgeport! Change cars for the Naugatuck Railroad!" shouted the conductor of the New York and Boston Express Train, on the evening of May 27th, 1858. Indeed, he does it every night (Sundays excepted), for that matter; but as this story refers especially to Mr. J. Edward Johnson, who was a passenger on that train, on the aforesaid evening, I make special mention of the fact. Mr. Johnson, carpet-bag in hand, jumped upon the platform, entered the office, purchased a ticket for Waterbury, and was soon whirling in the Naugatuck train towards his destination.

On reaching Waterbury, in the soft spring twilight, Mr. Johnson walked up and down in front of the station, curiously scanning the faces of the assembled crowd. Presently he noticed a gentleman who was performing the same operation upon the faces of the alighting passengers. Throwing himself directly in the way of the latter, the two exchanged a steady gaze.

"Is your name Billings?" "Is your name Johnson?" were simultaneous questions, followed by the simultaneous exclamations—"Ned!" "Enos!"

Then there was a crushing grasp of hands, repeated after a pause, in testimony of ancient friendship, and Mr. Billings, returning to practical life, asked—

"Is that all your baggage? Come, I have a buggy here: Eunice has heard the whistle, and she'll be impatient to welcome you."

The impatience of Eunice (Mrs. Billings, of course,) was not of long duration, for in five minutes thereafter she stood at the door of her husband's chocolate-colored villa, receiving his friend.

While these three persons are comfortably seated at the tea-table, enjoying their waffles, cold tongue, and canned peaches, and asking and answering questions helter-skelter in the delightful confusion of reunion after long separation, let us briefly inform the reader who and what they are.

Mr. Enos Billings, then, was part owner of a manufactory of metal buttons, forty years old, of middling height, ordinarily quiet and rather shy, but with a large share of latent warmth and enthusiasm in his nature. His hair was brown, slightly streaked with gray, his eyes a soft, dark hazel, forehead square, eyebrows straight, nose of no very marked character, and a mouth moderately full, with a tendency to twitch a little at the corners. His voice was undertoned, but mellow and agreeable.

Mrs. Eunice Billings, of nearly equal age, was a good specimen of the wide-awake New-England woman. Her face had a piquant smartness of expression, which might have been refined into a sharp edge, but for her natural hearty good-humor. Her head was smoothly formed, her face a full oval, her hair and eyes blond and blue in a strong light, but brown and steel-gray at other times, and her complexion of that ripe fairness into which a ruddier color will sometimes fade. Her form, neither plump nor square, had yet a firm, elastic compactness, and her slightest movement conveyed a certain impression of decision and self-reliance.

As for J. Edward Johnson, it is enough to say that he was a tall, thin gentleman of forty-five, with an aquiline nose, narrow face, and military whiskers, which swooped upwards and met under his nose in a glossy black mustache. His complexion was dark, from the bronzing of fifteen summers in New Orleans. He was a member of a wholesale hardware firm in that city, and had now revisited his native North for the first time since his departure. A year before, some letters relating to invoices of metal buttons signed, "Foster, Kirkup, & Co., per Enos Billings," had accidentally revealed to him the whereabouts of the old friend of his youth, with whom we now find him domiciled. The first thing he did, after attending to some necessary business matters in New York, was to take the train for Waterbury.

"Enos," said he, as he stretched out his hand for the third cup of tea (which he had taken only for the purpose of prolonging the pleasant table-chat), "I wonder which of us is most changed."

"You, of course," said Mr. Billings, "with your brown face and big mustache. Your own brother wouldn't have known you if he had seen you

536

last, as I did, with smooth cheeks and hair of unmerciful length. Why, not even your voice is the same!"

"That is easily accounted for," replied Mr. Johnson. "But in your case, Enos, I am puzzled to find where the difference lies. Your features seem to be but little changed, now that I can examine them at leisure; yet it is not the same face. But, really, I never looked at you for so long a time, in those days. I beg pardon; you used to be so—so remarkably shy."

Mr. Billings blushed slightly, and seemed at a loss what to answer.

His wife, however, burst into a merry laugh, exclaiming—

"Oh, that was before the days of the A. C.!"

He, catching the infection, laughed also; in fact Mr. Johnson laughed, but without knowing why.

"The 'A. C.'!" said Mr. Billings. "Bless me, Eunice! how long it is since we have talked of that summer! I had almost forgotten that there ever was an A. C."

"Enos, COULD you ever forget Abel Mallory and the beer?—or that scene between Hollins and Shelldrake?—or" (here SHE blushed the least bit) "your own fit of candor?" And she laughed again, more heartily than ever.

"What a precious lot of fools, to be sure!" exclaimed her husband.

Mr. Johnson, meanwhile, though enjoying the cheerful humor of his hosts, was not a little puzzled with regard to its cause.

"What is the A. C.?" he ventured to ask.

Mr. and Mrs. Billings looked at each other, and smiled without replying.

"Really, Ned," said the former, finally, "the answer to your question involves the whole story."

"Then why not tell him the whole story, Enos?" remarked his wife.

"You know I've never told it yet, and it's rather a hard thing to do, seeing that I'm one of the heroes of the farce—for it wasn't even genteel comedy, Ned," said Mr. Billings. "However," he continued, "absurd as the story may seem, it's the only key to the change in my life, and I must run the risk of being laughed at."

"I'll help you through, Enos," said his wife, encouragingly; "and besides, my role in the farce was no better than yours. Let us resuscitate, for to-night only, the constitution of the A. C."

"Upon my word, a capital idea! But we shall have to initiate Ned."

Mr. Johnson merrily agreeing, he was blindfolded and conducted into another room. A heavy arm-chair, rolling on casters, struck his legs in the rear, and he sank into it with lamb-like resignation.

"Open your mouth!" was the command, given with mock solemnity.

He obeyed.

"Now shut it!"

And his lips closed upon a cigar, while at the same time the handkerchief was whisked away from his eyes. He found himself in Mr. Billing's library.

"Your nose betrays your taste, Mr. Johnson," said the lady, "and I am not hard-hearted enough to deprive you of the indulgence. Here are matches."

"Well," said he, acting upon the hint, "if the remainder of the ceremonies are equally agreeable, I should like to be a permanent member of your order."

By this time Mr. and Mrs. Billings, having between them lighted the lamp, stirred up the coal in the grate, closed the doors, and taken possession of comfortable chairs, the latter proclaimed—

"The Chapter (isn't that what you call it?) will now be held!"

"Was it in '43 when you left home, Ned?" asked Mr. B.

"Yes."

"Well, the A. C. culminated in '45. You remember something of the society of Norridgeport, the last winter you were there? Abel Mallory, for instance?"

"Let me think a moment," said Mr. Johnson reflectively. "Really, it seems like looking back a hundred years. Mallory—wasn't that the sentimental young man, with wispy hair, a tallowy skin, and big, sweaty hands, who used to be spouting Carlyle on the 'reading evenings' at Shelldrake's? Yes, to be sure; and there was Hollins, with his clerical face and infidel talk,—and Pauline Ringtop, who used to say, 'The Beautiful is the Good.' I can still hear her shrill voice, singing, 'Would that I were beautiful, would that I were fair!'"

There was a hearty chorus of laughter at poor Miss Ringtop's expense. It harmed no one, however; for the tar-weed was already thick over her Californian grave.

"Oh, I see," said Mr. Billings, "you still remember the absurdities of those days. In fact, I think you partially saw through them then. But I was younger, and far from being so clear-headed, and I looked upon those evenings at Shelldrake's as being equal, at least, to the symposia of Plato. Something in Mallory always repelled me. I detested the sight of his thick nose, with the flaring nostrils, and his coarse, half-formed lips, of the bluish color of raw corned-beef. But I looked upon these feelings as unreasonable prejudices, and strove to conquer them, seeing the admiration which he received from others. He was an oracle on the subject of 'Nature.' Having eaten nothing for two years, except Graham bread, vegetables without salt, and fruits, fresh or dried, he considered himself to have attained an antediluvian purity of health—or that he would attain it, so soon as two pimples on his left temple should have healed. These pimples he looked upon as the last feeble stand made by the pernicious juices left from the meat he had formerly eaten and the coffee he had drunk. His theory was, that through a body so purged and purified none but true and natural impulses could find access to the soul. Such, indeed, was the theory we all held. A Return to Nature was the near Millennium, the dawn of which we already beheld in the sky. To be sure there was a difference in our individual views as to how this should be achieved, but we were all agreed as to what the result should be.

"I can laugh over those days now, Ned; but they were really happy while they lasted. We were the salt of the earth; we were lifted above those grovelling instincts which we saw manifested in the lives of others. Each contributed his share of gas to inflate the painted balloon to which we all clung, in the expectation that it would presently soar with us to the stars. But it only went up over the out-houses, dodged backwards and forwards two or three times, and finally flopped down with us into a swamp."

"And that balloon was the A. C.?" suggested Mr. Johnson.

"As President of this Chapter, I prohibit questions," said Eunice. "And, Enos, don't send up your balloon until the proper time. Don't anticipate the programme, or the performance will be spoiled."

"I had almost forgotten that Ned is so much in the dark," her obedient husband answered. "You can have but a slight notion," he continued, turning to his friend, "of the extent to which this sentimental, or transcendental, element in the little circle at Shelldrake's increased after you left Norridgeport. We read the 'Dial,' and Emerson; we believed in Alcott as the 'purple Plato' of modern times; we took psychological works out of the library, and would listen for hours to Hollins while he read Schelling or Fichte, and then go home with a misty impression of having imbibed infinite wisdom. It was, perhaps, a natural, though very eccentric rebound from the hard, practical, unimaginative New-England mind which surrounded us; yet I look back upon it with a kind of wonder. I was then, as you know, unformed mentally, and might have been so still, but for the experiences of the A. C."

Mr. Johnson shifted his position, a little impatiently. Eunice looked at him with laughing eyes, and shook her finger with a mock threat.

"Shelldrake," continued Mr. Billings, without noticing this by-play, "was a man of more pretence than real cultivation, as I afterwards discovered. He was in good circumstances, and always glad to receive us at his house, as this made him, virtually, the chief of our tribe, and the outlay for refreshments involved only the apples from his own orchard and water from his well. There was an entire absence of conventionality at our meetings, and this, compared with the somewhat stiff society of the village, was really an attraction. There was a mystic bond of union in our ideas: we discussed life, love, religion,

540

and the future state, not only with the utmost candor, but with a warmth of feeling which, in many of us, was genuine. Even I (and you know how painfully shy and bashful I was) felt myself more at home there than in my father's house; and if I didn't talk much, I had a pleasant feeling of being in harmony with those who did.

"Well, 'twas in the early part of '45—I think in April,—when we were all gathered together, discussing, as usual, the possibility of leading a life in accordance with Nature. Abel Mallory was there, and Hollins, and Miss Ringtop, and Faith Levis, with her knitting,—and also Eunice Hazleton, a lady whom you have never seen, but you may take my wife at her representative—"

"Stick to the programme, Enos," interrupted Mrs. Billings.

"Eunice Hazleton, then. I wish I could recollect some of the speeches made on that occasion. Abel had but one pimple on his temple (there was a purple spot where the other had been), and was estimating that in two or three months more he would be a true, unspoiled man. His complexion, nevertheless, was more clammy and whey-like than ever.

"'Yes,' said he, 'I also am an Arcadian! This false dual existence which I have been leading will soon be merged in the unity of Nature. Our lives must conform to her sacred law. Why can't we strip off these hollow Shams,' (he made great use of that word,) 'and be our true selves, pure, perfect, and divine?'

"Miss Ringtop heaved a sigh, and repeated a stanza from her favorite poet:

> "*Ah, when wrecked are my desires*
>
> *On the everlasting Never,*
>
> *And my heart with all its fires*
>
> *Out forever,*
>
> *In the cradle of Creation*
>
> *Finds the soul resuscitation!*

"Shelldrake, however, turning to his wife, said—

"'Elviry, how many up-stairs rooms is there in that house down on the Sound?'

"'Four,—besides three small ones under the roof. Why, what made you think of that, Jesse?' said she.

"'I've got an idea, while Abel's been talking,' he answered. 'We've taken a house for the summer, down the other side of Bridgeport, right on the water, where there's good fishing and a fine view of the Sound. Now, there's room enough for all of us—at least all that can make it suit to go. Abel, you and Enos, and Pauline and Eunice might fix matters so that we could all take the place in partnership, and pass the summer together, living a true and beautiful life in the bosom of Nature. There we shall be perfectly free and untrammelled by the chains which still hang around us in Norridgeport. You know how often we have wanted to be set on some island in the Pacific Ocean, where we could build up a true society, right from the start. Now, here's a chance to try the experiment for a few months, anyhow.'

"Eunice clapped her hands (yes, you did!) and cried out—

"'Splendid! Arcadian! I'll give up my school for the summer.'

"Miss Ringtop gave her opinion in another quotation:

"'*The rainbow hues of the Ideal*

*Condense to gems, and form the Real!*'

"Abel Mallory, of course, did not need to have the proposal repeated. He was ready for any thing which promised indulgence, and the indulgence of his sentimental tastes. I will do the fellow the justice to say that he was not a hypocrite. He firmly believed both in himself and his ideas—especially the former. He pushed both hands through the long wisps of his drab-colored hair, and threw his head back until his wide nostrils resembled a double door to his brain.

"'Oh Nature!' he said, 'you have found your lost children! We shall

542

obey your neglected laws! we shall hearken to your divine whispers I we shall bring you back from your ignominious exile, and place you on your ancestral throne!'

"'Let us do it!' was the general cry.

"A sudden enthusiasm fired us, and we grasped each other's hands in the hearty impulse of the moment. My own private intention to make a summer trip to the White Mountains had been relinquished the moment I heard Eunice give in her adhesion. I may as well confess, at once, that I was desperately in love, and afraid to speak to her.

"By the time Mrs. Sheldrake brought in the apples and water we were discussing the plan as a settled thing. Hollins had an engagement to deliver Temperance lectures in Ohio during the summer, but decided to postpone his departure until August, so that he might, at least, spend two months with us. Faith Levis couldn't go—at which, I think, we were all secretly glad. Some three or four others were in the same case, and the company was finally arranged to consist of the Shelldrakes, Hollins, Mallory, Eunice, Miss Ringtop, and myself. We did not give much thought, either to the preparations in advance, or to our mode of life when settled there. We were to live near to Nature: that was the main thing.

"'What shall we call the place?' asked Eunice.

"'Arcadia!' said Abel Mallory, rolling up his large green eyes.

"'Then,' said Hollins, 'let us constitute ourselves the Arcadian Club!'"

"Aha!" interrupted Mr. Johnson, "I see! The A. C.!"

"Yes, you can see the A. C. now," said Mrs. Billings; "but to understand it fully, you should have had a share in those Arcadian experiences."

"I am all the more interested in hearing them described. Go on, Enos."

"The proposition was adopted. We called ourselves The Arcadian Club; but in order to avoid gossip, and the usual ridicule, to which we were all more or less sensitive, in case our plan should become generally known, it was agreed that the initials only should be used. Besides, there was an agreeable air of mystery about it: we thought of Delphi, and Eleusis, and Samothrace: we should discover that Truth which the dim eyes of worldly men and women were unable to see, and the day of disclosure would be the day of Triumph. In one sense we were truly Arcadians: no suspicion of impropriety, I verily believe, entered any of our minds. In our aspirations after what we called a truer life there was no material taint. We were fools, if you choose, but as far as possible from being sinners. Besides, the characters of Mr. and Mrs. Shelldrake, who naturally became the heads of our proposed community were sufficient to preserve us from slander or suspicion, if even our designs had been publicly announced.

"I won't bore you with an account of our preparations. In fact, there was very little to be done. Mr. Shelldrake succeeded in hiring the house, with most of its furniture, so that but a few articles had to be supplied. My trunk contained more books than boots, more blank paper than linen.

"'Two shirts will be enough,' said Abel: 'you can wash one of them any day, and dry it in the sun.'

"The supplies consisted mostly of flour, potatoes, and sugar. There was a vegetable-garden in good condition, Mr. Shelldrake said, which would be our principal dependence.

"'Besides, the clams!' I exclaimed unthinkingly.

"'Oh, yes!' said Eunice, 'we can have chowder-parties: that will be delightful!'

"'Clams! chowder! oh, worse than flesh!' groaned Abel. 'Will you reverence Nature by outraging her first laws?'

"I had made a great mistake, and felt very foolish. Eunice and I looked at each other, for the first time."

"Speak for yourself only, Enos," gently interpolated his wife.

"It was a lovely afternoon in the beginning of June when we first approached Arcadia. We had taken two double teams at Bridgeport, and drove slowly forward to our destination, followed by a cart containing our trunks and a few household articles. It was a bright, balmy day: the wheat-fields were rich and green, the clover showed faint streaks of ruby mist along slopes leaning southward, and the meadows were yellow with buttercups. Now and then we caught glimpses of the Sound, and, far beyond it, the dim Long Island shore. Every old white farmhouse, with its gray-walled garden, its clumps of lilacs, viburnums, and early roses, offered us a picture of pastoral simplicity and repose. We passed them, one by one, in the happiest mood, enjoying the earth around us, the sky above, and ourselves most of all.

"The scenery, however, gradually became more rough and broken. Knobs of gray gneiss, crowned by mournful cedars, intrenched upon the arable land, and the dark-blue gleam of water appeared through the trees. Our road, which had been approaching the Sound, now skirted the head of a deep, irregular inlet, beyond which extended a beautiful promontory, thickly studded with cedars, and with scattering groups of elm, oak and maple trees. Towards the end of the promontory stood a house, with white walls shining against the blue line of the Sound.

"'There is Arcadia, at last!' exclaimed Mr. Shelldrake.

"A general outcry of delight greeted the announcement. And, indeed, the loveliness of the picture surpassed our most poetic anticipations. The low sun was throwing exquisite lights across the point, painting the slopes of grass of golden green, and giving a pearly softness to the gray rocks. In the back-ground was drawn the far-off water-line, over which a few specks of sail glimmered against the sky. Miss Ringtop, who, with Eunice, Mallory, and myself, occupied one carriage, expressed her 'gushing' feelings in the usual manner:

> "*Where the turf is softest, greenest,*
>
> *Doth an angel thrust me on,—*
>
> *Where the landscape lies serenest,*
>
> *In the journey of the sun!'*

"'Don't, Pauline!' said Eunice; 'I never like to hear poetry flourished in the face of Nature. This landscape surpasses any poem in the world. Let us enjoy the best thing we have, rather than the next best.'

"'Ah, yes!' sighed Miss Ringtop, ''tis true!

"*'They sing to the ear; this sings to the eye!'*

"Thenceforward, to the house, all was childish joy and jubilee. All minor personal repugnances were smoothed over in the general exultation. Even Abel Mallory became agreeable; and Hollins, sitting beside Mrs. Shelldrake on the back seat of the foremost carriage, shouted to us, in boyish lightness of heart.

"Passing the head of the inlet, we left the country-road, and entered, through a gate in the tottering stone wall, on our summer domain. A track, open to the field on one side, led us past a clump of deciduous trees, between pastures broken by cedared knolls of rock, down the centre of the peninsula, to the house. It was quite an old frame-building, two stories high, with a gambrel roof and tall chimneys. Two slim Lombardy poplars and a broad-leaved catalpa shaded the southern side, and a kitchen-garden, divided in the centre by a double row of untrimmed currant-bushes, flanked it on the east. For flowers, there were masses of blue flags and coarse tawny-red lilies, besides a huge trumpet-vine which swung its pendent arms from one of the gables. In front of the house a natural lawn of mingled turf and rock sloped steeply down to the water, which was not more than two hundred yards distant. To the west was another and broader inlet of the Sound, out of which our Arcadian promontory rose bluff and bold, crowned with a thick fringe of pines. It was really a lovely spot which Shelldrake had chosen—so secluded, while almost surrounded by the winged and moving life of the Sound, so simple, so pastoral and home-like. No one doubted the success of our experiment, for that evening at least.

"Perkins Brown, Shelldrake's boy-of-all-work, awaited us at the door. He had been sent on two or three days in advance, to take charge of the house, and seemed to have had enough of hermit-life, for he hailed us with a wild whoop, throwing his straw hat half-way up one of the poplars. Perkins was a boy of fifteen, the child of poor parents, who were satisfied to get him off their hands, regardless as to what humanitarian theories might be tested upon him. As the Arcadian Club recognized no such thing as caste, he was always admitted to our meetings, and understood just enough of our conversation to excite a silly ambition in his slow mind. His animal nature was predominant, and this led him to be deceitful. At that time, however, we all looked upon him as a proper young Arcadian, and hoped that he would develop into a second Abel Mallory.

"After our effects had been deposited on the stoop, and the carriages had driven away, we proceeded to apportion the rooms, and take possession. On the first floor there were three rooms, two of which would serve us as dining and drawing rooms, leaving the third for the Shelldrakes. As neither Eunice and Miss Ringtop, nor Hollins and Abel showed any disposition to room together, I quietly gave up to them the four rooms in the second story, and installed myself in one of the attic chambers. Here I could hear the music of the rain close above my head, and through the little gable window, as I lay in bed, watch the colors of the morning gradually steal over the distant shores. The end was, we were all satisfied.

"'Now for our first meal in Arcadia!' was the next cry. Mrs. Shelldrake, like a prudent housekeeper, marched off to the kitchen, where Perkins had already kindled a fire. We looked in at the door, but thought it best to allow her undisputed sway in such a narrow realm. Eunice was unpacking some loaves of bread and paper bags of crackers; and Miss Ringtop, smiling through her ropy curls, as much as to say, 'You see, I also can perform the coarser tasks of life!' occupied herself with plates and cups. We men, therefore, walked out to the garden, which we found in a promising condition. The usual vegetables had been planted and were growing finely, for the season was yet scarcely warm enough for the weeds to make much headway. Radishes, young onions, and lettuce formed our contribution to the table. The Shelldrakes, I should explain, had not yet advanced to the antediluvian point, in diet: nor, indeed, had either Eunice or myself. We acknowledged the fascination of tea, we saw a very mitigated evil in milk and butter, and we were conscious of stifled longings after the abomination of meat. Only Mallory, Hollins, and Miss Ringtop had reached that loftiest round on the ladder of progress where the material nature loosens the last fetter of the spiritual. They looked down upon us, and we meekly admitted their right to do so.

"Our board, that evening, was really tempting. The absence of meat was compensated to us by the crisp and racy onions, and I craved only a little salt, which had been interdicted, as a most pernicious substance. I sat at one corner of the table, beside Perkins Brown, who took an opportunity, while the others were engaged in conversation, to jog my elbow gently. As I turned towards him, he said nothing, but dropped his eyes significantly. The little rascal had the lid of a blacking-box, filled with salt, upon his knee, and was privately seasoning his onions and radishes.

I blushed at the thought of my hypocrisy, but the onions were so much better that I couldn't help dipping into the lid with him.

"'Oh,' said Eunice, 'we must send for some oil and vinegar! This lettuce is very nice.'

"'Oil and vinegar?' exclaimed Abel.

"'Why, yes,' said she, innocently: 'they are both vegetable substances.'

"Abel at first looked rather foolish, but quickly recovering himself, said—

"'All vegetable substances are not proper for food: you would not taste the poison-oak, or sit under the upas-tree of Java.'

"'Well, Abel,' Eunice rejoined, 'how are we to distinguish what is best for us? How are we to know WHAT vegetables to choose, or what animal and mineral substances to avoid?'

"'I will tell you,' he answered, with a lofty air. 'See here!' pointing to his temple, where the second pimple—either from the change of air, or because, in the excitement of the last few days, he had forgotten it—was actually healed. 'My blood is at last pure. The struggle between the natural and the unnatural is over, and I am beyond the depraved influences of my former taste. My instincts are now, therefore, entirely pure also. What is good for man to eat, that I shall have a natural desire to eat: what is bad will be naturally repelled.

How does the cow distinguish between the wholesome and the poisonous herbs of the meadow? And is man less than a cow, that he cannot cultivate his instincts to an equal point? Let me walk through the woods and I can tell you every berry and root which God designed for food, though I know not its name, and have never seen it before. I shall make use of my time, during our sojourn here, to test, by my purified instinct, every substance, animal, mineral, and vegetable, upon which the human race subsists, and to create a catalogue of the True Food of Man!'

"Abel was eloquent on this theme, and he silenced not only Eunice, but the rest of us. Indeed, as we were all half infected with the same delusions, it was not easy to answer his sophistries.

"After supper was over, the prospect of cleaning the dishes and putting things in order was not so agreeable; but Mrs. Shelldrake and Perkins undertook the work, and we did not think it necessary to interfere with them. Half an hour afterwards, when the full moon had risen, we took our chairs upon the sloop, to enjoy the calm, silver night, the soft sea-air, and our summer's residence in anticipatory talk.

"'My friends,' said Hollins (and HIS hobby, as you may remember, Ned, was the organization of Society, rather than those reforms which apply directly to the Individual),—'my friends, I think we are sufficiently advanced in progressive ideas to establish our little Arcadian community upon what I consider the true basis: not Law, nor Custom, but the uncorrupted impulses of our nature. What Abel said in regard to dietetic reform is true; but that alone will not regenerate the race. We must rise superior to those conventional ideas of Duty whereby Life is warped and crippled. Life must not be a prison, where each one must come and go, work, eat, and sleep, as the jailer commands. Labor must not be a necessity, but a spontaneous joy. 'Tis true, but little labor is required of us here: let us, therefore, have no set tasks, no fixed rules, but each one work, rest, eat, sleep, talk or be silent, as his own nature prompts.'

"Perkins, sitting on the steps, gave a suppressed chuckle, which I think no one heard but myself. I was vexed with his levity, but, nevertheless, gave him a warning nudge with my toe, in payment for the surreptitious salt.

"'That's just the notion I had, when I first talked of our coming here,' said Shelldrake. 'Here we're alone and unhindered; and if the plan shouldn't happen to work well (I don't see why it shouldn't though), no harm will be done. I've had a deal of hard work in my life, and I've been badgered and bullied so much by your strait-laced professors, that I'm glad to get away from the world for a spell, and talk and do rationally, without being laughed at.'

"'Yes,' answered Hollins, 'and if we succeed, as I feel we shall, for I think I know the hearts of all of us here, this may be the commencement of a new Epoch for the world. We may become the turning-point between two dispensations: behind us every thing false and unnatural, before us every thing true, beautiful, and good.'

"'Ah,' sighed Miss Ringtop, 'it reminds me of Gamaliel J. Gawthrop's beautiful lines:

"*Unrobed man is lying hoary*

*In the distance, gray and dead;*

*There no wreaths of godless glory*

*To his mist-like tresses wed,*

*And the foot-fall of the Ages*

*Reigns supreme, with noiseless tread.'*

"'I am willing to try the experiment,' said I, on being appealed to by Hollins; 'but don't you think we had better observe some kind of order, even in yielding every thing to impulse? Shouldn't there be, at least, a platform, as the politicians call it—an agreement by which we shall all be bound, and which we can afterwards exhibit as the basis of our success?'

"He meditated a few moments, and then answered—

"'I think not. It resembles too much the thing we are trying to overthrow. Can you bind a man's belief by making him sign certain articles of Faith? No: his thought will be free, in spite of it; and I would have Action—Life—as free as Thought. Our platform—to adopt your image—has but one plank: Truth.

Let each only be true to himself: BE himself, ACT himself, or herself with the uttermost candor. We can all agree upon that.'

"The agreement was accordingly made. And certainly no happier or more hopeful human beings went to bed in all New England that night.

"I arose with the sun, went into the garden, and commenced weeding, intending to do my quota of work before breakfast, and then devote the day to reading and conversation. I was presently joined by Shelldrake and Mallory, and between us we finished the onions and radishes, stuck the peas, and cleaned the alleys. Perkins, after milking the cow and turning her out to pasture, assisted Mrs. Shelldrake in the kitchen. At breakfast we were joined by Hollins, who made no excuse for his easy morning habits; nor was one expected. I may as well tell you now, though, that his natural instincts never led him to work. After a week, when a second crop of weeds was coming on, Mallory fell off also, and thenceforth Shelldrake and myself had the entire charge of the garden. Perkins did the rougher work, and was always on hand when he was wanted. Very soon, however, I noticed that he was in the habit of disappearing for two or three hours in the afternoon.

"Our meals preserved the same Spartan simplicity. Eunice, however, carried her point in regard to the salad; for Abel, after tasting and finding it very palatable, decided that oil and vinegar might be classed in the catalogue of True Food. Indeed, his long abstinence from piquant flavors gave him such an appetite for it that our supply of lettuce was soon exhausted. An embarrassing accident also favored us with the use of salt. Perkins happening to move his knee at the moment I was dipping an onion into the blacking-box lid, our supply was knocked upon the floor. He picked it up, and we both hoped the accident might pass unnoticed. But Abel, stretching his long neck across the corner of the table, caught a glimpse of what was going on.

"'What's that?' he asked.

"'Oh, it's—it's only,' said I, seeking for a synonyme, 'only chloride of sodium!'

"'Chloride of sodium! what do you do with it?'

"'Eat it with onions,' said I, boldly: 'it's a chemical substance, but I believe it is found in some plants.'

"Eunice, who knew something of chemistry (she taught a class, though you wouldn't think it), grew red with suppressed fun, but the others were as ignorant as Abel Mallory himself.

"'Let me taste it,' said he, stretching out an onion.

"I handed him the box-lid, which still contained a portion of its contents. He dipped the onion, bit off a piece, and chewed it gravely.

"'Why,' said he, turning to me, 'it's very much like salt.'

"Perkins burst into a spluttering yell, which discharged an onion-top he had just put between his teeth across the table; Eunice and I gave way at the same moment; and the others, catching the joke, joined us. But while we were laughing, Abel was finishing his onion, and the result was that Salt was added to the True Food, and thereafter appeared regularly on the table.

"The forenoons we usually spent in reading and writing, each in his or her chamber. (Oh, the journals, Ned!—but you shall not see mine.) After a midday meal,—I cannot call it dinner,—we sat upon the stoop, listening while one of us read aloud, or strolled down the shores on either side, or, when the sun was not too warm, got into a boat, and rowed or floated lazily around the promontory.

"One afternoon, as I was sauntering off, past the garden, towards the eastern inlet, I noticed Perkins slipping along behind the cedar knobs, towards the little woodland at the end of our domain. Curious to find out the cause of his mysterious disappearances, I followed cautiously. From the edge of the wood I saw him enter a little gap between the rocks, which led down to the water. Presently a thread of blue smoke stole up. Quietly creeping along, I got upon the nearer bluff and looked down. There was a sort of hearth built up at the base of the rock, with a brisk little fire burning upon it, but Perkins had disappeared. I stretched myself out upon the moss, in the shade, and waited. In about half an hour up came Perkins, with a large fish in one hand and a lump of clay in the other. I now understood the mystery. He carefully imbedded the fish in a thin layer of clay, placed it on the coals, and then went down to the shore to wash his hands. On his return he found me watching the fire.

"'Ho, ho, Mr. Enos!' said he, 'you've found me out; But you won't say nothin'. Gosh! you like it as well I do. Look 'ee there!'—breaking open the clay, from which arose 'a steam of rich distilled perfumes,'—'and, I say, I've got the box-lid with that 'ere stuff in it,—ho! ho!'—and the scamp roared again.

"Out of a hole in the rock he brought salt and the end of a loaf, and between us we finished the fish. Before long, I got into the habit of disappearing in the afternoon.

"Now and then we took walks, alone or collectively, to the nearest village, or even to Bridgeport, for the papers or a late book. The few purchases we required were made at such times, and sent down in a cart, or, if not too heavy, carried by Perkins in a basket. I noticed that Abel, whenever we had occasion to visit a grocery, would go sniffing around, alternately attracted or repelled by the various articles: now turning away with a shudder from a ham,—now inhaling, with a fearful delight and uncertainty, the odor of smoked herrings. 'I think herrings must feed on sea-weed,' said he, 'there is such a vegetable attraction about them.' After his violent vegetarian harangues, however, he hesitated about adding them to his catalogue.

"But, one day, as we were passing through the village, he was reminded by the sign of 'WARTER CRACKERS' in the window of an obscure grocery that he required a supply of these articles, and we therefore entered. There was a splendid Rhode Island cheese on the counter, from which the shop-mistress was just cutting a slice for a customer. Abel leaned over it, inhaling the rich, pungent fragrance.

"'Enos,' said he to me, between his sniffs, 'this impresses me like flowers—like marigolds. It must be—really—yes, the vegetable element is predominant. My instinct towards it is so strong that I cannot be mistaken. May I taste it, ma'am?'

"The woman sliced off a thin corner, and presented it to him on the knife.

"'Delicious!' he exclaimed; 'I am right,—this is the True Food. Give me two pounds—and the crackers, ma'am.'

"I turned away, quite as much disgusted as amused with this charlatanism. And yet I verily believe the fellow was sincere—self-deluded only. I had by this time lost my faith in him, though not in the great Arcadian principles. On reaching home, after an hour's walk, I found our household in unusual commotion. Abel was writhing in intense pain: he had eaten the whole two pounds of cheese, on his way home! His stomach, so weakened by years of unhealthy abstinence from true nourishment, was now terribly tortured by this sudden stimulus. Mrs. Shelldrake, fortunately, had some mustard among her stores, and could therefore administer a timely emetic. His life was saved, but he was very ill for two or three days. Hollins did not fail to take advantage of this circumstance to overthrow the authority which Abel had gradually acquired on the subject of food. He was so arrogant in his nature that he could not tolerate the same quality in another, even where their views coincided.

"By this time several weeks had passed away. It was the beginning of July, and the long summer heats had come. I was driven out of my attic during the middle hours of the day, and the others found it pleasanter on the doubly shaded stoop than in their chambers. We were thus thrown more together than usual—a circumstance which made our life more monotonous to the others, as I could see; but to myself, who could at last talk to Eunice, and who was happy at the very sight of her, this 'heated term' seemed borrowed from Elysium.

"I read aloud, and the sound of my own voice gave me confidence; many passages suggested discussions, in which I took a part; and you may judge, Ned, how fast I got on, from the fact that I ventured to tell Eunice of my fish-bakes with Perkins, and invite her to join them. After that, she also often disappeared from sight for an hour or two in the afternoon."

——"Oh, Mr. Johnson," interrupted Mrs. Billings, "it wasn't for the fish!"

"Of course not," said her husband; "it was for my sake."

"No, you need not think it was for you. Enos," she added, perceiving the feminine dilemma into which she had been led, "all this is not necessary to the story."

"Stop!" he answered. "The A. C. has been revived for this night only. Do you remember our platform, or rather no-platform? I must follow my impulses, and say whatever comes uppermost."

"Right, Enos," said Mr. Johnson; "I, as temporary Arcadian, take the same ground. My instinct tells me that you, Mrs. Billings, must permit the confession."

She submitted with a good grace, and her husband continued:

"I said that our lazy life during the hot weather had become a little monotonous. The Arcadian plan had worked tolerably well, on the whole, for there was very little for any one to do—Mrs. Shelldrake and Perkins Brown excepted. Our conversation, however, lacked spirit and variety. We were, perhaps unconsciously, a little tired of hearing and assenting to the same sentiments. But one evening, about this time, Hollins struck upon a variation, the consequences of which he little foresaw. We had been reading one of Bulwer's works (the weather was too hot for Psychology), and came upon this paragraph, or something like it:

"'Ah, Behind the Veil! We see the summer smile of the Earth—enamelled meadow and limpid stream,—but what hides she in her sunless heart? Caverns of serpents, or grottoes of priceless gems? Youth, whose soul sits on thy countenance, thyself wearing no mask, strive not to lift the masks of others! Be content with what thou seest; and wait until Time and Experience shall teach thee to find jealousy behind the sweet smile, and hatred under the honeyed word!'

"This seemed to us a dark and bitter reflection; but one or another of us recalled some illustration of human hypocrisy, and the evidences, by the simple fact of repetition, gradually led to a division of opinion—Hollins, Shelldrake, and Miss Ringtop on the dark side, and the rest of us on the bright. The last, however, contented herself with quoting from her favorite poet, Gamaliel J. Gawthrop:

> *"I look beyond thy brow's concealment!*
>
> *I see thy spirit's dark revealment!*
>
> *Thy inner self betrayed I see:*
>
> *Thy coward, craven, shivering ME!'*

"'We think we know one another,' exclaimed Hollins; 'but do we? We see the faults of others, their weaknesses, their disagreeable qualities, and we keep silent. How much we should gain, were candor as universal as concealment! Then each one, seeing himself as others see him, would truly know himself. How much misunderstanding might be avoided—how much hidden shame be removed—hopeless, because unspoken, love made glad—honest admiration cheer its object—uttered sympathy mitigate misfortune—in short, how much brighter and happier the world would become if each one expressed, everywhere and at all times, his true and entire feeling! Why, even Evil would lose half its power!'

"There seemed to be so much practical wisdom in these views that we were all dazzled and half-convinced at the start. So, when Hollins, turning towards me, as he continued, exclaimed—'Come, why should not this candor be adopted in our Arcadia? Will any one—will you, Enos—commence at once by telling me now—to my face—my principal faults?' I answered after a moment's reflection—'You have a great deal of intellectual arrogance, and you are, physically, very indolent'

"He did not flinch from the self-invited test, though he looked a little surprised.

"'Well put,' said he, 'though I do not say that you are entirely correct. Now, what are my merits?'

"'You are clear-sighted,' I answered, 'an earnest seeker after truth, and courageous in the avowal of your thoughts.'

"This restored the balance, and we soon began to confess our own private

556

faults and weaknesses. Though the confessions did not go very deep,—no one betraying anything we did not all know already,—yet they were sufficient to strength Hollins in his new idea, and it was unanimously resolved that Candor should thenceforth be the main charm of our Arcadian life. It was the very thing I wanted, in order to make a certain communication to Eunice; but I should probably never have reached the point, had not the same candor been exercised towards me, from a quarter where I least expected it.

"The next day, Abel, who had resumed his researches after the True Food, came home to supper with a healthier color than I had before seen on his face.

"'Do you know,' said he, looking shyly at Hollins, 'that I begin to think Beer must be a natural beverage? There was an auction in the village to-day, as I passed through, and I stopped at a cake-stand to get a glass of water, as it was very hot. There was no water—only beer: so I thought I would try a glass, simply as an experiment. Really, the flavor was very agreeable. And it occurred to me, on the way home, that all the elements contained in beer are vegetable. Besides, fermentation is a natural process. I think the question has never been properly tested before.'

"'But the alcohol!' exclaimed Hollins.

"'I could not distinguish any, either by taste or smell. I know that chemical analysis is said to show it; but may not the alcohol be created, somehow, during the analysis?'

"'Abel,' said Hollins, in a fresh burst of candor, 'you will never be a Reformer, until you possess some of the commonest elements of knowledge.'

"The rest of us were much diverted: it was a pleasant relief to our monotonous amiability.

"Abel, however, had a stubborn streak in his character. The next day he sent Perkins Brown to Bridgeport for a dozen bottles of 'Beer.' Perkins, either intentionally or by mistake, (I always suspected the former,) brought pint-bottles of Scotch ale, which he placed in the coolest part of the cellar. The evening happened to be exceedingly hot and sultry, and, as we were all fanning ourselves and talking languidly, Abel bethought him of his beer. In his thirst, he drank the contents of the first bottle, almost at a single draught.

"'The effect of beer,' said he, 'depends, I think, on the commixture of the nourishing principle of the grain with the cooling properties of the water. Perhaps, hereafter, a liquid food of the same character may be invented, which shall save us from mastication and all the diseases of the teeth.'

"Hollins and Shelldrake, at his invitation, divided a bottle between them, and he took a second. The potent beverage was not long in acting on a brain so unaccustomed to its influence. He grew unusually talkative and sentimental, in a few minutes.

"'Oh, sing, somebody!' he sighed in a hoarse rapture: 'the night was made for Song.'

"Miss Ringtop, nothing loath, immediately commenced, 'When stars are in the quiet skies;' but scarcely had she finished the first verse before Abel interrupted her.

"'Candor's the order of the day, isn't it?' he asked.

"'Yes!' 'Yes!' two or three answered.

"'Well then,' said he, 'candidly, Pauline, you've got the darn'dest squeaky voice'—

"Miss Ringtop gave a faint little scream of horror.

"'Oh, never mind!' he continued. 'We act according to impulse, don't we? And I've the impulse to swear; and it's right. Let Nature have her way. Listen! Damn, damn, damn, damn! I never knew it was so easy. Why, there's a pleasure in it! Try it, Pauline! try it on me!'

"'Oh-ooh!' was all Miss Ringtop could utter.

"'Abel! Abel!' exclaimed Hollins, 'the beer has got into your head.'

"'No, it isn't Beer,—it's Candor!' said Abel. 'It's your own proposal, Hollins. Suppose it's evil to swear: isn't it better I should express it, and be done with it, than keep it bottled up to ferment in my mind? Oh, you're a precious, consistent old humbug, you are!'

"And therewith he jumped off the stoop, and went dancing awkwardly down towards the water, singing in a most unmelodious voice, ''Tis home where'er the heart is.'

"'Oh, he may fall into the water!' exclaimed Eunice, in alarm.

"'He's not fool enough to do that,' said Shelldrake. 'His head is a little light, that's all. The air will cool him down presently.'

"But she arose and followed him, not satisfied with this assurance. Miss Ringtop sat rigidly still. She would have received with composure the news of his drowning.

"As Eunice's white dress disappeared among the cedars crowning the shore, I sprang up and ran after her. I knew that Abel was not intoxicated, but simply excited, and I had no fear on his account: I obeyed an involuntary impulse. On approaching the water, I heard their voices—hers in friendly persuasion, his in sentimental entreaty,—then the sound of oars in the row-locks. Looking out from the last clump of cedars, I saw them seated in the boat, Eunice at the stern, while Abel, facing her, just dipped an oar now and then to keep from drifting with the tide. She had found him already in the boat, which was loosely chained to a stone. Stepping on one of the forward thwarts in her eagerness to persuade him to return, he sprang past her, jerked away the chain, and pushed off before she could escape. She would have fallen, but he caught her and placed her in the stern, and then seated himself at the oars. She must have been somewhat alarmed, but there was only indignation in her voice. All this had transpired before my arrival, and the first words I heard bound me to the spot and kept me silent.

"'Abel, what does this mean?' she asked

"'It means Fate—Destiny!' he exclaimed, rather wildly. 'Ah, Eunice, ask the night, and the moon,—ask the impulse which told you to follow me! Let us be candid like the old Arcadians we imitate. Eunice, we know that we love each other: why should we conceal it any longer? The Angel of Love comes down from the stars on his azure wings, and whispers to our hearts. Let us confess to each other! The female heart should not be timid, in this pure and beautiful atmosphere of Love which we breathe. Come, Eunice! we are alone: let your heart speak to me!'

"Ned, if you've ever been in love, (we'll talk of that after a while,) you will easily understand what tortures I endured, in thus hearing him speak. That HE should love Eunice! It was a profanation to her, an outrage to me. Yet the assurance with which he spoke! COULD she love this conceited, ridiculous, repulsive fellow, after all? I almost gasped for breath, as I clinched the prickly boughs of the cedars in my hands, and set my teeth, waiting to hear her answer.

"'I will not hear such language! Take me back to the shore!' she said, in very short, decided tones.

"'Oh, Eunice,' he groaned, (and now, I think he was perfectly sober,) 'don't you love me, indeed? I love you,—from my heart I do: yes, I love you. Tell me how you feel towards me.'

"'Abel,' said she, earnestly, 'I feel towards you only as a friend; and if you wish me to retain a friendly interest in you, you must never again talk in this manner. I do not love you, and I never shall. Let me go back to the house.'

"His head dropped upon his breast, but he rowed back to the shore, drew the bow upon the rocks, and assisted her to land. Then, sitting down, he groaned forth—

"'Oh, Eunice, you have broken my heart!' and putting his big hands to his face, began to cry.

"She turned, placed one hand on his shoulder, and said in a calm, but kind tone—

"'I am very sorry, Abel, but I cannot help it.'

"I slipped aside, that she might not see me, and we returned by separate paths.

"I slept very little that night. The conviction which I chased away from

560

my mind as often as it returned, that our Arcadian experiment was taking a ridiculous and at the same time impracticable development, became clearer and stronger. I felt sure that our little community could not hold together much longer without an explosion. I had a presentiment that Eunice shared my impressions. My feelings towards her had reached that crisis where a declaration was imperative: but how to make it? It was a terrible struggle between my shyness and my affection. There was another circumstance in connection with this subject, which troubled me not a little. Miss Ringtop evidently sought my company, and made me, as much as possible, the recipient of her sentimental outpourings. I was not bold enough to repel her—indeed I had none of that tact which is so useful in such emergencies,—and she seemed to misinterpret my submission. Not only was her conversation pointedly directed to me, but she looked at me, when singing, (especially, 'Thou, thou, reign'st in this bosom!') in a way that made me feel very uncomfortable. What if Eunice should suspect an attachment towards her, on my part. What if— oh, horror!—I had unconsciously said or done something to impress Miss Ringtop herself with the same conviction? I shuddered as the thought crossed my mind. One thing was very certain: this suspense was not to be endured much longer.

"We had an unusually silent breakfast the next morning. Abel scarcely spoke, which the others attributed to a natural feeling of shame, after his display of the previous evening. Hollins and Shelldrake discussed Temperance, with a special view to his edification, and Miss Ringtop favored us with several quotations about 'the maddening bowl,'—but he paid no attention to them. Eunice was pale and thoughtful. I had no doubt in my mind, that she was already contemplating a removal from Arcadia. Perkins, whose perceptive faculties were by no means dull, whispered to me, 'Shan't I bring up some porgies for supper?' but I shook my head. I was busy with other thoughts, and did not join him in the wood, that day.

"The forenoon was overcast, with frequent showers. Each one occupied his or her room until dinner-time, when we met again with something of the old geniality. There was an evident effort to restore our former flow of good feeling. Abel's experience with the beer was freely discussed. He insisted

561

strongly that he had not been laboring under its effects, and proposed a mutual test. He, Shelldrake, and Hollins were to drink it in equal measures, and compare observations as to their physical sensations. The others agreed,—quite willingly, I thought,—but I refused. I had determined to make a desperate attempt at candor, and Abel's fate was fresh before my eyes.

"My nervous agitation increased during the day, and after sunset, fearing lest I should betray my excitement in some way, I walked down to the end of the promontory, and took a seat on the rocks. The sky had cleared, and the air was deliciously cool and sweet. The Sound was spread out before me like a sea, for the Long Island shore was veiled in a silvery mist. My mind was soothed and calmed by the influences of the scene, until the moon arose. Moonlight, you know, disturbs—at least, when one is in love. (Ah, Ned, I see you understand it!) I felt blissfully miserable, ready to cry with joy at the knowledge that I loved, and with fear and vexation at my cowardice, at the same time.

"Suddenly I heard a rustling beside me. Every nerve in my body tingled, and I turned my head, with a beating and expectant heart. Pshaw! It was Miss Ringtop, who spread her blue dress on the rock beside me, and shook back her long curls, and sighed, as she gazed at the silver path of the moon on the water.

"'Oh, how delicious!' she cried. 'How it seems to set the spirit free, and we wander off on the wings of Fancy to other spheres!'

"'Yes,' said I, 'It is very beautiful, but sad, when one is alone.'

"I was thinking of Eunice.

"'How inadequate,' she continued, 'is language to express the emotions which such a scene calls up in the bosom! Poetry alone is the voice of the spiritual world, and we, who are not poets, must borrow the language of the gifted sons of Song. Oh, Enos, I WISH you were a poet! But you FEEL poetry, I know you do. I have seen it in your eyes, when I quoted the burning lines of Adeliza Kelley, or the soul-breathings of Gamaliel J. Gawthrop. In HIM, particularly, I find the voice of my own nature. Do you know his

'Night-Whispers?' How it embodies the feelings of such a scene as this!

> *"Star-drooping bowers bending down the spaces,*
>
> *And moonlit glories sweep star-footed on;*
>
> *And pale, sweet rivers, in their shining races,*
>
> *Are ever gliding through the moonlit places,*
>
> *With silver ripples on their tranced faces,*
>
> *And forests clasp their dusky hands, with low and sullen moan!'*

"'Ah!' she continued, as I made no reply, 'this is an hour for the soul to unveil its most secret chambers! Do you not think, Enos, that love rises superior to all conventionalities? that those whose souls are in unison should be allowed to reveal themselves to each other, regardless of the world's opinions?'

"'Yes!' said I, earnestly.

"'Enos, do you understand me?' she asked, in a tender voice—almost a whisper.

"'Yes,' said I, with a blushing confidence of my own passion.

"'Then,' she whispered, 'our hearts are wholly in unison. I know you are true, Enos. I know your noble nature, and I will never doubt you. This is indeed happiness!'

"And therewith she laid her head on my shoulder, and sighed—

> *"'Life remits his tortures cruel,*
>
> *Love illumes his fairest fuel,*
>
> *When the hearts that once were dual*
>
> *Meet as one, in sweet renewal!'*

"'Miss Ringtop!' I cried, starting away from her, in alarm, 'you don't mean that—that—'

"I could not finish the sentence.

"'Yes, Enos, DEAR Enos! henceforth we belong to each other.'

"The painful embarrassment I felt, as her true meaning shot through my mind, surpassed anything I had imagined, or experienced in anticipation, when planning how I should declare myself to Eunice. Miss Ringtop was at least ten years older than I, far from handsome (but you remember her face,) and so affectedly sentimental, that I, sentimental as I was then, was sick of hearing her talk. Her hallucination was so monstrous, and gave me such a shock of desperate alarm, that I spoke, on the impulse of the moment, with great energy, without regarding how her feelings might be wounded.

"'You mistake!' I exclaimed. 'I didn't mean that,—I didn't understand you. Don't talk to me that way,—don't look at me in that way, Miss Ringtop! We were never meant for each other—I wasn't——You're so much older—I mean different. It can't be—no, it can never be! Let us go back to the house: the night is cold.'

"I rose hastily to my feet. She murmured something,—what, I did not stay to hear,—but, plunging through the cedars, was hurrying with all speed to the house, when, half-way up the lawn, beside one of the rocky knobs, I met Eunice, who was apparently on her way to join us.

"In my excited mood, after the ordeal through which I had passed, everything seemed easy. My usual timidity was blown to the four winds. I went directly to her, took her hand, and said—

"'Eunice, the others are driving me mad with their candor; will you let me be candid, too?'

"'I think you are always candid, Enos,' she answered.

"Even then, if I had hesitated, I should have been lost. But I went on, without pausing—

"'Eunice, I love you—I have loved you since we first met. I came here that I might be near you; but I must leave you forever, and to-night, unless you can trust your life in my keeping. God help me, since we have been together I have lost my faith in almost everything but you. Pardon me, if I am impetuous—different from what I have seemed. I have struggled so hard to speak! I have been a coward, Eunice, because of my love. But now I have spoken, from my heart of hearts. Look at me: I can bear it now. Read the truth in my eyes, before you answer.'

"I felt her hand tremble while I spoke. As she turned towards me her face, which had been averted, the moon shone full upon it, and I saw that tears were upon her cheeks. What was said—whether anything was said—I cannot tell. I felt the blessed fact, and that was enough. That was the dawning of the true Arcadia."

Mrs. Billings, who had been silent during this recital, took her husband's hand and smiled. Mr. Johnson felt a dull pang about the region of his heart. If he had a secret, however, I do not feel justified in betraying it.

"It was late," Mr. Billings continued, "before we returned to the house. I had a special dread of again encountering Miss Ringtop, but she was wandering up and down the bluff, under the pines, singing, 'The dream is past.' There was a sound of loud voices, as we approached the stoop. Hollins, Shelldrake and his wife, and Abel Mallory were sitting together near the door. Perkins Brown, as usual, was crouched on the lowest step, with one leg over the other, and rubbing the top of his boot with a vigor which betrayed to me some secret mirth. He looked up at me from under his straw hat with the grin of a malicious Puck, glanced towards the group, and made a curious gesture with his thumb. There were several empty pint-bottles on the stoop.

"'Now, are you sure you can bear the test?' we heard Hollins ask, as we approached.

"'Bear it? Why to be sure!' replied Shelldrake; 'if I couldn't bear it, or if YOU couldn't, your theory's done for. Try! I can stand it as long as you can.'

"'Well, then,' said Hollins, 'I think you are a very ordinary man. I derive no intellectual benefit from my intercourse with you, but your house is convenient to me. I'm under no obligations for your hospitality, however, because my company is an advantage to you. Indeed if I were treated according to my deserts, you couldn't do enough for me.'

"Mrs. Shelldrake was up in arms.

"'Indeed,' she exclaimed, 'I think you get as good as you deserve, and more too.'

"'Elvira,' said he, with a benevolent condescension, 'I have no doubt you think so, for your mind belongs to the lowest and most material sphere. You have your place in Nature, and you fill it; but it is not for you to judge of intelligences which move only on the upper planes.'

"'Hollins,' said Shelldrake, 'Elviry's a good wife and a sensible woman, and I won't allow you to turn up your nose at her.'

"'I am not surprised,' he answered, 'that you should fail to stand the test. I didn't expect it.'

"'Let me try it on YOU!' cried Shelldrake. 'You, now, have some intellect,—I don't deny that,—but not so much, by a long shot, as you think you have. Besides that, you're awfully selfish in your opinions. You won't admit that anybody can be right who differs from you. You've sponged on me for a long time; but I suppose I've learned something from you, so we'll call it even. I think, however, that what you call acting according to impulse is simply an excuse to cover your own laziness.'

"'Gosh! that's it!' interrupted Perkins, jumping up; then, recollecting himself, he sank down on the steps again, and shook with a suppressed 'Ho! ho! ho!'

"Hollins, however, drew himself up with an exasperated air.

"'Shelldrake,' said he, 'I pity you. I always knew your ignorance, but I thought you honest in your human character. I never suspected you of envy and malice. However, the true Reformer must expect to be misunderstood and misrepresented by meaner minds. That love which I bear to all creatures teaches me to forgive you. Without such love, all plans of progress must fail. Is it not so, Abel?'

"Shelldrake could only ejaculate the words, 'Pity!' 'Forgive?' in his most contemptuous tone; while Mrs. Shelldrake, rocking violently in her chair, gave utterance to that peculiar clucking, 'TS, TS, TS, TS,' whereby certain women express emotions too deep for words.

"Abel, roused by Hollins's question, answered, with a sudden energy—

"'Love! there is no love in the world. Where will you find it? Tell me, and I'll go there. Love! I'd like to see it! If all human hearts were like mine, we might have an Arcadia; but most men have no hearts. The world is a miserable, hollow, deceitful shell of vanity and hypocrisy. No: let us give up. We were born before our time: this age is not worthy of us.'

"Hollins stared at the speaker in utter amazement. Shelldrake gave a long whistle, and finally gasped out—

"'Well, what next?'

"None of us were prepared for such a sudden and complete wreck of our Arcadian scheme. The foundations had been sapped before, it is true; but we had not perceived it; and now, in two short days, the whole edifice tumbled about our ears. Though it was inevitable, we felt a shock of sorrow, and a silence fell upon us. Only that scamp of a Perkins Brown, chuckling and rubbing his boot, really rejoiced. I could have kicked him.

"We all went to bed, feeling that the charm of our Arcadian life was over. I was so full of the new happiness of love that I was scarcely conscious of regret. I seemed to have leaped at once into responsible manhood, and a glad rush of courage filled me at the knowledge that my own heart was a better oracle than those—now so shamefully overthrown—on whom I had so long implicitly relied. In the first revulsion of feeling, I was perhaps unjust to my associates. I see now, more clearly, the causes of those vagaries, which originated in a genuine aspiration, and failed from an ignorance of the true nature of Man, quite as much as from the egotism of the individuals. Other attempts at reorganizing Society were made about the same time by men of culture and experience, but in the A. C. we had neither. Our leaders had caught a few half-truths, which, in their minds, were speedily warped into errors. I can laugh over the absurdities I helped to perpetrate, but I must confess that the experiences of those few weeks went far towards making a man of me."

"Did the A. C. break up at once?" asked Mr. Johnson.

"Not precisely; though Eunice and I left the house within two days, as we had agreed. We were not married immediately, however. Three long years—years of hope and mutual encouragement—passed away before that happy consummation. Before our departure, Hollins had fallen into his old manner, convinced, apparently, that Candor must be postponed to a better age of the world. But the quarrel rankled in Shelldrake's mind, and especially in that of his wife. I could see by her looks and little fidgety ways that his further stay would be very uncomfortable. Abel Mallory, finding himself gaining in weight and improving in color, had no thought of returning. The day previous, as I afterwards learned, he had discovered Perkins Brown's secret kitchen in the woods.

"'Golly!' said that youth, in describing the circumstance to me, 'I had to ketch TWO porgies that day.'

"Miss Ringtop, who must have suspected the new relation between Eunice and myself, was for the most part rigidly silent. If she quoted, it was from the darkest and dreariest utterances of her favorite Gamaliel.

"What happened after our departure I learned from Perkins, on the return of the Shelldrakes to Norridgeport, in September. Mrs. Shelldrake stoutly persisted in refusing to make Hollins's bed, or to wash his shirts. Her brain was dull, to be sure; but she was therefore all the more stubborn in her resentment. He bore this state of things for about a week, when his engagements to lecture in Ohio suddenly called him away. Abel and Miss Ringtop were left to wander about the promontory in company, and to exchange lamentations on the hollowness of human hopes or the pleasures of despair. Whether it was owing to that attraction of sex which would make any man and any woman, thrown together on a desert island, finally become mates, or whether she skilfully ministered to Abel's sentimental vanity, I will not undertake to decide: but the fact is, they were actually betrothed, on leaving Arcadia. I think he would willingly have retreated, after his return to the world; but that was not so easy. Miss Ringtop held him with an inexorable clutch. They were not married, however, until just before his departure for California, whither she afterwards followed him. She died in less than a year, and left him free."

"And what became of the other Arcadians?" asked Mr. Johnson.

"The Shelldrakes are still living in Norridgeport. They have become Spiritualists, I understand, and cultivate Mediums. Hollins, when I last heard of him, was a Deputy-Surveyor in the New York Custom-House. Perkins Brown is our butcher here in Waterbury, and he often asks me—'Do you take chloride of soda on your beefsteaks?' He is as fat as a prize ox, and the father of five children."

"Enos!" exclaimed Mrs. Billings, looking at the clock, "it's nearly midnight! Mr. Johnson must be very tired, after such a long story.

"The Chapter of the A. C. is hereby closed!"

# FRIEND ELI'S DAUGHTER.

## I.

The mild May afternoon was drawing to a close, as Friend Eli Mitchenor reached the top of the long hill, and halted a few minutes, to allow his horse time to recover breath. He also heaved a sigh of satisfaction, as he saw again the green, undulating valley of the Neshaminy, with its dazzling squares of young wheat, its brown patches of corn-land, its snowy masses of blooming orchard, and the huge, fountain like jets of weeping willow, half concealing the gray stone fronts of the farm-houses. He had been absent from home only six days, but the time seemed almost as long to him as a three years' cruise to a New Bedford whaleman. The peaceful seclusion and pastoral beauty of the scene did not consciously appeal to his senses; but he quietly noted how much the wheat had grown during his absence, that the oats were up and looking well, that Friend Comly's meadow had been ploughed, and Friend Martin had built his half of the line-fence along the top of the hill-field. If any smothered delight in the loveliness of the spring-time found a hiding-place anywhere in the well-ordered chambers of his heart, it never relaxed or softened the straight, inflexible lines of his face. As easily could his collarless drab coat and waistcoat have flushed with a sudden gleam of purple or crimson.

Eli Mitchenor was at peace with himself and the world—that is, so much of the world as he acknowledged. Beyond the community of his own sect, and a few personal friends who were privileged to live on its borders, he neither knew nor cared to know much more of the human race than if it belonged to a planet farther from the sun. In the discipline of the Friends he was perfect; he was privileged to sit on the high seats, with the elders of the Society; and the travelling brethren from other States, who visited Bucks County, invariably blessed his house with a family-meeting. His farm was one of the best on the banks of the Neshaminy, and he also enjoyed the annual interest of a few thousand dollars, carefully secured by mortgages on real estate. His wife, Abigail, kept even pace with him in the consideration she enjoyed within the limits of the sect; and his two children, Moses and Asenath, vindicated the paternal training by the strictest sobriety of dress and conduct. Moses wore the plain coat, even when his ways led him among "the world's people;" and Asenath had never been known to wear, or to express a desire for, a ribbon of a brighter tint than brown or fawn-color. Friend Mitchenor had thus gradually ripened to his sixtieth year in an atmosphere of life utterly placid and serene, and looked forward with confidence to the final change, as a translation into a deeper calm, a serener quiet, a prosperous eternity of mild voices, subdued colors, and suppressed emotions.

He was returning home, in his own old-fashioned "chair," with its heavy square canopy and huge curved springs, from the Yearly Meeting of the Hicksite Friends, in Philadelphia. The large bay farm-horse, slow and grave in his demeanor, wore his plain harness with an air which made him seem, among his fellow-horses, the counterpart of his master among men. He would no more have thought of kicking than the latter would of swearing a huge oath. Even now, when the top of the hill was gained, and he knew that he was within a mile of the stable which had been his home since colthood, he showed no undue haste or impatience, but waited quietly, until Friend Mitchenor, by a well-known jerk of the lines, gave him the signal to go on. Obedient to the motion, he thereupon set forward once more, jogging soberly down the eastern slope of the hill,—across the covered bridge, where, in spite of the tempting level of the hollow-sounding floor, he was as careful to abstain from trotting as if he had read the warning notice,—along the wooded edge of the green meadow, where several cows of his acquaintance were grazing,— and finally, wheeling around at the proper angle, halted squarely in front of the gate which gave entrance to the private lane.

The old stone house in front, the spring-house in a green little hollow just below it, the walled garden, with its clumps of box and lilac, and the vast barn on the left, all joining in expressing a silent welcome to their owner, as he drove up the lane. Moses, a man of twenty-five, left his work in the garden, and walked forward in his shirt-sleeves.

571

"Well, father, how does thee do?" was his quiet greeting, as they shook hands.

"How's mother, by this time?" asked Eli.

"Oh, thee needn't have been concerned," said the son. "There she is. Go in: I'll tend to the horse."

Abigail and her daughter appeared on the piazza. The mother was a woman of fifty, thin and delicate in frame, but with a smooth, placid beauty of countenance which had survived her youth. She was dressed in a simple dove-colored gown, with book-muslin cap and handkerchief, so scrupulously arranged that one might have associated with her for six months without ever discovering a spot on the former, or an uneven fold in the latter. Asenath, who followed, was almost as plainly attired, her dress being a dark-blue calico, while a white pasteboard sun-bonnet, with broad cape, covered her head.

"Well, Abigail, how art thou?" said Eli, quietly giving his hand to his wife.

"I'm glad to see thee back," was her simple welcome.

No doubt they had kissed each other as lovers, but Asenath had witnessed this manifestation of affection but once in her life—after the burial of a younger sister. The fact impressed her with a peculiar sense of sanctity and solemnity: it was a caress wrung forth by a season of tribulation, and therefore was too earnest to be profaned to the uses of joy. So far, therefore, from expecting a paternal embrace, she would have felt, had it been given, like the doomed daughter of the Gileadite, consecrated to sacrifice.

Both she and her mother were anxious to hear the proceedings of the meeting, and to receive personal news of the many friends whom Eli had seen; but they asked few questions until the supper-table was ready and Moses had come in from the barn. The old man enjoyed talking, but it must be in his own way and at his own good time. They must wait until the communicative spirit should move him. With the first cup of coffee the inspiration came. Hovering at first over indifferent details, he gradually approached those of more importance,—told of the addresses which had been made, the points of

572

discipline discussed, the testimony borne, and the appearance and genealogy of any new Friends who had taken a prominent part therein. Finally, at the close of his relation, he said—

"Abigail, there is one thing I must talk to thee about. Friend Speakman's partner,—perhaps thee's heard of him, Richard Hilton,—has a son who is weakly. He's two or three years younger than Moses. His mother was consumptive, and they're afraid he takes after her. His father wants to send him into the country for the summer—to some place where he'll have good air, and quiet, and moderate exercise, and Friend Speakman spoke of us. I thought I'd mention it to thee, and if thee thinks well of it, we can send word down next week, when Josiah Comly goes"

"What does THEE think?" asked his wife, after a pause

"He's a very quiet, steady young man, Friend Speakman says, and would be very little trouble to thee. I thought perhaps his board would buy the new yoke of oxen we must have in the fall, and the price of the fat ones might go to help set up Moses. But it's for thee to decide."

"I suppose we could take him," said Abigail, seeing that the decision was virtually made already; "there's the corner room, which we don't often use. Only, if he should get worse on our hands—"

"Friend Speakman says there's no danger. He is only weak-breasted, as yet, and clerking isn't good for him. I saw the young man at the store. If his looks don't belie him, he's well-behaved and orderly."

So it was settled that Richard Hilton the younger was to be an inmate of Friend Mitchenor's house during the summer.

## II.

At the end of ten days he came.

In the under-sized, earnest, dark-haired and dark-eyed young man of three-and-twenty, Abigail Mitchenor at once felt a motherly interest. Having received him as a temporary member of the family, she considered him entitled to the same watchful care as if he were in reality an invalid son. The

573

ice over an hereditary Quaker nature is but a thin crust, if one knows how to
break it; and in Richard Hilton's case, it was already broken before his arrival.
His only embarrassment, in fact, arose from the difficulty which he naturally
experienced in adapting himself to the speech and address of the Mitchenor
family. The greetings of old Eli, grave, yet kindly, of Abigail, quaintly familiar
and tender, of Moses, cordial and slightly condescending, and finally of
Asenath, simple and natural to a degree which impressed him like a new
revelation in woman, at once indicated to him his position among them. His
city manners, he felt, instinctively, must be unlearned, or at least laid aside
for a time. Yet it was not easy for him to assume, at such short notice, those
of his hosts. Happening to address Asenath as "Miss Mitchenor," Eli turned
to him with a rebuking face.

"We do not use compliments, Richard," said he; "my daughter's name
is Asenath.

"I beg pardon. I will try to accustom myself to your ways, since you have
been so kind as to take me for a while," apologized Richard Hilton.

"Thee's under no obligation to us," said Friend Mitchenor, in his strict
sense of justice; "thee pays for what thee gets."

The finer feminine instinct of Abigail led her to interpose.

"We'll not expect too much of thee, at first, Richard," she remarked,
with a kind expression of face, which had the effect of a smile: "but our ways
are plain and easily learned. Thee knows, perhaps, that we're no respecters of
persons."

It was some days, however, before the young man could overcome his
natural hesitation at the familiarity implied by these new forms of speech.
"Friend Mitchenor" and "Moses" were not difficult to learn, but it seemed
a want of respect to address as "Abigail" a woman of such sweet and serene
dignity as the mother, and he was fain to avoid either extreme by calling
her, with her cheerful permission, "Aunt Mitchenor." On the other hand, his
own modest and unobtrusive nature soon won the confidence and cordial
regard of the family. He occasionally busied himself in the garden, by way of

exercise, or accompanied Moses to the corn-field or the woodland on the hill, but was careful never to interfere at inopportune times, and willing to learn silently, by the simple process of looking on.

One afternoon, as he was idly sitting on the stone wall which separated the garden from the lane, Asenath, attired in a new gown of chocolate-colored calico, with a double-handled willow work-basket on her arm, issued from the house. As she approached him, she paused and said—

"The time seems to hang heavy on thy hands, Richard. If thee's strong enough to walk to the village and back, it might do thee more good than sitting still."

Richard Hilton at once jumped down from the wall.

"Certainly I am able to go," said he, "if you will allow it."

"Haven't I asked thee?" was her quiet reply.

"Let me carry your basket," he said, suddenly, after they had walked, side by side, some distance down the lane.

"Indeed, I shall not let thee do that. I'm only going for the mail, and some little things at the store, that make no weight at all. Thee mustn't think I'm like the young women in the city, who, I'm told, if they buy a spool of Cotton, must have it sent home to them. Besides, thee mustn't over-exert thy strength."

Richard Hilton laughed merrily at the gravity with which she uttered the last sentence.

"Why, Miss—Asenath, I mean—what am I good for; if I have not strength enough to carry a basket?"

"Thee's a man, I know, and I think a man would almost as lief be thought wicked as weak. Thee can't help being weakly-inclined, and it's only right that thee should be careful of thyself. There's surely nothing in that that thee need be ashamed of."

While thus speaking, Asenath moderated her walk, in order,

unconsciously to her companion, to restrain his steps.

"Oh, there are the dog's-tooth violets in blossom?" she exclaimed, pointing to a shady spot beside the brook; "does thee know them?"

Richard immediately gathered and brought to her a handful of the nodding yellow bells, trembling above their large, cool, spotted leaves.

"How beautiful they are!" said he; "but I should never have taken them for violets."

"They are misnamed," she answered. "The flower is an Erythronium; but I am accustomed to the common name, and like it. Did thee ever study botany?"

"Not at all. I can tell a geranium, when I see it, and I know a heliotrope by the smell. I could never mistake a red cabbage for a rose, and I can recognize a hollyhock or a sunflower at a considerable distance. The wild flowers are all strangers to me; I wish I knew something about them."

"If thee's fond of flowers, it would be very easy to learn. I think a study of this kind would pleasantly occupy thy mind. Why couldn't thee try? I would be very willing to teach thee what little I know. It's not much, indeed, but all thee wants is a start. See, I will show thee how simple the principles are."

Taking one of the flowers from the bunch, Asenath, as they slowly walked forward, proceeded to dissect it, explained the mysteries of stamens and pistils, pollen, petals, and calyx, and, by the time they had reached the village, had succeeded in giving him a general idea of the Linnaean system of classification. His mind took hold of the subject with a prompt and profound interest. It was a new and wonderful world which suddenly opened before him. How surprised he was to learn that there were signs by which a poisonous herb could be detected from a wholesome one, that cedars and pine-trees blossomed, that the gray lichens on the rocks belonged to the vegetable kingdom! His respect for Asenath's knowledge thrust quite out of sight the restraint which her youth and sex had imposed upon him. She was teacher, equal, friend; and the simple candid manner which was the natural expression of her dignity and purity thoroughly harmonized with this relation.

Although, in reality, two or three years younger than he, Asenath had a gravity of demeanor, a calm self-possession, a deliberate balance of mind, and a repose of the emotional nature, which he had never before observed, except in much older women. She had had, as he could well imagine, no romping girlhood, no season of careless, light-hearted dalliance with opening life, no violent alternation even of the usual griefs and joys of youth. The social calm in which she had expanded had developed her nature as gently and securely as a sea-flower is unfolded below the reach of tides and storms.

She would have been very much surprised if any one had called her handsome: yet her face had a mild, unobtrusive beauty which seemed to grow and deepen from day to day. Of a longer oval than the Greek standard, it was yet as harmonious in outline; the nose was fine and straight, the dark-blue eyes steady and untroubled, and the lips calmly, but not too firmly closed. Her brown hair, parted over a high white forehead, was smoothly laid across the temples, drawn behind the ears, and twisted into a simple knot. The white cape and sun-bonnet gave her face a nun-like character, which set her apart, in the thoughts of "the world's people" whom she met, as one sanctified for some holy work. She might have gone around the world, repelling every rude word, every bold glance, by the protecting atmosphere of purity and truth which inclosed her.

The days went by, each bringing some new blossom to adorn and illustrate the joint studies of the young man and maiden. For Richard Hilton had soon mastered the elements of botany, as taught by Priscilla Wakefield,— the only source of Asenath's knowledge,—and entered, with her, upon the text-book of Gray, a copy of which he procured from Philadelphia. Yet, though he had overtaken her in his knowledge of the technicalities of the science, her practical acquaintance with plants and their habits left her still his superior. Day by day, exploring the meadows, the woods, and the clearings, he brought home his discoveries to enjoy her aid in classifying and assigning them to their true places. Asenath had generally an hour or two of leisure from domestic duties in the afternoons, or after the early supper of summer was over; and sometimes, on "Seventh-days," she would be his guide to some locality where the rarer plants were known to exist. The parents saw this community of interest and exploration without a thought of misgiving. They trusted their daughter as themselves; or, if any possible fear had flitted across their hearts, it was allayed by the absorbing delight with which Richard Hilton pursued his study. An earnest discussion as to whether a certain leaf was ovate or lanceolate, whether a certain plant belonged to the species scandens or canadensis, was, in their eyes, convincing proof that the young brains were touched, and therefore NOT the young hearts.

But love, symbolized by a rose-bud, is emphatically a botanical emotion. A sweet, tender perception of beauty, such as this study requires, or develops, is at once the most subtile and certain chain of communication between impressible natures. Richard Hilton, feeling that his years were numbered, had given up, in despair, his boyish dreams, even before he understood them: his fate seemed to preclude the possibility of love. But, as he gained a little strength from the genial season, the pure country air, and the release from gloomy thoughts which his rambles afforded, the end was farther removed, and a future—though brief, perhaps, still a FUTURE—began to glimmer before him. If this could be his life,—an endless summer, with a search for new plants every morning, and their classification every evening, with Asenath's help on the shady portico of Friend Mitchenor's house,—he could forget his doom, and enjoy the blessing of life unthinkingly.

The azaleas succeeded to the anemones, the orchis and trillium followed, then the yellow gerardias and the feathery purple pogonias, and finally the growing gleam of the golden-rods along the wood-side and the red umbels of the tall eupatoriums in the meadow announced the close of summer. One evening, as Richard, in displaying his collection, brought to view the blood-red leaf of a gum-tree, Asenath exclaimed—

"Ah, there is the sign! It is early, this year."

"What sign?" he asked.

"That the summer is over. We shall soon have frosty nights, and then nothing will be left for us except the asters and gentians and golden-rods."

Was the time indeed so near? A few more weeks, and this Arcadian life would close. He must go back to the city, to its rectilinear streets, its close brick walls, its artificial, constrained existence. How could he give up the peace, the contentment, the hope he had enjoyed through the summer? The question suddenly took a more definite form in his mind: How could he give up Asenath? Yes—the quiet, unsuspecting girl, sitting beside him, with her lap full of the September blooms he had gathered, was thenceforth a part of his inmost life. Pure and beautiful as she was, almost sacred in his regard, his heart dared to say—"I need her and claim her!"

"Thee looks pale to-night, Richard," said Abigail, as they took their seats at the supper-table. "I hope thee has not taken cold."

## III.

"Will thee go along, Richard? I know where the rudbeckias grow," said Asenath, on the following "Seventh-day" afternoon.

They crossed the meadows, and followed the course of the stream, under its canopy of magnificent ash and plane trees, into a brake between the hills. It was an almost impenetrable thicket, spangled with tall autumnal flowers. The eupatoriums, with their purple crowns, stood like young trees, with an undergrowth of aster and blue spikes of lobelia, tangled in a golden mesh of dodder. A strong, mature odor, mixed alike of leaves and flowers, and very different from the faint, elusive sweetness of spring, filled the air. The creek, with a few faded leaves dropped upon its bosom, and films of gossamer streaming from its bushy fringe, gurgled over the pebbles in its bed. Here and there, on its banks, shone the deep yellow stars of the flower they sought.

Richard Hilton walked as in a dream, mechanically plucking a stem of rudbeckia, only to toss it, presently, into the water.

"Why, Richard! what's thee doing?" cried Asenath; "thee has thrown away the very best specimen."

"Let it go," he answered, sadly. "I am afraid everything else is thrown away."

"What does thee mean?" she asked, with a look of surprised and anxious inquiry.

"Don't ask me, Asenath. Or—yes, I WILL tell you. I must say it to you now, or never afterwards. Do you know what a happy life I've been leading since I came here?—that I've learned what life is, as if I'd never known it before? I want to live, Asenath,—and do you know why?"

"I hope thee will live, Richard," she said, gently and tenderly, her deep-blue eyes dim with the mist of unshed tears.

"But, Asenath, how am I to live without you? But you can't understand that, because you do not know what you are to me. No, you never guessed that all this while I've been loving you more and more, until now I have no other idea of death than not to see you, not to love you, not to share your life!"

"Oh, Richard!"

"I knew you would be shocked, Asenath. I meant to have kept this to myself. You never dreamed of it, and I had no right to disturb the peace of your heart. The truth is told now,—and I cannot take it back, if I wished. But if you cannot love, you can forgive me for loving you—forgive me now and every day of my life."

He uttered these words with a passionate tenderness, standing on the edge of the stream, and gazing into its waters. His slight frame trembled with the violence of his emotion. Asenath, who had become very pale as he commenced to speak, gradually flushed over neck and brow as she listened. Her head drooped, the gathered flowers fell from her hands, and she hid her face. For a few minutes no sound was heard but the liquid gurgling of the water, and the whistle of a bird in the thicket beside them. Richard Hilton at last turned, and, in a voice of hesitating entreaty, pronounced her name—

"Asenath!"

She took away her hands, and slowly lifted her face. She was pale, but her eyes met his with a frank, appealing, tender expression, which caused his heart to stand still a moment. He read no reproach, no faintest thought of blame; but—was it pity?—was it pardon?—or——

"We stand before God, Richard," said she, in a low, sweet, solemn tone.

580

"He knows that I do not need to forgive thee. If thee requires it, I also require His forgiveness for myself."

Though a deeper blush now came to cheek and brow, she met his gaze with the bravery of a pure and innocent heart. Richard, stunned with the sudden and unexpected bliss, strove to take the full consciousness of it into a being which seemed too narrow to contain it. His first impulse was to rush forward, clasp her passionately in his arms, and hold her in the embrace which encircled, for him, the boundless promise of life; but she stood there, defenceless, save in her holy truth and trust, and his heart bowed down and gave her reverence.

"Asenath," said he, at last, "I never dared to hope for this. God bless you for those words! Can you trust me?—can you indeed love me?"

"I can trust thee,—I DO love thee!"

They clasped each other's hands in one long, clinging pressure. No kiss was given, but side by side they walked slowly up the dewy meadows, in happy and hallowed silence. Asenath's face became troubled as the old farmhouse appeared through the trees.

"Father and mother must know of this, Richard," said she. "I am afraid it may be a cross to them."

The same fear had already visited his own mind, but he answered, cheerfully—

"I hope not. I think I have taken a new lease of life, and shall soon be strong enough to satisfy them. Besides, my father is in prosperous business."

"It is not that," she answered; "but thee is not one of us."

It was growing dusk when they reached the house. In the dim candle-light Asenath's paleness was not remarked; and Richard's silence was attributed to fatigue.

The next morning the whole family attended meeting at the neighboring Quaker meeting-house, in the preparation for which, and the various special occupations of their "First-day" mornings, the unsuspecting parents overlooked that inevitable change in the faces of the lovers which they must otherwise have observed. After dinner, as Eli was taking a quiet walk in the garden, Richard Hilton approached him.

"Friend Mitchenor," said he, "I should like to have some talk with thee."

"What is it, Richard?" asked the old man, breaking off some pods from a seedling radish, and rubbing them in the palm of his hand.

"I hope, Friend Mitchenor," said the young man, scarcely knowing how to approach so important a crisis in his life, "I hope thee has been satisfied with my conduct since I came to live with thee, and has no fault to find with me as a man."

"Well," exclaimed Eli, turning around and looking up, sharply, "does thee want a testimony from me? I've nothing, that I know of, to say against thee."

"If I were sincerely attached to thy daughter, Friend Mitchenor, and she returned the attachment, could thee trust her happiness in my hands?"

"What!" cried Eli, straightening himself and glaring upon the speaker, with a face too amazed to express any other feeling.

"Can you confide Asenath's happiness to my care? I love her with my whole heart and soul, and the fortune of my life depends on your answer."

The straight lines in the old man's face seemed to grow deeper and more rigid, and his eyes shone with the chill glitter of steel. Richard, not daring to say a word more, awaited his reply in intense agitation.

"So!" he exclaimed at last, "this is the way thee's repaid me! I didn't expect THIS from thee! Has thee spoken to her?"

"I have."

"Thee has, has thee? And I suppose thee's persuaded her to think as thee does. Thee'd better never have come here. When I want to lose my daughter, and can't find anybody else for her, I'll let thee know."

"What have you against me, Friend Mitchenor?" Richard sadly asked, forgetting, in his excitement, the Quaker speech he had learned.

"Thee needn't use compliments now! Asenath shall be a Friend while I live; thy fine clothes and merry-makings and vanities are not for her. Thee belongs to the world, and thee may choose one of the world's women."

"Never!" protested Richard; but Friend Mitchenor was already ascending the garden-steps on his way to the house.

The young man, utterly overwhelmed, wandered to the nearest grove and threw himself on the ground. Thus, in a miserable chaos of emotion, unable to grasp any fixed thought, the hours passed away. Towards evening, he heard a footstep approaching, and sprang up. It was Moses.

The latter was engaged, with the consent of his parents and expected to "pass meeting" in a few weeks. He knew what had happened, and felt a sincere sympathy for Richard, for whom he had a cordial regard. His face was very grave, but kind.

"Thee'd better come in, Richard," said he; "the evenings are damp, and I v'e brought thy overcoat. I know everything, and I feel that it must be a great cross for thee. But thee won't be alone in bearing it."

"Do you think there is no hope of your father relenting?" he asked, in a tone of despondency which anticipated the answer.

"Father's very hard to move," said Moses; "and when mother and Asenath can't prevail on him, nobody else need try. I'm afraid thee must make up thy mind to the trial. I'm sorry to say it, Richard, but I think thee'd better go back to town."

"I'll go to-morrow,—go and die!" he muttered hoarsely, as he followed Moses to the house.

Abigail, as she saw his haggard face, wept quietly. She pressed his hand tenderly, but said nothing. Eli was stern and cold as an Iceland rock. Asenath did not make her appearance. At supper, the old man and his son exchanged a few words about the farm-work to be done on the morrow, but nothing else was said. Richard soon left the room and went up to his chamber to spend his last, his only unhappy night at the farm. A yearning, pitying look from Abigail accompanied him.

"Try and not think hard of us!" was her farewell the next morning, as he stepped into the old chair, in which Moses was to convey him to the village where he should meet the Doylestown stage. So, without a word of comfort from Asenath's lips, without even a last look at her beloved face, he was taken away.

## IV.

True and firm and self-reliant as was the nature of Asenath Mitchenor, the thought of resistance to her father's will never crossed her mind. It was fixed that she must renounce all intercourse with Richard Hilton; it was even sternly forbidden her to see him again during the few hours he remained in the house; but the sacred love, thus rudely dragged to the light and outraged, was still her own. She would take it back into the keeping of her heart, and if a day should ever come when he would be free to return and demand it of her, he would find it there, unwithered, with all the unbreathed perfume hoarded in its folded leaves. If that day came not, she would at the last give it back to God, saying, "Father, here is Thy most precious gift, bestow it as Thou wilt."

As her life had never before been agitated by any strong emotion, so it was not outwardly agitated now. The placid waters of her soul did not heave and toss before those winds of passion and sorrow: they lay in dull, leaden calm, under a cold and sunless sky. What struggles with herself she underwent no one ever knew. After Richard Hilton's departure, she never mentioned his name, or referred, in any way, to the summer's companionship with him. She performed her household duties, if not cheerfully, at least as punctually and carefully as before; and her father congratulated himself that the unfortunate attachment had struck no deeper root. Abigail's finer sight, however, was not deceived by this external resignation. She noted the faint shadows under the eyes, the increased whiteness of the temples, the unconscious traces of pain which sometimes played about the dimpled corners of the mouth, and watched her daughter with a silent, tender solicitude.

The wedding of Moses was a severe test of Asenath's strength, but she

584

stood the trial nobly, performing all the duties required by her position with such sweet composure that many of the older female Friends remarked to Abigail, "How womanly Asenath has grown!" Eli Mitchenor noted, with peculiar satisfaction, that the eyes of the young Friends—some of them of great promise in the sect, and well endowed with worldly goods—followed her admiringly.

"It will not be long," he thought, "before she is consoled."

Fortune seemed to favor his plans, and justify his harsh treatment of Richard Hilton. There were unfavorable accounts of the young man's conduct. His father had died during the winter, and he was represented as having become very reckless and dissipated. These reports at last assumed such a definite form that Friend Mitchenor brought them to the notice of his family.

"I met Josiah Comly in the road," said he, one day at dinner. "He's just come from Philadelphia, and brings bad news of Richard Hilton. He's taken to drink, and is spending in wickedness the money his father left him. His friends have a great concern about him, but it seems he's not to be reclaimed."

Abigail looked imploringly at her husband, but he either disregarded or failed to understand her look. Asenath, who had grown very pale, steadily met her father's gaze, and said, in a tone which he had never yet heard from her lips—

"Father, will thee please never mention Richard Hilton's name when I am by?"

The words were those of entreaty, but the voice was that of authority. The old man was silenced by a new and unexpected power in his daughter's heart: he suddenly felt that she was not a girl, as heretofore, but a woman, whom he might persuade, but could no longer compel.

"It shall be as thee wishes, Asenath," he said; "we had best forget him."

Of their friends, however, she could not expect this reserve, and she was doomed to hear stories of Richard which clouded and embittered her thoughts of him. And a still severer trial was in store. She accompanied her father, in obedience to his wish, and against her own desire, to the Yearly Meeting in Philadelphia. It has passed into a proverb that the Friends, on these occasions, always bring rain with them; and the period of her visit was no exception to the rule. The showery days of "Yearly Meeting Week" glided by, until the last, and she looked forward with relief to the morrow's return to Bucks County, glad to have escaped a meeting with Richard Hilton, which might have confirmed her fears and could but have given her pain in any case.

As she and her father joined each other, outside the meeting-house, at the close of the afternoon meeting, a light rain was falling. She took his arm, under the capacious umbrella, and they were soon alone in the wet streets, on their way to the house of the Friends who entertained them. At a crossing, where the water pouring down the gutter towards the Delaware, caused them to halt a man, plashing through the flood, staggered towards them. Without an umbrella, with dripping, disordered clothes, yet with a hot, flushed face, around which the long black hair hung wildly, he approached, singing to himself with maudlin voice a song that would have been sweet and tender in a lover's mouth. Friend Mitchenor drew to one side, lest his spotless drab should be brushed by the unclean reveller; but the latter, looking up, stopped suddenly face to face with them.

"Asenath!" he cried, in a voice whose anguish pierced through the confusion of his senses, and struck down into the sober quick of his soul.

"Richard!" she breathed, rather than spoke, in a low, terrified voice.

It was indeed Richard Hilton who stood before her, or rather—as she afterwards thought, in recalling the interview—the body of Richard Hilton possessed by an evil spirit. His cheeks burned with a more than hectic red, his eyes were wild and bloodshot, and though the recognition had suddenly sobered him, an impatient, reckless devil seemed to lurk under the set mask of his features.

"Here I am, Asenath," he said at length, hoarsely. "I said it was death, didn't I? Well, it's worse than death, I suppose; but what matter? You can't be more lost to me now than you were already. This is THY doing, Friend

586

Eli," he continued, turning to the old man, with a sneering emphasis on the "THY." "I hope thee's satisfied with thy work!"

Here he burst into a bitter, mocking laugh, which it chilled Asenath's blood to hear.

The old man turned pale. "Come away, child!" said he, tugging at her arm. But she stood firm, strengthened for the moment by a solemn feeling of duty which trampled down her pain.

"Richard," she said, with the music of an immeasurable sorrow in her voice, "oh, Richard, what has thee done? Where the Lord commands resignation, thee has been rebellious; where he chasteneth to purify, thee turns blindly to sin. I had not expected this of thee, Richard; I thought thy regard for me was of the kind which would have helped and uplifted thee,—not through me, as an unworthy object, but through the hopes and the pure desires of thy own heart. I expected that thee would so act as to justify what I felt towards thee, not to make my affection a reproach,—oh, Richard, not to cast over my heart the shadow of thy sin!"

The wretched young man supported himself against the post of an awning, buried his face in his hands, and wept passionately. Once or twice he essayed to speak, but his voice was choked by sobs, and, after a look from the streaming eyes which Asenath could scarcely bear to meet, he again covered his face. A stranger, coming down the street, paused out of curiosity. "Come, come!" cried Eli, once more, eager to escape from the scene. His daughter stood still, and the man slowly passed on.

Asenath could not thus leave her lost lover, in his despairing grief. She again turned to him, her own tears flowing fast and free.

"I do not judge thee, Richard, but the words that passed between us give me a right to speak to thee. It was hard to lose sight of thee then, but it is still harder for me to see thee now. If the sorrow and pity I feel could save thee, I would be willing never to know any other feelings. I would still do anything for thee except that which thee cannot ask, as thee now is, and I could not give. Thee has made the gulf between us so wide that it cannot be crossed. But

587

I can now weep for thee and pray for thee as a fellow-creature whose soul is still precious in the sight of the Lord. Fare thee well!"

He seized the hand she extended, bowed down, and showered mingled tears and kisses upon it. Then, with a wild sob in his throat, he started up and rushed down the street, through the fast-falling rain. The father and daughter walked home in silence. Eli had heard every word that was spoken, and felt that a spirit whose utterances he dared not question had visited Asenath's tongue.

She, as year after year went by, regained the peace and patience which give a sober cheerfulness to life. The pangs of her heart grew dull and transient; but there were two pictures in her memory which never blurred in outline or faded in color: one, the brake of autumn flowers under the bright autumnal sky, with bird and stream making accordant music to the new voice of love; the other a rainy street, with a lost, reckless man leaning against an awning-post, and staring in her face with eyes whose unutterable woe, when she dared to recall it, darkened the beauty of the earth, and almost shook her trust in the providence of God.

## V.

Year after year passed by, but not without bringing change to the Mitchenor family. Moses had moved to Chester County soon after his marriage, and had a good farm of his own. At the end of ten years Abigail died; and the old man, who had not only lost his savings by an unlucky investment, but was obliged to mortgage his farm, finally determined to sell it and join his son. He was getting too old to manage it properly, impatient under the unaccustomed pressure of debt, and depressed by the loss of the wife to whom, without any outward show of tenderness, he was, in truth, tenderly attached. He missed her more keenly in the places where she had lived and moved than in a neighborhood without the memory of her presence. The pang with which he parted from his home was weakened by the greater pang which had preceded it.

It was a harder trial to Asenath. She shrank from the encounter with new faces, and the necessity of creating new associations. There was a quiet

588

satisfaction in the ordered, monotonous round of her life, which might be the same elsewhere, but here alone was the nook which held all the morning sunshine she had ever known. Here still lingered the halo of the sweet departed summer,—here still grew the familiar wild-flowers which THE FIRST Richard Hilton had gathered. This was the Paradise in which the Adam of her heart had dwelt, before his fall. Her resignation and submission entitled her to keep those pure and perfect memories, though she was scarcely conscious of their true charm. She did not dare to express to herself, in words, that one everlasting joy of woman's heart, through all trials and sorrows—"I have loved, I have been beloved."

On the last "First-day" before their departure, she walked down the meadows to the lonely brake between the hills. It was the early spring, and the black buds of the ash had just begun to swell. The maples were dusted with crimson bloom, and the downy catkins of the swamp-willow dropped upon the stream and floated past her, as once the autumn leaves. In the edges of the thickets peeped forth the blue, scentless violet, the fairy cups of the anemone, and the pink-veined bells of the miskodeed. The tall blooms through which the lovers walked still slept in the chilly earth; but the sky above her was mild and blue, and the remembrance of the day came back to her with a delicate, pungent sweetness, like the perfume of the trailing arbutus in the air around her. In a sheltered, sunny nook, she found a single erythronium, lured forth in advance of its proper season, and gathered it as a relic of the spot, which she might keep without blame. As she stooped to pluck it, her own face looked up at her out of a little pool filled by the spring rains. Seen against the reflected sky, it shone with a soft radiance, and the earnest eyes met hers, as if it were her young self, evoked from the past, to bid her farewell. "Farewell!" she whispered, taking leave at once, as she believed, of youth and the memory of love.

During those years she had more than once been sought in marriage, but had steadily, though kindly, refused. Once, when the suitor was a man whose character and position made the union very desirable in Eli Mitchenor's eyes, he ventured to use his paternal influence. Asenath's gentle resistance was overborne by his arbitrary force of will, and her protestations were of no avail.

"Father," she finally said, in the tone which he had once heard and still remembered, "thee can take away, but thee cannot give."

He never mentioned the subject again.

Richard Hilton passed out of her knowledge shortly after her meeting with him in Philadelphia. She heard, indeed, that his headlong career of dissipation was not arrested,—that his friends had given him up as hopelessly ruined,—and, finally, that he had left the city. After that, all reports ceased. He was either dead, or reclaimed and leading a better life, somewhere far away. Dead, she believed—almost hoped; for in that case might he not now be enjoying the ineffable rest and peace which she trusted might be her portion? It was better to think of him as a purified spirit, waiting to meet her in a holier communion, than to know that he was still bearing the burden of a soiled and blighted life. In any case, her own future was plain and clear. It was simply a prolongation of the present—an alternation of seed-time and harvest, filled with humble duties and cares, until the Master should bid her lay down her load and follow Him.

Friend Mitchenor bought a small cottage adjacent to his son's farm, in a community which consisted mostly of Friends, and not far from the large old meeting-house in which the Quarterly Meetings were held. He at once took his place on the upper seat, among the elders, most of whom he knew already, from having met them, year after year, in Philadelphia. The charge of a few acres of ground gave him sufficient occupation; the money left to him after the sale of his farm was enough to support him comfortably; and a late Indian summer of contentment seemed now to have come to the old man. He was done with the earnest business of life. Moses was gradually taking his place, as father and Friend; and Asenath would be reasonably provided for at his death. As his bodily energies decayed, his imperious temper softened, his mind became more accessible to liberal influences, and he even cultivated a cordial friendship with a neighboring farmer who was one of "the world's people." Thus, at seventy-five he was really younger, because tenderer of heart and more considerate, than he had been at sixty.

Asenath was now a woman of thirty-five, and suitors had ceased to

590

approach her. Much of her beauty still remained, but her face had become thin and wasted, and the inevitable lines were beginning to form around her eyes. Her dress was plainer than ever, and she wore the scoop-bonnet of drab silk, in which no woman can seem beautiful, unless she be very old. She was calm and grave in her demeanor, save that her perfect goodness and benevolence shone through and warmed her presence; but, when earnestly interested, she had been known to speak her mind so clearly and forcibly that it was generally surmised among the Friends that she possessed "a gift," which might, in time, raise her to honor among them. To the children of Moses she was a good genius, and a word from "Aunt 'Senath" oftentimes prevailed when the authority of the parents was disregarded. In them she found a new source of happiness; and when her old home on the Neshaminy had been removed a little farther into the past, so that she no longer looked, with every morning's sun, for some familiar feature of its scenery, her submission brightened into a cheerful content with life.

It was summer, and Quarterly-Meeting Day had arrived. There had been rumors of the expected presence of "Friends from a distance," and not only those of the district, but most of the neighbors who were not connected with the sect, attended. By the by-road, through the woods, it was not more than half a mile from Friend Mitchenor's cottage to the meeting-house, and Asenath, leaving her father to be taken by Moses in his carriage, set out on foot. It was a sparkling, breezy day, and the forest was full of life. Squirrels chased each other along the branches of the oaks, and the air was filled with fragrant odors of hickory-leaves, sweet fern, and spice-wood. Picking up a flower here and there, Asenath walked onward, rejoicing alike in shade and sunshine, grateful for all the consoling beauty which the earth offers to a lonely heart. That serene content which she had learned to call happiness had filled her being until the dark canopy was lifted and the waters took back their transparency under a cloudless sky.

Passing around to the "women's side" of the meeting-house, she mingled with her friends, who were exchanging information concerning the expected visitors. Micajah Morrill had not arrived, they said, but Ruth Baxter had spent the last night at Friend Way's, and would certainly be there. Besides, there were Friend Chandler, from Nine Partners, and Friend Carter, from Maryland: they had been seen on the ground. Friend Carter was said to have a wonderful gift,—Mercy Jackson had heard him once, in Baltimore. The Friends there had been a little exercised about him, because they thought he was too much inclined to "the newness," but it was known that the Spirit had often manifestly led him. Friend Chandler had visited Yearly Meeting once, they believed. He was an old man, and had been a personal friend of Elias Hicks.

At the appointed hour they entered the house. After the subdued rustling which ensued upon taking their seats, there was an interval of silence, shorter than usual, because it was evident that many persons would feel the promptings of the Spirit. Friend Chandler spoke first, and was followed by Ruth Baxter, a frail little woman, with a voice of exceeding power. The not unmelodious chant in which she delivered her admonitions rang out, at times, like the peal of a trumpet. Fixing her eyes on vacancy, with her hands on the wooden rail before her, and her body slightly swaying to and fro, her voice soared far aloft at the commencement of every sentence, gradually dropping, through a melodious scale of tone, to the close. She resembled an inspired prophetess, an aged Deborah, crying aloud in the valleys of Israel.

The last speaker was Friend Carter, a small man, not more than forty years of age. His face was thin and intense in its expression, his hair gray at the temples, and his dark eye almost too restless for a child of "the stillness and the quietness." His voice, though not loud, was clear and penetrating, with an earnest, sympathetic quality, which arrested, not the ear alone, but the serious attention of the auditor. His delivery was but slightly marked by the peculiar rhythm of the Quaker preachers; and this fact, perhaps, increased the effect of his words, through the contrast with those who preceded him.

His discourse was an eloquent vindication of the law of kindness, as the highest and purest manifestation of true Christian doctrine.

The paternal relation of God to man was the basis of that religion which appealed directly to the heart: so the fraternity of each man with his fellow was its practical application. God pardons the repentant sinner: we can also pardon, where we are offended; we can pity, where we cannot pardon. Both the good and the bad principles generate their like in others. Force begets force; anger excites a corresponding anger; but kindness awakens the slumbering emotions even of an evil heart. Love may not always be answered by an equal love, but it has never yet created hatred. The testimony which Friends bear against war, he said, is but a general assertion, which has no value except in so far as they manifest the principle of peace in their daily lives—in the exercise of pity, of charity, of forbearance, and Christian love.

The words of the speaker sank deeply into the hearts of his hearers. There was an intense hush, as if in truth the Spirit had moved him to speak, and every sentence was armed with a sacred authority. Asenath Mitchenor looked at him, over the low partition which divided her and her sisters from the men's side, absorbed in his rapt earnestness and truth. She forgot that other hearers were present: he spake to her alone. A strange spell seemed to seize upon her faculties and chain them at his feet: had he beckoned to her, she would have arisen and walked to his side.

Friend Carter warmed and deepened as he went on. "I feel moved to-day," he said,—"moved, I know not why, but I hope for some wise purpose,— to relate to you an instance of Divine and human kindness which has come directly to my own knowledge. A young man of delicate constitution, whose lungs were thought to be seriously affected, was sent to the house of a Friend in the country, in order to try the effect of air and exercise."

Asenath almost ceased to breathe, in the intensity with which she gazed and listened. Clasping her hands tightly in her lap to prevent them from trembling, and steadying herself against the back of the seat, she heard the story of her love for Richard Hilton told by the lips of a stranger!—not merely of his dismissal from the house, but of that meeting in the street, at which only she and her father were present! Nay, more, she heard her own words repeated, she heard Richard's passionate outburst of remorse described in language that brought his living face before her! She gasped for breath—his face WAS before her! The features, sharpened by despairing grief, which her memory recalled, had almost anticipated the harder lines which fifteen years had made, and which now, with a terrible shock and choking leap of the

heart, she recognized. Her senses faded, and she would have fallen from her
seat but for the support of the partition against which she leaned. Fortunately,
the women near her were too much occupied with the narrative to notice her
condition. Many of them wept silently, with their handkerchiefs pressed over
their mouths.

The first shock of death-like faintness passed away, and she clung to the
speaker's voice, as if its sound alone could give her strength to sit still and
listen further.

"Deserted by his friends, unable to stay his feet on the evil path," he
continued, "the young man left his home and went to a city in another State.
But here it was easier to find associates in evil than tender hearts that might
help him back to good. He was tired of life, and the hope of a speedier death
hardened him in his courses. But, my friends, Death never comes to those
who wickedly seek him. The Lord withholds destruction from the hands that
are madly outstretched to grasp it, and forces His pity and forgiveness on the
unwilling soul. Finding that it was the principle of LIFE which grew stronger
within him, the young man at last meditated an awful crime. The thought of
self-destruction haunted him day and night. He lingered around the wharves,
gazing into the deep waters, and was restrained from the deed only by the
memory of the last loving voice he had heard. One gloomy evening, when
even this memory had faded, and he awaited the approaching darkness to
make his design secure, a hand was laid on his arm. A man in the simple garb
of the Friends stood beside him, and a face which reflected the kindness of
the Divine Father looked upon him. 'My child,' said he, 'I am drawn to thee
by the great trouble of thy mind. Shall I tell thee what it is thee meditates?'
The young man shook his head. 'I will be silent, then, but I will save thee. I
know the human heart, and its trials and weaknesses, and it may be put into
my mouth to give thee strength.' He took the young man's hand, as if he had
been a little child, and led him to his home. He heard the sad story, from
beginning to end; and the young man wept upon his breast, to hear no word
of reproach, but only the largest and tenderest pity bestowed upon him. They
knelt down, side by side, at midnight; and the Friend's right hand was upon
his head while they prayed.

"The young man was rescued from his evil ways, to acknowledge still further the boundless mercy of Providence. The dissipation wherein he had recklessly sought death was, for him, a marvellous restoration to life. His lungs had become sound and free from the tendency to disease. The measure of his forgiveness was almost more than he could bear. He bore his cross thenceforward with a joyful resignation, and was mercifully drawn nearer and nearer to the Truth, until, in the fulness of his convictions, he entered into the brotherhood of the Friends.

"I have been powerfully moved to tell you this story." Friend Carter concluded, "from a feeling that it may be needed, here, at this time, to influence some heart trembling in the balance. Who is there among you, my friends, that may not snatch a brand from the burning! Oh, believe that pity and charity are the most effectual weapons given into the hands of us imperfect mortals, and leave the awful attribute of wrath in the hands of the Lord!"

He sat down, and dead silence ensued. Tears of emotion stood in the eyes of the hearers, men as well as women, and tears of gratitude and thanksgiving gushed warmly from those of Asenath. An ineffable peace and joy descended upon her heart.

When the meeting broke up, Friend Mitchenor, who had not recognized Richard Hilton, but had heard the story with feelings which he endeavored in vain to control, approached the preacher.

"The Lord spoke to me this day through thy lips," said he; "will thee come to one side, and hear me a minute?"

"Eli Mitchenor!" exclaimed Friend Carter; "Eli! I knew not thee was here! Doesn't thee know me?"

The old man stared in astonishment. "It seems like a face I ought to know," he said, "but I can't place thee." They withdrew to the shade of one of the poplars. Friend Carter turned again, much moved, and, grasping the old man's hands in his own, exclaimed—

"Friend Mitchenor, I was called upon to-day to speak of myself. I am—

595

or, rather, I WAS—the Richard Hilton whom thee knew."

Friend Mitchenor's face flushed with mingled emotions of shame and joy, and his grasp on the preacher's hands tightened.

"But thee calls thyself Carter?" he finally said.

"Soon after I was saved," was the reply, "an aunt on the mother's side died, and left her property to me, on condition that I should take her name. I was tired of my own then, and to give it up seemed only like losing my former self; but I should like to have it back again now."

"Wonderful are the ways of the Lord, and past finding out!" said the old man. "Come home with me, Richard,—come for my sake, for there is a concern on my mind until all is clear between us. Or, stay,—will thee walk home with Asenath, while I go with Moses?"

"Asenath?"

"Yes. There she goes, through the gate. Thee can easily overtake her. I 'm coming, Moses!"—and he hurried away to his son's carriage, which was approaching.

Asenath felt that it would be impossible for her to meet Richard Hilton there. She knew not why his name had been changed; he had not betrayed his identity with the young man of his story; he evidently did not wish it to be known, and an unexpected meeting with her might surprise him into an involuntary revelation of the fact. It was enough for her that a saviour had arisen, and her lost Adam was redeemed,—that a holier light than the autumn sun's now rested, and would forever rest, on the one landscape of her youth. Her eyes shone with the pure brightness of girlhood, a soft warmth colored her cheek and smoothed away the coming lines of her brow, and her step was light and elastic as in the old time.

Eager to escape from the crowd, she crossed the highway, dusty with its string of returning carriages, and entered the secluded lane. The breeze had died away, the air was full of insect-sounds, and the warm light of the sinking sun fell upon the woods and meadows. Nature seemed penetrated with a sympathy with her own inner peace.

But the crown of the benignant day was yet to come. A quick footstep followed her, and ere long a voice, near at hand, called her by name.

She stopped, turned, and for a moment they stood silent, face to face.

"I knew thee, Richard!" at last she said, in a trembling voice; "may the Lord bless thee!"

Tears were in the eyes of both.

"He has blessed me," Richard answered, in a reverent tone; "and this is His last and sweetest mercy. Asenath, let me hear that thee forgives me."

"I have forgiven thee long ago, Richard—forgiven, but not forgotten."

The hush of sunset was on the forest, as they walked onward, side by side, exchanging their mutual histories. Not a leaf stirred in the crowns of the tall trees, and the dusk, creeping along between their stems, brought with it a richer woodland odor. Their voices were low and subdued, as if an angel of God were hovering in the shadows, and listening, or God Himself looked down upon them from the violet sky.

At last Richard stopped.

"Asenath," said he, "does thee remember that spot on the banks of the creek, where the rudbeckias grew?"

"I remember it," she answered, a girlish blush rising to her face.

"If I were to say to thee now what I said to thee there, what would be thy answer?"

Her words came brokenly.

"I would say to thee, Richard,—'I can trust thee,—I DO love thee!'"

"Look at me, Asenath."

Her eyes, beaming with a clearer light than even then when she first confessed, were lifted to his. She placed her hands gently upon his shoulders, and bent her head upon his breast. He tenderly lifted it again, and, for the first time, her virgin lips knew the kiss of man.

# MISS BARTRAM'S TROUBLE.

## I.

It was a day of unusual excitement at the Rambo farm-house. On the farm, it is true, all things were in their accustomed order, and all growths did their accustomed credit to the season. The fences were in good repair; the cattle were healthy and gave promise of the normal increase, and the young corn was neither strangled with weeds nor assassinated by cut-worms. Old John Rambo was gradually allowing his son, Henry, to manage in his stead, and the latter shrewdly permitted his father to believe that he exercised the ancient authority. Leonard Clare, the strong young fellow who had been taken from that shiftless adventurer, his father, when a mere child, and brought up almost as one of the family, and who had worked as a joiner's apprentice during the previous six months, had come back for the harvest work; so the Rambos were forehanded, and probably as well satisfied as it is possible for Pennsylvania farmers to be.

In the house, also, Mrs. Priscilla Rambo was not severely haunted by the spectre of any neglected duty. The simple regular routine of the household could not be changed under her charge; each thing had its appropriate order of performance, must be done, and WAS done. If the season were backward, at the time appointed for whitewashing or soap-making, so much the worse for the season; if the unhatched goslings were slain by thunder, she laid the blame on the thunder. And if—but no, it is quite impossible to suppose that, outside of those two inevitable, fearful house-cleaning weeks in each year, there could have been any disorder in the cold prim, varnish-odored best rooms, sacred to company.

It was Miss Betty Rambo, whose pulse beat some ten strokes faster than its wont, as she sat down with the rest to their early country dinner. Whether her brother Henry's participated in the accelerated movement could not be guessed from his demeanor. She glanced at him now and then, with bright eyes and flushed cheeks, eager to speak yet shrinking from the half magisterial air which was beginning to supplant his old familiar banter. Henry was changing with his new responsibility, as she admitted to herself with a sort of dismay; he had the airs of an independent farmer, and she remained only a farmer's daughter,—without any acknowledged rights, until she should acquire them all, at a single blow, by marriage.

Nevertheless, he must have felt what was in her mind; for, as he cut out the quarter of a dried apple pie, he said carelessly:

"I must go down to the Lion, this afternoon. There's a fresh drove of Maryland cattle just come."

"Oh Harry!" cried Betty, in real distress.

"I know," he answered; "but as Miss Bartram is going to stay two weeks, she'll keep. She's not like a drove, that's here one day, and away the next. Besides, it is precious little good I shall have of her society, until you two have used up all your secrets and small talk. I know how it is with girls. Leonard will drive over to meet the train."

"Won't I do on a pinch?" Leonard asked.

"Oh, to be sure," said Betty, a little embarrassed, "only Alice—Miss Bartram—might expect Harry, because her brother came for me when I went up."

"If that's all, make yourself easy, Bet," Henry answered, as he rose from the table. "There's a mighty difference between here and there. Unless you mean to turn us into a town family while she stays—high quality, eh?"

"Go along to your cattle! there's not much quality, high or low, where you are."

Betty was indignant; but the annoyance exhausted itself healthfully while she was clearing away the dishes and restoring the room to its order, so that when Leonard drove up to the gate with the lumbering, old-fashioned carriage two hours afterwards, she came forth calm, cheerful, fresh as a pink in her pink muslin, and entirely the good, sensible country-girl she was.

Two or three years before, she and Miss Alice Bartram, daughter of the distinguished lawyer in the city, had been room-mates at the Nereid Seminary for Young Ladies. Each liked the other for the contrast to her own self; both were honest, good and lovable, but Betty had the stronger nerves and a practical sense which seemed to be admirable courage in the eyes of Miss Alice, whose instincts were more delicate, whose tastes were fine and high, and who could not conceive of life without certain luxurious accessories. A very cordial friendship sprang up between them,—not the effusive girl-love, with its iterative kisses, tears, and flow of loosened hair, but springing from the respect inspired by sound and positive qualities.

The winter before, Betty had been invited to visit her friend in the city, and had passed a very excited and delightful week in the stately Bartram mansion. If she were at first a little fluttered by the manners of the new world, she was intelligent enough to carry her own nature frankly through it, instead of endeavoring to assume its character. Thus her little awkwardnesses became originalities, and she was almost popular in the lofty circle when she withdrew from it. It was therefore, perhaps, slightly inconsistent in Betty, that she was not quite sure how Miss Bartram would accept the reverse side of this social experience. She imagined it easier to look down and make allowances, as a host, than as a guest; she could not understand that the charm of the change might be fully equal.

It was lovely weather, as they drove up the sweet, ever-changing curves of the Brandywine valley. The woods fairly laughed in the clear sunlight, and the soft, incessant, shifting breezes. Leonard, in his best clothes, and with a smoother gloss on his brown hair, sang to himself as he urged the strong-boned horses into a trot along the levels; and Betty finally felt so quietly happy that she forgot to be nervous. When they reached the station they walked up and down the long platform together, until the train from the city thundered up, and painfully restrained its speed. Then Betty, catching sight of a fawn-colored travelling dress issuing from the ladies' car, caught hold of Leonard's arm, and cried: "There she is!"

Miss Bartram heard the words, and looked down with a bright, glad expression on her face. It was not her beauty that made Leonard's heart suddenly stop beating; for she was not considered a beauty, in society. It was something rarer than perfect beauty, yet even more difficult to describe,—a serene, unconscious grace, a pure, lofty maturity of womanhood, such as our souls bow down to in the Santa Barbara of Palma Vecchio. Her features were not "faultlessly regular," but they were informed with the finer harmonies of her character. She was a woman, at whose feet a noble man might kneel, lay his forehead on her knee, confess his sins, and be pardoned.

She stepped down to the platform, and Betty's arms were about her. After a double embrace she gently disengaged herself, turned to Leonard, gave him her hand, and said, with a smile which was delightfully frank and cordial: "I will not wait for Betty's introduction, Mr. Rambo. She has talked to me so much of her brother Harry, that I quite know you already."

Leonard could neither withdraw his eyes nor his hand. It was like a double burst of warmth and sunshine, in which his breast seemed to expand, his stature to grow, and his whole nature to throb with some new and wonderful force. A faint color came into Miss Bartram's cheeks, as they stood thus, for a moment, face to face. She seemed to be waiting for him to speak, but of this he never thought; had any words come to his mind, his tongue could not have uttered them.

"It is not Harry," Betty explained, striving to hide her embarrassment. "This is Leonard Clare, who lives with us."

"Then I do not know you so well as I thought," Miss Bartram said to him; "it is the beginning of a new acquaintance, after all."

"There isn't no harm done," Leonard answered, and instantly feeling the awkwardness of the words, blushed so painfully that Miss Bartram felt the inadequacy of her social tact to relieve so manifest a case of distress. But she did, instinctively, what was really best: she gave Leonard the check for her trunk, divided her satchels with Betty, and walked to the carriage.

He did not sing, as he drove homewards down the valley. Seated on the trunk, in front, he quietly governed the horses, while the two girls, on the seat behind him, talked constantly and gaily. Only the rich, steady tones of Miss Bartram's voice WOULD make their way into his ears, and every light, careless sentence printed itself upon his memory. They came to him as if from some inaccessible planet. Poor fellow! he was not the first to feel "the desire of the moth for the star."

When they reached the Rambo farm-house, it was necessary that he should give his hand to help her down from the clumsy carriage. He held it but a moment; yet in that moment a gentle pulse throbbed upon his hard palm, and he mechanically set his teeth, to keep down the impulse which made him wild to hold it there forever. "Thank you, Mr. Clare!" said Miss Bartram, and passed into the house. When he followed presently, shouldering her trunk into the upper best-room, and kneeling upon the floor to unbuckle the straps, she found herself wondering: "Is this a knightly service, or the menial duty of a porter? Can a man be both sensitive and ignorant, chivalrous and vulgar?"

The question was not so easily decided, though no one guessed how much Miss Bartram pondered it, during the succeeding days. She insisted, from the first, that her coming should make no change in the habits of the household; she rose in the cool, dewy summer dawns, dined at noon in the old brown room beside the kitchen, and only differed from the Rambos in sitting at her moonlit window, and breathing the subtle odors of a myriad leaves, long after Betty was sleeping the sleep of health.

It was strange how frequently the strong, not very graceful figure of Leonard Clare marched through these reveries. She occasionally spoke to him at the common table, or as she passed the borders of the hay-field, where he and Henry were at work: but his words to her were always few and constrained. What was there in his eyes that haunted her? Not merely a most reverent admiration of her pure womanly refinement, although she read that also; not a fear of disparagement, such as his awkward speech implied, but something which seemed to seek agonizingly for another language than that of the lips,—something which appealed to her from equal ground, and asked for an answer.

One evening she met him in the lane, as she returned from the meadow.

602

She carried a bunch of flowers, with delicate blue and lilac bells, and asked him the name.

"Them's Brandywine cowslips," he answered; "I never heard no other name.

"May I correct you?" she said, gently, and with a smile which she meant to be playful. "I suppose the main thing is to speak one's thought, but there are neat and orderly ways, and there are careless ways." Thereupon she pointed out the inaccuracies of his answer, he standing beside her, silent and attentive. When she ceased, he did not immediately reply.

"You will take it in good part, will you not?" she continued. "I hope I have not offended you."

"No!" he exclaimed, firmly, lifting his head, and looking at her. The inscrutable expression in his dark gray eyes was stronger than before, and all his features were more clearly drawn. He reminded her of a picture of Adam which she had once seen: there was the same rather low forehead, straight, even brows, full yet strong mouth, and that broader form of chin which repeats and balances the character of the forehead. He was not positively handsome, but from head to foot he expressed a fresh, sound quality of manhood.

Another question flashed across Miss Bartram's mind: Is life long enough to transform this clay into marble? Here is a man in form, and with all the dignity of the perfect masculine nature: shall the broad, free intelligence, the grace and sweetness, the taste and refinement, which the best culture gives, never be his also? If not, woman must be content with faulty representations of her ideal.

So musing, she walked on to the farm-house. Leonard had picked up one of the blossoms she had let fall, and appeared to be curiously examining it. If he had apologized for his want of grammar, or promised to reform it, her interest in him might have diminished; but his silence, his simple, natural obedience to some powerful inner force, whatever it was, helped to strengthen that phantom of him in her mind, which was now beginning to be a serious trouble.

Once again, the day before she left the Rambo farmhouse to return to
the city, she came upon him, alone. She had wandered off to the Brandywine,
to gather ferns at a rocky point where some choice varieties were to be found.
There were a few charming clumps, half-way up a slaty cliff, which it did not
seem possible to scale, and she was standing at the base, looking up in vain
longing, when a voice, almost at her ear, said:

"Which ones do you want?"

Afterwards, she wondered that she did not start at the voice. Leonard
had come up the road from one of the lower fields: he wore neither coat nor
waistcoat, and his shirt, open at the throat, showed the firm, beautiful white
of the flesh below the strong tan of his neck. Miss Bartram noticed the sinewy
strength and elasticity of his form, yet when she looked again at the ferns, she
shook her head, and answered:

"None, since I cannot have them."

Without saying a word, he took off his shoes, and commenced climbing
the nearly perpendicular face of the cliff. He had done it before, many a time;
but Miss Bartram, although she was familiar with such exploits from the
pages of many novels, had never seen the reality, and it quite took away her
breath.

When he descended with the ferns in his hand, she said: "It was a great
risk; I wish I had not wanted them."

"It was no risk for me," he answered.

"What can I send you in return?" she asked, as they walked forwards. "I
am going home to-morrow."

"Betty told me," Leonard said; "please, wait one minute."

He stepped down to the bank of the stream, washed his hands carefully
in the clear water, and came back to her, holding them, dripping, at his sides.

"I am very ignorant," he then continued,—"ignorant and rough. You
are good, to want to send me something, but I want nothing. Miss Bartram,

you are very good."

He paused; but with all her tact and social experience, she did not know what to say.

"Would you do one little thing for me—not for the ferns, that was nothing—no more than you do, without thinking, for all your friends?"

"Oh, surely!" she said.

"Might I—might I—now,—there'll be no chance tomorrow,—shake hands with you?"

The words seemed to be forced from him by the strength of a fierce will. Both stopped, involuntarily.

"It's quite dry, you see," said he, offering his hand. Her own sank upon it, palm to palm, and the fingers softly closed over each, as if with the passion and sweetness of a kiss. Miss Bartram's heart came to her eyes, and read, at last, the question in Leonard's. It was: "I as man, and you, as woman, are equals; will you give me time to reach you?" What her eyes replied she knew not. A mighty influence drew her on, and a mighty doubt and dread restrained her. One said: "Here is your lover, your husband, your cherished partner, left by fate below your station, yet whom you may lift to your side! Shall man, alone, crown the humble maiden,—stoop to love, and, loving, ennoble? Be you the queen, and love him by the royal right of womanhood!" But the other sternly whispered: "How shall your fine and delicate fibres be knit into this coarse texture? Ignorance, which years cannot wash away,—low instincts, what do YOU know?—all the servile side of life, which is turned from you,—what madness to choose this, because some current of earthly magnetism sets along your nerves? He loves you: what of that? You are a higher being to him, and he stupidly adores you. Think,—yes, DARE to think of all the prosaic realities of life, shared with him!"

Miss Bartram felt herself growing dizzy. Behind the impulse which bade her cast herself upon his breast swept such a hot wave of shame and pain that her face burned, and she dropped her eyelids to shut out the sight of his face. But, for one endless second, the sweeter voice spoke through their clasped hands. Perhaps he kissed hers; she did not know; she only heard herself murmur:

"Good-bye! Pray go on; I will rest here."

She sat down upon a bank by the roadside, turned away her head, and closed her eyes. It was long before the tumult in her nature subsided. If she reflected, with a sense of relief, "nothing was said," the thought immediately followed, "but all is known." It was impossible,—yes, clearly impossible; and then came such a wild longing, such an assertion of the right and truth and justice of love, as made her seem a miserable coward, the veriest slave of conventionalities.

Out of this struggle dawned self-knowledge, and the strength which is born of it. When she returned to the house, she was pale and weary, but capable of responding to Betty Rambo's constant cheerfulness. The next day she left for the city, without having seen Leonard Clare again.

## II.

Henry Rambo married, and brought a new mistress to the farm-house. Betty married, and migrated to a new home in another part of the State. Leonard Clare went back to his trade, and returned no more in harvest-time. So the pleasant farm by the Brandywine, having served its purpose as a background, will be seen no more in this history.

Miss Bartram's inmost life, as a woman, was no longer the same. The point of view from which she had beheld the world was shifted, and she was obliged to remodel all her feelings and ideas to conform to it. But the process was gradual, and no one stood near enough to her to remark it. She was occasionally suspected of that "eccentricity" which, in a woman of five-and-twenty, is looked upon as the first symptom of a tendency to old-maidenhood, but which is really the sign of an earnest heart struggling with the questions of life. In the society of cities, most men give only the shallow, flashy surface of their natures to the young women they meet, and Miss Bartram, after that revelation of the dumb strength of an ignorant man, sometimes grew very impatient of the platitudes and affectations which came to her clad in elegant words, and accompanied by irreproachable manners.

606

She had various suitors; for that sense of grace and repose and sweet feminine power, which hung around her like an atmosphere, attracted good and true men towards her. To some, indeed, she gave that noble, untroubled friendship which is always possible between the best of the two sexes, and when she was compelled to deny the more intimate appeal, it was done with such frank sorrow, such delicate tenderness, that she never lost the friend in losing the lover. But, as one year after another went by, and the younger members of her family fell off into their separate domestic orbits, she began to shrink a little at the perspective of a lonely life, growing lonelier as it receded from the Present.

By this time, Leonard Clare had become almost a dream to her. She had neither seen him nor heard of him since he let go her hand on that memorable evening beside the stream. He was a strange, bewildering chance, a cypher concealing a secret which she could not intelligently read. Why should she keep the memory of that power which was, perhaps, some unconscious quality of his nature (no, it was not so! something deeper than reason cried:), or long since forgotten, if felt, by him?

The man whom she most esteemed came back to her. She knew the ripeness and harmony of his intellect, the nobility of his character, and the generosity of a feeling which would be satisfied with only a partial return. She felt sure, also, that she should never possess a sentiment nearer to love than that which pleaded his cause in her heart. But her hand lay quiet in his, her pulses were calm when he spoke, and his face, manly and true as it was, never invaded her dreams. All questioning was vain; her heart gave no solution of the riddle. Perhaps her own want was common to all lives: then she was cherishing a selfish ideal, and rejecting the positive good offered to her hands.

After long hesitation she yielded. The predictions of society came to naught; instead of becoming an "eccentric" spinster, Miss Bartram was announced to be the affianced bride of Mr. Lawrie. A few weeks and months rolled around, and when the wedding-day came, she almost hailed it as the port of refuge, where she should find a placid and peaceful life.

They were married by an aged clergyman, a relative of the bridegroom.

607

The cross-street where his chapel stood, fronting a Methodist church—both of the simplest form of that architecture fondly supposed to be Gothic,—was quite blocked up by the carriages of the party. The pews were crowded with elegant guests, the altar was decorated with flowers, and the ceremony lacked nothing of its usual solemn beauty. The bride was pale, but strikingly calm and self-possessed, and when she moved towards the door as Mrs. Lawrie, on her husband's arm, many matrons, recalling their own experience, marvelled at her unflurried dignity.

Just as they passed out the door, and the bridal carriage was summoned, a singular thing happened. Another bridal carriage drew up from the opposite side, and a newly wedded pair came forth from the portal of the Methodist church. Both parties stopped, face to face, divided only by the narrow street. Mrs. Lawrie first noticed the flushed cheeks of the other bride, her white dress, rather showy than elegant, and the heavy gold ornaments she wore. Then she turned to the bridegroom. He was tall and well-formed, dressed like a gentleman, but like one who is not yet unconscious of his dress, and had the air of a man accustomed to exercise some authority.

She saw his face, and instantly all other faces disappeared. From the opposite brink of a tremendous gulf she looked into his eyes, and their blended ray of love and despair pierced her to the heart.

There was a roaring in her ears, followed a long sighing sound, like that of the wind on some homeless waste; she leaned more heavily on her husband's arm, leaned against his shoulder, slid slowly down into his supporting clasp, and knew no more.

"She's paying for her mock composure, after all," said the matrons.

"It must have been a great effort."

### III.

Ten years afterwards, Mrs. Lawrie went on board a steamer at Southampton, bound for New York. She was travelling alone, having been called suddenly from Europe by the approaching death of her aged father. For two or three days after sailing, the thick, rainy spring weather kept all below, except a few hardy gentlemen who crowded together on the lee of the smoke-stack, and kept up a stubborn cheerfulness on a very small capital of comfort. There were few cabin-passengers on board, but the usual crowd of emigrants in the steerage.

Mrs. Lawrie's face had grown calmer and colder during these years. There was yet no gray in her hair, no wrinkles about her clear eyes; each feature appeared to be the same, but the pale, monotonous color which had replaced the warm bloom of her youth, gave them a different character. The gracious dignity of her manner, the mellow tones of her voice, still expressed her unchanging goodness, yet those who met her were sure to feel, in some inexplicable way, that to be good is not always to be happy. Perhaps, indeed, her manner was older than her face and form: she still attracted the interest of men, but with a certain doubt and reserve.

Certain it is that when she made her appearance on deck, glad of the blue sky and sunshine, and threw back her hood to feel the freshness of the sea air, all eyes followed her movements, except those of a forlorn individual, who, muffled in his cloak and apparently sea-sick, lay upon one of the benches. The captain presently joined her, and the gentlemen saw that she was bright and perfectly self-possessed in conversation: some of them immediately resolved to achieve an acquaintance. The dull, passive existence of the beginning of every voyage, seemed to be now at an end. It was time for the little society of the vessel to awake, stir itself, and organize a life of its own, for the few remaining days.

That night, as Mrs. Lawrie was sleeping in her berth, she suddenly awoke with a singular feeling of dread and suspense. She listened silently, but for some time distinguished none other than the small sounds of night on shipboard—the indistinct orders, the dragging of ropes, the creaking of timbers, the dull, regular jar of the engine, and the shuffling noise of feet overhead. But, ere long, she seemed to catch faint, distant sounds, that seemed like cries; then came hurry and confusion on deck; then voices in the cabin, one of which said: "they never can get it under, at this rate!"

She rose, dressed herself hastily, and made her way through pale and excited stewards, and the bewildered passengers who were beginning to rush from their staterooms, to the deck. In the wild tumult which prevailed, she might have been thrown down and trampled under foot, had not a strong arm seized her around the waist, and borne her towards the stern, where there were but few persons.

"Wait here!" said a voice, and her protector plunged into the crowd.

She saw, instantly, the terrible fate which had fallen upon the vessel. The bow was shrouded in whirls of smoke, through which dull red flashes began to show themselves; and all the length and breadth of the deck was filled with a screaming, struggling, fighting mass of desperate human beings. She saw the captain, officers, and a few of the crew working in vain against the disorder: she saw the boats filled before they were lowered, and heard the shrieks as they were capsized; she saw spars and planks and benches cast overboard, and maddened men plunging after them; and then, like the sudden opening of the mouth of Hell, the relentless, triumphant fire burst through the forward deck and shot up to the foreyard.

She was leaning against the mizen shrouds, between the coils of rope. Nobody appeared to notice her, although the quarter-deck was fast filling with persons driven back by the fire, yet still shrinking from the terror and uncertainty of the sea. She thought: "It is but death—why should I fear? The waves are at hand, to save me from all suffering." And the collective horror of hundreds of beings did not so overwhelm her as she had both fancied and feared; the tragedy of each individual life was lost in the confusion, and was she not a sharer in their doom?

Suddenly, a man stood before her with a cork life-preserver in his hands, and buckled it around her securely, under the arms. He was panting and almost exhausted, yet he strove to make his voice firm, and even cheerful, as he said:

"We fought the cowardly devils as long as there was any hope. Two boats are off, and two capsized; in ten minutes more every soul must take to the water. Trust to me, and I will save you or die with you!"

"What else can I do?" she answered.

610

With a few powerful strokes of an axe, he broke off the top of the pilot-house, bound two or three planks to it with ropes, and dragged the mass to the bulwarks.

"The minute this goes," he then said to her, "you go after it, and I follow. Keep still when you rise to the surface."

She left the shrouds, took hold of the planks at his side, and they heaved the rude raft into the sea. In an instant she was seized and whirled over the side; she instinctively held her breath, felt a shock, felt herself swallowed up in an awful, fathomless coldness, and then found herself floating below the huge towering hull which slowly drifted away.

In another moment there was one at her side. "Lay your hand on my shoulder," he said; and when she did so, swam for the raft, which they soon reached. While she supported herself by one of the planks he so arranged and bound together the pieces of timber that in a short time they could climb upon them and rest, not much washed by the waves. The ship drifted further and further, casting a faint, though awful, glare over the sea, until the light was suddenly extinguished, as the hull sank.

The dawn was in the sky by this time, and as it broadened they could see faint specks here and there, where others, like themselves, clung to drifting spars. Mrs. Lawrie shuddered with cold and the reaction from an excitement which had been far more powerful than she knew at the time.

Her preserver then took off his coat, wrapped it around her, and produced a pocket-flask, saying; "this will support us the longest; it is all I could find, or bring with me."

She sat, leaning against his shoulder, though partly turned away from him: all she could say was: "you are very good."

After awhile he spoke, and his voice seemed changed to her ears. "You must be thinking of Mr. Lawrie. It will, indeed, be terrible for him to hear of the disaster, before knowing that you are saved."

"God has spared him that distress," she answered. "Mr. Lawrie died, a

611

year ago."

She felt a start in the strong frame upon which she leaned. After a few minutes of silence, he slowly shifted his position towards her, yet still without facing her, and said, almost in a whisper:

"You have said that I am very good. Will you put your hand in mine?"

She stretched hers eagerly and gratefully towards him. What had happened? Through all the numbness of her blood, there sprang a strange new warmth from his strong palm, and a pulse, which she had almost forgotten as a dream of the past, began to beat through her frame. She turned around all a-tremble, and saw his face in the glow of the coming day.

"Leonard Clare!" she cried.

"Then you have not forgotten me?"

"Could one forget, when the other remembers?"

The words came involuntarily from her lips. She felt what they implied, the moment afterwards, and said no more. But he kept her hand in his.

"Mrs. Lawrie," he began, after another silence, "we are hanging by a hair on the edge of life, but I shall gladly let that hair break, since I may tell you now, purely and in the hearing of God, how I have tried to rise to you out of the low place in which you found me. At first you seemed too far; but you yourself led me the first step of the way, and I have steadily kept my eyes on you, and followed it. When I had learned my trade, I came to the city. No labor was too hard for me, no study too difficult. I was becoming a new man, I saw all that was still lacking, and how to reach it, and I watched you, unknown, at a distance. Then I heard of your engagement: you were lost, and something of which I had begun to dream, became insanity. I determined to trample it out of my life. The daughter of the master-builder, whose first assistant I was, had always favored me in her society; and I soon persuaded her to love me. I fancied, too, that I loved her as most married men seemed to love their wives; the union would advance me to a partnership in her father's business, and my fortune would then be secured. You know what happened;

612

but you do not know how the sight of your face planted the old madness again in my life, and made me a miserable husband, a miserable man of wealth, almost a scoffer at the knowledge I had acquired for your sake.

"When my wife died, taking an only child with her, there was nothing left to me except the mechanical ambition to make myself, without you, what I imagined I might have become, through you. I have studied and travelled, lived alone and in society, until your world seemed to be almost mine: but you were not there!"

The sun had risen, while they sat, rocking on their frail support. Her hand still lay in his, and her head rested on his shoulder. Every word he spoke sank into her heart with a solemn sweetness, in which her whole nature was silent and satisfied. Why should she speak? He knew all.

Yes, it seemed that he knew. His arm stole around her, and her head was drawn from his shoulder to the warm breadth of his breast.

Something hard pressed her cheek, and she lifted her hand to move it aside. He drew forth a flat medallion case; and to the unconscious question in her face, such a sad, tender smile came to his lips, that she could not repress a sudden pain. Was it the miniature of his dead wife?

He opened the case, and showed her, under the glass, a faded, pressed flower.

"What is it?" she asked.

"The Brandywine cowslip you dropped, when you spoke to me in the lane. Then it was that you showed me the first step of the way."

She laid her head again upon his bosom. Hour after hour they sat, and the light swells of the sea heaved them aimlessly to and fro, and the sun burned them, and the spray drenched their limbs. At last Leonard Clare roused himself and looked around: he felt numb and faint, and he saw, also, that her strength was rapidly failing.

"We cannot live much longer, I fear," he said, clasping her closely in his arms. "Kiss me once, darling, and then we will die."

She clung to him and kissed him.

"There is life, not death, in your lips!" he cried. "Oh, God, if we should live!"

He rose painfully to his feet, stood, tottering? on the raft, and looked across the waves. Presently he began to tremble, then to sob like a child, and at last spoke, through his tears:

"A sail! a sail!—and heading towards us!"

# MRS. STRONGITHARM'S REPORT.

Mr. Editor,—If you ever read the "Burroak Banner" (which you will find among your exchanges, as the editor publishes your prospectus for six weeks every year, and sends no bill to you) my name will not be that of a stranger. Let me throw aside all affectation of humility, and say that I hope it is already and not unfavorably familiar to you. I am informed by those who claim to know that the manuscripts of obscure writers are passed over by you editors without examination—in short, that I must first have a name, if I hope to make one. The fact that an article of three hundred and seventy-five pages, which I sent, successively, to the "North American Review," the "Catholic World," and the "Radical," was in each case returned to me with MY knot on the tape by which it was tied, convinces me that such is indeed the case. A few years ago I should not have meekly submitted to treatment like this; but late experiences have taught me the vanity of many womanly dreams.

You are acquainted with the part I took (I am SURE you must have seen it in the "Burroak Banner" eight years ago) in creating that public sentiment in our favor which invested us with all the civil and political rights of men. How the editors of the "Revolution," to which I subscribe, and the conventions in favor of the equal rights of women, recently held in Boston and other cities, have failed to notice our noble struggle, is a circumstance for which I will not try to account. I will only say—and it is a hint which SOME PERSONS will understand—that there are other forms of jealousy than those which spring from love.

It is, indeed, incredible that so little is known, outside the State of Atlantic, of the experiment—I mean the achievement—of the last eight years. While the war lasted, we did not complain that our work was ignored; but now that our sisters in other States are acting as if in complete unconsciousness of what WE have done—now that we need their aid and they need ours (but in different ways), it is time that somebody should speak. Were Selina Whiston living, I should leave the task to her pen; she never recovered from the shock and mortification of her experiences in the State Legislature, in '64—but I will not anticipate the history. Of all the band of female iconoclasts, as the Hon. Mr. Screed called us in jest—it was no jest afterwards, HIS image being the first to go down—of all, I say, "some are married, and some are dead," and there is really no one left so familiar with the circumstances as I am, and equally competent to give a report of them.

Mr. Spelter (the editor of the "Burroak Banner") suggests that I must be brief, if I wish my words to reach the ears of the millions for whom they are designed; and I shall do my best to be so. If I were not obliged to begin at the very beginning, and if the interests of Atlantic had not been swallowed up, like those of other little States, in the whirlpool of national politics, I should have much less to say. But if Mr. George Fenian Brain and Mrs. Candy Station do not choose to inform the public of either the course or the results of our struggle, am I to blame? If I could have attended the convention in Boston, and had been allowed to speak—and I am sure the distinguished Chairwoman would have given me a chance—it would have been the best way, no doubt, to set our case before the world.

I must first tell you how it was that we succeeded in forcing the men to accept our claims, so much in advance of other States. We were indebted for it chiefly to the skill and adroitness of Selina Whiston. The matter had been agitated, it is true, for some years before, and as early as 1856, a bill, drawn up by Mrs. Whiston herself, had been introduced into the Legislature, where it received three votes. Moreover, we had held meetings in almost every election precinct in the State, and our Annual Fair (to raise funds) at Gaston, while the Legislature was in session, was always very brilliant and successful. So the people were not entirely unprepared.

Although our State had gone for Fremont in 1856, by a small majority, the Democrats afterwards elected their Governor; and both parties, therefore, had hopes of success in 1860. The canvass began early, and was very animated. Mrs. Whiston had already inaugurated the custom of attending political meetings, and occasionally putting a question to the stump orator—no matter of which party; of sometimes, indeed, taking the stump herself, after the others had exhausted their wind. She was very witty, as you know, and

616

her stories were so good and so capitally told, that neither Democrat nor Republican thought of leaving the ground while she was upon the stand.

Now, it happened that our Congressional District was one of the closest. It happened, also, that our candidate (I am a Republican, and so is Mr. Strongitharm) was rather favorably inclined to the woman's cause. It happened, thirdly—and this is the seemingly insignificant pivot upon which we whirled into triumph—that he, Mr. Wrangle, and the opposing candidate, Mr. Tumbrill, had arranged to hold a joint meeting at Burroak. This meeting took place on a magnificent day, just after the oats-harvest; and everybody, for twenty miles around, was there. Mrs. Whiston, together with Sarah Pincher, Olympia Knapp, and several other prominent advocates of our cause, met at my house in the morning; and we all agreed that it was time to strike a blow. The rest of us magnanimously decided to take no part in the concerted plan, though very eager to do so. Selina Whiston declared that she must have the field to herself; and when she said that, we knew she meant it.

It was generally known that she was on the ground. In fact, she spent most of the time while Messrs. Wrangle and Tumbrill were speaking, in walking about through the crowds—so after an hour apiece for the gentlemen, and then fifteen minutes apiece for a rejoinder, and the Star Spangled Banner from the band, for both sides, we were not a bit surprised to hear a few cries of "Whiston!" from the audience. Immediately we saw the compact gray bonnet and brown serge dress (she knew what would go through a crowd without tearing!) splitting the wedge of people on the steps leading to the platform. I noticed that the two Congressional candidates looked at each other and smiled, in spite of the venomous charges they had just been making.

Well—I won't attempt to report her speech, though it was her most splendid effort (as people WILL say, when it was no effort to her at all). But the substance of it was this: after setting forth woman's wrongs and man's tyranny, and taxation without representation, and an equal chance, and fair-play, and a struggle for life (which you know all about from the other conventions), she turned squarely around to the two candidates and said:

"Now to the practical application. You, Mr. Wrangle, and you, Mr.

Tumbrill, want to be elected to Congress. The district is a close one: you have both counted the votes in advance (oh, I know your secrets!) and there isn't a difference of a hundred in your estimates. A very little will turn the scale either way. Perhaps a woman's influence—perhaps my voice—might do it. But I will give you an equal chance. So much power is left to woman, despite what you withhold, that we, the women of Putnam, Shinnebaug, and Rancocus counties, are able to decide which of you shall be elected. Either of you would give a great deal to have a majority of the intelligent women of the District on your side: it would already be equivalent to success. Now, to show that we understand the political business from which you have excluded us— to prove that we are capable of imitating the noble example of MEN—we offer to sell our influence, as they their votes, to the highest bidder!"

There was great shouting and cheering among the people at this, but the two candidates, somehow or other, didn't seem much amused.

"I stand here," she continued, "in the interest of my struggling sisters, and with authority to act for them. Which of you will bid the most—not in offices or material advantages, as is the way of your parties, but in the way of help to the Woman's Cause? Which of you will here publicly pledge himself to say a word for us, from now until election-day, whenever he appears upon the stump?"

There was repeated cheering, and cries of "Got 'em there!" (Men are so vulgar).

"I pause for a reply. Shall they not answer me?" she continued, turning to the audience.

Then there were tremendous cries of "Yes! yes! Wrangle! Tumbrill!"

Mr. Wrangle looked at Mr. Tumbrill, and made a motion with his head, signifying that he should speak. Then Mr. Tumbrill looked at Mr. Wrangle, and made a motion that HE should speak. The people saw all this, and laughed and shouted as if they would never finish.

Mr. Wrangle, on second thoughts (this is my private surmise), saw that boldness would just then be popular; so he stepped forward.

"Do I understand," he said, "that my fair and eloquent friend demands perfect political and civil equality for her sex?"

"I do!" exclaimed Selina Whiston, in her firmest manner.

"Let me be more explicit," he continued. "You mean precisely the same rights, the same duties, the same obligations, the same responsibilities?"

She repeated the phrases over after him, affirmatively, with an emphasis which I never heard surpassed.

"Pardon me once more," said Mr. Wrangle; "the right to vote, to hold office, to practise law, theology, medicine, to take part in all municipal affairs, to sit on juries, to be called upon to aid in the execution of the law, to aid in suppressing disturbances, enforcing public order, and performing military duty?"

Here there were loud cheers from the audience; and a good many voices cried out: "Got her there!" (Men are so very vulgar.)

Mrs. Whiston looked troubled for a moment, but she saw that a moment's hesitation would be fatal to our scheme, so she brought out her words as if each one were a maul-blow on the butt-end of a wedge:

"All—that—we—demand!"

"Then," said Mr. Wrangle, "I bid my support in exchange for the women's! Just what the speaker demands, without exception or modification—equal privileges, rights, duties and obligations, without regard to the question of sex! Is that broad enough?"

I was all in a tremble when it came to that. Somehow Mr. Wrangle's acceptance of the bid did not inspire me, although it promised so much. I had anticipated opposition, dissatisfaction, tumult. So had Mrs. Whiston, and I could see, and the crowd could see, that she was not greatly elated.

Mr. Wrangle made a very significant bow to Mr. Tumbrill, and then sat down. There were cries of "Tumbrill!" and that gentleman—none of us, of course, believing him sincere, for we knew his private views—came forward and made exactly the same pledge. I will do both parties the justice to say that they faithfully kept their word; nay, it was generally thought the repetition of their brief pleas for woman, at some fifty meetings before election came, had gradually conducted them to the belief that they were expressing their own personal sentiments. The mechanical echo in public thus developed into an opinion in private. My own political experience has since demonstrated to me that this is a phenomenon very common among men.

The impulse generated at that meeting gradually spread all over the State. We—the leaders of the Women's Movement—did not rest until we had exacted the same pledge from all the candidates of both parties; and the nearer it drew towards election-day, the more prominence was given, in the public meetings, to the illustration and discussion of the subject. Our State went for Lincoln by a majority of 2763 (as you will find by consulting the "Tribune Almanac"), and Mr. Wrangle was elected to Congress, having received a hundred and forty-two more votes than his opponent. Mr. Tumbrill has always attributed his defeat to his want of courage in not taking up at once the glove which Selina Whiston threw down.

I think I have said enough to make it clear how the State of Atlantic came to be the first to grant equal civil and political rights to women. When the Legislature of 1860-'61 met at Gaston, we estimated that we might count upon fifty-three out of the seventy-one Republican Senators and Assemblymen, and on thirty-four out of the sixty-five Democrats. This would give a majority of twenty-eight in the House, and ten in the Senate. Should the bill pass, there was still a possibility that it might be vetoed by the Governor, of whom we did not feel sure. We therefore arranged that our Annual Fair should be held a fortnight later than usual, and that the proceeds (a circumstance known only to the managers) should be devoted to a series of choice suppers, at which we entertained, not only the Governor and our friends in both Houses, but also, like true Christians, our legislatorial enemies. Olympia Knapp, who, you know, is so very beautiful, presided at these entertainments. She put forth all her splendid powers, and with more effect than any of us suspected. On the day before the bill reached its third reading, the Governor made her an offer of marriage. She came to the managers in great agitation, and laid the matter before them, stating that she was overwhelmed with surprise (though Sarah Pincher always maintained that she wasn't in the least), and asking their advice. We discussed the question for four hours, and finally decided that the interests of the cause would oblige her to accept the Governor's hand. "Oh, I am so glad!" cried Olympia, "for I accepted him at once." It was a brave, a noble deed!

Now, I would ask those who assert that women are incapable of conducting the business of politics, to say whether any set of men, of either party, could have played their cards more skilfully? Even after the campaign was over we might have failed, had it not been for the suppers. We owed this idea, like the first, to the immortal Selina Whiston. A lucky accident—as momentous in its way as the fall of an apple to Newton, or the flying of a kite to Dr. Franklin—gave her the secret principle by which the politics of men are directed. Her house in Whittletown was the half of a double frame building, and the rear-end of the other part was the private office of—but no, I will not mention the name—a lawyer and a politician. He was known as a "wirepuller," and the other wire-pullers of his party used to meet in his office and discuss matters. Mrs. Whiston always asserted that there was a mouse-hole through the partition; but she had energy enough to have made a hole herself, for the sake of the cause.

She never would tell us all she overheard. "It is enough," she would say, "that I know how the thing is done."

I remember that we were all considerably startled when she first gave us an outline of her plan. On my saying that I trusted the dissemination of our principles would soon bring us a great adhesion, she burst out with:

"Principles! Why if we trust to principles, we shall never succeed! We must rely upon INFLUENCES, as the men do; we must fight them with their own weapons, and even then we are at a disadvantage, because we cannot very well make use of whiskey and cigars."

We yielded, because we had grown accustomed to be guided by her; and, moreover, we had seen, time and again, how she could succeed—as, for instance, in the Nelson divorce case (but I don't suppose you ever heard of that), when the matter seemed nigh hopeless to all of us. The history of 1860 and the following winter proves that in her the world has lost a stateswoman. Mr. Wrangle and Governor Battle have both said to me that they never knew a measure to be so splendidly engineered both before the public and in the State Legislature.

After the bill had been passed, and signed by the Governor, and so had become a law, and the grand Women's Jubilee had been held at Gaston, the excitement subsided. It would be nearly a year to the next State election, and none of the women seemed to care for the local and municipal elections in the spring. Besides, there was a good deal of anxiety among them in regard to the bill, which was drawn up in almost the exact terms used by Mr. Wrangle at the political meeting. In fact, we always have suspected that he wrote it. The word "male" was simply omitted from all laws. "Nothing is changed," said Mrs. Whiston, quoting Charles X., "there are only 201,758 more citizens in Atlantic!"

This was in January, 1861, you must remember; and the shadow of the coming war began to fall over us. Had the passage of our bill been postponed a fortnight it would have been postponed indefinitely, for other and (for the men) more powerful excitements followed one upon the other. Even our jubilee was thinly attended, and all but two of the members on whom we relied for speeches failed us. Governor Battle, who was to have presided, was at Washington, and Olympia, already his wife, accompanied him. (I may add that she has never since taken any active part with us. They have been in Europe for the last three years.)

Most of the women—here in Burroak, at least—expressed a feeling of disappointment that there was no palpable change in their lot, no sense of extended liberty, such as they imagined would come to transform them into brighter and better creatures. They supposed that they would at once gain in importance in the eyes of the men; but the men were now so preoccupied by the events at the South that they seemed to have forgotten our political value. Speaking for myself, as a good Union woman, I felt that I must lay aside, for a time, the interests of my sex. Once, it is true, I proposed to accompany Mr. Strongitharm to a party caucus at the Wrangle House; but he so suddenly discovered that he had business in another part of the town, that I withdrew my proposition.

As the summer passed over, and the first and second call for volunteers had been met, and more than met, by the patriotic men of the State (how we blessed them!) we began to take courage, and to feel, that if our new civil position brought us no very tangible enjoyment, at least it imposed upon us no very irksome duties.

The first practical effect of the new law came to light at the August term of our County Court. The names of seven women appeared on the list of jurors, but only three of them answered to their names. One, the wife of a poor farmer, was excused by the Judge, as there was no one to look after six small children in her absence; another was a tailoress, with a quantity of work on hand, some of which she proposed bringing with her into Court, in order to save time; but as this could not be allowed, she made so much trouble that she was also finally let off. Only one, therefore, remained to serve; fortunately for the credit of our sex, she was both able and willing to do so; and we afterward made a subscription, and presented her with a silver fish-knife, on account of her having tired out eleven jurymen, and brought in a verdict of $5,000 damages against a young man whom she convicted of seduction. She told me that no one would ever know what she endured during those three days; but the morals of our county have been better ever since.

Mr. Spelter told me that his State exchanges showed that there had been difficulties of the same kind in all the other counties. In Mendip (the county-town of which is Whittletown, Mrs. Whiston's home) the immediate result had been the decision, on the part of the Commissioners, to build an addition at the rear of the Court-House, with large, commodious and well-furnished jury-rooms, so arranged that a comfortable privacy was secured to the jury-women. I did my best to have the same improvement adopted here, but, alas! I have not the ability of Selina Whiston in such matters, and there is nothing to this day but the one vile, miserable room, properly furnished in no particular except spittoons.

The nominating Conventions were held in August, also, and we were therefore called upon to move at once, in order to secure our fair share. Much valuable time had been lost in discussing a question of policy, namely, whether we should attach ourselves to the two parties already in existence, according to our individual inclinations, or whether we should form a third party for ourselves. We finally accepted the former proposition, and I think wisely; for the most of us were so ignorant of political tricks and devices, that we still needed to learn from the men, and we could not afford to draw upon us the hostility of both parties, in the very infancy of our movement.

Never in my life did I have such a task, as in drumming up a few women to attend the primary township meeting for the election of delegates. It was impossible to make them comprehend its importance. Even after I had done my best to explain the technicalities of male politics, and fancied that I had made some impression, the answer would be: "Well, I'd go, I'm sure, just to oblige you, but then there's the tomatoes to be canned"—or, "I'm so behindhand with my darning and patching"—or, "John'll be sure to go, and there's no need of two from the same house"—and so on, until I was mightily discouraged. There were just nine of us, all told, to about a hundred men. I won't deny that our situation that night, at the Wrangle House, was awkward and not entirely agreeable. To be sure the landlord gave us the parlor, and most of the men came in, now and then, to speak to us; but they managed the principal matters all by themselves, in the bar-room, which was such a mess of smoke and stale liquor smells, that it turned my stomach when I ventured in for two minutes.

I don't think we should have accomplished much, but for a 'cute idea of Mrs. Wilbur, the tinman's wife. She went to the leaders, and threatened them that the women's vote should be cast in a body for the Democratic candidates, unless we were considered in making up the ticket. THAT helped: the delegates were properly instructed, and the County Convention afterward nominated two men and one woman as candidates for the Assembly. That woman was— as I need hardly say, for the world knows it—myself. I had not solicited the honor, and therefore could not refuse, especially as my daughter Melissa was then old enough to keep house in my absence. No woman had applied for the nomination for Sheriff, but there were seventeen schoolmistresses anxious for the office of County Treasurer. The only other nomination given to the women, however, was that of Director (or rather, Directress) of the Poor, which was conferred on Mrs. Bassett, wife of a clergyman.

Mr. Strongitharm insisted that I should, in some wise, prepare myself for my new duties, by reading various political works, and I conscientiously tried to do so—but, dear me! it was much more of a task than I supposed. We had all read the debate on our bill, of course; but I always skipped the dry, stupid stuff about the tariff, and finance, and stay laws and exemption laws, and railroad company squabbles; and for the life of me I can't see, to this day, what connection there is between these things and Women's Rights. But, as I said, I did my best, with the help of Webster's Dictionary; although the further I went the less I liked it.

As election-day drew nearer, our prospects looked brighter. The Republican ticket, under the editorial head of the "Burroak Banner," with my name and Mrs. Bassett's among the men's, was such an evidence, that many women, notably opposed to the cause, said: "We didn't want the right, but since we have it, we shall make use of it." This was exactly what Mrs. Whiston had foretold. We estimated that—taking the County tickets all over the State—we had about one-twentieth of the Republican, and one-fiftieth of the Democratic, nominations. This was far from being our due, but still it was a good beginning.

My husband insisted that I should go very early to the polls. I could scarcely restrain a tear of emotion as I gave my first ballot into the hands of the judges. There were not a dozen persons present, and the act did not produce the sensation which I expected. One man cried out: "Three cheers for our Assemblywoman!" and they gave them; and I thereupon returned home in the best spirits. I devoted the rest of the day to relieving poorer women, who could not have spared the time to vote, if I had not, meanwhile, looked after their children. The last was Nancy Black, the shoemaker's wife in our street, who kept me waiting upon her till it was quite dark. When she finally came, the skirt of her dress was ripped nearly off, her hair was down and her comb broken; but she was triumphant, for Sam Black was with her, and SOBER. "The first time since we were married, Mrs. Strongitharm!" she cried. Then she whispered to me, as I was leaving: "And I've killed HIS vote, anyhow!"

When the count was made, our party was far ahead. Up to this time, I think, the men of both parties had believed that only a few women, here and there, would avail themselves of their new right—but they were roundly mistaken. Although only ten per cent. of the female voters went to the polls, yet three-fourths of them voted the Republican ticket, which increased the majority of that party, in the State, about eleven thousand.

It was amazing what an effect followed this result. The whole country would have rung with it, had we not been in the midst of war. Mr. Wrangle declared that he had always been an earnest advocate of the women's cause. Governor Battle, in his next message, congratulated the State on the signal success of the experiment, and the Democratic masses, smarting under their defeat, cursed their leaders for not having been sharp enough to conciliate the new element. The leaders themselves said nothing, and in a few weeks the rank and file recovered their cheerfulness. Even Mrs. Whiston, with all her experience, was a little puzzled by this change of mood. Alas! she was far from guessing the correct explanation.

It was a great comfort to me that Mrs. Whiston was also elected to the Legislature. My husband had just then established his manufactory of patent self-scouring knife-blades (now so celebrated), and could not leave; so I was obliged to go up to Gaston all alone, when the session commenced. There were but four of us Assemblywomen, and although the men treated us with great courtesy, I was that nervous that I seemed to detect either commiseration or satire everywhere. Before I had even taken my seat, I was addressed by fifteen or twenty different gentlemen, either great capitalists, or great engineers, or distinguished lawyers, all interested in various schemes for developing the resources of our State by new railroads, canals or ferries. I then began to comprehend the grandeur of the Legislator's office. My voice could assist in making possible these magnificent improvements, and I promised it to all. Mr. Filch, President of the Shinnebaug and Great Western Consolidated Line, was so delighted with my appreciation of his plan for reducing the freight on grain from Nebraska, that he must have written extravagant accounts of me to his wife; for she sent me, at Christmas, one of the loveliest shawls I ever beheld.

I had frequently made short addresses at our public meetings, and was considered to have my share of self-possession; but I never could accustom myself to the keen, disturbing, irritating atmosphere of the Legislature. Everybody seemed wide-awake and aggressive, instead of pleasantly receptive; there were so many "points of order," and what not; such complete disregard, among the members, of each other's feelings; and, finally—a thing I could never understand, indeed—such inconsistency and lack of principle in the intercourse of the two parties. How could I feel assured of their sincerity, when I saw the very men chatting and laughing together, in the lobbies, ten minutes after they had been facing each other like angry lions in the debate?

Mrs. Whiston, also, had her trials of the same character. Nothing ever annoyed her so much as a little blunder she made, the week after the opening of the session. I have not yet mentioned that there was already a universal dissatisfaction among the women, on account of their being liable to military service. The war seemed to have hardly begun, as yet, and conscription was already talked about; the women, therefore, clamored for an exemption on account of sex. Although we all felt that this was a retrograde movement, the pressure was so great that we yielded. Mrs. Whiston, reluctant at first, no sooner made up her mind that the thing must be done, than she furthered it with all her might. After several attempts to introduce a bill, which were always cut off by some "point of order," she unhappily lost her usual patience.

I don't know that I can exactly explain how it happened, for what the men call "parliamentary tactics" always made me fidgetty. But the "previous question" turned up (as it always seemed to me to do, at the wrong time), and cut her off before she had spoken ten words.

"Mr. Speaker!" she protested; "there is no question, previous to this, which needs the consideration of the house! This is first in importance, and demands your immediate—"

"Order! order!" came from all parts of the house.

"I am in order—the right is always in order!" she exclaimed, getting

627

more and more excited. "We women are not going to be contented with the mere show of our rights on this floor; we demand the substance—"

And so she was going on, when there arose the most fearful tumult. The upshot of it was, that the speaker ordered the sergeant-at-arms to remove Mrs. Whiston; one of the members, more considerate, walked across the floor to her, and tried to explain in what manner she was violating the rules; and in another minute she sat down, so white, rigid and silent that it made me shake in my shoes to look at her.

"I have made a great blunder," she said to me, that evening; "and it may set us back a little; but I shall recover my ground." Which she did, I assure you. She cultivated the acquaintance of the leaders of both parties, studied their tactics, and quietly waited for a good opportunity to bring in her bill. At first, we thought it would pass; but one of the male members presently came out with a speech, which dashed our hopes to nothing. He simply took the ground that there must be absolute equality in citizenship; that every privilege was balanced by a duty, every trust accompanied with its responsibility. He had no objection to women possessing equal rights with men—but to give them all civil rights and exempt them from the most important obligation of service, would be, he said, to create a privileged class—a female aristocracy. It was contrary to the spirit of our institutions. The women had complained of taxation without representation; did they now claim the latter without the former?

The people never look more than half-way into a subject, and so this speech was immensely popular. I will not give Mrs. Whiston's admirable reply; for Mr. Spelter informs me that you will not accept an article, if it should make more than seventy or eighty printed pages. It is enough that our bill was "killed," as the men say (a brutal word); and the women of the State laid the blame of the failure upon us. You may imagine that we suffered under this injustice; but worse was to come.

As I said before, a great many things came up in the Legislature which I did not understand—and, to be candid, did not care to understand. But I was obliged to vote, nevertheless, and in this extremity I depended pretty much on Mrs. Whiston's counsel. We could not well go to the private nightly confabs of the members—indeed, they did not invite us; and when it came to the issue of State bonds, bank charters, and such like, I felt as if I were blundering along in the dark.

One day, I received, to my immense astonishment, a hundred and more letters, all from the northern part of our county. I opened them, one after the other, and—well, it is beyond my power to tell you what varieties of indignation and abuse fell upon me. It seems that I had voted against the bill to charter the Mendip Extension Railroad Co. I had been obliged to vote for or against so many things, that it was impossible to recollect them all. However, I procured the printed journal, and, sure enough! there, among the nays, was "Strongitharm." It was not a week after that—and I was still suffering in mind and body—when the newspapers in the interest of the Rancocus and Great Western Consolidated accused me (not by name, but the same thing—you know how they do it) of being guilty of taking bribes. Mr. Filch, of the Shinnebaug Consolidated had explained to me so beautifully the superior advantages of his line, that the Directors of the other company took their revenge in this vile, abominable way.

That was only the beginning of my trouble. What with these slanders and longing for the quiet of our dear old home at Burroak, I was almost sick; yet the Legislature sat on, and sat on, until I was nearly desperate. Then one morning came a despatch from my husband: "Melissa is drafted—come home!" How I made the journey I can't tell; I was in an agony of apprehension, and when Mr. Strongitharm and Melissa both met me at the Burroak Station, well and smiling, I fell into a hysterical fit of laughing and crying, for the first time in my life.

Billy Brandon, who was engaged to Melissa, came forward and took her place like a man; he fought none the worse, let me tell you, because he represented a woman, and (I may as well say it now) he came home a Captain, without a left arm—but Melissa seems to have three arms for his sake.

You have no idea what a confusion and lamentation there was all over the State. A good many women were drafted, and those who could neither get substitutes for love nor money, were marched to Gaston, where the recruiting Colonel was considerate enough to give them a separate camp. In a week, however, the word came from Washington that the Army Regulations of the United States did not admit of their being received; and they came home blessing Mr. Stanton. This was the end of drafting women in our State.

Nevertheless, the excitement created by the draft did not subside at once. It was seized upon by the Democratic leaders, as part of a plan already concocted, which they then proceeded to set in operation. It succeeded only too well, and I don't know when we shall ever see the end of it.

We had more friends among the Republicans at the start, because all the original Abolitionists in the State came into that party in 1860. Our success had been so rapid and unforeseen that the Democrats continued their opposition even after female suffrage was an accomplished fact; but the leaders were shrewd enough to see that another such election as the last would ruin their party in the State. So their trains were quietly laid, and the match was not applied until all Atlantic was ringing with the protestations of the unwilling conscripts and the laments of their families. Then came, like three claps of thunder in one, sympathy for the women, acquiescence in their rights, and invitations to them, everywhere, to take part in the Democratic caucuses and conventions. Most of the prominent women of the State were deluded for a time by this manifestation, and acted with the party for the sake of the sex.

I had no idea, however, what the practical result of this movement would be, until, a few weeks before election, I was calling upon Mrs. Buckwalter, and happened to express my belief that we Republicans were going to carry the State again, by a large majority.

"I am very glad of it," said she, with an expression of great relief, "because then my vote will not be needed."

"Why!" I exclaimed; "you won't decline to vote, surely?"

"Worse than that," she answered, "I am afraid I shall have to vote with the other side."

630

Now as I knew her to be a good Republican, I could scarcely believe my ears. She blushed, I must admit, when she saw my astonished face.

"I'm so used to Bridget, you know," she continued, "and good girls are so very hard to find, nowadays. She has as good as said that she won't stay a day later than election, if I don't vote for HER candidate; and what am I to do?"

"Do without!" I said shortly, getting up in my indignation.

"Yes, that's very well for you, with your wonderful PHYSIQUE," said Mrs. Buckwalter, quietly, "but think of me with my neuralgia, and the pain in my back! It would be a dreadful blow, if I should lose Bridget."

Well—what with torch-light processions, and meetings on both sides, Burroak was in such a state of excitement when election came, that most of the ladies of my acquaintance were almost afraid to go to the polls. I tried to get them out during the first hours after sunrise, when I went myself, but in vain. Even that early, I heard things that made me shudder. Those who came later, went home resolved to give up their rights rather than undergo a second experience of rowdyism. But it was a jubilee for the servant girls. Mrs. Buckwalter didn't gain much by her apostasy, for Bridget came home singing "The Wearing of the Green," and let fall a whole tray full of the best china before she could be got to bed.

Burroak, which, the year before, had a Republican majority of three hundred, now went for the Democrats by more than five hundred. The same party carried the State, electing their Governor by near twenty thousand. The Republicans would now have gladly repealed the bill giving us equal rights, but they were in a minority, and the Democrats refused to co-operate. Mrs. Whiston, who still remained loyal to our side, collected information from all parts of the State, from which it appeared that four-fifths of all the female citizens had voted the Democratic ticket. In New Lisbon, our great manufacturing city, with its population of nearly one hundred thousand, the party gained three thousand votes, while the accessions to the Republican ranks were only about four hundred.

Mrs. Whiston barely escaped being defeated; her majority was reduced from seven hundred to forty-three. Eleven Democratic Assemblywomen and four Senatoresses were chosen, however, so that she had the consolation of knowing that her sex had gained, although her party had lost. She was still in good spirits: "It will all right itself in time," she said.

You will readily guess, after what I have related, that I was not only not re-elected to the Legislature, but that I was not even a candidate. I could have born the outrageous attacks of the opposite party; but the treatment I had received from my own "constituents" (I shall always hate the word) gave me a new revelation of the actual character of political life. I have not mentioned half the worries and annoyances to which I was subjected—the endless, endless letters and applications for office, or for my influence in some way—the abuse and threats when I could not possibly do what was desired—the exhibitions of selfishness and disregard of all great and noble principles—and finally, the shameless advances which were made by what men call "the lobby," to secure my vote for this, that, and the other thing.

Why, it fairly made my hair stand on end to hear the stories which the pleasant men, whom I thought so grandly interested in schemes for "the material development of the country," told about each other. Mrs. Filch's shawl began to burn my shoulders before I had worn it a half a dozen times. (I have since given it to Melissa, as a wedding-present).

Before the next session was half over, I was doubly glad of being safe at home. Mrs. Whiston supposed that the increased female representation would give her more support, and indeed it seemed so, at first. But after her speech on the Bounty bill, only two of the fifteen Democratic women would even speak to her, and all hope of concord of action in the interests of women was at an end. We read the debates, and my blood fairly boiled when I found what taunts and sneers, and epithets she was forced to endure. I wondered how she could sit still under them.

To make her position worse, the adjoining seat was occupied by an Irishwoman, who had been elected by the votes of the laborers on the new Albemarle Extension, in the neighborhood of which she kept a grocery store. Nelly Kirkpatrick was a great, red-haired giant of a woman, very illiterate, but with some native wit, and good-hearted enough, I am told, when she was in her right mind. She always followed the lead of Mr. Gorham (whose name, you see, came before hers in the call), and a look from him was generally sufficient to quiet her when she was inclined to be noisy.

When the resolutions declaring the war a failure were introduced, the party excitement ran higher than ever. The "lunch-room" (as they called it—I never went there but once, the title having deceived me) in the basement-story of the State House was crowded during the discussion, and every time Nelly Kirkpatrick came up, her face was a shade deeper red. Mr. Gorham's nods and winks were of no avail—speak she would, and speak she did, not so very incoherently, after all, but very abusively. To be sure, you would never have guessed it, if you had read the quiet and dignified report in the papers on her side, the next day.

THEN Mrs. Whiston's patience broke down. "Mr. Speaker," she exclaimed, starting to her feet, "I protest against this House being compelled to listen to such a tirade as has just been delivered. Are we to be disgraced before the world—"

"Oh, hoo! Disgraced, is it?" yelled Nelly Kirkpatrick, violently interrupting her, "and me as dacent a woman as ever she was, or ever will be! Disgraced, hey? Oh, I'll larn her what it is to blaggard her betters!"

And before anybody could imagine what was coming, she pounced upon Mrs. Whiston, with one jerk ripped off her skirt (it was silk, not serge, this time), seized her by the hair, and gave her head such a twist backwards, that the chignon not only came off in her hands, but as her victim opened her mouth too widely in the struggle, the springs of her false teeth were sprung the wrong way, and the entire set flew out and rattled upon the floor.

Of course there were cries of "Order! Order!" and the nearest members—Mr. Gorham among the first—rushed in; but the mischief was done. Mrs. Whiston had always urged upon our minds the necessity of not only being dressed according to the popular fashion, but also as elegantly and becomingly as possible. "If we adopt the Bloomers," she said, "we shall never get our rights, while the world stands. Where it is necessary to influence men, we must be wholly and truly WOMEN, not semi-sexed nondescripts; we must employ every charm Nature gives us and Fashion adds, not hide them under a forked extinguisher!" I give her very words to show you her way of looking at things. Well, now imagine this elegant woman, looking not a day over forty, though she was—but no, I have no right to tell it,—imagine her, I say, with only her scanty natural hair hanging over her ears, her mouth dreadfully fallen in, her skirt torn off, all in open day, before the eyes of a hundred and fifty members (and I am told they laughed immensely, in spite of the scandal that it was), and, if you are human beings, you will feel that she must have been wounded to the very heart.

There was a motion made to expel Nelly Kirkpatrick, and perhaps it might have succeeded—but the railroad hands, all over the State, made a heroine of her, and her party was afraid of losing five or six thousand votes; so only a mild censure was pronounced. But there was no end to the caricatures, and songs, and all sorts of ribaldry, about the occurrence; and even our party said that, although Mrs. Whiston was really and truly a martyr, yet the circumstance was an immense damage to THEM. When she heard THAT, I believe it killed her. She resigned her seat, went home, never appeared again in public, and died within a year. "My dear friend," she wrote to me, not a month before her death, "I have been trying all my life to get a thorough knowledge of the masculine nature, but my woman's plummet will not reach to the bottom of that chaotic pit of selfishness and principle, expedience and firmness for the right, brutality and tenderness, gullibility and devilish shrewdness, which I have tried to sound. Only one thing is clear—we women cannot do without what we have sometimes, alas! sneered at as THE CHIVELRY OF THE SEX. The question of our rights is as clear to me as ever; but we must find a plan to get them without being forced to share, or even to SEE, all that men do in their political lives. We have only beheld some Principle riding aloft, not the mud through which her chariot wheels are dragged. The ways must be swept before we can walk in them—but how and by whom shall this be done?"

For my part, I can't say, and I wish somebody would tell me.

Well—after seeing our State, which we used to be proud of, delivered over for two years to the control of a party whose policy was so repugnant to all our feelings of loyalty, we endeavored to procure, at least a qualification of intelligence for voters. Of course, we didn't get it: the exclusion from suffrage of all who were unable to read and write might have turned the scales again, and given us the State. After our boys came back from the war, we might have succeeded—but their votes were over-balanced by those of the servant-girls, every one of whom turned out, making a whole holiday of the election.

I thought, last fall, that my Maria, who is German, would have voted with us. I stayed at home and did the work myself, on purpose that she might hear the oration of Carl Schurz; but old Hammer, who keeps the lager-beer saloon in the upper end of Burroak, gave a supper and a dance to all the German girls and their beaux, after the meeting, and so managed to secure nine out of ten of their votes for Seymour. Maria proposed going away a week before election, up into Decatur County, where, she said, some relations, just arrived from Bavaria, had settled. I was obliged to let her go, or lose her altogether, but I was comforted by the thought that if her vote were lost for Grant, at least it could not be given to Seymour. After the election was over, and Decatur County, which we had always managed to carry hitherto, went against us, the whole matter was explained. About five hundred girls, we were informed, had been COLONIZED in private families, as extra help, for a fortnight, and of course Maria was one of them. (I have looked at the addresses of her letters, ever since, and not one has she sent to Decatur). A committee has been appointed, and a report made on the election frauds in our State, and we shall see, I suppose, whether any help comes of it.

Now, you mustn't think, from all this, that I am an apostate from the principle of Women's Rights. No, indeed! All the trouble we have had, as I think will be evident to the millions who read my words, comes from THE MEN. They have not only made politics their monopoly, but they have fashioned it into a tremendous, elaborate system, in which there is precious little of either principle or honesty. We can and we MUST "run the machine" (to use another of their vulgar expressions) with them, until we get a chance to knock off the useless wheels and thingumbobs, and scour the whole concern, inside and out. Perhaps the men themselves would like to do this, if they only knew how: men have so little talent for cleaning-up. But when it comes to making a litter, they're at home, let me tell you!

Meanwhile, in our State, things are about as bad as they can be. The women are drawn for juries, the same as ever, but (except in Whittletown, where they have a separate room,) no respectable woman goes, and the fines come heavy on some of us. The demoralization among our help is so bad, that we are going to try Co-operative Housekeeping. If that don't succeed, I shall get brother Samuel, who lives in California, to send me two Chinamen, one for cook and chamber-boy, and one as nurse for Melissa. I console myself with thinking that the end of it all must be good, since the principle is right: but, dear me! I had no idea that I should be called upon to go through such tribulation.

Now the reason I write—and I suppose I must hurry to the end, or you will be out of all patience—is to beg, and insist, and implore my sisters in other States to lose no more time, but at once to coax, or melt, or threaten the men into accepting their claims. We are now so isolated in our rights that we are obliged to bear more than our proper share of the burden. When the States around us shall be so far advanced, there will be a chance for new stateswomen to spring up, and fill Mrs. Whiston's place, and we shall then, I firmly believe, devise a plan to cleanse the great Augean stable of politics by turning into it the river of female honesty and intelligence and morality. But they must do this, somehow or other, without letting the river be tainted by the heaps of pestilent offal it must sweep away. As Lord Bacon says (in that play falsely attributed to Shakespeare)—"Ay, there's the rub!"

If you were to ask me, NOW, what effect the right of suffrage, office, and all the duties of men has had upon the morals of the women of our State, I should be puzzled what to say. It is something like this—if you put a chemical purifying agent into a bucket of muddy water, the water gets clearer, to be sure, but the chemical substance takes up some of the impurity. Perhaps that's rather too strong a comparison; but if you say that men are worse than women, as most people do, then of course we improve them by closer political intercourse, and lose a little ourselves in the process. I leave you to decide the relative loss and gain. To tell you the truth, this is a feature of the question which I would rather not discuss; and I see, by the reports of the recent Conventions, that all the champions of our sex feel the same way.

Well, since I must come to an end somewhere, let it be here. To quote Lord Bacon again, take my "round, unvarnished tale," and perhaps the world will yet acknowledge that some good has been done by

Yours truly,

JANE STRONGITHARM.

## FOOTNOTE:

[1] [ Little Boris.]

# JOSEPH AND HIS FRIEND

The better angel is a man right fair;

The worser spirit a woman colour'd ill.

SHAKSPEARE: Sonnets.

# CHAPTER I. JOSEPH.

Rachel Miller was not a little surprised when her nephew Joseph came to the supper-table, not from the direction of the barn and through the kitchen, as usual, but from the back room up stairs, where he slept. His work-day dress had disappeared; he wore his best Sunday suit, put on with unusual care, and there were faint pomatum odors in the air when he sat down to the table.

Her face said—and she knew it—as plain as any words, "What in the world does this mean?" Joseph, she saw, endeavored to look as though coming down to supper in that costume were his usual habit; so she poured out the tea in silence. Her silence, however, was eloquent; a hundred interrogation-marks would not have expressed its import; and Dennis, the hired man, who sat on the other side of the table, experienced very much the same apprehension of something forthcoming, as when he had killed her favorite speckled hen by mistake.

Before the meal was over, the tension between Joseph and his aunt had so increased by reason of their mutual silence, that it was very awkward and oppressive to both; yet neither knew how to break it easily. There is always a great deal of unnecessary reticence in the intercourse of country people, and in the case of these two it had been specially strengthened by the want of every relationship except that of blood. They were quite ignorant of the fence, the easy thrust and parry of society, where talk becomes an art; silence or the bluntest utterance were their alternatives, and now the one had neutralized the other. Both felt this, and Dennis, in his dull way, felt it too. Although not a party concerned, he was uncomfortable, yet also internally conscious of a desire to laugh.

The resolution of the crisis, however, came by his aid. When the meal was finished and Joseph betook himself to the window, awkwardly drumming upon the pane, while his aunt gathered the plates and cups together, delaying to remove them as was her wont, Dennis said, with his hand on the door-knob: "Shall I saddle the horse right off?"

"I guess so," Joseph answered, after a moment's hesitation.

Rachel paused, with the two silver spoons in her hand. Joseph was still drumming upon the window, but with very irregular taps. The door closed upon Dennis.

"Well," said she, with singular calmness, "a body is not bound to dress particularly fine for watching, though I would as soon show him that much respect, if need be, as anybody else. Don't forget to ask Maria if there's anything I can do for her."

Joseph turned around with a start, a most innocent surprise on his face.

"Why, aunt, what are you talking about?"

"You are not going to Warne's to watch? They have nearer neighbors, to be sure, but when a man dies, everybody is free to offer their services. He was always strong in the faith."

Joseph knew that he was caught, without suspecting her manœuvre. A brighter color ran over his face, up to the roots of his hair. "Why, no!" he exclaimed; "I am going to Warriner's to spend the evening. There's to be a little company there,—a neighborly gathering. I believe it's been talked of this long while, but I was only invited to-day. I saw Bob, in the road-field."

Rachel endeavored to conceal from her nephew's eye the immediate impression of his words. A constrained smile passed over her face, and was instantly followed by a cheerful relief in his.

"Isn't it rather a strange time of year for evening parties?" she then asked, with a touch of severity in her voice.

"They meant to have it in cherry-time, Bob said, when Anna's visitor had come from town."

"That, indeed! I see!" Rachel exclaimed. "It's to be a sort of celebration for—what's-her-name? Blessing, I know,—but the other? Anna Warriner was there last Christmas, and I don't suppose the high notions are out of her head yet. Well, I hope it'll be some time before they take root here! Peace and quiet, peace and quiet, that's been the token of the neighborhood; but town ways are the reverse."

"All the young people are going," Joseph mildly suggested, "and so—"

"O, I don't say you shouldn't go, this time," Rachel interrupted him; "for you ought to be able to judge for yourself what's fit and proper, and what is not. I should be sorry, to be sure, to see you doing anything and going anywhere that would make your mother uneasy if she were living now. It's so hard to be conscientious, and to mind a body's bounden duty, without seeming to interfere."

She heaved a deep sigh, and just touched the corner of her apron to her eyes. The mention of his mother always softened Joseph, and in his earnest desire to live so that his life might be such as to give her joy if she could share it, a film of doubt spread itself over the smooth, pure surface of his mind. A vague consciousness of his inability to express himself clearly upon the question without seeming to slight her memory affected his thoughts.

"But, remember, Aunt Rachel," he said, at last, "I was not old enough, then, to go into society. She surely meant that I should have some independence, when the time came. I am doing no more than all the young men of the neighborhood."

"Ah, yes, I know," she replied, in a melancholy tone; "but they've got used to it by degrees, and mostly in their own homes, and with sisters to caution them; whereas you're younger according to your years, and innocent of the ways and wiles of men, and—and girls."

Joseph painfully felt that this last assertion was true. Suppressing the impulse to exclaim, "Why am I younger 'according to my years?' why am I so much more 'innocent'—which is, ignorant—than others?" he blundered out, with a little display of temper, "Well, how am I ever to learn?"

"By patience, and taking care of yourself. There's always safety in waiting. I don't mean you shouldn't go this evening, since you've promised it, and made yourself smart. But, mark my words, this is only the beginning. The season makes no difference; townspeople never seem to know that there's such things as hay-harvest and corn to be worked. They come out for merry-makings in the busy time, and want us country folks to give up everything for their pleasure. The tired plough-horses must be geared up for 'em, and the cows wait an hour or two longer to be milked while they're driving around; and the chickens killed half-grown, and the washing and baking put off when it comes in their way. They're mighty nice and friendly while it lasts; but go back to 'em in town, six months afterwards, and see whether they'll so much as ask you to take a meal's victuals!"

Joseph began to laugh. "It is not likely," he said, "that I shall ever go to the Blessings for a meal, or that this Miss Julia—as they call her—will ever interfere with our harvesting or milking."

"The airs they put on!" Rachel continued. "She'll very likely think that she's doing you a favor by so much as speaking to you. When the Bishops had boarders, two years ago, one of 'em said,—Maria told me with her own mouth,—'Why don't all the farmers follow your example? It would be so refining for them!' They may be very well in their place, but, for my part, I should like them to stay there."

"There comes the horse," said Joseph. "I must be on the way. I expect to meet Elwood Withers at the lane-end. But—about waiting, Aunt—you hardly need—"

"O, yes, I'll wait for you, of course. Ten o'clock is not so very late for me."

"It might be a little after," he suggested.

"Not much, I hope; but if it should be daybreak, wait I will! Your mother couldn't expect less of me."

When Joseph whirled into the saddle, the thought of his aunt, grimly waiting for his return, was already perched like an imp on the crupper, and clung to his sides with claws of steel. She, looking through the window, also felt that it was so; and, much relieved, went back to her household duties.

He rode very slowly down the lane, with his eyes fixed on the ground.

There was a rich orange flush of sunset on the hills across the valley; masses of burning cumuli hung, self-suspended, above the farthest woods, and such depths of purple-gray opened beyond them as are wont to rouse the slumbering fancies and hopes of a young man's heart; but the beauty and fascination, and suggestiveness of the hour could not lift his downcast, absorbed glance. At last his horse, stopping suddenly at the gate, gave a whinny of recognition, which was answered.

Elwood Withers laughed. "Can you tell me where Joseph Asten lives?" he cried,—"an old man, very much bowed and bent."

Joseph also laughed, with a blush, as he met the other's strong, friendly face. "There is plenty of time," he said, leaning over his horse's neck and lifting the latch of the gate.

"All right; but you must now wake up. You're spruce enough to make a figure to-night."

"O, no doubt!" Joseph gravely answered; "but what kind of a figure?"

"Some people, I've heard say," said Elwood, "may look into their looking-glass every day, and never know how they look. If you appeared to yourself as you appear to me, you wouldn't ask such a question as that."

"If I could only not think of myself at all, Elwood,—if I could be as unconcerned as you are—"

"But I'm not, Joseph, my boy!" Elwood interrupted, riding nearer and laying a hand on his friend's shoulder. "I tell you, it weakens my very marrow to walk into a room full o' girls, even though I know every one of 'em. They know it, too, and, shy and quiet as they seem, they're un-merciful. There they sit, all looking so different, somehow,—even a fellow's own sisters and cousins,—filling up all sides of the room, rustling a little and whispering a little, but you feel that every one of 'em has her eyes on you, and would be so glad to see you flustered. There's no help for it, though; we've got to grow case-hardened to that much, or how ever could a man get married?"

"Elwood!" Joseph asked, after a moment's silence, "were you ever in love?"

"Well,"—and Elwood pulled up his horse in surprise,—"well, you do come out plump. You take the breath out of my body. Have I been in love? Have I committed murder? One's about as deadly a secret as the other!"

The two looked each other in the face. Elwood's eyes answered the question, but Joseph's,—large, shy, and utterly innocent,—could not read the answer.

"It's easy to see you've never been," said the former, dropping his voice to a grave gentleness. "If I should say Yes, what then?"

"Then, how do you know it,—I mean, how did you first begin to find it out? What is the difference between that and the feeling you have towards any pleasant girl whom you like to be with?"

"All the difference in the world!" Elwood exclaimed with energy; then paused, and knitted his brows with a perplexed air; "but I'll be shot if I know exactly what else to say; I never thought of it before. How do I know that I am Elwood Withers? It seems just as plain as that,—and yet—well, for one thing, she's always in your mind, and you think and dream of just nothing but her; and you'd rather have the hem of her dress touch you than kiss anybody else; and you want to be near her, and to have her all to yourself, yet it's hard work to speak a sensible word to her when you come together,—but, what's the use? A fellow must feel it himself, as they say of experiencing religion; he must get converted, or he'll never know. Now, I don't suppose you've understood a word of what I've said!"

"Yes!" Joseph answered; "indeed, I think so. It's only an increase of what we all feel towards some persons. I have been hoping, latterly, that it might come to me, but—but—"

"But your time will come, like every man's," said Elwood; "and, maybe, sooner than you think. When it does, you won't need to ask anybody; though I think you're bound to tell me of it, after pumping my own secret out of me."

Joseph looked grave.

650

"Never mind; I wasn't obliged to let you have it. I know you're close-mouthed and honest-hearted, Joseph; but I'll never ask your confidence unless you can give it as freely as I give mine to you."

"You shall have it, Elwood, if my time ever comes. And I can't help wishing for the time, although it may not be right. You know how lonely it is on the farm, and yet it's not always easy for me to get away into company. Aunt Rachel stands in mother's place to me, and maybe it's only natural that she should be over-concerned; any way, seeing what she has done for my sake, I am hindered from opposing her wishes too stubbornly. Now, to-night, my going didn't seem right to her, and I shall not get it out of my mind that she is waiting up, and perhaps fretting, on my account."

"A young fellow of your age mustn't be so tender," Elwood said. "If you had your own father and mother, they'd allow you more of a range. Look at me, with mine! Why, I never as much as say 'by your leave.' Quite the contrary; so long as the work isn't slighted, they're rather glad than not to have me go out; and the house is twice as lively since I bring so much fresh gossip into it. But then, I've had a rougher bringing up."

"I wish I had had!" cried Joseph. "Yet, no, when I think of mother, it is wrong to say just that. What I mean is, I wish I could take things as easily as you,—make my way boldly in the world, without being held back by trifles, or getting so confused with all sorts of doubts. The more anxious I am to do right, the more embarrassed I am to know what is the right thing. I don't believe you have any such troubles."

"Well, for my part, I do about as other fellows; no worse, I guess, and likely no better. You must consider, also, that I'm a bit rougher made, besides the bringing up, and that makes a deal of difference. I don't try to make the scales balance to a grain; if there's a handful under or over, I think it's near enough. However, you'll be all right in a while. When you find the right girl and marry her, it'll put a new face on to you. There's nothing like a sharp, wide-awake wife, so they say, to set a man straight. Don't make a mountain of anxiety out of a little molehill of inexperience. I'd take all your doubts and more, I'm sure, if I could get such a two-hundred-acre farm with them."

651

"Do you know," cried Joseph eagerly, his blue eyes flashing through the gathering dusk, "I have often thought very nearly the same thing! If I were to love,—if I were to marry—"

"Hush!" interrupted Elwood; "I know you don't mean others to hear you. Here come two down the branch road."

The horsemen, neighboring farmers' sons, joined them. They rode together up the knoll towards the Warriner mansion, the lights of which glimmered at intervals through the trees. The gate was open, and a dozen vehicles could be seen in the enclosure between the house and barn. Bright, gliding forms were visible on the portico.

"Just see," whispered Elwood to Joseph; "what a lot of posy-colors! You may be sure they're every one watching us. No flinching, mind; straight to the charge! We'll walk up together, and it won't be half as hard for you."

# CHAPTER II. MISS BLESSING.

To consider the evening party at Warriner's a scene of "dissipation"—as some of the good old people of the neighborhood undoubtedly did—was about as absurd as to call butter-milk an intoxicating beverage. Anything more simple and innocent could not well be imagined. The very awkwardness which everybody felt, and which no one exactly knew how to overcome, testified of virtuous ignorance. The occasion was no more than sufficed for the barest need of human nature. Young men and women must come together for acquaintance and the possibilities of love, and, fortunately, neither labor nor the severer discipline of their elders can prevent them.

Where social recreation thus only exists under discouraging conditions, ease and grace and self-possession cannot be expected. Had there been more form, in fact, there would have been more ease. A conventional disposition of the guests would have reduced the loose elements of the company to some sort of order; the shy country nature would have taken refuge in fixed laws, and found a sense of freedom therein. But there were no generally understood rules; the young people were brought together, delighted yet uncomfortable, craving yet shrinking from speech and jest and song, and painfully working their several isolations into a warmer common atmosphere.

On this occasion, the presence of a stranger, and that stranger a lady, and that lady a visitor from the city, was an additional restraint. The dread of a critical eye is most keenly felt by those who secretly acknowledge their own lack of social accomplishment. Anna Warriner, to be sure, had been loud in her praises of "dear Julia," and the guests were prepared to find all possible beauty and sweetness; but they expected, none the less, to be scrutinized and judged.

Bob Warriner met his friends at the gate and conducted them to the parlor, whither the young ladies, who had been watching the arrival, had retreated. They were disposed along the walls, silent and cool, except Miss Blessing, who occupied a rocking-chair in front of the mantel-piece, where her figure was in half-shadow, the lamplight only touching some roses in her hair. As the gentlemen were presented, she lifted her face and smiled upon each, graciously offering a slender hand. In manner and attitude, as in dress, she seemed a different being from the plump, ruddy, self-conscious girls on the sofas. Her dark hair fell about her neck in long, shining ringlets; the fairness of her face heightened the brilliancy of her eyes, the lids of which were slightly drooped as if kindly veiling their beams; and her lips, although thin, were very sweetly and delicately curved. Her dress, of some white, foamy texture, hung about her like a trailing cloud, and the cluster of rosebuds on her bosom lay as if tossed there.

The young men, spruce as they had imagined themselves to be, suddenly felt that their clothes were coarse and ill-fitting, and that the girls of the neighborhood, in their neat gingham and muslin dresses, were not quite so airy and charming as on former occasions. Miss Blessing, descending to them out of an unknown higher sphere, made their deficiencies unwelcomely evident; she attracted and fascinated them, yet was none the less a disturbing influence. They made haste to find seats, after which a constrained silence followed.

There could be no doubt of Miss Blessing's amiable nature. She looked about with a pleasant expression, half smiled—but deprecatingly, as if to say, "Pray, don't be offended!"—at the awkward silence, and then said, in a clear, carefully modulated voice: "It is beautiful to arrive at twilight, but how charming it must be to ride home in the moonlight; so different from our lamps!"

The guests looked at each other, but as she had seemed to address no one in particular, so each hesitated, and there was no immediate reply.

"But is it not awful, tell me, Elizabeth, when you get into the shadows of the forests? we are so apt to associate all sorts of unknown dangers with forests, you know," she continued.

The young lady thus singled out made haste to answer: "O, no! I rather like it, when I have company."

Elwood Withers laughed. "To be sure!" he exclaimed; "the shade is full

654

of opportunities."

Then there were little shrieks, and some giggling and blushing. Miss Blessing shook her fan warningly at the speaker.

"How wicked in you! I hope you will have to ride home alone to-night, after that speech. But you are all courageous, compared with us. We are really so restricted in the city, that it's a wonder we have any independence at all. In many ways, we are like children."

"O Julia, dear!" protested Anna Warriner, "and such advantages as you have! I shall never forget the day Mrs. Rockaway called—her husband's cashier of the Commercial Bank" (this was said in a parenthesis to the other guests)—"and brought you all the news direct from head-quarters, as she said."

"Yes," Miss Blessing answered, slowly, casting down her eyes, "there must be two sides to everything, of course; but how much we miss until we know the country! Really, I quite envy you."

Joseph had found himself, almost before he knew it, in a corner, beside Lucy Henderson. He felt soothed and happy, for of all the girls present he liked Lucy best. In the few meetings of the young people which he had attended, he had been drawn towards her by an instinct founded, perhaps, on his shyness and the consciousness of it; for she alone had the power, by a few kindly, simple words, to set him at ease with himself. The straightforward glance of her large brown eyes seemed to reach the self below the troubled surface. However much his ears might have tingled afterwards, as he recalled how frankly and freely he had talked with her, he could only remember the expression of an interest equally frank, upon her face. She never dropped one of those amused side-glances, or uttered one of those pert, satirical remarks, the recollection of which in other girls stung him to the quick.

Their conversation was interrupted, for when Miss Blessing spoke, the others became silent. What Elwood Withers had said of the phenomena of love, however, lingered in Joseph's mind, and he began, involuntarily, to examine the nature of his feeling for Lucy Henderson. Was she not often in his thoughts? He had never before asked himself the question, but now he suddenly became conscious that the hope of meeting her, rather than any curiosity concerning Miss Blessing, had drawn him to Warriner's. Would he rather touch the edge of her dress than kiss anybody else? That question drew his eyes to her lips, and with a soft shock of the heart, he became aware of their freshness and sweetness as never before. To touch the edge of her dress! Elwood had said nothing of the lovelier and bolder desire which brought the blood swiftly to his cheeks. He could not help it that their glances met,—a moment only, but an unmeasured time of delight and fear to him,—and then Lucy quickly turned away her head. He fancied there was a heightened color on her face, but when she spoke to him a few minutes afterwards it was gone, and she was as calm and composed as before.

In the mean time there had been other arrivals; and Joseph was presently called upon to give up his place to some ladies from the neighboring town. Many invitations had been issued, and the capacity of the parlor was soon exhausted. Then the sounds of merry chat on the portico invaded the stately constraint of the room; and Miss Blessing, rising gracefully and not too rapidly, laid her hands together and entreated Anna Warriner,—

"O, do let us go outside! I think we are well enough acquainted now to sit on the steps together."

She made a gesture, slight but irresistibly inviting, and all arose. While they were cheerfully pressing out through the hall, she seized Anna's arm and drew her back into the dusky nook under the staircase.

"Quick, Anna!" she whispered; "who is the roguish one they call Elwood? What is he?"

"A farmer; works his father's place on shares."

"Ah!" exclaimed Miss Blessing, in a peculiar tone; "and the blue-eyed, handsome one, who came in with him? He looks almost like a boy."

"Joseph Asten? Why, he's twenty-two or three. He has one of the finest properties in the neighborhood, and money besides, they say; lives alone, with an old dragon of an aunt as housekeeper. Now, Julia dear, there's a

656

chance for you!"

"Pshaw, you silly Anna!" whispered Miss Blessing, playfully pinching her ear; "you know I prefer intellect to wealth."

"As for that"—Anna began, but her friend was already dancing down the hall towards the front door, her gossamer skirts puffing and floating out until they brushed the walls on either side. She hummed to herself, "O Night! O lovely Night!" from the Désert, skimmed over the doorstep, and sank, subsiding into an ethereal heap, against one of the pillars of the portico. Her eyelids were now fully opened, and the pupils, the color of which could not be distinguished in the moonlight, seemed wonderfully clear and brilliant.

"Now, Mr. Elwood—O, excuse me, I mean Mr. Withers," she began, "you must repeat your joke for my benefit. I missed it, and I feel so foolish when I can't laugh with the rest."

Anna Warriner, standing in the door, opened her eyes very wide at what seemed to her to be the commencement of a flirtation; but before Elwood Withers could repeat his rather stupid fun, she was summoned to the kitchen by her mother, to superintend the preparation of the refreshments.

Miss Blessing made her hay while the moon shone. She so entered into the growing spirit of the scene and accommodated herself to the speech and ways of the guests, that in half an hour it seemed as if they had always known her. She laughed with their merriment, and flattered their sentiment with a tender ballad or two, given in a veiled but not unpleasant voice, and constantly appealed to their good-nature by the phrase: "Pray, don't mind me at all; I'm like a child let out of school!" She tapped Elizabeth Fogg on the shoulder, stealthily tickled Jane McNaughton's neck with a grass-blade, and took the roses from her hair to stick into the buttonholes of the young men.

"Just see Julia!" whispered Anna Warriner to her half-dozen intimates; "didn't I tell you she was the life of society?"

Joseph had quite lost his uncomfortable sense of being watched and criticized; he enjoyed the unrestraint of the hour as much as the rest. He was rather relieved to notice that Elwood Withers seemed uneasy, and almost willing to escape from the lively circle around Miss Blessing. By and by the company broke into smaller groups, and Joseph again found himself near the pale pink dress which he knew. What was it that separated him from her? What had slipped between them during the evening? Nothing, apparently; for Lucy Henderson, perceiving him, quietly moved nearer. He advanced a step, and they were side by side.

"Do you enjoy these meetings, Joseph?" she asked.

"I think I should enjoy everything," he answered, "if I were a little older, or—or—"

"Or more accustomed to society? Is not that what you meant? It is only another kind of schooling, which we must all have. You and I are in the lowest class, as we once were,—do you remember?"

"I don't know why," said he, "—but I must be a poor scholar. See Elwood, for instance!"

"Elwood!" Lucy slowly repeated; "he is another kind of nature, altogether."

There was a moment's silence. Joseph was about to speak, when something wonderfully soft touched his cheek, and a delicate, violet-like odor swept upon his senses. A low, musical laugh sounded at his very ear.

"There! Did I frighten you?" said Miss Blessing. She had stolen behind him, and, standing on tiptoe, reached a light arm over his shoulder, to fasten her last rosebud in the upper buttonhole of his coat.

"I quite overlooked you, Mr. Asten," she continued. "Please turn a little towards me. Now!—has it not a charming effect? I do like to see some kind of ornament about the gentlemen, Lucy. And since they can't wear anything in their hair,—but, tell me, wouldn't a wreath of flowers look well on Mr. Asten's head?"

"I can't very well imagine such a thing," said Lucy.

"No? Well, perhaps I am foolish: but when one has escaped from the tiresome conventionalities of city life, and comes back to nature, and delightful natural society, one feels so free to talk and think! Ah, you don't know what a luxury it is, just to be one's true self!"

Joseph's eyes lighted up, and he turned towards Miss Blessing, as if eager that she should continue to speak.

"Lucy," said Elwood Withers, approaching; "you came with the McNaughtons, didn't you?"

"Yes: are they going?"

"They are talking of it now; but the hour is early, and if you don't mind riding on a pillion, you know my horse is gentle and strong—"

"That's right, Mr. Withers!" interrupted Miss Blessing. "I depend upon you to keep Lucy with us. The night is at its loveliest, and we are all just fairly enjoying each other's society. As I was saying, Mr. Asten, you cannot conceive what a new world this is to me: oh, I begin to breathe at last!"

Therewith she drew a long, soft inspiration, and gently exhaled it again, ending with a little flutter of the breath, which made it seem like a sigh. A light laugh followed.

"I know, without looking at your face, that you are smiling at me," said she. "But you have never experienced what it is to be shy and uneasy in company; to feel that you are expected to talk, and not know what to say, and when you do say something, to be startled at the sound of your voice; to stand, or walk, or sit, and imagine that everybody is watching you; to be introduced to strangers, and be as awkward as if both spoke different languages, and were unable to exchange a single thought. Here, in the country, you experience nothing of all this."

"Indeed, Miss Blessing," Joseph replied, "it is just the same to us—to me—as city society is to you."

"How glad I am!" she exclaimed, clasping her hands. "It is very selfish in me to say it, but I can't help being sincere towards the Sincere. I shall now feel ever so much more freedom in talking with you, Mr. Asten, since we have one experience in common. Don't you think, if we all knew each other's natures truly, we should be a great deal more at ease,—and consequently happier?"

She spoke the last sentence in a low, sweet, penetrating tone, lifted her face to meet his gaze a moment, the eyes large, clear, and appealing in their expression, the lips parted like those of a child, and then, without waiting for his answer, suddenly darted away, crying, "Yes, Anna dear!"

"What is it, Julia?" Anna Warriner asked.

"O, didn't you call me? Somebody surely called some Julia, and I'm the only one, am I not? I've just arranged Mr. Asten's rosebud so prettily, and now all the gentlemen are decorated. I'm afraid they think I take great liberties for a stranger, but then, you all make me forget that I am strange. Why is it that everybody is so good to me?"

She turned her face upon the others with a radiant expression. Then, there were earnest protestations from the young men, and a few impulsive hugs from the girls, which latter Miss Blessing returned with kisses.

Elwood Withers sat beside Lucy Henderson, on the steps of the portico. "Why, we owe it to you that we're here to-night, Miss Blessing!" he exclaimed. "We don't come together half often enough as it is; and what better could we do than meet again, somewhere else, while you are in the country?"

"O, how delightful! how kind!" she cried. "And while the lovely moonlight lasts! Shall I really have another evening like this?"

The proposition was heartily seconded, and the only difficulty was, how to choose between the three or four invitations which were at once proffered. There was nothing better to do than to accept all, in turn, and the young people pledged themselves to attend. The new element which they had dreaded in advance, as a restraint, had shown itself to be the reverse: they had never been so free, so cheerfully excited. Miss Blessing's unconscious ease of manner, her grace and sweetness, her quick, bright sympathy with country ways, had so warmed and fused them, that they lost the remembrance of their stubborn selves and yielded to the magnetism of the hour. Their manners, moreover, were greatly improved, simply by their forgetting that they were expected to have any.

Joseph was one of the happiest sharers in this change. He eagerly gave his word to be present at the entertainments to come: his heart beat with delight at the prospect of other such evenings. The suspicion of a tenderer feeling towards Lucy Henderson, the charm of Miss Blessing's winning frankness, took equal possession of his thoughts; and not until he had said good night did he think of his companion on the homeward road. But Elwood Withers had already left, carrying Lucy Henderson on a pillion behind him.

"Is it ten o'clock, do you think?" Joseph asked of one of the young men, as they rode out of the gate.

The other answered with a chuckle: "Ten? It's nigher morning than evening!"

The imp on the crupper struck his claws deep into Joseph's sides. He urged his horse into a gallop, crossed the long rise in the road and dashed along the valley-level, with the cool, dewy night air whistling in his locks. After entering the lane leading upward to his home, he dropped the reins and allowed the panting horse to choose his own gait. A light, sparkling through the locust-trees, pierced him with the sting of an unwelcome external conscience, in which he had no part, yet which he could not escape.

Rachel Miller looked wearily up from her knitting as he entered the room. She made a feeble attempt to smile, but the expression of her face suggested imminent tears.

"Aunt, why did you wait?" said he, speaking rapidly. "I forgot to look at my watch, and I really thought it was no more than ten—"

He paused, seeing that her eyes were fixed. She was looking at the tall old-fashioned clock. The hand pointed to half-past twelve, and every cluck of the ponderous pendulum said, distinctly, "Late! late! late!"

He lighted a candle in silence, said, "Good night, Aunt!" and went up to his room.

"Good night, Joseph!" she solemnly responded, and a deep, hollow sigh reached his ear before the door was closed.

# CHAPTER III. THE PLACE AND PEOPLE.

Joseph Asten's nature was shy and sensitive, but not merely from a habit of introversion. He saw no deeper into himself, in fact, than his moods and sensations, and thus quite failed to recognize what it was that kept him apart from the society in which he should have freely moved. He felt the difference of others, and constantly probed the pain and embarrassment it gave him, but the sources wherefrom it grew were the last which he would have guessed.

A boy's life may be weakened for growth, in all its fibres, by the watchfulness of a too anxious love, and the guidance of a too exquisitely nurtured conscience. He may be so trained in the habits of goodness, and purity, and duty, that every contact with the world is like an abrasion upon the delicate surface of his soul. Every wind visits him too roughly, and he shrinks from the encounters which brace true manliness, and strengthen it for the exercise of good.

The rigid piety of Joseph's mother was warmed and softened by her tenderness towards him, and he never felt it as a yoke. His nature instinctively took the imprint of hers, and she was happy in seeing so clear a reflection of herself in his innocent young heart. She prolonged his childhood, perhaps without intending it, into the years when the unrest of approaching manhood should have led him to severer studies and lustier sports. Her death transferred his guardianship to other hands, but did not change its character. Her sister Rachel was equally good and conscientious, possibly with an equal capacity for tenderness, but her barren life had restrained the habit of its expression. Joseph could not but confess that she was guided by the strictest sense of duty, but she seemed to him cold, severe, unsympathetic. There were times when the alternative presented itself to his mind, of either allowing her absolute control of all his actions, or wounding her to the heart by asserting a moderate amount of independence.

He was called fortunate, but it was impossible for him consciously to feel his fortune. The two hundred acres of the farm, stretching back over the softly swelling hills which enclosed the valley on the east, were as excellent soil as the neighborhood knew; the stock was plentiful; the house, barn, and all the appointments of the place were in the best order, and he was the sole owner of all. The work of his own hands was not needed, but it was a mechanical exhaustion of time,—an enforced occupation of body and mind, which he followed in the vague hope that some richer development of life might come afterwards. But there were times when the fields looked very dreary,—when the trees, rooted in their places, and growing under conditions which they were powerless to choose or change, were but tiresome types of himself,— when even the beckoning heights far down the valley failed to touch his fancy with the hint of a broader world. Duty said to him, "You must be perfectly contented in your place!" but there was the miserable, ungrateful, inexplicable fact of discontent.

Furthermore, he had by this time discovered that certain tastes which he possessed were so many weaknesses—if not, indeed, matters of reproach—in the eyes of his neighbors. The delight and the torture of finer nerves—an inability to use coarse and strong phrases, and a shrinking from all display of rude manners—were peculiarities which he could not overcome, and must endeavor to conceal. There were men of sturdy intelligence in the community; but none of refined culture, through whom he might have measured and understood himself; and the very qualities, therefore, which should have been his pride, gave him only a sense of shame.

Two memories haunted him, after the evening at Warriner's; and, though so different, they were not to be disconnected. No two girls could be more unlike than Lucy Henderson and Miss Julia Blessing; he had known one for years, and the other was the partial acquaintance of an evening; yet the image of either one was swiftly followed by that of the other. When he thought of Lucy's eyes, Miss Julia's hand stole over his shoulder; when he recalled the glossy ringlets of the latter, he saw, beside them, the faintly flushed cheek and the pure, sweet mouth which had awakened in him his first daring desire.

Phantoms as they were, they seemed to have taken equal possession of the house, the garden, and the fields. While Lucy sat quietly by the window, Miss Julia skipped lightly along the adjoining hall. One lifted a fallen rose-branch on the lawn, the other snatched the reddest blossom from it. One leaned against the trunk of the old hemlock-tree, the other fluttered in and out among the clumps of shrubbery; but the lonely green was wonderfully brightened by these visions of pink and white, and Joseph enjoyed the fancy without troubling himself to think what it meant.

The house was seated upon a gentle knoll, near the head of a side-valley sunk like a dimple among the hills which enclosed the river-meadows, scarcely a quarter of a mile away. It was nearly a hundred years old, and its massive walls were faced with checkered bricks, alternately red and black, to which the ivy clung with tenacious feet wherever it was allowed to run. The gables terminated in broad double chimneys, between which a railed walk, intended for a look-out, but rarely used for that or any other purpose, rested on the peak of the roof. A low portico paved with stone extended along the front, which was further shaded by two enormous sycamore-trees as old as the house itself. The evergreens and ornamental shrubs which occupied the remainder of the little lawn denoted the taste of a later generation. To the east, an open turfy space, in the centre of which stood a superb weeping-willow, divided the house from the great stone barn with its flanking cribs and "over-shoots;" on the opposite side lay the sunny garden, with gnarled grape-vines clambering along its walls, and a double row of tall old box-bushes, each grown into a single solid mass, stretching down the centre.

The fields belonging to the property, softly rising and following the undulations of the hills, limited the landscape on three sides; but on the south there was a fair view of the valley of the larger stream, with its herd-speckled meadows, glimpses of water between the fringing trees, and farm-houses sheltered among the knees of the farther hills. It was a region of peace and repose and quiet, drowsy beauty, and there were few farms which were not the ancestral homes of the families who held them. The people were satisfied, for they lived upon a bountiful soil; and if but few were notably rich, still fewer were absolutely poor. They had a sluggish sense of content, a half-conscious feeling that their lines were cast in pleasant places; they were orderly, moral, and generally honest, and their own types were so constantly reproduced and fixed, both by intermarriage and intercourse, that any variation therein was a thing to be suppressed if possible. Any sign of an unusual taste, or a different view of life, excited their suspicion, and the most of them were incapable of discriminating between independent thought on moral and social questions, and "free-thinking" in the religious significance which they attached to the word. Political excitements, it is true, sometimes swept over the neighborhood, but in a mitigated form; and the discussions which then took place between neighbors of opposite faith were generally repetitions of the arguments furnished by their respective county papers.

To one whose twofold nature conformed to the common mould,—into whom, before his birth, no mysterious element had been infused, to be the basis of new sensations, desires, and powers,—the region was a paradise of peaceful days. Even as a boy the probable map of his life was drawn: he could behold himself as young man, as husband, father, and comfortable old man, by simply looking upon these various stages in others.

If, however, his senses were not sluggish, but keen; if his nature reached beyond the ordinary necessities, and hungered for the taste of higher things; if he longed to share in that life of the world, the least part of which was known to his native community; if, not content to accept the mechanical faith of passive minds, he dared to repeat the long struggle of the human race in his own spiritual and mental growth; then,—why, then, the region was not a paradise of peaceful days.

Rachel Miller, now that the dangerous evening was over, was shrewd enough to resume her habitual manner towards her nephew. Her curiosity to know what had been done, and how Joseph had been affected by the merry-making, rendered her careful not to frighten him from the subject by warnings or reproaches. He was frank and communicative, and Rachel found, to her surprise, that the evening at Warriner's was much, and not wholly unpleasantly, in her thoughts during her knitting-hours. The farm-work was briskly forwarded; Joseph was active in the field, and decidedly brighter in the house; and when he announced the new engagement, with an air which hinted that his attendance was a matter of course, she was only able to say:—

"I'm very much mistaken if that's the end. Get agoing once, and there's no telling where you'll fetch up. I suppose that town's girl won't stay much longer,—the farm-work of the neighborhood couldn't stand it,—and so she means to have all she can while her visit lasts."

"Indeed, Aunt," Joseph protested, "Elwood Withers first proposed it, and the others all agreed."

"And ready enough they were, I'll be bound."

"Yes, they were," Joseph replied, with a little more firmness than usual. "All of them. And there was no respectable family in the neighborhood that wasn't represented."

Rachel made an effort and kept silence. The innovation might be temporary, and in that case it were prudent to take no further notice; or it might be the beginning of a change in the ways of the young people, and if so, she needed further knowledge in order to work successfully against it in Joseph's case.

She little suspected how swiftly and closely the question would be brought to her own door.

A week afterwards the second of the evening parties was held, and was even more successful than the first. Everybody was there, bringing a cheerful memory of the former occasion, and Miss Julia Blessing, no longer dreaded as an unknown scrutinizing element, was again the life and soul of the company. It was astonishing how correctly she retained the names and characteristics of all those whom she had already met, and how intelligently she seemed to enjoy the gossip of the neighborhood. It was remarked that her dress was studiously simple, as if to conform to country ways, yet the airy, graceful freedom of her manner gave it a character of elegance which sufficiently distinguished her from the other girls.

Joseph felt that she looked to him, as by an innocent natural instinct, for a more delicate and intimate recognition than she expected to find elsewhere. Fragments of sentences, parenthetical expressions, dropped in her lively talk, were always followed by a quick glance which said to him: "We have one feeling in common; I know that you understand me." He was fascinated,

666

but the experience was so new that it was rather bewildering. He was drawn to catch her seemingly random looks,—to wait for them, and then shrink timidly when they came, feeling all the while the desire to be in the quiet corner, outside the merry circle of talkers, where sat Lucy Henderson.

When, at last, a change in the diversions of the evening brought him to Lucy's side, she seemed to him grave and preoccupied. Her words lacked the pleasant directness and self-possession which had made her society so comfortable to him. She no longer turned her full face towards him while speaking, and he noticed that her eyes were wandering over the company with a peculiar expression, as if she were trying to listen with them. It seemed to him, also, that Elwood Withers, who was restlessly moving about the room, was watching some one, or waiting for something.

"I have it!" suddenly cried Miss Blessing, floating towards Joseph and Lucy; "it shall be you, Mr. Asten!"

"Yes," echoed Anna Warriner, following; "if it could be, how delightful!"

"Hush, Anna dear! Let us keep the matter secret!" whispered Miss Blessing, assuming a mysterious air; "we will slip away and consult; and, of course, Lucy must come with us."

"Now," she resumed, when the four found themselves alone in the old-fashioned dining-room, "we must, first of all, explain everything to Mr. Asten. The question is, where we shall meet, next week. McNaughtons are building an addition (I believe you call it) to their barn, and a child has the measles at another place, and something else is wrong somewhere else. We cannot interfere with the course of nature; but neither should we give up these charming evenings without making an effort to continue them. Our sole hope and reliance is on you, Mr. Asten."

She pronounced the words with a mock solemnity, clasping her hands, and looking into his face with bright, eager, laughing eyes.

"If it depended on myself—" Joseph began.

"O, I know the difficulty, Mr. Asten!" she exclaimed; "and really, it's unpardonable in me to propose such a thing. But isn't it possible—just possible—that Miss Miller might be persuaded by us?"

"Julia dear!" cried Anna Warriner, "I believe there's nothing you'd be afraid to undertake."

Joseph scarcely knew what to say. He looked from one to the other, coloring slightly, and ready to turn pale the next moment, as he endeavored to imagine how his aunt would receive such an astounding proposition.

"There is no reason why she should be asked," said Lucy. "It would be a great annoyance to her."

"Indeed?" said Miss Blessing; "then I should be so sorry! But I caught a glimpse of your lovely place the other day as we were driving up the valley. It was a perfect picture,—and I have such a desire to see it nearer!"

"Why will you not come, then?" Joseph eagerly asked. Lucy's words seemed to him blunt and unfriendly, although he knew they had been intended for his relief.

"It would be a great pleasure; yet, if I thought your aunt would be annoyed—"

"I am sure she will be glad to make your acquaintance," said Joseph, with a reproachful side-glance at Lucy.

Miss Blessing noticed the glance. "I am more sure," she said, playfully, "that she will be very much amused at my ignorance and inexperience. And I don't believe Lucy meant to frighten me. As for the party, we won't think of that now; but you will go with us, Lucy, won't you,—with Anna and myself, to make a neighborly afternoon call?"

Lucy felt obliged to accede to a request so amiably made, after her apparent rudeness. Yet she could not force herself to affect a hearty acquiescence, and Joseph thought her singularly cold.

He did not doubt but that Miss Blessing, whose warm, impulsive nature seemed to him very much what his own might be if he dared to show it, would fulfil her promise. Neither did he doubt that so much innocence and sweetness as she possessed would make a favorable impression upon his aunt; but he judged it best not to inform the latter of the possible visit.

# CHAPTER IV. MISS BLESSING CALLS ON RACHEL MILLER.

On the following Saturday afternoon, Rachel Miller sat at the front window of the sitting-room, and arranged her light task of sewing and darning, with a feeling of unusual comfort. The household work of the week was over; the weather was fine and warm, with a brisk drying breeze for the hay on the hill-field, the last load of which Joseph expected to have in the barn before his five o'clock supper was ready. As she looked down the valley, she noticed that the mowers were still swinging their way through Hunter's grass, and that Cunningham's corn sorely needed working. There was a different state of things on the Asten place. Everything was done, and well done, up to the front of the season. The weather had been fortunate, it was true; but Joseph had urged on the work with a different spirit. It seemed to her that he had taken a new interest in the farm; he was here and there, even inspecting with his own eyes the minor duties which had been formerly intrusted to his man Dennis. How could she know that this activity was the only outlet for a restless heart?

If any evil should come of his social recreation, she had done her duty; but no evil seemed likely. She had always separated his legal from his moral independence; there was no enactment establishing the period when the latter commenced, and it could not be made manifest by documents, like the former. She would have admitted, certainly, that her guardianship must cease at some time, but the thought of making preparation for that time had never entered her head. She only understood conditions, not the adaptation of characters to them. Going back over her own life, she could recall but little difference between the girl of eighteen and the woman of thirty. There was the same place in her home, the same duties, the same subjection to the will of her parents—no exercise of independence or self-reliance anywhere, and no growth of those virtues beyond what a passive maturity brought with it.

Even now she thought very little about any question of life in connection with Joseph. Her parents had trained her in the discipline of a rigid sect, and she could not dissociate the idea of morality from that of solemn renunciation. She could not say that social pleasures were positively wrong, but they always seemed to her to be enjoyed on the outside of an open door labelled "Temptation;" and who could tell what lay beyond? Some very good people, she knew, were fond of company, and made merry in an innocent fashion; they were of mature years and settled characters, and Joseph was only a boy. The danger, however, was not so imminent: no fault could be found with his attention to duty, and a chance so easily escaped was a comfortable guaranty for the future.

In the midst of this mood (we can hardly say train of thought), she detected the top of a carriage through the bushes fringing the lane. The vehicle presently came into view: Anna Warriner was driving, and there were two other ladies on the back seat. As they drew up at the hitching-post on the green, she recognized Lucy Henderson getting out; but the airy creature who sprang after her,—the girl with dark, falling ringlets,—could it be the stranger from town? The plain, country-made gingham dress, the sober linen collar, the work-bag on her arm—could they belong to the stylish young lady whose acquaintance had turned Anna's head?

A proper spirit of hospitality required her to meet the visitors at the gate; so there was no time left for conjecture. She was a little confused, but not dissatisfied at the chance of seeing the stranger.

"We thought we could come for an hour this afternoon, without disturbing you," said Anna Warriner. "Mother has lost your receipt for pickling cherries, and Bob said you were already through with the hay-harvest; and so we brought Julia along—this is Julia Blessing."

"How do you do?" said Miss Blessing, timidly extending her hand, and slightly dropping her eyelids. She then fell behind Anna and Lucy, and spoke no more until they were all seated in the sitting-room.

"How do you like the country by this time?" Rachel asked, feeling that a little attention was necessary to a new guest.

"So well that I think I shall never like the city again," Miss Blessing answered. "This quiet, peaceful life is such a rest; and I really never before knew what order was, and industry, and economy."

She looked around the room as she spoke, and glanced at the barn through the eastern window.

"Yes, your ways in town are very different," Rachel remarked.

"It seems to me, now, that they are entirely artificial. I find myself so ignorant of the proper way of living that I should be embarrassed among you, if you were not all so very kind. But I am trying to learn a little."

"O, we don't expect too much of town's-folks," said Rachel, in a much more friendly tone, "and we're always glad to see them willing to put up with our ways. But not many are."

"Please don't count me among those!" Miss Blessing exclaimed.

"No, indeed, Miss Rachel!" said Anna Warriner; "you'd be surprised to know how Julia gets along with everything—don't she, Lucy?"

"Yes, she's very quick," Lucy Henderson replied.

Miss Blessing cast down her eyes, smiled, and shook her head.

Rachel Miller asked some questions which opened the sluices of Miss Warriner's gossip—and she had a good store of it. The ways and doings of various individuals were discussed, and Miss Blessing's occasional remarks showed a complete familiarity with them. Her manner was grave and attentive, and Rachel was surprised to find so much unobtrusive good sense in her views. The reality was so different from her previously assumed impression, that she felt bound to make some reparation. Almost before she was aware of it, her manner became wholly friendly and pleasant.

"May I look at your trees and flowers?" Miss Blessing asked, when the gossip had been pretty well exhausted.

They all arose and went out on the lawn. Rose and woodbine, phlox and verbena, passed under review, and then the long, rounded walls of box attracted Miss Blessing's eye. This was a feature of the place in which Rachel

672

Miller felt considerable pride, and she led the way through the garden gate. Anna Warriner, however, paused, and said:—

"Lucy, let us go down to the spring-house. We can get back again before Julia has half finished her raptures."

Lucy hesitated a moment. She looked at Miss Blessing, who laughed and said, "O, don't mind me!" as she took her place at Rachel's side.

The avenue of box ran the whole length of the garden, which sloped gently to the south. At the bottom the green walls curved outward, forming three-fourths of a circle, spacious enough to contain several seats. There was a delightful view of the valley through the opening.

"The loveliest place I ever saw!" exclaimed Miss Blessing, taking one of the rustic chairs. "How pleasant it must be, when you have all your neighbors here together!"

Rachel Miller was a little startled; but before she could reply, Miss Blessing continued:—

"There is such a difference between a company of young people here in the country, and what is called 'a party' in the city. There it is all dress and flirtation and vanity, but here it is only neighborly visiting on a larger scale. I have enjoyed the quiet company of all your folks so much the more, because I felt that it was so very innocent. Indeed, I don't see how anybody could be led into harmful ways here."

"I don't know," said Rachel: "we must learn to mistrust our own hearts."

"You are right! The best are weak—of themselves; but there is more safety where all have been brought up unacquainted with temptation. Now, you will perhaps wonder at me when I say that I could trust the young men— for instance, Mr. Asten, your nephew—as if they were my brothers. That is, I feel a positive certainty of their excellent character. What they say they mean: it is otherwise in the city. It is delightful to see them all together, like members of one family. You must enjoy it, I should think, when they meet here."

Rachel Miller's eyes opened wide, and there was both a puzzled and a searching expression in the look she gave Miss Blessing. The latter, with an air of almost infantine simplicity, her lips slightly parted, accepted the scrutiny with a quiet cheerfulness which seemed the perfection of candor.

"The truth is," said Rachel, slowly, "this is a new thing. I hope the merry-makings are as innocent as you think; but I'm afraid they unsettle the young people, after all."

"Do you, really?" exclaimed Miss Blessing. "What have you seen in them which leads you to think so? But no—never mind my question; you may have reasons which I have no right to ask. Now, I remember Mr. Asten telling Anna and Lucy and myself, how much he should like to invite his friends here, if it were not for a duty which prevented it; and a duty, he said, was more important to him than a pleasure."

"Did Joseph say that?" Rachel exclaimed.

"O, perhaps I oughtn't to have told it," said Miss Blessing, casting down her eyes and blushing in confusion: "in that case, please don't say anything about it! Perhaps it was a duty towards you, for he told me that he looked upon you as a second mother."

Rachel's eyes softened, and it was a little while before she spoke. "I've tried to do my duty by him," she faltered at last, "but it sometimes seems an unthankful business, and I can't always tell how he takes it. And so he wanted to have a company here?"

"I am so sorry I said it!" cried Miss Blessing. "I never thought you were opposed to company, on principle. Miss Chaffinch, the minister's daughter, you know, was there the last time; and, really, if you could see it—But it is presumptuous in me to say anything. Indeed, I am not a fair judge, because these little gatherings have enabled me to make such pleasant acquaintances. And the young men tell me that they work all the better after them."

"It's only on his account," said Rachel.

"Nay, I'm sure that the last thing Mr. Asten would wish would be your giving up a principle for his sake! I know, from his face, that his own character

674

is founded on principle. And, besides, here in the country, you don't keep count of hospitality, as they do in the city, and feel obliged to return as much as you receive. So, if you will try to forget what I have said—"

Rachel interrupted her. "I meant something different. Joseph knows why I objected to parties. He must not feel under obligations which I stand in the way of his repaying. If he tells me that he should like to invite his friends to this place, I will help him to entertain them."

"You are his second mother, indeed," Miss Blessing murmured, looking at her with a fond admiration. "And now I can hope that you will forgive my thoughtlessness. I should feel humiliated in his presence, if he knew that I had repeated his words. But he will not ask you, and this is the end of any harm I may have done."

"No," said Rachel, "he will not ask me; but won't I be an offence in his mind?"

"I can understand how you feel—only a woman can judge a woman's heart. Would you think me too forward if I tell you what might be done, this once?"

She stole softly up to Rachel as she spoke, and laid her hand gently upon her arm.

"Perhaps I am wrong—but if you were first to suggest to your nephew that if he wished to make some return for the hospitality of his neighbors,—or put it in whatever form you think best,—would not that remove the 'offence' (though he surely cannot look at it in that light), and make him grateful and happy?"

"Well," said Rachel, after a little reflection, "if anything is done, that would be as good a way as any."

"And, of course, you won't mention me?"

"There is no call to do it—as I can see."

"Julia, dear!" cried Anna from the gate; "come and see the last load of hay hauled into the barn!"

"I should like to see it, if you will excuse me," said Miss Blessing to Rachel; "I have taken quite an interest in farming."

As they were passing the porch, Rachel paused on the step and said to Anna: "You'll bide and get your suppers?"

"I don't know," Anna replied: "we didn't mean to; but we stayed longer than we intended—"

"Then you can easily stay longer still."

There was nothing unfriendly in Rachel's blunt manner. Anna laughed, took Miss Blessing by the arm, and started for the barn. Lucy Henderson quietly turned and entered the house, where, without any offer of services, she began to assist in arranging the table.

The two young ladies took their stand on the green, at a safe distance, as the huge fragrant load approached. The hay overhung and concealed the wheels, as well as the hind quarters of the oxen, and on the summit stood Joseph, in his shirt-sleeves and leaning on a pitch-fork. He bent forward as he saw them, answering their greetings with an eager, surprised face.

"O, take care, take care!" cried Miss Blessing, as the load entered the barn-door; but Joseph had already dropped upon his knees and bent his shoulders. Then the wagon stood upon the barn-floor; he sprang lightly upon a beam, descended the upright ladder, and the next moment was shaking hands with them.

"We have kept our promise, you see," said Miss Blessing.

"Have you been in the house yet?" Joseph asked, looking at Anna.

"O, for an hour past, and we are going to take supper with you."

"Dennis!" cried Joseph, turning towards the barn, "we will let the load stand to-night."

"How much better a man looks in shirt-sleeves than in a dress-coat!"

676

remarked Miss Blessing aside to Anna Warriner, but not in so low a tone as to prevent Joseph from hearing it.

"Why, Julia, you are perfectly countrified! I never saw anything like it!" Anna replied.

Joseph turned to them again, with a bright flush on his face. He caught Miss Blessing's eyes, full of admiration, before the lids fell modestly over them.

"So you've seen my home, already?" he said, as they walked slowly towards the house.

"O, not the half yet!" she answered, in a low, earnest tone. "A place so lovely and quiet as this cannot be appreciated at once. I almost wish I had not seen it: what shall I do when I must go back to the hot pavements, and the glaring bricks, and the dust, and the hollow, artificial life?" She tried to check a sigh, but only partially succeeded; then, with a sudden effort, she laughed lightly, and added: "I wonder if everybody doesn't long for something else? Now, Anna, here, would think it heavenly to change places with me."

"Such privileges as you have!" Anna protested.

"Privileges?" Miss Blessing echoed. "The privilege of hearing scandal, of being judged by your dress, of learning the forms and manners, instead of the good qualities, of men and women? No! give me an independent life."

"Alone?" suggested Miss Warriner.

Joseph looked at Miss Blessing, who made no reply. Her head was turned aside, and he could well understand that she must feel hurt at Anna's indelicacy.

In the house Rachel Miller and Lucy had, in the mean time, been occupied with domestic matters. The former, however, was so shaken out of her usual calm by the conversation in the garden, that in spite of prudent resolves to keep quiet, she could not restrain herself from asking a question or two.

"Lucy," said she, "how do you find these evening parties you've been attending?"

"They are lively and pleasant,—at least every one says so."

"Are you going to have any more?"

"It seems to be the wish," said Lucy, suddenly hesitating, as she found Rachel's eyes intently fixed upon her face.

The latter was silent for a minute, arranging the tea-service; but she presently asked again: "Do you think Joseph would like to invite the young people here?"

"She has told you!" Lucy exclaimed, in unfeigned irritation. "Miss Rachel, don't let it trouble you a moment: nobody expects it of you!"

Lucy felt, immediately, that her expression had been too frankly positive; but even the consciousness thereof did not enable her to comprehend its effect.

Rachel straightened herself a little, and said "Indeed?" in anything but an amiable tone. She went to the cupboard and returned before speaking again. "I didn't say anybody told me," she continued; "it's likely that Joseph might think of it, and I don't see why people should expect me to stand in the way of his wishes."

Lucy was so astonished that she could not immediately reply; and the entrance of Joseph and the two ladies cut off all further opportunity of clearing up what she felt to be an awkward misunderstanding.

"I must help, too!" cried Miss Blessing, skipping into the kitchen after Rachel. "That is one thing, at least, which we can learn in the city. Indeed, if it wasn't for housekeeping, I should feel terribly useless."

Rachel protested against her help, but in vain. Miss Blessing had a laugh and a lively answer for every remonstrance, and flitted about in a manner which conveyed the impression that she was doing a great deal.

Joseph could scarcely believe his eyes, when he came down from his room in fresh attire, and beheld his aunt not only so assisted, but seeming to enjoy it. Lucy, who appeared to be ill at ease, had withdrawn from the table, and was sitting silently beside the window. Recalling their conversation a few evenings before, he suspected that she might be transiently annoyed on his aunt's account; she had less confidence, perhaps, in Miss Blessing's winning, natural manners. So Lucy's silence threw no shadow upon his cheerfulness: he had never felt so happy, so free, so delighted to assume the character of a host.

After the first solemnity which followed the taking of seats at the table, the meal proceeded with less than the usual decorum. Joseph, indeed, so far forgot his duties, that his aunt was obliged to remind him of them from time to time. Miss Blessing was enthusiastic over the cream and butter and marmalade, and Rachel Miller found it exceedingly pleasant to have her handiwork appreciated. Although she always did her best, for Joseph's sake, she knew that men have very ignorant, indifferent tastes in such matters.

When the meal was over, Anna Warriner said: "We are going to take Lucy on her way as far as the cross-roads; so there will not be more than time to get home by sunset."

Before the carriage was ready, however, another vehicle drove up the lane. Elwood Withers jumped out, gave Joseph a hearty grip of his powerful hand, greeted the others rapidly, and then addressed himself specially to Lucy: "I was going to a township-meeting at the Corner," said he; "but Bob Warriner told me you were here with Anna, so I thought I could save her a roundabout drive by taking you myself."

"Thank you; but I'm sorry you should go so far out of your road," said Lucy. Her face was pale, and there was an evident constraint in the smile which accompanied the words.

"O, he'd go twice as far for company," Anna Warriner remarked. "You know I'd take you, and welcome, but Elwood has a good claim on you, now."

"I have no claim, Lucy," said Elwood, rather doggedly.

"Let us go, then," were Lucy's words.

She rose, and the four were soon seated in the two vehicles. They drove away in the low sunshine, one pair chatting and laughing merrily as long as they were within hearing, the other singularly grave and silent.

# CHAPTER V. ELWOOD'S EVENING, AND JOSEPH'S.

For half a mile Elwood Withers followed the carriage containing Anna Warriner and her friend; then, at the curve of the valley, their roads parted, and Lucy and he were alone. The soft light of the delicious summer evening was around them; the air, cooled by the stream which broadened and bickered beside their way, was full of all healthy meadow odors, and every farm in the branching dells they passed was a picture of tranquil happiness. Yet Lucy had sighed before she was aware of it,—a very faint, tremulous breath, but it reached Elwood's sensitive ear.

"You don't seem quite well, Lucy," he said.

"Because I have talked so little?" she asked.

"Not just that, but—but I was almost afraid my coming for you was not welcome. I don't mean—" But here he grew confused, and did not finish the sentence.

"Indeed, it was very kind of you," said she. This was not an answer to his remark, and both felt that it was not.

Elwood struck the horse with his whip, then as suddenly drew the reins on the startled animal. "Pshaw!" he exclaimed, in a tone that was almost fierce, "what's the use o' my beating about the bush in this way?"

Lucy caught her breath, and clenched her hands under her shawl for one instant. Then she became calm, and waited for him to say more.

"Lucy!" he continued, turning towards her, "you have a right to think me a fool. I can talk to anybody else more freely than to you, and the reason is, I want to say more to you than to any other woman! There's no use in my being a coward any longer; it's a desperate venture I'm making, but it must be made. Have you never guessed how I feel towards you?"

"Yes," she answered, very quietly.

"Well, what do you say to it?" He tried to speak calmly, but his breath came thick and hard, and the words sounded hoarsely.

"I will say this, Elwood," said she, "that because I saw your heart, I have watched your ways and studied your character. I find you honest and manly in everything, and so tender and faithful that I wish I could return your affection in the same measure."

A gleam, as of lightning, passed over his face.

"O, don't misunderstand me!" she cried, her calmness forsaking her, "I esteem, I honor you, and that makes it harder for me to seem ungrateful, unfeeling,—as I must. Elwood, if I could, I would answer you as you wish, but I cannot."

"If I wait?" he whispered.

"And lose your best years in a vain hope! No, Elwood, my friend,—let me always call you so,—I have been cowardly also. I knew an explanation must come, and I shrank from the pain I should feel in giving you pain. It is hard; and better for both of us that it should not be repeated!"

"There's something wrong in this world!" he exclaimed, after a long pause. "I suppose you could no more force yourself to love me than I could force myself to love Anna Warriner or that Miss Blessing. Then what put it into my heart to love you? Was it God or the Devil!"

"Elwood!"

"How can I help myself? Can I help drawing my breath? Did I set about it of my own will? Here I see a life that belongs to my own life,—as much a part of it as my head or heart; but I can't reach it,—it draws away from me, and maybe joins itself to some one else forever! O my God!"

Lucy burst into such a violent passion of weeping, that Elwood forgot himself in his trouble for her. He had never witnessed such grief, as it seemed to him, and his honest heart was filled with self-reproach at having caused it.

"Forgive me, Lucy!" he said, very tenderly encircling her with his arm, and drawing her head upon his shoulder; "I spoke rashly and wickedly, in my disappointment. I thought only of myself, and forgot that I might hurt you by my words. I'm not the only man who has this kind of trouble to bear; and perhaps if I could see clearer—but I don't know; I can only see one thing."

She grew calmer as he spoke. Lifting her head from his shoulder, she took his hand, and said: "You are a true and a noble man, Elwood. It is only a grief to me that I cannot love you as a wife should love her husband. But my will is as powerless as yours."

"I believe you, Lucy," he answered, sadly. "It's not your fault,—but, then, it isn't mine, either. You make me feel that the same rule fits both of us, leastways so far as helping the matter is concerned. You needn't tell me I may find another woman to love; the very thought of it makes me sick at heart. I'm rougher than you are, and awkward in my ways—"

"It is not that! O, believe me, it is not that!" cried Lucy, interrupting him. "Have you ever sought for reasons to account for your feeling toward me? Is it not something that does not seem to depend upon what I am,— upon any qualities that distinguish me from other women?"

"How do you know so much?" Elwood asked. "Have you—" He commenced, but did not finish the question. He leaned silently forward, urged on the horse, and Lucy could see that his face was very stern.

"They say," she began, on finding that he was not inclined to speak,— "they say that women have a natural instinct which helps them to understand many things; and I think it must be true. Why can you not spare me the demand for reasons which I have not? If I were to take time, and consider it, and try to explain, it would be of no help to you: it would not change the fact. I suppose a man feels humiliated when this trouble comes upon him. He shows his heart, and there seems to be a claim upon the woman of his choice to show hers in return. The sense of injustice is worse than humiliation, Elwood. Though I cannot, cannot do otherwise, I shall always have the feeling that I have wronged you."

"O Lucy," he murmured, in a very sad, but not reproachful voice, "every word you say, in showing me that I must give you up, only makes it more impossible to me. And it is just impossible,—that's the end of the matter! I know how people talk about trials being sent us for our good, and its being the will of God, and all that. It's a trial, that's true: whether it's for my good or not, I shall learn after a while; but I can find out God's will only by trying the strength of my own. Don't be afeared, Lucy! I've no notion of saying or doing anything from this time on to disturb you, but here you are" (striking his breast with his clenched hand), "and here you will be when the day comes, as I feel that it must and shall come, to bring us together!"

She could see the glow of his face in the gathering dusk, as he turned towards her and offered his hand. How could she help taking it? If some pulse in her own betrayed the thrill of admiring recognition of the man's powerful and tender nature, which suddenly warmed her oppressed blood, she did not fear that he would draw courage from the token. She wished to speak, but found no words which, coming after his, would not have seemed either cold and unsympathetic, or too near the verge of the hope which she would gladly have crushed.

Elwood was silent for a while, and hardly appeared to be awaiting an answer. Meanwhile the road left the valley, climbing the shoulders of its enclosing hills, where the moist meadow fragrance was left behind, and dry, warm breezes, filled with the peculiar smell of the wheat-fields, blew over them. It was but a mile farther to the Corner, near which Lucy's parents resided.

"How came you three to go to Joseph's place this afternoon?" he asked. "Wasn't it a dodge of Miss Blessing's?"

"She proposed it,—partly in play, I think; and when she afterwards insisted on our going, there seemed to be no good reason for refusing."

"O, of course not," said Elwood; "but tell me now, honestly, Lucy, what do you make out of her?"

Lucy hesitated a moment. "She is a little wilful in her ways, perhaps, but we mustn't judge too hastily. We have known her such a short time. Her manner is very amiable."

"I don't know about that," Elwood remarked. "It reminds me of one of her dresses,—so ruffled, and puckered, and stuck over with ribbons and things, that you can't rightly tell what the stuff is. I'd like to be sure whether she has an eye to Joseph."

"To him!" Lucy exclaimed.

"Him first and foremost! He's as innocent as a year-old baby. There isn't a better fellow living than Joseph Asten, but his bringing up has been fitter for a girl than a boy. He hasn't had his eye-teeth cut yet, and it's my opinion that she has."

"What do you mean by that?"

"No harm. Used to the world, as much as anything else. He don't know how to take people; he thinks th' outside color runs down to the core. So it does with him; but I can't see what that girl is, under her pleasant ways, and he won't guess that there's anything else of her. Between ourselves, Lucy,— you don't like her. I saw that when you came away, though you were kissing each other at the time."

"What a hypocrite I must be!" cried Lucy, rather fiercely.

"Not a bit of it. Women kiss as men shake hands. You don't go around, saying, 'Julia dear!' like Anna Warriner."

Lucy could not help laughing. "There," she said, "that's enough, Elwood! I'd rather you would think yourself in the right than to say anything more about her this evening."

She sighed wearily, not attempting to conceal her fatigue and depression.

"Well, well!" he replied; "I'll pester you no more with disagreeable subjects. There's the house, now, and you'll soon be rid of me. I won't tell you, Lucy, that if you ever want for friendly service, you must look to me,— because I'm afeared you won't feel free to do it; but you'll take all I can find to do without your asking."

684

Without waiting for an answer he drew up his horse at the gate of her home, handed her out, said "Good night!" and drove away.

Such a singular restlessness took possession of Joseph, after the departure of his guests, that the evening quiet of the farm became intolerable. He saddled his horse and set out for the village, readily inventing an errand which explained the ride to himself as well as to his aunt.

The regular movements of the animal did not banish the unquiet motions of his mind, but it relieved him by giving them a wider sweep and a more definite form. The man who walks is subject to the power of his Antæus of a body, moving forwards only by means of the weight which holds it to the earth. There is a clog upon all his thoughts, an ever-present sense of restriction and impotence. But when he is lifted above the soil, with the air under his foot-soles, swiftly moving without effort, his mind, a poising Mercury, mounts on winged heels. He feels the liberation of new and nimble powers; wider horizons stretch around his inward vision; obstacles are measured or overlooked; the brute strength under him charges his whole nature with a more vigorous electricity.

The fresh, warm, healthy vital force which filled Joseph's body to the last embranchment of every nerve and vein—the hum of those multitudinous spirits of life, which, while building their glorious abode, march as if in triumphant procession through its secret passages, and summon all the fairest phantoms of sense to their completed chambers—constituted, far more than he suspected, an element of his disturbance. This was the strong pinion on which his mind and soul hung balanced, above the close atmosphere which he seemed to ride away from, as he rode. The great joy of human life filled and thrilled him; all possibilities of action and pleasure and emotion swam before his sight; all he had read or heard of individual careers in all ages, climates, and conditions of the race—dazzling pictures of the myriad-sided earth, to be won by whosoever dared arbitrarily to seize the freedom waiting for his grasp—floated through his brain.

Hitherto a conscience not born of his own nature,—a very fair and saintly-visaged jailer of thought, but a jailer none the less,—had kept strict guard over every outward movement of his mind, gently touching hope and desire and conjecture when they reached a certain line, and saying, "No; no farther: it is prohibited." But now, with one strong, involuntary throb, he found himself beyond the line, with all the ranges ever trodden by man stretching forward to a limitless horizon. He rose in his stirrups, threw out his arms, lifted his face towards the sky, and cried, "God! I see what I am!"

It was only a glimpse,—like that of a landscape struck in golden fire by lightning, from the darkness. "What is it," he mused, "that stands between me and this vision of life? Who built a wall of imaginary law around these needs, which are in themselves inexorable laws? The World, the Flesh, and the Devil, they say in warning. Bright, boundless world, my home, my playground, my battle-field, my kingdom to be conquered! And this body they tell me to despise,—this perishing house of clay, which is so intimately myself that its comfort and delight cheer me to the inmost soul: it is a dwelling fit for an angel to inhabit! Shall not its hungering senses all be fed? Who shall decide for me—if not myself—on their claims?—who can judge for me what strength requires to be exercised, what pleasure to be enjoyed, what growth to be forwarded? All around me, everywhere, are the means of gratification,—I have but to reach forth my hand and grasp; but a narrow cell, built ages ago, encloses me wherever I go!"

Such was the vague substance of his thoughts. It was the old struggle between life—primitive, untamed life, as the first man may have felt it—and its many masters: assertion, and resistance, all the more fierce because so many influences laid their hands upon its forces. As he came back to his usual self, refreshed by this temporary escape, Joseph wondered whether other men shared the same longing and impatience; and this turned his musings into another channel. "Why do men so carefully conceal what is deepest and strongest in their natures? Why is so little of spiritual struggle and experience ever imparted? The convert publicly admits his sinful experience, and tries to explain the entrance of grace into his regenerated nature; the reformed drunkard seems to take a positive delight in making his former condition degraded and loathsome; but the opening of the individual life to the knowledge of power and passion and all the possibilities of the world is kept more secret than sin. Love is hidden as if it were a reproach; friendship watched, lest it express its warmth too frankly; joy and grief and doubt and anxiety repressed as much as possible. A great lid is shut down upon the human race. They must painfully stoop and creep, instead of standing erect with only God's heaven over their heads. I am lonely, but I know not how to cry for companionship; my words would not be understood, or, if they were, would not be answered. Only one gate is free to me,—that leading to the love of woman. There, at least, must be such an intense, intimate sympathy as shall make the reciprocal revelation of the lives possible!"

Full of this single certainty, which, the more he pondered upon it, seemed to be his nearest chance of help, Joseph rode slowly homewards. Rachel Miller, who had impatiently awaited his coming, remarked the abstraction of his face, and attributed it to a very different cause. She was thereby wonderfully strengthened to make her communication in regard to the evening company; nevertheless, the subject was so slowly approached and so ambiguously alluded to, that Joseph could not immediately understand it.

"That is something! That is a step!" he said to himself; then turning towards her with a genuine satisfaction in his face, added: "Aunt, do you know that I have never really felt until now that I am the owner of this property? It will be more of a home to me after I have received the neighborhood as my guests. It has always controlled me, but now it must serve me."

He laughed in great good-humor, and Rachel Miller, in her heart, thanked Miss Julia Blessing.

# CHAPTER VI. IN THE GARDEN.

Rachel Miller was not a woman to do a thing by halves. As soon as the question was settled, she gave her heart and mind to the necessary preparations. There might have been a little surprise in some quarters, when the fact became known in the neighborhood through Joseph's invitation, but no expression of it reached the Asten place. Mrs. Warriner, Anna's mother, called to inquire if she could be of service, and also to suggest, indirectly, her plan of entertaining company. Rachel detected the latter purpose, and was a little more acquiescent than could have been justified to her own conscience, seeing that at the very moment when she was listening with much apparent meekness, she was mentally occupied with plans for outdoing Mrs. Warriner. Moreover, the Rev. Mr. Chaffinch had graciously signified his willingness to be present, and the stamp of strictest orthodoxy was thus set upon the entertainment. She was both assured and stimulated, as the time drew near, and even surprised Joseph by saying: "If I was better acquainted with Miss Blessing, she might help me a good deal in fixing everything just as it should be. There are times, it seems, when it's an advantage to know something of the world."

"I'll ask her!" Joseph exclaimed.

"You! And a mess you'd make of it, very likely; men think they've only to agree to invite a company, and that's all! There's a hundred things to be thought of that women must look to; you couldn't even understand 'em. As for speaking to her,—she's one of the invites, and it would never do in the world."

Joseph said no more, but he silently determined to ask Miss Blessing on her arrival; there would still be time. She, with her wonderful instinct, her power of accommodating people to each other, and the influence which she had already acquired with his aunt, would certainly see at a glance how the current was setting, and guide it in the proper direction.

But, as the day drew near, he grew so restless and uneasy that there seemed nothing better to do than to ride over to Warriner's in the hope of catching a moment's conference with her, in advance of the occasion.

He was entirely fortunate. Anna was apparently very busy with household duties, and after the first greetings left him alone with Miss Blessing. He had anticipated a little difficulty in making his message known, and was therefore much relieved when she said: "Now, Mr. Asten, I see by your face that you have something particular to say. It's about to-morrow night, isn't it? You must let me help you, if I can, because I am afraid I have been, without exactly intending it, the cause of so much trouble to you and your aunt."

Joseph opened his heart at once. All that he had meant to say came easily and naturally to his lips, because Miss Blessing seemed to feel and understand the situation, and met him half-way in her bright, cheerful acquiescence. Almost before he knew it, he had made her acquainted with what had been said and done at home. How easily she solved the absurd doubts and difficulties which had so unnecessarily tormented him! How clearly, through her fine female instinct, she grasped little peculiarities of his aunt's nature, which he, after years of close companionship, had failed to define! Miss Rachel, she said, was both shy and inexperienced, and it was only the struggle to conceal these conscious defects which made her seem—not unamiable, exactly, but irregular in her manner. Her age, and her character in the neighborhood, did not permit her to appear incompetent to any emergency; it was a very natural pride, and must be treated very delicately and tenderly.

Would Joseph trust the matter entirely to her, Miss Blessing? It was a great deal to ask, she knew, comparative stranger as she was; but she believed that a woman, when her nature had not been distorted by the conventionalities of life, had a natural talent for smoothing difficulties, and removing obstacles for others. Her friends had told her that she possessed this power; and it was a great happiness to think so. In the present case, she was sure she should make no mistake. She would endeavor not to seem to suggest anything, but merely to assist in such a way that Miss Rachel would of herself see what else was necessary to be done.

"Now," she remarked, in conclusion, "this sounds like vanity in me; but

I really hope it is not. You must remember that in the city we are obliged to know all the little social arts,—and artifices, I am afraid. It is not always to our credit, but then, the heart may be kept fresh and uncorrupted."

She sighed, and cast down her eyes. Joseph felt the increasing charm of a nature so frank and so trustful, constantly luring to the surface the maiden secrets of his own. The confidence already established between them was wholly delightful, because their sense of reciprocity increased as it deepened. He felt so free to speak that he could not measure the fitness of his words, but exclaimed, without a pause for thought:—

"Tell me, Miss Julia, did you not suggest this party to Aunt Rachel?"

"Don't give me too much credit!" she answered; "it was talked about, and I couldn't help saying Ay. I longed so much to see you—all—again before I go away."

"And Lucy Henderson objected to it?"

"Lucy, I think, wanted to save your aunt trouble. Perhaps she did not guess that the real objection was inexperience, and not want of will to entertain company. And very likely she helped to bring it about, by seeming to oppose it; so you must not be angry with Lucy,—promise me!"

She looked at him with an irresistibly entreating expression, and extended her hand, which he seized so warmly as to give her pain. But she returned the pressure, and there was a moment's silence, which Anna Warriner interrupted at the right time.

The next day, on the Asten farm, all the preparations were quietly and successfully made long in advance of the first arrivals. The Rev. Mr. Chaffinch and a few other specially chosen guests made their appearance in the afternoon. To Joseph's surprise, the Warriners and Miss Blessing speedily joined them. It was, in reality, a private arrangement which his aunt had made, in order to secure at the start the very assistance which he had been plotting to render. One half the secret of the ease and harmony which he felt was established was thus unknown to him. He looked for hints or indications of management on Miss Blessing's part, but saw none. The two women, meeting

690

each other half-way, needed no words in order to understand each other, and Miss Rachel, gradually made secure in her part of hostess, experienced a most unaccustomed sense of triumph.

At the supper-table Mr. Chaffinch asked a blessing with fervor; a great, balmy dish of chickens stewed in cream was smoking before his nostrils, and his fourth cup of tea made Rachel Miller supremely happy. The meal was honored in silence, as is the case where there is much to eat and a proper desire and capacity to do it; only towards its close were the tongues of the guests loosened, and content made them cheerful.

"You have entertained us almost too sumptuously, Miss Miller," said the clergyman. "And now let us go out on the portico, and welcome the young people as they arrive."

"I need hardly ask you, then, Mr. Chaffinch," said she, "whether you think it right for them to come together in this way."

"Decidedly!" he answered; "that is, so long as their conversation is modest and becoming. It is easy for the vanities of the world to slip in, but we must watch,—we must watch."

Rachel Miller took a seat near him, beholding the gates of perfect enjoyment opened to her mind. Dress, the opera, the race-course, literature, stocks, politics, have their fascination for so many several classes of the human race; but to her there was nothing on this earth so delightful as to be told of temptation and backsliding and sin, and to feel that she was still secure. The fact that there was always danger added a zest to the feeling; she gave herself credit for a vigilance which had really not been exercised.

The older guests moved their chairs nearer, and listened, forgetting the sweetness of sunset which lay upon the hills down the valley. Anna Warriner laid her arm around Miss Chaffinch's waist, and drew her towards the mown field beyond the barn; and presently, by a natural chance, as it seemed, Joseph found himself beside Miss Blessing, at the bottom of the lawn.

All the western hills were covered with one cool, broad shadow. A rich orange flush touched the tops of the woods to the eastward, and brightened as the sky above them deepened into the violet-gray of coming dusk. The moist, delicious freshness which filled the bed of the valley slowly crept up the branching glen, and already tempered the air about them. Now and then a bird chirped happily from a neighboring bush, or the low of cattle was heard from the pasture-fields.

"Ah!" sighed Miss Blessing, "this is too sweet to last: I must learn to do without it."

She looked at him swiftly, and then glanced away. It seemed that there were tears in her eyes.

Joseph was about to speak, but she laid her hand on his arm. "Hush!" she said; "let us wait until the light has faded."

The glow had withdrawn to the summits of the distant hills, fringing them with a thin, wonderful radiance. But it was only momentary. The next moment it broke on the irregular topmost boughs, and then disappeared, as if blown out by a breeze which came with the sudden lifting of the sky. She turned away in silence, and they walked slowly together towards the house. At the garden gate she paused.

"That superb avenue of box!" she exclaimed; "I must see it again, if only to say farewell."

They entered the garden, and in a moment the dense green wall, breathing an odor seductive to heart and senses, had hidden them from the sight—and almost from the hearing—of the guests on the portico. Looking down through the southern opening of the avenue, they seemed alone in the evening valley.

Joseph's heart was beating fast and strong; he was conscious of a wild fear, so interfused with pleasure, that it was impossible to separate the sensations. Miss Blessing's hand was on his arm, and he fancied that it trembled.

"If life were as beautiful and peaceful as this," she whispered, at last, "we should not need to seek for truth and—and—sympathy: we should find them everywhere."

692

"Do you not think they are to be found?" he asked.

"O, in how few hearts! I can say it to you, and you will not misunderstand me. Until lately I was satisfied with life as I found it: I thought it meant diversion, and dress, and gossip, and common daily duties, but now—now I see that it is the union of kindred souls!"

She clasped both her hands over his arm as she spoke, and leaned slightly towards him, as if drawing away from the dreary, homeless world. Joseph felt all that the action expressed, and answered in an unsteady voice:—

"And yet—with a nature like yours—you must surely find them."

She shook her head sadly, and answered: "Ah, a woman cannot seek. I never thought I should be able to say—to any human being—that I have sought, or waited for recognition. I do not know why I should say it now. I try to be myself—my true self—with all persons; but it seems impossible: my nature shrinks from some and is drawn towards others. Why is this? What is the mystery that surrounds us?"

"Do you believe," Joseph asked, "that two souls may be so united that they shall dare to surrender all knowledge of themselves to each other, as we do, helplessly, before God?"

"O," she murmured, "it is my dream! I thought I was alone in cherishing it! Can it ever be realized?"

Joseph's brain grew hot: the release he had invoked sprang to life and urged him forward. Words came to his lips, he knew not how.

"If it is my dream and yours,—if we both have come to the faith and the hope we find in no others, and which alone will satisfy our lives, is it not a sign that the dream is over and the reality has begun?"

She hid her face in her hands. "Do not tempt me with what I had given up, unless you can teach me to believe again?" she cried.

"I do not tempt you," he answered breathlessly. "I tempt myself. I believe."

She turned suddenly, laid a hand upon his shoulder, lifted her face and looked into his eyes with an expression of passionate eagerness and joy. All her attitude breathed of the pause of the wave that only seems to hesitate an instant before throwing itself upon the waiting strand. Joseph had no defence, knew of none, dreamed of none. The pale-brown eyes, now dark, deep, and almost tearful, drew him with irresistible force: the sense of his own shy reticent self was lost, dissolved in the strength of an instinct which possessed him body and soul,—which bent him nearer to the slight form, which stretched his arms to answer its appeal, and left him, after one dizzy moment, with Miss Blessing's head upon his breast.

"I should like to die now," she murmured: "I never can be so happy again."

"No, no," said he, bending over her; "live for me!"

She raised herself, and kissed him again and again, and this frank, almost childlike betrayal of her heart seemed to claim from Joseph the full surrender of his own. He returned her caresses with equal warmth, and the twilight deepened around them as they stood, still half-embracing.

"Can I make you happy, Joseph?"

"Julia, I am already happier than I ever thought it possible to be."

With a sudden impulse she drew away from him. "Joseph!" she whispered, "will you always bear in mind what a cold, selfish, worldly life mine has been? You do not know me; you cannot understand the school in which I have been taught. I tell you, now, that I have had to learn cunning and artifice and equivocation. I am dark beside a nature so pure and good as yours! If you must ever learn to hate me, begin now! Take back your love: I have lived so long without the love of a noble human heart, that I can live so to the end!"

She again covered her face with her hands, and her frame shrank, as if dreading a mortal blow. But Joseph caught her back to his breast, touched and even humiliated by such sharp self-accusation. Presently she looked up: her eyes were wet, and she said, with a pitiful smile:—

"I believe you do love me."

"And I will not give you up," said Joseph, "though you should be full of evil as I am, myself."

She laughed, and patted his cheek: all her frank, bright, winning manner returned at once. Then commenced those reciprocal expressions of bliss, which are so inexhaustibly fresh to lovers, so endlessly monotonous to everybody else; and Joseph, lost to time, place, and circumstance, would have prolonged them far into the night, but for Miss Julia's returning self-possession.

"I hear wheels," she warned; "the evening guests are coming, and they will expect you to receive them, Joseph. And your dear, good old aunt will be looking for me. O, the world, the world! We must give ourselves up to it, and be as if we had never found each other. I shall be wild unless you set me an example of self-control. Let me look at you once,—one full, precious, perfect look, to carry in my heart through the evening!"

Then they looked in each other's faces; and looking was not enough; and their lips, without the use of words, said the temporary farewell. While Joseph hurried across the bottom of the lawn, to meet the stream of approaching guests which filled the lane, Miss Julia, at the top of the garden, plucked amaranth leaves for a wreath which would look well upon her dark hair, and sang, in a voice loud enough to be heard from the portico:—

"Ever be happy, light as thou art,

Pride of the pirate's heart!"

Everybody who had been invited—and quite a number who had not been, availing themselves of the easy habits of country society—came to the Asten farm that evening. Joseph, as host, seemed at times a little confused and flurried, but his face bloomed, his blue eyes sparkled, and even his nearest acquaintances were astonished at the courage and cordiality with which he performed his duties. The presence of Mr. Chaffinch kept the gayety of the company within decorous bounds; perhaps the number of detached groups appeared to form too many separate circles, or atmospheres of talk, but they easily dissolved, or gave to and took from each other. Rachel Miller was not inclined to act the part of a moral detective in the house which she managed; she saw nothing which the strictest sense of propriety could condemn.

Early in the evening, Joseph met Lucy Henderson in the hall. He could not see the graver change in her face; he only noticed that her manner was not so quietly attractive as usual. Yet on meeting her eyes he felt the absurd blood rushing to his cheeks and brow, and his tongue hesitated and stammered. This want of self-possession vexed him; he could not account for it; and he cut short the interview by moving abruptly away.

Lucy half turned, and looked after him, with an expression rather of surprise than of pain. As she did so she felt that there was an eye upon her, and by a strong effort entered the room without encountering the face of Elwood Withers.

When the company broke up, Miss Blessing, who was obliged to leave with the Warriners, found an opportunity to whisper to Joseph: "Come soon!" There was a long, fervent clasp of hands under her shawl, and then the carriage drove away. He could not see how the hand was transferred to that of Anna Warriner, which received from it a squeeze conveying an entire narrative to that young lady's mind.

Joseph's duties to his many guests prevented him from seeing much of Elwood during the evening; but, when the last were preparing to leave, he turned to the latter, conscious of a tenderer feeling of friendship than he had ever before felt, and begged him to stay for the night. Elwood held up the lantern, with which he had been examining the harness of a carriage that had just rolled away, and let its light fall upon Joseph's face.

"Do you really mean it?" he then asked.

"I don't understand you, Elwood."

"Perhaps I don't understand myself." But the next moment he laughed, and then added, in his usual tone: "Never mind; I'll stay."

They occupied the same room; and neither seemed inclined to sleep.

After the company had been discussed, in a way which both felt to be awkward and mechanical, Elwood said: "Do you know anything more about love, by this time?"

Joseph was silent, debating with himself whether he should confide the wonderful secret. Elwood suddenly rose up in his bed, leaned forward, and whispered: "I see,—you need not answer. But tell me this one thing: is it Lucy Henderson?"

"No; O, no!"

"Does she know of it? Your face told some sort of a tale when you met her to-night."

"Not to her,—surely not to her!" Joseph exclaimed.

"I hope not," Elwood quietly said: "I love her."

With a bound Joseph crossed the room and sat down on the edge of his friend's bed. "Elwood!" he cried; "and you are happy, too! O, now I can tell you all,—it is Julia Blessing!"

"Ha! ha!" Elwood laughed,—a short, bitter laugh, which seemed to signify anything but happiness. "Forgive me, Joseph!" he presently added, "but there's a deal of difference between a mitten and a ring. You will have one and I have the other. I did think for a little while that you stood between Lucy and me; but I suppose disappointment makes men fools."

Something in Joseph's breast seemed to stop the warm flood of his feelings. He could only stammer, after a long pause: "But I am not in your way."

"So I see,—and perhaps nobody is, except myself. We won't talk of this any more; there's many a roundabout road that comes out into the straight one at last. But you,—I can't understand the thing at all. How did she—did you come to love her?"

"I don't know; I hardly guessed it until this evening."

"Then, Joseph, go slowly, and feel your way. I'm not the one to advise, after what has happened to me; but maybe I know a little more of womankind than you. It's best to have a longer acquaintance than yours has been; a fellow can't always tell a sudden fancy from a love that has the grip of death."

"Now I might turn your own words against you, Elwood, for you tried to tell me what love is."

"I did; and before I knew the half. But come, Joseph: promise me that you won't let Miss Blessing know how much you feel until—"

"Elwood," Joseph breathlessly interrupted, "she knows it now! We were together this evening."

Elwood fell back on the pillow with a groan. "I'm a poor friend to you," he said: "I want to wish you joy, but I can't,—not to-night. The way things are fixed in this world stumps me, out and out. Nothing fits as it ought, and if I didn't take my head in my own hands and hold it towards the light by main force, I'd only see blackness, and death, and hell."

Joseph stole back to his bed, and lay there silently. There was a subtle chill in the heart of his happiness, which all the remembered glow of that tender scene in the garden could not thaw.

# CHAPTER VII. THE BLESSING FAMILY.

Joseph's secret was not suspected by any of the company. Elwood's manner towards him next morning was warmer and kinder than ever; the chill of the past night had been forgotten, and the betrothal, which then almost seemed like a fetter upon his future, now gave him a sense of freedom and strength. He would have gone to Warriner's at once, but for the fear lest he should betray himself. Miss Blessing was to return to the city in three days more, and a single farewell call might be made with propriety; so he controlled his impatience and allowed another day to intervene.

When, at last, the hour of meeting came, Anna Warriner proved herself an efficient ally. Circumstances were against her, yet she secured the lovers a few minutes in which they could hold each other's hands, and repeat their mutual delight, with an exquisite sense of liberty in doing so. Miss Blessing suggested that nothing should be said until she had acquainted her parents with the engagement; there might be some natural difficulties to overcome; it was so unexpected, and the idea of losing her would possibly be unwelcome, at first. She would write in a few days, and then Joseph must come and make the acquaintance of her family.

"Then," she added, "I shall have no fear. When they have once seen you all difficulties will vanish. There will be no trouble with ma and sister Clementina; but pa is sometimes a little peculiar, on account of his connections. There! don't look so serious, all at once; it is my duty, you know, to secure you a loving reception. You must try to feel already that you have two homes, as I do."

Joseph waited very anxiously for the promised letter, and in ten days it came; it was brief, but satisfactory. "Would you believe it, dear Joseph," she commenced, "pa makes no difficulty! he only requires some assurances which you can very easily furnish. Ma, on the other hand, don't like the idea of giving me up. I can hardly say it without seeming to praise myself; but Clementina never took very kindly to housekeeping and managing, and even if I were only indifferent in those branches, I should be missed. It really went to my heart when ma met me at the door, and cried out, 'Now I shall have a little rest!' You may imagine how hard it was to tell her. But she is a dear, good mother, and I know she will be so happy to find a son in you—as she certainly will. Come, soon,—soon! They are all anxious to know you."

The city was not so distant as to make a trip thither an unusual event for the young farmers of the neighborhood. Joseph had frequently gone there for a day in the interest of his sales of stock and grain, and he found no difficulty in inventing a plausible reason for the journey. The train at the nearest railway station transported him in two or three hours to the commencement of the miles of hot, dusty, rattling pavements, and left him free to seek for the brick nest within which his love was sheltered.

Yet now, so near the point whence his new life was to commence, a singular unrest took possession of him. He distinctly felt the presence of two forces, acting against each other with nearly equal power, but without neutralizing their disturbing influence. He was developing faster than he guessed, yet, to a nature like his, the last knowledge that comes is the knowledge of self. Some occult instinct already whispered that his life thenceforth would be stronger, more independent, but also more disturbed; and this was what he had believed was wanting. If the consciousness of loving and being loved were not quite the same in experience as it had seemed to his ignorant fancy, it was yet a positive happiness, and wedlock would therefore be its unbroken continuance. Julia had prepared for his introduction into her family; he must learn to accept her parents and sister as his own; and now the hour and the opportunity were at hand.

What was it, then, that struck upon his breast almost like a physical pressure, and mysteriously resisted his errand? When he reached the cross-street, in which, many squares to the northward, the house was to be found, he halted for some minutes, and then, instead of turning, kept directly onward toward the river. The sight of the water, the gliding sails, the lusty life and labor along the piers, suddenly refreshed him. Men were tramping up and down the gangways of the clipper-ships; derricks were slowly swinging over the sides the bales and boxes which had been brought up from the holds; drays were clattering to and fro: wherever he turned he saw a picture of strength, courage, reality, solid work. The men that went and came took life simply as a succession of facts, and if these did not fit smoothly into each other, they either gave themselves no trouble about the rough edges, or drove them out of sight with a few sturdy blows. What Lucy Henderson had said about going to school was recalled to Joseph's mind. Here was a class where he would be apt to stand at the foot for many days. Would any of those strapping forms comprehend the disturbance of his mind?—they would probably advise him to go to the nearest apothecary-shop and purchase a few blue-pills. The longer he watched them, the more he felt the contagion of their unimaginative, face to face grapple with life; the manly element in him, checked so long, began to push a vigorous shoot towards the light.

"It is only the old cowardice, after all," he thought. "I am still shrinking from the encounter with new faces! A lover, soon to be a husband, and still so much of a green youth! It will never do. I must learn to handle my duty as that stevedore handles a barrel,—take hold with both hands, push and trundle and guide, till the weight becomes a mere plaything. There!—he starts a fresh one,—now for mine!"

Therewith he turned about, walked sternly back to the cross-street, and entered it without pausing at the corner. It was still a long walk; and the street, with its uniform brick houses, with white shutters, green interior blinds, and white marble steps, grew more silent and monotonous. There was a mixed odor of salt-fish, molasses, and decaying oranges at every corner; dark wenches lowered the nozzles of their jetting hose as he passed, and girls in draggled calico frocks turned to look at him from the entrances of gloomy tunnels leading into the back yards. A man with something in a cart uttered from time to time a piercing unintelligible cry; barefooted youngsters swore over their marbles on the sidewalk; and, at rare intervals, a marvellous moving fabric of silks and colors and glosses floated past him. But he paused for none of these. His heart beat faster, and the strange resistance seemed to increase with the increasing numbers of houses, now rapidly approaching The One— then it came!

There was an entire block of narrow three-storied dwellings, with

701

crowded windows and flat roofs. If Joseph had been familiar with the city, he would have recognized the air of cheap gentility which exhaled from them, and which said, as plainly as if the words had been painted on their fronts, "Here we keep up appearances on a very small capital." He noticed nothing, however, except the marble steps and the front doors, all of which were alike to him until he came upon a brass plate inscribed "B. Blessing." As he looked up a mass of dark curls vanished with a start from the window. The door suddenly opened before he could touch the bell-pull, and two hands upon his own drew him into the diminutive hall.

The door instantly closed again, but softly: then two arms were flung around his neck, and his willing lips received a subdued kiss. "Hush!" she said; "it is delightful that you have arrived, though we didn't expect you so immediately. Come into the drawing-room, and let us have a minute together before I call ma."

She tripped lightly before him, and they were presently seated side by side, on the sofa.

"What could have brought me to the window just at that moment?" she whispered; "it must have been presentiment."

Joseph's face brightened with pleasure. "And I was long on the way," he answered. "What will you think of me, Julia? I was a little afraid."

"I know you were, Joseph," she said. "It is only the cold, insensible hearts that are never agitated."

Their eyes met, and he remarked, for the first time, their peculiar pale-brown, almost tawny clearness. The next instant her long lashes slowly fell and half concealed them; she drew away slightly from him, and said: "I should like to be beautiful, for your sake; I never cared about it before."

Without giving him time to reply, she rose and moved towards the door, then looked back, smiled, and disappeared.

Joseph, left alone, also rose and walked softly up and down the room. To his eyes it seemed an elegant, if rather chilly apartment. It was long and narrow, with a small, delusive fireplace of white marble (intended only for hot air) in the middle, a carpet of many glaring colors on the floor, and a paper brilliant with lilac-bunches on the walls. There was a centre-table, with some lukewarm literature cooling itself on the marble top; an étagère, with a few nondescript cups and flagons, and a cottage piano, on which lay several sheets of music by Verdi and Balfe. The furniture, not very abundant, was swathed in a nankeen summer dress. There were two pictures on the walls, portraits of a gentleman and lady, and when once Joseph had caught the fixed stare of their lustreless eyes, he found it difficult to turn away. The imperfect light which came through the bowed window-shutters revealed a florid, puffy-faced young man, whose head was held up by a high black satin stock. He was leaning against a fluted pillar, apparently constructed of putty, behind which fell a superb crimson curtain, lifted up at one corner to disclose a patch of stormy sky. The long locks, tucked in at the temples, the carefully-delineated whiskers, and the huge signet-ring on the second finger of the one exposed hand, indicated that a certain "position" in society was either possessed or claimed of right by the painted person. Joseph could hardly doubt that this was a representation of "B. Blessing," as he appeared twenty or thirty years before.

He turned to the other picture. The lady was slender, and meant to be graceful, her head being inclined so that the curls on the left side rolled in studied disorder upon her shoulder. Her face was thin and long, with well-marked and not unpleasant features. There was rather too positive a bloom upon her cheeks, and the fixed smile on the narrow mouth scarcely harmonized with the hard, serious stare of the eyes. She was royally attired in purple, and her bare white arm—much more plumply rounded than her face would have given reason to suspect—hung with a listless grace over the end of a sofa.

Joseph looked from one face to the other with a curious interest, which the painted eyes seemed also to reflect, as they followed him. They were strangers, out of a different sphere of life, yet they must become, nay, were already, a part of his own! The lady scrutinized him closely, in spite of her smile; but the indifference of the gentleman, blandly satisfied with himself,

703

seemed less assuring to his prospects.

Footsteps in the hall interrupted his revery, and he had barely time to slip into his seat when the door opened and Julia entered, followed by the original of one of the portraits. He recognized her, although the curls had disappeared, the dark hair was sprinkled with gray, and deep lines about the mouth and eyes gave them an expression of care and discontent. In one respect she differed from her daughter: her eyes were gray.

She bent her head with a stately air as Joseph rose, walked past Julia, and extended her hand, with the words,—

"Mr. Asten, I am glad to see you. Pray be seated."

When all had taken seats, she resumed: "Excuse me if I begin by asking a question. You must consider that I have only known you through Julia, and her description could not, under the circumstances, be very clear. What is your age?"

"I shall be twenty-three next birthday," Joseph replied.

"Indeed! I am happy to hear it. You do not look more than nineteen. I have reason to dread very youthful attachments, and am therefore reassured to know that you are fully a man and competent to test your feelings. I trust that you have so tested them. Again I say, excuse me if the question seems to imply a want of confidence. A mother's anxiety, you know—"

Julia clasped her hands and bent down her head.

"I am quite sure of myself," Joseph said, "and would try to make you as sure, if I knew how to do it."

"If you were one of us,—of the city, I mean,—I should be able to judge more promptly. It is many years since I have been outside of our own select circle, and I am therefore not so competent as once to judge of men in general. While I will never, without the most sufficient reason, influence my daughters in their choice, it is my duty to tell you that Julia is exceedingly susceptible on the side of her affections. A wound there would be incurable to her. We are alike in that; I know her nature through my own."

704

Julia hid her face upon her mother's shoulder: Joseph was moved, and vainly racked his brain for some form of assurance which might remove the maternal anxiety.

"There," said Mrs. Blessing; "we will say no more about it now. Go and bring your sister!"

"There are some other points, Mr. Asten," she continued, "which have no doubt already occurred to your mind. Mr. Blessing will consult with you in relation to them. I make it a rule never to trespass upon his field of duty. As you were not positively expected to-day, he went to the Custom-House as usual; but it will soon be time for him to return. Official labors, you understand, cannot be postponed. If you have ever served in a government capacity, you will appreciate his position. I have sometimes wished that we had not become identified with political life; but, on the other hand, there are compensations."

Joseph, impressed more by Mrs. Blessing's important manner than the words she uttered, could only say, "I beg that my visit may not interfere in any way with Mr. Blessing's duties."

"Unfortunately," she replied, "they cannot be postponed. His advice is more required by the Collector than his special official services. But, as I said, he will confer with you in regard to the future of our little girl. I call her so, Mr. Asten, because she is the youngest, and I can hardly yet realize that she is old enough to leave me. Yes: the youngest, and the first to go. Had it been Clementina, I should have been better prepared for the change. But a mother should always be ready to sacrifice herself, where the happiness of a child is at stake."

Mrs. Blessing gently pressed a small handkerchief to the corner of each eye, then heaved a sigh, and resumed her usual calm dignity of manner. The door opened, and Julia re-entered, followed by her sister.

"This is Miss Blessing," said the mother.

The young lady bowed very formally, and therewith would have finished her greeting, but Joseph had already risen and extended his hand.

She thereupon gave him the tips of four limp fingers, which he attempted to grasp and then let go.

Clementina was nearly a head taller than her sister, and amply proportioned. She had a small, petulant mouth, small gray eyes, a low, narrow forehead, and light brown hair. Her eyelids and cheeks had the same puffy character as her father's, in his portrait on the wall; yet there was a bloom and brilliancy about her complexion which suggested beauty. A faint expression of curiosity passed over her face, on meeting Joseph, but she uttered no word of welcome. He looked at Julia, whose manner was suddenly subdued, and was quick enough to perceive a rivalry between the sisters. The stolidity of Clementina's countenance indicated that indifference which is more offensive than enmity. He disliked her from the first moment.

Julia kept modestly silent, and the conversation, in spite of her mother's capacity to carry it on, did not flourish. Clementina spoke only in monosyllables, which she let fall from time to time with a silver sweetness which startled Joseph, it seemed so at variance with her face and manner. He felt very much relieved when, after more than one significant glance had been exchanged with her mother, the two arose and left the room. At the door Mrs. Blessing said: "Of course you will stay and take a family tea with us, Mr. Asten. I will order it to be earlier served, as you are probably not accustomed to our city hours."

Julia looked up brightly after the door had closed, and exclaimed: "Now! when ma says that, you may be satisfied. Her housekeeping is like the laws of the Medes and Persians. She probably seemed rather formal to you, and it is true that a certain amount of form has become natural to her; but it always gives way when she is strongly moved. Pa is to come yet, but I am sure you will get on very well with him; men always grow acquainted in a little while. I'm afraid that Clementina did not impress you very—very genially; she is, I may confess it to you, a little peculiar."

"She is very quiet," said Joseph, "and very unlike you."

"Every one notices that. And we seem to be unlike in character, as much so as if there were no relationship between us. But I must say for Clementina, that she is above personal likings and dislikings; she looks at people abstractly. You are only a future brother-in-law to her, and I don't believe she can tell whether your hair is black or the beautiful golden brown that it is."

Joseph smiled, not ill-pleased with Julia's delicate flattery. "I am all the more delighted," he said, "that you are different. I should not like you, Julia, to consider me an abstraction."

"You are very real, Joseph, and very individual," she answered, with one of her loveliest smiles.

Not ten minutes afterwards, Julia, whose eyes and ears were keenly on the alert, notwithstanding her gay, unrestrained talk, heard the click of a latch-key. She sprang up, laid her forefinger on her lips, gave Joseph a swift, significant glance, and darted into the hall. A sound of whispering followed, and there was no mistaking the deep, hoarse murmur of one of the voices.

Mr. Blessing, without the fluted pillar and the crimson curtain, was less formidable than Joseph had anticipated. The years had added to his body and taken away from his hair; yet his face, since high stocks were no longer in fashion, had lost its rigid lift, and expressed the chronic cordiality of a popular politician. There was a redness about the rims of his eyes, and a fulness of the under lid, which also denoted political habits. However, despite wrinkles, redness, and a general roughening and coarsening of the features, the resemblance to the portrait was still strong; and Joseph, feeling as if the presentation had already been made, offered his hand as soon as Mr. Blessing entered the room.

"Very happy to see you, Mr. Asten," said the latter. "An unexpected pleasure, sir."

He removed the glove from his left hand, pulled down his coat and vest, felt the tie of his cravat, twitched at his pantaloons, ran his fingers through his straggling gray locks, and then threw himself into a chair, exclaiming: "After business, pleasure, sir! My duties are over for the day. Mrs. Blessing probably informed you of my official capacity; but you can have no conception of the vigilance required to prevent evasion of the revenue laws. We are the country's watch-dogs, sir."

"I can understand," Joseph said, "that an official position carries with it much responsibility."

"Quite right, sir, and without adequate remuneration. Figuratively speaking, we handle millions, and we are paid by dimes. Were it not for the consciousness of serving and saving for the nation—but I will not pursue the subject. When we have become better acquainted, you can judge for yourself whether preferment always follows capacity. Our present business is to establish a mutual understanding,—as we say in politics, to prepare a platform,—and I think you will agree with me that the circumstances of the case require frank dealing, as between man and man."

"Certainly!" Joseph answered; "I only ask that, although I am a stranger to you, you will accept my word until you have the means of verifying it."

"I may safely do that with you, sir. My associations—duties, I may say—compel me to know many persons with whom it would not be safe. We will forget the disparity of age and experience between us. I can hardly ask you to imagine yourself placed in my situation, but perhaps we can make the case quite as clear if I state to you, without reserve, what I should be ready to do, if our present positions were reversed: Julia, will you look after the tea?"

"Yes, pa," said she, and slipped out of the drawing-room.

"If I were a young man from the country, and had won the affections of a young lady of—well, I may say it to you—of an old family, whose parents were ignorant of my descent, means, and future prospects in life, I should consider it my first duty to enlighten those parents upon all these points. I should reflect that the lady must be removed from their sphere to mine; that, while the attachment was, in itself, vitally important to her and to me, those parents would naturally desire to compare the two spheres, and assure themselves that their daughter would lose no material advantages by the transfer. You catch my meaning?"

"I came here," said Joseph, "with the single intention of satisfying you— at least, I came hoping that I shall be able to do so—in regard to myself. It will be easy for you to test my statements."

"Very well. We will begin, then, with the subject of Family. Understand me, I mention this solely because, in our old communities, Family is the stamp of Character. An established name represents personal qualities, virtues. It is indifferent to me whether my original ancestor was a De Belsain (though beauty and health have always been family characteristics); but it is important that he transmitted certain traits which—which others, perhaps, can better describe. The name of Asten is not usual; it has, in fact, rather a distinguished sound; but I am not acquainted with its derivation."

Joseph restrained a temptation to smile, and replied: "My great-grandfather came from England more than a hundred years ago: that is all I positively know. I have heard it said that the family was originally Danish."

"You must look into the matter, sir: a good pedigree is a bond for good behavior. The Danes, I have been told, were of the same blood as the Normans. But we will let that pass. Julia informs me you are the owner of a handsome farm, yet I am so ignorant of values in the country,—and my official duties oblige me to measure property by such a different standard,—that, really, unless you could make the farm evident to me in figures, I—"

He paused, but Joseph was quite ready with the desired intelligence. "I have two hundred acres," he said, "and a moderate valuation of the place would be a hundred and thirty dollars an acre. There is a mortgage of five thousand dollars on the place, the term of which has not yet expired; but I have nearly an equal amount invested, so that the farm fairly represents what I own."

"H'm," mused Mr. Blessing, thrusting his thumbs into the arm-holes of his waistcoat, "that is not a great deal here in the city, but I dare say it is a handsome competence in the country. It doubtless represents a certain annual income!"

"It is a very comfortable home, in the first place," said Joseph; "the farm ought to yield, after supplying nearly all the wants of a family, an annual return of a thousand to fifteen hundred dollars, according to the season."

"Twenty-six thousand dollars!—and five per cent!" Mr. Blessing exclaimed. "If you had the farm in money, and knew how to operate with it, you might pocket ten—fifteen—twenty per cent. Many a man, with less than that to set him afloat, has become a millionnaire in five years' time. But it takes pluck and experience, sir!"

"More of both than I can lay claim to," Joseph remarked; "but what there is of my income is certain. If Julia were not so fond of the country, and already so familiar with our ways, I might hesitate to offer her such a plain, quiet home, but—"

"O, I know!" Mr. Blessing interrupted. "We have heard of nothing but cows and spring-houses and willow-trees since she came back. I hope, for your sake, it may last; for I see that you are determined to suit each other. I have no inclination to act the obdurate parent. You have met me like a man, sir: here's my hand; I feel sure that, as my son-in-law, you will keep up the reputation of the family!"

# CHAPTER VIII. A CONSULTATION.

The family tea was served in a small dining-room in the rear. Mr. Blessing, who had become more and more cordial with Joseph after formally accepting him, led the way thither, and managed to convey a rapid signal to his wife before the family took their seats at the table. Joseph was the only one who did not perceive the silent communication of intelligence; but its consequences were such as to make him speedily feel at ease in the Blessing mansion. Even Clementina relented sufficiently to say, in her most silvery tones, "May I offer you the butter, Mr. Asten?"

The table, it is true, was very unlike the substantial suppers of the country. There was a variety of diminutive dishes, containing slices so delicate that they mocked rather than excited the appetite; yet Julia, (of course it was she!) had managed to give the repast an air of elegance which was at least agreeable to a kindred sense. Joseph took the little cup, the thin tea, the five drops of milk, and the fragment of sugar, without asking himself whether the beverage were palatable: he divided a leaf-like piece of flesh and consumed several wafers of bread, blissfully unconscious whether his stomach were satisfied. He felt that he had been received into The Family. Mr. Blessing was magnificently bland, Mrs. Blessing was maternally interested, Clementina recognized his existence, and Julia,—he needed but one look at her sparkling eyes, her softly flushed cheeks, her bewitching excitement of manner, to guess the relief of her heart. He forgot the vague distress which had preceded his coming, and the embarrassment of his first reception, in the knowledge that Julia was so happy, and through the acquiescence of her parents, in his love.

It was settled that he should pass the night there. Mrs. Blessing would take no denial; he must now consider their house as his home. She would also call him "Joseph," but not now,—not until she was entitled to name him "son." It had come suddenly upon her, but it was her duty to be glad, and in a little while she would become accustomed to the change.

All this was so simply and cordially said, that Joseph quite warmed to the stately woman, and unconsciously decided to accept his fortune, whatever features it might wear. Until the one important event, at least; after that it would be in his own hands—and Julia's.

After tea, two or three hours passed away rather slowly. Mr. Blessing sat in the pit of a back yard and smoked until dusk; then the family collected in the "drawing-room," and there was a little music, and a variety of gossip, with occasional pauses of silence, until Mrs. Blessing said: "Perhaps you had better show Mr. Asten to his room, Mr. Blessing. We may have already passed over his accustomed hour for retiring. If so, I know he will excuse us; we shall soon become familiar with each other's habits."

When Mr. Blessing returned, he first opened the rear window, drew an arm-chair near it, took off his coat, seated himself, and lit another cigar. His wife closed the front shutters, slipped the night-bolts of the door, and then seated herself beside him. Julia whirled around on her music-stool to face the coming consultation, and Clementina gracefully posed herself in the nearest corner of the sofa.

"How do you like him, Eliza?" Mr. Blessing asked, after several silent, luxurious whiffs.

"He is handsome, and seems amiable, but younger than I expected. Are you sure of his—his feelings, Julia?"

"O ma!" Julia exclaimed; "what a question! I can only judge them by my own."

Clementina curled her lip in a singular fashion, but said nothing.

"It seems like losing Julia entirely," Mrs. Blessing resumed. "I don't know how she will be able to retain her place in our circle, unless they spend a part of the winter in the city, and whether he has means enough—"

She paused, and looked inquisitively at her husband.

"You always look at the establishment," said he, "and never consider the chances. Marriage is a deal, a throw, a sort of kite-flying, in fact (except in our case, my dear), and, after all I've learned of our future son-in-law, I must say that Julia hasn't a bad hand."

"I knew you'd like him, pa!" cried the delighted Julia.

Mr. Blessing looked at her steadily a moment, and then winked; but she took no notice of it.

"There is another thing," said his wife. "If the wedding comes off this fall, we have but two months to prepare; and how will you manage about the—the money? We can save afterwards, to be sure, but there will be an immediate and fearful expense. I've thought, perhaps, that a simple and private ceremony,—married in travelling-dress, you know, just before the train leaves, and no cards,—it is sometimes done in the highest circles."

"It won't do!" exclaimed Mr. Blessing, waving his right hand. "Julia's husband must have an opportunity of learning our standing in society. I will invite the Collector, and the Surveyor, and the Appraiser. The money must be raised. I should be willing to pawn—"

He looked around the room, inspecting the well-worn carpet, the nankeen-covered chairs, the old piano, and finally the two pictures.

"—Your portrait, my dear; but, unless it were a Stuart, I couldn't get ten dollars on it. We must take your set of diamonds, and Julia's rubies, and Clementina's pearls."

He leaned back, and laughed with great glee. The ladies became rigid and grave.

"It is wicked, Benjamin," Mrs. Blessing severely remarked, "to jest over our troubles at such a time as this. I see nothing else to do, but to inform Mr. Asten, frankly, of our condition. He is yet too young, I think, to be repelled by poverty."

"Ma, it would break my heart," said Julia. "I could not bear to be humiliated in his eyes."

"Decidedly the best thing to do," warbled Clementina, speaking for the first time.

"That's the way with women,—flying from one extreme to the other. If you can't have white, you turn around and say there's no other color than black. When all devices are exhausted, a man of pluck and character goes to work and constructs a new one. Upon my soul, I don't know where the money is to come from; but give me ten days, and Julia shall have her white satin. Now, girls, you had better go to bed."

Mr. Blessing smoked silently until the sound of his daughters' footsteps had ceased on the stairs; then, bringing down his hand emphatically upon his thigh, he exclaimed, "By Jove, Eliza, if I were as sharp as that girl, I'd have had the Collectorship before this!"

"What do you mean? She seems to be strongly attached to him."

"O, no doubt! But she has a wonderful talent for reading character. The young fellow is pretty green wood still; what he'll season into depends on her. Honest as the day,—there's nothing like a country life for that. But it's a pity that such a fund for operations should lie idle; he has a nest-egg that might hatch out millions!"

"I hope, Benjamin, that after all your unfortunate experience—"

"Pray don't lament in advance, and especially now, when a bit of luck comes to us. Julia has done well, and I'll trust her to improve her opportunities. Besides, this will help Clementina's chances; where there is one marriage in a family, there is generally another. Poor girl! she has waited a long while. At thirty-three, the market gets v-e-r-y flat."

"And yet Julia is thirty," said Mrs. Blessing; "and Clementina's complexion and manners have been considered superior."

"There's just her mistake. A better copy of Mrs. Halibut's airs and attitudes was never produced, and it was all very well so long as Mrs. Halibut gave the tone to society; but since she went to Europe, and Mrs. Bass has somehow crept into her place, Clementina is quite—I may say—obsolete. I don't object to her complexion, because that is a standing fashion, but she is expected to be chatty, and witty, and instead of that she stands about like a Venus of Milo. She looks like me, and she can't lack intelligence and tact.

Why couldn't she unbend a little more to Asten, whether she likes him or not?"

"You know I never seemed to manage Clementina," his wife replied; "if she were to dispute my opinion sometimes, I might, perhaps, gain a little influence over her: but she won't enter into a discussion."

"Mrs. Halibut's way. It was new, then, and, with her husband's money to back it, her 'grace' and 'composure' and 'serenity' carried all before her. Give me fifty thousand a year, and I'll put Clementina in the same place! But, come,—to the main question. I suppose we shall need five hundred dollars!"

"Three hundred, I think, will be ample," said Mrs. Blessing.

"Three or five, it's as hard to raise one sum as the other. I'll try for five, and if I have luck with the two hundred over—small, careful operations, you know, which always succeed—I may have the whole amount on hand, long before it's due."

Mrs. Blessing smiled in a melancholy, hopeless way, and the consultation came to an end.

When Joseph was left alone in his chamber, he felt no inclination to sleep. He sat at the open window, and looked down into the dim, melancholy street, the solitude of which was broken about once every quarter of an hour by a forlorn pedestrian, who approached through gloom and lamplight, was foreshortened to his hat, and then lengthened away on the other side. The new acquaintances he had just made remained all the more vividly in his thoughts from their nearness; he was still within their atmosphere. They were unlike any persons he knew, and therefore he felt that he might do them injustice by a hasty estimate of their character. Clementina, however, was excluded from this charitable resolution. Concentrating his dislike on her, he found that her parents had received him with as much consideration as a total stranger could expect. Moreover, whatever they might be, Julia was the same here, in her own home, as when she was a guest in the country. As playful, as winning, and as natural; and he began to suspect that her present life was not congenial to such a nature. If so, her happiness was all the more assured

715

by their union.

This thought led him into a pictured labyrinth of anticipation, in which his mind wandered with delight. He was so absorbed in planning the new household, that he did not hear the sisters entering the rear room on the same floor, which was only separated by a thin partition from his own.

"White satin!" he suddenly heard Clementina say: "of course I shall have the same. It will become me better than you."

"I should think you might be satisfied with a light silk," Julia said; "the expenses will be very heavy."

"We'll see," Clementina answered shortly, pacing up and down the room.

After a long pause, he heard Julia's voice again. "Never mind," she said, "I shall soon be out of your way."

"I wonder how much he knows about you!" Clementina exclaimed. "Your arts were new there, and you played an easy game." Here she lowered her voice, and Joseph only distinguished a detached word now and then. He rose, indignant at this unsisterly assault, and wishing to hear no more; but it seemed that the movement was not noticed, for Julia replied, in smothered, excited tones, with some remark about "complexion."

"Well, there is one thing," Clementina continued,—"one thing you will keep very secret, and that is your birthday. Are you going to tell him that you are—"

Joseph had seized the back of a chair and with a sudden impulse tilted it and let it fall on the floor. Then he walked to the window, closed it, and prepared to go to rest,—all with more noise than was habitual with him. There were whispers and hushed movements in the next room, but not another audible word was spoken. Before sleeping he came to the conclusion that he was more than Julia's lover: he was her deliverer. The idea was not unwelcome: it gave a new value and significance to his life.

However curious Julia might have been to discover how much he had overheard, she made no effort to ascertain the fact. She met him next morning with a sweet unconsciousness of what she had endured, which convinced him that such painful scenes must have been frequent, or she could not have forgotten so easily. His greeting to Clementina was brief and cold, but she did not seem to notice it in the least.

It was decided, before he left, that the wedding should take place in October.

## CHAPTER IX. JOSEPH AND HIS FRIEND.

The train moved slowly along through the straggling and shabby suburbs, increasing its speed as the city melted gradually into the country; and Joseph, after a vain attempt to fix his mind upon one of the volumes he had procured for his slender library at home, leaned back in his seat and took note of his fellow-travellers. Since he began to approach the usual destiny of men, they had a new interest for him. Hitherto he had looked upon strange faces very much as on a strange language, without a thought of interpreting them; but now their hieroglyphics seemed to suggest a meaning. The figures around him were so many sitting, silent histories, so many locked-up records of struggle, loss, gain, and all the other forces which give shape and color to human life. Most of them were strangers to each other, and as reticent (in their railway conventionality) as himself; yet, he reflected, the whole range of passion, pleasure, and suffering was probably illustrated in that collection of existences. His own troublesome individuality grew fainter, so much of it seemed to be merged in the common experience of men.

There was the portly gentleman of fifty, still ruddy and full of unwasted force. The keenness and coolness of his eyes, the few firmly marked lines on his face, and the color and hardness of his lips, proclaimed to everybody: "I am bold, shrewd, successful in business, scrupulous in the performance of my religious duties (on the Sabbath), voting with my party, and not likely to be fooled by any kind of sentimental nonsense." The thin, not very well-dressed man beside him, with the irregular features and uncertain expression, announced as clearly, to any who could read: "I am weak, like others, but I never consciously did any harm. I just manage to get along in the world, but if I only had a chance, I might make something better of myself." The fresh, healthy fellow, in whose lap a child was sleeping, while his wife nursed a younger one,—the man with ample mouth, large nostrils, and the hands of a mechanic,—also told his story: "On the whole, I find life a comfortable thing. I don't know much about it, but I take it as it comes, and never worry over what I can't understand."

The faces of the younger men, however, were not so easy to decipher. On them life was only beginning its plastic task, and it required an older eye to detect the delicate touches of awakening passions and hopes. But Joseph consoled himself with the thought that his own secret was as little to be discovered as any they might have. If they were still ignorant, of the sweet experience of love, he was already their superior; if they were sharers in it, though strangers, they were near to him. Had he not left the foot of the class, after all?

All at once his eye was attracted by a new face, three or four seats from his own. The stranger had shifted his position, so that he was no longer seen in profile. He was apparently a few years older than Joseph, but still bright with all the charm of early manhood. His fair complexion was bronzed from exposure, and his hands, graceful without being effeminate, were not those of the idle gentleman. His hair, golden in tint, thrust its short locks as it pleased about a smooth, frank forehead; the eyes were dark gray, and the mouth, partly hidden by a mustache, at once firm and full. He was moderately handsome, yet it was not of that which Joseph thought; he felt that there was more of developed character and a richer past history expressed in those features than in any other face there. He felt sure—and smiled at himself, notwithstanding, for the impression—that at least some of his own doubts and difficulties had found their solution in the stranger's nature. The more he studied the face, the more he was conscious of its attraction, and his instinct of reliance, though utterly without grounds, justified itself to his mind in some mysterious way.

It was not long before the unknown felt his gaze, and, turning slowly in his seat, answered it. Joseph dropped his eyes in some confusion, but not until he had caught the full, warm, intense expression of those that met them. He fancied that he read in them, in that momentary flash, what he had never before found in the eyes of strangers,—a simple, human interest, above curiosity and above mistrust. The usual reply to such a gaze is an unconscious defiance: the unknown nature is on its guard: but the look which seems to answer, "We are men, let us know each other!" is, alas! too rare in this world.

While Joseph was fighting the irresistible temptation to look again,

719

there was a sudden thud of the car-wheels. Many of the passengers started
from their seats, only to be thrown into them again by a quick succession of
violent jolts. Joseph saw the stranger springing towards the bell-rope; then
he and all others seemed to be whirling over each other; there was a crash, a
horrible grinding and splintering sound, and the end of all was a shock, in
which his consciousness left him before he could guess its violence.

After a while, out of some blank, haunted by a single lost, wandering
sense of existence, he began to awaken slowly to life. Flames were still dancing
in his eyeballs, and waters and whirlwinds roaring in his ears; but it was
only a passive sensation, without the will to know more. Then he felt himself
partly lifted and his head supported, and presently a soft warmth fell upon
the region of his heart. There were noises all about him, but he did not listen
to them; his effort to regain his consciousness fixed itself on that point alone,
and grew stronger as the warmth calmed the confusion of his nerves.

"Dip this in water!" said a voice, and the hand (as he now knew it to be)
was removed from his heart.

Something cold came over his forehead, and at the same time warm
drops fell upon his cheek.

"Look out for yourself: your head is cut!" exclaimed another voice.

"Only a scratch. Take the handkerchief out of my pocket and tie it up;
but first ask yon gentleman for his flask!"

Joseph opened his eyes, knew the face that bent over his, and then closed
them again. Gentle and strong hands raised him, a flask was set to his lips,
and he drank mechanically, but a full sense of life followed the draught. He
looked wistfully in the stranger's face.

"Wait a moment," said the latter; "I must feel your bones before you try
to move. Arms and legs all right,—impossible to tell about the ribs. There!
now put your arm around my neck, and lean on me as much as you like,
while I lift you."

Joseph did as he was bidden, but he was still weak and giddy, and after a few steps, they both sat down together upon a bank. The splintered car lay near them upside down; the passengers had been extricated from it, and were now busy in aiding the few who were injured. The train had stopped and was waiting on the track above. Some were very pale and grave, feeling that Death had touched without taking them; but the greater part were concerned only about the delay to the train.

"How did it happen?" asked Joseph: "where was I? how did you find me?"

"The usual story,—a broken rail," said the stranger. "I had just caught the rope when the car went over, and was swung off my feet so luckily that I somehow escaped the hardest shock. I don't think I lost my senses for a moment. When we came to the bottom you were lying just before me; I thought you dead until I felt your heart. It is a severe shock, but I hope nothing more."

"But you,—are you not badly hurt?"

The stranger pushed up the handkerchief which was tied around his head, felt his temple, and said: "It must have been one of the splinters; I know nothing about it. But there is no harm in a little blood-letting except"—he added, smiling—"except the spots on your face."

By this time the other injured passengers had been conveyed to the train; the whistle sounded a warning of departure.

"I think we can get up the embankment now," said the stranger. "You must let me take care of you still: I am travelling alone."

When they were seated side by side, and Joseph leaned his head back on the supporting arm, while the train moved away with them, he felt that a new power, a new support, had come to his life. The face upon which he looked was no longer strange; the hand which had rested on his heart was warm with kindred blood. Involuntarily he extended his own; it was taken and held, and the dark gray, courageous eyes turned to him with a silent assurance which he felt needed no words.

"It is a rough introduction," he then said: "my name is Philip Held. I was on my way to Oakland Station; but if you are going farther—"

"Why, that is my station also!" Joseph exclaimed, giving his name in return.

"Then we should have probably met, sooner or later, in any case. I am bound for the forge and furnace at Coventry, which is for sale. If the company who employ me decide to buy it,—according to the report I shall make,—the works will be placed in my charge."

"It is but six miles from my farm," said Joseph, "and the road up the valley is the most beautiful in our neighborhood. I hope you can make a favorable report."

"It is only too much to my own interest to do so. I have been mining and geologizing in Nevada and the Rocky Mountains for three or four years, and long for a quiet, ordered life. It is a good omen that I have found a neighbor in advance of my settlement. I have often ridden fifty miles to meet a friend who cared for something else than horse-racing or monte; and your six miles,—it is but a step!"

"How much you have seen!" said Joseph. "I know very little of the world. It must be easy for you to take your own place in life."

A shade passed over Philip Held's face. "It is only easy to a certain class of men," he replied,—"a class to which I should not care to belong. I begin to think that nothing is very valuable, the light to which a man don't earn,—except human love, and that seems to come by the grace of God."

"I am younger than you are,—not yet twenty-three," Joseph remarked. "You will find that I am very ignorant."

"And I am twenty-eight, and just beginning to get my eyes open, like a nine-days' kitten. If I had been frank enough to confess my ignorance, five years ago, as you do now, it would have been better for me. But don't let us measure ourselves or our experience against each other. That is one good thing we learn in Rocky Mountain life; there is no high or low, knowledge or ignorance, except what applies to the needs of men who come together.

So there are needs which most men have, and go all their lives hungering for, because they expect them to be supplied in a particular form. There is something," Philip concluded, "deeper than that in human nature."

Joseph longed to open his heart to this man, every one of whose words struck home to something in himself. But the lassitude which the shock left behind gradually overcame him. He suffered his head to be drawn upon Philip Held's shoulder, and slept until the train reached Oakland Station. When the two got upon the platform, they found Dennis waiting for Joseph, with a light country vehicle. The news of the accident had reached the station, and his dismay was great when he saw the two bloody faces. A physician had already been summoned from the neighboring village, but they had little need of his services. A prescription of quiet and sedatives for Joseph, and a strip of plaster for his companion, were speedily furnished, and they set out together for the Asten place.

It is unnecessary to describe Rachel Miller's agitation when the party arrived; or the parting of the two men who had been so swiftly brought near to each other; or Philip Held's farther journey to the forge that evening. He resisted all entreaty to remain at the farm until morning, on the ground of an appointment made with the present proprietor of the forge. After his departure Joseph was sent to bed, where he remained for a day or two, very sore and a little feverish. He had plenty of time for thought,—not precisely of the kind which his aunt suspected, for out of pure, honest interest in his welfare, she took a step which proved to be of doubtful benefit. If he had not been so innocent,—if he had not been quite as unconscious of his inner nature as he was over-conscious of his external self,—he would have perceived that his thoughts dwelt much more on Philip Held than on Julia Blessing. His mind seemed to run through a swift, involuntary chain of reasoning, to account to himself for his feeling towards her, and her inevitable share in his future; but towards Philip his heart sprang with an instinct beyond his control. It was impossible to imagine that the latter also would not be shot, like a bright thread, through the web of his coming days.

On the third morning, when he had exchanged the bed for an arm-chair, a letter from the city was brought to him. "Dearest Joseph," it ran, "what a fright and anxiety we have had! When pa brought the paper home, last night, and I read the report of the accident, where it said, 'J. Asten, severe contusions,' my heart stopped beating for a minute, and I can only write now (as you see) with a trembling hand. My first thought was to go directly to you; but ma said we had better wait for intelligence. Unless our engagement were generally known, it would give rise to remarks,—in short, I need not repeat to you all the worldly reasons with which she opposed me; but, oh, how I longed for the right to be at your side, and assure myself that the dreadful, dreadful danger has passed! Pa was quite shaken with the news: he felt hardly able to go to the Custom-House this morning. But he sides with ma about my going, and now, when my time as a daughter with them is growing so short, I dare not disobey. I know you will understand my position, yet, dear and true as you are, you cannot guess the anxiety with which I await a line from your hand, the hand that was so nearly taken from me forever!"

Joseph read the letter twice and was about to commence it for the third time, when a visitor was announced. He had barely time to thrust the scented sheet into his pocket; and the bright eyes and flushed face with which he met the Rev. Mr. Chaffinch convinced both that gentleman and his aunt, as she ushered the latter into the room, that the visit was accepted as an honor and a joy.

On Mr. Chaffinch's face the air of authority which he had been led to believe belonged to his calling had not quite succeeded in impressing itself; but melancholy, the next best thing, was strongly marked. His dark complexion and his white cravat intensified each other; and his eyes, so long uplifted above the concerns of this world, had ceased to vary their expression materially for the sake of any human interest. All this had been expected of him, and he had simply done his best to meet the requirements of the flock over which he was placed. Any of the latter might have easily been shrewd enough to guess, in advance, very nearly what the pastor would say, upon a given occasion; but each and all of them would have been both disappointed and disturbed if he had not said it.

After appropriate and sympathetic inquiries concerning Joseph's bodily condition, he proceeded to probe him spiritually.

"It was a merciful preservation. I hope you feel that it is a solemn thing to look Death in the face."

"I am not afraid of death," Joseph replied.

"You mean the physical pang. But death includes what comes after it,—judgment. That is a very awful thought."

"It may be to evil men; but I have done nothing to make me fear it."

"You have never made an open profession of faith; yet it may be that grace has reached you," said Mr. Chaffinch. "Have you found your Saviour?"

"I believe in him with all my soul!" Joseph exclaimed; "but you mean something else by 'finding' him. I will be candid with you, Mr. Chaffinch. The last sermon I heard you preach, a month ago, was upon the nullity of all good works, all Christian deeds; you called them 'rags, dust, and ashes,' and declared that man is saved by faith alone. I have faith, but I can't accept a doctrine which denies merit to works; and you, unless I accept it, will you admit that I have 'found' Christ?"

"There is but One Truth!" exclaimed Mr. Chaffinch, very severely.

"Yes," Joseph answered, reverently, "and that is only perfectly known to God."

The clergyman was more deeply annoyed than he cared to exhibit. His experience had been confined chiefly to the encouragement of ignorant souls, willing to accept his message, if they could only be made to comprehend it, or to the conflict with downright doubt and denial. A nature so seemingly open to the influences of the Spirit, yet inflexibly closed to certain points of doctrine, was something of a problem to him. He belonged to a class now happily becoming scarce, who, having been taught to pace a reasoned theological round, can only efficiently meet those antagonists who voluntarily come inside of their own ring.

His habit of control, however, enabled him to say, with a moderately friendly manner, as he took leave: "We will talk again when you are stronger. It is my duty to give spiritual help to those who seek it."

To Rachel Miller he said: "I cannot say that he is dark. His mind is cloudy, but we find that the vanities of youth often obscure the true light for a time."

Joseph leaned back in his arm-chair, closed his eyes, and meditated earnestly for half an hour. Rachel Miller, uncertain whether to be hopeful or discouraged by Mr. Chaffinch's words, stole into the room, but went about on tiptoe, supposing him to be asleep. Joseph was fully conscious of all her movements, and at last startled her by the sudden question:—

"Aunt, why do you suppose I went to the city?"

"Goodness, Joseph! I thought you were sound asleep. I suppose to see about the fall prices for grain and cattle."

"No, aunt," said he, speaking with determination, though the foolish blood ran rosily over his face, "I went to get a wife!"

She stood pale and speechless, staring at him. But for the rosy sign on his cheeks and temples she could not have believed his words.

"Miss Blessing?" she finally uttered, almost in a whisper.

Joseph nodded his head. She dropped into the nearest chair, drew two or three long breaths, and in an indescribable tone ejaculated, "Well!"

"I knew you would be surprised," said he; "because it is almost a surprise to myself. But you and she seemed to fall so easily into each other's ways, that I hope—"

"Why, you're hardly acquainted with her!" Rachel exclaimed. "It is so hasty! And you are so young!"

"No younger than father was when he married mother; and I have learned to know her well in a short time. Isn't it so with you, too, aunt?—you certainly liked her?"

"I'll not deny that, nor say the reverse now: but a farmer's wife should be a farmer's daughter."

"But suppose, aunt, that the farmer doesn't happen to love any farmer's

726

daughter, and does love a bright, amiable, very intelligent girl, who is delighted with country life, eager and willing to learn, and very fond of the farmer's aunt (who can teach her everything)?"

"Still, it seems to me a risk," said Rachel; but she was evidently relenting.

"There is none to you," he answered, "and I am not afraid of mine. You will be with us, for Julia couldn't do without you, if she wished. If she were a farmer's daughter, with different ideas of housekeeping, it might bring trouble to both of us. But now you will have the management in your own hands until you have taught Julia, and afterwards she will carry it on in your way."

She did not reply; but Joseph could see that she was becoming reconciled to the prospect. After awhile she came across the room, leaned over him, kissed him upon the forehead, and then silently went away.

# CHAPTER X. APPROACHING FATE.

Only two months intervened until the time appointed for the marriage, and the days rolled swiftly away. A few lines came to Joseph from Philip Held, announcing that he was satisfied with the forge and furnace, and the sale would doubtless be consummated in a short time. He did not, however, expect to take charge of the works before March, and therefore gave Joseph his address in the city, with the hope that the latter would either visit or write to him.

On the Sunday after the accident Elwood Withers came to the farm. He seemed to have grown older in the short time which had elapsed since they had last met; after his first hearty rejoicing over Joseph's escape and recovery, he relapsed into a silent but not unfriendly mood. The two young men climbed the long hill behind the house and seated themselves under a noble pin-oak on the height, whence there was a lovely view of the valley for many miles to the southward.

They talked mechanically, for a while, of the season, and the crops, and the other usual subjects which farmers never get to the end of discussing; but both felt the impendence of more important themes, and, nevertheless, were slow to approach them. At last Elwood said: "Your fate is settled by this time, I suppose?"

"It is arranged, at least," Joseph replied. "But I can't yet make clear to myself that I shall be a married man in two months from now."

"Does the time seem long to you?"

"No," Joseph innocently answered; "it is very short."

Elwood turned away his head to conceal a melancholy smile; it was a few minutes before he spoke again.

"Joseph," he then said, "are you sure, quite sure, you love her?"

"I am to marry her."

"I meant nothing unfriendly," Elwood remarked, in a gentle tone. "My thought was this,—if you should ever find a still stronger love growing upon you,—something that would make the warmth you feel now seem like ice compared to it,—how would you be able to fight it? I asked the question of myself for you. I don't think I'm much different from most soft-hearted men,—except that I keep the softness so well stowed away that few persons know of it,—but if I were in your place, within two months of marriage to the girl I love, I should be miserable!"

Joseph turned towards him with wide, astonished eyes.

"Miserable from hope and fear," Elwood went on; "I should be afraid of fever, fire, murder, thunderbolts! Every hour of the day I should dread lest something might come between us; I should prowl around her house day after day, to be sure that she was alive! I should lengthen out the time into years; and all because I'm a great, disappointed, soft-hearted fool!"

The sad, yearning expression of his eyes touched Joseph to the heart. "Elwood," he said, "I see that it is not in my power to comfort you; if I give you pain unknowingly, tell me how to avoid it! I meant to ask you to stand beside me when I am married; but now you must consider your own feeling in answering, not mine. Lucy is not likely to be there."

"That would make no difference," Elwood answered. "Do you suppose it is a pain for me to see her, because she seems lost to me? No; I'm always a little encouraged when I have a chance to measure myself with her, and to guess—sometimes this and sometimes that—what it is that she needs to find in me. Force of will is of no use; as to faithfulness,—why, what it's worth can't be shown unless something turns up to try it. But you had better not ask me to be your groomsman. Neither Miss Blessing nor her sister would be overly pleased."

"Why so?" Joseph asked; "Julia and you are quite well acquainted, and she was always friendly towards you."

Elwood was silent and embarrassed. Then, reflecting that silence, at that moment, might express even more than speech, he said: "I've got the notion in my head; maybe it's foolish, but there it is. I talked a good deal with Miss Blessing, it's true, and yet I don't feel the least bit acquainted. Her manner to me was very friendly, and yet I don't think she likes me."

"Well!" exclaimed Joseph, forcing a laugh, though he was much annoyed, "I never gave you credit for such a lively imagination. Why not be candid, and admit that the dislike is on your side? I am sorry for it, since Julia will so soon be in the house there as my wife. There is no one else whom I can ask, unless it were Philip Held—"

"Held! To be sure, he took care of you. I was at Coventry the day after, and saw something of him." With these words, Elwood turned towards Joseph and looked him squarely in the face. "He'll have charge there in a few months, I hear," he then said, "and I reckon it as a piece of good luck for you. I've found that there are men, all, maybe, as honest and outspoken as they need be; yet two of 'em will talk at different marks and never fully understand each other, and other two will naturally talk right straight at the same mark and never miss. Now, Held is the sort that can hit the thing in the mind of the man they're talking to; it's a gift that comes o' being knocked about the world among all classes of people. What we learn here, always among the same folks, isn't a circumstance."

"Then you think I might ask him?" said Joseph, not fully comprehending all that Elwood meant to express.

"He's one of those men that you're safe in asking to do anything. Make him spokesman of a committee to wait on the President, arbitrator in a crooked lawsuit, overseer of a railroad gang, leader in a prayer-meeting (if he'd consent), or whatever else you choose, and he'll do the business as if he was used to it! It's enough for you that I don't know the town ways, and he does; it's considered worse, I've heard, to make a blunder in society than to commit a real sin."

He rose, and they loitered down the hill together. The subject was quietly dropped, but the minds of both were none the less busy. They felt the stir and pressure of new experiences, which had come to one through disappointment and to the other through success. Not three months had passed since they

730

rode together through the twilight to Warriner's, and already life was opening to them,—but how differently! Joseph endeavored to make the most kindly allowance for his friend's mood, and to persuade himself that his feelings were unchanged. Elwood, however, knew that a shadow had fallen between. It was nothing beside the cloud of his greater trouble: he also knew the cost of his own justification to Joseph, and prayed that it might never come.

That evening, on taking leave, he said: "I don't know whether you meant to have the news of your engagement circulated; but I guess Anna Warriner has heard, and that amounts to—"

"To telling it to the whole neighborhood, doesn't it?" Joseph answered. "Then the mischief is already done, if it is a mischief. It is well, therefore, that the day is set: the neighborhood will have little time for gossip."

He smiled so frankly and cheerfully, that Elwood seized his hand, and with tears in his eyes, said: "Don't remember anything against me, Joseph. I've always been honestly your friend, and mean to stay so."

He went that evening to a homestead where he knew he should find Lucy Henderson. She looked pale and fatigued, he thought; possibly his presence had become a restraint. If so, she must bear his unkindness: it was the only sacrifice he could not make, for he felt sure that his intercourse with her must either terminate in hate or love. The one thing of which he was certain was, that there could be no calm, complacent friendship between them.

It was not long before one of the family asked him whether he had heard the news; it seemed that they had already discussed it, and his arrival revived the flow of expression. In spite of his determination, he found it impossible to watch Lucy while he said, as simply as possible, that Joseph Asten seemed very happy over the prospect of the marriage; that he was old enough to take a wife; and if Miss Blessing could adapt herself to country habits, they might get on very well together. But later in the evening he took a chance of saying to her: "In spite of what I said, Lucy, I don't feel quite easy about Joseph's marriage. What do you think of it?"

She smiled faintly, as she replied: "Some say that people are attracted by mutual unlikeness. This seems to me to be a case of the kind; but they are free choosers of their own fates."

"Is there no possible way of persuading him—them—to delay?"

"No!" she exclaimed, with unusual energy; "none whatever!"

Elwood sighed, and yet felt relieved.

Joseph lost no time in writing to Philip Held, announcing his approaching marriage, and begging him—with many apologies for asking such a mark of confidence on so short an acquaintance—to act the part of nearest friend, if there were no other private reasons to prevent him.

Four or five days later the following answer arrived:—

My dear Asten:—Do you remember that curious whirling, falling sensation, when the car pitched over the edge of the embankment? I felt a return of it on reading your letter; for you have surprised me beyond measure. Not by your request, for that is just what I should have expected of you; and as well now, as if we had known each other for twenty years; so the apology is the only thing objectionable—But I am tangling my sentences; I want to say how heartily I return the feeling which prompted you to ask me, and yet how embarrassed I am that I cannot unconditionally say, "Yes, with all my heart!" My great, astounding surprise is, to find you about to be married to Miss Julia Blessing,—a young lady whom I once knew. And the embarrassment is this: I knew her under circumstances (in which she was not personally concerned, however) which might possibly render my presence now, as your groomsman, unwelcome to the family: at least, it is my duty—and yours, if you still desire me to stand beside you—to let Miss Blessing and her family decide the question. The circumstances to which I refer concern them rather than myself. I think your best plan will be simply to inform them of your request and my reply, and add that I am entirely ready to accept whatever course they may prefer.

Pray don't consider that I have treated your first letter to me ungraciously. I am more grieved than you can imagine that it happens so.

You will probably come to the city a day before the wedding, and I insist that you shall share my bachelor quarters, in any case.

Always your friend,

PHILIP HELD.

This letter threw Joseph into a new perplexity. Philip a former acquaintance of the Blessings! Formerly, but not now; and what could those mysterious "circumstances" have been, which had so seriously interrupted their intercourse? It was quite useless to conjecture; but he could not resist the feeling that another shadow hung over the aspects of his future. Perhaps he had exaggerated Elwood's unaccountable dislike to Julia, which had only been implied, not spoken; but here was a positive estrangement on the part of the man who was so suddenly near and dear to him. He never thought of suspecting Philip of blame; the candor and cheery warmth of the letter rejoiced his heart. There was evidently nothing better to do than to follow the advice contained in it, and leave the question to the decision of Julia and her parents.

Her reply did not come by the return mail, nor until nearly a week afterwards; during which time he tormented himself by imagining the wildest reasons for her silence. When the letter at last arrived, he had some difficulty in comprehending its import.

"Dearest Joseph," she said, "you must really forgive me this long trial of your patience. Your letter was so unexpected,—I mean its contents,—and it seems as if ma and pa and Clementina would never agree what was best to be done. For that matter, I cannot say that they agree now; we had no idea that you were an intimate friend of Mr. Held, (I can't think how ever you should have become acquainted!) and it seems to break open old wounds,—none of mine, fortunately, for I have none. As Mr. Held leaves the question in our hands, there is, you will understand, all the more necessity that we should be careful. Ma thinks he has said nothing to you about the unfortunate occurrence, or you would have expressed an opinion. You never can know how happy your fidelity makes me; but I felt that, the first moment we met.

"Ma says that at very private (what pa calls informal) weddings there need not be bridesmaids or groomsmen. Miss Morrisey was married that way, not long ago; it is true that she is not of our circle, nor strictly a first family (this is ma's view, not mine, for I understand the hollowness of society); but we could very well do the same. Pa would be satisfied with a reception afterwards; he wants to ask the Collector, and the Surveyor, and the Appraiser. Clementina won't say anything now, but I know what she thinks, and so does ma; however, Mr. Held has so dropped out of city life that it is not important. I suppose everything must be dim in his memory now; you do not write to me much that he related. How strange that he should be your friend! They say my dress is lovely, but I am sure I should like a plain muslin just as well. I shall only breathe freely when I get back to the quiet of the country, (and your—our charming home, and dear, good Aunt Rachel!) and away from all these conventional forms. Ma says if there is one groomsman there ought to be two; either very simple, or according to custom. In a matter so delicate, perhaps, Mr. Held would be as competent to decide as we are; at least I am quite willing to leave it to his judgment. But how trifling is all this discussion, compared with the importance of the day to us! It is now drawing very near, but I have no misgivings, for I confide in you wholly and forever!"

After reading the letter with as much coolness as was then possible to him, Joseph inferred three things: that his acquaintance with Philip Held was not entirely agreeable to the Blessing family; that they would prefer the simplest style of a wedding, and this was in consonance with his own tastes; and that Julia clung to him as a deliverer from conditions with which her nature had little sympathy. Her incoherence, he fancied, arose from an agitation which he could very well understand, and his answer was intended to soothe and encourage her. It was difficult to let Philip know that his services would not be required, without implying the existence of an unfriendly feeling towards him; and Joseph, therefore, all the more readily accepted his invitation. He was assured that the mysterious difficulty did not concern Julia; even if it were so, he was not called upon to do violence, without cause, to so welcome a friendship.

The September days sped by, not with the lingering, passionate uncertainty of which Elwood Withers spoke, but almost too swiftly. In the

734

hurry of preparation, Joseph had scarcely time to look beyond the coming event and estimate its consequences. He was too ignorant of himself to doubt: his conscience was too pure and perfect to admit the possibility of changing the course of his destiny. Whatever the gossip of the neighborhood might have been, he heard nothing of it that was not agreeable. His aunt was entirely reconciled to a wife who would not immediately, and probably not for a long time, interfere with her authority; and the shadows raised by the two men whom he loved best seemed, at last, to be accidentally thrown from clouds beyond the horizon of his life. This was the thought to which he clung, in spite of a vague, utterly formless apprehension, which he felt lurking somewhere in the very bottom of his heart.

Philip met him on his arrival in the city, and after taking him to his pleasant quarters, in a house looking on one of the leafy squares, good-naturedly sent him to the Blessing mansion, with a warning to return before the evening was quite spent. The family was in a flutter of preparation, and though he was cordially welcomed, he felt that, to all except Julia, he was subordinate in interest to the men who came every quarter of an hour, bringing bouquets, and silver spoons with cards attached, and pasteboard boxes containing frosted cakes. Even Julia's society he was only allowed to enjoy by scanty instalments; she was perpetually summoned by her mother or Clementina, to consult about some indescribable figment of dress. Mr. Blessing was occupied in the basement, with the inspection of various hampers. He came to the drawing-room to greet Joseph, whom he shook by both hands, with such incoherent phrases that Julia presently interposed. "You must not forget, pa," she said, "that the man is waiting: Joseph will excuse you, I know." She followed him to the basement, and he returned no more.

Joseph left early in the evening, cheered by Julia's words: "We can't complain of all this confusion, when it's for our sakes; but we'll be happier when it's over, won't we?"

He gave her an affirmative kiss, and returned to Philip's room. That gentleman was comfortably disposed in an arm-chair, with a book and a cigar. "Ah!" he exclaimed, "you find that a house is more agreeable any evening than that before the wedding?"

"There is one compensation," said Joseph; "it gives me two or three hours with you."

"Then take that other arm-chair, and tell me how this came to pass. You see I have the curiosity of a neighbor, already."

He listened earnestly while Joseph related the story of his love, occasionally asking a question or making a suggestive remark, but so gently that it seemed to come as an assistance. When all had been told, he rose and commenced walking slowly up and down the room. Joseph longed to ask, in turn, for an explanation of the circumstances mentioned in Philip's letter; but a doubt checked his tongue.

As if in response to his thought, Philip stopped before him and said: "I owe you my story, and you shall have it after a while, when I can tell you more. I was a young fellow of twenty when I knew the Blessings, and I don't attach the slightest importance, now, to anything that happened. Even if I did, Miss Julia had no share in it. I remember her distinctly; she was then about my age, or a year or two older; but hers is a face that would not change in a long while."

Joseph stared at his friend in silence. He recalled the latter's age, and was startled by the involuntary arithmetic which revealed Julia's to him. It was unexpected, unwelcome, yet inevitable.

"Her father had been lucky in some of his 'operations,'" Philip continued, "but I don't think he kept it long. I hardly wonder that she should come to prefer a quiet country life to such ups and downs as the family has known. Generally, a woman don't adapt herself so readily to a change of surroundings as a man: where there is love, however, everything is possible."

"There is! there is!" Joseph exclaimed, certifying the fact to himself as much as to his friend. He rose and stood beside him.

Philip looked at him with grave, tender eyes.

"What can I do?" he said.

"What should you do?" Joseph asked.

"This!" Philip exclaimed, laying his hands on Joseph's shoulders,—"this, Joseph! I can be nearer than a brother. I know that I am in your heart as you are in mine. There is no faith between us that need be limited, there is no truth too secret to be veiled. A man's perfect friendship is rarer than a woman's love, and most hearts are content with one or the other: not so with yours and mine! I read it in your eyes, when you opened them on my knee: I see it in your face now. Don't speak: let us clasp hands."

But Joseph could not speak.

# CHAPTER XI. A CITY WEDDING.

There was not much of the happy bridegroom to be seen in Joseph's face when he arose the next morning. To Philip's eyes he appeared to have suddenly grown several years older; his features had lost their boyish softness and sweetness, which would thenceforth never wholly come back again. He spoke but little, and went about his preparation with an abstracted, mechanical air, which told how much his mind was preoccupied. Philip quietly assisted, and when all was complete, led him before the mirror.

"There!" he said; "now study the general effect; I think nothing more is wanting."

"It hardly looks like myself," Joseph remarked, after a careless inspection.

"In all the weddings I have seen," said Philip, "the bridegrooms were pale and grave, the brides flushed and trembling. You will not make an exception to the rule; but it is a solemn thing, and I—don't misunderstand me, Joseph—I almost wish you were not to be married to-day."

"Philip!" Joseph exclaimed, "let me think, now, at least,—now, at the last moment,—that it is best for me! If you knew how cramped, restricted, fettered, my life has been, and how much emancipation has already come with this—this love! Perhaps my marriage is a venture, but it is one which must be made; and no consequence of it shall ever come between us!"

"No; and I ought not to have spoken a word that might imply a doubt. It may be that your emancipation, as you rightly term it, can only come in this way. My life has been so different, that I am unconsciously putting myself in your place, instead of trying to look with your eyes. When I next go to Coventry Forge, I shall drive over and dine with you, and I hope your Julia will be as ready to receive me as a friend as I am to find one in her. There is the carriage at the door, and you had better arrive a little before the appointed hour. Take only my good wishes, my prayers for your happiness, along with you,—and now, God bless you, Joseph!"

The carriage rolled away. Joseph, in full wedding costume, was painfully conscious of the curious glances which fell upon him, and presently pulled down the curtains. Then, with an impatient self-reprimand, he pulled them up again, lowered the window, and let the air blow upon his hot cheeks. The house was speedily reached, and he was admitted by a festive waiter (hired for the occasion) before he had been exposed for more than five seconds to the gaze of curious eyes in all the windows around.

Mrs. Blessing, resplendent in purple, and so bedight that she seemed almost as young as her portrait, swept into the drawing-room. She inspected him rapidly, and approved, while advancing; otherwise he would scarcely have received the thin, dry kiss with which she favored him.

"It lacks half an hour," she said; "but you have the usual impatience of a bridegroom. I am accustomed to it. Mr. Blessing is still in his room; he has only just commenced arranging his cambric cravat, which is a work of time. He cannot forget that he was distinguished for an elegant tie in his youth. Clementina,"—as that young lady entered the room,—"is the bride completely attired?"

"All but her gloves," replied Clementina, offering three-fourths of her hand to Joseph. "And she don't know what ear-rings to wear."

"I think we might venture," Mrs. Blessing remarked, "as there seems to be no rule applicable to the case, to allow Mr. Asten a sight of his bride. Perhaps his taste might assist her in the choice."

Thereupon she conducted Joseph up stairs, and, after some preliminary whispering, he was admitted to the room. He and Julia were equally surprised at the change in each other's appearance: he older, paler, with a grave and serious bearing; she younger, brighter, rounder, fresher, and with the loveliest pink flush on her cheeks. The gloss of her hair rivalled that of the white satin which draped her form and gave grace to its outlines; her neck and shoulders were slight, but no one could have justly called them lean; and even the thinness of her lips was forgotten in the vivid coral of their color, and the nervous life which hovered about their edges. At that moment she was certainly beautiful, and a stranger would have supposed her to be young.

She looked into Joseph's face with a smile in which some appearance of maiden shyness yet lingered. A shrewder bridegroom would have understood its meaning, and would have said, "How lovely you are!" Joseph, it is true, experienced a sense of relief, but he knew not why, and could not for his life have put it into words. His eyes dwelt upon and followed her, and she seemed to be satisfied with that form of recognition. Mrs. Blessing inspected the dress with a severe critical eye, pulling out a fold here and smoothing a bit of lace there, until nothing further could be detected. Then, the adornment of the victim being completed, she sat down and wept moderately.

"O ma, try to bear up!" Julia exclaimed, with the very slightest touch of impatience in her voice; "it is all to come yet."

There was a ring at the door.

"It must be your aunt," said Mrs. Blessing, drying her eyes. "My sister," she added, turning to Joseph,—Mrs. Woollish, with Mr. Woollish and their two sons and one daughter. He's in the—the leather trade, so to speak, which has thrown her into a very different circle; but, as we have no nearer relations in the city, they will be present at the ceremony. He is said to be wealthy. I have no means of knowing; but one would scarcely think so, to judge from his wedding-gift to Julia."

"Ma, why should you mention it?"

"I wish to enlighten Mr. Asten. Six pairs of shoes!—of course all of the same pattern; and the fashion may change in another year!"

"In the country we have no fashions in shoes," Joseph suggested.

"Certainly!" said Julia. "I find Uncle Woollish's present very practical indeed."

Mrs. Blessing looked at her daughter, and said nothing.

Mr. Blessing, very red in the face, but with triumphant cambric about his throat, entered the room, endeavoring to get his fat hands into a pair of No. 9 gloves. A strong smell of turpentine or benzine entered with him.

"Eliza," said he, "you must find me some eau de cologne. The odor

740

left from my—my rheumatic remedy is still perceptible. Indeed, patchouly would be better, if it were not the scent peculiar to parvenus."

Clementina came to say that the clergyman's carriage had just reached the door, and Mr. Blessing was hurried down stairs, mopping his gloves and the collar of his coat with liquid fragrance by the way. Mrs. Blessing and Clementina presently followed.

"Julia," said Joseph when they were quite alone, "have you thought that this is for life?"

She looked up with a tender smile, but something in his face arrested it on her lips.

"I have lived ignorantly until now," he continued,—"innocently and ignorantly. From this time on I shall change more than you, and there may be, years hence, a very different Joseph Asten from the one whose name you will take to-day. If you love me with the love I claim from you,—the love that grows with and through all new knowledge and experience,—there will be no discord in our lives. We must both be liberal and considerate towards each other; it has been but a short time since we met, and we have still much to learn."

"O, Joseph!" she murmured, in a tone of gentle reproach, "I knew your nature at first sight."

"I hope you did," he answered gravely, "for then you will be able to see its needs, and help me to supply them. But, Julia, there must not the shadow of concealment come between us: nothing must be reserved. I understand no love that does not include perfect trust. I must draw nearer, and be drawn nearer to you, constantly, or—"

He paused; it was no time to utter the further sentence in his mind. Julia glided to him, clasped her arms about his waist, and laid her head against his shoulder. Although she said nothing, the act was eloquent. It expressed acquiescence, trust, fidelity, the surrender of her life to his, and no man in his situation could have understood it otherwise. A tenderness, which seemed to be the something hitherto lacking to his love, crept softly over his heart, and

741

the lurking unrest began to fade from his face.

There was a rustle on the stairs; Clementina and Miss Woollish made their appearance. "Mr. Bogue has arrived," whispered the former, "and ma thinks you should come down soon. Are you entirely ready? I don't think you need the salts, Julia; but you might carry the bottle in your left hand: brides are expected to be nervous."

She gave a light laugh, like the purl and bubble of a brook; but Joseph shrank, with an inward chill, from the sound.

"So! shall we go? Fanny and I—(I beg pardon; Mr. Asten—Miss Woollish)—will lead the way. We will stand a little in the rear, not beside you, as there are no groomsmen. Remember, the farther end of the room!"

They rustled slowly downward, in advance, and the bridal pair followed. The clergyman, Mr. Bogue, suddenly broke off in the midst of an oracular remark about the weather, and, standing in the centre of the room, awaited them. The other members of the two families were seated, and very silent.

Joseph heard the introductory remarks, the ceremony, and the final benediction, as in a dream. His lips opened mechanically, and a voice which did not exactly seem to be his own uttered the "I will!" at the proper time; yet, in recalling the experience afterwards, he was unable to decide whether any definite thought or memory or hope had passed through his mind. From his entrance into the room until his hand was violently shaken by Mr. Blessing, there was a blank.

Of course there were tears, but the beams of congratulation shone through them, and they saddened nobody. Miss Fanny Woollish assured the bridal pair, in an audible whisper, that she had never seen a sweeter wedding; and her mother, a stout, homely little body, confirmed the opinion with, "Yes, you both did beautifully!" Then the marriage certificate was produced and signed, and the company partook of wine and refreshments to strengthen them for the reception.

Until there had been half a dozen arrivals, Mrs. Blessing moved about restlessly, and her eyes wandered to the front window. Suddenly three or four carriages came rattling together up the street, and Joseph heard her whisper to her husband: "There they are! it will be a success!" It was not long before the little room was uncomfortably crowded, and the presentations followed so rapidly that Joseph soon became bewildered. Julia, however, knew and welcomed every one with the most bewitching grace, being rewarded with kisses by the gorgeous young ladies and compliments by the young men with weak mouths and retreating chins.

In the midst of the confusion Mr. Blessing, with a wave of his hand, presented "Mr. Collector Twining" and "Mr. Surveyor Knob" and "Mr. Appraiser Gerrish," all of whom greeted Joseph with a bland, almost affectionate, cordiality. The door of the dining-room was then thrown open, and the three dignitaries accompanied the bridal pair to the table. Two servants rapidly whisked the champagne-bottles from a cooling-tub in the adjoining closet, and Mr. Blessing commenced stirring and testing a huge bowl of punch. Collector Twining made a neat little speech, proposing the health of bride and bridegroom, with a pun upon the former's name, which was received with as much delight as if it had never been heard before. Therefore Mr. Surveyor Knob repeated it in giving the health of the bride's parents. The enthusiasm of the company not having diminished, Mr. Appraiser Gerrish improved the pun in a third form, in proposing "the Ladies." Then Mr. Blessing, although his feelings overcame him, and he was obliged to use a handkerchief smelling equally of benzine and eau de cologne, responded, introducing the collector's and surveyor's names with an ingenuity which was accepted as the inspiration of genius. His peroration was especially admired.

"On this happy occasion," he said, "the elements of national power and prosperity are represented. My son-in-law, Mr. Asten, is a noble specimen of the agricultural population,—the free American yeomanry; my daughter, if I may be allowed to say it in the presence of so many bright eyes and blooming cheeks, is a representative child of the city, which is the embodiment of the nation's action and enterprise. The union of the two is the movement of our life. The city gives to the country as the ocean gives the cloud to the mountain-springs: the country gives to the city as the streams flow back to the ocean. ["Admirable!" Mr. Collector Twining exclaimed.] Then we have, as our highest honor, the representatives of the political system under which city and country flourish alike. The wings of our eagle must be extended over this fortunate house to-day, for here are the strong Claws which seize and guard its treasures!"

The health of the Claws was drunk enthusiastically. Mr. Blessing was congratulated on his eloquence; the young gentlemen begged the privilege of touching their glasses to his, and every touch required that the contents be replenished; so that the bottom of the punch-bowl was nearly reached before the guests departed.

When Joseph came down in his travelling-dress, he found the drawing-room empty of the crowd; but leaves, withered flowers, crumbs of cake, and crumpled cards scattered over the carpet, indicated what had taken place. In the dining-room Mr. Blessing, with his cravat loosened, was smoking a cigar at the open window.

"Come, son-in-law!" he cried, "take another glass of punch before you start."

Joseph declined, on the plea that he was not accustomed to the beverage.

"Nothing could have gone off better!" said Mr. Blessing. "The collector was delighted: by the by, you're to go to the St. Jerome, when you get to New York this evening. He telegraphed to have the bridal-chamber reserved for you. Tell Julia: she won't forget it. That girl has a deuced sharp intellect: if you'll be guided by her in your operations—"

"Pa, what are you saying about me?" Julia, asked, hastily entering the room.

"Only that you have a deuced sharp intellect, and to-day proves it. Asten is one of us now, and I may tell him of his luck."

He winked and laughed stupidly, and Joseph understood and obeyed his wife's appealing glance. He went to his mother-in-law in the drawing-room.

Julia lightly and swiftly shut the door. "Pa," she said, in a strong, angry whisper; "if you are not able to talk coherently, you must keep your tongue

744

still. What will Joseph think of me, to hear you?"

"What he'll think anyhow, in a little while," he doggedly replied. "Julia, you have played a keen game, and played it well; but you don't know much of men yet. He'll not always be the innocent, white-nosed lamb he is now, nibbling the posies you hold out to him. Wait till he asks for stronger feed, and see whether he'll follow you!"

She was looking on the floor, pale and stern. Suddenly one of her gloves burst, across the back of the hand. "Pa," she then said, "it's very cruel to say such things to me, now when I'm leaving you."

"So it is!" he exclaimed, tearfully contrite; "I am a wretch! They flattered my speech so much,—the collector was so impressed by me,—and said so many pleasant things, that—I don't feel quite steady. Don't forget the St. Jerome; the bridal-chamber is ordered, and I'll see that Mumm writes a good account for the 'Evening Mercury.' I wish you could be here to remember my speech for me. O, I shall miss you! I shall miss you!"

With these words, and his arm lovingly about his daughter, they joined the family. The carriage was already at the door, and the coachman was busy with the travelling-trunks. There were satchels, and little packages,—an astonishing number it seemed to Joseph,—to be gathered together, and then the farewells were said.

As they rolled through the streets towards the station, Julia laid her head upon her husband's shoulder, drew a long, deep breath, and said, "Now all our obligations to society are fulfilled, and we can rest awhile. For the first time in my life I am a free woman,—and you have liberated me!"

He answered her in glad and tender words; he was equally grateful that the exciting day was over. But, as they sped away from the city through the mellow October landscapes, Philip's earnest, dark gray eyes, warm with more than brotherly love, haunted his memory, and he knew that Philip's faithful thoughts followed him.

# CHAPTER XII. CLOUDS.

There are some days when the sun comes slowly up, filling the vapory air with diffused light, in advance of his coming; when the earth grows luminous in the broad, breezeless morning; when nearer objects shine and sparkle, and the distances melt into dim violet and gold; when the vane points to the southwest, and the blood of man feels neither heat nor cold, but only the freshness of that perfect temperature wherein the limits of the body are lost, and the pulses of its life beat in all the life of the world. But ere long the haze, instead of thinning into blue, gradually thickens into gray; the vane creeps southward, swinging to southeast in brief, rising flaws of the air; the horizon darkens; the enfranchised life of the spirit creeps back to its old isolation, shorn of all its rash delight, and already foreboding the despondency which comes with the east wind and the chilly rains.

Some such variation of the atmospheric influences attended Joseph Asten's wedding-travel. The mellow, magical glory of his new life diminished day by day; the blue of his sky became colder and grayer. Yet he could not say that his wife had changed: she was always ready with her smiles, her tender phrases, her longings for quiet and rest, and simple, natural life, away from the conventionalities and claims of Society. But, even as, looking into the pale, tawny-brown of her eyes, he saw no changing depth below the hard, clear surface, so it also seemed with her nature; he painfully endeavored to penetrate beyond expressions, the repetition of which it was hard not to find tiresome, and to reach some spring of character or feeling; yet he found nothing. It was useless to remember that he had been content with those expressions before marriage had given them his own eager interpretation, independent of her will and knowledge; that his duty to her remained the same, for she had not deceived him.

On the other hand, she was as tender and affectionate as he could desire. Indeed, he would often have preferred a less artless manifestation of her fondness; but she playfully insisted on his claiming the best quarters at every stopping-place, on the ground of their bridal character, and was sometimes a little petulant when she fancied that they had not been sufficiently honored. Joseph would have willingly escaped the distinction, allowing himself to be confounded with the prosaic multitude, but she would not permit him to try the experiment.

"The newly married are always detected," she would say, "and they are only laughed at when they try to seem like old couples. Why not be frank and honest, and meet half-way the sympathy which I am sure everybody has for us?"

To this he could make no reply, except that it was not agreeable to exact a special attention.

"But it is our right!" was her answer.

In every railway-car they entered she contrived, in a short time, to impress the nature of their trip upon the other travellers; yet it was done with such apparent unconsciousness, such innocent, impulsive manifestations of her happiness in him, that he could not, in his heart, charge her with having intentionally brought upon him the discomfort of being curiously observed. He could have accustomed himself to endure the latter, had it been inevitable; the suspicion that he owed it to her made it an increasing annoyance. Yet, when the day's journey was over, and they were resting together in their own private apartment, she would bring a stool to his feet, lay her head on his knee, and say: "Now we can talk as we please,—there are none watching and listening."

At such times he was puzzled to guess whether some relic of his former nervous shyness were not remaining, and had made him over-sensitive to her ways. The doubt gave him an additional power of self-control; he resolved to be more slow and cautious of judgment, and observe men and women more carefully than he had been wont to do. Julia had no suspicion of what was passing in his mind: she took it for granted that his nature was still as shallow and transparent as when she first came in contact with it.

After nearly a fortnight this flying life came to an end. They returned to the city for a day, before going home to the farm. The Blessing mansion received them with a hearty welcome; yet, in spite of it, a depressing atmosphere seemed to fill the house. Mrs. Blessing looked pinched and care-worn, Clementina discontented, and Mr. Blessing as melancholy as was possible to so bouyant a politician.

"What's the matter? I hope pa hasn't lost his place," Julia remarked in an undertone to her mother.

"Lost my place!" Mr. Blessing exclaimed aloud; "I'd like to see how the collection of customs would go on without me. But a man may keep his place, and yet lose his house and home."

Clementina vanished, Mrs. Blessing followed, with her handkerchief to her eyes, and Julia hastened after them, crying: "Ma! dear ma!"

"It's only on their account," said Mr. Blessing, pointing after them and speaking to Joseph. "A plucky man never desponds, sir; but women, you'll find, are upset by every reverse."

"May I ask what has happened?"

"A delicate regard for you," Mr. Blessing replied, "would counsel me to conceal it, but my duty as your father-in-law leaves me no alternative. Our human feelings prompt us to show only the bright side of life to those whom we love; principle, however,—conscience, commands us not to suppress the shadows. I am but one out of the many millions of victims of mistaken judgment. The case is simply this; I will omit certain legal technicalities touching the disposition of property, which may not be familiar to you, and state the facts in the most intelligible form; securities which I placed as collaterals for the loan of a sum, not a very large amount, have been very unexpectedly depreciated, but only temporarily so, as all the market knows. If I am forced to sell them at such an untoward crisis, I lose the largest part of my limited means; if I retain them, they will ultimately recover their full value."

"Then why not retain them?" Joseph asked.

"The sum advanced upon them must be repaid, and it so happens—the

748

market being very tight—that every one of my friends is short. Of course, where their own paper is on the street, I can't ask them to float mine for three months longer, which is all that is necessary. A good indorsement is the extent of my necessity; for any one who is familiar with the aspects of the market can see that there must be a great rebound before three months."

"If it were not a very large amount," Joseph began.

"Only a thousand! I know what you were going to say it is perfectly natural: I appreciate it, because, if our positions were reversed, I should have done the same thing. But, although it is a mere form, a temporary fiction, which has the force of reality, and, therefore, so far as you are concerned, I should feel entirely easy, yet it might subject me to very dishonoring suspicions! It might be said that I had availed myself of your entrance into my family to beguile you into pecuniary entanglements; the amount might be exaggerated, the circumstance misrepresented,—no, no! rather than that, let me make the sacrifice like a man! I'm no longer young, it is true; but the feeling that I stand on principle will give me strength to work."

"On the other hand, Mr. Blessing," said Joseph, "very unpleasant things might be said of me, if I should permit you to suffer so serious a loss, when my assistance would prevent it."

"I don't deny it. You have made a two-horned dilemma out of a one-sided embarrassment. Would that I had kept the secret in my own breast! The temptation is strong, I confess, for the mere use of your name for a few months is all I should require. Either the securities will rise to their legitimate value, or some of the capitalists with whom I have dealings will be in a position to accommodate me. I have frequently tided over similar snags and sand-bars in the financial current; they are familiar even to the most skilful operators,—navigators, I might say, to carry out the figure,—and this is an instance where an additional inch of water will lift me from wreck to flood-tide. The question is, should I allow what I feel to be a just principle, a natural suggestion of delicacy, to intervene between my necessity and your generous proffer of assistance?"

"Your family—" Joseph began.

749

"I know! I know!" Mr. Blessing cried, leaning his head upon his hand. "There is my vulnerable point,—my heel of Achilles! There would be no alternative,—better sell this house than have my paper dishonored! Then, too, I feel that this is a turning-point in my fortunes: if I can squeeze through this narrow pass, I shall find a smooth road beyond. It is not merely the sum which is at stake, but the future possibilities into which it expands. Should I crush the seed while it is germinating? Should I tear up the young tree, with an opening fruit-bud on every twig? You see the considerations that sway me: unless you withdraw your most generous proffer, what can I do but yield and accept it?"

"I have no intention of withdrawing it," Joseph answered, taking his words literally; "I made the offer freely and willingly. If my indorsement is all that is necessary now, I can give it at once."

Mr. Blessing grasped him by the hand, winked hard three or four times, and turned away his head without speaking. Then he drew a large leather pocket-book from his breast, opened it, and produced a printed promissory note.

"We will make it payable at your county bank," said he, "because your name is known there, and upon acceptance—which can be procured in two days—the money will be drawn here. Perhaps we had better say four months, in order to cover all contingencies."

He went to a small writing-desk, at the farther end of the room, and filled the blanks in the note, which Joseph then endorsed. When it was safely lodged in his breast-pocket, he said: "We will keep this entirely to ourselves. My wife, let me whisper to you, is very proud and sensitive, although the De l'Hotels (Doolittles now) were never quite the equals of the De Belsains; but women see matters in a different light. They can't understand the accommodation of a name, but fancy that it implies a kind of humiliation, as if one were soliciting charity."

He laughed and rubbed his hands. "I shall soon be in a position," he said, "to render you a favor in return. My long experience, and, I may add, my intimate knowledge of the financial field, enables me to foresee many splendid opportunities. There are, just now, some movements which are not yet perceptible on the surface. Mark my words! we shall shortly have a new excitement, and a cool, well-seasoned head is a fortune at such times."

"In the country," Joseph replied, "we only learn enough to pay off our debts and invest our earnings. We are in the habit of moving slowly and cautiously. Perhaps we miss opportunities; but if we don't see them, we are just as contented as if they had not been. I have enough for comfort, and try to be satisfied."

"Inherited ideas! They belong to the community in which you live. Are you satisfied with your neighbors' ways of living and thinking? I do not mean to disparage them, but have you no desire to rise above their level? Money,—as I once said at a dinner given to a distinguished railroad man,—money is the engine which draws individuals up the steepest grades of society; it is the lubricating oil which makes the truck of life run easy; it is the safety-break which renders collision and wreck impossible! I have long been accustomed to consider it in the light of power, not of property, and I classify men according as they take one or the other view. The latter are misers; but the former, sir, are philosophers!"

Joseph scarcely knew how to answer this burst of eloquence. But there was no necessity for it; the ladies entered the room at that moment, each one, in her own way, swiftly scrutinizing the two gentlemen. Mrs. Blessing's face lost its woe-worn expression, while a gleam of malicious satisfaction passed over Clementina's.

The next day, on their journey to the country, Julia suddenly said, "I am sure, Joseph, that pa made use of your generosity; pray don't deny it!"

There was the faintest trace of hardness in her voice, which he interpreted as indicating dissatisfaction with his failure to confide the matter to her.

"I have no intention of denying anything, Julia," he answered. "I was not called upon to exercise generosity; it was simply what your father would term an 'accommodation.'"

"I understand. How much?"

"An endorsement of his note for a thousand dollars, which is little, when it will prevent him from losing valuable securities."

Julia was silent for at least ten minutes; then, turning towards him with a sternness which she vainly endeavored to conceal under a "wreathed smile," she said: "In future, Joseph, I hope you will always consult me in any pecuniary venture. I may not know much about such matters, but it is my duty to learn. I have been obliged to hear a great deal of financial talk from pa and his friends, and could not help guessing some things which I think I can apply for your benefit. We are to have no secrets from each other, you know."

His own words! After all, what she said was just and right, and he could not explain to himself why he should feel annoyed. Perhaps he missed a frank expression of delight in the assistance he had so promptly given; but why should he suspect that it was unwelcome to her? He tried to banish the feeling, to hide it under self-reproach and shame, but it clung to him most uncomfortably.

Nevertheless, he forgot everything in the pleasure of the homeward drive from the station. The sadness of late autumn lay upon the fields, but spring already said, "I am coming!" in the young wheat; the houses looked warm and cosey behind their sheltering fir-trees; cattle still grazed on the meadows, and the corn was not yet deserted by the huskers. The sun gave a bright edge to the sombre colors of the landscape, and to Joseph's eyes it was beautiful as never before. Julia leaned back in the carriage, and complained of the cold wind.

"There!" cried Joseph, as a view of the valley opened below them, with the stream flashing like steel between the leafless sycamores,—"there is home-land! Do you know where to look for our house?"

Julia made an effort, leaned forward, smiled, and pointed silently across the shoulder of a hill to the eastward. "You surely didn't suppose I could forget," she murmured.

Rachel Miller awaited them at the gate, and Julia had no sooner alighted than she flung herself into her arms. "Dear Aunt Rachel!" she cried: "you

752

must now take my mother's place; I have so much to learn from you! It is doubly a home since you are here. I feel that we shall all be happy together!"

Then there were kisses, of which Joseph received his share, and the first evening lapsed away in perfect harmony. Everything was delightful: the room, the furniture, the meal, even the roar of the wind in the dusky trees. While Julia lay in the cushioned rocking-chair, Rachel gave her nephew an account of all that had been done on the farm; but Joseph only answered her from the surface of his mind. Under the current of his talk ran a graver thought, which said: "You wanted independence and a chance of growth for your life; you fancied they would come in this form. Lo, now! here are the conditions which you desired to establish; from this hour begins the new life of which you dreamed. Whether you have been wise or rash, you can change nothing. You are limited, as before, though within a different circle. You may pace it to its fullest extent, but all the lessons you have yet learned require you to be satisfied within it."

# CHAPTER XIII. PRESENTIMENTS.

The autumn lapsed into winter, and the household on the Asten farm began to share the isolation of the season. There had been friendly visits from all the nearest neighbors and friends, followed by return visits, and invitations which Julia willingly accepted. She was very amiable, and took pains to confirm the favorable impression which she knew she had made in the summer. Everybody remarked how she had improved in appearance, how round and soft her neck and shoulders, how bright and fresh her complexion. She thanked them, with many grateful expressions to which they were not accustomed, for their friendly reception, which she looked upon as an adoption into their society; but at home, afterwards, she indulged in criticisms of their manners and habits which were not always friendly. Although these were given in a light, playful tone, and it was sometimes impossible not to be amused, Rachel Miller always felt uncomfortable when she heard them.

Then came quiet, lonely days, and Julia, weary of her idle life, undertook to master the details of the housekeeping. She went from garret to cellar, inspecting every article in closet and pantry, wondering much, censuring occasionally, and only praising a little when she found that Rachel was growing tired and irritable. Although she made no material changes, it was soon evident that she had very stubborn views of her own upon many points, and possessed a marked tendency for what the country people call "nearness." Little by little she diminished the bountiful, free-handed manner of provision which had been the habit of the house. One could not say that anything needful was lacking, and Rachel would hardly have been dissatisfied, had she not felt that the innovation was an indirect blame.

In some directions Julia seemed the reverse of "near," persuading Joseph into expenditures which the people considered very extravagant. When the snow came, his new and elegant sleigh, with the wolf-skin robe, the silver-mounted harness, and the silver-sounding bells, was the envy of all the young men, and an abomination to the old. It was a splendor which he could easily afford, and he did not grudge her the pleasure; yet it seemed to change his relation to the neighbors, and some of them were very free in hinting that they felt it so. It would be difficult to explain why they should resent this or any other slight departure from their fashions, but such had always been their custom.

In a few days the snow vanished and a tiresome season of rain and thaw succeeded. The south-eastern winds, blowing from the Atlantic across the intervening lowlands, rolled interminable gray masses of fog over the hills and blurred the scenery of the valley; dripping trees, soaked meadows, and sodden leaves were the only objects that detached themselves from the general void, and became in turn visible to those who travelled the deep, quaking roads. The social intercourse of the neighborhood ceased perforce, though the need of it were never so great: what little of the main highway down the valley was visible from the windows appeared to be deserted.

Julia, having exhausted the resources of the house, insisted on acquainting herself with the barn and everything thereto belonging. She laughingly asserted that her education as a farmer's wife was still very incomplete; she must know the amount of the crops, the price of grain, the value of the stock, the manner of work, and whatever else was necessary to her position. Although she made many pretty blunders, it was evident that her apprehension was unusually quick, and that whatever she acquired was fixed in her mind as if for some possible future use. She never wearied of the most trivial details, while Joseph, on the other hand, would often have willingly shortened his lessons. His mind was singularly disturbed between the desire to be gratified by her curiosity, and the fact that its eager and persistent character made him uncomfortable.

When an innocent, confiding nature begins to suspect that its confidence has been misplaced, the first result is a preternatural stubbornness to admit the truth. The clearest impressions are resisted, or half-consciously misinterpreted, with the last force of an illusion which already foresees its own overthrow. Joseph eagerly clung to every look and word and action which confirmed his sliding faith in his wife's sweet and simple character, and repelled—though a deeper instinct told him that a day would come when it must be admitted—the evidence of her coldness and selfishness. Yet, even while almost fiercely asserting to his own heart that he had every reason to be happy, he was consumed with a secret fever of unrest, doubt, and dread.

The horns of the growing moon were still turned downwards, and cold, dreary rains were poured upon the land. Julia's patience, in such straits, was wonderful, if the truth had been known, but she saw that some change was necessary for both of them. She therefore proposed, not what she most desired, but what her circumstances prescribed,—a visit from her sister Clementina. Joseph found the request natural enough: it was an infliction, but one which he had anticipated; and after the time had been arranged by letter, he drove to the station to meet the westward train from the city.

Clementina stepped upon the platform, so cloaked and hooded that he only recognized her by the deliberate grace of her movements. She extended her hand, giving his a cordial pressure, which was explained by the brass baggage-checks thus transferred to his charge.

"I will wait in the ladies' room," was all she said.

At the same moment Joseph's arm was grasped.

"What a lucky chance!" exclaimed Philip: then, suddenly pausing in his greeting, he lifted his hat and bowed to Clementina, who nodded slightly as she passed into the room.

"Let me look at you!" Philip resumed, laying his hands on Joseph's shoulders. Their eyes met and lingered, and Joseph felt the blood rise to his face as Philip's gaze sank more deeply into his heart and seemed to fathom its hidden trouble; but presently Philip smiled and said: "I scarcely knew, until this moment, that I had missed you so much, Joseph!"

"Have you come to stay?" Joseph asked.

"I think so. The branch railway down the valley, which you know was projected, is to be built immediately; but there are other reasons why the furnaces should be in blast. If it is possible, the work—and my settlement with it—will begin without any further delay. Is she your first family visit?"

He pointed towards the station.

756

"She will be with us a fortnight; but you will come, Philip?"

"To be sure!" Philip exclaimed. "I only saw her face indistinctly through the veil, but her nod said to me, 'A nearer approach is not objectionable.' Certainly, Miss Blessing; but with all the conventional forms, if you please!"

There was something of scorn and bitterness in the laugh which accompanied these words, and Joseph looked at him with a puzzled air.

"You may as well know now," Philip whispered, "that when I was a spoony youth of twenty, I very nearly imagined myself in love with Miss Clementina Blessing, and she encouraged my greenness until it spread as fast as a bamboo or a gourd-vine. Of course, I've long since congratulated myself that she cut me up, root and branch, when our family fortune was lost. The awkwardness of our intercourse is all on her side. Can she still have faith in her charms and my youth, I wonder? Ye gods! that would be a lovely conclusion of the comedy!"

Joseph could only join in the laugh as they parted. There was no time to reflect upon what had been said. Clementina, nevertheless, assumed a new interest in his eyes; and as he drove her towards the farm, he could not avoid connecting her with Philip in his thoughts. She, too, was evidently preoccupied with the meeting, for Philip's name soon floated to the surface of their conversation.

"I expect a visit from him soon," said Joseph. As she was silent, he ventured to add: "You have no objections to meeting with him, I suppose?"

"Mr. Held is still a gentleman, I believe," Clementina replied, and then changed the subject of conversation.

Julia flew at her sister with open arms, and showered on her a profusion of kisses, all of which were received with perfect serenity, Clementina merely saying, as soon as she could get breath: "Dear me, Julia, I scarcely recognize you! You are already so countrified!"

Rachel Miller, although a woman, and notwithstanding her recent experience, found herself greatly bewildered by this new apparition.

Clementina's slow, deliberate movements and her even-toned, musical utterance impressed her with a certain respect; yet the qualities of character they suggested never manifested themselves. On the contrary, the same words, in any other mouth, would have often expressed malice or heartlessness. Sometimes she heard her own homely phrases repeated, as if by the most unconscious purposeless imitation, and had Julia either smiled or appeared annoyed her suspicions might have been excited; as it was, she was constantly and sorely puzzled.

Once only, and for a moment, the two masks were slightly lifted. At dinner, Clementina, who had turned the conversation upon the subject of birthdays, suddenly said to Joseph: "By the way, Mr. Asten, has Julia told you her age?"

Julia gave a little start, but presently looked up, with an expression meant to be artless.

"I knew it before we were married," Joseph quietly answered.

Clementina bit her lip. Julia, concealing her surprise, flashed a triumphant glance at her sister, then a tender one at Joseph, and said: "We will both let the old birthdays go; we will only have one and the same anniversary from this time on!"

Joseph felt, through some natural magnetism of his nature rather than from any perceptible evidence, that Clementina was sharply and curiously watching the relation between himself and his wife. He had no fear of her detecting misgivings which were not yet acknowledged to himself, but was instinctively on his guard in her presence.

It was not many days before Philip called. Julia received him cordially, as the friend of her husband, while Clementina bowed with an impassive face, without rising from her seat. Philip, however, crossed the room and gave her his hand, saying cheerily: "We used to be old friends, Miss Blessing. You have not forgotten me?"

"We cannot forget when we have been asked to do so," she warbled.

Philip took a chair. "Eight years!" he said: "I am the only one who has changed in that time."

Julia, looked at her sister, but the latter was apparently absorbed in comparing some zephyr tints.

"The whirligig of time!" he exclaimed: "who can foresee anything? Then I was an ignorant, petted young aristocrat,—an expectant heir; now behold me, working among miners and puddlers and forgemen! It's a rough but wholesome change. Would you believe it, Mrs. Asten, I've forgotten the mazurka!"

"I wish to forget it," Julia replied: "the spring-house is as important to me as the furnace to you."

"Have you seen the Hopetons lately?" Clementina asked.

Joseph saw a shade pass over Philip's face, and he seemed to hesitate a moment before answering: "I hear they will be neighbors of mine next summer. Mr. Hopeton is interested in the new branch down the valley, and has purchased the old Calvert property for a country residence."

"Indeed? Then you will often see them."

"I hope so: they are very agreeable people. But I shall also have my own little household: my sister will probably join me."

"Not Madeline!" exclaimed Julia.

"Madeline," Philip answered. "It has long been her wish, as well as mine. You know the little cottage on the knoll, at Coventry, Joseph! I have taken it for a year."

"There will be quite a city society," murmured Clementina, in her sweetest tones. "You will need no commiseration, Julia. Unless, indeed, the country people succeed in changing you all into their own likeness. Mrs. Hopeton will certainly create a sensation. I am told that she is very extravagant, Mr. Held?"

"I have never seen her husband's bank account," said Philip, dryly.

He rose presently, and Joseph accompanied him to the lane. Philip, with

759

the bridle-rein over his arm, delayed to mount his horse, while the mechanical commonplaces of speech, which, somehow, always absurdly come to the lips when graver interests have possession of the heart, were exchanged by the two. Joseph felt, rather than saw, that Philip was troubled. Presently the latter said: "Something is coming over both of us,—not between us. I thought I should tell you a little more, but perhaps it is too soon. If I guess rightly, neither of us is ready. Only this, Joseph, let us each think of the other as a help and a support!"

"I do, Philip!" Joseph answered. "I see there is some influence at work which I do not understand, but I am not impatient to know what it is. As for myself, I seem to know nothing at all; but you can judge,—you see all there is."

Even as he pronounced these words Joseph felt that they were not strictly sincere, and almost expected to find an expression of reproof in Philip's eyes. But no: they softened until he only saw a pitying tenderness. Then he knew that the doubts which he had resisted with all the force of his nature were clearly revealed to Philip's mind.

They shook bands, and parted in silence; and Joseph, as he looked up to the gray blank of heaven, asked himself: "Is this all? Has my life already taken the permanent imprint of its future?"

# CHAPTER XIV. THE AMARANTH.

Clementina returned to the city without having made any very satisfactory discovery. Her parting was therefore conventionally tender: she even thanked Joseph for his hospitality, and endeavored to throw a little natural emphasis into her words as she expressed the hope of being allowed to renew her visit in the summer.

During her stay it seemed to Joseph that the early harmony of his household had been restored. Julia's manner had been so gentle and amiable, that, on looking back, he was inclined to believe that the loneliness of her new life was alone responsible for any change. But after Clementina's departure his doubts were reawakened in a more threatening form. He could not guess, as yet, the terrible chafing of a smiling mask; of a restraint which must not only conceal itself, but counterfeit its opposite; of the assumption by a narrow, cold, and selfish nature of virtues which it secretly despises. He could not have foreseen that the gentleness, which had nearly revived his faith in her, would so suddenly disappear. But it was gone, like a glimpse of the sun through the winter fog. The hard, watchful expression came back to Julia's face; the lowered eyelids no longer gave a fictitious depth to her shallow, tawny pupils; the soft roundness of her voice took on a frequent harshness, and the desire of asserting her own will in all things betrayed itself through her affected habits of yielding and seeking counsel.

She continued her plan of making herself acquainted with all the details of the farm business. When the roads began to improve, in the early spring, she insisted in driving to the village alone, and Joseph soon found that she made good use of these journeys in extending her knowledge of the social and pecuniary standing of all the neighboring families. She talked with farmers, mechanics, and drovers; became familiar with the fluctuations in the prices of grain and cattle; learned to a penny the wages paid for every form of service; and thus felt, from week to week, the ground growing more secure under her feet.

Joseph was not surprised to see that his aunt's participation in the direction of the household gradually diminished. Indeed, he scarcely noticed the circumstance at all, but he was at last forced to remark her increasing silence and the trouble of her face. To all appearance the domestic harmony was perfect, and if Rachel Miller felt some natural regret at being obliged to divide her sway, it was a matter, he thought, wherein he had best not interfere. One day, however, she surprised him by the request:—

"Joseph, can you take or send me to Magnolia to-morrow?"

"Certainly, Aunt!" he replied. "I suppose you want to visit Cousin Phebe; you have not seen her since last summer."

"It was that,—and something more." She paused a moment, and then added, more firmly: "She has always wished that I should make my home with her, but I couldn't think of any change so long as I was needed here. It seems to me that I am not really needed now."

"Why, Aunt Rachel!" Joseph exclaimed, "I meant this to be your home always, as much as mine! Of course you are needed,—not to do all that you have done heretofore, but as a part of the family. It is your right."

"I understand all that, Joseph. But I've heard it said that a young wife should learn to see to everything herself, and Julia, I'm sure, doesn't need either my help or my advice."

Joseph's face became very grave. "Has she—has she—?" he stammered.

"No," said Rachel, "she has not said it—in words. Different persons have different ways. She is quick, O very quick!—and capable. You know I could never sit idly by, and look on; and it's hard to be directed. I seem to belong to the place and everything connected with it; yet there's times when what a body ought to do is plain."

In endeavoring to steer a middle course between her conscience and her tender regard for her nephew's feelings Rachel only confused and troubled him. Her words conveyed something of the truth which she sought to hide under them. She was both angered and humiliated; the resistance

762

with which she had attempted to meet Julia's domestic innovations was no match for the latter's tactics; it had gone down like a barrier of reeds and been contemptuously trampled under foot. She saw herself limited, opposed, and finally set aside by a cheerful dexterity of management which evaded her grasp whenever she tried to resent it. Definite acts, whereon to base her indignation, seemed to slip from her memory, but the atmosphere of the house became fatal to her. She felt this while she spoke, and felt also that Joseph must be spared.

"Aunt Rachel," said he, "I know that Julia is very anxious to learn everything which she thinks belongs to her place,—perhaps a little more than is really necessary. She's an enthusiastic nature, you know. Maybe you are not fully acquainted yet; maybe you have misunderstood her in some things: I would like to think so."

"It is true that we are different, Joseph,—very different. I don't say, therefore, that I'm always right. It's likely, indeed, that any young wife and any old housekeeper like myself would have their various notions. But where there can be only one head, it's the wife's place to be that head. Julia has not asked it of me, but she has the right. I can't say, also, that I don't need a little rest and change, and there seems to be some call on me to oblige Phebe. Look at the matter in the true light," she continued, seeing that Joseph remained silent, "and you must feel that it's only natural."

"I hope so," he said at last, repressing a sigh; "all things are changing."

"What can we do?" Julia asked, that evening, when he had communicated to her his aunt's resolution; "it would be so delightful if she would stay, and yet I have had a presentiment that she would leave us—for a little while only, I hope. Dear, good Aunt Rachel! I couldn't help seeing how hard it was for her to allow the least change in the order of housekeeping. She would be perfectly happy if I would sit still all day and let her tire herself to death; but how can I do that, Joseph? And no two women have exactly the same ways and habits. I've tried to make everything pleasant for her: if she would only leave many little matters entirely to me, or at least not think of them,—but I fear she cannot. She manages to see the least that I do, and secretly worries about it, in the very kindness of her heart. Why can't women carry on partnerships in housekeeping as men do in business? I suppose we are too particular; perhaps I am just as much so as Aunt Rachel. I have no doubt she thinks a little hardly of me, and so it would do her good—we should really come nearer again—if she had a change. If she will go, Joseph, she must at least leave us with the feeling that our home is always hers, whenever she chooses to accept it."

Julia bent over Joseph's chair, gave him a rapid kiss, and then went off to make her peace with Aunt Rachel. When the two women came to the tea-table the latter had an uncertain, bewildered air, while the eyelids of the former were red,—either from tears or much rubbing.

A fortnight afterwards Rachel Miller left the farm and went to reside with her widowed niece, in Magnolia.

The day after her departure another surprise came to Joseph in the person of his father-in-law. Mr. Blessing arrived in a hired vehicle from the station. His face was so red and radiant from the March winds, and perhaps some private source of satisfaction, that his sudden arrival could not possibly be interpreted as an omen of ill-fortune. He shook hands with the Irish groom who had driven him over, gave him a handsome gratuity in addition to the hire of the team, extracted an elegant travelling-satchel from under the seat, and met Joseph at the gate, with a breezy burst of feeling:—

"God bless you, son-in-law! It does my heart good to see you again! And then, at last, the pleasure of beholding your ancestral seat; really, this is quite—quite manorial!"

Julia, with a loud cry of "O pa!" came rushing from the house.

"Bless me, how wild and fresh the child looks!" cried Mr. Blessing, after the embrace. "Only see the country roses on her cheeks! Almost too young and sparkling for Lady Asten, of Asten Hall, eh? As Dryden says, 'Happy, happy, happy pair!' It takes me back to the days when I was a gay young lark; but I must have a care, and not make an old fool of myself. Let us go in and subside into soberness: I am ready both to laugh and cry."

When they were seated in the comfortable front room, Mr. Blessing

764

opened his satchel and produced a large leather-covered flask. Julia was probably accustomed to his habits, for she at once brought a glass from the sideboard.

"I am still plagued with my old cramps," her father said to Joseph, as he poured out a stout dose. "Physiologists, you know, have discovered that stimulants diminish the wear and tear of life, and I find their theories correct. You, in your pastoral isolation and pecuniary security, can form no conception of the tension under which we men of office and of the world live, Beatus ille, and so forth,—strange that the only fragment of Latin which I remember should be so appropriate! A little water, if you please, Julia."

In the evening, when Mr. Blessing, slippered, sat before the open fireplace, with a cigar in his mouth, the object of his sudden visit crept by slow degrees to the light. "Have you been dipping into oil?" he asked Joseph.

Julia made haste to reply. "Not yet, but almost everybody in the neighborhood is ready to do so now, since Clemson has realized his fifty thousand dollars in a single year. They are talking of nothing else in the village. I heard yesterday, Joseph, that Old Bishop has taken three thousand dollars' worth of stock in a new company."

"Take my advice, and don't touch 'em!" exclaimed Mr. Blessing.

"I had not intended to," said Joseph.

"There is this thing about these excitements," Mr. Blessing continued: "they never reach the rural districts until the first sure harvest is over. The sharp, intelligent operators in the large cities—the men who are ready to take up soap, thimbles, hand-organs, electricity, or hymn-books, at a moment's notice—always cut into a new thing before its value is guessed by the multitude. Then the smaller fry follow and secure their second crop, while your quiet men in the country are shaking their heads and crying 'humbug!' Finally, when it really gets to be a humbug, in a speculative sense, they just begin to believe in it, and are fair game for the bummers and camp-followers of the financial army. I respect Clemson, though I never heard of him before; as for Old Bishop, he may be a very worthy man, but he'll never see the color of his three thousand dollars again."

"Pa!" cried Julia, "how clear you do make everything. And to think that I was wishing—O, wishing so much!—that Joseph would go into oil."

She hung her head a little, looking at Joseph with an affectionate, penitent glance. A quick gleam of satisfaction passed over Mr. Blessing's face; he smiled to himself, puffed rapidly at his cigar for a minute, and then resumed: "In such a field of speculation everything depends on being initiated. There are men in the city—friends of mine—who know every foot of ground in the Alleghany Valley. They can smell oil, if it's a thousand feet deep. They never touch a thing that isn't safe,—but, then, they know what's safe. In spite of the swindling that's going on, it takes years to exhaust the good points; just so sure as your honest neighbors here will lose, just so sure will these friends of mine gain. There are millions in what they have under way, at this moment."

"What is it?" Julia breathlessly asked, while Joseph's face betrayed that his interest was somewhat aroused.

Mr. Blessing unlocked his satchel, and took from it a roll of paper, which he began to unfold upon his knee. "Here," he said, "you see this bend of the river, just about the centre of the oil region, which is represented by the yellow color. These little dots above the bend are the celebrated Fluke Wells; the other dots below are the equally celebrated Chowder Wells. The distance between the two is nearly three miles. Here is an untouched portion of the treasure,—a pocket of Pactolus waiting to be rifled. A few of us have acquired the land, and shall commence boring immediately."

"But," said Joseph, "it seems to me that either the attempt must have been made already, or that the land must command such an enormous price as to lessen the profits."

"Wisely spoken! It is the first question which would occur to any prudent mind. But what if I say that neither is the case? And you, who are familiar with the frequent eccentricities of old farmers, can understand the explanation. The owner of the land was one of your ignorant, stubborn men, who took such a dislike to the prospectors and speculators, that he refused

766

to let them come near him. Both the Fluke and Chowder Companies tried their best to buy him out, but he had a malicious pleasure in leading them on to make immense offers, and then refusing. Well, a few months ago he died, and his heirs were willing enough to let the land go; but before it could be regularly offered for sale, the Fluke and Chowder Wells began to flow less and less. Their shares fell from 270 to 95; the supposed value of the land fell with them, and finally the moment arrived when we could purchase for a very moderate sum. I see the question in your mind; why should we wish to buy when the other wells were giving out? There comes in the secret, which is our veritable success. Consider it whispered in your ears, and locked in your bosoms,—torpedoes! It was not then generally exploded (to carry out the image), so we bought at the low figure, in the very nick of time. Within a week the Fluke and Chowder Wells were torpedoed, and came back to more than their former capacity; the shares rose as rapidly as they had fallen, and the central body we hold—to which they are, as it were, the two arms—could now be sold for ten times what it cost us!"

Here Mr. Blessing paused, with his finger on the map, and a light of merited triumph in his eyes. Julia clapped her hands, sprang to her feet, and cried: "Trumps at last!"

"Ay," said he, "wealth, repose for my old days,—wealth for us all, if your husband will but take the hand I hold out to him. You now know, son-in-law, why the endorsement you gave me was of such vital importance; the note, as you are aware, will mature in another week. Why should you not charge yourself with the payment, in consideration of the transfer to you of shares of the original stock, already so immensely appreciated in value? I have delayed making any provision, for the sake of offering you the chance."

Julia was about to speak, but restrained herself with an apparent effort.

"I should like to know," Joseph said, "who are associated with you in the undertaking?"

"Well done, again! Where did you get your practical shrewdness? The best men in the city!—not only the Collector and the Surveyor, but Congressman Whaley, E. D. Stokes, of Stokes, Pirricutt and Company, and even the Reverend Doctor Lellifant. If I had not been an old friend of Kanuck, the agent who negotiated the purchase, my chance would have been impalpably small. I have all the documents with me. There has been no more splendid opportunity since oil became a power! I hesitate to advise even one so near to me in such matters; but if you knew the certainties as I know them, you would go in with all your available capital. The excitement, as you say, has reached the country communities, which are slow to rise and equally slow to subside; all oil stock will be in demand, but the Amaranth,—'The Blessing,' they wished to call it, but I was obliged to decline, for official reasons,—the Amaranth shares will be the golden apex of the market!"

Julia looked at Joseph with eager, hungry eyes. He, too, was warmed and tempted by the prospect of easy profit which the scheme held out to him; only the habit of his nature resisted, but with still diminishing force. "I might venture the thousand," he said.

"It is no venture!" Julia cried. "In all the speculations I have heard discussed by pa and his friends, there was nothing so admirably managed as this. Such a certainty of profit may never come again. If you will be advised by me, Joseph, you will take shares to the amount of five or ten thousand."

"Ten thousand is exactly the amount I hold open," Mr. Blessing gravely remarked. "That, however, does not represent the necessary payment, which can hardly amount to more than twenty-five per cent. before we begin to realize. Only ten per cent. has yet been called, so that your thousand at present will secure you an investment of ten thousand. Really, it seems like a fortunate coincidence."

He went on, heating himself with his own words, until the possibilities of the case grew so splendid that Joseph felt himself dazzled and bewildered. Mr. Blessing was a master in the art of seductive statement. Even where he was only the mouthpiece of another, a few repetitions led him to the profoundest belief. Here there could be no doubt of his sincerity, and, moreover, every movement from the very inception of the scheme, every statistical item, all collateral influences, were clear in his mind and instantly accessible. Although he began by saying, "I will make no estimate of the profits, because it is not prudent to fix our hopes on a positive sum," he was soon carried far away from this resolution, and most luxuriously engaged, pencil in hand, in figuring out results which drove Julia wild with desire, and almost took away Joseph's breath. The latter finally said, as they rose from the session, late at night:—

"It is settled that I take as much as the thousand will cover; but I would rather think over the matter quietly for a day or two before venturing further."

"You must," replied Mr. Blessing, patting him on the shoulder. "These things are so new to your experience, that they disturb and—I might almost say—alarm you. It is like bringing an increase of oxygen into your mental atmosphere. (Ha! a good figure: for the result will be, a richer, fuller life. I must remember it.) But you are a healthy organization, and therefore you are certain to see clearly: I can wait with confidence."

The next morning Joseph, without declaring his purpose, drove to Coventry Forge to consult Philip. Mr. Blessing and Julia, remaining at home, went over the shining ground again, and yet again, confirming each other in the determination to secure it. Even Joseph, as he passed up the valley in the mild March weather, taking note of the crimson and gold of the flowering spice-bushes and maple-trees, could not prevent his thoughts from dwelling on the delights of wealth,—society, books, travel, and all the mellow, fortunate expansion of life. Involuntarily, he hoped that Philip's counsel might coincide with his father-in-law's offer.

But Philip was not at home. The forge was in full activity, the cottage on the knoll was repainted and made attractive in various ways, and Philip would soon return with his sister to establish a permanent home. Joseph found the sign-spiritual of his friend in numberless little touches and changes; it seemed to him that a new soul had entered into the scenery of the place.

A mile or two farther up the valley, a company of mechanics and laborers were apparently tearing the old Calvert mansion inside out. House, barn, garden, and lawn were undergoing a complete transformation. While he paused at the entrance of the private lane, to take a survey of the operations, Mr. Clemson rode down to him from the house. The Hopetons, he said, would migrate from the city early in May: work had already commenced on the new railway, and in another year a different life would come upon the whole neighborhood.

In the course of the conversation Joseph ventured to sound Mr. Clemson in regard to the newly formed oil companies. The latter frankly confessed that he had withdrawn from further speculation, satisfied with his fortune; he preferred to give no opinion, further than that money was still to be made, if prudently placed. Tho Fluke and Chowder Wells, he said, were old, well known, and profitable. The new application of torpedoes had restored their failing flow, and the stock had recovered from its temporary depreciation. His own venture had been made in another part of the region.

The atmosphere into which Joseph entered, on returning home, took away all further power of resistance. Tempted already, and impressed by what he had learned, he did what his wife and father-in-law desired.

# CHAPTER XV. A DINNER PARTY.

Having assumed the payment of Mr. Blessing's note, as the first instalment upon his stock, Joseph was compelled to prepare himself for future emergencies. A year must still elapse before the term of the mortgage upon his farm would expire, but the sums he had invested for the purpose of meeting it when due must be held ready for use. The assurance of great and certain profit in the mean time rendered this step easy; and, even at the worst, he reflected, there would be no difficulty in procuring a now mortgage whereby to liquidate the old. A notice which he received at this time, that a second assessment of ten per cent. on the Amaranth stock had been made, was both unexpected and disquieting. Mr. Blessing, however, accompanied it with a letter, making clear not only the necessity, but the admirable wisdom of a greater present outlay than had been anticipated. So the first of April—the usual business anniversary of the neighborhood—went smoothly by. Money was plenty, the Asten credit had always been sound, and Joseph tasted for the first time a pleasant sense of power in so easily receiving and transferring considerable sums.

One result of the venture was the development of a new phase in Julia's nature. She not only accepted the future profit as certain, but she had apparently calculated its exact amount and framed her plans accordingly. If she had been humiliated by the character of Joseph's first business transaction with her father, she now made amends for it. "Pa" was their good genius. "Pa" was the agency whereby they should achieve wealth and social importance. Joseph now had the clearest evidence of the difference between a man who knew the world and was of value in it, and their slow, dull-headed country neighbors. Indeed, Julia seemed to consider the Asten property as rather contemptible beside the splendor of the Blessing scheme. Her gratitude for a quiet home, her love of country life, her disparagement of the shams and exactions of "society," were given up as suddenly and coolly as if she had never affected them. She gave herself no pains to make the transition gradual, and thus lessen its shock. Perhaps she supposed that Joseph's fresh, unsuspicious nature was so plastic that it had already sufficiently taken her impress, and that he would easily forget the mask she had worn. If so, she was seriously mistaken.

He saw, with a deadly chill of the heart, the change in her manner,—a change so complete that another face confronted him at the table, even as another heart beat beside his on the dishallowed marriage-bed. He saw the gentle droop vanish from the eyelids, leaving the cold, flinty pupils unshaded; the soft appeal of the half-opened lips was lost in the rigid, almost cruel compression which now seemed habitual to them; all the slight dependent gestures, the tender airs of reference to his will or pleasure, had rapidly transformed themselves into expressions of command or obstinate resistance. But the patience of a loving man is equal to that of a loving woman: he was silent, although his silence covered an ever-increasing sense of outrage.

Once it happened, that after Julia had been unusually eloquent concerning "what pa is doing for us," and what use they should make of "pa's money, as I call it," Joseph quietly remarked:—

"You seem to forget, Julia, that without my money not much could have been done."

An angry color came into her face; but, on second thought, she bent her head, and murmured in an offended voice: "It is very mean and ungenerous in you to refer to our temporary poverty. You might forget, by this time, the help pa was compelled to ask of you."

"I did not think of that!" he exclaimed. "Besides, you did not seem entirely satisfied with my help, at the time."

"O, how you misunderstand me!" she groaned. "I only wished to know the extent of his need. He is so generous, so considerate towards us, that we only guess his misfortune at the last moment."

The possibility of being unjust silenced Joseph. There were tears in Julia's voice, and he imagined they would soon rise to her eyes. After a long, uncomfortable pause, he said, for the sake of changing the subject: "What can have become of Elwood Withers? I have not seen him for months."

"I don't think you need care to know," she remarked. "He's a rough, vulgar fellow: it's just as well if he keeps away from us."

"Julia! he is my friend, and must always be welcome to me. You were friendly enough towards him, and towards all the neighborhood, last summer: how is it that you have not a good word to say now?"

He spoke warmly and indignantly. Julia, however, looked at him with a calm, smiling face. "It is very simple," she said. "You will agree with me, in another year. A guest, as I was, must try to see only the pleasant side of people: that's our duty; and so I enjoyed—as much as I could—the rusticity, the awkwardness, the ignorance, the (now, don't be vexed, dear!)—the vulgarity of your friend. As one of the society of the neighborhood, as a resident, I am not bound by any such delicacy. I take the same right to judge and select as I should take anywhere. Unless I am to be hypocritical, I cannot—towards you, at least—conceal my real feelings. How shall I ever get you to see the difference between yourself and these people, unless I continually point it out? You are modest, and don't like to acknowledge your own superiority."

She rose from the table, laughing, and went out of the room humming a lively air, leaving Joseph to make the best of her words.

A few days after this the work on the branch railway, extending down the valley, reached a point where it could be seen from the Asten farm. Joseph, on riding over to inspect the operations, was surprised to find Elwood, who had left his father's place and become a sub-contractor. The latter showed his hearty delight at their meeting.

"I've been meaning to come up," he said, "but this is a busy time for me. It's a chance I couldn't let slip, and now that I've taken hold I must hold on. I begin to think this is the thing I was made for, Joseph."

"I never thought of it before," Joseph answered, "and yet I'm sure you are right. How did you hit upon it?"

"I didn't; it was Mr. Held."

"Philip?"

"Him. You know I've been hauling for the Forge, and so it turned up by degrees, as I may say. He's at home, and, I expect, looking for you. But how are you now, really?"

Elwood's question meant a great deal more than he knew how to say. Suddenly, in a flash of memory, their talk of the previous year returned to Joseph's mind; he saw his friend's true instincts and his own blindness as never before. But he must dissemble, if possible, with that strong, rough, kindly face before him.

"O," he said, attempting a cheerful air, "I am one of the old folks now. You must come up—"

The recollection of Julia's words cut short the invitation upon his lips. A sharp pang went through his heart, and the treacherous blood crowded to his face all the more that he tried to hold it back.

"Come, and I'll show you where we're going to make the cutting," Elwood quietly said, taking him by the arm. Joseph fancied, thenceforth, that there was a special kindness in his manner, and the suspicion seemed to rankle in his mind as if he had been slighted by his friend.

As before, to vary the tedium of his empty life, so now, to escape from the knowledge which he found himself more and more powerless to resist, he busied himself beyond all need with the work of the farm. Philip had returned with his sister, he knew, but after the meeting with Elwood he shrank with a painful dread from Philip's heart-deep, intimate eye. Julia, however, all the more made use of the soft spring weather to survey the social ground, and choose where to take her stand. Joseph scarcely knew, indeed, how extensive her operations had been, until she announced an invitation to dine with the Hopetons, who were now in possession of the renovated Calvert place. She enlarged, more than was necessary, on the distinguished city position of the family, and the importance of "cultivating" its country members. Joseph's single brief meeting with Mr. Hopeton—who was a short, solid man, in ripe middle age, of a thoroughly cosmopolitan, though not a remarkably intellectual stamp—had been agreeable, and he recognized the obligation to be neighborly. Therefore he readily accepted the invitation on his own grounds.

When the day arrived, Julia, after spending the morning over her toilet, came forth resplendent in rosy silk, bright and dazzling in complexion, and with all her former grace of languid eyelids and parted lips. The void in Joseph's heart grew wider at the sight of her; for he perceived, as never before, her consummate skill in assuming a false character. It seemed incredible that he should have been so deluded. For the first time a feeling of repulsion, which was almost disgust, came upon him as he listened to her prattle of delight in the soft weather, and the fragrant woods, and the blossoming orchards. Was not, also, this delight assumed? he asked himself: false in one thing, false in all, was the fatal logic which then and there began its torment.

The most that was possible in such a short time had been achieved on the Calvert place. The house had been brightened, surrounded by light, airy verandas, and the lawn and garden, thrown into one and given into the hands of a skilful gardener, were scarcely to be recognized. A broad, solid gravel-walk replaced the old tan-covered path; a pretty fountain tinkled before the door; thick beds of geranium in flower studded the turf, and veritable thickets of rose-trees were waiting for June. Within the house, some rooms had been thrown together, the walls richly yet harmoniously colored, and the sumptuous furniture thus received a proper setting. In contrast to the houses of even the wealthiest farmers, which expressed a nicely reckoned sufficiency of comfort, the place had an air of joyous profusion, of a wealth which delighted in itself.

Mr. Hopeton met them with the frank, offhand manner of a man of business. His wife followed, and the two guests made a rapid inspection of her as she came down the hall. Julia noticed that her crocus-colored dress was high in the neck, and plainly trimmed; that she wore no ornaments, and that the natural pallor of her complexion had not been corrected by art. Joseph remarked the simple grace of her movement, the large, dark, inscrutable eyes, the smooth bands of her black hair, and the pure though somewhat lengthened oval of her face. The gentle dignity of her manner more than refreshed, it soothed him. She was so much younger than her husband that Joseph involuntarily wondered how they should have come together.

The greetings were scarcely over before Philip and Madeline Held arrived. Julia, with the least little gush of tenderness, kissed the latter, whom Philip then presented to Joseph for the first time. She had the same wavy hair as her brother, but the golden hue was deepened nearly into brown, and her eyes were a clear hazel. It was also the same frank, firm face, but her woman's smile was so much the sweeter as her lips were lovelier than the man's. Joseph seemed to clasp an instant friendship in her offered hand.

There was but one other guest, who, somewhat to his surprise, was Lucy Henderson. Julia concealed whatever she might have felt, and made so much reference to their former meetings as might satisfy Lucy without conveying to Mrs. Hopeton the impression of any special intimacy. Lucy looked thin and worn, and her black silk dress was not of the latest fashion: she seemed to be the poor relation of the company. Joseph learned that she had taken one of the schools in the valley, for the summer. Her manner to him was as simple and friendly as ever, but he felt the presence of some new element of strength and self-reliance in her nature.

His place at dinner was beside Mrs. Hopeton, while Lucy—apparently by accident—sat upon the other side of the hostess. Philip and the host led the conversation, confining it too exclusively to the railroad and iron interests; but those finally languished, and gave way to other topics in which all could take part. Joseph felt that while the others, except Lucy and himself, were fashioned under different aspects of life, some of which they shared in common, yet that their seeming ease and freedom of communication touched, here and there, some invisible limit, which they were careful not to pass. Even Philip appeared to be beyond his reach, for the time.

The country and the people, being comparatively new to them, naturally came to be discussed.

"Mr. Held, or Mr. Asten,—either of you know both,"—Mr. Hopeton asked, "what are the principal points of difference between society in the city and in the country?"

"Indeed, I know too little of the city," said Joseph.

"And I know too little of the country,—here, at least," Philip added. "Of course the same passions and prejudices come into play everywhere. There are circles, there are jealousies, ups and downs, scandals, suppressions, and rehabilitations: it can't be otherwise."

"Are they not a little worse in the country," said Julia, "because—I may ask the question here, among us—there is less refinement of manner?"

"If the external forms are ruder," Philip resumed, "it may be an advantage, in one sense. Hypocrisy cannot be developed into an art."

Julia bit her lip, and was silent.

"But are the country people, hereabouts, so rough?" Mrs. Hopeton asked. "I confess that they don't seem so to me. What do you say, Miss Henderson?"

"Perhaps I am not an impartial witness," Lucy answered. "We care less about what is called 'manners' than the city people. We have no fixed rules for dress and behavior,—only we don't like any one to differ too much from the rest of us."

"That's it!" Mr. Hopeton cried; "the tyrannical levelling sentiment of an imperfectly developed community! Fortunately, I am beyond its reach."

Julia's eyes sparkled: she looked across the table at Joseph, with a triumphant air.

Philip suddenly raised his head. "How would you correct it? Simply by resistance?" he asked.

Mr. Hopeton laughed. "I should no doubt get myself into a hornet's-nest. No; by indifference!"

Then Madeline Held spoke. "Excuse me," she said; "but is indifference possible, even if it were right? You seem to take the levelling spirit for granted, without looking into its character and causes; there must be some natural sense of justice, no matter how imperfectly society is developed. We are members of this community,—at least, Philip and I certainly consider ourselves so,—and I am determined not to judge it without knowledge, or to offend what may be only mechanical habits of thought, unless I can see a sure advantage in doing so."

Lucy Henderson looked at the speaker with a bright, grateful face. Joseph's eyes wandered from her to Julia, who was silent and watchful.

"But I have no time for such conscientious studies," Mr. Hopeton resumed. "One can be satisfied with half a dozen neighbors, and let the mass go. Indifference, after all, is the best philosophy. What do you say, Mr. Held?"

"Indifference!" Philip echoed. A dark flush came into his face, and he was silent a moment. "Yes: our hearts are inconvenient appendages. We suffer a deal from unnecessary sympathies, and from imagining, I suppose, that others feel them as we do. These uneasy features of society are simply the effort of nature to find some occupation for brains otherwise idle—or empty. Teach the people to think, and they will disappear."

Joseph stared at Philip, feeling that a secret bitterness was hidden under his careless, mocking air. Mrs. Hopeton rose, and the company left the table. Madeline Held had a troubled expression, but there was an eager, singular brightness in Julia's eyes.

"Emily, let us have coffee on the veranda," said Mr. Hopeton, leading the way. He had already half forgotten the subject of conversation: his own expressions, in fact, had been made very much at random, for the sole purpose of keeping up the flow of talk. He had no very fixed views of any kind, beyond the sphere of his business activity.

Philip, noticing the impression he had made on Joseph, drew him to one side. "Don't seriously remember my words against me," he said; "you were sorry to hear them, I know. All I meant was, that an over-sensitive tenderness towards everybody is a fault. Besides, I was provoked to answer him in his own vein."

"But, Philip!" Joseph whispered, "such words tempt me! What if they were true?"

Philip grasped his arm with a painful force. "They never can be true to you, Joseph," he said.

Gay and pleasant as the company seemed to be, each one felt a secret sense of relief when it came to an end. As Joseph drove homewards, silently recalling what had been said, Julia interrupted his reflections with: "Well, what do you think of the Hopetons?"

"She is an interesting woman," he answered.

"But reserved; and she shows very little taste in dress. However, I suppose you hardly noticed anything of the kind. She kept Lucy Henderson beside her as a foil: Madeline Held would have been damaging."

Joseph only partly guessed her meaning; it was repugnant, and he determined to avoid its further discussion.

"Hopeton is a shrewd business man," Julia continued, "but he cannot compare with her for shrewdness—either with her or—Philip Held!"

"What do you mean?"

"I made a discovery before the dinner was over, which you—innocent, unsuspecting man that you are—might have before your eyes for years, without seeing it. Tell me now, honestly, did you notice nothing?"

"What should I notice, beyond what was said?" he asked.

"That was the least!" she cried; "but, of course, I knew you couldn't. And perhaps you won't believe me, when I tell you that Philip Held,— your particular friend, your hero, for aught I know your pattern of virtue and character, and all that is manly and noble,—that Philip Held, I say, is furiously in love with Mrs. Hopeton!"

Joseph started as if he had been shot, and turned around with an angry red on his brow. "Julia!" he said, "how dare you speak so of Philip!"

She laughed. "Because I dare to speak the truth, when I see it. I thought I should surprise you. I remembered a certain rumor I had heard before she was married,—while she was Emily Marrable,—and I watched them closer than they guessed. I'm certain of Philip: as for her, she's a deep creature, and

779

she was on her guard; but they are near neighbors."

Joseph was thoroughly aroused and indignant. "It is your own fancy!" he exclaimed. "You hate Philip on account of that affair with Clementina; but you ought to have some respect for the woman whose hospitality you have accepted!"

"Bless me! I have any quantity of respect both for her and her furniture. By the by, Joseph, our parlor would furnish better than hers; I have been thinking of a few changes we might make, which would wonderfully improve the house. As for Philip, Clementina was a fool. She'd be glad enough to have him now, but in these matters, once gone is gone for good. Somehow, people who marry for love very often get rich afterwards,—ourselves, for instance."

It was some time before Joseph's excitement subsided. He had resented Julia's suspicion as dishonorable to Philip, yet he could not banish the conjecture of its possible truth. If Philip's affected cynicism had tempted him, Julia's unblushing assumption of the existence of a passion which was forbidden, and therefore positively guilty, seemed to stain the pure texture of his nature. The lightness with which she spoke of the matter was even more abhorrent to him than the assertion itself; the malicious satisfaction in the tones of her voice had not escaped his ear.

"Julia," he said, just before they reached home, "do not mention your fancy to another soul than me. It would reflect discredit on you."

"You are innocent," she answered. "And you are not complimentary. If I have any remarkable quality, it is tact. Whenever I speak, I shall know the effect before-hand; even pa, with all his official experience, is no match for me in this line. I see what the Hopetons are after, and I mean to show them that we were first in the field. Don't be concerned, you good, excitable creature, you are no match for such well-drilled people. Let me alone, and before the summer is over we will give the law to the neighborhood!"

# CHAPTER XVI. JOSEPH'S TROUBLE, AND PHILIP'S.

The bare, repulsive, inexorable truth was revealed at last. There was no longer any foothold for doubt, any possibility of continuing his desperate self-deceit. From that day all the joy, the trust, the hope, seemed to fade out of Joseph's life. What had been lost was irretrievable: the delusion of a few months had fixed his fate forever.

His sense of outrage was so strong and keen—so burned upon his consciousness as to affect him like a dull physical pain—that a just and temperate review of his situation was impossible. False in one thing, false in all: that was the single, inevitable conclusion. Of course she had never even loved him. Her coy maiden airs, her warm abandonment to feeling, her very tears and blushes, were artfully simulated: perhaps, indeed, she had laughed in her heart, yea, sneered, at his credulous tenderness! Her assumption of rule, therefore, became an arrogance not to be borne. What right had she, guilty of a crime for which there is no name and no punishment, to reverse the secret justice of the soul, and claim to be rewarded?

So reasoned Joseph to himself, in his solitary broodings; but the spell was not so entirely broken as he imagined. Sternly as he might have resolved in advance, there was a glamour in her mask of cheerfulness and gentleness, which made his resolution seem hard and cruel. In her presence he could not clearly remember his wrongs: the past delusion had been a reality, nevertheless; and he could make no assertion which did not involve his own miserable humiliation. Thus the depth and vital force of his struggle could not be guessed by Julia. She saw only irritable moods, the natural male resistance which she had often remarked in her father,—perhaps, also, the annoyance of giving up certain "romantic" fancies, which she believed to be common to all young men, and never permanent. Even an open rupture could not have pushed them apart so rapidly as this hollow external routine of life.

Joseph took the earliest opportunity of visiting Philip, whom he found busy in forge and foundry. "This would be the life for you!" he said: "we deal only with physical forces, human and elemental: we direct and create power, yet still obey the command to put money in our purses."

"Is that one secret of your strength?" Joseph asked.

"Who told you that I had any?"

"I feel it," said Joseph; and even as he said it he remembered Julia's unworthy suspicion.

"Come up and see Madeline a moment, and the home she has made for me. We get on very well, for brother and sister—especially since her will is about as stubborn as mine."

Madeline was very bright and cheerful, and Joseph, certainly, saw no signs of a stubborn will in her fair face. She was very simply dressed, and busy with some task of needle-work, which she did not lay aside.

"You might pass already for a member of our community," he could not help saying.

"I think your most democratic farmers will accept me," she answered, "when they learn that I am Philip's housekeeper. The only dispute we have had, or are likely to have, is in relation to the salary."

"She is an inconsistent creature, Joseph," said Philip. "I was obliged to offer her as much as she earned by her music-lessons before she would come at all, and now she can't find work enough to balance it."

"How can I, Philip, when you tempt me every day with walks and rides, botany, geology, and sketching from nature?"

So much frank, affectionate confidence showed itself through the playful gossip of the two, that Joseph was at once comforted and pained. "If I had only had a sister!" he sighed to Philip, as they walked down the knoll.

The friends took the valley road, Joseph leading his horse by the bridle. The stream was full to its banks, and crystal clear: shoals of young fishes passed like drifted leaves over the pebbly ground, and the fragrant water-beetles skimmed the surface of the eddies. Overhead the vaults of the great

782

elms and sycamores were filled with the green, delicious illumination of the tender foliage. It was a scene and a season for idle happiness.

Yet the first words Philip spoke, after a long silence, were: "May I speak now?" There was infinite love and pity in his voice. He took Joseph by the hand.

"Yes," the latter whispered.

"It has come," Philip continued; "you cannot hide it from yourself any longer. My pain is that I did not dare to warn you, though at the risk of losing your friendship. There was so little time—"

"You did try to warn me, Philip! I have recalled your words, and the trouble in your face as you spoke, a thousand times. I was a fool, a blind, miserable fool, and my folly has ruined my life!"

"Strange," said Philip, musingly, "that only a perfectly good and pure nature can fall into such a wretched snare. And yet 'Virtue is its own reward,' is dinned into our ears! It is Hell for a single fault: nay, not even a fault, an innocent mistake! But let us see what can be done: is there no common ground whereon your natures can stand together? If there should be a child—"

Joseph shuddered. "Once it seemed too great, too wonderful a hope," he said, "but now, I don't dare to wish for it. Philip, I am too sorely hurt to think clearly: there is nothing to do but to wait. It is a miserable kind of comfort to me to have your sympathy, but I fear you cannot help me."

Philip saw that he could bear no more: his face was pale to the lips and his hands trembled. He led him to the bank, sat down beside him, and laid his arm about his neck. The silence and the caress were more soothing to Joseph than any words; he soon became calm, and remembered an important part of his errand, which was to acquaint Philip with the oil speculation, and to ask his advice.

They discussed the matter long and gravely. With all his questions, and the somewhat imperfect information which Joseph was able to give, Philip could not satisfy himself whether the scheme was a simple swindle or a well-considered business venture. Two or three of the names were respectable, but the chief agent, Kanuck, was unknown to him; moreover, Mr. Blessing's apparent prominence in the undertaking did not inspire him with much confidence.

"How much have you already paid on the stock?" he asked.

"Three instalments, which, Mr. Blessing thinks, is all that will be called for. However, I have the money for a fourth, should it be necessary. He writes to me that the stock has already risen a hundred per cent. in value."

"If that is so," said Philip, "let me advise you to sell half of it, at once. The sum received will cover your liabilities, and the half you retain, as a venture, will give you no further anxiety."

"I had thought of that; yet I am sure that my father-in-law will oppose such a step with all his might. You must know him, Philip; tell me, frankly, your opinion of his character."

"Blessing belongs to a class familiar enough to me," Philip answered; "yet I doubt whether you will comprehend it. He is a swaggering, amiable, magnificent adventurer; never purposely dishonest, I am sure, yet sometimes engaged in transactions that would not bear much scrutiny. His life has been one of ups and downs. After a successful speculation, he is luxurious, open-handed, and absurdly self-confident; his success is soon flung away: he then good-humoredly descends to poverty, because he never believes it can last long. He is unreliable, from his over-sanguine temperament; and yet this very temperament gives him a certain power and influence. Some of our best men are on familiar terms with him. They are on their guard against his pecuniary approaches, they laugh at his extravagant schemes, but they now and then find him useful. I heard Gray, the editor, once speak of him as a man 'filled with available enthusiasms,' and I guess that phrase hits both his strength and his weakness."

On the whole, Joseph felt rather relieved than disquieted. The heart was lighter in his breast as he mounted his horse and rode homewards.

Philip slowly walked forwards, yielding his mind to thoughts wherein

Joseph was an important but not the principal figure. Was there a positive strength, he asked himself, in a wider practical experience of life? Did such experience really strengthen the basis of character which must support a man, when some unexpected moral crisis comes upon him? He knew that he seemed strong, to Joseph; but the latter, so far, was bearing his terrible test with a patience drawn from some source of elemental power. Joseph had simply been ignorant: he had been proud, impatient, and—he now confessed to himself—weakly jealous. In both cases, a mistake had passed beyond the plastic stage where life may still be remoulded: it had hardened into an inexorable fate. What was to be the end of it all?

A light footstep interrupted his reflections. He looked up, and almost started, on finding himself face to face with Mrs. Hopeton.

Her face was flushed from her walk and the mellow warmth of the afternoon. She held a bunch of wild-flowers,—pink azaleas, delicate sigillarias, valerian, and scarlet painted-cup. She first broke the silence by asking after Madeline.

"Busy with some important sewing,—curtains, I fancy. She is becoming an inveterate housekeeper," Philip said.

"I am glad, for her sake, that she is here. And it must be very pleasant for you, after all your wanderings."

"I must look on it, I suppose," Philip answered, "as the only kind of a home I shall ever have,—while it lasts. But Madeline's life must not be mutilated because mine happens to be."

The warm color left Mrs. Hopeton's face. She strove to make her voice cold and steady, as she said: "I am sorry to see you growing so bitter, Mr. Held."

"I don't think it is my proper nature, Mrs. Hopeton. But you startled me out of a retrospect which had exhausted my capacity for self-reproach, and was about to become self-cursing. There is no bitterness quite equal to that of seeing how weakly one has thrown away an irrecoverable fortune."

She stood before him, silent and disturbed. It was impossible not to understand, yet it seemed equally impossible to answer him. She gave one glance at his earnest, dark gray eyes, his handsome manly face, and the sprinkled glosses of sunshine on his golden hair, and felt a chill strike to her heart. She moved a step, as if to end the interview.

"Only one moment, Mrs. Hopeton—Emily!" Philip cried. "We may not meet again—thus—for years. I will not needlessly recall the past. I only mean to speak of my offence,—to acknowledge it, and exonerate you from any share in the misunderstanding which—made us what we are. You cannot feel the burden of an unpardoned fault; but will you not allow me to lighten mine?"

A softer change came over her stately form. Her arm relaxed, and the wild-flowers fell upon the ground.

"I was wrong, first," Philip went on, "in not frankly confiding to you the knowledge of a boyish illusion and disappointment. I had been heartlessly treated: it was a silly affair, not worth the telling now; but the leaven of mistrust it left behind was not fully worked out of my nature. Then, too, I had private troubles, which my pride—sore, just then, from many a trifling prick, at which I should now laugh—led me to conceal. I need not go over the appearances which provoked me into a display of temper as unjust as it was unmanly,—it is enough to say that all circumstances combined to make me impatient, suspicious, fiercely jealous. I never paused to reflect that you could not know the series of aggravations which preceded our misunderstanding. I did not guess how far I was giving expression to them, and unconsciously transferring to you the offences of others. Nay, I exacted a completer surrender of your woman's pride, because a woman had already chosen to make a plaything of my green boy-love. There is no use in speaking of any of the particulars of our quarrel; for I confess to you that I was recklessly, miserably wrong. But the time has come when you can afford to be generous, when you can allow yourself to speak my forgiveness. Not for the sake of anything I might have been to you, but as a true woman, dealing with her brother-man, I ask your pardon!"

Mrs. Hopeton could not banish the memory of the old tenderness which pleaded for Philip in her heart. He had spoken no word which could offend or alarm her: they were safely divided by a gulf which might never be bridged, and perhaps it was well that a purely human reconciliation should now clarify what was turbid in the past, and reunite them by a bond pure, though eternally sad. She came slowly towards him, and gave him her hand.

"All is not only pardoned, Philip," she said, "but it is now doubly my duty to forget it. Do not suppose, however, that I have had no other than reproachful memories. My pride was as unyielding as yours, for it led me to the defiance which you could not then endure. I, too, was haughty and imperious. I recall every word I uttered, and I know that you have not forgotten them. But let there be equal and final justice between us: forget my words, if you can, and forgive me!"

Philip took her hand, and held it softly in his own. No power on earth could have prevented their eyes from meeting. Out of the far-off distance of all dead joys, over all abysses of fate, the sole power which time and will are powerless to tame, took swift possession of their natures. Philip's eyes were darkened and softened by a film of gathering tears: he cried in a broken voice:—

"Yes, pardon!—but I thought pardon might be peace. Forget? Yes, it would be easy to forget the past, if,—O Emily, we have never been parted until now!"

She had withdrawn her hand, and covered her face. He saw, by the convulsive tremor of her frame, that she was fiercely suppressing her emotion. In another moment she looked up, pale, cold, and almost defiant.

"Why should you say more?" she asked. "Mutual forgiveness is our duty, and there the duty ends. Leave me now!"

Philip knew that he had betrayed himself. Not daring to speak another word he bowed and walked rapidly away. Mrs. Hopeton stood, with her hand pressed upon her bosom, until he had disappeared among the farther trees: then she sat down, and let her withheld tears flow freely.

Presently the merry whoops and calls of children met her ear. She gathered together the fallen flowers, rose and took her way across the meadows towards a little stone schoolhouse, at the foot of the nearest hill. Lucy Henderson already advanced to meet her. There was still an hour or two of sunshine, but the mellow, languid heat of the day was over, and the breeze winnowing down the valley brought with it the smell of the blossoming vernal grass.

The two women felt themselves drawn towards each other, though neither had as yet divined the source of their affectionate instinct. Now, looking upon Lucy's pure, gently firm, and reliant face, Mrs. Hopeton, for the second or third time in her life, yielded to a sudden, powerful impulse, and said: "Lucy, I foresee that I shall need the love and the trust of a true woman: where shall I find it if not in you?"

"If mine will content you," said Lucy.

"O my dear!" Mrs. Hopeton cried; "none of us can stand alone. God has singular trials for us, sometimes, and the use and the conquest of a trouble may both become clear in the telling of it. The heart can wear itself out with its own bitterness. You see, I force my confidence upon you, but I know you are strong to receive it."

"At least," Lucy answered, gravely, "I have no claim to strength unless I am willing to have it tested."

"Then let me make the severest test at once: I shall have less courage if I delay. Can you comprehend the nature of a woman's trial, when her heart resists her duty?"

A deep blush overspread Lucy's face, but she forced herself to meet Mrs. Hopeton's gaze. The two women were silent a moment; then the latter threw her arms around Lucy's neck and kissed her.

"Let us walk!" she said. "We shall both find the words we need."

They moved away over the fragrant, shining meadows. Down the valley, at the foot of the blue cape which wooed their eyes, and perhaps suggested to their hearts that mysterious sense of hope which lies in landscape distances, Elwood Withers was directing his gang of workmen. Over the eastern hill,

Joseph Asten stood among his fields, hardly recognizing their joyous growth. The smoke of Philip's forge rose above the trees to the northward. So many disappointed hearts, so many thwarted lives! What strand stall be twisted out of the broken threads of these destinies, thus drawn so near to each other? What new forces—fatal or beneficent—shall be developed from these elements?

Mr. Hopeton, riding homewards along the highway, said to himself: "It's a pleasant country, but what slow, humdrum lives the people lead!"

# CHAPTER XVII. A STORM.

"I have a plan," said Julia, a week or two later. "Can you guess it? No, I think not; yet you might! O, how lovely the light falls on your hair: it is perfect satin!"

She had one hand on his shoulder, and ran the fingers of the other lightly through his brown locks. Her face, sparkling all over with a witching fondness, was lifted towards his. It was the climax of an amiable mood which had lasted three days.

What young man can resist a playful, appealing face, a soft, caressing touch? Joseph smiled as he asked,—

"Is it that I shall wear my hair upon my shoulders, or that we shall sow plaster on the clover-field, as old Bishop advised you the other day?"

"Now you are making fun of my interest in farming; but wait another year! I am trying earnestly to understand it, but only so that ornament—beauty—what was the word in those lines you read last night?—may grow out of use. That's it—Beauty out of Use! I know I've bored you a little sometimes——just a little, now, confess it!—with all my questions; but this is something different. Can't you think of anything that would make our home, O so much more beautiful?"

"A grove of palm-trees at the top of the garden? Or a lake in front, with marble steps leading down to the water?"

"You perverse Joseph! No: something possible, something practicable, something handsome, something profitable! Or, are you so old-fashioned that you think we must drudge for thirty years, and only take our pleasure after we grow rheumatic?"

Joseph looked at her with a puzzled, yet cheerful face.

"You don't understand me yet!" she exclaimed. "And indeed, indeed, I dread to tell you, for one reason: you have such a tender regard for old associations,—not that I'd have it otherwise, if I could. I like it: I trust I have the same feeling; yet a little sentiment sometimes interferes practically with the improvement of our lives."

Joseph's curiosity was aroused. "What do you mean, Julia?" he asked.

"No!" she cried; "I will not tell you until I have read part of pa's letter, which came this afternoon. Take the arm-chair, and don't interrupt me."

She seated herself on the window-sill and opened the letter. "I saw," she said, "how uneasy you felt when the call came for the fourth instalment of ten per cent. on the Amaranth shares, especially after I had so much difficulty in persuading you not to sell the half. It surprised me, although I knew that, where pa is concerned, there's a good reason for everything. So I wrote to him the other day, and this is what he says,—you remember, Kanuck is the company's agent on the spot:—

"'Tell Joseph that in matters of finance there's often a wheel within a wheel. Blenkinsop, of the Chowder Company, managed to get a good grab of our shares through a third party, of whom we had not the slightest suspicion. I name no name at present, from motives of prudence. We only discovered the circumstance after the third party left for Europe. Looking upon the Chowder as a rival, it is our desire, of course, to extract this entering wedge before it has been thrust into our vitals, and we can only accomplish the end by still keeping secret the discovery of the torpedoes (an additional expense, I might remark), and calling for fresh instalments from all the stockholders. Blenkinsop, not being within the inside ring,—and no possibility of his getting in!—will naturally see only the blue of disappointment where we see the rose of realized expectations. Already, so Kanuck writes to me, negotiations are on foot which will relieve our Amaranth of this parasitic growth, and a few weeks—days—hours, in fact, may enable us to explode and triumph! I was offered, yesterday, by one of our shrewdest operators, who has been silently watching us, ten shares of the Sinnemahoning Hematite for eight of ours. Think of that,—the Sinnemahoning Hematite! No better stock in the market, if you remember the quotations! Explain the significance of the figures to your husband, and let him see that he has—but no, I will restrain myself and make no estimate. I will only mention, under the seal of the profoundest secrecy, that the number of shafts now sinking (or being sunk) will give an enormous flowing capacity when the electric spark fires the mine, and I should not wonder if our shares then soared high over the pinnacles of all previous speculation!'

"No, nor I!" Julia exclaimed, as she refolded the letter; "it is certain,—positively certain! I have never known the Sinnemahoning Hematite to be less than 147. What do you say, Joseph?"

"I hope it may be true," he answered. "I can't feel so certain, while an accident—the discovery of the torpedo-plan, for instance—might change the prospects of the Amaranth. It will be a great relief when the time comes to 'realize,' as your father says."

"You only feel so because it is your first experience; but for your sake I will consent that it shall be the last. We shall scarcely need any more than this will bring us; for, as pa says, a mere competence in the city is a splendid fortune in the country. You need leisure for books and travel and society, and you shall have it. Now, let us make a place for both!"

Thereupon she showed him how the parlor and rear bed-room might be thrown into one; where there were alcoves for bookcases and space for a piano; how a new veranda might be added to the western end of the house; how the plastering might be renewed, a showy cornice supplied, and an air of elegant luxury given to the new apartment. Joseph saw and listened, conscious at once of a pang at changing the ancient order of things, and a temptation to behold a more refined comfort in its place. He only asked to postpone the work; but Julia pressed him so closely, with such a multitude of unanswerable reasons, that he finally consented to let a mechanic look at the house, and make an estimate of the expense.

In such cases, the man who deliberates is lost.

His consent once reluctantly exacted, Julia insisting that she would take the whole charge of directing the work, a beginning was made without delay, and in a few days the ruin was so complete that the restoration became a matter of necessity.

Julia kept her word only too faithfully. With a lively, playful manner in the presence of the workmen, but with a cold, inflexible obstinacy when they were alone, she departed from the original plan, adding showy and expensive features, every one of which, Joseph presently saw, was devised to surpass the changes made by the Hopetons in their new residence. His remonstrances produced no effect, and he was precluded from a practical interference by the fear of the workmen guessing his domestic trouble. Thus the days dragged on, and the breach widened without an effort on either side to heal it.

The secret of her temporary fondness gave him a sense of positive disgust when it arose in his memory. He now suspected a selfish purpose in her caresses, and sought to give her no chance of repeating them, but in the company of others he was forced to endure a tenderness which, he was surprised to find, still half deceived him, as it wholly deceived his neighbors. He saw, too,—and felt himself powerless to change the impression,—that Julia's popularity increased with her knowledge of the people, while their manner towards him was a shade less frank and cordial than formerly. He knew that the changes in his home were so much needless extravagance, to them; and that Julia's oft-repeated phrase (always accompanied with a loving look), "Joseph is making the old place so beautiful for me!" increased their mistrust, while seeming to exalt him as a devoted husband.

It is not likely that she specially intended this result; while, on the other hand, he somewhat exaggerated its character. Her object was simply to retain her growing ascendency: within the limits where her peculiar faculties had been exercised she was nearly perfect; but she was indifferent to tracing the consequences of her actions beyond those limits. When she ascertained Mr. Chaffinch's want of faith in Joseph's entire piety, she became more regular in her attendance at his church, not so much to prejudice her husband by the contrast, as to avoid the suspicion which he had incurred. To Joseph, however, in the bitterness of his deception, these actions seemed either hostile or heartless; he was repelled from the clearer knowledge of a nature so foreign to his own. So utterly foreign: yet how near beyond all others it had once seemed!

It was not a jealousy of the authority she assumed which turned his heart from her: it was the revelation of a shallowness and selfishness not at all rare in the class from which she came, but which his pure, guarded youth had never permitted him to suspect in any human being. A man familiar with men and women, if he had been caught in such toils, would have soon discovered some manner of controlling her nature, for the very shrewdest and falsest have their vulnerable side. It gave Joseph, however, so much keen spiritual pain to encounter her in her true character, that such a course was simply impossible.

Meanwhile the days went by; the expense of labor and material had already doubled the estimates made by the mechanics; bills were presented for payment, and nothing was heard from the Amaranth. Money was a necessity, and there was no alternative but to obtain a temporary loan at a county town, the centre of transactions for all the debtors and creditors of the neighboring country. It was a new and disagreeable experience for Joseph to appear in the character of a borrower, and he adopted it most reluctantly; yet the reality was a greater trial than he had suspected. He found that the most preposterous stories of his extravagance were afloat. He was transforming his house into a castle: he had made, lost, and made again a large fortune in petroleum; he had married a wealthy wife and squandered her money; he drove out in a carriage with six white horses; he was becoming irregular in his habits and heretical in his religious views; in short, such marvellous powers of invention had been exercised that the Arab story-tellers were surpassed by the members of that quiet, sluggish community.

It required all his self-control to meet the suspicions of the money-agents, and convince them of the true state of his circumstances. The loan was obtained, but after such a wear and tear of flesh and spirit as made it seem a double burden.

When he reached home, in the afternoon, Julia instantly saw, by his face, that all had not gone right. A slight effort, however, enabled her to say carelessly and cheerfully,—

"Have you brought me my supplies, dear?"

794

"Yes," he answered curtly.

"Here is a letter from pa," she then said. "I opened it, because I knew what the subject must be. But if you're tired, pray don't read it now, for then you may be impatient. There's a little more delay."

"Then I'll not delay to know it," he said, taking the letter from her hand. A printed slip, calling upon the stockholders of the Amaranth to pay a fifth instalment, fell out of the envelope. Accompanying it there was a hasty note from B. Blessing: "Don't be alarmed, my dear son-in-law! Probably a mere form. Blenkinsop still holds on, but we think this will bring him at once. If it don't, we shall very likely have to go on with him, even if it obliges us to unite the Amaranth and the Chowder. In any case, we shall ford or bridge this little Rubicon within a fortnight. Have the money ready, if convenient, but do not forward unless I give the word. We hear, through third parties, that Clementina (who is now at Long Branch) receives much attention from Mr. Spelter, a man of immense wealth, but, I regret to say, no refinement."

Joseph smiled grimly when he finished the note. "Is there never to be an end of humbug?" he exclaimed.

"There, now!" cried Julia; "I knew you'd be impatient. You are so unaccustomed to great operations. Why, the Muchacho Land Grant—I remember it, because pa sold out just at the wrong time—hung on for seven years!"

"D——curse the Muchacho Land Grant, and the Amaranth too!"

"Aren't you ashamed!" exclaimed Julia, taking on a playful air of offence; "but you're tired and hungry, poor fellow!" Therewith she put her hands on his shoulders, and raised herself on tiptoe to kiss him.

Joseph, unable to control his sudden instinct, swiftly turned away his head.

"O you wicked husband, you deserve to be punished!" she cried, giving him what was meant to be a light tap on the cheek.

It was a light tap, certainly; but perhaps a little of the annoyance which she banished from her face had lodged, unconsciously, in her fingers. They left just sting enough to rouse Joseph's heated blood. He started back a step, and looked at her with flaming eyes.

"No more of that, Julia! I know, now, how much your arts are worth. I am getting a vile name in the neighborhood,—losing my property,—losing my own self-respect,—because I have allowed you to lead me! Will you be content with what you have done, or must you go on until my ruin is complete?"

Before he had finished speaking she had taken rapid counsel with herself, and decided. "Oh, oh! such words to me!" she groaned, hiding her face between her hands. "I never thought you could be so cruel! I had such pleasure in seeing you rich and free, in trying to make your home beautiful; and now this little delay, which no business man would think anything of, seems to change your very nature! But I will not think it's your true self: something has worried you to-day,—you have heard some foolish story—"

"It is not the worry of to-day," he interrupted, in haste to state his whole grievance, before his weak heart had time to soften again,—"it is the worry of months past! It is because I thought you true and kind-hearted, and I find you selfish and hypocritical! It is very well to lead me into serious expenses, while so much is at stake, and now likely to be lost,—it is very well to make my home beautiful, especially when you can outshine Mrs. Hopeton! It is easy to adapt yourself to the neighbors, and keep on the right side of them, no matter how much your husband's character may suffer in the process!"

"That will do!" said Julia, suddenly becoming rigid. She lifted her head, and apparently wiped the tears from her eyes. "A little more and it would be too much for even me! What do I care for 'the neighbors'? persons whose ideas and tastes and habits of life are so different from mine? I have endeavored to be friendly with them for your sake: I have taken special pains to accommodate myself to their notions, just because I intended they should justify you in choosing me! I believed—for you told me so—that there was no calculation in love, that money was dross in comparison; and how could I imagine that you would so soon put up a balance and begin to weigh the two? Am I your wife or your slave? Have I an equal share in what is yours, or am I here merely to increase it? If there is to be a question of dollars and cents between us, pray have my allowance fixed, so that I may not overstep it, and may save myself from such reproaches! I knew you would be disappointed in pa's letter: I have been anxious and uneasy since it came, through my sympathy with you, and was ready to make any sacrifice that might relieve your mind; and now you seem to be full of unkindness and injustice! What shall I do, O what shall I do?

She threw herself upon a sofa, weeping hysterically.

"Julia!" he cried, both shocked and startled by her words, "you purposely misunderstand me. Think how constantly I have yielded to you, against my own better judgment! When have you considered my wishes?"

"When?" she repeated: then, addressing the cushion with a hopeless, melancholy air, "he asks, when! How could I misunderstand you? your words were as plain as daggers. If you were not aware how sharp they were, call them back to your mind when these mad, unjust suspicions have left you! I trusted you so perfectly, I was looking forward to such a happy future, and now—now, all seems so dark! It is like a flash of lightning: I am weak and giddy: leave me,—I can bear no more!"

She covered her face, and sobbed wretchedly.

"I am satisfied that you are not as ignorant as you profess to be," was all Joseph could say, as he obeyed her command, and left the room. He was vanquished, he knew, and a little confused by his wife's unexpected way of taking his charges in flank instead of meeting them in front, as a man would have done. Could she be sincere? he asked himself. Was she really so ignorant of herself, as to believe all that she had uttered? There seemed to be not the shadow of hypocrisy in her grief and indignation. Her tears were real: then why not her smiles and caresses? Either she was horribly, incredibly false,—worse than he dared dream her to be,—or so fatally unconscious of her nature that nothing short of a miracle could ever enlighten her. One thing only was certain: there was now no confidence between them, and there might never be again.

He walked slowly forth from the house, seeing nothing, and unconscious whither his feet were leading him.

# CHAPTER XVIII. ON THE RAILROAD TRACK.

Still walking, with bent head, and a brain which vainly strove to work its way to clearness through the perplexities of his heart, Joseph went on. When, wearied at last, though not consciously calmer, he paused and looked about him, it was like waking from a dream. Some instinct had guided him on the way to Philip's forge: the old road had been moved to accommodate the new branch railway, and a rapid ring of hammers came up from the embankment below. It was near the point of the hill where Lucy's schoolhouse stood, and even as he looked she came, accompanied by her scholars, to watch the operation of laying the track. Elwood Withers, hale, sunburnt, full of lusty life, walked along the sleepers directing the workmen.

"He was right,—only too right!" muttered Joseph to himself. "Why could I not see with his eyes? 'It's the bringing up,' he would say; but that is not all. I have been an innocent, confiding boy, and thought that years and acres had made me a man. O, she understood me—she understands me now; but in spite of her, God helping me, I shall yet be a man."

Elwood ran down the steep side of the embankment, greeted Lucy, and helped her to the top, the children following with whoops and cries.

"Would it have been different," Joseph further soliloquized, "if Lucy and I had loved and married? It is hardly treating Elwood fairly to suppose such a thing, yet—a year ago—I might have loved her. It is better as it is: I should have stepped upon a true man's heart. Have they drawn nearer? and if so, does he, with his sturdier nature, his surer knowledge, find no flaw in her perfections?"

A morbid curiosity to watch the two suddenly came upon him. He clambered over the fence, crossed the narrow strip of meadow, and mounted the embankment. Elwood's back was towards him, and he was just saying: "It all comes of taking an interest in what you're doing. The practical part is easy enough, when you once have the principles. I can manage the theodolite already, but I need a little showing when I come to the calculations. Somehow, I never cared much about study before, but here it's all applied as soon as you've learned it, and that fixes it, like, in your head."

Lucy was listening with an earnest, friendly interest on her face. She scarcely saw Joseph until he stood before her. After the first slight surprise, her manner towards him was quiet and composed: Elwood's eyes were bright, and there was a fresh intelligence in his appearance. The habit of command had already given him a certain dignity.

"How can I get knowledge which may be applied as soon as learned?" Joseph asked, endeavoring to assume the manner furthest from his feelings. "I'm still at the foot of the class, Lucy," he added, turning to her.

"How?" Elwood replied. "I should say by going around the world alone. That would be about the same for you as what these ten miles I'm overseeing are to me. A little goes a great way with me, for I can only pick up one thing at a time."

"What kind of knowledge are you looking for, Joseph?" Lucy gravely asked.

"Of myself," said he, and his face grew dark.

"That's a true word!" Elwood involuntarily exclaimed. He then caught Lucy's eye, and awkwardly added: "It's about what we all want, I take it."

Joseph recovered himself in a moment, and proposed looking over the work. They walked slowly along the embankment, listening to Elwood's account of what had been done and what was yet to do, when the Hopeton carriage came up the highway, near at hand. Mrs. Hopeton sat in it alone.

"I was looking for you, Lucy," she called. "If you are going towards the cutting, I will join you there."

She sent the coachman home with the carriage, and walked with them on the track. Joseph felt her presence as a relief, but Elwood confessed to himself that he was a little disturbed by the steady glance of her dark eyes. He had already overcome his regret at the interruption of his rare and welcome chance of talking with Lucy, but then Joseph knew his heart, while this stately lady looked as if she were capable of detecting what she had no right to know. Nevertheless, she was Lucy's friend, and that fact had great weight with Elwood.

"It's rather a pity to cut into the hills and bank up the meadows in this way, isn't it?" he asked.

"And to disturb my school with so much hammering," Lucy rejoined; "when the trains come I must retreat."

"None too soon," said Mrs. Hopeton. "You are not strong, Lucy, and the care of a school is too much for you."

Elwood thanked her with a look, before he knew what he was about.

"After all," said Joseph, "why shouldn't nature be cut up? I suppose everything was given up to us to use, and the more profit the better the use, seems to be the rule of the world. 'Beauty grows out of Use,' you know."

His tone was sharp and cynical, and grated unpleasantly on Lucy's sensitive ear.

"I believe it is a rule in art," said Mrs. Hopeton, "that mere ornament, for ornament's sake, is not allowed. It must always seem to answer some purpose, to have a necessity for its existence. But, on the other hand, what is necessary should be beautiful, if possible."

"A loaf of bread, for instance," suggested Elwood.

They all laughed at this illustration, and the conversation took a lighter turn. By this time they had entered the narrower part of the valley, and on passing around a sharp curve of the track found themselves face to face with Philip and Madeline Held.

If Mrs. Hopeton's heart beat more rapidly at the unexpected meeting, she preserved her cold, composed bearing. Madeline, bright and joyous, was the unconscious agent of unconstraint, in whose presence each of the others felt immediately free.

800

"Two inspecting committees at once!" cried Philip. "It is well for you, Withers, that you didn't locate the line. My sister and I have already found several unnecessary curves and culverts."

"And we have found a great deal of use and no beauty," Lucy answered.

"Beauty!" exclaimed Madeline. "What is more beautiful than to see one's groceries delivered at one's very door? Or to have the opera and the picture-gallery brought within two hours' distance? How far are we from a lemon, Philip?"

"You were a lemon, Mad, in your vegetable, pre-human state; and you are still acid and agreeable."

"Sweets to the sweet!" she gayly cried. "And what, pray, was Miss Henderson?"

"Don't spare me, Mr. Held," said Lucy, as he looked at her with a little hesitation.

"An apple."

"And Mrs. Hopeton?"

"A date-palm," said Philip, fixing his eyes upon her face.

She did not look up, but an expression which he could not interpret just touched her lips and faded.

"Now, it's your turn, Miss Held," Elwood remarked: "what were we men?"

"O, Philip a prickly pear, of course; and you, well, some kind of a nut; and Mr. Asten—"

"A cabbage," said Joseph.

"What vanity! Do you imagine that you are all head,—or that your heart is in your head? Or that you keep the morning dew longer than the rest of us?"

"It might well be," Joseph answered; and Madeline felt her arm gently

801

pinched by Philip, from behind. She had tact enough not to lower her pitch of gayety too suddenly, but her manner towards Joseph became grave and gentle. Mrs. Hopeton said but little: she looked upon the circling hills, as if studying their summer beauty, while the one desire in her heart was to be away from the spot,—away from Philip's haunting eyes.

After a little while, Philip seemed to be conscious of her feeling. He left his place on the opposite side of the track, took Joseph's arm and led him a little aside from the group.

"Philip, I want you!" Joseph whispered; "but no, not quite yet. There is no need of coming to you in a state of confusion. In a day or two more I shall have settled a little."

"You are right," said Philip: "there is no opiate like time, be there never so little of it. I felt the fever of your head in your hand. Don't come to me, until you feel that it is the one thing which must be done! I think you know why I say so."

"I do!" Joseph exclaimed. "I am just now more of an ostrich than anything else; I should like to stick my head in the sand, and imagine myself invisible. But—Philip—here are six of us together. One other, I know, has a secret wound, perhaps two others: is it always so in life? I think I am selfish enough to be glad to know that I am not specially picked out for punishment."

Philip could not help smiling. "Upon my soul," he said, "I believe Madeline is the only one of the six who is not busy with other thoughts than those we all seem to utter. Specially picked out? There is no such thing as special picking out, in this world! Joseph, it may seem hard and schoolmaster-like in me again to say 'wait!' yet that is the only word I can say."

"Good evening, all!" cried Elwood. "I must go down to my men; but I'd be glad of such an inspection as this, a good deal oftener."

"I'll go that far with you," said Joseph.

Mrs. Hopeton took Lucy's arm with a sudden, nervous movement. "If you are not too tired, let us walk over the hill," she said; "I want to find the right point of view for sketching our house."

The company dissolved. Philip, as he walked up the track with his sister, said to himself: "Surely she was afraid of me. And what does her fear indicate? What, if not that the love she once bore for me still lives in her heart, in spite of time and separated fates? I should not, dare not think of her; I shall never again speak a word to her which her husband might not hear; but I cannot tear from me the dream of what she might be, the knowledge of what she is, false, hopeless, fatal, as it all may be!"

"Elwood," said Joseph, when they had walked a little distance in silence, "do you remember the night you spent with me, a year ago?"

"I'm not likely to forget it."

"Let me ask you one question, then. Have you come nearer to Lucy Henderson?"

"If no further off means nearer, and it almost seems so in my case,—yes!"

"And you see no difference in her,—no new features of character, which you did not guess, at first?"

"Indeed, I do!" Elwood emphatically answered. "To me she grows less and less like any other woman,—so right, so straightforward, so honest in all her ways and thoughts! If I am ever tempted to do anything—well, not exactly mean, you know, but such as a man might as well leave undone, I have only to say to myself: 'If you're not thoroughly good, my boy, you'll lose her!' and that does the business, right away. Why, Joseph, I'm proud of myself, that I mean to deserve her!"

"Ah!" A sigh, almost a groan, came from Joseph's lips. "What will you think of me?" he said. "I was about to repeat your own words,—to warn you to be cautious, and take time, and test your feelings, and not to be too sure of her perfection! What can a young man know about women? He can only discover the truth after marriage, and then—they are indifferent how it affects him—their fortunes are made!"

"I know," answered Elwood, turning his head away slightly; "but there's a difference between the women you seek, and work to get, and the women who seek, and work to get you."

"I understand you."

"Forgive me for saying it!" Elwood cried, instantly repenting his words. "I couldn't help seeing and feeling what you know now. But what man—leastways, what friend—could ha' said it to you with any chance of being believed? You were like a man alone in a boat above a waterfall; only you could bring yourself to shore. If I stood on the bank and called, and you didn't believe me, what then? The Lord knows, I'd give this right arm, strong as it is, to put you back where you were a year ago."

"I've been longing for frankness, and I ought to bear it better," said Joseph. "Put the whole subject out of your thoughts, and come and see me as of old. It is quite time I should learn to manage my own life."

He grasped Elwood's hand convulsively, sprang down the embankment, and took to the highway. Elwood looked after him a minute, then slowly shook his head and walked onward towards the men.

Meanwhile, Mrs. Hopeton and Lucy had climbed the hill, and found themselves on the brow of a rolling upland, which fell on the other side towards the old Calvert place. The day was hot. Mrs. Hopeton's knees trembled under her, and she sank on the soft grass at the foot of a tree. Lucy took a seat beside her.

"You know so much of my trouble," said the former, when the coolness and rest had soothed her, "and I trust you so perfectly, that I can tell you all, Lucy. Can you guess the man whom I loved, but must never love again?"

"I have sometimes thought—" but here Lucy hesitated.

"Speak the name in your mind, or, let me say 'Philip Held' for you! Lucy, what am I to do? he loves me still: he told me so, just now, where we were all together below there!"

Lucy turned with a start, and gazed wonderingly upon her friend's face.

804

"Why does he continue telling me what I must not hear? with his eyes, Lucy! in the tones of his voice, in common words which I am forced to interpret by his meaning! I had learned to bear my inevitable fate, for it is not an unhappy one; I can bear even his presence, if he were generous enough to close his heart as I do,—either that, or to avoid me; for I now dread to meet him again."

"Is it not," Lucy asked, "because the trial is new, and takes you by surprise and unprepared? May you not be fearing more than Mr. Held has expressed, or, at least, intended?"

"The speech that kills, or makes alive, needs no words. What I mean is, there is no resistance in his face. I blush for myself, I am indignant at my own pitiful weakness, but something in his look to-day made me forget everything that has passed since we were parted. While it lasted, I was under a spell,—a spell which it humiliates me to remember. Your voices sounded faint and far-off; all that I have, and hold, seemed to be slipping from me. It was only for a moment, but, Lucy, it frightened me. My will is strong, and I think I can depend upon it; yet what if some influence beyond my control were to paralyze it?"

"Then you must try to win the help of a higher will; our souls always win something of that which they wrestle and struggle to reach. Dear Mrs. Hopeton, have you never thought that we are still as children who cannot have all they cry for? Now that you know what you fear, do not dread to hold it before your mind and examine what it is: at least, I think that would be my instinct,—to face a danger at once when I found I could not escape it."

"I have no doubt you are right, Lucy," said Mrs. Hopeton; but her tone was sad, as if she acquiesced without clearly believing.

"It seems very hard," Lucy continued, "when we cannot have the one love of all others that we need, harder still when we must put it forcibly from our hearts. But I have always felt that, when we can bring ourselves to renounce cheerfully, a blessing will follow. I do not know how, but I must believe it. Might it not come at last through the love that we have, though it now seems imperfect?"

Mrs. Hopeton lifted her head from her knees, and sat erect. "Lucy," she said, "I do not believe you are a woman who would ask another to bear what is beyond your own strength. Shall I put you to the test?"

Lucy, though her face became visibly paler, replied: "I did not mean to compare my burden with yours; but weigh me, if you wish. If I am found wanting, you will show me wherein."

"Your one love above all others is lost to you. Have you conquered the desire for it?"

"I think I have. If some soreness remains, I try to believe that it is the want of the love which I know to be possible, not that of the—the person."

"Then could you be happy with what you call an imperfect love?"

Lucy blushed a little, in spite of herself. "I am still free," she answered, "and not obliged to accept it. If I were bound, I hope I should not neglect my duty."

"What if another's happiness depended on your accepting it? Lucy, my eyes have been made keen by what I have felt. I saw to-day that a man's heart follows you, and I guess that you know it. Here is no imperfect love on his part: were you his wife, could you learn to give him so much that your life might become peaceful and satisfied?"

"You do, indeed, test me!" Lucy murmured. "How can I know? What answer can I make? I have shrunk from thinking of that, and I cannot feel that my duty lies there. Yet, if it were so, if I were already bound, irrevocably, surely all my present faith must be false if happiness in some form did not come at last!"

"I believe it would, to you!" cried Mrs. Hopeton. "Why not to me? Do you think I have ever looked for love in my husband? It seems, now, that I have been content to know that he was proud of me. If I seek, perhaps I may find more than I have dreamed of; and if I find,—if indeed and truly I find,—I shall never more lack self-possession and will!"

She rose to her full height, and a flush came over the pallor of her cheeks.

806

"Yes," she continued, "rather than feel again the humiliation of to-day, I will trample all my nature down to the level of an imperfect love!"

"Better," said Lucy, rising also,—"better to bend only for a while to the imperfect, that you may warm and purify and elevate it, until it shall take the place of the perfect in your heart."

The two women kissed each other, and there were tears on the cheeks of both.

## CHAPTER XIX. THE "WHARF-RAT."

On his way home Joseph reviewed the quarrel with a little more calmness, and, while admitting his own rashness and want of tact, felt relieved that it had occurred. Julia now knew, at least, how sorely he had been grieved by her selfishness, and she had thus an opportunity, if she really loved him, of showing whether her nature were capable of change. He determined to make no further reference to the dissension, and to avoid what might lead to a new one. He did not guess, as he approached the house, that his wife had long been watching at the front window, in an anxious, excited state, and that she only slipped back to the sofa and covered her head just before he reached the door.

For a day or two she was silent, and perhaps a little sullen; but the payment of the most pressing bills, the progress of the new embellishments, and the necessity of retaining her affectionate playfulness in the presence of the workmen, brought back her customary manner. Now and then a sharp, indirect allusion showed that she had not forgotten, and had not Joseph closed his teeth firmly upon his tongue, the household atmosphere might have been again disturbed.

Not many days elapsed before a very brief note from Mr. Blessing announced that the fifth instalment would be needed. He wrote in great haste, he said, and would explain everything by a later mail.

Joseph was hardly surprised now. He showed the note to Julia, merely saying: "I have not the money, and if I had, he could scarcely expect me to pay it without knowing the necessity. My best plan will be to go to the city at once."

"I think so, too," she answered. "You will be far better satisfied when you have seen pa, and he can also help you to raise the money temporarily, if it is really inevitable. He knows all the capitalists."

"I shall do another thing, Julia. I shall sell enough of the stock to pay the instalment; nay, I shall sell it all, if I can do so without loss."

"Are you—" she began fiercely, but, checking herself, merely added, "see pa first, that's all I stipulate."

Mr. Blessing had not returned from the Custom-House when Joseph reached the city. He had no mind to sit in the dark parlor and wait; so he plunged boldly into the labyrinth of clerks, porters, inspectors, and tide-waiters. Everybody knew Blessing, but nobody could tell where he was to be found. Finally some one, more obliging than the rest, said: "Try the Wharf-Rat!"

The Wharf-Rat proved to be a "saloon" in a narrow alley behind the Custom-House. On opening the door, a Venetian screen prevented the persons at the bar from being immediately seen, but Joseph recognized his father-in-law's voice, saying, "Straight, if you please!" Mr. Blessing was leaning against one end of the bar, with a glass in his hand, engaged with an individual of not very prepossessing appearance. He remarked to the latter, almost in a whisper (though the words reached Joseph's ears), "You understand, the collector can't be seen every day; it takes time, and—more or less capital. The doorkeeper and others expect to be fed."

As Joseph approached, he turned towards him with an angry, auspicious look, which was not changed into one of welcome so soon that a flash of uncomfortable surprise did not intervene. But the welcome once there, it deepened and mellowed, and became so warm and rich that only a cold, contracted nature could have refused to bathe in its effulgence.

"Why!" he cried, with extended hands, "I should as soon have expected to see daisies growing in this sawdust, or to find these spittoons smelling like hyacinths! Mr. Tweed, one of our rising politicians, Mr. Asten, my son-in-law! Asten, of Asten Hall, I might almost say, for I hear that your mansion is assuming quite a palatial aspect. Another glass, if you please: your throat must be full of dust, Joseph,—pulvis faucibus hæsit, if I might be allowed to change the classic phrase."

Joseph tried to decline, but was forced to compromise on a moderate glass of ale; while Mr. Blessing, whose glass was empty, poured something into it from a black bottle, nodded to Mr. Tweed, and saying, "Always straight!" drank it off.

"You would not suppose," he then said to Joseph, "that this little room, dark as it is, and not agreeably fragrant, has often witnessed the arrangement of political manœuvres which have decided the City, and through the City the State. I have seen together at that table, at midnight, Senator Slocum, and the Honorables Whitstone, Hacks, and Larruper. Why, the First Auditor of the Treasury was here no later than last week! I frequently transact some of the confidential business of the Custom-House within these precincts, as at present."

"Shall I wait for you outside?" Joseph asked.

"I think it will not be necessary. I have stated the facts, Mr. Tweed, and if you accept them, the figures can be arranged between us at any time. It is a simple case of algebra: by taking x, you work out the unknown quantity."

With a hearty laugh at his own smartness, he shook the "rising politician's" hand, and left the Wharf-Rat with Joseph.

"We can talk here as well as in the woods," he said. "Nobody ever hears anything in this crowd. But perhaps we had better not mention the Amaranth by name, as the operation has been kept so very close. Shall we say 'Paraguay' instead, or—still better—'Reading,' which is a very common stock? Well, then, I guess you have come to see me in relation to the Reading?"

Joseph, as briefly as possible, stated the embarrassment he suffered, on account of the continued calls for payment, the difficulty of raising money for the fifth instalment, and bluntly expressed his doubts of the success of the speculation. Mr. Blessing heard him patiently to the end, and then, having collected himself, answered:—

"I understand, most perfectly, your feeling in the matter. Further, I do not deny that in respect to the time of realizing from the Am—Reading, I should say—I have also been disappointed. It has cost me no little trouble to keep my own shares intact, and my stake is so much greater than yours, for it is my all! I am ready to unite with the Chowder, at once: indeed, as one of the directors, I mentioned it at our last meeting, but the proposition, I regret to say, was not favorably entertained. We are dependent, in a great measure, on Kanuck, who is on the spot superintending the Reading; he has been telegraphed to come on, and promises to do so as soon as the funds now called for are forthcoming. My faith, I hardly need intimate, is firm."

"My only resource, then," said Joseph, "will be to sell a portion of my stock, I suppose?"

"There is one drawback to that course, and I am afraid you may not quite understand my explanation. The—Reading has not been introduced in the market, and its real value could not be demonstrated without betraying the secret lever by which we intend hoisting it to a fancy height. We could only dispose of a portion of it to capitalists whom we choose to take into our confidence. The same reason would be valid against hypothecation."

"Have you paid this last instalment?" Joseph suddenly asked.

"N—no; not wholly; but I anticipate a temporary accommodation. If Mr. Spelter deprives me of Clementina, as I hear (through third parties) is daily becoming more probable, my family expenses will be so diminished that I shall have an ample margin; indeed, I shall feel like a large paper copy, with my leaves uncut!"

He rubbed his hands gleefully; but Joseph was too much disheartened to reply.

"This might be done," Mr. Blessing continued. "It is not certain that all the stockholders have yet paid. I will look over the books, and if such be the case, your delay would not be a sporadic delinquency. If otherwise, I will endeavor to gain the consent of my fellow-directors to the introduction of a new capitalist, to whom a small portion of your interest may be transferred. I trust you perceive the relevancy of this caution. We do not mean that our flower shall always blush unseen, and waste its sweetness on the oleaginous air; we only wish to guard against its being 'untimely ripped' (as Shakespeare says) from its parent stalk. I can well imagine how incomprehensible all this may appear to you. In all probability much of your conversation at home, relative to crops and the like, would be to me an unknown dialect. But I should not, therefore, doubt your intelligence and judgment in such matters."

Joseph began to grow impatient. "Do I understand you to say, Mr. Blessing," he asked, "that the call for the fifth instalment can be met by the sale of a part of my stock?"

"In an ordinary case it might not—under the peculiar circumstances of our operation—be possible. But I trust I do not exaggerate my own influence when I say that it is within my power to arrange it. If you will confide it to my hands, you understand, of course, that a slight formality is necessary,—a power of attorney?"

Joseph, in his haste and excitement, had not considered this, or any other legal point: Mr. Blessing was right.

"Then, supposing the shares to be worth only their par value," he said, "the power need not apply to more than one-tenth of my stock?"

Mr. Blessing came into collision with a gentleman passing him. Mutual wrath was aroused, followed by mutual apologies. "Let us turn into the other street," he said to Joseph; "really, our lives are hardly safe in this crowd; it is nearly three o'clock, and the banks will soon be closed."

"It would be prudent to allow a margin," he resumed, after their course had been changed: "the money market is very tight, and if a necessity were suspected, most capitalists are unprincipled enough to exact according to the urgency of the need. I do not say—nor do I at all anticipate—that it would be so in your case; still, the future is a sort of dissolving view, and my suggestion is that of the merest prudence. I have no doubt that double the amount—say one-fifth of your stock—would guard us against all contingencies. If you prefer not to intrust the matter to my hands, I will introduce you to Honeyspoon Brothers, the bankers,—the elder Honeyspoon being a director,—who will be very ready to execute your commission."

What could Joseph do? It was impossible to say to Mr. Blessing's face that he mistrusted him: yet he certainly did not trust! He was weary of plausible

812

phrases, the import of which he was powerless to dispute, yet which were so at variance with what seemed to be the facts of the case. He felt that he was lifted aloft into a dazzling, secure atmosphere, but as often as he turned to look at the wings which upheld him, their plumage shrivelled into dust, and he fell an immense distance before his feet touched a bit of reality.

The power of attorney was given. Joseph declined Mr. Blessing's invitation to dine with him at the Universal Hotel, the Blessing table being "possibly a little lean to one accustomed to the bountiful profusion of the country," on the plea that he must return by the evening train; but such a weariness and disgust came over him that he halted at the Farmers' Tavern, and took a room for the night. He slept until long into the morning, and then, cheered in spirit through the fresh vigor of all his physical functions, started homewards.

# CHAPTER XX. A CRISIS.

Joseph had made half the distance between Oakland Station and his farm, walking leisurely, when a buggy, drawn by an aged and irreproachable gray horse, came towards him. The driver was the Reverend Mr. Chaffinch. He stopped as they met.

"Will you turn back, as far as that tree?" said the clergyman, after greetings had been exchanged. "I have a message to deliver."

"Now," he continued, reining up his horse in the shade, "we can talk without interruption. I will ask you to listen to me with the spiritual, not the carnal ear. I must not be false to my high calling, and the voice of my own conscience calls me to awaken yours."

Joseph said nothing, but the flush upon his face was that of anger, not of confusion, as Mr. Chaffinch innocently supposed.

"It is hard for a young man, especially one wise in his own conceit, to see how the snares of the Adversary are closing around him. We cannot plead ignorance, however, when the Light is there, and we wilfully turn our eyes from it. You are walking on a road, Joseph Asten, it may seem smooth and fair to you, but do you know where it leads? I will tell you: to Death and Hell!"

Still Joseph was silent.

"It is not too late! Your fault, I fear, is that you attach merit to works, as if works could save you! You look to a cold, barren morality for support, and imagine that to do what is called 'right' is enough for God! You shut your eyes to the blackness of your own sinful heart, and are too proud to acknowledge the vileness and depravity of man's nature; but without this acknowledgment your morality (as you call it) is corrupt, your good works (as you suppose them to be) will avail you naught. You are outside the pale of Grace, and while you continue there, knowing the door to be open, there is no Mercy for you!"

The flush on Joseph's face faded, and he became very pale, but he still waited. "I hope," Mr. Chaffinch continued, after a pause, "that your silence is the beginning of conviction. It only needs an awakening, an opening of the eyes in them that sleep. Do you not recognize your guilt, your miserable condition of sin?"

"No!"

Mr. Chaffinch started, and an ugly, menacing expression came into his face.

"Before you speak again," said Joseph, "tell me one thing! Am I indebted for this Catechism to the order—perhaps I should say the request—of my wife?"

"I do not deny that she has expressed a Christian concern for your state; but I do not wait for a request when I see a soul in peril. If I care for the sheep that willingly obey the shepherd, how much more am I commanded to look after them which stray, and which the wolves and bears are greedy to devour!"

"Have you ever considered, Mr. Chaffinch," Joseph rejoined, lifting his head and speaking with measured clearness, "that an intelligent man may possibly be aware that he has an immortal soul,—that the health and purity and growth of that soul may possibly be his first concern in life,—that no other man can know, as he does, its imperfections its needs, its aspirations which rise directly towards God; and that the attempt of a stranger to examine and criticise, and perhaps blacken, this most sacred part of his nature, may possibly be a pious impertinence?"

"Ah, the natural depravity of the heart!" Mr. Chaffinch groaned.

"It is not the depravity, it is the only pure quality which the hucksters of doctrine, the money-changers in God's temple of Man, cannot touch! Shall I render a reckoning to you on the day when souls are judged? Are you the infallible agent of the Divine Mercy? What blasphemy!"

Mr. Chaffinch shuddered. "I wash my hands of you!" he cried. "I have had to deal with many sinners in my day, but I have found no sin which came so directly from the Devil as the pride of the mind. If you were rotten in all your members from the sins of the flesh, I might have a little hope. Verily, it shall go easier with the murderer and the adulterer on that day than with such as ye!"

He gave the horse a more than saintly stroke, and the vehicle rattled away. Joseph could not see the predominance of routine in all that Mr. Chaffinch had said. He was too excited to remember that certain phrases are transmitted, and used without a thought of their tremendous character; he applied every word personally, and felt it as an outrage in all the sensitive fibres of his soul. And who had invoked the outrage? His wife: Mr. Chaffinch had confessed it. What representations had she made?—he could only measure them by the character of the clergyman's charges. He sat down on the bank, sick at heart; it was impossible to go home and meet her in his present frame of mind.

Presently he started up, crying aloud: "I will go to Philip! He cannot help me, I know, but I must have a word of love from a friend, or I shall go mad!"

He retraced his steps, took the road up the valley, and walked rapidly towards the Forge. The tumult in his blood gradually expended its force, but it had carried him along more swiftly than he was aware. When he reached the point where, looking across the valley, now narrowed to a glen, he could see the smoke of the Forge near at hand, and even catch a glimpse of the cottage on the knoll, he stopped. Up to this moment he had felt, not reflected; and a secret instinct told him that he should not submit his trouble to Philip's riper manhood until it was made clear and coherent in his own mind. He must keep Philip's love, at all hazards; and to keep it he must not seem simply a creature of moods and sentiments, whom his friend might pity, but could not respect.

He left the road, crossed a sloping field on the left, and presently found himself on a bank overhanging the stream. Under the wood of oaks and hemlocks the laurel grew in rich, shining clumps; the current, at this point deep, full, and silent, glimmered through the leaves, twenty feet below; the

816

opposite shore was level, and green with an herbage which no summer could wither. He leaned against a hemlock bole, and tried to think, but it was not easy to review the past while his future life overhung him like a descending burden which he had not the strength to lift. Love betrayed, trust violated, aspiration misinterpreted, were the spiritual aspects; a divided household, entangling obligations, a probability of serious loss, were the material evils which accompanied them. He was so unprepared for the change that he could only rebel, not measure, analyze, and cast about for ways of relief.

It was a miserable strait in which he found himself; and the more he thought—or, rather, seemed to think—the less was he able to foresee any other than an unfortunate solution. What were his better impulses, if men persisted in finding them evil? What was life, yoked to such treachery and selfishness? Life had been to him a hope, an inspiration, a sound, enduring joy; now it might never be so again! Then what a release were death!

He walked forward to the edge of the rock. A few pebbles, dislodged by his feet, slid from the brink, and plunged with a bubble and a musical tinkle into the dark, sliding waters. One more step, and the release which seemed so fair might be attained. He felt a morbid sense of delight in playing with the thought. Gathering a handful of broken stones, he let them fall one by one, thinking, "So I hold my fate in my hand." He leaned over and saw a shifting, quivering image of himself projected against the reflected sky, and a fancy, almost as clear as a voice, said: "This is your present self: what will you do with it beyond the gulf, where only the soul superior to circumstances here receives a nobler destiny?"

He was still gazing down at the flickering figure, when a step came upon the dead leaves. He turned and saw Philip, moving stealthily towards him, pale, with outstretched hand. They looked at each other for a moment without speaking.

"I guess your thought, Philip," Joseph then said. "But the things easiest to do are sometimes the most impossible."

"The bravest man may allow a fancy to pass through his mind, Joseph, which only the coward will carry into effect."

817

"I am not a coward!" Joseph exclaimed.

Philip took his hand, drew him nearer, and flinging his arms around him, held him to his heart.

Then they sat down, side by side.

"I was up the stream, on the other side, trolling for trout," said Philip, "when I saw you in the road. I was welcoming your coming, in my heart: then you stopped, stood still, and at last turned away. Something in your movements gave me a sudden, terrible feeling of anxiety: I threw down my rod, came around by the bridge at the Forge, and followed you here. Do not blame me for my foolish dread."

"Dear, dear friend," Joseph cried, "I did not mean to come to you until I seemed stronger and more rational in my own eyes. If that were a vanity, it is gone now: I confess my weakness and ignorance. Tell me, if you can, why this has come upon me? Tell me why nothing that I have been taught, why no atom of the faith which I still must cling to, explains, consoles, or remedies any wrong of my life!"

"Faiths, I suspect," Philip answered, "are, like laws, adapted to the average character of the human race. You, in the confiding purity of your nature, are not an average man: you are very much above the class, and if virtue were its own reward, you would be most exceptionally happy. Then the puzzle is, what's the particular use of virtue?"

"I don't know, Philip, but I don't like to hear you ask the question. I find myself so often on the point of doubting all that was my Truth a little while ago; and yet, why should my misfortunes, as an individual, make the truth a lie? I am only one man among millions who must have faith in the efficacy of virtue. Philip, if I believed the faith to be false, I think I should still say, 'Let it be preached!'"

Joseph related to Philip the whole of his miserable story, not sparing himself, nor concealing the weakness which allowed him to be entangled to such an extent. Philip's brow grew dark as he listened, but at the close of the recital his face was calm, though stern.

818

"Now," said he,—"now put this aside for a little while, and give your ear (and your heart too, Joseph) to my story. Do not compare my fortune with yours, but let us apply to both the laws which seem to govern life, and see whether justice is possible."

Joseph had dismissed his wife's suspicion, after the dinner at Hopeton's, so immediately from his memory, that he had really forgotten it; and he was not only startled, but also a little shocked, by Philip's confession. Still, he saw that it was only the reverse form of his own experience, not more strange, perhaps not more to be condemned, yet equally inevitable.

"Is there no way out of this labyrinth of wrong?" Philip exclaimed. "Two natures, as far apart as Truth and Falsehood, monstrously held together in the most intimate, the holiest of bonds,—two natures destined for each other monstrously kept apart by the same bonds! Is life to be so sacrificed to habit and prejudice? I said that Faith, like Law, was fashioned for the average man: then there must be a loftier faith, a juster law, for the men—and the women—who cannot shape themselves according to the common-place pattern of society,—who were born with instincts, needs, knowledge, and rights—ay, rights!—of their own!"

"But, Philip," said Joseph, "we were both to blame: you through too little trust, I through too much. We have both been rash and impatient: I cannot forget that; and how are we to know that the punishment, terrible as it seems, is disproportioned to the offence?"

"We know this, Joseph,—and who can know it and be patient?— that the power which controls our lives is pitiless, unrelenting! There is the same punishment for an innocent mistake as for a conscious crime. A certain Nemesis follows ignorance, regardless how good and pure may be the individual nature. Had you even guessed your wife's true character just before marriage, your very integrity, your conscience, and the conscience of the world, would have compelled the union, and Nature would not have mitigated her selfishness to reward you with a tolerable life. O no! You would still have suffered as now. Shall a man with a heart feel this horrible injustice, and not rebel? Grant that I am rightly punished for my impatience, my pride, my jealousy, how have you been rewarded for your stainless youth, your innocent trust, your almost miraculous goodness? Had you known the world better, even though a part of your knowledge might have been evil, you would have escaped this fatal marriage. Nothing can be more certain; and will you simply groan and bear? What compensating fortune have you, or can you ever expect to find?"

Joseph was silent at first; but Philip could see, from the trembling of his hands, and his quick breathing, that he was profoundly agitated. "There is something within me," he said, at last, "which accepts everything you say; and yet, it alarms me. I feel a mighty temptation in your words: they could lead me to snap my chains, break violently away from my past and present life, and surrender myself to will and appetite. O Philip, if we could make our lives wholly our own! If we could find a spot—"

"I know such a spot!" Philip cried, interrupting him,—"a great valley, bounded by a hundred miles of snowy peaks; lakes in its bed; enormous hillsides, dotted with groves of ilex and pine; orchards of orange and olive; a perfect climate, where it is bliss enough just to breathe, and freedom from the distorted laws of men, for none are near enough to enforce them! If there is no legal way of escape for you, here, at least, there is no force which can drag you back, once you are there: I will go with you, and perhaps—perhaps—"

Philip's face glowed, and the vague alarm in Joseph's heart took a definite form. He guessed what words had been left unspoken.

"If we could be sure!" he said.

"Sure of what? Have I exaggerated the wrong in your case? Say we should be outlaws there, in our freedom!—here we are fettered outlaws."

"I have been trying, Philip, to discover a law superior to that under which we suffer, and I think I have found it. If it be true that ignorance is equally punished with guilt; if causes and consequences, in which there is neither pity nor justice, govern our lives,—then what keeps our souls from despair but the infinite pity and perfect justice of God? Yes, here is the difference between human and divine law! This makes obedience safer than rebellion. If you and

I, Philip, stand above the level of common natures, feeling higher needs and claiming other rights, let us shape them according to the law which is above, not that which is below us!"

Philip grew pale. "Then you mean to endure in patience, and expect me to do the same?" he asked.

"If I can. The old foundations upon which my life rested are broken up, and I am too bewildered to venture on a random path. Give me time; nay, let us both strive to wait a little. I see nothing clearly but this: there is a Divine government, on which I lean now as never before. Yes, I say again, the very wrong that has come upon us makes God necessary!"

It was Philip's turn to be agitated. There was a simple, solemn conviction in Joseph's voice which struck to his heart. He had spoken from the heat of his passion, it is true, but he had the courage to disregard the judgment of men, and make his protest a reality. Both natures shared the desire, and were enticed by the daring of his dream; but out of Joseph's deeper conscience came a whisper, against which the cry of passion was powerless.

"Yes, we will wait," said Philip, after a long pause. "You came to me, Joseph, as you said, in weakness and confusion: I have been talking of your innocence and ignorance. Let us not measure ourselves in this way. It is not experience alone which creates manhood. What will become of us I cannot tell, but I will not, I dare not, say you are wrong!"

They took each other's hands. The day was fading, the landscape was silent, and only the twitter of nesting birds was heard in the boughs above them. Each gave way to the impulse of his manly love, rarer, alas! but as tender and true as the love of woman, and they drew nearer and kissed each other. As they walked back and parted on the highway, each felt that life was not wholly unkind, and that happiness was not yet impossible.

# CHAPTER XXI. UNDER THE WATER.

Joseph said nothing that evening concerning the result of his trip to the city, and Julia, who instantly detected the signs which a powerful excitement had left upon his face, thought it prudent to ask no immediate questions. She was purposely demonstrative in little arrangements for his comfort, but spared him her caresses; she did not intend to be again mistaken in choosing the time and occasion of bestowing them.

The next morning, when he felt that he could speak calmly, Joseph told her what he had done, carefully avoiding any word that might seem to express disappointment, or even doubt.

"I hope you are satisfied that pa will make it easy for you?" she ventured to say.

"He thinks so." Then Joseph could not help adding: "He depends, I imagine, upon your sister Clementina marrying a Mr. Spelter,—'a man of immense wealth, but, I regret to say, no refinement.'"

Julia bit her lip, and her eyes assumed that hard, flinty look which her husband knew so well. "If Clementina marries immense wealth," she exclaimed, with a half-concealed sneer, "she will become simply insufferable! But what difference can that make in pa's business affairs?"

The answer tingled on Joseph's tongue: "Probably he expects Mr. Spelter to indorse a promissory note"; but he held it back. "What I have resolved to do is this," he said. "In a day or two—as soon as I can arrange to leave—I shall make a journey to the oil region, and satisfy myself where and what the Amaranth is. Your own practical instincts will tell you, Julia, that this intention of mine must be kept secret, even from your father."

She leaned her head upon her hand, and appeared to reflect. When she looked up her face had a cheerful, confiding expression.

"I think you are right," she then said. "If—if things should not happen to be quite as they are represented, you can secure yourself against any risk—and pa, too—before the others know of it. You will have the inside track; that is, if there is one. On the other hand, if all is right, pa can easily manage, if some of the others are shaky in their faith, to get their stock at a bargain. I am sure he would have gone out there himself, if his official services were not so important to the government."

It was a hard task for Joseph to keep his feelings to himself.

"And now," she continued,—"now I know you will agree to a plan of mine, which I was going to propose. Lucy Henderson's school closes this week, and Mrs. Hopeton tells me she is a little overworked and ailing. It would hardly help her much to go home, where she could not properly rest, as her father is a hard, avaricious man, who can't endure idleness, except, I suppose, in a corpse (so these people seem to me). I want to ask Lucy to come here. I think you always liked her" (here Julia shot a swift, stealthy glance at Joseph), "and so she will be an agreeable guest for both of us. She shall just rest and grow strong. While you are absent, I shall not seem quite so lonely. You may be gone a week or more, and I shall find the separation very hard to bear, even with her company."

"Why has Mrs. Hopeton not invited her?" Joseph asked.

"The Hopetons are going to the sea-shore in a few days. She would take Lucy as a guest, but there is one difficulty in the way. She thinks Lucy would accept the trip and the stay there as an act of hospitality, but that she cannot (or thinks she cannot) afford the dresses that would enable her to appear in Mrs. Hopeton's circle. But it is just as well: I am sure Lucy would feel more at home here."

"Then by all means ask her!" said Joseph. "Lucy Henderson is a noble girl, for she has forced a true-hearted man to love her, without return."

"Ind-e-e-d!"

Julia's drawl denoted surprise and curiosity, but Joseph felt that once more he had spoken too quickly. He endeavored to cover his mistake by a hearty acquiescence in the plan, which was speedily arranged between them, in all its details, Lucy's consent being taken for granted.

It required, however, the extreme of Julia's powers of disguise, aided by Joseph's frank and hearty words and Mrs. Hopeton's influence, to induce Lucy to accept the invitation. Unable to explain wholly to herself, much less mention to any other, the instinct which held her back, she found herself, finally, placed in a false position, and then resolved to blindly trust that she was doing right, inasmuch as she could not make it clear that she was doing wrong. Her decision once taken, she forcibly banished all misgivings, and determined to find nothing but a cheerful and restful holiday before her.

And, indeed, the first day or two of her residence at the farm, before Joseph's departure, brought her a more agreeable experience than she had imagined. Both host and hostess were busy, the latter in the household and the former in the fields, and when they met at meals or in the evening, her presence was an element which compelled an appearance of harmony. She was surprised to find so quiet and ordered a life in two persons whom she had imagined to be miserably unfitted for each other, and began to suspect that she had been seriously mistaken.

After Joseph left, the two women were much together. Julia insisted that she should do nothing, and amiably protested at first against Lucy giving her so much of her society; but, little by little, the companionship was extended and became more frank and intimate. Lucy was in a charitable mood, and found it very easy to fancy that Julia's character had been favorably affected by the graver duties which had come with her marriage. Indeed, Julia found many indirect ways of hinting as much: she feared she had seemed flighty (perhaps a little shallow); looking back upon her past life she could see that such a charge would not be unjust. Her education had been so superficial; all city education of young women was false; they were taught to consider external appearances, and if they felt a void in their nature which these would not fill, whither could they turn for counsel or knowledge?

Her face was sad and thoughtful while she so spoke; but when, shaking her dark curls with a pretty impatience, she would lift her head and ask, with a smile: "But it is not too late, in my case, is it? I'm really an older child, you know,"—Lucy could only answer: "Since you know what you need, it can never be too late. The very fact that you do know, proves that it will be easy for you."

Then Julia would shake her head again, and say, "O, you are too kind, Lucy; you judge my nature by your own."

When the friendly relation between them had developed a little further, Julia became—though still with a modest reticence—more confiding in relation to Joseph.

"He is so good, so very, very true and good," she said, one day, "that it grieves me, more than I can tell, to be the cause of a little present anxiety of his. As it is only a business matter, some exaggerated report of which you have probably heard (for I know there have been foolish stories afloat in the neighborhood), I have no hesitation about confiding it to you. Perhaps you can advise me how to atone for my error; for, if it was an error, I fear it cannot be remedied now; if not, it will be a relief to me to confess it."

Thereupon she gave a minute history of the Amaranth speculation, omitting the energy of her persuasion with Joseph, and presenting very strongly her father's views of a sure and splendid success soon to follow. "It was for Joseph's sake," she concluded, "rather than my own, that I advised the investment; though, knowing his perfect unselfishness, I fear he complied only for mine. He had guessed already, it seems to me now, that we women like beauty as well as comfort about our lives; otherwise, he would hardly have undertaken these expensive improvements of our home. But, Lucy, it terrifies me to think that pa and Joseph and I may have been deceived! The more I shut my mind against the idea the more it returns to torment me. I, who brought so little to him, to be the instrument of such a loss! O, if you were not here, how could I endure the anxiety and the absence?"

She buried her face in her handkerchief, and sobbed.

"I know Joseph to be good and true," said Lucy, "and I believe that he will bear the loss cheerfully, if it should come. But it is never good to 'borrow trouble,' as we say in the country. Neither the worst nor the best things which we imagine ever come upon us."

"You are wrong!" cried Julia, starting up and laughing gleefully; "I have the best thing, in my husband! And yet, you are right, too: no worst thing can come to me, while I keep him!"

Lucy wished to visit the Hopetons before their departure for the sea-shore, and Julia was quite ready to accompany her. Only, with the wilfulness common to all selfish natures, she determined to arrange the matter in her own way. She drove away alone the next morning to the post-office, with a letter for Joseph, but never drew rein until she had reached Coventry Forge. Philip being absent, she confided to Madeline Held her wish (and Lucy's) that they should all spend an afternoon together, on the banks of the stream,—a free society in the open air instead of a formal one within doors. Madeline entered into the plan with joyous readiness, accepting both for herself and for Philip. They all met together too rarely, she said: a lunch or a tea under the trees would be delightful: there was a little skiff which might be borrowed, and they might even catch and cook their own fish, as the most respectable people did in the Adirondacks.

Julia then drove to the Hopetons in high spirits. Mr. Hopeton found the proposed party very pleasant, and said at once to his wife: "We have still three days, my dear: we can easily spare to-morrow?"

"Mrs. Asten is very kind," she replied; "and her proposition is tempting: but I should not like to go without you, and I thought your business might—"

"O, there is nothing pressing," he interrupted. "I shall enjoy it exceedingly, especially the boat, and the chance of landing a few trout."

So it was settled. Lucy, it is true, felt a dissatisfaction which she could scarcely conceal, and possibly did not, to Julia's eyes; but it was not for her own sake. She must seem grateful for a courtesy meant to favor both herself and her friend, and a little reflection reconciled her to the plan. Mrs. Hopeton dared not avoid Philip Held, and it might be well if she carried away with her to the sea-shore a later and less alarming memory of him. Lucy's own desire for a quiet talk with the woman in whom she felt such a loving interest was of no consequence, if this was the result.

They met in the afternoon, on the eastern side of the stream, just below the Forge, where a little bay of level shore, shaded by superb trees, was left between the rocky bluffs. Stumps and a long-fallen trunk furnished them with rough tables and seats; there was a natural fireplace among some huge tumbled stones; a spring of icy crystal gushed out from the foot of the bluff; and the shimmering, murmuring water in front, with the meadows beyond burning like emerald flame in the sunshine, offered a constant delight to the senses.

All were enchanted with the spot, which Philip and Madeline claimed as their discovery. The gypsy spirit awoke in them, and while they scattered here and there, possessed with the influences of the place, and constantly stumbling upon some new charm or convenience, Lucy felt her heart grow light for her friend, and the trouble of her own life subside. For a time no one seemed to think of anything but the material arrangements. Mr. Hopeton's wine-flasks were laid in the spring to cool; Philip improvised a rustic table upon two neighboring stumps; rough seats were made comfortable, dry sticks collected for fire-wood, stores unpacked and placed in readiness, and every little preliminary of labor, insufferable in a kitchen, took on its usual fascination in that sylvan nook.

Then they rested from their work. Mr. Hopeton and Philip lighted cigars and sat to leeward, while the four ladies kept their fingers busy with bunches of maiden-hair and faint wildwood blossoms, as they talked. It really seemed as if a peace and joy from beyond their lives had fallen upon them. Madeline believed so, and Lucy hoped so: let us hope so, too, and not lift at once the veil which was folded so closely over two restless hearts!

Mr. Hopeton threw away the stump of his cigar, adjusted his fishing-tackle, and said: "If we are to have a trout supper, I must begin to troll at once."

"May I go with you?" his wife asked.

"Yes," he answered, smiling, "if you will not be nervous. But I hardly need to make that stipulation with you, Emily."

Philip assisted her into the unsteady little craft, which was fastened to a tree. Mr. Hopeton seated himself carefully, took the two light, short oars, and held himself from the shore, while Philip loosened the rope.

"I shall row up stream," he said, "and then float back to you, trolling as I come. When I see you again, I hope I can ask you to have the coals ready."

Slowly, and not very skilfully, he worked his way against the current, and passed out of sight around a bend in the stream. Philip watched Mrs. Hopeton's slender figure as she sat in the stern, listlessly trailing one hand in the water. "Does she feel that my eyes, my thoughts, are following her?" he asked; but she did not once turn her head.

"Philip!" cried Madeline, "here are three forlorn maidens, and you the only Sir Isumbras, or whoever is the proper knight! Are you looking into the stream, expecting the 'damp woman' to arise? She only rises for fishermen: she will come up and drag Mr. Hopeton down. Let me invoke the real nymph of this stream!" She sang:—

> "Sabrina fair,
>
> Listen where thou art sitting
>
> Under the glassy, cool, translucent wave,
>
> In twisted braids of lilies knitting
>
> The loose train of thy amber-dropping hair;
>
> Listen for dear honor's sake,
>
> Goddess of the silver lake,
>
> Listen and save!"

Madeline did not know what she was doing. She could not remark Philip's paleness in the dim green light where they sat, but she was struck by the startled expression of his eyes.

"One would think you really expected Sabrina to come," she laughed.

"Miss Henderson, too, looks as if I had frightened her. You and I, Mrs. Asten, are the only cool, unimaginative brains in the party. But perhaps it was all owing to my poor voice? Come now, confess it! I don't expect you to say,—

'Can any mortal mixture of earth's mould

Breathe such divine, enchanting ravishment?'"

"I was trying to place the song," said Lucy; "I read it once."

"If any one could evoke a spirit, Madeline," Philip replied, "it would be you. But the spirit would be no nymph; it would have little horns and hoofs, and you would be glad to get rid of it again."

They all laughed at this, and presently, at Julia's suggestion, arranged the wood they had collected, and kindled a fire. It required a little time and patience to secure a strong blaze, and in the great interest which the task called forth the Hopetons were forgotten.

At last Philip stepped back, heated and half stifled, for a breath of fresher air, and, turning, saw the boat between the trees gliding down the stream. "There they are!" he cried; "now, to know our luck!"

Tho boat was in midstream, not far from a stony strip which rose above the water. Mrs. Hopeton sat musing with her hands in her lap, while her husband, resting on his knees and one hand, leaned over the bow, watching the fly which trailed at the end of his line. He seemed to be quite unconscious that an oar, which had slowly loosened itself from the lock, was floating away behind the boat.

"You are losing your oars!" Philip cried.

Mr. Hopeton started, as from a dream of trout, dropped his line and stretched forward suddenly to grasp the oar. The skiff was too light and unbalanced to support the motion. It rocked threateningly; Mrs. Hopeton, quite forgetting herself, started to her feet, and, instantly losing her equilibrium, was thrown headlong into the deeper water. The skiff whirled back, turned over, and before Mr. Hopeton was aware of what had happened, he plunged full length, face downwards, into the shallower current.

It was all over before Madeline and Lucy reached the bank, and Philip was already in the stream. A few strokes brought him to Mrs. Hopeton, who struggled with the current as she rose to the surface, but made no outcry. No sooner had she touched Philip than she seized and locked him in her arms, and he was dragged down again with her. It was only the physical clinging to life: if some feeble recognition at that moment told her whose was the form she held and made powerless, it could not have abated an atom of her frantic, instinctive force.

Philip felt that they had drifted into water beyond his depth. With great exertion he freed his right arm and sustained himself and her a moment at the surface. Mrs. Hopeton's head was on his shoulder; her hair drifted against his face, and even the desperation of the struggle could not make him insensible to the warmth of her breast upon his own. A wild thought flashed upon and stung his brain: she was his at last—his in death, if not in life!

His arm slackened, and they sank slowly together. Heart and brain were illuminated with blinding light, and the swift succession of his thoughts compressed an age into the fragment of a second. Yes, she was his now: clasping him as he clasped, their hearts beating against each other, with ever slower pulsations, until they should freeze into one. The world, with its wrongs and prejudices, lay behind them; the past was past, and only a short and painless atonement intervened between the immortal possession of souls! Better that it should end thus: he had not sought this solution, but he would not thrust it from him.

But, even as his mind accepted it, and with a sense of perfect peace, He heard Joseph's voice, saying, "We must shape our lives according to the law which is above, not that which is below us." Through the air and the water, on the very rock which now overhung his head, he again saw Joseph bending, and himself creeping towards him with outstretched hand. Ha! who was the coward now? And again Joseph spake, and his words were: "The very wrong that has come upon us makes God necessary." God? Then how would God in his wisdom fashion their future life? Must they sweep eternally, locked in an unsevering embrace, like Paolo and Francesca, around some dreary circle of hell? Or must the manner of entering that life together be the act to separate them eternally? Only the inevitable act dare ask for pardon; but here, if not will or purpose, was at least submission without resistance! Then it seemed to him that Madeline's voice came again to him, ringing like a trumpet through the waters, as she sang:—

"Listen for dear honor's sake,

Goddess of the silver lake,

Listen and save!"

He pressed his lips to Mrs. Hopeton's unconscious brow, his heart saying, "Never, never again!" released himself by a sudden, powerful effort, seized her safely, as a practised swimmer, shot into light and air, and made for the shallower side of the stream. The upturned skiff was now within reach, and all danger was over.

Who could guess that the crisis of a soul had been reached and passed in that breath of time under the surface? Julia's long, shrill scream had scarcely come to an end; Mr. Hopeton, bewildered by his fall, was trying to run towards them through water up to his waist, and Lucy and Madeline looked on, holding their breath in an agony of suspense. In another moment Philip touched bottom, and raising Mrs. Hopeton in his arms, carried her to the opposite bank.

She was faint and stunned, but not unconscious. She passively allowed Philip to support her until Mr. Hopeton, struggling through the shallows, drew near with an expression of intense terror and concern on his broad face. Then, breaking from Philip, she half fell, half flung herself into his arms, laid her head upon his shoulder, and burst into a fit of hysterical weeping.

Tears began to run down the honest man's cheeks, and Philip, turning away, busied himself with righting the boat and recovering the oars.

"O, my darling!" said Mr. Hopeton, "what should I do if I had lost you?"

"Hold me, keep me, love me!" she cried. "I must not leave you!"

He held her in his arms, he kissed her, he soothed her with endearing words. She grew calm, lifted her head, and looked in his eyes with a light which he had never yet seen in them. The man's nature was moved and stirred: his lips trembled, and the tears still slowly trickled from his eyes.

"Let me set you over!" Philip called from the stream. "The boat is wet, but then neither of us is dry. We have, fortunately, a good fire until the carriage can be brought for Mrs. Hopeton, and your wine will be needed at once."

They had no trout, nor indeed any refreshment, except the wine. Philip tried to rally the spirits of the party, but Julia was the only one who at all seconded his efforts; the others had been too profoundly agitated. Mr. and Mrs. Hopeton were grave; it seemed scarcely possible for them to speak, and yet, as Lucy remarked with amazement, the faces of both were bright and serene.

"I shall never invoke another water-nymph," said Madeline, as they were leaving the spot.

"Yes!" Philip cried, "always invoke Sabrina, and the daughter of Locrine will arise for you, as she arose to-day."

"That is, not at all?"

"No," said Philip, "she arose."

# CHAPTER XXII. KANUCK.

When he set forth upon his journey, Joseph had enough of natural shrewdness to perceive that his own personal interest in the speculation were better kept secret. The position of the Amaranth property, inserted like a wedge between the Fluke and Chowder Companies, was all the geography he needed; and he determined to assume the character of a curious traveller,—at least for a day or two,—to keep his eyes and ears open, and learn as much as might be possible to one outside the concentric "rings" of oil operations.

He reached Corry without adventure, and took passage in the train to Oil City, intending to make the latter place the starting-point of his investigations. The car was crowded, and his companion on the seat was a keen, witty, red-faced man, with an astonishing diamond pin and a gold watch-chain heavy enough to lift an anchor. He was too restless, too full of "operative" energy, to travel in silence, as is the universal and most dismal American habit; and before they passed three stations he had extracted from Joseph the facts that he was a stranger, that he intended visiting the principal wells, and that he might possibly (Joseph allowing the latter point to be inferred) be tempted to invest something, if the aspects were propitious.

"You must be sure to take a look at my wells," said the stranger; "not that any of our stock is in the market,—it is never offered to the public, unless accidentally,—but they will give you an illustration of the magnitude of the business. All wells, you know, sink after a while to what some people call the normal flowing capacity (we oilers call it 'the everidge run'), and so it was reported of ourn. But since we've begun to torpedo them, it's almost equal to the first tapping, though I don't suppose it'll hold out so long."

"Are the torpedoes generally used?" Joseph asked, in some surprise.

"They're generally tried, anyhow. The cute fellow who first hit upon the idea meant to keep it dark, but the oilers, you'll find, have got their teeth skinned, and what they can't find out isn't worth finding out! Lord! I torpedoed my wells at midnight, and it wasn't a week before the Fluke was at it, bustin' and bustin' all their dry auger-holes!"

"The what!" Joseph exclaimed.

"Fluke. Queer name, isn't it? But that's nothing: we have the Crinoline, the Pipsissaway, the Mud-Lark, and the Sunburst, between us and Tideoute."

"What is the name of your company, if I may ask?"

"About as queer as any of 'em,—the Chowder."

Joseph started, in spite of himself. "It seems to me I have heard of that company," he managed to say.

"O no doubt," replied the stranger. "'T isn't often quoted in the papers, but it's known. I'm rather proud of it, for I got it up. I was boring—boss, though—at three dollars a day, two years ago, and now I have my forty thousand a year, 'free of income tax,' as the Insurance Companies say. But then, where one is lucky like the Chowder, a hundred busts."

Joseph rapidly collected himself while the man was speaking. "I should very much like to see your wells," he said. "Will you be there a day or two from now? My name is Asten,—not that you have ever heard of it before."

"Shall be glad to hear it again, though, and to see you," said the man. "My name is Blenkinsop."

Again it was all that Joseph could do to restrain his astonishment.

"I suppose you are the President of the Chowder?" he ventured to say.

"Yes," Mr. Blenkinsop answered, "since it's a company. It was all mine at the start, but I wanted capital, and I had to work 'em."

"What other important companies are there near you?"

"None of any account, except the Fluke and the Depravity. They flow tolerable now, after torpedoing. To be sure, there are kites and catches with all sorts o' names,—the Penny-royal, the Ruby, the Wallholler (whatever that is), and the Amaranth,—ha, ha!"

834

"I think I have heard of the Amaranth," Joseph mildly remarked.

"Lord! are you bit already?" Mr. Blenkinsop exclaimed, fixing his small, sharp eyes on Joseph's face.

"I—I really don't know what you mean."

"No offence: I thought it likely, that's all. The Amaranth is Kanuck's last dodge. He keeps mighty close, but if he don't feather his nest in a hurry, at somebody's expense, I ain't no judge o' men!"

Joseph did not dare to mention the Amaranth again. He parted with Mr. Blenkinsop at Tarr Farm, and went on to Oil City, where he spent a day in unprofitable wanderings, and then set out up the river, first to seek the Chowder wells, and afterwards to ascertain whether there was any perennial beauty in the Amaranth.

The first thing which he remarked was the peculiar topography of the region. The Chowder property was a sloping bottom, gradually rising from the river to a range of high hills a quarter of a mile in the rear. Just above this point the river made a sharp horseshoe bend, washing the foot of the hills for a considerable distance, and then curving back again, with a second tract of bottom-land beyond. On the latter, he was informed, the Fluke wells were located. The inference was therefore irresistible that the Amaranth Company must be the happy possessor of the lofty section of hills dividing the two.

"Do they get oil up there?" he asked of Blenkinsop's foreman, pointing to the ragged, barren heights.

"They may get skunk oil, or rattlesnake oil," the man answered. "Them'll do to peddle, but you can't fill tanks with 'em. I hear they've got a company for that place,—th' Amaranth, they call it,—but any place'll do for derned fools. Why, look 'ee here! We've got seven hundred feet to bore: now, jest put twelve hundred more atop o' that, and guess whether they can even pump oil, with the Chowder and Fluke both sides of 'em! But it does for green 'uns, as well as any other place."

Joseph laughed,—a most feeble, unnatural, ridiculous laugh.

"I'll walk over that way to the Fluke," he said. "I should like to see how such things are managed."

"Then be a little on your guard with Kanuck, if you meet him," the man good-naturedly advised. "Don't ask him too many questions."

It was a hot, wearisome climb to the timber-skeletons on the summit (more like gibbets than anything else), which denoted shafts to the initiated as well as the ignorant eye. There were a dozen or more, but all were deserted.

Joseph wandered from one to the other, asking himself, as he inspected each, "Is this the splendid speculation?" What was there in that miserable, shabby, stony region, a hundred acres of which would hardly pasture a cow, whence wealth should come? Verily, as stony and as barren were the natures of the men, who on this wretched basis built their cheating schemes!

A little farther on he came to a deep ravine, cleaving the hills in twain. There was another skeleton in its bed, but several shabby individuals were gathered about it,—the first sign of life or business he had yet discovered.

He hastened down the steep declivity, the warning of the Chowder foreman recurring to his mind, yet it seemed so difficult to fix his policy in advance that he decided to leave everything to chance. As he approached he saw that the men were laborer's, with the exception of a tall, lean individual, who looked like an unfortunate clergyman. He had a sallow face, lighted by small, restless, fiery eyes, which reminded Joseph, when they turned upon him, of those of a black snake. His greeting was cold and constrained, and his manner said plainly, "The sooner you leave the better I shall be satisfied."

"This is a rough country for walking," said Joseph; "how much farther is it to the Fluke wells?"

"Just a bit," said one of the workmen.

Joseph took a seat on a stone, with the air of one who needed rest. "This well, I suppose," he remarked, "belongs to the Amaranth?"

"Who told you so?" asked the lean, dark man.

"They said below, at the Chowder, that the Amaranth was up here."

836

"Did Blenkinsop send you this way?" the man asked again.

"Nobody sent me," Joseph replied. "I am a stranger, taking a look at the oil country. I have never before been in this part of the State."

"May I ask your name?"

"Asten," said Joseph, unthinkingly.

"Asten! I think I know where that name belongs. Let me see."

The man pulled out a large dirty envelope from his breast-pocket, ran over several papers, unfolded one, and presently asked,—

"Joseph Asten?"

"Yes." (Joseph set his teeth, and silently cursed his want of forethought.)

"Proprietor of ten thousand dollars' worth of stock in the Amaranth! Who sent you here?"

His tone, though meant to be calm, was fierce and menacing. Joseph rose, scanned the faces of the workmen, who listened with a malicious curiosity, and finally answered, with a candor which seemed to impress, while it evidently disappointed the questioner:—

"No one sent me, and no one, beyond my own family, knows that I am here. I am a farmer, not a speculator. I was induced to take the stock from representations which have not been fulfilled, and which, I am now convinced, never will be fulfilled. My habit is, when I cannot get the truth from others, to ascertain it for myself. I presume you are Mr. Kanuck?"

The man did not answer immediately, but the quick, intelligent glance of one of the workmen showed Joseph that his surmise was correct. Mr. Kanuck conversed apart with the men, apparently giving private orders, and then, said, with a constrained civility:—

"If you are bound for the Fluke, Mr. Asten, I will join you. I am also going in that direction, and we can talk on the way."

They toiled up the opposite side of the ravine in silence. When they had reached the top and taken breath, Mr. Kanuck commenced:—

"I must infer that you have little faith in anything being realized from the Amaranth. Any man, ignorant of the technicalities of boring, might be discouraged by the external appearance of things; and I shall therefore not endeavor to explain to you my grounds of hope, unless you will agree to join me for a month or two and become practically acquainted with the locality and the modes of labor."

"That is unnecessary," Joseph replied.

"You being a farmer, of course I could not expect it. On the other hand, I think I can appreciate your,—disappointment, if we must call it so, and I should be willing, under certain conditions, to save you, not from positive loss, because I do not admit the possibility of that, but from what, at present, may seem loss to you. Do I make my meaning clear?"

"Entirely," Joseph replied, "except as to the conditions."

"We are dealing on the square, I take it?"

"Of course."

"Then," said Mr. Kanuck, "I need only intimate to you how important it is that I should develop our prospects. To do this, the faith of the principal stockholders must not be disturbed, otherwise the funds without which the prospects cannot be developed may fail me at the critical moment. Your hasty and unintelligent impressions, if expressed in a reckless manner, might do much to bring about such a catastrophe. I must therefore stipulate that you keep such impressions to yourself. Let me speak to you as man to man, and ask you if your expressions, not being founded on knowledge, would be honest? So far from it, you will be bound in all fairness, in consideration of my releasing you and restoring you what you have ventured, to adopt and disseminate the views of an expert,—namely, mine."

"Let me put it into fewer words," said Joseph. "You will buy my stock, repaying me what I have disbursed, if, on my return, I say nothing of what I have seen, and express my perfect faith (adopting your views) in the success of the Amaranth?"

"You have stated the conditions a little barely, perhaps, but not incorrectly. I only ask for perfect fairness, as between man and man."

"One question first, Mr. Kanuck. Does Mr. Blessing know the real prospects of the Amaranth?"

"No man more thoroughly, I assure you, Mr. Asten. Indeed, without Mr. Blessing's enthusiastic concurrence in the enterprise, I doubt whether we could have carried the work so far towards success. His own stock, I may say to you,—since we understand each other,—was earned by his efforts. If you know him intimately, you know also that he has no visible means of support. But he has what is much more important to us,—a thorough knowledge of men and their means."

He rubbed his hands, and laughed softly. They had been walking rapidly during the conversation, and now came suddenly upon the farthest crest of the hills, where the ridge fell away to the bottom occupied by the Fluke wells. Both paused at this point.

"On the square, then!" said Mr. Kanuck, offering his hand. "Tell me where you will be to-morrow morning, and our business can be settled in five minutes. You will carry out your part of the bargain, as man to man, when you find that I carry out mine."

"Do you take me for an infernal scoundrel?" cried Joseph, boiling over with disgust and rage.

Mr. Kanuck stepped back a pace or two. His sallow face became livid, and there was murder in his eyes. He put his hand into his breast, and Joseph, facing him, involuntarily did the same. Not until long afterwards, when other experiences had taught him the significance of the movement, did he remember what it then meant.

"So! that's your game, is it?" his antagonist said, hissing the words through his teeth. "A spy, after all! Or a detective, perhaps? I was a fool to trust a milk-and-water face: but one thing I tell you,—you may get away, but come back again if you dare!"

Joseph said nothing, but gazed steadily in the man's eyes, and did not move from his position so long as he was within sight. Then, breathing deeply, as if relieved from the dread of an unknown danger, he swiftly descended the hill.

That evening, as he sat in the bar-room of a horrible shanty (called a hotel), farther up the river, he noticed a pair of eyes fixed intently upon him: they belonged to one of the workmen in the Amaranth ravine. The man made an almost imperceptible signal, and left the room. Joseph followed him.

"Hush!" whispered the former. "Don't come back to the hill; and get away from here to-morrow morning, if you can!" With these words he darted off and disappeared in the darkness.

The counsel was unnecessary. Joseph, with all his inexperience of the world, saw plainly that his only alternatives were loss—or connivance. Nothing was to be gained by following the vile business any further. He took the earliest possible train, and by the afternoon of the following day found himself again in the city.

He was conscious of no desire to meet Mr. Blessing, yet the pressure of his recent experience seemed to drive him irresistibly in that direction. When he rang the bell, it was with the hope that he should find nobody at home. Mr. Blessing, however, answered the summons, and after the first expression of surprise, ushered him into the parlor.

"I am quite alone," he said; "Mrs. Blessing is passing the evening with her sister, Mrs. Woollish, and Clementina is still at Long Branch. I believe it is as good as settled that we are to lose her; at least she has written to inquire the extent of my available funds, which, in her case, is tantamount to—very much more."

Joseph determined to avoid all digressions, and insist on the Amaranth speculation, once for all, being clearly discussed. He saw that his father-in-law became more uneasy and excited as he advanced in the story of his journey, and, when it was concluded, did not seem immediately prepared to reply. His suspicions, already aroused by Mr. Kanuck's expressions, were confirmed, and a hard, relentless feeling of hostility took possession of his heart.

"I—I really must look into this," Mr. Blessing stammered, at last. "It seems incredible: pardon me, but I would doubt the statements, did they come from other lips than yours. It is as if I had nursed a dove in my bosom, and unexpectedly found it to be a—a basilisk!"

"It can be no serious loss to you," said Joseph, "since you received your stock in return for services."

"That is true: I was not thinking of myself. The real sting of the cockatrice is, that I have innocently misled you."

"Yet I understood you to say you had ventured your all?"

"My all of hope—my all of expectation!" Mr. Blessing cried. "I dreamed I had overtaken the rainbow at last; but this—this is senna—-quassia—aloes! My nature is so confiding that I accept the possibilities of the future as present realities, and build upon them as if they were Quincy granite. And yet, with all my experience, my acknowledged sagacity, my acquaintance with the hidden labyrinths of finance, it seems impossible that I can be so deceived! There must be some hideous misunderstanding: I have calculated all the elements, prognosticated all the planetary aspects, so to speak, and have not found a whisper of failure!"

"You omitted one very important element," Joseph said.

"What is that? I might have employed a detective, it is true—"

"No!" Joseph replied. "Honesty!"

Mr. Blessing fell back in his chair, weeping bitterly.

"I deserve this!" he exclaimed. "I will not resent it. I forgive you in advance of the time when you shall recognize my sincere, my heartfelt wish to serve you! Go, go: let me not recriminate! I meant to be, and still mean to be, your friend: but spare my too confiding child!"

Without a word of good-by, Joseph took his hat and hastened from the house. At every step the abyss of dishonesty seemed to open deeper before his feet. Spare the too confiding child! Father and daughter were alike: both mean, both treacherous, both unpardonably false to him.

With such feelings he left the city next morning, and made his way homewards.

# CHAPTER XXIII. JULIA'S EXPERIMENT.

In the mean time the Hopetons had left for the sea-shore, and the two women, after a drive to Magnolia, remained quietly on the farm. Julia employed the days in studying Lucy with a soft, stealthy, unremitting watchfulness which the latter could not suspect, since, in the first place, it was a faculty quite unknown to her, and, secondly, it would have seemed absurd because inexplicable. Neither could she guess with what care Julia's manner and conversation were adapted to her own. She was only surprised to find so much earnest desire to correct faults, such artless transparency of nature. Thus an interest quite friendly took the place of her former repulsion of feeling, of which she began to be sincerely ashamed.

Moreover, Julia's continual demonstration of her love for Joseph, from which Lucy at first shrank with a delicate tremor of the heart, soon ceased to affect her. Nay, it rather seemed to interpose a protecting barrier between her present and the painful memory of her past self. She began to suspect that all regret was now conquered, and rejoiced in the sense of strength which could only thus be made clear to her mind. Her feeling towards Joseph became that of a sister or a dear woman friend; there could be no harm in cherishing it; she found a comfort in speaking to Julia of his upright, unselfish character, his guilelessness and kindness of heart.

The work upon the house was nearly finished, but new and more alarming bills began to come in; and worse was in store. There was a chimney-piece, "the loveliest ivory veins through the green marble," Julia said, which she had ordered from the city; there were boxes and packages of furniture already on hand, purchased without Joseph's knowledge and with entire faith in the virtues of the Amaranth. Although she still clung to that faith with a desperate grip, the sight of the boxes did not give her the same delight as she had felt in ordering them. She saw the necessity of being prepared, in advance, for either alternative. It was not in her nature to dread any scene or circumstance of life (although she had found the appearance of timidity very available, and could assume it admirably); the question which perplexed her was, how to retain and strengthen her ascendency over Joseph?

It is needless to say that the presence of Lucy Henderson was a part of her plan, although she held a more important service in reserve. Lucy's warm, frank expressions of friendship for Joseph gave her great satisfaction, and she was exhaustless in inventing ways to call them forth.

"You look quite like another person, Lucy," she would say; "I really think the rest has done you good."

"I am sure of it," Lucy answered.

"Then you must be in no hurry to leave. We must build you up, as the doctors say; and, besides, if—if this speculation should be unfortunate—O, I don't dare to think of it!—there will be such a comfort to me, and I am sure to Joseph also, in having you here until we have learned to bear it. We should not allow our minds to dwell on it so much, you know; we should make an exertion to hide our disappointment in your presence, and that would be such a help! Now you will say I am borrowing trouble, but do, pray, make allowances for me, Lucy! Think how everything has been kept from me that I ought to have known!"

"Of course, I will stay a little while for your sake," Lucy answered; "but Joseph is a man, and most men bear bad luck easily. He would hardly thank me for condoling with him."

"O, no, no!" Julia cried; "he thinks everything of you! He was so anxious for you to come here! he said to me, 'Lucy Henderson is a noble, true-hearted girl, and you will love her at once,' as I did, Lucy, when I first saw you, but without knowing why, as I now do."

A warm color came into Lucy's face, but she only shook her head and said nothing.

The two women had just risen from the breakfast-table the next morning, when a shadow fell into the room through the front window, and a heavy step was heard on the stone pavement of the veranda. Julia gave a little start and shriek, and seized Lucy's arm. The door opened and Joseph was there. He had risen before daybreak and taken the earliest train from the city. He had scarcely slept for two nights; his face was stern and haggard, and the fatigue, instead of exhausting, had only added to his excitement.

Julia sprang forward, threw her arm around, him, and kissed him repeatedly. He stood still and passively endured the caress, without returning it; then, stepping forward, he gave his hand to Lucy. She felt that it was cold and moist; and she did not attempt to repress the quick sympathy which came into her face and voice.

Julia guessed something of the truth instantly, and nothing but the powerful necessity of continuing to play her part enabled her to conceal the bitter anger which the contrast between Joseph's greeting to her and to Lucy aroused in her heart. She stood for a moment as if paralyzed, but in reality to collect herself; then, approaching her husband, she stammered forth: "O, Joseph—I'm afraid—I don't dare to ask you what—what news you bring. You didn't write—I've been so uneasy—and now I see from your face—that something is wrong."

He did not answer.

"Don't tell me all at once, if it's very bad!" she then cried: "but, no! it's my duty to hear it, my duty to bear it,—Lucy has taught me that,—tell me all, tell me all, this moment!"

"You and your father have ruined me: that is all."

"Joseph!" The word sounded like the essence of tender protest, of heartbreaking reproach. Lucy rose quietly and moved towards the door.

"Don't leave me, Lucy!" was Julia's appeal.

"It is better that I should go," Lucy answered, in a faint voice, and left the room.

"But, Joseph," Julia resumed, with a wild, distracted air, "why do you say such terrible things? I really do not know what you mean. What have you learned? what have you seen?"

"I have seen the Amaranth!"

"Well! Is there no oil?"

"O yes, plenty of oil!" he laughed; "skunk oil and rattlesnake oil! It is one of the vilest cheats that the Devil ever put into the minds of bad men."

"O, poor pa!" Julia cried; "what a terrible blow to him!"

"'Poor pa!' Yes, my discovery of the cheat is a terrible blow to 'poor pa,'—he did not calculate on its being found out so soon. When I learned from Kanuck that all the stock he holds was given to him for services,—that is, for getting the money out of the pockets of innocents like myself,—you may judge how much pity I feel for poor pa! I told him the fact to his face, last night, and he admitted it."

"Then," said Julia, "if the others know nothing, he may be able to sell his stock to-day,—his and yours; and we may not lose much after all."

"I should have sent you to the oil region, instead of going myself," Joseph answered, with a sneer. "You and Kanuck would soon have come to terms. He offered to take my stock off my hands, provided I would go back to the city and make such a report of the speculation as he would dictate."

"And you didn't do it?" Julia's voice rose almost to a scream, as the words burst involuntarily from her lips.

The expression on Joseph's face showed her that she had been rash; but the words were said, and she could only advance, not recede.

"It is perfectly legitimate in business," she continued. "Every investment in the Amaranth was a venture,—every stockholder knew that he risked losing his money! There is not one that would not save himself in that way, if he had the chance. But you pride yourself on being so much better than other men! Mr. Chaffinch is right; you have what he calls a 'moral pride'! You—"

"Stop!" Joseph interrupted. "Who was it that professed such concern about my faith? Who sent Mr. Chaffinch to insult me?"

"Faith and business are two different things: all the churches know that.

846

There was Mr. Sanctus, in the city: he subscribed ten thousand dollars to the Church of the Acceptance: he couldn't pay it, and they levied on his property, and sold him out of house and home! Really, you are as ignorant of the world as a baby!"

"God keep me so, then!" he exclaimed.

"However," she resumed, after a pause, "since you insist on our bearing the loss, I shall expect of your moral pride that you bear it patiently, if not cheerfully. It is far from being ruin to us. The rise in property will very likely balance it, and you will still be worth what you were."

"That is not all," he said. "I will not mention my greatest loss, for you are incapable of understanding it; but how much else have you saddled me with? Let me have a look at it!"

He crossed the hall and entered the new apartment, Julia following. Joseph inspected the ceiling, the elaborate and overladen cornices, the marble chimney-piece, and finally peered into the boxes and packages, not trusting himself to speak while the extent of the absurd splendor to which she had committed him grew upon his mind. Finally he said, striving to make his voice calm, although it trembled in his throat: "Since you were so free to make all these purchases, perhaps you will tell me how they are to be paid for?"

"Let me manage it, then," she answered. "There is no hurry. These country mechanics are always impatient,—I should call them impertinent, and I should like to teach them a lesson. Sellers are under obligations to the buyers, and they are bound to be accommodating. They have so many bills which are never paid, that an extension of time is the least they can do. Why, they will always wait a year, two years, three years, rather than lose."

"I suppose so."

"Then," said Julia, deceived by Joseph's quiet tone, "their profits are so enormous, that it would only be fair to reduce the bills. I am sure, that if I were to mention that you were embarrassed by heavy losses, and press them hard, they would compromise with me on a moderate amount. You know they allow what is called a margin for losses,—pa told me, but I forget how much,—they always expect to lose a certain percentage; and, of course, it can make no difference by whom they lose it. You understand, don't you?"

"Yes: it is very plain."

"Pa could help me to get both a reduction and an extension of time. The bills have not all been sent, and it will be better to wait two or three months after they have come in. If the dealers are a little uneasy in advance, they will be all the readier to compromise afterwards."

Joseph walked up and down the hollow room, with his hands clasped behind his back and his eyes fixed upon the floor. Suddenly he stopped before her and said: "There is another way."

"Not a better one, I am certain."

"The furniture has not yet been unpacked, and can be returned to them uninjured. Then the bills need not be paid at all."

"And we should be the laughing-stock of the neighborhood!" she cried, her eyes flashing. "I never heard of anything so ridiculous! If the worst comes to the worst, you can sell Bishop those fifty acres over the hill, which he stands ready to take, any day. But you'd rather have a dilapidated house,—no parlor,—guests received in the dining-room and the kitchen,—the Hopetons and your friends, the Helds, sneering at us behind our backs! And what would your credit be worth? We shall not even get trusted for groceries at the village store, if you leave things as they are!"

Joseph groaned, speaking to himself rather than answering her: "Is there no way out of this? What is done is done; shall I submit to it, and try to begin anew? or—"

He did not finish the sentence. Julia turned her head, so that only the chimney-piece and the furniture could see the sparkle of triumph in her eyes. She felt that she had maintained her position; and, what was far more, she now clearly saw the course by which she could secure it.

She left the room, drawing a full breath of relief as the door closed behind her. The first shock of the evil news was over, and it had not fallen quite so heavily as she had feared. There were plenty of devices in store whereby all that was lost might be recovered. Had not her life at home been an unbroken succession of devices? Was she not seasoned to all manner of ups and downs, and wherefore should this first failure disconcert her? The loss of the money was, in reality, much less important to her than the loss of her power over Joseph. Weak as she had supposed him to he, he had shown a fierce and unexpected resistance, which must be suppressed now, or it might crush her whole plan of life. It seemed to her that he was beginning to waver: should she hasten a scheme by which she meant to entrap him into submission,—a subtle and dangerous scheme, which must either wholly succeed, or, wholly failing, involve her in its failure?

Rapidly turning over the question in her mind, she entered her bed-room. Locking the door, she walked directly to the looking-glass; the curtain was drawn from the window, and a strong light fell upon her face.

"This will never do!" she said to herself. "The anxiety and excitement have made me thin again, and I seem to have no color." She unfastened her dress, bared her neck, and pushed the ringlets behind her ears. "I look pinched; a little more, and I shall look old. If I were a perfect brunette or a perfect blonde, there would be less difficulty; but I have the most provoking, unmanageable complexion! I must bring on the crisis at once, and then see if I can't fill out these hollows."

She heard the front door opening, and presently saw Joseph on the lawn. He looked about for a moment, with a heavy, bewildered air, and then slowly turned towards the garden. She withdrew from the window, hesitated a moment, murmured to herself, "I will try, there cannot be a better time!" and then, burying her face in her hands and sobbing, rushed to Lucy's room.

"O Lucy!" she cried, "help me, or I am lost! How can I tell you? it is harder than I ever dreamed!"

"Is the loss so very serious,—so much more than you feared?" Lucy asked.

"Not that—O, if that were all! But Joseph—" Here Julia's sobs became almost hysterical. "He is so cruel; I did advise him, as I told you, for his sake, and now he says that pa and I have combined to cheat him! I don't think he knows how dreadful his words are. I would sooner die than hear any more of them! Go to him, Lucy; he is in the garden; perhaps he will listen to you. I am afraid, and I never thought I should be afraid of him!"

"It is very, very sad," said Lucy. "But if he is in such an excited condition he will surely resent my coming. What can I say?"

"Say only what you heard me speak! Tell him of my anxiety, my self-reproach! Tell him that even if he will believe that pa meant to deceive him, he must not believe it of me! You know, Lucy, how he wrongs me in his thoughts; if you knew how hard it is to be wronged by a husband, you would pity me!"

"I do pity you, Julia, from my very heart; and the proof of it is, that I will try to do what you ask, against my own sense of its prudence. If Joseph repels my interference, I shall not blame him."

"Heaven bless you, Lucy! He will not repel you, he cannot!" Julia sobbed. "I will lie down and try to grow calm." She rose from the bed, upon which she had flung herself, and tottered through the door. When she had reached her own room, she again looked at her image in the glass, nodded and smiled.

Lucy walked slowly along the garden paths, plucking a flower or two, and irresolute how to approach Joseph. At last, descending the avenue of box, she found him seated in the semicircular enclosure, gazing steadfastly down the valley, but (she was sure) not seeing the landscape. As he turned his head at her approach, she noticed that his eyelids were reddened and his lips compressed with an expression of intense pain.

"Sit down, Lucy; I am a grim host, to-day," he said, with a melancholy attempt at a smile.

Lucy had come to him with a little womanly indignation, for Julia's sake, in her heart; but it vanished utterly, and the tears started into her eyes. For a moment she found it impossible to speak.

"I shall not talk of my ignorance any more, as I once did," Joseph

850

continued. "If there is a class in the school of the world, graded according to experience of human meanness and treachery and falsehood, I ought to stand at the head."

Lucy stretched out her hand in protest. "Do not speak so bitterly, Joseph; it pains me to hear you."

"How would you have me speak?"

"As a man who will not see ruin before him because a part of his property happens to slip from him,—nay, if all were lost! I always took you to be liberal, Joseph, never careful of money for money's sake, and I cannot understand how your nature should be changed now, even though you have been the victim of some dishonesty."

"'Some dishonesty'! You are thinking only of money: what term would you give to the betrayal of a heart, the ruin of a life?"

"Surely, Joseph, you do not, you cannot mean—"

"My wife, of course. It needed no guessing."

"Joseph!" Lucy cried, seizing the opportunity, "indeed you do her wrong! I know what anxiety she has suffered during your absence. She blamed herself for having advised you to risk so much in an uncertain speculation, dreaded your disappointment, resolved to atone for it, if she could! She may have been rash and thoughtless, but she never meant to deceive you. If you are disappointed in some qualities, you should not shut your eyes and refuse to see others. I know, now, that I have myself not been fair in my judgment of Julia. A nearer acquaintance has led me to conceive what disadvantages of education, for which she is not responsible, she is obliged to overcome: she sees, she admits them, and she will overcome them. You, as her husband, are bound to show her a patient kindness—"

"Enough!" Joseph interrupted; "I see that you have touched pitch, also. Lucy, your first instinct was right. The woman whom I am bound to look upon as my wife is false and selfish in every fibre of her nature; how false and selfish I only can know, for to me she takes off her mask!"

851

"Do you believe me, then?" Lucy's words were slightly defiant. She had
not quite understood the allusion to touching pitch, and Joseph's indifference
to her advocacy seemed to her unfeeling.

"I begin to fear that Philip was right," said Joseph, not heeding her
question. "Life is relentless: ignorance or crime, it is all the same. And if God
cares less about our individual wrongs than we flatter ourselves He does, what
do we gain by further endurance? Here is Lucy Henderson, satisfied that my
wife is a suffering angel; thinks my nature is changed, that I am cold-hearted
and cruel, while I know Lucy to be true and noble, and deceived by the very
goodness of her own heart!"

He lifted his head, looked in her face a moment, and then went on:—

"I am sick of masks; we all wear them. Do you want to know the truth,
Lucy? When I look back I can see it very clearly, now. A little more than a year
ago the one girl who began to live in my thoughts was you! Don't interrupt
me: I am only speaking of what was. When I went to Warriner's, it was in
the hope of meeting you, not Julia Blessing. It was not yet love that I felt,
but I think it would have grown to that, if I had not been led away by the
cunningest arts ever a woman devised. I will not speculate on what might
have been: if I had loved you, perhaps there would have been no return: had
there been, I should have darkened the life of a friend. But this I say; I honor
and esteem you, Lucy, and the loss of your friendship, if I now lose it, is
another evil service which my wife has done me."

Joseph little suspected how he was torturing Lucy. She must have been
more than woman, had not a pang of wild regret for the lost fortune, and a
sting of bitter resentment against the woman who had stolen it, wrung her
heart. She became deadly pale, and felt that her whole body was trembling.

"Joseph," she said, "you should not, must not, speak so to me."

"I suppose not," he answered, letting his head sink wearily; "it is
certainly not conventional; but it is true, for all that! I could tell you the
whole story, for I can read it backwards, from now to the beginning, without
misunderstanding a word. It would make no difference; she is simple, natural,

artless, amiable, for all the rest of the world, while to me—"

There was such despondency in his voice and posture, that Lucy, now longing more than ever to cheer him, and yet discouraged by the failure of her first attempt, felt sorely troubled.

"You mistake me, Joseph," she said, at last, "if you think you have lost my friendship, my sincerest sympathy. I can see that your disappointment is a bitter one, and my prayer is that you will not make it bitterer by thrusting from you the hopeful and cheerful spirit you once showed. We all have our sore trials."

Lucy found her own words very mechanical, but they were the only ones, that came to her lips. Joseph did not answer; he still sat, stooping, with his elbows on his knees, and his forehead resting on his palms.

"If I am deceived in Julia," she began again, "it is better to judge too kindly than too harshly. I know you cannot change your sentence against her now, nor, perhaps, very soon. But you are bound to her for life, and you must labor—it is your sacred duty—to make that life smoother and brighter for both. I do not know how, and I have no right to condemn you if you fail. But, Joseph, make the attempt now, when the most unfortunate experience that is likely to come to you is over; make it, and it may chance that, little by little, the old confidence will return, and you will love her again."

Joseph started to his feet. "Love her!" he exclaimed, with suppressed passion,—"love her! I hate her!"

There was a hissing, rattling sound, like that of some fierce animal at bay. The thick foliage of two of the tall box-trees was violently parted. The branches snapped and gave way: Julia burst through, and stood before them.

# CHAPTER XXIV. FATE.

The face that so suddenly glared upon them was that of a Gorgon. The ringlets were still pushed behind her ears and the narrowness of the brow was entirely revealed; her eyes were full of cold, steely light; the nostrils were violently drawn in, and the lips contracted, as if in a spasm, so that the teeth were laid bare. Her hands were clenched, and there was a movement in her throat as of imprisoned words or cries; but for a moment no words came.

Lucy, who had started to her feet at the first sound, felt the blood turn chill in her veins, and fell, rather than sank, upon the seat again.

Joseph was hardly surprised, and wholly reckless. This eavesdropping was nothing worse than he already knew; indeed, there was rather a comfort in perceiving that he had not overestimated her capacity for treachery. There was now no limit; anything was possible.

"There is one just law, after all," he said, "the law that punishes listeners. You have heard the truth, for once. You have snared and trapped me, but I don't take to my captor more kindly than any other animal. From this moment I choose my own path, and if you still wish to appear as my wife, you must adapt your life to mine!"

"You mean to brazen it out, do you!" Julia cried, in a strange, hoarse, unnatural voice. "That's not so easy! I have not listened to no purpose: I have a hold upon your precious 'moral pride' at last!"

Joseph laughed scornfully.

"Yes, laugh, but it is in my hands to make or break you! There is enough decent sentiment in this neighborhood to crush a married man who dares to make love to an unmarried girl! As to the girl who sits still and listens to it, I say nothing; her reputation is no concern of mine!"

Lucy uttered a faint cry of horror.

"If you choose to be so despicable," said Joseph, "you will force me to set my truth against your falsehood. Wherever you tell your story, I shall follow with mine. It will be a wretched, a degrading business; but for the sake of Lucy's good name, I have no alternative. I have borne suspicion, misrepresentation, loss of credit,—brought upon me by you,—patiently, because they affected only myself; but since I am partly responsible in bringing to this house a guest for your arts to play upon and entrap, I am doubly bound to protect her against you. But I tell you, Julia, beware! I am desperate; and it is ill meddling with a desperate man! You may sneer at my moral pride, but you dare not forget that I have another quality,—manly self-respect,—which it will be dangerous to offend."

If Julia did not recognize, in that moment, that her subject had become her master, it was because the real, unassumed rage which convulsed her did not allow her to perceive anything clearly. Her first impulse was to scream and shriek, that servant and farm-hand might hear her, and then to repeat her accusation before them; but Joseph's last words, and the threatening sternness of his voice withheld her.

"So?" she said, at last; "this is the man who was all truth, and trust, and honor! With you the proverb seems to be reversed; it's off with the new love and on with the old. You can insult and threaten me in her presence! Well— go on: play out your little love-scene: I shall not interrupt you. I have heard enough to darken my life from this day!"

She walked away from them, up the avenue. Her dress was torn, her arms scratched and bleeding. She had played her stake and failed,—miserably, hopelessly failed. Her knees threatened to give way under her at every step, but she forced herself to walk erect, and thus reached the house without once looking back.

Joseph and Lucy mechanically followed her with their eyes. Then they turned and gazed at each other a moment without speaking. Lucy was very pale, and the expression of horror had not yet left her face.

"She told me to come to you," she stammered. "She begged me, with tears, to try and soften your anger against her; and then—oh, it is monstrous!"

"Now I see the plan!" Joseph exclaimed; "and I, in my selfish recklessness, saying what there was no need to utter, have almost done as she calculated,—have exposed you to this outrage! Why should I have recalled the past at all? I was not taking off a mask, I was only showing a scar—no, not even a scar, but a bruise!—which I ought to have forgotten. Forget it, too, Lucy, and, if you can, forgive me!"

"It is easy to forgive—everything but my own blindness," Lucy answered. "But there is one thing which I must do immediately: I must leave this house!"

"I see that," said Joseph, sadly. Then, as if speaking to himself, he murmured: "Who knows what friends will come to it in the future? Well, I will hear what can be borne; and afterwards,—there is Philip's valley. A free outlaw is better than a fettered outlaw!"

Lucy feared that his mind was wandering. He straightened himself to his full height, drew a deep breath, and exclaimed: "Action is a sedative in such cases, isn't it? Dennis has gone to the mill; I will get the other horse from the field and drive you home. Or, stay! will you not go to Philip Held's cottage for a day or two? I think his sister asked you to come."

"No, no!" cried Lucy; "you must not go! I will wait for Dennis."

"No one must suspect what has happened here this morning, unless Julia compels me to make it known, and I don't think she will. It is, therefore, better that I should take you. It will put me, I hope, in a more rational frame of mind. Go quietly to your room and make your preparations. I will see Julia, and if there is no further scene now, there will be none of the kind henceforth. She is cunning when she is calm."

On reaching the house Joseph went directly to his wife's bed-room. The necessity of an immediate interview could not be avoided, since Lucy was to leave. When he opened the door, Julia, who was bending over an open drawer of her bureau, started up with a little cry of alarm. She closed the drawer hastily, and began to arrange her hair at the mirror. Her face in the glass was flushed, but its expression was sullen and defiant.

"Julia," he said, as coolly as possible, "I am going to take Lucy home. Of course you understand that she cannot stay here an hour longer. You overheard my words to her, and you know just how much they were worth. I expect now, that—for your sake as much as hers or mine—you will behave towards her at parting in such a way that the servants may find no suggestions of gossip or slander."

"And if I don't choose to obey you?"

"I am not commanding. I propose a course which your own mind must find sensible. You have 'a deuced sharp intellect,' as your father said, on our wedding-day."

Joseph bit his tongue: he felt that he might have omitted this sting. But he was so little accustomed to victory, that he did not guess how thoroughly he had already conquered.

"Pa loved me, nevertheless," she said, and burst into tears.

Her emotion seemed real, but he mistrusted it.

"What can I do?" she sobbed: "I will try. I thought I was your wife, but I am not much more than your slave."

The foolish pity again stole into Joseph's heart, although he set his teeth and clenched his hands against it. "I am going for the horse," he said, in a kinder tone. "When I come back from this drive, this afternoon, I hope I shall find you willing to discuss our situation dispassionately, as I mean to do. We have not known each other fairly before to-day, and our plan of life must be rearranged."

It was a relief to walk forth, across the silent, sunny fields; and Joseph had learned to accept a slight relief as a substitute for happiness. The feeling that the inevitable crisis was over, gave him, for the first time in months, a sense of liberation. There was still a dreary and painful task before him, and he hardly knew why he should be so cheerful; but the bright, sweet currents of his blood were again in motion, and the weight upon his heart was lifted by some impatient, joyous energy.

The tempting vision of Philip's valley, which had haunted him from time to time, faded away. The angry tumult through which he had passed appeared to him like a fever, and he rejoiced consciously in the beginning of his spiritual convalescence. If he could simply suspend Julia's active interference in his life, he might learn to endure his remaining duties. He was yet young; and how much strength and knowledge had come to him—through sharpest pain, it was true—in a single year! Would he willingly return to his boyish innocence of the world, if that year could be erased from his life? He was not quite sure. Yet his nature had not lost the basis of that innocent time, and he felt that he must still build his future years upon it.

Thus meditating, he caught the obedient horse, led him to the barn, and harnessed him to the light carriage which Julia was accustomed to use. His anxiety concerning her probable demeanor returned as he entered the house. The two servant-women were both engaged, in the hall, in some sweeping or scouring operation, and might prove to be very inconvenient witnesses. The workmen in the new parlor—fortunately, he thought—were absent that day.

Lucy Henderson, dressed for the journey, sat in the dining-room. "I think I will go to Madeline Held for a day or two," she said; "I made a half-promise to visit her after your return."

"Where is Julia?"

"In her bed-room. I have not seen her. I knocked at the door, but there was no answer."

Joseph's trouble returned. "I will see her myself," he said, sternly; "she forgets what is due to a guest."

"No, I will go again," Lucy urged, rising hastily; "perhaps she did not hear me."

She followed him into the hall. Scarcely had he set his foot upon the first step of the staircase, when the bed-room door above suddenly burst open, and Julia, with a shriek of mortal terror, tottered down to the landing. Her face was ashy, and the dark-blue rings around her sunken eyes made them seem almost like the large sockets of a skull. She leaned against the railing, breathing short and hard.

Joseph sprang up the steps, but as he approached her she put out her right hand, and pushed against his breast with all her force, crying out: "Go away! You have killed me!"

The next moment She fell senseless upon the landing.

Joseph knelt and tried to lift her. "Good God! she is dead!" he exclaimed.

"No," said Lucy, after taking Julia's wrist, "it is only a fainting fit. Bring some water, Susan."

The frightened woman, who had followed them, rushed down the stairs.

"But she must be ill, very ill," Lucy continued. "This is not an ordinary swoon. Perhaps the violent excitement has brought about some internal injury. You must send for a physician as soon as possible."

"And Dennis not here! I ought not to leave her; what shall I do?"

"Go yourself, and instantly! The carriage is ready. I will stay and do all that can be done during your absence."

Joseph delayed until, under the influence of air and water, Julia began to recover consciousness. Then he understood Lucy's glance,—the women were present and she dared not speak,—that he should withdraw before Julia could recognize him.

He did not spare the horse, but the hilly road tried his patience. It was between two and three miles to the house of the nearest physician, and he only arrived, anxious and breathless, to find that the gentleman had been called away to attend another patient. Joseph was obliged to retrace part of his road, and drive some distance in the opposite direction, in order to summon a second. Here, however, he was more fortunate. The physician was just sitting down to an early dinner, which he persisted in finishing, assuring Joseph, after ascertaining such symptoms of the case as the latter was able to describe, that it was probably a nervous attack, "a modified form of hysteria." Notwithstanding he violated his own theory of digestion by eating rapidly, the minutes seemed intolerably long. Then his own horse must be harnessed to his own sulky, during which time he prepared a few doses of valerian, belladonna, and other palliatives, which he supposed might be needed.

Meanwhile, Lucy and the woman had placed Julia in her own bed, and applied such domestic restoratives as they could procure, but without any encouraging effect. Julia appeared to be conscious, but she shook her head when they spoke to her, and even, so Lucy imagined, attempted to turn it away. She refused the tea, the lavender and ginger they brought, and only drank water in long, greedy draughts. In a little while she started up, with clutchings and incoherent cries, and then slowly sank back again, insensible.

The second period of unconsciousness was longer and more difficult to overcome. Lucy began to be seriously alarmed as an hour, two hours, passed by, and Joseph did not return. Dennis was despatched in search of him, carrying also a hastily pencilled note to Madeline Held, and then Lucy, finding that she could do nothing more, took her seat by the window and watched the lane, counting the seconds, one by one, as they were ticked off by the clock in the hall.

Finally a horse's head appeared above the hedge, where it curved around the shoulder of the hill: then the top of a carriage,—Joseph at last! The physician's sulky was only a short distance in the rear. Lucy hurried down and met Joseph at the gate.

"No better,—worse, I fear," she said, answering his look.

"Dr. Hartman," he replied,—"Worrall was away from home,—thinks it is probably a nervous attack. In that case it can soon be relieved."

"I hope so, but I fancy there is danger."

The doctor now arrived, and after hearing Lucy's report, shook his head. "It is not an ordinary case of hysteria," he remarked; "let me see her at once."

When they entered the room Julia opened her eyes languidly, fixed them on Joseph, and slowly lifted her hand to her head. "What has happened to me?" she murmured, in a hardly audible whisper.

"You had a fainting fit," he answered, "and I have brought the doctor. This is Dr. Hartman; you do not know him, but he will help you; tell him how you feel, Julia!"

"Cold!" she said, "cold! Sinking down somewhere! Will he lift me up?"

The physician made a close examination, but seemed to become more perplexed as he advanced. He administered only a slight stimulant, and then withdrew from the bedside. Lucy and the servant left the room, at his request, to prepare some applications.

"There is something unusual here," he whispered, drawing Joseph aside. "She has been sinking rapidly since the first attack. The vital force is very low: it is in conflict with some secret enemy, and it cannot resist much longer, unless we discover that enemy at once. I will do my best to save her, but I do not yet see how."

He was interrupted by a noise from the bed. Julia was vainly trying to rise: her eyes were wide and glaring. "No, no!" came from her lips, "I will not die! I heard you. Joseph, I will try—to be different—but—I must live—for that!"

Then her utterance became faint and indistinct, and she relapsed into unconsciousness. The physician re-examined her with a grave, troubled face. "She need not be conscious," he said, "for the next thing I shall do. I will not interrupt this syncope at once; it may, at least, prolong the struggle. What have they been giving her?"

He picked up, one by one, the few bottles of the household pharmacy which stood upon the bureau. Last of all, he found an empty glass shoved behind one of the supports of the mirror. He looked into it, held it against the light, and was about to set it down again, when he fancied that there was a misty appearance on the bottom, as if from some delicate sediment. Stepping to the window, he saw that he had not been mistaken. He collected a few of the minute granulations on the tip of his forefinger, touched them to his tongue, and, turning quickly to Joseph, whispered:—

"She is poisoned!"

"Impossible!" Joseph exclaimed; "she could not have been so mad!"

"It is as I tell you! This form of the operation of arsenic is very unusual, and I did not suspect it; but now I remember that it is noted in the books. Repeated syncopes, utter nervous prostration, absence of the ordinary burning and vomiting, and signs of rapid dissolution; it fits the case exactly! If I had some oxy-hydrate of iron, there might still be a possibility, but I greatly fear—"

"Do all you can!" Joseph interrupted. "She must have been insane! Do not tell me that you have no antidote!"

"We must try an emetic, though it will now be very dangerous. Then oil, white of egg,"—and the doctor hastened down to the kitchen.

Joseph walked up and down the room, wringing his hands. Here was a horror beyond anything he had imagined. His only thought was to save the life which she, in the madness of passion, must have resolved to take; she must not, must not, die now; and yet she seemed to be already in some region on the very verge of darkness, some region where it was scarcely possible to reach and pull her back. What could be done? Human science was baffled; and would God, who had allowed him to be afflicted through her, now answer his prayer to continue that affliction? But, indeed, the word "affliction" was not formed in his mind; the only word which he consciously grasped was "Life! life!"

He paused by the bedside and gazed upon her livid skin, her sunken features: she seemed already dead. Then, sinking on his knees, he tried to pray, if that was prayer which was the single intense appeal of all his confused feelings. Presently he heard a faint sigh; she slightly moved; consciousness was evidently returning.

She looked at him with half-opened eyes, striving to fix upon something which evaded her mind. Then she said, in the faintest broken whisper: "I did love you—I did—and do—love you! But—you—you hate me!"

A pang sharper than a knife went through Joseph's heart. He cried, through his tears: "I did not know what I said! Give me your forgiveness, Julia! Pardon me, not because I ask it, but freely, from your heart, and I will bless you!"

She did not speak, but her eyes softened, and a phantom smile hovered upon her lips. It was no mask this time: she was sacredly frank and true. Joseph bent over her and kissed her.

"O Julia!" he said, "why did you do it? Why did you not wait until I could speak with you? Did you think you would take a burden off yourself or me?"

Her lips moved, but no voice came. He lifted her head, supported her, and bent his ear to her mouth. It was like the dream of a voice:—

"I—did—not—mean—"

There it stopped. The doctor entered the room, followed by Lucy.

"First the emetic," said the former.

"For God's sake, be silent!" Joseph cried, with his ear still at Julia's lips. The doctor stepped up softly and looked, at her. Then, seating himself on the bed beside Joseph, he laid his hand upon her heart. For several minutes there was silence in the room.

Then the doctor removed his hand, took Julia's head out of Joseph's arms, and laid it softly upon the pillow.

She was dead.

# CHAPTER XXV. THE MOURNERS.

"It cannot be!" cried Joseph, looking at the doctor with an agonized face; "it is too dreadful!"

"There is no room for doubt in relation to the cause. I suspect that her nervous system has been subjected to a steady and severe tension, probably for years past. This may have induced a condition, or at least a temporary paroxysm, during which she was—you understand me—not wholly responsible for her actions. You must have noticed whether such a condition preceded this catastrophe."

Lucy looked from one to the other, and back to the livid face on the pillow, unable to ask a question, and not yet comprehending that the end had come. Joseph arose at the doctor's words.

"That is my guilt," he said. "I was excited and angry, for I had been bitterly deceived. I warned her that her life must henceforth conform to mine: my words were harsh and violent. I told her that we had at last ascertained each other's true natures, and proposed a serious discussion for the purpose of arranging our common future, this afternoon. Can she have misunderstood my meaning? It was not separation, not divorce: I only meant to avoid the miserable strife of the last few weeks. Who could imagine that this would follow?"

Even as he spoke the words Joseph remembered the tempting fancy which had passed through his own mind,—and the fear of Philip,—as he stood on the brink of the rock, above the dark, sliding water. He covered his face with his hands and sat down. What right had he to condemn her, to pronounce her mad? Grant that she had been blinded by her own unbalanced, excitable nature rather than consciously false; grant that she had really loved him, that the love survived under all her vain and masterful ambition,—and how could he doubt it after the dying words and looks?—it was then easy to guess how sorely she had been wounded, how despair should follow her fierce excitement! Her words, "Go away! you have killed me!" were now explained. He groaned in the bitterness of his self-accusation. What were all the trials he had endured to this? How light seemed the burden from which he was now free! how gladly would he bear it, if the day's words and deeds could be unsaid and undone!

Tho doctor, meanwhile, had explained the manner of Julia's death to Lucy Henderson. She, almost overcome with this last horror, could only agree with his conjecture, for her own evidence confirmed it. Joseph had forborne to mention her presence in the garden, and she saw no need of repeating his words to her; but she described Julia's convulsive excitement, and her refusal to admit her to her room, half an hour before the first attack of the poison. The case seemed entirely clear to both.

"For the present," said the doctor, "let us say nothing about the suicide. There is no necessity for a post-mortem examination: the symptoms, and the presence of arsenic in the glass, are quite sufficient to establish the cause of death. You know what a foolish idea of disgrace is attached to families here in the country when such a thing happens, and Mr. Asten is not now in a state to bear much more. At least, we must save him from painful questions until after the funeral is over. Say as little as possible to him: he is not in a condition to listen to reason: he believes himself guilty of her death."

"What shall I do?" cried Lucy: "will you not stay until the man Dennis returns? Mr. Asten's aunt must be fetched immediately."

It was not a quarter of an hour before Dennis arrived, followed by Philip and Madeline Held.

Lucy, who had already despatched Dennis, with a fresh horse, to Magnolia, took Philip and Madeline into the dining-room, and hurriedly communicated to them the intelligence of Julia's death. Philip's heart gave a single leap of joy; then he compelled himself to think of Joseph and the exigencies of the situation.

"You cannot stay here alone," he said. "Madeline must keep you company. I will go up and take care of Joseph: we must think of both the living and the dead."

No face could have been half so comforting in the chamber of death as Philip's. The physician had, in the mean time, repeated to Joseph the words he had spoken to Lucy, and now Joseph said, pointing to Philip, "Tell him everything!"

Philip, startled as he was, at once comprehended the situation. He begged Dr. Hartman to leave all further arrangements to him, and to summon Mrs. Bishop, the wife of one of Joseph's near neighbors, on his way home. Then, taking Joseph by the arm, he said:—

"Now come with me. We will leave this room awhile to Lucy and Madeline; but neither must you be alone. If I am anything to you, Joseph, now is the time when my presence should be some slight comfort. We need not speak, but we will keep together."

Joseph clung the closer to his friend's arm, without speaking, and they passed out of the house. Philip led him, mechanically, towards the garden, but as they drew near the avenue of box-trees Joseph started back, crying out:—

"Not there!—O, not there!"

Philip turned in silence, conducted him past the barn into the grass-field, and mounted the hill towards the pin-oak on its summit. From this point the house was scarcely visible behind the fir-trees and the huge weeping-willow, but the fair hills around seemed happy under the tender sky, and the melting, vapory distance, seen through the southern opening of the valley, hinted of still happier landscapes beyond. As Joseph contemplated the scene, the long strain upon his nerves relaxed: he leaned upon Philip's shoulder, as they sat side by side, and wept passionately.

"If she had not died!" he murmured, at last.

Philip was hardly prepared for this exclamation, and he did not immediately answer.

"Perhaps it is better for me to talk," Joseph continued. "You do not know the whole truth, Philip. You have heard of her madness, but not of my guilt. What was it I said when we last met? I cannot recall it now: but I know that I feared to call my punishment unjust. Since then I have deserved it all, and more. If I am a child, why should I dare to handle fire? If I do not understand life, why should I dare to set death in motion?"

He began, and related everything that had passed since they parted on the banks of the stream. He repeated the words that had been spoken in the house and in the garden, and the last broken sentences that came from Julia's lips. Philip listened with breathless surprise and attention. The greater part of the narrative made itself clear to his mind; his instinctive knowledge of Julia's nature enabled him to read much further than was then possible to Joseph; but there was a mystery connected with the suicide which he could not fathom. Her rage he could easily understand; her apparent submission to Joseph's request, however,—her manifest desire to live, on overhearing the physician's fears,—her last incomplete sentence, "I—did—not—mean—" indicated no such fatal intention, but the reverse. Moreover, she was too inherently selfish, even in the fiercest paroxysm of disappointment, to take her own life, he believed. All the evidence justified him in this view of her nature, yet at the same time rendered her death more inexplicable.

It was no time to mention these doubts to Joseph. His only duty was to console and encourage.

"There is no guilt in accident," he said. "It was a crisis which must have come, and you took the only course possible to a man. If she felt that she was defeated, and her mad act was the consequence, think of your fate had she felt herself victorious!"

"It could have been no worse than it was," Joseph answered. "And she might have changed: I did not give her time. I have accused my own mistaken education, but I had no charity, no pity for hers!"

When they descended the hill Mrs. Bishop had arrived, and the startled household was reduced to a kind of dreary order. Dennis, who had driven with speed, brought Rachel Miller at dusk, and Philip and Madeline then departed, taking Lucy Henderson with them. Rachel was tearful, but composed; she said little to her nephew, but there was a quiet, considerate tenderness in her manner which soothed him more than any words.

The reaction from so much fatigue and excitement almost prostrated him. When he went to bed in his own guest-room, feeling like a stranger in a strange house, he lay for a long time between sleep and waking, haunted by all the scenes and personages of his past life. His mother's face, so faded in memory, came clear and fresh from the shadows; a boy whom he had loved in his school-days floated with fair, pale features just before his closed eyes; and around and between them there was woven a web of twilights and moonlights, and sweet sunny days, each linked to some grief or pleasure of the buried years. It was a keen, bitter joy, a fascinating torment, from which he could not escape. He was caught and helplessly ensnared by the phantoms, until, late in the night, the strong claim of nature drove them away and left him in a dead, motionless, dreamless slumber.

Philip returned in the morning, and devoted the day not less to the arrangements which must necessarily be made for the funeral than to standing between Joseph and the awkward and inquisitive sympathy of the neighbors. Joseph's continued weariness favored Philip's exertions, while at the same time it blunted the edge of his own feelings, and helped him over that cold, bewildering, dismal period, during which a corpse is lord of the mansion and controls the life of its inmates.

Towards evening Mr. and Mrs. Blessing, who had been summoned by telegraph, made their appearance. Clementina did not accompany them. They were both dressed in mourning: Mrs. Blessing was grave and rigid, Mr. Blessing flushed and lachrymose. Philip conducted them first to the chamber of the dead and then to Joseph.

"It is so sudden, so shocking!" Mrs. Blessing sobbed; "and Julia always seemed so healthy! What have you done to her, Mr. Asten, that she should be cut off in the bloom of her youth?"

"Eliza!" exclaimed her husband, with his handkerchief to his eyes; "do not say anything which might sound like a reproach to our heart-broken son! There are many foes in the citadel of life: they may be undermining our—our

868

foundations at this very moment!"

"No," said Joseph; "you, her father and mother, must hear the truth. I would give all I have in the world if I were not obliged to tell it."

It was, at the best, a painful task; but it was made doubly so by exclamations, questions, intimations, which he was forced to hear. Finally, Mrs. Blessing asked, in a tone of alarm:—

"How many persons know of this?"

"Only the physician and three of my friends," Joseph answered.

"They must be silent! It might ruin Clementina's prospects if it were generally known. To lose one daughter and to have the life of another blasted would be too much."

"Eliza," said her husband, "we must, try to accept whatever is inevitable. It seems to me that I no more recognize Julia's usually admirable intellect in her—yes, I must steel myself to say the word!—her suicide, than I recognized her features just now! unless Decay's effacing fingers have already swept the lines where beauty lingers. I warned her of the experiment, for such I felt it to be; yet in this last trying experience I do not complain of Joseph's disappointment, and his temporary—I trust it is only temporary—suspicion. We must not forget that he has lost more than we have."

"Where is—" Joseph began, endeavoring to turn the conversation from this point.

"Clementina? I knew you would find her absence unaccountable. We instantly forwarded a telegram to Long Branch; the answer said, 'My grief is great, but it is quite impossible to come.' Why impossible she did not particularize, and we can only conjecture. When I consider her age and lost opportunities, and the importance which a single day, even a fortunate situation, may possess for her at present, it seems to remove some of the sharpness of the serpent's tooth. Neither she nor we are responsible for Julia's rash taking off; yet it is always felt as a cloud which lowers upon the family. There was a similar case among the De Belsains, during the Huguenot times, but we never mention it. For your sake silence is rigidly imposed upon us; since the preliminary—what shall I call it?—dis-harmony of views?—would probably become a part of the narrative."

"Pray do not speak of that now!" Joseph groaned.

"Pardon me; I will not do so again. Our minds naturally become discursive under the pressure of grief. It is easier for me to talk at such times than to be silent and think. My power of recuperation seems to be spiritual as well as physical; it is congenital, and therefore exposes me to misconceptions. But we can close over the great abyss of our sorrow, and hide it from view in the depth of our natures, without dancing on the platform which covers it."

Philip turned away to hide a smile, and even Mrs. Blessing exclaimed: "Really, Benjamin, you are talking heartlessly!"

"I do not mean it so," he said, melting into tears, "but so much has come upon me all at once! If I lose my buoyancy, I shall go to the bottom like a foundered ship! I was never cut out for the tragic parts of life; but there are characters who smile on the stage and weep behind the scenes. And, you know, the Lord loveth a cheerful giver."

He was so touched by the last words he spoke, that he leaned his head upon his arms and wept bitterly.

Then Mrs. Blessing, weeping also, exclaimed: "O, don't take on so, Benjamin!"

Philip put an end to the scene, which was fast becoming a torment to Joseph. But, later in the evening, Mr. Blessing again sought the latter, softly apologizing for the intrusion, but declaring that he was compelled, then and there, to make a slight explanation.

"When you called the other evening," he said, "I was worn out, and not competent to grapple with such an unexpected revelation of villainy. I had been as ignorant of Kanuck's real character as you were. All our experience of the world is sometimes at fault; but where the Reverend Dr. Lellifant was first deceived, my own case does not seem so flagrant. Your early information, however, enabled me (through third parties) to secure a partial sale of the stock held by yourself and me,—at something of a sacrifice, it is true; but I prefer not to dissociate myself entirely from the enterprise. I do not pretend to be more than the merest tyro in geology; nevertheless, as I lay awake last night,—being, of course, unable to sleep after the shock of the telegram,—I sought relief in random scientific fancies. It occurred to mo that since the main Chowder wells are 'spouting,' their source or reservoir must be considerably higher than the surface. Why might not that source be found under the hills of the Amaranth? If so, the Chowder would be tapped at the fountain-head and the flow of Pactolean grease would be ours! When I return to the city I shall need instantly—after the fearful revelations of to-day—some violently absorbing occupation; and what could be more appropriate? If anything could give repose to Julia's unhappy shade, it would be the knowledge that her faith in the Amaranth was at last justified! I do not presume to awaken your confidence: it has been too deeply shaken; all I ask is, that I may have the charge of your shares, in order—without calling upon you for the expenditure of another cent, you understand—to rig a jury-mast on the wreck, and, D. V., float safely into port!"

"Why should I refuse to trust you with what is already worthless?" said Joseph.

"I will admit even that, if you desire. 'Exitus acta probat' was Washington's motto; but I don't consider that we have yet reached the exitus! Thank you, Joseph! Your question has hardly the air of returning confidence, but I will force myself to consider it as such, and my labor will be to deserve it."

He wrung Joseph's hand, shed a few more tears, and betook himself to his wife's chamber. "Eliza, let us be calm: we never know our strength until it has been tried," he said to her, as he opened his portmanteau and took from it the wicker-covered flask.

Then came the weariest and dreariest day of all,—when the house must be thrown open to the world; when in one room the corpse must be displayed for solemn stares and whispered comments, while in another the preparation of the funeral meats absorbs all the interest of half a dozen busy women; when

871

the nearest relatives of the dead sit together in a room up stairs, hungering
only for the consolations of loneliness and silence; when all talk under their
voices, and uncomfortably fulfil what they believe to be their solemn duty;
and when even Nature is changed to all eyes, and the mysterious gloom of an
eclipse seems to fall from the most unclouded sun.

There was a general gathering of the neighbors from far and near. The
impression seemed to be—and Philip was ready to substantiate it—that Julia
had died in consequence of a violent convulsive spasm, which some attributed
to one cause and some to another.

The Rev. Mr. Chaffinch made his way, as by right, to the chamber of the
mourners. Rachel Miller was comforted in seeing him, Mr. and Mrs. Blessing
sadly courteous, and Joseph strengthened himself to endure with patience
what might follow. After a few introductory words, and a long prayer, the
clergyman addressed himself to each, in turn, with questions or remarks
which indicated a fierce necessity of resignation.

"I feel for you, brother," he said, as he reached Joseph and bent over his
chair. "It is an inscrutable visitation, but I trust you submit, in all obedience?"

Joseph bowed silently.

"He has many ways of searching the heart," Mr. Chaffinch continued.
"Your one precious comfort must be that she believed, and that she is now in
glory. O, if you would but resolve to follow in her footsteps! He shows His
love, in that He chastens you: it is a stretching out of His hand, a visible offer
of acceptance, this on one side, and the lesson of our perishing mortality on
the other! Do you not feel your heart awfully and tenderly moved to approach
Him?"

Joseph sat, with bowed head, listening to the smooth, unctuous, dismal
voice at his ear, until the tension of his nerves became a positive physical pain.
He longed to cry aloud, to spring up and rush away; his heart was moved, but
not awfully and tenderly. It had been yearning towards the pure Divine Light
in which all confusions of the soul are disentangled; but now some opaque
foreign substance intervened, and drove him back upon himself. How long

the torture lasted he did not know. He spake no word, and made no further sign.

Then Philip took him and Rachel Miller down, for the last conventional look at the stony, sunken face. He was seated here and led there; he was dimly conscious of a crowd, of murmurs and steadfast faces; he heard some one whisper, "How dreadfully pale he looks!" and wondered whether the words could possibly refer to him. Then there was the welcome air and the sunshine, and Dennis driving them slowly down the lane, following a gloomy vehicle, in which something—not surely the Julia whom he knew—was carried.

He recalled but one other such stupor of the senses: it was during the performance of the marriage ceremony.

But the longest day wears out at last; and when night came only Philip was beside him. The Blessings had been sent to Oakland Station for the evening train to the city, and Joseph's shares in the Amaranth Company were in their portmanteau.

# CHAPTER XXVI. THE ACCUSATION.

For a few days it almost seemed to Joseph that the old order of his existence had been suddenly restored, and the year of his betrothal and marriage had somehow been intercalated into his life simply as a test and trial. Rachel Miller was back again, in her old capacity, and he did not yet see— what would have been plain to any other eyes—that her manner towards him was far more respectful and considerate than formerly. But, in fact, she made a wide distinction between the "boy" that he had been and the man and widower which he had come to be. At first, she had refused to see the dividing line: having crossed it, her new course soon became as natural and fixed as the old. She was the very type of a mechanically developed old maid,—inflexibly stern towards male youth, devotedly obedient to male maturity.

Joseph had been too profoundly moved to lose at once the sense of horror which the manner of Julia's death had left in his heart. He could not forgive himself for having, though never so ignorantly, driven her to madness. He was troubled, restless, unhappy; and the mention of his loss was so painful that he made every effort to avoid hearing it. Some of his neighbors, he imagined, were improperly curious in their inquiries. He felt bound, since the doctor had suggested it, since Philip and Lucy had acquiesced, and Mrs. Blessing had expressed so much alarm lest it might become known, to keep the suicide a secret; but he was driven so closely by questions and remarks that his task became more and more difficult.

Had the people taken offence at his reticence? It seemed so; for their manner towards him was certainly changed. Something in the look and voice; an indefinable uneasiness at meeting him; an awkward haste and lame excuses for it,—all these things forced themselves upon his mind. Elwood Withers, alone, met him as of old, with even a tenderer though a more delicately veiled affection; yet in Elwood's face he detected the signs of a grave trouble. It could not be possible, he thought, that Elwood had heard some surmise, or distorted echo, of his words to Lucy in the garden,—that there had been another listener besides Julia!

There were times, again, when he doubted all these signs, when he ascribed them to his own disturbed mind, and decided to banish them from his memory. He would stay quietly at home, he resolved, and grow into a healthier mood: he would avoid the society of men, until he should cease to wrong them by his suspicions.

First, however, he would see Philip; but on reaching the Forge he found Philip absent. Madeline received him with a subdued kindness in which he felt her sympathy; but it was also deeper, he acknowledged to himself, than he had any right to claim.

"You do not see much of your neighbors, I think, Mr. Asten?" she asked. The tone of her voice indicated a slight embarrassment.

"No," he answered; "I have no wish to see any but my friends."

"Lucy Henderson has just left us. Philip took her to her father's, and was intending to call at your place on his way home. I hope you will not miss him. That is," she added, while a sudden flush of color spread over her face, "I want you to see him to-day. I beg you won't take my words as intended for a dismissal."

"Not now, certainly," said Joseph. But he rose from his seat as he spoke.

Madeline looked both confused and pained. "I know that I spoke awkwardly," she said, "but indeed I was very anxious. It was also Lucy's wish. We have been talking about you this morning."

"You are very kind. And yet—I ought to wish you a more cheerful subject."

What was it in Madeline's face that haunted Joseph on his way home? The lightsome spirit was gone from her eyes, and they were troubled as if by the pressure of tears, held back by a strong effort. Her assumed calmness at parting seemed to cover a secret anxiety; he had never before seen her bright, free nature so clouded.

Philip, meanwhile, had reached the farm, where he was received by

Rachel Miller.

"I am glad to find that Joseph is not at home," he said; "there are some things which I need to discuss with you, before I see him. Can you guess what they are? Have you heard nothing,—no stories?"

Rachel's face grew pale, yet there was a strong fire of indignation in her eyes. "Dennis told me an outrageous report he had heard in the village," she said: "if you mean the same thing, you did well to see me first. You can help me to keep this insult from Joseph's knowledge."

"If I could I would, Miss Rachel. I share your feeling about it; but suppose the report were now so extended—and of course in a more exaggerated form the farther it goes—that we cannot avoid its probable consequences? This is not like a mere slander, which can be suffered to die of itself. It is equivalent to a criminal charge, and must be faced."

She clasped her hands, and stared at him in terror.

"But why," she faltered—"why does any one dare to make such a charge? And against the best, the most innocent—"

"The fact of the poisoning cannot be concealed," said Philip. "It appears, moreover, that one of the women who was in the house on the day of Julia's death heard her cry out to Joseph: 'Go away,—you have killed me!' I need not take up the reports any further; there is enough in these two circumstances to excite the suspicions of those who do not know Joseph as we do. It is better, therefore, to meet those suspicions before they come to us in a legal form."

"What can we do?" cried Rachel; "it is terrible!"

"One course is clear, if it is possible. We must try to discover not only the cause of Julia's suicide, but the place where she procured the poison, and her design in procuring it. She must have had it already in the house."

"I never thought of that. And her ways were so quiet and sly! How shall we ever find it out? O, to think that, dead and gone as she is, she can yet bring all this upon Joseph!"

"Try to be calm, Miss Rachel," said Philip. "I want your help, and

876

you must have all your wits about you. First, you must make a very careful examination of her clothing and effects, even to the merest scrap of paper. A man's good name—a man's life, sometimes—hangs upon a thread, in the most literal sense. There is no doubt that Julia meant to keep a secret, and she must have had a strong reason; but we have a stronger one, now, to discover it. First, as to the poison; was there any arsenic in the house when Julia came?"

"Not a speck! I never kept it, even for rats."

"Then we shall begin with ascertaining where she bought it. Let us make our investigations secretly, and as speedily as possible. Joseph need not know, at present, what we have undertaken, but he must know the charge that hangs over him. Unless I tell him, he may learn it in a more violent way. I sent Elwood Withers to Magnolia yesterday, and his report leaves me no choice of action."

Rachel Miller felt, from the stern gravity of Philip's manner, that he had not exaggerated Joseph's danger. She consented to be guided by him in all things; and this point being settled, they arranged a plan of action and communication, which was tolerably complete by the time Joseph returned.

As gently as possible Philip broke the unwelcome news; but, lightly as he pretended to consider it, Joseph's instinct saw at once what might be the consequences. The circumstances were all burned upon his consciousness, and it needed no reflection to show him how completely he was entangled in them.

"There is no alternative," he said, at last. "It was a mistake to conceal the cause of her death from the public: it is easy to misunderstand her exclamation, and make my crime out of her madness. I see the whole connection! This suspicion will not stop where it is. It will go further; and therefore I must anticipate it. I must demand a legal inquiry before the law forces one upon me. If it is not my only method of defence, it is certainly my best!"

"You are right!" Philip exclaimed. "I knew this would be your decision; I said so to Madeline this morning."

Now Madeline's confused manner became intelligible to Joseph. Yet a doubt still lingered in his mind. "Did she, did Madeline question it?" he asked.

"Neither she nor Lucy Henderson. If you do this, I cannot see how it will terminate without a trial. Lucy may then happen to be an important witness."

Joseph started. "Must that be!" he cried. "Has not Lucy been already forced to endure enough for my sake? Advise me, Philip! Is there any other way than that I have proposed?"

"I see no other. But your necessity is far greater than that for Lucy's endurance. She is a friend, and there can be no sacrifice in so serving you. What are we all good for, if not to serve you in such a strait?"

"I would like to spare her, nevertheless," said Joseph, gloomily. "I meant so well towards all my friends, and my friendship seems to bring only disgrace and sorrow."

"Joseph!" Philip exclaimed, "you have saved one friend from more than disgrace and sorrow! I do not know what might have come, but you called me back from the brink of an awful, doubtful eternity! You have given me an infinite loss and an infinite gain! I only ask you, in return, to obey your first true, proud instinct of innocence, and let me, and Lucy, and Elwood be glad to take its consequences, for your sake!"

"I cannot help myself," Joseph answered. "My rash impatience and injustice will come to light, and that may be the atonement I owe. If Lucy will spare herself, and report me truly, as I must have appeared to her, she will serve me best."

"Leave that, now! The first step is what most concerns us. When will you be ready to demand a legal investigation?"

"At once!—to-morrow!"

"Then we will go together to Magnolia. I fear we cannot change the ordinary forms of procedure, and there must be bail for your appearance at the proper time."

878

"Already on the footing of a criminal?" Joseph murmured, with a sinking of the heart. He had hardly comprehended, up to this moment, what his position would be.

The next day they drove to the county town. The step had not been taken a moment too soon, for such representations had been made that a warrant for Joseph's arrest was in the hands of the constable, and would have been served in a few hours. Philip and Mr. Hopeton, who also happened to be in the town by a fortunate chance (though Philip knew how the chance came), offered to accept whatever amount of bail might be demanded. The matter was arranged as privately as possible, but it leaked out in some way, and Philip was seriously concerned lest the curiosity—perhaps, even, the ill-will—of a few persons might be manifested towards Joseph. He visited the offices of the county papers, and took care that the voluntary act should be stated in such a manner as to set its character properly before the people. Everything, he felt, depended on securing a fair and unprejudiced judgment of the case.

This, indeed, was far more important than even he suspected. In a country where the press is so entirely free, and where, owing to the lazy, indifferent habit of thought—or, rather, habit of no thought—of the people, the editorial views are accepted without scrutiny, a man's good name or life may depend on the coloring given to his acts by a few individual minds, it is especially necessary to keep the balance even, to offset one statement by another, and prevent a partial presentation of the case from turning the scales in advance. The same phenomena were as likely to present themselves here, before a small public, as in the large cities, where the whole population of the country become a more or less interested public. The result might hinge, not upon Joseph's personal character as his friends knew it, but upon the political party with which he was affiliated, the church to which he belonged,—nay, even upon the accordance of his personal sentiments with the public sentiment of the community in which he lived. If he had dared to defy the latter, asserting the sacred right of his own mind to the largest liberty, he was already a marked man. Philip did not understand the extent and power of the external influences which control what we complacently call "justice," but he

knew something of the world, and acted in reality more prudently than he
supposed.

He was calm and cheerful for Joseph's sake; yet, now that the matter
was irrevocably committed to the decision of a new, uninterested tribunal, he
began to feel the gravity of his friend's position.

"I almost wish," Joseph said, as they drove homewards, "that no bail
had been granted. Since the court meets in October, a few weeks of seclusion
would do me no harm; whereas now I am a suspected person to nearly all
whom I may meet."

"It is not agreeable," Philip answered, "but the discipline may be useful.
The bail terminates when the trial commences, you understand, and you will
have a few nights alone, as it is,—quite enough, I imagine, to make you
satisfied with liberty under suspicion. However I have one demand to make,
Joseph! I have thought over all possible lines of defence; I have secured legal
assistance for you, and we are agreed as to the course to be adopted. I do not
think you can help us at all. If we find that you can, we will call upon you; in
the mean time, wait and hope!"

"Why should I not?" Joseph asked. "I have nothing to fear, Philip."

"No!" But Philip's emphatic answer was intended to deceive. He was
purposely false, knew himself to be so, and yet his conscience never troubled
him less!

When they reached the farm, Philip saw by Rachel Miller's face that
she had a communication to make. It required a little management to secure
an interview with her without Joseph's knowledge; but some necessity for
his presence at the barn favored his friend. No sooner were they alone than
Rachel approached Philip hastily and said, in a hurried whisper:—

"Here! I have found something, at last! It took a mighty search: I thought
I never should come upon the least bit that we could make anything of: but
this was in the upper part of a box where she kept her rings and chains, and
such likes! Take it,—it makes me uncomfortable to hold it in my fingers!"

She thrust a small paper into his hand.

It was folded very neatly, and there was an apothecary's label on the back. Philip read: "Ziba Linthicum's Drug store, No. 77 Main St., Magnolia." Under this printed address was written in large letters the word "Arsenic." On unfolding the paper he saw that a little white dust remained in the creases: quite enough to identify the character of the drug.

"I shall go back to-morrow!" he said. "Thank Heaven, we have got one clew to the mystery! Joseph must know nothing of this until all is explained; but while I am gone make another and more thorough search! Leave no corner unexplored: I am sure we shall find something more."

"I'd rip up her dresses!" was Rachel's emphatic reply. "That is, if it would do any good. But perhaps feeling of the lining and the hems might be enough. I'll take every drawer out, and move the furniture! But I must wait for daylight: I'm not generally afeared, but there is some things, you know, which a body would as lief not do by night, with cracks and creaks all around you, which you don't seem to hear at other times."

# CHAPTER XXVII. THE LABELS.

The work at Coventry Forge was now so well organized that Philip could easily give the most of his time to Joseph's vindication. He had secured the services of an excellent country lawyer, but he also relied much upon the assistance of two persons,—his sister Madeline and Elwood Withers: Madeline, from her rapid, clear insight, her shrewd interpretation of circumstances; and Elwood as an active, untiring practical agent.

The latter, according to agreement, had ridden up from his section of the railway, and was awaiting Philip when he returned home.

Philip gave them the history of the day,—this time frankly, with all the signs and indications which he had so carefully kept from Joseph's knowledge. Both looked aghast; and Elwood bent an ivory paper-cutter so suddenly in his hands that it snapped in twain. He colored like a girl.

"It serves me right," he said. "Whenever my hands are idle, Satan finds mischief for 'em,—as the spelling-book says. But just so the people bend and twist Joseph Asten's character, and just so unexpectedly his life may snap in their hands!"

"May the omen be averted!" Madeline cried. "Put down the pieces, Mr. Withers! You frighten me."

"No, it is reversed!" said Philip. "Just so Joseph's friends will snap this chain of circumstances. If you begin to be superstitious, I must look out for other aids. The tracing of the poison is a more fortunate step than I hoped, at the start. I cannot at all guess to what it may lead, but there is a point beyond which even the most malignant fate has no further power over an innocent man. Thus far we have met nothing but hostile circumstances: there seems to be more than Chance in the game, and I have an idea that the finding of this paper will break the evil spell. Come now, Madeline, and you, Withers, give me your guesses as to what my discovery shall be to-morrow!"

After a pause, Madeline answered: "It must have been purchased—

perhaps even by Mr. Asten—for rats or mice; and she may have swallowed the drug in a fit of passion."

"I think," said Elwood, "that she bought it for the purpose of poisoning Joseph! Then, may be, the glasses were changed, as I've heard tell of a man whose wife changed his coffee-cup because there was a fly in it, giving him hers, and thereby innocently killed him when he meant to ha' killed her."

"Ha!" Philip cried; "the most incredible things, apparently, are sometimes the most natural! I had not thought of this explanation."

"O Philip!" said Madeline, "that would be a new horror! Pray, let us not think of it: indeed, indeed, we must not guess any more."

Philip strove to put the idea from his mind: he feared lest it might warp his judgment and mislead him in investigations which it required a cool, sharp intellect to prosecute. But the idea would not stay away: it haunted him precisely on account of its enormity, and he rode again to Magnolia the next day with a foreboding sense of some tragic secret about to be revealed.

But he never could have anticipated the actual revelation.

There was no difficulty in finding Ziba Linthicum's Drug store. The proprietor was a lank, thin-faced man, with projecting, near-sighted eyes, and an exceedingly prim, pursed mouth. His words, uttered in the close, wiry twang peculiar to Southern Pennsylvania, seemed to give him a positive relish: one could fancy that his mouth watered slightly as he spoke. His long, lean lips had a settled smirk at the corner, and the skin was drawn so tightly over his broad, concave chin-bone that it shone, as if polished around the edges.

He was waiting upon a little girl when Philip entered; but he looked up from his scales, bowed, smiled, and said: "In a moment, if you please."

Philip leaned upon the glass case, apparently absorbed in the contemplation of the various soaps and perfumes under his eyes, but thinking only of the paper in his pocket-book.

"Something in this line, perhaps?"

883

Mr. Linthicum, with a still broader smile, began to enumerate: "These are from the Society Hygiennick—"

"No," said Philip, "my business is especially private. I take it for granted that you have many little confidential matters intrusted to you."

"Oh, undoubtedly, sir! Quite as much so as a physician."

"You are aware also that mistakes sometimes occur in making up prescriptions, or in using them afterwards?"

"Not by me, I should hope. I keep a record of every dangerous ingredient which goes out of my hands."

"Ah!" Philip exclaimed. Then he paused, uncertain how much to confide to Mr. Linthicum's discretion. But, on mentioning his name and residence, he found that both himself and Mr. Hopeton were known—and favorably, it seemed—to the apothecary. He knew the class of men to which the latter belonged,—prim, fussy, harmlessly vain persons, yet who take as good care of their consciences as of their cravats and shirt-bosoms. He produced the paper without further delay.

"That was bought here, certainly," said Mr. Linthicum. "The word 'Arsenic' is written in my hand. The date when, and the person by whom it was purchased, must be in my register. Will you go over it with me?"

He took a volume from a drawer, and beginning at the last entry, they went slowly backward over the names, the apothecary saying: "This is confidential: I rely upon your seeing without remembering."

They had not gone back more than two or three weeks before Philip came upon a name that made his heart stand still. There was a record in a single line:—

"Miss Henderson. Arsenic."

He waited a few seconds, until he felt sure of his voice. Then he asked: "Do you happen to know Miss Henderson?"

"Not at all! A perfect stranger."

884

"Can you, perhaps, remember her appearance?"

"Let me see," said Mr. Linthicum, biting the end of his forefinger; "that must have been the veiled lady. The date corresponds. Yes, I feel sure of it, as all the other poison customers are known to me."

"Pray describe her then!" Philip exclaimed.

"Really, I fear that I cannot. Dressed in black, I think; but I will not be positive. A soft, agreeable voice, I am sure."

"Was she alone? Or was any one else present?"

"Now I do recall one thing," the apothecary answered. "There was an agent of a wholesale city firm—a travelling agent, you understand—trying to persuade me into an order on his house. He stepped on one side as she came to the counter, and he perhaps saw her face more distinctly, for he laughed as she left, and said something about a handsome girl putting her lovers out of their misery."

But Mr. Linthicum could remember neither the name of the agent nor that of the firm which he represented. All Philip's questioning elicited no further particulars, and he was obliged to be satisfied with the record of the day and probable hour of the purchase, and with the apothecary's promise of the strictest secrecy.

He rode immediately home, and after a hasty consultation with Madeline, remounted his horse and set out to find Lucy Henderson. He was fortunate enough to meet her on the highway, on her way to call upon a neighbor. Springing from his horse he walked beside her, and announced his discovery at once.

Lucy remembered the day when she had accompanied Julia to Magnolia, during Joseph's absence from home. The time of the day, also, corresponded to that given by the apothecary.

"Did you visit the drug-store?" Philip asked.

"No," she answered, "and I did not know that Julia had. I paid two or three visits to acquaintances, while she did her shopping, as she told me."

"Then try and remember, not only the order of those visits, but the time occupied by each," said Philip. "Write to your friends, and ask them to refresh their memories. It has become an important point, for—the poison was purchased in your name!"

"Impossible!" Lucy cried. She gazed at Philip with such amazement that her innocence was then fixed in his mind, if it had not been so before.

"Yes, I say 'impossible!' too," he answered. "There is only one explanation. Julia Asten gave your name instead of her own when she purchased it."

"Oh!" Lucy's voice sounded like a hopeless personal protest against the collective falsehood and wickedness of the world.

"I have another chance to reach the truth," said Philip. "I shall find the stranger,—the travelling agent,—if it obliges me to summon every such agent of every wholesale drug-house in the city! It is at least a positive fortune that we have made this discovery now."

He looked at his watch. "I have just time to catch the evening train," he said, hurriedly, "but I should like to send a message to Elwood Withers. If you pass through that wood on the right, you will see the track just below you. It is not more than half a mile from here; and you are almost sure to find him at or near the unfinished tunnel. Tell him to see Rachel Miller, and if anything further has been found, to inform my sister Madeline at once. That is all. I make no apology for imposing the service on you: good-by, and keep up your faith, Lucy!"

He pressed her hand, sprang into the saddle, and cantered briskly away.

Lucy, infected by his haste, crossed the field, struggled through the under-growth of the wild belt of wood, and descended to the railway track, without giving herself time to think. She met a workman near the mouth of the tunnel, and not daring to venture in, sent by him a summons to Elwood. It was not many minutes before he appeared.

"Something has happened, Lucy? he exclaimed.

"Philip thinks he has made a discovery," she answered, "and I come to you as his messenger." She then repeated Philip's words.

"Is that all?" Elwood asked, scanning her face anxiously. "You do not seem quite like your real self, Lucy."

She sat down upon the hank. "I am out of breath," she said; "I must have walked faster than I thought."

"Wait a minute!" said he. He ran up the track, to where a little side-glen crossed it, sprang down among the bushes, and presently reappeared with a tin cup full of cold, pure spring water.

The draught seemed to revive her at once. "It is not all, Elwood," she said. "Joseph is not the only one, now, who is implicated by the same circumstances."

"Who else?—not Philip Held!"

"No," she answered, very quietly, "it is a woman. Her name is Lucy Henderson."

Before Elwood could speak, she told him all that she had heard from Philip. He could scarcely bring his mind to accept its truth.

"Oh, the—" he began; "but, no! I will keep the words to myself. There is something deeper in this than any of us has yet looked for! Depend upon it, Lucy, she had a plan in getting you there!"

Lucy was silent. She fancied she knew Julia's plan already.

"Did she mean to poison Joseph herself, and throw the suspicion on you? And now by her own death, after all, she accomplishes her chief end! It is a hellish tangle, whichever way I look; but they say that the truth will sooner or later put down any amount of lies, and so it must be, here. We must get at the truth, the whole truth, and nothing but the truth! Do you not say so, Lucy?"

"Yes!" she answered firmly, looking him in the face.

"Ay, though all should come to light! We can't tell what it may be

887

necessary to say. They may go to work and unravel Joseph's life, and yours, and mine, and hold up the stuff for everybody to look at. Well, let 'em! say I. If there are dark streaks in mine, I guess they'll look tolerably fair beside that one black heart. We're here alone, Lucy; there may not be a chance to say it soon again, so I'll say now, that if need comes to publish what I said to you one night a year ago,—to publish it for Joseph's sake, or your sake,—don't keep back a single word! The worst would be, some men or women might think me conceited."

"No, Elwood!" she exclaimed: "that reproach would fall on me! You once offered me your help, and I—I fear I spurned it; but I will take it now. Nay, I beg you to offer it to me again, and I will accept it with gratitude!"

She rose, and stretched out her hand.

Elwood clasped it tenderly, held it a moment, and seemed about to speak. But although his lips parted, and there was a movement of the muscles of his throat, he did not utter a word. In another moment he turned, walked a few yards up the track, and then came back to her.

"No one could mistake you for Julia Asten," he said. "You are at least half a head taller than she was. Your voice is not at all the same: the apothecary will surely notice the difference! Then an alibi, as they call it, can be proved."

"So Philip Held thought. But if my friends should not remember the exact time,—what should I then do?"

"Lucy, don't ask yourself the question now! It seems to me that the case stands this way: one evil woman has made a trap, fallen into it herself, and taken the secret of its make away with her. There is nothing more to be invented, and so we hold all that we gain. While we are mining, where's the counter-mining to come from? Who is to lie us out of our truth? There isn't much to stand on yet, I grant; but another step—the least little thing—may give us all the ground we want!"

He spoke so firmly and cheerily that Lucy's despondent feeling was charmed away. Besides, nothing could have touched her more than Elwood's heroic self-control. After the miserable revelation which Philip had made, it was unspeakably refreshing to be brought into contact with a nature so sound and sweet and strong. When he had led her by an easier path up the hill, and they had parted at the end of the lane leading to her father's house, she felt, as never before, the comfort of relying so wholly on a faithful man friend.

Elwood took his horse and rode to the Asten farm. Joseph's face brightened at his appearance, and they talked as of old, avoiding the dark year that lay between their past intimacy and its revival. As in Philip's case, it was difficult to communicate secretly with Rachel Miller; but Elwood, with great patience, succeeded in looking his wish to speak with her, and uniting her efforts with his own. She adroitly turned the conversation upon a geological work which Joseph had been reading.

"I've been looking into the subject myself," Elwood said. "Would you let me see the book: it may be the thing I want."

"It is on the book-shelf in your bed-room, Joseph," Rachel remarked.

There was time enough for Elwood to declare his business, and for Rachel to answer: "Mr. Held said every scrap, and it is but a scrap, with half a name on it. I found it behind and mostly under the lower drawer in the same box. I'll get it before you leave, and give it to you when we shake hands. Be careful, for he may make something out of it, after all. Tell him there isn't a stitch in a dress but I've examined, and a mortal work it was!"

It was late before Elwood could leave; nevertheless, he rode to Coventry Forge. The scrap of paper had been successfully transferred, and his pressing duty was to deliver it into the hands of Madeline Held. He found her anxiously waiting, in accordance with Philip's instructions.

When they looked at the paper, it seemed, truly, to be a worthless fragment. It had the character, also, of an apothecary's label, but the only letters remaining were those forming the end of the name, apparently —ers, and a short distance under them —Sts.

"Behind and mostly under the lower drawer of her jewel-case," said Madeline, musingly. "I think I might guess how it came there. She had seen the label, which had probably been forgotten, and then, as she supposed, had snatched it away and destroyed it, without noticing that this piece, caught behind the drawer, had been torn off. But there is no evidence—and perhaps none can be had—that the paper contained poison."

"Can you make anything out of the letters?" Elwood asked.

"The 'Sts' certainly means 'Streets'—now I see! It is a corner house! This makes the place a little mare easy to be identified. If Philip cannot find it, I am sure a detective can. I will write to him at once."

"Then I'll wait and ride to the office with the letter," said Elwood.

Madeline rose, and commenced walking up and down the room: she appeared to be suddenly and unusually excited.

"I have a new suspicion," she said, at last. "Perhaps I am in too much of a hurry to make conjectures, because Philip thinks I have a talent for it,—and yet, this grows upon me every minute! I hope—oh, I hope I am right!"

She spoke with so much energy that Elwood began to share her excitement without knowing its cause. She noticed the eager, waiting expression of his face.

"You must really pardon, me, Mr. Withers. I believe I was talking to myself rather than to you; I will not mention my fancy until Philip decides whether it is worth acting upon. There will be no harm if each of us finds a different clew, and follows it. Philip will hardly leave the city to-morrow. I shall not write, but go down with the first train in the morning!"

Elwood took his leave, feeling hopeful and yet very restless.

It was a long while before Madeline encountered Philip. He was busily employed in carrying out his plan of tracing the travelling agent,—not yet successful, but sanguine of success. He examined the scrap of paper which Madeline brought, listened to her reasons for the new suspicion which had crossed her mind, and compared them with the little evidence already collected.

"Do not let us depend too seriously on this," he then said; "there is about an even chance that you are right. We will keep it as an additional and independent test, but we dare not lose sight of the fact that the law will assume Joseph's guilt, and we must establish his innocence, first of all. Nay, if we can simply prove that Julia, and not Lucy, purchased the poison, we shall save both! But, at the same time, I will try to find this —ers, who lives in a corner house, and I will have a talk with old Blessing this very evening."

"Why not go now?"

"Patience, you impetuous girl! I mean to take no step without working out every possible result in advance. If I were not here in the city, I would consult with Mr. Pinkerton before proceeding further. Now I shall take you to the train: you must return to Coventry, and watch and wait there."

When Philip called at the Blessing mansion, in the evening, he found only Mrs. Blessing at home. She was rigid and dreary in her mourning, and her reception of him was almost repellant in its stiff formality.

"Mr. Blessing is absent," she explained, inviting Philip to a seat by a wave of her hand. "His own interests rendered a trip to the Oil Regions imperative; it is a mental distraction which I do not grudge him. This is a cheerless household, sir,—one daughter gone forever, and another about to leave us. How does Mr. Asten bear his loss?"

Philip thereupon, as briefly and forcibly as possible, related all that had occurred. "I wish to consult Mr. Blessing," he concluded, "in relation to the possibility of his being able to furnish any testimony on his son-in-law's side. Perhaps you, also—"

"No!" she interrupted. "I know nothing whatever! If the trial (which I think most unnecessary and shocking) gets into the city papers, it will be a terrible scandal for us. When will it come on, did you say?"

"In two or three weeks"

"There will be barely time!" she cried.

"For that reason," said he, "I wish to secure the evidence at once. All the preparations for the defence must be completed within that time."

"Clementina," Mrs. Blessing continued, without heeding his words, "will be married about the first of October. Mr. Spelter has been desirous of making a bridal tour in Europe. She did not favor the plan; but it seems to me like an inter-position of Heaven!"

Philip rose, too disgusted to speak. He bowed in silence, and left the house.

# CHAPTER XXVIII. THE TRIAL.

As the day of trial drew nigh, the anxiety and activity of Joseph's friends increased, so that even the quiet atmosphere wherein he lived was disturbed by it. He could not help knowing that they were engaged in collecting evidence, but inasmuch as Philip always said, "You can do nothing!" he forced himself to wait with such patience as was possible. Rachel Miller, who had partly taken the hired man, Dennis, into her confidence, hermetically sealed the house to the gossip of the neighborhood; but her greatest triumph was in concealing her alarm, as the days rolled by and the mystery was not yet unravelled.

There was not much division of opinion in the neighborhood, however. The growing discord between husband and wife had not been generally remarked: they were looked upon as a loving and satisfied couple. Joseph's integrity of character was acknowledged, and, even had it been doubted, the people saw no motive for crime. His action in demanding a legal investigation also operated favorably upon public opinion.

The quiet and seclusion were beneficial to him. His mind became calmer and clearer; he was able to survey the past without passion, and to contemplate his own faults with a sense of wholesome bitterness rather than pain. The approaching trial was not a pleasant thing to anticipate, but the worst which he foresaw was the probability of so much of his private life being laid bare to the world. Here, again, his own words returned to condemn him. Had he not said to Lucy, on the morning of that fatal day, "I am sick of masks!" Had he not threatened to follow Julia with his own miserable story? The system of checks which restrain impulse, and the whirl of currents and counter-currents which govern a man's movement through life, began to arrange themselves in his mind. True wisdom, he now felt, lay in understanding these, and so employing them as to reach individual liberty of action through law, and not outside of it. He had been shallow and reckless, even in his good impulses; it was now time to endure quietly for a season what their effect had been.

The day previous to the trial Philip had a long consultation with Mr. Pinkerton. He had been so far successful that the name and whereabouts of the travelling agent had been discovered: the latter had been summoned, but he could not possibly arrive before the next day. Philip had also seen Mr. Blessing, who entered with great readiness into his plans, promised his assistance in ascertaining the truth of Madeline's suspicion, and would give his testimony as soon as he could return from New York, whither he had gone to say farewell to Mrs. Clementina Spelter, before her departure for Paris on a bridal journey. These were the two principal witnesses for the defence, and it was yet uncertain what kind of testimony they would be able to give.

"We must finish the other witnesses," Mr. Pinkerton said, "(who, in spite of all we can do, will strengthen the prosecution), by the time you reach here. If Spenham gives us trouble, as I am inclined to suspect, we cannot well spare you the first day, but I suppose it cannot be helped."

"I will send a telegram to Blessing, in New York, to make sure," Philip answered. "Byle and Glanders answer for their agent, and I can try him with the photograph on the way out. If that succeeds, Blessing's failure will be of less consequence."

"If only they do not reach Linthicum in the mean time! I will prolong the impanelling of the jury, and use every other liberty of delay allowed me; yet I have to be cautious. This is Spenham's first important case, and he is ambitious to make capital."

Mr. Spenham was the prosecuting attorney, who had just been elected to his first term of service in that capacity. He had some shrewdness as a criminal lawyer, and a great deal of experience of the subterranean channels of party politics. This latter acquirement, in fact, was the secret of his election, for he was known to be coarse, unscrupulous, and offensive. Mr. Pinkerton was able to foresee his probable line of attack, and was especially anxious, for that reason, to introduce testimony which would shorten the trial.

When the hour came, and Joseph found that Philip was inevitably absent, the strength he had summoned to his heart seemed to waver for an instant. All his other friends were present, however: Lucy Henderson and

894

Madeline came with the Hopetons, and Elwood Withers stood by his side so boldly and proudly that he soon recovered his composure.

The court-room was crowded, not only by the idlers of the town, but also many neighbors from the country. They were grave and silent, and Joseph's appearance in the place allotted to the accused seemed to impress them painfully. The preliminaries occupied some time, and it was nearly noon before the first witness was called.

This was the physician. He stated, in a clear, business-like manner, the condition in which he found Julia, his discovery of the poison, and the unusual character of its operation, adding his opinion that the latter was owing to a long-continued nervous tension, culminating in hysterical excitement. Mr. Spenham questioned him very closely as to Joseph's demeanor, and his expressions before and after the death. The point of attack which he selected was Julia's exclamation: "Joseph, I will try to be different, but I must live for that!"

"These words," he said, "indicate a previous threat on the part of the accused. His helpless victim—"

Mr. Pinkerton protested against the epithet. But his antagonist found numberless ways of seeming to take Joseph's guilt for granted, and thus gradually to mould the pliant minds of a not very intelligent jury. The physician was subjected to a rigid cross-examination, in the course of which he was led to state that he, himself, had first advised that the fact of the poisoning should not be mentioned until after the funeral. The onus of the secrecy was thus removed from Joseph, and this was a point gained.

The next witness was the servant-woman, who had been present in the hall when Julia fell upon the landing of the staircase. She had heard the words, "Go away! you have killed me!" spoken in a shrill, excited voice. She had already guessed that something was wrong between the two. Mr. Asten came home looking quite wild and strange; he didn't seem to speak in his usual voice; he walked about in a restless way, and then went into the garden. Miss Lucy followed him, and then Mrs. Asten; but in a little while she came back, with her dress torn and her arms scratched; she, the witness, noticed this as Mrs. Asten passed through the hall, tottering as she went and with her fists shut tight.

Then Mr. Asten went up stairs to her bed-room; heard them speaking, but not the words; said to Sally, who was in the kitchen, "It's a real tiff and no mistake," and Sally remarked, "They're not used to each other yet, as they will be in a year or two."

The witness was with difficulty kept to a direct narrative. She had told the tale so often that every particular had its fixed phrases of description, and all the questioning on both sides called forth only repetitions. Joseph listened with a calm, patient air; nothing had yet occurred for which he was not prepared. The spectators, however, began to be deeply interested, and a sharp observer might have noticed that they were already taking sides.

Mr. Pinkerton soon detected that, although the woman's statements told against Joseph, she possessed no friendly feeling for Julia. He endeavored to make the most of this; but it was not much.

When Lucy Henderson's name was called, there was a stir of curiosity in the audience. They knew that the conference in the garden, from which Julia had returned in such an excited condition, must now be described. Mr. Spenham pricked up his red ears, ran his hand through his stubby hair, and prepared himself for battle; while Mr. Pinkerton, already in possession of all the facts, felt concerned only regarding the manner in which Lucy might give them. This was a case where so much depended on the impression produced by the individual!

By the time Lucy was sworn she appeared to be entirely composed; her face was slightly pale, but calm, and her voice steady. Mrs. Hopeton and Madeline Held sat near her, and Elwood Withers, leaning against a high railing, was nearly opposite.

There was profound silence as she began, and the interest increased as she approached the time of Joseph's return. She described his appearance, repeated the words she had heard, reproduced the scene in her own chamber, and so came, step by step, to the interview in the garden. The trying nature

896

of her task now became evident. She spoke slowly, and with longer pauses; but whichever way she turned in her thought, the inexorable necessity of the whole truth stared her in the face.

"Must I repeat everything?" she asked. "I am not sure of recollecting the words precisely as they were spoken."

"You can certainly give the substance," said Mr. Spenham. "And be careful that you omit nothing: you are on your oath, and you ought to know what that means."

His words were loud and harsh. Lucy looked at the impassive face of the judge, at Elwood's earnest features, at the attentive jurymen, and went on.

When she came to Joseph's expression of the love that might have been possible, she gave also his words: "Had there been, I should have darkened the life of a friend."

"Ha!" exclaimed Mr. Spenham, "we are coming upon the motive of the murder."

Again Mr. Pinkerton protested, and was sustained by the court.

"Tell the jury," said Mr. Spenham, "whether there had been any interchange of such expressions between you and the accused previous to his marriage!"

This question was objected to, but the objection was overruled.

"None whatever!" was the answer.

Julia's sudden appearance, the accusation she made, and the manner in which Joseph met it, seemed to turn the current of sympathy the other way. Lucy's recollection of this scene was very clear and complete: had she wished it, she could not have forgotten a word or a look. In spite of Mr. Spenham's angry objections, she was allowed to go on and relate the conversation between Joseph and herself after Julia's return to the house. Mr. Pinkerton made the best use of this portion of the evidence, and it seemed that his side was strengthened, in spite of all unfavorable appearances.

"This is not all!" exclaimed the prosecuting attorney. "A married man does not make a declaration of love—"

"Of a past possible love," Mr. Pinkerton interrupted.

"A very fine hair-splitting indeed! A 'possible' love and a 'possible' return, followed by a 'possible' murder and a 'possible' remarriage! Our duty is to remove possibilities and establish facts. The question is, Was there no previous affection between the witness and the accused? This is necessary to prove a motive. I ask, then, the woman—I beg pardon, the lady—what were her sentiments towards the husband of the poisoned before his marriage, at the time of the conversation in the garden, and now?"

Lucy started, and could not answer. Mr. Pinkerton came to her aid. He protested strongly against such a question, though he felt that there was equal danger in answering it or leaving it unanswered. A portion of the spectators, sympathizing with Lucy, felt indignant at Mr. Spenham's demand; another portion, hungry for the most private and intimate knowledge of all the parties concerned, eagerly hoped that it would be acceded to.

Lucy half turned, so that she caught a glimpse of Joseph. He was calm, but his eyes expressed a sympathetic trouble. Then she felt her gaze drawn to Elwood, who had become a shade paler, and who met her eyes with a deep, inscrutable expression. Was he thinking of his recent words to her,—"If need comes to publish what I said to you, don't keep back a single word!" She felt sure of it, for all that he said was in her mind. Her decision was made: for truth's sake, and under the eye of God, she would speak. Having so resolved, she shut her mind to all else, for she needed the greatest strength of either woman or man.

The judge had decided that she was not obliged to answer the question. There was a murmur, here and there, among the spectators.

"Then I will use my freedom of choice," said Lucy, in a firm voice, "and answer it."

She kept her eyes on Elwood as she spoke, and compelled him to face her. She seemed to forget judge, jury, and the curious public, and to speak

898

only to his ear.

"I am here to tell the whole truth, God helping me," she said. "I do not know how what I am required to say can touch the question of Joseph Asten's guilt or innocence; but I cannot pause to consider that. It is not easy for a woman to lay bare her secret heart to the world; I would like to think that every man who hears me has a wife, a sister, or a beloved girl of his choice, and that he will try to understand my heart through his knowledge of hers. I did cherish a tenderness which might have been love—I cannot tell—for Joseph Asten before his betrothal. I admit that his marriage was a grief to me at the time, for, while I had not suffered myself to feel any hope, I could not keep the feeling of disappointment out of my heart. It was both my blame and shame: I wrestled with it, and with God's help I overcame it."

There was a simple pathos in Lucy's voice, which pierced directly to the hearts of her hearers. She stood before them as pure as Godiva in her helpful nakedness. She saw on Elwood's cheek the blush which did not visit hers, and the sparkle of an unconscious tear. Joseph had hidden his face in his hands for a moment, but now looked up with a sadness which no man there could misinterpret.

Lucy had paused, as if waiting to be questioned, but the effect of her words had been so powerful and unexpected that Mr. Spenham was not quite ready. She went on:—

"When I say that I overcame it, I think I have answered everything. I went to him in the garden against my own wish, because his wife begged me with tears and sobs to intercede for her: I could not guess that he had ever thought of me otherwise than as a friend. I attributed his expressions to his disappointment in marriage, and pardoned him when he asked me to forget them—"

"O, no doubt!" Mr. Spenham interrupted, looking at the jury; "after all we have heard, they could not have been very disagreeable!"

Elwood made a rapid step forward; then, recollecting himself, resumed his position against the railing. Very few persons noticed the movement.

"They were very unwelcome," Lucy replied: "under any other circumstances, it would not have been easy to forgive them."

"And this former—'tenderness,' I think you called it," Mr. Spenham persisted, "—do you mean to say that you feel nothing of it at present?"

There was a murmur of indignation all over the room. If there is anything utterly incomprehensible to a vulgar nature, it is the natural delicacy of feeling towards women, which is rarely wanting even to the roughest and most ignorant men. The prosecution had damaged itself, and now the popular sympathy was wholly and strongly with Lucy.

"I have already answered that question," she said. "For the holy sake of truth, and of my own free-will, I have opened my heart. I did it, believing that a woman's first affection is pure, and would be respected; I did it, hoping that it might serve the cause of an innocent man; but now, since it has brought upon me doubt and insult, I shall avail myself of the liberty granted to me by the judge, and speak no word more!"

The spectators broke into applause, which the judge did not immediately check. Lucy's strength suddenly left her; she dropped into her seat and burst into tears.

"I have no further question to ask the witness," said Mr. Pinkerton.

Mr. Spenham inwardly cursed himself for his blunder,—not for his vulgarity, for of that he was sublimely unconscious,—and was only too ready to be relieved from Lucy's presence.

She rose to leave the court, Mrs. Hopeton accompanying her; but Elwood Withers was already at her side, and she leaned upon his arm as they passed through the crowd. The people fell back to make a way, and not a few whispered some honest word of encouragement. Elwood breathed heavily, and the veins on his forehead were swollen.

Not a word was spoken until they reached the hotel. Then Lucy, taking Elwood's hand, said: "Thank you, true, dear friend! I can say no more now. Go back, for Joseph's sake, and when the day is over come here and tell me, if

900

you can, that I have not injured him in trying to help him."

When Elwood returned to the court-room, Rachel Miller was on the witness stand. Her testimony confirmed the interpretation of Julia's character which had been suggested by Lucy Henderson's. The sweet, amiable, suffering wife began to recede into the background, and the cold, false, selfish wife to take her place.

All Mr. Spenham's cross-examination failed to give the prosecution any support until he asked the question:—

"Have you discovered nothing whatever, since your return to the house, which will throw any light upon Mrs. Asten's death?"

Mr. Pinkerton, Elwood, and Madeline all felt that the critical moment had come. Philip's absence threatened to be a serious misfortune.

"Yes," Rachel Miller answered.

"Ah!" exclaimed the prosecuting attorney, rubbing his hair; "what was it?"

"The paper in which the arsenic was put up."

"Will you produce that paper?" he eagerly asked.

"I cannot now," said Rachel; "I gave it to Mr. Philip Held, so that he might find out something more."

Joseph listened with a keen, undisguised interest. After the first feeling of surprise that such an important event had been kept from his knowledge, his confidence in Philip's judgment reassured him.

"Has Mr. Philip Held destroyed that paper?" Mr. Spenham asked.

"He retains it, and will produce it before this court to-morrow," Mr. Pinkerton replied.

"Was there any mark, or label, upon it, which indicated the place where the poison had been procured?"

"Yes," said Rachel Miller.

"State what it was."

"Ziba Linthicum's Drug store, No. 77 Main Street, Magnolia," she replied, as if the label were before her eyes.

"Let Ziba Linthicum be summoned at once!" Mr. Spenham cried.

Mr. Pinkerton, however, arose and stated that the apothecary's testimony required that of another person who was present when the poison was purchased. This other person had been absent in a distant part of the country, but had been summoned, and would arrive, in company with Mr. Philip Held, on the following morning. He begged that Mr. Linthicum's evidence might be postponed until then, when he believed that the mystery attending the poisoning would be wholly explained.

Mr. Spenham violently objected, but he again made the mistake of speaking for nearly half an hour on the subject,—an indiscretion into which he was led by his confirmed political habits. By the time the question was decided, and in favor of the defence, the afternoon was well advanced, and the court adjourned until the next day.

# CHAPTER XXIX. NEW EVIDENCE.

Elwood accompanied Joseph to the prison where he was obliged to spend the night, and was allowed to remain with him until Mr. Pinkerton (who was endeavoring to reach Philip by telegraph) should arrive.

Owing to Rachel Miller's forethought, the bare room was sufficiently furnished. There was a clean bed, a chair or two, and a table, upon which stood a basket of provisions.

"I suppose I must eat," said Joseph, "as a matter of duty. If you will sit down and join me, Elwood, I will try."

"If I could have that fellow Spenham by the throat for a minute," Elwood growled, "it would give me a good appetite. But I will take my share, as it is: I never can think rightly when I'm hungry. Why, there is enough for a picnic! sandwiches, cold chicken, pickles, cakes, cheese, and two bottles of coffee, as I live! Just think that we're in a hotel, Joseph! It's all in one's notion, leastways for a single night; for you can go where you like to-morrow!"

"I hope so," said Joseph, as he took his seat. Elwood set the provisions before him, but he did not touch them. After a moment of hesitation he stretched out his hand and laid it on Elwood's shoulder.

"Now, old boy!" Elwood cried: "I know it. What you mean is unnecessary, and I won't have it!"

"Let me speak!"

"I don't see why I should, Joseph. It's no more than I guessed. She didn't love me: you were tolerably near together once, and if you should now come nearer—"

But he could not finish the sentence; the words stuck in his throat.

"Great Heaven!" Joseph exclaimed, starting to his feet; "what are you thinking of? Don't you see that Lucy Henderson and I are parted forever by what has happened to-day? Didn't you hear her say that she overcame the tenderness which might have become love, as I overcame mine for her? Neither of us can recall that first feeling, any more than we can set our lives again in the past. I shall worship her as one of the purest and noblest souls that breathe; but love her? make her my wife? It could never, never be! No, Elwood! I was wondering whether you could pardon me the rashness which has exposed her to to-day's trial."

Elwood began to laugh strangely. "You are foolish, Joseph," he said. "Pshaw! I can't hold my knife. These sudden downs and then ups are too much for a fellow! Pardon you? Yes, on one condition—that you empty your plate before you speak another word to me!"

They were both cheerful after this, and the narrow little room seemed freer and brighter to their eyes. It was late before Mr. Pinkerton arrived: he had waited in vain for an answer from Philip. Elwood's presence was a relief to him, for he did not wish to excite Joseph by a statement of what he expected to prove unless the two witnesses had been really secured. He adroitly managed, however, to say very little while seeming to say a great deal, and Joseph was then left to such rest as his busy memory might allow him.

Next morning there was an even greater crowd in the court-room. All Joseph's friends were there, with the exception of Lucy Henderson, who, by Mr. Pinkerton's advice, remained at the hotel. Philip had not arrived, but had sent a message saying that all was well, and he would come in the morning train.

Mr. Spenham, the evening before, had ascertained the nature of Mr. Linthicum's evidence. The apothecary, however, was only able to inform him of Philip's desire to discover the travelling agent, without knowing his purpose. In the name recorded as that of the purchaser of the poison Mr. Spenham saw a weapon which would enable him to repay Lucy for his discomfiture, and to indicate, if not prove, a complicity of crime, in which Philip Held also, he suspected, might be concerned.

The court opened at nine o'clock, and Philip could not be on hand before ten. Mr. Pinkerton endeavored to procure the examination of Dennis, and another subordinate witness, before the apothecary; but he only succeeded in gaining fifteen minutes' time by the discussion. Mr. Ziba Linthicum was then called and sworn. He carried a volume under his arm.

As Philip possessed the label, Mr. Linthicum could only testify to the fact that a veiled lady had purchased so many grains of arsenic of him on a certain day; that he kept a record of all sales of dangerous drugs; and that the lady's name was recorded in the book which he had brought with him. He then read the entry:—

"Miss Henderson. Arsenic."

Although Mr. Pinkerton had whispered to Joseph, "Do not be startled when he reads the name!" it was all the latter could do to suppress an exclamation. There was a murmur and movement through the whole court.

"We have now both the motive and the co-agent of the crime," said Mr. Spenham, rising triumphantly. "After the evidence which was elicited yesterday, it will not be difficult to connect the two. If the case deepens in enormity as it advances, we may be shocked, but we have no reason to be surprised. The growth of free-love sentiments, among those who tear themselves loose from the guidance of religious influences, naturally leads to crime; and the extent to which this evil has been secretly developed is not suspected by the public. Testimony can be adduced to show that the accused, Joseph Asten, has openly expressed his infidelity; that he repelled with threats and defiance a worthy minister of the Gospel, whom his own pious murdered wife had commissioned to lead him into the true path. The very expression which the woman Lucy Henderson testified to his having used in the garden,—'I am sick of masks,'—what does it mean? What but unrestrained freedom of the passions,—the very foundation upon which the free-lovers build up their pernicious theories? The accused cannot complain if the law lifts the mask from his countenance, and shows his nature in all its hideous deformity. But another mask, also, must be raised: I demand the arrest of the woman Lucy Henderson!"

Mr. Pinkerton sprang to his feet. In a measured, solemn voice, which contrasted strongly with the loud, sharp tones of the prosecuting attorney, he stated that Mr. Linthicum's evidence was already known to him; that it required an explanation which would now be given in a few minutes, and which would completely exonerate Miss Henderson from the suspicion of having purchased the poison, or even having any knowledge of its purchase. He demanded that no conclusion should be drawn from evidence which would mislead the minds of the jury: he charged the prosecuting attorney with most unjustly assailing the characters of both Joseph Asten and Lucy Henderson, and invoked, in the name of impartial justice, the protection of the court.

He spoke both eloquently and earnestly; but the spectators noticed that he looked at his watch from minute to minute. Mr. Spenham interrupted him, but he continued to repeat his statements, until there came a sudden movement in the crowd, near the outer door of the hall. Then he sat down.

Philip led the way, pressing the crowd to right and left in his eagerness. He was followed by a tall young man, with a dark moustache and an abundance of jewelry, while Mr. Benjamin Blessing, flushed and perspiring, brought up the rear. The spectators were almost breathless in their hushed, excited interest.

Philip seized Joseph's hand, and, bending nearer, whispered, "You are free!" His eyes sparkled and his face glowed.

Room was made for the three witnesses, and after a brief whispered consultation between Philip and Mr. Pinkerton, Elwood was despatched to bring Lucy Henderson to the court.

"May it please the Court," said Mr. Pinkerton, "I am now able to fulfil that promise which I this moment made. The evidence which was necessary to set forth the manner of Mrs. Asten's death, and which will release the court from any further consideration of the present case, is in my hands. I therefore ask leave to introduce this evidence without any further delay."

After a little discussion the permission was granted, and Philip Held was placed upon the stand.

He first described Joseph's genuine sorrow at his wife's death, and his self-accusation of having hastened it by his harsh words to her in the morning. He related the interview at which Joseph, on learning of the reports concerning him, had immediately decided to ask for a legal investigation, and in a simple, straightforward way, narrated all that had been done up to the time of consulting Ziba Linthicum's poison record.

"As I knew it to be quite impossible that Miss Lucy Henderson could have been the purchaser," he began—

Mr. Spenham instantly objected, and the expression was ruled out by the Court.

"Then," Philip resumed, "I determined to ascertain who had purchased the arsenic. Mr. Linthicum's description of the lady was too vague to be recognized. It was necessary to identify the travelling agent who was present; for this purpose I went to the city, ascertained the names and addresses of all the travelling agents of all the wholesale drug firms, and after much time and correspondence discovered the man,—Mr. Case, who is here present. He was in Persepolis, Iowa, when the summons reached him, and would have been here yesterday but for an accident on the Erie Railway.

"In the mean time I had received the small fragment of another label, and by the clew which the few letters gave me I finally identified the place as the drug-store of Wallis and Erkers, at the corner of Fifth and Persimmon Streets. There was nothing left by which the nature of the drug could be ascertained, and therefore this movement led to nothing which could be offered as evidence in this court,—that is, by the druggists themselves, and they have not been summoned. It happened, however, by a coincidence which only came to light this morning, that—"

Here Philip was again interrupted. His further testimony was of less consequence. He was sharply cross-examined by Mr. Spenham as to his relations with Joseph, and his object in devoting so much time to procuring evidence for the defence; but he took occasion, in replying, to express his appreciation of Joseph's character so emphatically, that the prosecution lost rather than gained. Then the plan of attack was changed. He was asked whether he believed in the Bible, in future rewards and punishments, in the views of the so-called free-lovers, in facile divorce and polygamy. He was too shrewd, however, to lay himself open to the least misrepresentation, and the moral and mental torture which our jurisprudence has substituted for the rack, thumb-screws, and Spanish boots of the Middle Ages finally came to an end.

Then the tall young man, conscious of his own elegance, took his place. He gave his name and occupation as Augustus Fitzwilliam Case, commercial traveller for the house of Byle and Glanders, wholesale druggists.

"State whether you were in the drug-store of Ziba Linthicum, No. 77 Main Street, in this town, on the day of the entry in Mr. Linthicum's book."

"I was."

"Did you notice the person who called for arsenic?"

"I did."

"What led you specially to notice her?"

"It is my habit," said the witness. "I am impressible to beauty, and I saw at once that the lady had what I call—style. I recollect thinking, 'More style than could be expected in these little places.'"

"Keep your thoughts to yourself!" cried Mr. Spenham.

"Describe the lady as correctly as you can," said Mr. Pinkerton.

"Something under the medium size; a little thin, but not bad lines,—what I should call jimp, natty, or 'lissome,' in the Scotch dialect. A well-trained voice; no uncertainty about it,—altogether about as keen and wide-awake a woman as you'll find in a day's travel."

"You guessed all this from her figure?" Mr. Spenham asked, with a sneer.

"Not entirely. I saw her face. I suppose something in my appearance or attitude attracted her attention. While Mr. Linthicum was weighing the arsenic she leaned over the counter, let her veil fall forward slightly, and gave me a quick side-look. I bent a little at the same time, as if to examine the soaps, and saw her face in a three-quarter position, as the photographers say."

"Can you remember her features distinctly?"

"Quite so. In fact, it is difficult for me to forget a female face. Hers was just verging on the sharp, but still tolerably handsome. Hair quite dark, and worn in ringlets; eyebrows clean and straight; mouth a little too thin for my fancy; and eyes—well, I couldn't undertake to say exactly what color they were, for she seemed to have the trick—very common in the city—of letting the lids droop over them."

"Were you able to judge of her age?"

"Tolerably, I should say. There is a certain air of preservation which enables a practised eye to distinguish an old girl from a young one. She was certainly not to be called young,—somewhere between twenty-eight and thirty-five."

"You heard the name she gave Mr. Linthicum?"

"Distinctly. Mr. Linthicum politely stated that it was his custom to register the names of all those to whom he furnished either poisons or prescriptions requiring care in being administered. She said, 'You are very particular, sir;' and, a moment afterward, 'Pardon me, perhaps it is necessary.'—'What name, then?' he asked. I thought she hesitated a moment, but this I will not say positively; whether or not, the answer was, 'Miss Henderson.' She went out of the store with a light, brisk step."

"You are sure you would be able to recognize the lady?" Mr. Pinkerton asked.

"Quite sure." And Mr. Augustus Fitzwilliam Case smiled patronizingly, as if the question were superfluous.

Mr. Pinkerton made a sign to Lucy, and she arose.

"Look upon this lady!" he said to the witness.

The latter made a slight, graceful inclination of his head, as much as to say, "Pardon me, I am compelled to stare." Lucy quietly endured his gaze.

"Consider her well," said the lawyer, "and then tell the jury whether she is the person."

"No considerment is necessary. This lady has not the slightest resemblance to Miss Henderson. She is younger, taller, and modelled upon a wholly different style."

"Will you now look at this photograph?"

"Ah!" the witness exclaimed; "you can yourself judge of the correctness of my memory! Here is Miss Henderson herself, and in three-quarter face, as I saw her!"

"That," said Mr. Pinkerton, addressing the judge and jury, "that is the photograph of Mrs. Julia Asten."

The spectators were astounded, and Mr. Spenham taken completely aback by this revelation. Joseph and Elwood both felt that a great weight had been lifted from their hearts. The testimony established Julia's falsehood at the same time, and there was such an instant and complete revulsion of opinion that many persons present at once suspected her of a design to poison Joseph.

"Before calling upon Mr. Benjamin Blessing, the father of the late Mrs. Asten, for his testimony," said Mr. Pinkerton,—"and I believe he will be the last witness necessary,—I wish to show that, although Miss Lucy Henderson accompanied Mrs. Asten to Magnolia, she could not have visited Mr. Linthicum's Drug store at the time indicated; nor, indeed, at any time during that day. She made several calls upon friends, each of whom is now in attendance, and their joint evidence will account for every minute of her stay in the place. The base attempt to blacken her fair name imperatively imposes this duty upon me."

No objection was made, and the witnesses were briefly examined in succession. Their testimony was complete.

"One mystery still remains to be cleared up," the lawyer continued; "the purpose of Mrs. Asten in purchasing the poison, and the probable explanation of her death. I say 'probable,' because absolute certainty is impossible. But I will not anticipate the evidence. Mr. Benjamin Blessing, step forward, if you please!"

# CHAPTER XXX. MR. BLESSING'S TESTIMONY.

On entering the court-room Mr. Blessing had gone to Joseph, given his hand a long, significant grasp, and looked in his face with an expression of triumph, almost of exultation. The action was not lost upon the spectators or the jury, and even Joseph felt that it was intended to express the strongest faith in his innocence.

When the name was called there was a movement in the crowd, and a temporary crush in some quarters, as the people thrust forward their heads to see and listen. Mr. Blessing, bland, dignified, serene, feeling that he was the central point of interest, waited until quiet had been restored, slightly turning his head to either side, as if to summon special attention to what he should say.

After being sworn, and stating his name, he thus described his occupation:—

"I hold a position under government; nominally, it is a Deputy Inspectorship in the Custom-House, yet it possesses a confidential—I might say, if modesty did not prevent, an advisory—character."

"In other words, a Ward Politician!" said Mr. Spenham.

"I must ask the prosecuting attorney," Mr. Blessing blandly suggested, "not to define my place according to his own political experiences."

There was a general smile at these words; and a very audible chuckle from spectators belonging to the opposite party.

"You are the father of the late Mrs. Julia Asten?"

"I am—her unhappy father, whom nothing but the imperious commands of justice, and the knowledge of her husband's innocence of the crime with which he stands charged, could have compelled to appear here, and reveal the painful secrets of a family, which—"

Here Mr. Spenham interrupted him.

"I merely wish to observe," Mr. Blessing continued, with a stately wave of his hand towards the judge and jury, "that the De Belsains and their descendants may have been frequently unfortunate, but were never dishonorable. I act in their spirit when I hold duty to the innocent living higher than consideration for the unfortunate dead."

Here he drew forth a handkerchief, and held it for a moment to his eyes.

"Did you know of any domestic discords between your daughter and her husband?"

"I foresaw that such might be, and took occasion to warn my daughter, on her wedding-day, not to be too sure of her influence. There was too much disparity of age, character, and experience. It could not be called crabbed age and rosy youth, but there was difference enough to justify Shakespeare's doubts. I am aware that the court requires ocular—or auricular—evidence. The only such I have to offer is my son-in-law's own account of the discord which preceded my daughter's death."

"Did this discord sufficiently explain to you the cause and manner of her death?"

"My daughter's nature—I do not mean to digress, but am accustomed to state my views clearly—my daughter's nature was impulsive. She inherited my own intellect, but modified by the peculiar character of the feminine nervous system. Hence she might succumb to a depression which I should resist. She appeared to be sure of her control over my son-in-law's nature, and of success in an enterprise, in which—I regret to say—my son-in-law lost confidence. I assumed, at the time, that her usually capable mind was unbalanced by the double disappointment, and that she had rushed, unaneled, to her last account. This, I say, was the conclusion forced upon me; yet I cannot admit that it was satisfactory. It seemed to disparage my daughter's intellectual power: it was not the act which I should have anticipated in any possible emergency."

"Had you no suspicion that her husband might have been instrumental?"

912

Mr. Spenham asked.

"He? he is simply incapable of that, or any crime!"

"We don't want assertions," said Mr. Spenham, sternly.

"I beg pardon of the court," remarked Mr. Blessing; "it was a spontaneous expression. The touch of nature cannot always be avoided."

"Go on, sir!"

"I need not describe the shock and sorrow following my daughter's death," Mr. Blessing continued, again applying his handkerchief. "In order to dissipate it, I obtained a leave of absence from my post,—the exigencies of the government fortunately admitting of it,—and made a journey to the Oil Regions, in the interest of myself and my son-in-law. While there I received a letter from Mr. Philip Held, the contents of which—"

"Will you produce the letter?" Mr. Spenham exclaimed.

"It can be produced, if necessary. I will state nothing further, since I perceive that this would not be admissible evidence. It is enough to say that I returned to the city without delay, in order to meet Mr. Philip Held. The requirements of justice were more potent with me than the suggestions of personal interest. Mr. Held had already, as you will have noticed from his testimony, identified the fragment of paper as having emanated from the drug-store of Wallis and Erkers, corner of Fifth and Persimmon Streets. I accompanied him to that drug-store, heard the statements of the proprietors, in answer to Mr. Held's questions,—statements which, I confess, surprised me immeasurably (but I could not reject the natural deductions to be drawn from them), and was compelled, although it overwhelmed me with a sense of unmerited shame, to acknowledge that there was plausibility in Mr. Held's conjectures. Since they pointed to my elder daughter, Clementina, now Mrs. Spelter, and at this moment tossing upon the ocean-wave, I saw that Mr. Held might possess a discernment superior to my own. But for a lamentable cataclysm, he might have been my son-in-law, and I need not say that I prefer that refinement of character which comes of good blood to the possession of millions—"

Here Mr. Blessing was again interrupted, and ordered to confine himself to the simple statement of the necessary facts.

"I acknowledge the justice of the rebuke," he said. "But the sentiment of the mens conscia recti will sometimes obtrude through the rigid formula of Themis. In short, Mr. Philip Held's representations—"

"State those representations at once, and be done with them!" Mr. Spenham cried.

"I am coming to them presently. The Honorable Court understands, I am convinced, that a coherent narrative, although moderately prolix, is preferable to a disjointed narrative, even if the latter were terse as Tacitus. Mr. Held's representations, I repeat, satisfied me that an interview with my daughter Clementina was imperative. There was no time to be lost, for the passage of the nuptial pair had already been taken in the Ville de Paris. I started at once, sending a telegram in advance, and in the same evening arrived at their palatial residence in Fifth Avenue. Clementina's nature, I must explain to the Honorable Court, is very different from that of her sister,— the reappearance, I suspect, of some lateral strain of blood. She is reticent, undemonstrative,—in short, frequently inscrutable. I suspected that a direct question might defeat my object; therefore, when I was alone with her the next morning,—my son-in-law, Mr. Spelter, being called to a meeting of Erie of which he is one of the directors,—I said to her: 'My child, you are perfectly blooming! Your complexion was always admirable, but now it seems to me incomparable!'"

"This is irrelevant!" cried Mr. Spenham.

"By no means! It is the very corpus delicti,—the foot of Hercules,—the milk (powder would be more appropriate) in the cocoa-nut!" Clementina smiled in her serene way, and made no reply. 'How do you keep it up now?' I asked, tapping her cheek; 'you must be careful, here: all persons are not so discreet as Wallis and Erkers.' She was astounded, stupefied, I might say, but I saw that I had reached the core of truth. 'Did you suppose I was ignorant of it?' I said, still very friendly and playfully. 'Then it was Julia who told you!' she exclaimed. 'And if she did,' I answered, 'what was the harm? I have no doubt

914

that Julia did the same thing.' 'She was always foolish,' Clementina then said; 'she envied me my complexion, and she watched me until she found out. I told her that it would not do for any except blondes, like myself, and her complexion was neither one thing nor the other. And I couldn't see that it improved much, afterwards.'"

Mr. Pinkerton saw that the jurymen were puzzled, and requested Mr. Blessing to explain the conversation to them.

"It is my painful duty to obey; yet a father's feelings may be pardoned if he shrinks from presenting the facts at once in their naked—unpleasantness. However, since the use of arsenic as a cosmetic is so general in our city, especially among blondes, as Wallis and Erkers assure me, my own family is not an isolated case. Julia commenced using the drug, so Clementina informed me, after her engagement with Mr. Asten, and only a short time before her marriage. To what extent she used it, after that event, I have no means of knowing; but, I suspect, less frequently, unless she feared that the disparity of age between her and her husband was becoming more apparent. I cannot excuse her duplicity in giving Miss Henderson's name instead of her own at Mr. Linthicum's Drug store, since the result might have been so fearfully fatal; yet I entreat you to believe that there may have been no inimical animus in the act. I attribute her death entirely to an over-dose of the drug, voluntarily taken, but taken in a moment of strong excitement."

The feeling of relief from suspense, not only among Joseph's friends, but throughout the crowded court-room, was clearly manifested: all present seemed to breathe a lighter and fresher atmosphere.

Mr. Blessing wiped his forehead and his fat cheeks, and looked benignly around. "There are a hundred little additional details," he said, "which will substantiate my evidence; but I have surely said sufficient for the ends of justice. The heavens will not fall because I have been forced to carve the emblems of criminal vanity upon the sepulchre of an unfortunate child,— but the judgment of an earthly tribunal may well be satisfied. However, I am ready," he added, turning towards Mr. Spenham; "apply all the engines of technical procedure, and I shall not wince."

The manner of the prosecuting attorney was completely changed. He answered respectfully and courteously, and his brief cross-examination was calculated rather to confirm the evidence for the defence than to invalidate it.

Mr. Pinkerton then rose and stated that he should call no other witnesses. The fact had been established that Mrs. Asten had been in the habit of taking arsenic to improve her complexion; also that she had purchased much more than enough of the drug to cause death, at the store of Mr. Ziba Linthicum, only a few days before her demise, and under circumstances which indicated a desire to conceal the purchase. There were two ways in which the manner of her death might be explained; either she had ignorantly taken an over-dose, or, having mixed the usual quantity before descending to the garden to overhear the conversation between Mr. Asten and Lucy Henderson, had forgotten the fact in the great excitement which followed, and thoughtlessly added as much more of the poison. Her last words to her husband, which could not be introduced as evidence, but might now be repeated, showed that her death was the result of accident, and not of design. She was thus absolved of the guilt of suicide, even as her husband of the charge of murder.

Mr. Spenham, somewhat to the surprise of those who were unacquainted with his true character, also stated that he should call no further witness for the prosecution. The testimonies of Mr. Augustus Fitzwilliam Case and Mr. Benjamin Blessing—although the latter was unnecessarily ostentatious and discursive—were sufficient to convince him that the prosecution could not make out a case. He had no doubt whatever of Mr. Joseph Asten's innocence. Lest the expressions which he had been compelled to use, in the performance of his duty, might be misunderstood, he wished to say that he had the highest respect for the characters of Mr. Asten and also of Miss Lucy Henderson. He believed the latter to be a refined and virtuous lady, an ornament to the community in which she resided. His language towards her had been professional,—by no means personal. It was in accordance with the usage of the most eminent lights of the bar; the ends of justice required the most searching examination, and the more a character was criminated the more brightly it would shine forth to the world after the test had been successfully endured. He was simply the agent of the law, and all respect of persons was prohibited to him while in the exercise of his functions.

The judge informed the jurymen that he did not find it necessary to give them any instructions. If they were already agreed upon their verdict, even the formality of retiring might be dispensed with.

There was a minute's whispering back and forth among the men, and the foreman then rose and stated that they were agreed.

The words "Not Guilty!" spoken loudly and emphatically, were the signal for a stormy burst of applause from the audience. In vain the court-crier, aided by the constables, endeavored to preserve order. Joseph's friends gathered around him with their congratulations; while Mr. Blessing, feeling that some recognition of the popular sentiment was required, rose and bowed repeatedly to the crowd. Philip led the way to the open air, and the others followed, but few words were spoken until they found themselves in the large parlor of the hotel.

Mr. Blessing had exchanged some mysterious whispers with the clerk, on arriving; and presently two negro waiters entered the room, bearing wine, ice, and other refreshments. When the glasses had been filled, Mr. Blessing lifted his with an air which imposed silence on the company, and thus spake: "'Out of the abundance of the heart the mouth speaketh.' There may be occasions when silence is golden, but to-day we are content with the baser metal. A man in whom we all confide, whom we all love, has been rescued from the labyrinth of circumstances; he comes to us as a new Theseus, saved from the Minotaur of the Law! Although Mr. Held, with the assistance of his fair sister, was the Ariadne who found the clew, it has been my happy lot to assist in unrolling it; and now we all stand together, like our classic models on the free soil of Crete, to chant a pæan of deliverance. While I propose the health and happiness and good-fortune of Joseph Asten, I beg him to believe that my words come ab imo pectore,—from my inmost heart: if any veil of mistrust, engendered by circumstances which I will not now recall, still hangs between him and myself, I entreat him to rend that veil, even as David rent his garments, and believe in my sincerity, if he cannot in my discretion!"

Philip was the only one, besides Joseph, who understood the last allusion.

He caught hold of Mr. Blessing's hand and exclaimed: "Spoken like a man!"

Joseph stepped instantly forward. "I have again been unjust," he said, "and I thank you for making me feel it. You have done me an infinite service, sacrificing your own feelings, bearing no malice against me for my hasty and unpardonable words, and showing a confidence in my character which—after what has passed between us—puts me to shame. I am both penitent and grateful: henceforth I shall know you and esteem you!"

Mr. Blessing took the offered hand, held it a moment, and then stammered, while the tears started from his eyes: "Enough! Bury the past a thousand fathoms deep! I can still say: foi de Belsain!"

"One more toast!" cried Philip. "Happiness and worldly fortune to the man whom misfortunes have bent but cannot break,—who has been often deceived, but who never purposely deceived in turn,—whose sentiment of honor has been to-day so nobly manifested,—Benjamin Blessing!"

While the happy company were pouring out but not exhausting their feelings, Lucy Henderson stole forth upon the upper balcony of the hotel. There was a secret trouble in her heart, which grew from minute to minute. She leaned upon the railing, and looked down the dusty street, passing in review the events of the two pregnant days, and striving to guess in what manner they would affect her coming life. She felt that she had done her simple duty: she had spoken no word which she was not ready to repeat; yet in her words there seemed to be the seeds of change.

After a while the hostler brought a light carriage from the stable, and Elwood Withers stepped into the street below her. He was about to take the reins, when he looked up, saw her, and remained standing. She noticed the intensely wistful expression of his face.

"Are you going, Elwood,—and alone?" she asked.

"Yes," he said eagerly; and waited.

"Then I will go with you,—that is, if you will take me." She tried to speak lightly and playfully.

In a few minutes they were out of town, passing between the tawny fields and under the russet woods. A sweet west wind fanned them with nutty and spicy odors, and made a crisp, cheerful music among the fallen leaves.

"What a delicious change!" said Lucy, "after that stifling, dreadful room."

"Ay, Lucy—and think how Joseph will feel it! And how near, by the chance of a hair, we came of missing the truth!"

"Elwood!" she exclaimed, "while I was giving my testimony, and I found your eyes fixed on me, were you thinking of the counsel you gave me, three weeks ago, when we met at the tunnel?"

"I was!"

"I knew it, and I obeyed. Do you now say that I did right?"

"Not for that reason," he answered. "It was your own heart that told you what to do. I did not mean to bend or influence you in any way: I have no right."

"You have the right of a friend," she whispered.

"Yes," said he, "I sometimes take more upon myself than I ought. But it's hard, in my case, to hit a very fine line."

"O, you are now unjust to yourself, Elwood. You are both strong and generous."

"I am not strong! I am this minute spoiling my good luck. It was a luck from Heaven to me, Lucy, when you offered to ride home with me, and it is, now—if I could only swallow the words that are rising into my mouth!"

She whispered again: "Why should you swallow them?"

"You are cruel! when you have forbidden me to speak, and I have promised to obey!"

"After all you have heard?" she asked.

"All the more for what I have heard."

She took his hand, and cried, in a trembling voice: "I have been cruel, in remaining blind to your nature. I resisted what would have been—what will be, if you do not turn away—my one happiness in this life! Do not speak—let me break the prohibition! Elwood, dear, true, noble heart,—Elwood, I love you!"

"Lucy!"

And she lay upon his bosom.

## CHAPTER XXXI. BEGINNING ANOTHER LIFE.

IT was hard for the company of rejoicing friends, at the hotel in Magnolia, to part from each other. Mr. Blessing had tact enough to decline Joseph's invitation, but he was sorely tempted by Philip's, in which Madeline heartily joined. Nevertheless, he only wavered for a moment; a mysterious resolution strengthened him, and taking Philip to one side, he whispered:—

"Will you allow me to postpone, not relinquish, the pleasure? Thanks! A grave duty beckons,—a task, in short, without which the triumph of to-day would be dramatically incomplete. I must speak in riddles, because this is a case in which a whisper might start the overhanging avalanche; but I am sure you will trust me."

"Of course I will!" Philip cried, offering his hand.

"Foi de Belsain!" was Mr. Blessing's proud answer, as he hurried away to reach the train for the city.

Joseph looked at Philip, as the horses were brought from the stable, and then at Rachel Miller, who, wrapped in her great crape shawl, was quietly waiting for him.

"We must not separate all at once," said Philip, stepping forward. "Miss Miller, will you invite my sister and myself to take tea with you this evening?"

Philip had become one of Rachel's heroes; she was sure that Mr. Blessing's testimony and Joseph's triumphant acquittal were owing to his exertions. The Asten farm could produce nothing good enough for his entertainment,—that was her only trouble.

"Do tell me the time o' day," she said to Joseph, as he drove out of town, closely followed by Philip's light carriage. "It's three days in one to me, and a deal more like day after to-morrow morning than this afternoon. Now, a telegraph would be a convenience; I could send word and have chickens killed and picked, against we got there."

Joseph answered her by driving as rapidly as the rough country roads permitted, without endangering horse and vehicle. It was impossible for him to think coherently, impossible to thrust back the single overwhelming prospect of relief and release which had burst upon his life. He dared to admit the fortune which had come to him through death, now that his own innocence of any indirect incitement thereto had been established. The future was again clear before him; and even the miserable discord of the past year began to recede and form only an indistinct background to the infinite pity of the death-scene. Mr. Blessing's testimony enabled him to look back and truly interpret the last appealing looks, the last broken words; his heart banished the remembrance of its accusations, and retained only—so long as it should beat among living men—a deep and tender commiseration. As for the danger he had escaped, the slander which had been heaped upon him, his thoughts were above the level of life which they touched. He was nearer than he suspected to that only true independence of soul which releases a man from the yoke of circumstances.

Rachel Miller humored his silence as long as she thought proper, and then suddenly and awkwardly interrupted it. "Yes," she exclaimed; "there's a little of the old currant wine in the cellar-closet! Town's-folks generally like it, and we used to think it good to stay a body's stomach for a late meal,—as it'll be apt to be. But I've not asked you how you relished the supper, though Elwood, to be sure, allowed that all was tolerable nice. And I see the Lord's hand in it, as I hope you do, Joseph; for the righteous is never forsaken. We can't help rejoice, where we ought to be humbly returning thanks, and owning our unworthiness; but Philip Held is a friend, if there ever was one; and the white hen's brood, though they are new-fashioned fowls, are plump enough by this time. I disremember whether I asked Elwood to stop—"

"There he is!" Joseph interrupted; "turning the corner of the wood before us! Lucy is with him,—and they must both come!"

He drove on rapidly, and soon overtook Elwood's lagging team. The horse, indeed, had had his own way, and the sound of approaching wheels awoke Elwood from a trance of incredible happiness. Before answering Joseph, he whispered to Lucy:—

922

"What shall we say? It'll be the heaviest favor I've ever been called upon to do a friend."

"Do it, then!" she said: "The day is too blessed to be kept for ourselves alone."

How fair the valley shone, as they came into it out of the long glen between the hills! What cheer there was, even in the fading leaves; what happy promise in the mellow autumn sky! The gate to the lane stood open; Dennis, with a glowing face, waited for the horse. He wanted to say something, but not knowing how, shook hands with Joseph, and then pretended to be concerned with the harness. Rachel, on entering the kitchen, found her neighbor, Mrs. Bishop, embarked on a full tide of preparation. Two plump fowls, scalded and plucked, lay upon the table!

This was too much for Rachel Miller. She had borne up bravely through the trying days, concealing her anxiety lest it might be misinterpreted, hiding even her grateful emotion, to make her faith in Joseph's innocence seem the stronger; and now Mrs. Bishop's thoughtfulness was the slight touch under which she gave way. She sat down and cried.

Mrs. Bishop, with a stew-pan in one hand, while she wiped her sympathetic eyes with the other, explained that her husband had come home an hour before, with the news; and that she just guessed help would be wanted, or leastways company, and so she had made bold to begin; for, though the truth had been made manifest, and the right had been proved, as anybody might know it would be, still it was a trial, and people needed to eat more and better under trials than at any other time. "You may not feel inclined for victuals; but there's the danger! A body's body must be supported, whether or no."

Meanwhile, Joseph and his guests sat on the veranda, in the still, mild air. He drew his chair near to Philip's, their hands closed upon each other, and they were entirely happy in the tender and perfect manly love which united them. Madeline sat in front, with a nimbus of sunshine around her hair, feeling also the embarrassment of speech at such a moment, yet bravely endeavoring to gossip with Lucy on other matters. But Elwood's face, so bright

923

that it became almost beautiful, caught her eye: she glanced at Philip, who answered with a smile; then at Lucy, whose cheek bloomed with the loveliest color; and, rising without a word, she went to the latter and embraced her.

Then, stretching her hand to Elwood, she said: "Forgive me, both of you, for showing how glad I am!"

"Philip!" Joseph cried, as the truth flashed upon him; "life is not always unjust! It is we who are impatient."

They both arose and gave hands of congratulation; and Elwood, though so deeply moved that he scarcely trusted himself to speak, was so frankly proud and happy,—so purely and honestly man in such a sacred moment,—that Lucy's heart swelled with an equally proud recognition of his feeling. Their eyes met, and no memory of a mistaken Past could ever again come like a cloud across the light of their mutual faith.

"The day was blessed already," said Philip; "but this makes it perfect."

No one knew how the time went by, or could afterwards recall much that was said. Rachel Miller, with many apologies, summoned them to a sumptuous meal; and when the moon hung chill and clear above the creeping mists of the valley, they parted.

The next evening, Joseph went to Philip at the Forge. It was well that he should breathe another atmosphere, and dwell, for a little while, within walls where no ghosts of his former life wandered. Madeline, the most hospitably observant of hostesses, seemed to have planned the arrangements solely for his and Philip's intercourse. The short evening of the country was not half over, before she sent them to Philip's room, where a genial wood-fire prattled and flickered on the hearth, with two easy-chairs before it.

Philip lighted a pipe and they sat down. "Now, Joseph," said he, "I'll answer 'Yes!' to the question in your mind."

"You have been talking with Bishop, Philip?"

"No; but I won't mystify you. As I rode up the valley, I saw you two standing on the hill, and could easily guess the rest. A large estate in this

924

country is only an imaginary fortune. You are not so much of a farmer, Joseph, that it will cut you to the heart and make you dream of ruin to part with a few fields; if you were, I should say get that weakness out of you at once! A man should possess his property, not be possessed by it."

"You are right," Joseph answered; "I have been fighting against an inherited feeling."

"The only question is, will the sale of those fifty acres relieve you of all present embarrassments?"

"So far, Philip, that a new mortgage of about half the amount will cover what remains."

"Bravo!" cried Philip. "This is better than I thought. Mr. Hopeton is looking for sure, steady investments, and will furnish whatever you need. So there is no danger of foreclosure."

"Things seem to shape themselves almost too easily now," Joseph answered. "I see the old, mechanical routine of my life coming back: it should be enough for me, but it is not; can you tell me why, Philip?"

"Yes: it never was enough. The most of our neighbors are cases of arrested development. Their intellectual nature only takes so many marks, like a horse's teeth; there is a point early in their lives, where its form becomes fixed. There is neither the external influence, nor the inward necessity, to drive them a step further. They find the Sphinx dangerous, and keep out of her way. Of course, as soon as they passively begin, to accept what is, all that was fluent or plastic in them soon hardens into the old moulds. Now, I am not very wise, but this appears to me to be truth; that life is a grand centrifugal force, forever growing from a wider circle towards one that is still wider. Your stationary men may be necessary, and even serviceable; but to me—and to you, Joseph—there is neither joy nor peace except in some kind of growth."

"If we could be always sure of the direction!" Joseph sighed.

"That's the point!" Philip eagerly continued. "If we stop to consider danger in advance, we should never venture a step. A movement is always clear after it has been made, not often before. It is enough to test one's intention; unless we are tolerably bad, something guides us, and adjusts the consequences of our acts. Why, we are like spiders, in the midst of a million gossamer threads, which we are all the time spinning without knowing it! Who are to measure our lives for us? Not other men with other necessities! and so we come back to the same point again, where I started. Looking back now, can you see no gain in your mistake?"

"Yes, a gain I can never lose. I begin to think that haste and weakness also are vices, and deserve to be punished. It was a dainty, effeminate soul you found, Philip,—a moral and spiritual Sybarite, I should say now. I must have expected to lie on rose-leaves, and it was right that I should find thorns."

"I think," said Philip, "the world needs a new code of ethics. We must cure the unfortunate tendencies of some qualities that seem good, and extract the good from others that seem evil. But it would need more than a Luther for such a Reformation. I confess I am puzzled, when I attempt to study moral causes and consequences in men's lives. It is nothing but a tangle, when I take them collectively. What if each of us were, as I half suspect, as independent as a planet, yet all held together in one immense system? Then the central force must be our close dependence on God, as I have learned to feel it through you."

"Through me!" Joseph exclaimed.

"Do you suppose we can be so near each other without giving and taking? Let us not try to get upon a common ground of faith or action: it is a thousand times more delightful to discover that we now and then reach the same point by different paths. This reminds me, Joseph, that our paths ought to separate now, for a while. It is you who should leave,—but only to come back again, 'in the fulness of time.' Heaven knows, I am merciless to myself in recommending it."

"You are right to try me. It is time that I should know something of the world. But to leave, now—so immediately—"

"It will make no difference," said Philip. "Whether you go or stay, there will be stories afloat. The bolder plan is the better."

The subject was renewed the next morning at breakfast. Madeline heartily seconded Philip's counsel, and took a lively part in the discussion.

"We were in Europe as children," she said to Joseph, "and I have very clear and delightful memories of the travel."

"I was not thinking especially of Europe," he answered. "I am hardly prepared for such a journey. What I should wish is, not to look idly at sights and shows, but to have some active interest or employment, which would bring me into contact with men. Philip knows my purpose."

"Then," said Madeline, "why not hunt on Philip's trail? I have no doubt you can track him from Texas to the Pacific by the traditions of his wild pranks and adventures! How I should enjoy getting hold of a few chapters of his history!"

"Madeline, you are a genius!" Philip cried. "How could I have forgotten Wilder's letter, a fortnight ago, you remember? One need not be a practical geologist to make the business report he wants; but Joseph has read enough to take hold, with the aid of the books I can give him! If it is not too late!"

"I was not thinking of that, Philip," Madeline answered. "Did you not say that the place was—"

She hesitated. "Dangerous?" said Philip. "Yes. But if Joseph goes there, he will come back to us again."

"O, don't invoke misfortune in that way!"

"Neither do I," he gravely replied; "but I can see the shadow of Joseph's life thrown ahead, as I can see my own."

"I think I should like to be sent into danger," said Joseph.

Philip smiled: "As if you had not just escaped the greatest! Well,—it was Madeline's guess which most helped to avert it, and now it is her chance word which will probably send you into another one."

Joseph looked up in astonishment. "I don't understand you, Philip," he said.

"O Philip!" cried Madeline.

"I had really forgotten," he answered, "that you knew nothing of the course by which we reached your defence. Madeline first suggested to me that the poison was sometimes used as a cosmetic, and on this hint, with Mr. Blessing's help, the truth was discovered."

"And I did not know how much I owe to you!" Joseph, exclaimed, turning towards her.

"Do not thank me," she said, "for Philip thinks the fortunate guess may be balanced by an evil one."

"No, no!" Joseph protested, noticing the slight tremble in her voice; "I will take it as a good omen. Now I know that danger will pass me by, if it comes!"

"If your experience should be anything like mine," said Philip, "you will only recognize the danger when you can turn and look back at it. But, come! Madeline has less superstition in her nature than she would have us believe. Wilder's offer is just the thing; I have his letter on file, and will write to him at once. Let us go down to my office at the Forge!"

The letter was from a capitalist who had an interest in several mines in Arizona and Nevada. He was not satisfied with the returns, and wished to send a private, confidential agent to those regions, to examine the prospects and operations of the companies and report thereupon. With the aid of a map the probable course of travel was marked out, and Joseph rejoiced at the broad field of activity and adventure which it opened to him.

He stayed with Philip a day or two longer, and every evening the fire made a cheery accompaniment to the deepest and sweetest confidences of their hearts, now pausing as if to listen, now rapidly murmuring some happy, inarticulate secret of its own. As each gradually acquired full possession of the other's past, the circles of their lives, as Philip said, were reciprocally widened; but as the horizon spread, it seemed to meet a clearer sky. Their eyes were

928

no longer fixed on the single point of time wherein they breathed. Whatever pain remained, melted before them and behind them into atmospheres of resignation and wiser patience. One gave his courage and experience, the other his pure instinct, his faith and aspiration; and a new harmony came from the closer interfusion of sweetness and strength.

When Joseph returned home, he at once set about putting his affairs in order, and making arrangements for an absence of a year or more. It was necessary that he should come in contact with most of his neighbors, and he was made aware of their good will without knowing that it was, in many cases, a reaction from suspicion and slanderous gossip. Mr. Chaffinch had even preached a sermon, in which no name was mentioned, but everybody understood the allusion. This was considered to be perfectly right, so long as the prejudices of the people were with him, and Julia was supposed to be the pious and innocent victim of a crime. When, however, the truth had been established, many who had kept silent now denounced the sermon, and another on the deceitfulness of appearances, which Mr. Chaffinch gave on the following Sabbath, was accepted as the nearest approach to an apology consistent with his clerical dignity.

Joseph was really ignorant of these proceedings, and the quiet, self-possessed, neighborly way in which he met the people gave them a new impression of his character. Moreover, he spoke of his circumstances, when it was necessary, with a frankness unusual among them; and the natural result was that his credit was soon established on as sound a basis as ever. When, through Philip's persistence, the mission to the Pacific coast was secured, but little further time was needed to complete the arrangements. By the sacrifice of one-fourth of his land, the rest was saved, and intrusted to good hands during his absence. Philip, in the mean time, had fortified him with as many hints and instructions as possible, and he was ready, with a light heart and a full head, to set out upon the long and uncertain journey.

# CHAPTER XXXII. LETTERS.

I. Joseph to Philip.

Camp ——, Arizona, October 19, 1868.

Since I wrote to you from Prescott, dear Philip, three months have passed, and I have had no certain means of sending you another letter. There was, first, Mr. Wilder's interest at ——, the place hard to reach, and the business difficult to investigate. It was not so easy, even with the help of your notes, to connect the geology of books with the geology of nature; these rough hills don't at all resemble the clean drawings of strata. However, I have learned all the more rapidly by not assuming to know much, and the report I sent contained a great deal more than my own personal experience. The duty was irksome enough, at times; I have been tempted by the evil spirits of ignorance, indolence, and weariness, and I verily believe that the fear of failing to make good your guaranty for my capacity was the spur which kept me from giving way. Now, habit is beginning to help me, and, moreover, my own ambition has something to stand on.

I had scarcely finished and forwarded my first superficial account of the business as it appeared to me, when a chance suddenly offered of joining a party of prospectors, some of whom I had already met: as you know, we get acquainted in little time, and with no introductions in these parts. They were bound, first, for some little-known regions in Eastern Nevada, and then, passing a point which Mr. Wilder wished me to visit (and which I could not have reached so directly from any other quarter), they meant to finish the journey at Austin. It was an opportunity I could not let go, though I will admit to you, Philip, that I also hoped to overtake the adventures, which had seemed to recede from me, rainbow-fashion, as I went on.

Some of the party were old Rocky Mountain men, as wary as courageous; yet we passed through one or two straits which tested all their endurance and invention. I won't say how I stood the test; perhaps I ought to be satisfied that I came through to the end, and am now alive and cheerful. To be sure, there are many other ways of measuring our strength. This experience wouldn't help me the least in a discussion of principles, or in organizing any of the machinery of society. It is rather like going back to the first ages of mankind, and being tried in the struggle for existence. To me, that is a great deal. I feel as if I had been taken out of civilization and set back towards the beginning, in order to work my way up again.

But what is the practical result of this journey? you will ask. I can hardly tell, at present: if I were to state that I have been acting on your system of life rather than my own,—that is, making ventures without any certainty of the consequences,—I think you would shake your head. Nevertheless, in these ten months of absence I have come out of my old skin and am a livelier snake than you ever knew me to be. No, I am wrong; it is hardly a venture after all, and my self-glorification is out of place. I have the prospect of winning a great deal where a very little has been staked, and the most timid man in the world might readily go that far. Again you will shake your head; you remember "The Amaranth." How I should like to hear what has become of that fearful and wonderful speculation!

Pray give me news of Mr. Blessing. All those matters seem to lie so far behind me, that they look differently to my eyes. Somehow, I can't keep the old impressions; I even begin to forget them. You said, Philip, that he was not intentionally dishonest, and something tells me you are right. We learn men's characters rapidly in this rough school, because we cannot get away from the close, rough, naked contact. What surprises me is that the knowledge is not only good for present and future use, but that I can take it with me into my past life. One weakness is left, and you will understand it. I blush to myself,—I am ashamed of my early innocence and ignorance. This is wrong; yet, Philip, I seem to have been so unmanly,—at least so unmasculine! I looked for love, and fidelity, and all the virtues, on the surface of life; believed that a gentle tongue was the sign of a tender heart; felt a wound when some strong and positive, yet differently moulded being approached me! Now, here are fellows prickly as a cactus, with something at the core as true and tender as you will find in a woman's heart. They would stake their lives for me sooner than some persons (whom we know) would lend me a hundred dollars, without security! Even your speculator, whom I have met in every form, is by no means the purely mercenary and dangerous man I had supposed.

In short, Philip, I am on very good terms with human nature; the other nature does not suit me so well. It is a grand thing to look down into the cañon of the Colorado, or to see a range of perfectly clear and shining snow-peaks across the dry sage-plains; but oh, for one acre of our green meadows! I dreamed of them, and the clover-fields, and the woods and running streams, through the terrific heat of the Nevada deserts, until the tears came. It is nearly a year since I left home: I should think it fifty years!

With this mail goes another report to Mr. Wilder. In three or four months my task will be at an end, and I shall then be free to return. Will you welcome the brown-faced, full bearded man, broad in cheeks and shoulders, as you would the—but how did I use to look, Philip? It was a younger brother you know; but he has bequeathed all of his love, and more, to the older.

## II. Philip To Joseph.

Coventry Forge; Christmas Day.

When Madeline hung a wreath of holly around your photograph this morning, I said to it as I say now: "A merry Christmas, Joseph, wherever you are!" It is a calm sunny day, and my view, as you know, reaches much further through the leafless trees; but only the meadow on the right is green. You, on the contrary, are enjoying something as near to Paradise in color, and atmosphere, and temperature (if you are, as I guess, in Southern California), as you will ever be likely to see.

Yes, I will welcome the new man, although I shall see more of the old one in him than you perhaps think,—nor would I have it otherwise.

We don't change the bases of our lives, after all: the forces are differently combined, otherwise developed, but they hang, I fancy, to the same roots. Nay, I'll leave preaching until I have you again at the old fireside. You want news from home, and no miserable little particular is unimportant. I've been there, and know what kind of letters are welcome.

The neighborhood (I like to hover around a while, before alighting) is still a land where all things always seem the same. The trains run up and down our valley, carrying a little of the world boxed up in shabby cars, but leaving no mark behind. In another year the people will begin to visit the city more frequently; in still another, the city people will find their way to us; in five years, population will increase and property will rise in value. This is my estimate, based on a plentiful experience.

Last week, Madeline and I attended the wedding of Elwood Withers. It was at the Hopeton's, and had been postponed a week or two, on account of the birth of a son to our good old business-friend. There are two events for you! Elwood, who has developed, as I knew he would, into an excellent director of men and material undertakings, has an important contract on the new road to the coal regions. He showed me the plans and figures the other day, and I see the beginning of wealth in them. Lucy, who is a born lady, will save him socially and intellectually. I have never seen a more justifiable marriage. He was pale and happy, she sweetly serene and confident; and the few words he said at the breakfast, in answer to the health which Hopeton gave in his choice Vin d'Aï, made the unmarried ladies envy the bride. Really and sincerely, I came away from the house more of a Christian than I went.

You know all, dearest friend: was it not a test of my heart to see that she was intimately, fondly happy? It was hardly any more the face I once knew. I felt the change in the touch of her hand. I heard it in the first word she spoke. I did not dare to look into my heart to see if something there were really dead, for the look would have called the dead to life. I made one heroic effort, heaved a stone over the place, and sealed it down forever. Then I felt your arm on my shoulder, your hand on my breast. I was strong and joyous; Lucy, I imagined, looked at me from time to time, but with a bright face, as if she divined what I had done. Can she have ever suspected the truth?

Time is a specific administered to us for all spiritual shocks; but change of habit is better. Why may I not change in quiet as you in action? It seams to me, sometimes, as I sit alone before the fire, with the pipe-stem between my teeth, that each of us is going backward through the other's experience. You will thus prove my results as I prove yours. Then, parted as we are, I see our souls lie open to each other in equal light and warmth, and feel that the way to God lies through the love of man.

Two years ago, how all our lives were tangled! Now, with so little agency of our own, how they are flowing into smoothness and grace! Yours and mine are not yet complete, but they are no longer distorted. One disturbing, yet most pitiable, nature has been removed; Elwood, Lucy, the Hopetons, are happy; you and I are healed of our impatience. Yes, there is something outside of our own wills that works for or against us, as we may decide. If I once forgot this, it is all the clearer now.

I have forgotten one other,—Mr. Blessing. The other day I visited him in the city. I found him five blocks nearer the fashionable quarter, in a larger house. He was elegantly dressed, and wore a diamond on his bosom. He came to meet me with an open letter in his hand.

"From Mrs. Spelter, my daughter," he said, waving it with a grand air,—"an account of her presentation to the Emperor Napoleon. The dress was—let me see—blue moiré and Chantilly lace; Eugénie was quite struck with her figure and complexion."

"The world seems to treat you well," I suggested.

"Another turn of the wheel. However, it showed me what I am capable of achieving, when a strong spur is applied. In this case the spur was, as you probably guess, Mr. Held,—honor. Sir, I prevented a cataclysm! You of course know the present quotations of the Amaranth stock, but you can hardly be aware of my agency in the matter. When I went to the Oil Region with the available remnant of funds, Kanuck had fled. Although the merest tyro in geology, I selected a spot back of the river-bluffs, in a hollow of the undulating table-land, sunk a shaft, and—succeeded! It was what somebody calls an inspired guess. I telegraphed instantly to a friend, and succeeded in purchasing a moderate portion of the stock—not so much as I desired—before its value was known. As for the result, si monumentum quaris, circumspice!"

I wish I could give you an idea of the air with which he said this, standing before me with his feet in position, and his arms thrown out in the attitude of Ajax defying the lightning.

I ventured to inquire after your interest. "The shares are here, sir, and safe," he said, "worth not a cent less than twenty-five thousand dollars."

I urged him to sell them and deposit the money to your credit, but this he refused to do without your authority. There was no possibility of depreciation, he said: very well, if so, this is your time to sell. Now, as I write, it occurs to me that the telegraph may reach you. I close this, therefore, at once, and post over to the office at Oakland.

Madeline says: "A merry Christmas from me!" It is fixed in her head that you are still exposed to some mysterious danger. Come back, shame her superstition, and make happy your

PHILIP.

III. JOSEPH TO PHILIP.

SAN FRANCISCO, June 3, 1869.

Philip, Philip, I have found your valley!

After my trip to Oregon, in March, I went southward, along the western base of the Sierra Nevada, intending at first to cross the range; but falling in with an old friend of yours, a man of the mountains and the sea, of books and men, I kept company with him, on and on, until the great wedges of snow lay behind us, and only a long, low, winding pass divided us from the sands of the Colorado Desert. From the mouth of this pass I looked on a hundred miles of mountains; there were lakes glimmering below; there were groves of ilex on the hillsides, an orchard of oranges, olives, and vines in the hollow, millions of flowers hiding the earth, pure winds, fresh waters, and remoteness from all conventional society. I have never seen a landscape so broad, so bright, so beautiful!

Yes, but we will only go there on one of these idle epicurean journeys of which we dream, and then to enjoy the wit and wisdom of our generous friend, not to seek a refuge from the perversions of the world! For I have learned another thing, Philip: the freedom we craved is not a thing to be found in this or that place. Unless we bring it with us, we shall not find it.

The news of the decline of the Amaranth stock, in your last, does not surprise me. How fortunate that my telegraphic order arrived in season! It was in Mr. Blessing's nature to hold on; but he will surely have something left. I mean to invest half of the sum in his wife's name, in any case; for the "prospecting" of which I wrote you, last fall, was a piece of more than, ordinary luck. You must have heard of White Pine, by this time. We were the discoverers, and reaped a portion of the first harvest, which is never equal to the second; but this way of getting wealth is so incredible to me, even after I have it, that I almost fear the gold will turn into leaves or pebbles, as in the fairy tales. I shall not tell you what my share is: let me keep one secret,—nay, two,—to carry home!

More incredible than anything else is now the circumstance that we are within a week of each other. This letter, I hope, will only precede me by a fortnight. I have one or two last arrangements to make, and then the locomotive will cross the continent too slowly for my eager haste. Why should I deny it? I am homesick, body and soul. Verily, if I were to meet Mr. Chaffinch in Montgomery Street, I should fling myself upon his neck, before coming to my sober senses. Even he is no longer an antipathy: I was absurd to make one of him. I have but one left; and Eugénie's admiration of her figure and complexion does not soften it in the least.

How happy Madeline's letter made me! After I wrote to her, I would have recalled mine, at any price; for I had obeyed an impulse, and I feared foolishly. What you said of her "superstition" might have been just, I thought. But I believe that a true-hearted woman always values impulses, because she is never at a loss to understand them. So now I obey another, in sending the enclosed. Do you know that her face is as clear in my memory as yours? and as—but why should I write, when I shall so soon be with you?

# CHAPTER XXXIII. ALL ARE HAPPY.

Three weeks after the date of Joseph's last letter Philip met him at the railroad station in the city. Brown, bearded, fresh, and full of joyous life after his seven days' journey across the continent, he sprang down from the platform to be caught in his friend's arms.

The next morning they went together to Mr. Blessing's residence. That gentleman still wore a crimson velvet dressing-gown, and the odor of the cigar, which he puffed in a rear room, called the library (the books were mostly Patent Office and Agricultural Reports, with Faublas and the Decamerone), breathed plainly of the Vuelte Abajo.

"My dear boy!" he cried, jumping up and extending his arms, "Asten of Asten Hall! After all your moving accidents by flood and field; back again! This is—is—what shall I say? compensation for many a blow of fate! And my brave Knight with the Iron Hand, sit down, though it be in Carthage, and let me refresh my eyes with your faces!"

"Not Carthage yet, I hope," said Joseph.

"Not quite, if I adhere strictly to facts," Mr. Blessing replied; "although it threatens to be my Third Punic War.

"There is even a slight upward tendency in the Amaranth shares, and if the company were in my hands, we should soon float upon the topmost wave. But what can I do? The Honorable Whaley and the Reverend Dr. Lellifant were retained on account of their names; Whaley made president, and I—being absent at the time developing the enterprise, not only pars magna but totus teres atque rotundus, ha! ha!—I was put off with a director's place. Now I must stand by, and see the work of my hands overthrown. But 'tis ever thus!"

He heaved a deep sigh. Philip, most heroically repressing a tendency to shriek with laughter, drew him on to state the particulars, and soon discovered, as he had already suspected, that Mr. Blessing's sanguine temperament was the real difficulty; it was still possible for him to withdraw, and secure a moderate success.

When this had been made clear, Joseph interposed.

"Mr. Blessing," said he, "I cannot forget how recklessly, in my disappointment, I charged you with dishonesty. I know also that you have not forgotten it. Will you give me an opportunity of atoning for my injustice?— not that you require it, but that I may, henceforth, have less cause for self-reproach."

"Your words are enough!" Mr. Blessing exclaimed. "I excused you long ago. You, in your pastoral seclusion—"

"But I have not been secluded for eighteen months past," said Joseph, smiling. "It is the better knowledge of men which has opened my eyes. Besides, you have no right to refuse me; it is Mrs. Blessing whom I shall have to consult."

He laid the papers on the table, explaining that half the amount realized from his shares of the Amaranth had been invested, on trust, for the benefit of Mrs. Eliza Blessing.

"You have conquered—vincisti!" cried Mr. Blessing, shedding tears. "What can I do? Generosity is so rare a virtue in the world, that it would be a crime to suppress it!"

Philip took advantage of the milder mood, and plied his arguments so skilfully that at last the exuberant pride of the De Belsain blood gave way.

"What shall I do, without an object,—a hope, a faith in possibilities?" Mr. Blessing cried. "The amount you have estimated, with Joseph's princely provision, is a competence for my old days; but how shall I fill out those days? The sword that is never drawn from the scabbard rusts."

"But," said Philip, gravely, "you forget the field for which you were destined by nature. These operations in stocks require only a low order of intellect; you were meant to lead and control multitudes of men. With your fluency of speech, your happy faculty of illustration, your power of presenting facts and probabilities, you should confine yourself exclusively to the higher arena of politics. Begin as an Alderman; then, a Member of the Assembly; then, the State Senate; then—"

"Member of Congress!" cried Mr. Blessing, rising, with flushed face and flashing eyes. "You are right! I have allowed the necessity of the moment to pull me down from my proper destiny! You are doubly right! My creature comforts once secured, I can give my time, my abilities, my power of swaying the minds of men,—come, let us withdraw, realize, consolidate, invest, at once!"

They took him at his word, and before night a future, free from want, was secured to him. While Philip and Joseph were on their way to the country by a late train, Mr. Blessing was making a speech of an hour and a half at one of the primary political meetings.

There was welcome through the valley when Joseph's arrival was known. For two or three days the neighbors flocked to the farm to see the man whose adventures, in a very marvellous form, had been circulating among them for a year past. Even Mr. Chaffinch called, and was so conciliated by his friendly reception, that he, thenceforth, placed Joseph in the ranks of those "impracticable" men, who might be nearer the truth than they seemed: it was not for us to judge.

Every evening, however, Joseph took his saddle-horse and rode up the valley to Philip's Forge. It was not only the inexpressible charm of the verdure to which he had so long been a stranger,—not only the richness of the sunset on the hills, the exquisite fragrance of the meadow-grasses in the cool air,— nay, not entirely the dear companionship of Philip which drew him thither. A sentiment so deep and powerful that it was yet unrecognized,—a hope so faint that it had not yet taken form,—was already in his heart. Philip saw, and was silent.

But, one night, when the moon hung over the landscape, edging with sparkling silver the summits of the trees below them, when the air was still and sweet and warm, and filled with the diffused murmurs of the stream, and Joseph and Madeline stood side by side, on the curving shoulder of the knoll, Philip, watching them from the open window, said to himself: "They are swiftly coming to the knowledge of each other; will it take Joseph further from my heart, or bring him nearer? It ought to fill me with perfect joy, yet there is a little sting of pain somewhere. My life had settled down so peacefully into what seemed a permanent form; with Madeline to make a home and brighten it for me, and Joseph to give me the precious intimacy of a man's love, so different from woman's, yet so pure and perfect! They have destroyed my life, although they do not guess it. Well, I must be vicariously happy, warmed in my lonely sphere by the far radiation of their nuptial bliss, seeing a faint reflection of some parts of myself in their children, nay, claiming and making them mine as well, if it is meant that my own blood should not beat in other hearts. But will this be sufficient? No! either sex is incomplete alone, and a man's full life shall be mine! Ah, you unconscious lovers, you simple-souled children, that know not what you are doing, I shall be even with you in the end! The world is a failure, God's wonderful system is imperfect, if there is not now living a noble woman to bless me with her love, strengthen me with her self-sacrifice, purify me with her sweeter and clearer faith! I will wait: but I shall find her!"

THE END.

# About Author

**Bayard Taylor** (January 11, 1825 – December 19, 1878) was an American poet, literary critic, translator, travel author, and diplomat.

## Life and work

Taylor was born on January 11, 1825, in Kennett Square in Chester County, Pennsylvania. He was the fourth son, the first to survive to maturity, of the Quaker couple, Joseph and Rebecca (née Way) Taylor. His father was a wealthy farmer. Bayard received his early instruction in an academy at West Chester, Pennsylvania, and later at nearby Unionville. At the age of seventeen, he was apprenticed to a printer in West Chester. The influential critic and editor Rufus Wilmot Griswold encouraged him to write poetry. The volume that resulted, Ximena, or the Battle of the Sierra Morena, and other Poems, was published in 1844 and dedicated to Griswold.

Using the money from his poetry and an advance for travel articles, he visited parts of England, France, Germany and Italy, making largely pedestrian tours for almost two years. He sent accounts of his travels to the Tribune, The Saturday Evening Post, and Gazette of the United States.

In 1846, a collection of his articles was published in two volumes as Views Afoot, or Europe seen with Knapsack and Staff. That publication resulted in an invitation to serve as an editorial assistant for Graham's Magazine for a few months in 1848. That same year, Horace Greeley, editor of the New York Tribune, hired Taylor and sent him to California to report on the gold rush. He returned by way of Mexico and published another two-volume collection of travel essays, El Dorado; or, Adventures in the Path of Empire (1850). Within two weeks of release, the books sold 10,000 copies in the U.S. and 30,000 in Great Britain.

In 1849 Taylor married Mary Agnew, who died of tuberculosis the next year. That same year, Taylor won a popular competition sponsored by P. T. Barnum to write an ode for the "Swedish Nightingale", singer Jenny Lind. His poem "Greetings to America" was set to music by Julius Benedict and performed by the singer at numerous concerts on her tour of the United States.

In 1851 he traveled to Egypt, where he followed the Nile River as far as 12° 30' N. He also traveled in Palestine and Mediterranean countries, writing poetry based on his experiences. Toward the end of 1852, he sailed from England to Calcutta, and then to China, where he joined the expedition of Commodore Matthew Calbraith Perry to Japan. The results of these journeys were published as A Journey to Central Africa; or, Life and Landscapes from Egypt to the Negro Kingdoms of the White Nile (1854); The Lands of the Saracen; or, Pictures of Palestine, Asia Minor, Sicily and Spain (1854); and A Visit to India, China and Japan in the Year 1853 (1855).

He returned to the U.S. on December 20, 1853, and undertook a successful public lecturer tour that extended from Maine to Wisconsin. After two years, he went to northern Europe to study Swedish life, language and literature. The trip inspired his long narrative poem Lars. His series of articles Swedish Letters to the Tribune were republished as Northern Travel: Summer and Winter Pictures (1857).

In Berlin in 1856, Taylor met the great German scientist Alexander von Humboldt, hoping to interview him for the New York Tribune. Humboldt was welcoming, and inquired whether they should speak English or German. Taylor planned to go to central Asia, where Humboldt had traveled in 1829. Taylor informed Humboldt of Washington Irving's death; Humboldt had met him in Paris. Taylor saw Humboldt again in 1857 at Potsdam.

In October 1857, he married Maria Hansen, the daughter of the Danish/German astronomer Peter Hansen. The couple spent the following winter in Greece. In 1859 Taylor returned to the American West and lectured at San Francisco.

In 1862, he was appointed to the U.S. diplomatic service as secretary of legation at St. Petersburg, and acting minister to Russia for a time during 1862-3 after the resignation of Ambassador Simon Cameron.

He published his first novel Hannah Thurston in 1863. The newspaper

The New York Times first praised him for "break new ground with such assured success". A second much longer appreciation in the same newspaper was thoroughly negative, describing "one pointless, aimless situation leading to another of the same stamp, and so on in maddening succession". It concluded: "The platitudes and puerilities which might otherwise only raise a smile, when confronted with such pompous pretensions, excite the contempt of every man who has in him the feeblest instincts of common honesty in literature." It proved successful enough for his publisher to announce another novel from him the next year.

In 1864 Taylor and his wife Maria returned to the U.S. In 1866, Taylor traveled to Colorado and made a large loop through the northern mountains on horseback with a group that included William Byers, editor of the newspaper Rocky Mountain News. His letters describing this adventure were later compiled and published as Colorado: A Summer Trip.

His late novel, Joseph and His Friend: A Story of Pennsylvania (1870), first serialized in the magazine The Atlantic, was described as a story of young man in rural Pennsylvania and "the troubles which arise from the want of a broader education and higher culture". It is believed to be based on the poets Fitz-Greene Halleck and Joseph Rodman Drake, and since the late 20th-century has been called America's first gay novel. Taylor spoke at the dedication of a monument to Halleck in his native town, Guilford, Connecticut. He said that in establishing this monument to an American poet "we symbolize the intellectual growth of the American people.... The life of the poet who sleeps here represents the long period of transition between the appearance of American poetry and the creation of an appreciative and sympathetic audience for it."

Taylor imitated and parodied the writings of various poets in Diversions of the Echo Club (London, 1873; Boston, 1876).In 1874 Taylor traveled to Iceland to report for the Tribune on the one thousandth anniversary of the first European settlement there.

During March 1878, the U.S. Senate confirmed his appointment as United States Minister to Prussia. Mark Twain, who traveled to Europe on the same ship, was envious of Taylor's command of German.

Taylor's travel writings were widely quoted by congressmen seeking to defend racial discrimination. Richard Townshend quoted passages from Taylor such as "the Chinese are morally, the most debased people on the face of the earth" and "A Chinese city is the greatest of all abominations."

A few months after arriving in Berlin, Taylor died there on December 19, 1878. His body was returned to the U.S. and buried in Kennett Square, Pennsylvania. The New York Times published his obituary on its front page, referring to him as "a great traveler, both on land and paper". Shortly after his death, Henry Wadsworth Longfellow wrote a memorial poem in Taylor's memory, at the urging of Oliver Wendell Holmes, Sr.

### Legacy and honors

Cedarcroft, Taylor's home from 1859 to 1874, which he built near Kennett Square, is preserved as a National Historic Landmark.

The Bayard Taylor School was added to the National Register of Historic Places in 1988.

The Bayard Taylor Memorial Library is in Kennett Square.

### Evaluations

Though he wanted to be known most as a poet, Taylor was mostly recognized as a travel writer during his lifetime. Modern critics have generally accepted him as technically skilled in verse, but lacking imagination and, ultimately, consider his work as a conventional example of 19th-century sentimentalism.

His translation of Faust, however, was recognized for its scholarly skill and remained in print through 1969. According to the 1920 edition of Encyclopedia Americana:

> It is by his translation of Faust, one of the finest attempts of the kind in any literature, that Taylor is generally known; yet as an original poet he stands well up in the second rank of Americans. His Poems of the Orient and his Pennsylvania ballads comprise his best work. His verse is finished and sonorous, but at times over-rhetorical.

According to the 1911 edition of Encyclopædia Britannica:

Taylor's most ambitious productions in poetry— his Masque of the Gods (Boston, 1872), Prince Deukalion; a lyrical drama (Boston, 1878), The Picture of St John (Boston, 1866), Lars; a Pastoral of Norway (Boston, 1873), and The Prophet; a tragedy (Boston, 1874)— are marred by a ceaseless effort to overstrain his power. But he will be remembered by his poetic and excellent translation of Goethe's Faust (2 vols, Boston, 1870-71) in the original metres.

Taylor felt, in all truth, the torment and the ecstasy of verse; but, as a critical friend has written of him, his nature was so ardent, so full-blooded, that slight and common sensations intoxicated him, and he estimated their effect, and his power to transmit it to others, beyond the true value. He had, from the earliest period at which he began to compose, a distinct lyrical faculty: so keen indeed was his ear that he became too insistently haunted by the music of others, pre-eminently of Tennyson. But he had often a true and fine note of his own. His best short poems are The Metempsychosis of the Pine and the well-known Bedouin love-song.

In his critical essays Bayard Taylor had himself in no inconsiderable degree what he wrote of as that pure poetic insight which is the vital spirit of criticism. The most valuable of these prose dissertations are the Studies in German Literature (New York, 1879).

In Appletons' Cyclopædia of American Biography of 1889, Edmund Clarence Stedman gives the following critique:

His poetry is striking for qualities that appeal to the ear and eye, finished, sonorous in diction and rhythm, at times too rhetorical, but rich in sound, color, and metrical effects. His early models were Byron and Shelley, and his more ambitious lyrics and dramas exhibit the latter's peculiar, often vague, spirituality. Lars, somewhat after the manner of Tennyson, is his longest and most attractive narrative poem. Prince Deukalion was designed for a masterpiece; its blank verse and choric interludes are noble in spirit and mould. Some of Taylor's songs, oriental idyls, and the true and tender Pennsylvanian ballads, have passed into lasting favor, and show the native quality of his poetic gift. His fame rests securely upon his unequalled rendering of Faust in the original metres, of which the first and second parts appeared in 1870 and 1871. His commentary upon Part II for the first time interpreted the motive and allegory of that unique structure. (source: wikipedia)

# NOTABLE WORKS

Ximena, or the Battle of the Sierra Morena, and other Poems (1844)

Views Afoot, or Europe seen with Knapsack and Staff (1846)

Rhymes of Travel: Ballads and Poems (1849)

El Dorado; or, Adventures in the Path of Empire (1850)

Romances, Lyrics, and Songs (1852)

Journey to Central Africa; or, Life and Landscapes from Egypt to the Negro Kingdoms of the White Nile, A (1854)

Lands of the Saracen; or, Pictures of Palestine, Asia Minor, Sicily and Spain, The (1854)

A visit to India, China, and Japan in the year 1853 (1855)

Lands of the Saracen; or, Pictures of Palestine, Asia Minor, Sicily and Spain, The (1855)

Poems of the Orient (Boston: Ticknor and Fields, 1855)

Poems of Home and Travel (1856)

Cyclopedia of Modern Travel (1856)

Northern Travel: Summer and Winter Pictures (1857)

View A-Foot, or Europe Seen with Knapsack and Staff (1859)

Life, Travels And Books Of Alexander Von Humboldt, The (1859)

At Home and Abroad, First Series: A Sketch-book of Life, Scenery, and Men (1859)

Cyclopaedia of Modern Travel Vol I (1861)

Prose Writings: India, China, and Japan (1862)

Travels in Greece and Russia, with an Excursion to Crete (1859)

Poet's Journal (1863)

Hanna Thurston (1863)

John Godfrey's Fortunes Related by Himself: A story of American Life (1864)

"Cruise On Lake Ladoga, A" (1864)

"The Poems of Bayard Taylor" (1865)

John Godrey's Fortunes Related By Himself - A story of American Life (1865)

The Story of Kennett (1866)

Visit To The Balearic Islands, Complete in Two Parts, A (1867)

Picture of St. John, The (1867)

Colorado: A Summer Trip (1867)

"Little Land Of Appenzell, The" (1867)

"Island of Maddalena with a Distant View of Caprera, The" (1868)

"Land Of Paoli, The" (1868)

"Catalonian Bridle-Roads" (1868)

"Kyffhauser And Its Legend, The" (1868)

By-Ways Of Europe (1869)

Joseph and His Friend: A Story of Pennsylvania (1870)

Ballad of Abraham Lincoln, The (1870)

"Sights In And Around Yedo" (1871)

Northern Travel (1871)

Japan in Our Day (1872)

Masque of the Gods, The (1872)

"Heart Of Arabia, The" (1872)

Travels in South Africa (1872)

At Home and Abroad: A Sketch-Book of Life, Scenery and Men (1872)

Diversions of the Echo Club (1873)

Lars: A Pastoral of Norway (1873)

Wonders of the Yellowstone - The Illustrated Library of Travel, Exploration and Adventure (with James Richardson) (1873)

Northern Travel: Summer and Winter Pictures - Sweden, Denmark and Lapland (1873).

Lake Regions of Central Africa (1873)

Prophet: A Tragedy, The. (1874)

Home Pastorals Ballads & Lyrics (1875)

Egypt And Iceland In The Year 1874 (1875)

Boys of Other Countries: Stories for American Boys (1876)

Echo Club and Other Literary Diversions (1876)

Picturesque Europe Part Thirty-Six (1877)

National Ode: The Memorial Freedom Poem, The (1877)

Bismarck: His Authentic Biography (1877)

"Assyrian Night-Song" (August 1877)

Prince Deukalion (1878)

Picturesque Europe (1878)

Studies in German Literature (1879)

Faust: A Tragedy translated in the Original Metres (1890)

Travels in Arabia (1892).

A school history of Germany (1882).

## EDITIONS

Collected editions of his Poetical Works and his Dramatic Works were published at Boston in 1888; his Life and Letters (Boston, 2 vols., 1884) were edited by his wife and Horace Scudder.

Marie Hansen Taylor translated into German Bayard's Greece (Leipzig, 1858), Hannah Thurston (Hamburg, 1863), Story of Kennett (Gotha, 1868), Tales of Home (Berlin, 1879), Studies in German Literature (Leipzig, 1880), and notes to Faust, both parts (Leipzig, 1881). After her husband's death, she edited, with notes, his Dramatic Works (1880), and in the same year his Poems in a "Household Edition", and brought together his Critical Essays and Literary Notes. In 1885 she prepared a school edition of Lars, with notes and a sketch of its author's life.